The Valiant Chronicles

VAL TOBIN

*To Marion,
always look up!
Val Tobin
Sept. 9/18.*

NOTE FROM THE AUTHOR

The Valiant Chronicles is a two-part story comprised of *The Experiencers* (book one) and *A Ring of Truth* (book two). *Earthbound* is a prequel to *The Experiencers* but was written after *A Ring of Truth*. If you would like to read events in chronological order, start with *Earthbound*. If you prefer to read in the order the books were written, start with *The Experiencers*. The advantage of reading the prequel last is that you read it knowing many of the characters, their secrets, and what happens to them. In my opinion, that makes it more fun.

The events in *Earthbound* are outside of what happens later though they lead into *The Experiencers*. For this reason, *Earthbound* was placed at the end as a bonus story.

Fiction often draws on real events or explores concepts drawn from reality. *The Valiant Chronicles* are no exception. For some interesting reading, investigate Rendlesham Forest in Suffolk, England and the UFO sightings there; Nikola Tesla and his death ray; the StarGate project; and project MKUltra.

The reading list below contains some non-fiction books that offer a unique perspective on "life, the universe, and everything" (as Douglas Adams would say):

Chaos and Harmony: Perspectives on Scientific Revolutions of the Twentieth Century by Trinh Xuan Thuan

Communion: A True Story by Whitley Strieber

Life after Life by Raymond A. Moody, Jr., M.D.

Limitless Mind: A Guide to Remote Viewing and Transformational Consciousness by Russell Targ

The End of Materialism: How Evidence of the Paranormal is Bringing Science and Spirit Together by Charles T. Tart, Ph.D.

UFO's: A Scientific Debate edited by Carl Sagan and Thornton Page.

CONTENTS

THE EXPERIENCERS

The Valiant Chronicles: Book I

by

Val Tobin

ACKNOWLEDGMENTS

Editing by Alan Annand (Sextile) sextile.com and Kelly Hartigan (XterraWeb) editing.xterraweb.com. Thank you, Alan and Kelly. Thanks to Patti Roberts of Paradox Cover Designs for the amazing cover.

To my husband, Bob Tobin, and all who gave love, support, or their expertise: Jenn Cunningham, Andrea Holmes, Val Cseh, Mark Tobin, Amanda David, Judy Flinn, Tania Gabor, Michelle Legere, Julie Marsh, Moses Leal, Peter Wolf, Sheila Trecartin, Kathy Rinaldo, Jennifer Fasciano, Bruce Greenaway, Dr. Maral, Sharon Reesor, Anne Collins, Angel Morgan, Erika Wolf, Diane King, Angela Swift, Jeff McQueen, Arla King, Blair Weeks, Tara VanderMeulen, Karen Stephenson, Kevin Barnum, Jim Smith, Dr. Alis Kennedy, Heather Tobin, James Borg, Joe Ryan, Brad Jones, staff at Algonquin Park, Archangel Michael, Archangel Gabriel, and my spirit guides.

CHAPTER 1

Michael "Mick" Valiant checked his watch and realized he was going to finish work early. The upside was he'd be home for dinner; the downside was he'd be home for dinner. He cringed. The thought of going home reminded him he might be getting separated soon, perhaps even the next time he was home long enough to see his wife before she went to bed. Jessica had something on her mind lately, and he suspected it was divorce.

He pulled his thoughts away from his marriage and refocused on the job. Michael sat behind the driver's seat in the back of a white van displaying a cable company logo on the side. The video monitor before him showed the inside of the sprawling brick bungalow across the street. His target, Patty Richards, was inside the house.

Aside from the stats he needed for the job, Michael knew little about Richards. He knew her only as a threat to the Extraterrestrial Alliance Project, or ETAP, as those involved referred to it, and any threat to the Project had to go.

Michael glanced over at his partner, Gerry "Torque" Muniz, who sat next to Michael, also staring at the monitor. Judging from the vacant look in Torque's eyes, he wasn't seeing what was there. Sweat beaded on Torque's broad forehead. Hair around his bald spot spiked up, reminding Michael of a porcupine with tiny black and grey quills.

"Why don't you take off that jacket?" Michael asked. "You're drenched."

1

Torque shook his head, eyes still unfocused. He continued to sit and stare, brows furrowed. Finally, he spoke. "I hate leaving them alive."

He meant Ralph Drummond. They'd forced him into a mental institution to silence him. It hadn't been their typical job. As if they hadn't had this conversation numerous times since they'd been handed Drummond's dossier, Michael said, "Then why did we?"

"Have you looked at the rest of the targets?"

This was new. In previous conversations, at this point, Torque would say, "I don't know," to which Michael would reply, "Then why worry about it?"

Michael did a job, following orders precisely, and then forgot about it. It helped him maintain his detachment and his sanity. The Drummond job had been no exception though his initial gut reaction to it had been different.

When he'd first read the file on Drummond, he'd felt uneasy, like something was off. But he'd ignored it and carried on. With Torque's reminder of Drummond and his file, the uneasiness returned.

He gave Torque a puzzled stare. "I've read the list."

"No," Torque said. "Have you looked at the list in detail?"

"What's your point?"

"I figured out why we didn't kill him and why we won't kill the other two either."

"Okay," Michael said. "Why?"

"They're abductees, and killing them would interfere with the experiments."

"Where did it say that?"

"It didn't. Not explicitly. They're all members of the same UFO group, except this next target. The ones we can't terminate are flagged as 'catch and release.' The aliens want them for their experiments. We have to get creative if we want to silence them. Drummond goes to the mental hospital; the other two are disappeared to the Agency."

"Why didn't I see that?"

"You wouldn't have noticed if you weren't looking for it."

"Carolyn Fairchild and Arnie Griffen. I saw they weren't to be terminated."

Michael didn't have the other files, but he picked up the Richards file and opened it. Torque was right. Nothing in the file

2

indicated she belonged to the same UFO group as the others. In fact, she wasn't a member of any UFO group. He saw on her schedule that tonight she was due to attend a concert at her daughter's school. Michael felt a twinge. She'd be dead by then. A note in the file stated Richards was Drummond's associate, maintained a blog, and travelled around North America doing speaking engagements.

"What's the blog about?" he asked.

Torque shrugged. "Doesn't matter."

Michael nodded, understanding. He removed his weapon from a pouch at his side and marvelled, not for the first time, at how something so small could be so deadly. The size and shape of a penlight or laser pointer, the weapon discharged a microwave beam that could penetrate walls and kill a person from over twenty metres away. Soon, when he deemed the time right, Richards's heart would stop, and the coroner would list it as natural causes.

In no hurry, he waited and watched. He ran his hand through his hair, an absent-minded gesture he'd repeat often when he was waiting to kill. He glanced at Torque, expecting a remark. Torque was back to staring vacantly at the screen and hadn't noticed.

Michael looked up when he heard the door to the house open. Two teenagers stepped onto the porch. Their light and jovial voices carried through the open windows of the van. The girl was Patty's daughter, Michelle. The male would be Ian, the daughter's boyfriend.

Ian said something too low for Michael to make out. It must have been funny because the girl burst out laughing. The hearty laugh jarred Torque out of his stupor, and he shifted his gaze from the monitor to Michael.

Michael continued to wait.

The two teens scampered down the porch steps and jumped into a black Volkswagen Jetta parked in the driveway. Sleek and shiny, the car couldn't have been more than a few months old. Had to be the kid's father's car. But perhaps not. Kids these days were spoiled. The car could very well be his.

Michael glanced at the clock on the dashboard and waited for the kids to pull out of the driveway. He'd have an hour before the husband returned. That would be plenty of time. Most of the neighbours were also at work.

The Jetta eased onto the road, the back end swinging past the van. Michael glimpsed Ian's face as the kid straightened the wheel and then accelerated the car down the street. Neither kid spared the van a glance.

Michael checked the monitor and changed the view to the kitchen. From his periphery, he saw Torque turn back to the monitor.

Richards, her long hair tied back in a ponytail, stood in front of the kitchen island, stirring something in a bowl. She resembled her daughter. It would be easy to mistake them for sisters even though Patty was more than twice her daughter's age.

Michael realized he was holding his breath and exhaled. Sweat trickled down his back, and he checked the thermometer: twenty-two Celsius. Hot, for the end of April in Southern Ontario, but not hot enough to make them roll up the windows and turn on the air conditioning. Fortunately, there was a breeze and only slight humidity.

He started to lift the weapon, but paused. His hand drifted back to rest on his thigh. This looked wrong. It felt wrong. But he had the right target. All the information he had bore that out, the clincher being the carefully installed surveillance equipment the grunts from the Agency had placed inside the house. Michael felt another twinge. This reminded him of the Drummond job—like someone had made a mistake and he was silencing the wrong person.

"What are you waiting for?" Torque's voice startled Michael, but he didn't flinch. He cleared his head and focused.

Michael lifted his weapon and pointed the business end of it in the direction that put the Richards woman in its path. He clicked a button and locked it into place, keeping the weapon on and trained at her. On the monitor, Richards swayed. She turned off the mixer, but before she could set it down, she collapsed, dragging bowl and mixer down with her.

The bowl shattered when it hit the floor. Batter and glass sprayed everywhere. The mixer plug yanked free of the outlet, the cord snaking down on top of her.

Michael waited.

She jittered and thrashed. Then she was still.

He waited.

She didn't move.

Michael took his cell phone from his jacket, which hung on the

4

back of the passenger seat behind him, and speed-dialled Jim Cornell, his boss. He heard a click, and Cornell's voicemail kicked in.

When the beep sounded, Michael cleared his throat and spoke. "Hi, Jim. Valiant here. We're done at the job site and on our way back."

He ended the call and returned the phone to his jacket.

A glance at the monitor verified Richards was still motionless. Michael stuck the weapon back into the pouch at his side. Mindful of the low ceiling, he climbed into the driver's seat. He started the van, anxious to leave, but waited while Torque shut down the equipment and climbed into the passenger seat.

When they reached the south end of Richmond Hill, Michael's cell phone rang. He punched the speaker button.

"Valiant here."

"Yeah, Mick. It's Jim. I got your message. Good job."

"I've gotta ask, Jim: what did these people do? They don't seem like our typical targets."

"You can ask, Mick, but trust me, they're a threat. And this isn't something we discuss over a cell phone."

"Right." He hung up the phone, but his doubts continued.

"I wouldn't question Cornell if I were you," said Torque. "If you want to ask someone anything, ask me. If I don't know the answer, it's because we're not supposed to know. Are we clear?"

Michael nodded, keeping his eyes on the road. Torque was right. But he persisted.

"Don't you think it's odd, though, that we're targeting housewives now?"

"Maybe they aren't just housewives. It's not our job to verify that the targets are correct. What's up with you? I've never known you to question an assignment."

"This feels different."

Torque stared at him, one eyebrow raised, his lips pursed.

"You going all new-agey on me? Have you been spending too much time on Carolyn Fairchild's file?"

Carolyn Fairchild, one of their catch-and-release targets, was a psychic medium running a holistic practice from her home.

Michael laughed, shaking his head. "Thanks for that. I needed a good chuckle."

"Let it go, Mick. Don't worry about if they've been properly vetted. You can be sure they have. Whoever the Agency targets, they no doubt earned the recognition."

Michael didn't reply. He exhaled, releasing tension. These were career-limiting thoughts. He needed to get over them, or risk, at the least, his career, at the most, his life and perhaps even Jessie's life.

Two hours later, Michael pulled the van into a reserved spot in a parking garage in downtown Toronto.

Torque scanned the van. "Don't forget your jacket."

Michael nodded, retrieved his jacket, and picked up his files. He locked the van and walked around to where Torque waited. Torque already had his ID badge clipped to his lapel. Michael pulled his own badge out of his pocket and pinned it on.

"Have time for a drink after we report to Cornell?" Michael asked.

"Still avoiding the home front?"

"I guess. I have to make it up to her, but I don't know how." Even as he said it, Michael knew he wouldn't have that drink with Torque, he wouldn't be home for dinner, and he wouldn't let it drop. He'd hole up in his office and do a little digging on that UFO group.

Michael mentally reviewed the list of remaining targets: John and Carolyn Fairchild, Shelly and Steven Rudolph, and Arnold Griffen. But first, he would find out why Ralph Drummond and Patty Richards were considered such threats they'd had to be silenced immediately.

CHAPTER 2

Before settling in at his desk, Michael delivered a hurried verbal report to Jim Cornell, who seemed by turns complacent and suspicious. When Michael tried to ask again about some background information on the targets, he swore Torque and Cornell exchanged looks. Michael knew he was pushing it, but somehow, the words kept spilling out of his mouth.

It was the way Richards had twitched on the floor, batter and glass speckling her body, and the sight of her daughter, who'd never again have her mother watch her in a school recital. A visceral need to know why compelled him to continue talking about it.

At first, there was stunned silence while Michael sputtered about hitting the wrong target. Then Cornell asked Michael to leave the room.

Now Michael hunched over the computer at his desk, Patty Richards's blog open on the screen. He scrolled through the page. Richards referenced Ralph Drummond often, and they frequently collaborated on speaking engagements. While Richards wasn't listed as a member of any UFO groups, she was often a guest speaker. Michael clicked on a link to see on what topic she'd last spoken.

The Government Conspiracy with Extraterrestrials to Plan the End of the World

Well, she wasn't far off the mark. Michael could see why it would attract attention. Where had she found her information? He checked her schedule. She'd spent the last four months touring North America and was slated to present more talks in early May. Obviously, it was too soon for the websites to be updated with information on her death.

Michael opened up a popular video site and searched for anything that might show one of her talks. He found a large collection, clicked on one, and let it play, immersing himself in it.

Ten minutes later, he heard someone in the outer office. He paused the recording and toggled the screen to a document with his report to Cornell.

Torque stuck his head in the door.

"What are you doing here, Mick? I thought you were going home for dinner."

"I stayed to finish some things."

"Such as?"

"Writing up that report for Cornell." He tried to sound bored. "I thought I'd wrap this up tonight."

"You mean you thought you'd avoid Jess tonight."

Michael flushed and averted his eyes. He glanced at the time. It was 7:00 PM. If he dropped everything and left now, it would take him at least an hour to get home. Jess would've had her dinner already, and he'd eat alone. But he wasn't leaving yet. At this point, he wouldn't get home tonight until after she was in bed.

Torque stepped into Michael's office and shut the door. "Listen. Cornell asked me to make sure you fall in line. This isn't a threat—yet. We've worked together a long time. You're doing well. Never mind what the targets are up to or why they were selected. Leave it alone. If you don't, you could find yourself on the list, and there'd be no questions asked by anyone about why you're on it. Go home. We have more jobs to do, and I expect you to carry them out the way you've always done. Will you do that?"

Without missing a beat, Michael said, "Sure. No worries. Did Cornell leave yet?"

"Yeah. Anything I can do?"

"No. I'll catch him in the morning."

Torque frowned. "Just remember what I said." He left, closing the door behind him.

Michael waited for a few moments, making sure his partner was gone, before he flipped back to the paused video and clicked "play." Richards's voice, impassioned, floated up.

"The facts I've presented point clearly to a coming catastrophe. Sadly, the whole thing is being orchestrated and accelerated by our government. And our government isn't alone in this. They're joined by covert agencies from the governments of other countries: The United States. The UK and member states of the European Union. Australia. The conspiracy is far-reaching, but it includes only a select number who will survive what comes."

Michael paused the video. He'd heard enough. So where had she found her information? She was right, up to a point. The conspiracy existed, the earth was in trouble, but the Agency wasn't accelerating the damage.

He had a horrifying thought. As far as he knew, the Agency wasn't accelerating it. Was that why they'd killed Richards? Was she exposing something even those who thought they were in on it didn't know?

Michael searched for Ralph Drummond's blog. When he found it, he saw immediately where Richards had gotten her information. Drummond was vocal. He also had links to videos of his talks about the conspiracy and the coming catastrophe, but he was talking as if he had first-hand knowledge.

Do we have a leak in one of the agencies? In this one?

No wonder Drummond had been silenced, and it made sense they wouldn't want Richards to keep talking. Was their source one of the others on the list? No. If the source were known, he or she would've been the first to go.

Drummond must've had evidence at his home, but the Agency would've removed whatever was there. His house was also bugged and loaded with hidden cameras. Drummond was paranoid—but he was one of the few paranoids who had a valid reason to be.

Michael opened a drawer in his desk and removed Drummond's file. Included in the dossier were the addresses of his home and a cottage he and his wife owned. It was possible Drummond stored backups of whatever he had at his cottage, but the Agency would've thought of that.

Only Ralph Drummond would be able to tell him anything, but he wouldn't willingly talk to Michael. He'd be suspicious of anyone trying to get information from him—particularly one of the men who'd helped lock him up. Perhaps the wife, Beth, would be helpful? But if Michael approached her, then Torque and Cornell would know he hadn't let it go.

Perhaps he could find what he was looking for at the Agency? Whatever they'd retrieved from the Drummond house would be in the evidence room in the basement. Michael had access, but only on Cornell's authority. However, there'd be no one there right now. The room had security cameras, but no one would have any reason to review the footage on the cameras if he left no evidence of tampering.

Michael slipped a lock-picking tool case and roll of packing tape into his briefcase. After verifying his digital camera and netbook were in there, he shut down his computer.

Ten minutes later, he was jimmying the lock on the storage room door, careful not to do any damage. Once inside, Michael switched on the lights and locked the door. An orange couch rested along the left wall, and two matching orange armchairs sat along the right wall.

The furniture in here always reminded him of a hippy commune in the nineteen-sixties—not that he was old enough to have seen one. But he'd never seen furniture more outdated and garish in his life, and it out-gassed a musty odour, like salvage from a flooded basement. The art wasn't any better. Dogs playing poker hung above the couch, and a velvet matador challenged a bull above the chairs.

An attendant usually sat behind the reception counter. A bulletproof glass pane, drawn across the counter, sealed off the space. When an agent came to retrieve something from storage, he or she would hold the requisition form and ID up to the window. If everything checked out, the attendant would open the door on the right of the counter to let the agent through.

Michael went directly to the door and jimmied the lock, again taking care not to damage the locking mechanism. After switching on the light in that room, he turned off the lights in the main reception area. He returned to the storage area and locked the door behind him.

A long table against the wall on the right, across from the attendant's desk, held the latest evidence to be catalogued and stored. He hoped whatever had been retrieved from Drummond still sat on this table and not on one of the hundreds of shelving units that filled the 700 square metres of the storage room. He didn't want to have to crack into the database to find it.

Michael started with the boxes brought in two days before and worked his way down the table. The third set of boxes looked likely. There were four boxes. One contained a laptop, external hard drive, and a few memory sticks. The others contained a digital camera, file folders with papers, and larger documents rolled up and secured with elastics.

He set his netbook on the table. While it booted up, he opened one of the file folders. When he spotted Drummond's name, he knew he'd found what he was looking for. The folder he held contained copies of Patty Richards's blog posts. He returned it to the box. Even if the site was shut down, and he expected it would be, he could still find copies online through an archiving website.

While files transferred from the memory sticks, he unrolled the scrolled documents. Maps. He flattened them onto the table, using nearby boxes to keep them from curling back up. A detail map of Algonquin Park showing canoe routes caught his eye.

A black, oval mark in an area near the centre of the park, north of Highway 60, indicated an alien underground base. He'd never seen this base before, and he was sure he'd been made privy to all the ones located in Ontario. Michael photographed everything but put the map with the base into his briefcase. The other maps returned to the boxes.

He picked up the next folder and opened it.

The next time Michael looked up, it was 9:00 PM. Surprised he hadn't heard from Jess yet, he reached for his cell phone, but realized he wouldn't have service down here. He'd have to retrieve any messages from Jess when he left. It also meant he wouldn't be able to call to let her know he'd been delayed. She'd just have to understand.

By the time he'd reviewed half the folders in the box, he'd copied everything from the memory sticks and had cracked the login to the laptop and hard drive. Drummond didn't store files on the laptop. That left only the external hard drive, so he started transferring the files over to his netbook.

Twenty file folders remained. It shouldn't take him long to go through all this since he wasn't reading everything. When he found something he thought would be useful, he took a photo of it to review later. He removed the next folder and opened it.

When he saw what was there, he wished he'd listened to Torque and gone home. He closed his eyes as if to try to un-see it.

CHAPTER 3

Jessica Valiant turned off the television and stared at the dirty dinner plate on the coffee table—another meal eaten alone in front of the TV with no word from Michael. Jess picked up her plate and took it to the kitchen. When her bare feet hit the cold linoleum of the kitchen floor, a shiver went through her.

It had felt good to strip down to the bare minimum when she'd first arrived home, hot and sweaty from her commute on the bus from Toronto, but now she felt chilly after sitting in the air-conditioned house. She checked the clock on the stove. It was already after nine.

She rinsed her plate and cutlery and put them in the dishwasher. Jess looked around the kitchen, wondering what to do next. She'd already tried calling Michael, but all she got was his voicemail. She'd left one message. The other two times she'd hung up. Frustration welled up.

They'd spent five years in Canada, and no matter how much Michael promised her things would be different up here, nothing changed. Her routine still consisted of coming home from work to an empty house, eating dinner alone, and then going to bed alone.

Her friends and family thought she was crazy for putting up with it. Most of them told her to get a life. There seemed to be an even split between those who told her to get a hobby and those who told her to get a divorce. She didn't want to get a hobby.

Jess was afraid if she went out and joined something, she'd meet someone else. She didn't want anyone else. She wanted Michael.

But, like her friend Sarah said, it didn't look like Michael wanted her as much as she wanted him. Still, she wasn't ready to leave him. She wanted to be with him. She loved him.

To be fair, he had a demanding job. An expert in climate change, the issues of the world consumed him. His concerns weren't limited to what happened locally. He wasn't having an affair—not with a woman. His job was his mistress.

When they'd first met, she too had been passionate about her work and spent all her time focusing on her career. It made them a perfect match, especially since she also was a scientist. Her specialty was nutritional research, and she was a formulator for one of the top vitamin manufacturers in North America.

Sometime over the last five years, Jess decided she needed more in her life, and reneged on a promise she'd made to Michael when they'd first married. She brought up the subject of having a baby. He balked, of course. He'd made it clear to her he didn't want to have children.

His work made him pessimistic about the future of the planet, and she understood how that might make him cautious about bringing a child into this world. But she was sure they could manage no matter what happened. Shouldn't life go on with optimism? So Jess decided to do what she wanted and hope for the best.

She'd stopped taking the pill a few months ago, but her opportunities to entice Michael into bed were rare. In what she concluded was masterful manipulation on her part, she'd inveigled her sister to let them use her cottage for a long weekend the month before. She'd calculated her most likely time to be fertile, insisted he take the break from work, and lured him out to the cottage.

He'd kicked and screamed about it but had gone along, and they'd had a wonderful time. They spent cool but sunny afternoons on the dock, Michael nursing a beer, Jess sipping a glass of red wine. They laughed a lot. Michael's dry sense of humour came out to play, and he'd made her laugh until her stomach hurt, as he used to when they were first dating.

When the sun went down, they retired to the cabin and snuggled by the fire. Jess made sure the snuggling escalated into something more. From sundown to well past sunup, they spent most of their time in bed. She'd had her Michael back and knew they were meant for each other. The ulterior plan had worked—

she'd received verification a week ago that she was pregnant—but she still hadn't told Michael. Her inability to share the news with him had made the last few days tense and unbearable. She didn't want to tell him when he came home late at night while she was half-asleep and feeling resentful. She couldn't say anything about it while they rushed to leave for work in the morning. The weekend was coming up, but he'd be working. He was on some kind of new assignment, and it was consuming him. Again.

When she'd suggested to him she wanted some time together to talk, he'd promised to give her that. So far, it hadn't materialized. If anything, he was away even more, and she sensed he was avoiding her. She snatched up the phone and called his cell. It went to voicemail. She hung up, slamming the receiver down a little harder than she'd intended.

She looked around the kitchen for something else to do. Everything looked spotless. Of course—she had nothing to do but clean. Jess wandered back into the spotless living room, eyed the novel she was currently reading, picked it up, and put it down. She was in no mood to read about romance that was so obviously missing from her own life. Sometimes that sufficed, but not now.

She could call her mom. They hadn't spoken in ages, and she was dying to talk about her pregnancy. It would only be just after six o'clock in California, but Mom would've finished her dinner.

Jess picked up the phone again and punched in her mom's number. She settled into the corner of the couch and curled her legs up, draping the quilt from the back of the couch over her lap.

Her mother answered on the second ring, and sounded like she was in a good mood, chattering on about her latest shopping spree and the good use she'd made of her seniors' discount.

Jess smiled. Her mother could justify shopping under any circumstances. Most of the time, all she needed to defend a purchase was her seniors' discount.

"That's great, Mom. I have some news I'd like to share. Don't tell anyone, okay? Just Dad?"

"I promise," her mother said quickly. "What is it? Is everything all right? You're not getting a divorce, are you?"

Always the optimist, huh, Mom? "No. I'm not getting a divorce. I'm going to have a baby." She paused to let it sink in.

"Oh, Jessica. That's wonderful. What does Michael say? He

14

doesn't want you to have an abortion, does he?"

"Perhaps you could've stopped at 'that's wonderful,'" Jess said, thinking she'd made a mistake. It was a pattern she'd followed all her life. She wanted to share exciting news with her mother, and her mother turned it into a catastrophe. Yet Jess continued to try to share good news with her. She was her mother, damn it. Couldn't she just once share her happiness, excitement, or enthusiasm?

"Oh, sweetie, I'm just worried about you two. You both always said you wanted to focus on your careers. You never told me you'd changed your mind. Of course, I'm excited to be a grandma again. I love my grandkids. But your sisters always wanted kids and so did their husbands. What made you and Michael decide to have a baby?"

How much should she tell her mother about what she'd done? Probably not much. She'd at least have to admit Michael didn't know she was pregnant. She didn't want her mother blurting it out to him—not that she was likely to be talking to him anytime soon.

"Jessie?"

"I'm here. Michael doesn't know yet. I only found out a few days ago, but he's been too busy at work for me to tell him."

"Jessica, was this an accident? I thought you were on the pill."

"I stopped a few months ago. Then we went to Angela's cottage, and, well, now I'm pregnant."

"What changed your minds?"

"I want more in my life than just work. I want to be a mother."

"And Michael? What made him change his mind? I know how adamant he was about not having children. He wasn't shy about sharing his views on that."

Jess didn't know what to say. She didn't want to lie, but she certainly didn't want to tell her mother the truth.

"Well," she said at last, "I guess he's doing it for me." That, she decided, was probably going to be the truth—or so she hoped.

CHAPTER 4

Michael stared at the reports in the folder, the shock of what he saw sending a wave of nausea through his gut. These reports, originating from agencies all over the world, were so highly classified that Michael had never seen them. How in hell had Drummond gotten hold of them? Michael reviewed them again. Each one by itself was damning. Collectively, they were lethal and terrifying.

They were proof that the environment was deteriorating to the point where it would no longer sustain life, and the Agency actively contributed to it. The wealthy group of elite and the covert government arm funding the Agency were investing in biotechnology, fuel oils, vaccines, big agribusiness, and similar industries, with the awareness that they were putting financial gain above humanity's survival.

In their quest for more money, power, and self-preservation, they wantonly destroyed the environment, contaminated the global food supply, indiscriminately killed species necessary for food production, and introduced DNA-mutating elements into the system.

Michael tried to process this. A crisis loomed. This wasn't news to him. But he'd thought that, at the very least, they were all working to slow it down. That they weren't, that what they were doing was destroying everything to acquire wealth, seemed insane. Why? Then it hit him. They behaved like property owners who don't care if they trash their home because they know it's going to be demolished.

They knew the earth was beyond the point of no return, and they wanted to cash in the maximum before going underground. Their goal wasn't to speed things up; they simply wanted to suck up as many resources as possible before the end. The acceleration was a by-product, and they considered it just another cost of doing business.

He still didn't know where the aliens fit in. Did they condone this, or did they not care what happened to the earth so long as they had their supply of humans for experimentation? Or were they about to expropriate the earth the way the government expropriated land to build new infrastructure? He photographed the reports, set them aside, and picked up the next folder.

When Michael checked his watch again, it was 11:30 PM. Jess would already be in bed, and he'd forgotten to eat dinner. He rummaged around in his briefcase, hoping for a protein bar to tide him over until he could get home and spotted one in one of the pockets. Michael grabbed for it, but froze when he heard someone at the outer door.

If the security guard caught him, he'd have no reasonable explanation for being here. He turned off the light, lowered the top of his netbook, and faced it towards the wall. He closed his briefcase to make it seem part of the evidence stash.

Michael crouched in front of the door. The netbook gave off a faint glow from the crack of screen left open so it would continue to transfer files, but with luck, the guard wouldn't get suspicious.

The light in the reception area went on. A flashlight beam shone through the window.

Michael flattened himself against the door.

The beam of light paused at the table with the boxes, shining on the netbook. It sat there for what seemed an eternity.

Michael realized he was holding his breath and let it out slowly.

The light scoured the room once more and vanished.

He listened for the sound of a key in the lock or for the sound of the outer door closing. Light from the waiting room illuminated the reception desk and the floor behind it, adding a soft glow to the surrounding area. Michael heard some shuffling and then nothing for an interminable time.

He stood. The light from the reception area was still on, so he was sure whoever had entered hadn't slipped out. He felt an urge to throw open the door. It was like staring into the rushing waters of Niagara Falls and wanting to jump in. He squashed it.

Michael craned his head so he could see through the window. To his amazement, Frank, one of the security guards, lay on the couch. He was on his side, his back to Michael. The guy had come in here to have a nap.

Son of a bitch. Now what?

He was stuck here until Frank finished his nap, and he'd have to go through the rest of the files in the dark. Turning on a light was out of the question. He didn't even want to risk opening his damn protein bar in case Frankie boy was still awake or a light sleeper.

Michael sank to the floor. He'd have to be careful to stay awake. Falling asleep would be the perfect end to his day—or rather, the perfect start to his tomorrow. He hoped Frank's partner would look for him soon. What if Frank slept the whole night away? Michael didn't think it'd be possible on that smelly old couch, especially with the light on, but maybe Frank was used to it. Michael fought the urge to pack up and leave and decided to at least complete the file transfer.

He hadn't touched Drummond's digital camera and left whatever was on it alone. He opened the next file folder, setting it and its contents on the floor in the light spilling in from the reception area. Most of it was conspiracy stuff that Michael discarded, either because it was ridiculous or because it had nothing to do with the Agency or ETAP. He'd probably get through the rest of the folders quickly if they were all like this.

In this way, he examined eight more folders. When he opened the next folder and started reading, he knew Drummond had found a keg of dynamite and lit the fuse with his big mouth. The first printout mentioned not only ETAP, but also Jim Cornell by name, and referenced agents who worked under Cornell by description. Michael recognized himself. He'd have to read this carefully.

Michael rose, squashed himself against the door, and peered out the window.

Frank lay on his back, snoring.

Michael looked down at the floor, considering. He didn't want to take out his camera and start taking pictures. It was bad enough he was rustling the odd paper though he tried to be silent. A camera click and flash might do him in. He lowered himself to the floor and closed the folder.

There were no labels other than what Drummond had stuck on it. Since it came from a box on the table, he knew it hadn't been examined and catalogued. He was sure no one would notice it missing.

Removing everything from the folder, he set it all in his briefcase. Then, in case someone had counted the folders, he took some of the documents from the previous folder and put them into the empty one. He placed the folder back in its box. Ten folders remained. He opened the first one.

The next time Michael looked up, he was on the last folder. His legs cramped, and he had to piss. The hard drive was silent. The file transfer had finished—Michael hadn't noticed when. He flipped through the last folder, dismissed its contents, and returned it to the box. He disconnected the hard drive from his netbook and put everything away.

With luck, Frank wouldn't notice the rearrangement, but it needed to be in order for the person arriving in the morning. Michael checked his watch. It was 2:00 AM. He wondered if Jess was asleep. It would be better for him if she was unaware he still hadn't come home.

The outer door opened. A male voice spoke, gentle and low. "Frank, hey, Frank. Get up."

Finally. Hopefully, Frank's buddy would wake him and the two would go away so Michael could leave.

"Frank, get up. It's my turn."

Oh, for God's sake. Now the other guy is going to have a nap? Are they kidding?

For a moment, Michael considered shooting them both and going home.

Frank yawned, sounding like he was giving himself a good stretch.

"Hey, Joe. I'm up. Thanks for covering. I'm starving. Want to grab a bite before your nap? I brought some extra dessert. Mary made some of her butter tarts. We could make coffee. What do you say?"

Michael couldn't believe what he was hearing. He hoped Joe thought Mary's butter tarts were irresistible.

"I don't think I should have coffee. It might keep me up."

Michael thought again about shooting those dumbasses. If his situation weren't so dire, he could at least go out there and knock their heads together. He hoped they'd cut him a break and leave.

"Skip the nap, Joe. Keep me company. We could play some cards after we do our rounds again."

"I guess I can't resist Mary's butter tarts. Okay."

Michael wanted to cheer. He waited while Frank got up from the couch and left with Joe. They turned off the lights on the way out, and Michael stood in the darkness, giving them a few minutes to get to the elevator. When he was sure they were gone, he turned on the lights in the storage area and verified everything was back the way he'd found it.

He scanned the place one more time. All clear. He picked up the roll of packing tape he'd use to relock the deadbolts and closed the briefcase. For the first time in a long time, he looked forward to getting home.

CHAPTER 5

By the time Shelly Rudolph wriggled out from under Steve, her husband, she'd already decided her affair with their friend, Arnie Griffen, would have to end. Lately, her conscience had been pricking her more than Arnie was. At no point had she thought that Steve deserved the betrayal, or that she didn't consider herself happily married. It was more that she deserved the fun, and Arnie made it so easy.

Shelly turned to face Steve, who was watching her, and said, "I'm going to have a quick shower before we leave for tonight's sky watch. Want to join me? I'm sure Arnie will be late since it's a work day, and he's the one with the equipment."

She meant camera equipment, of course. The sky watch tonight, at the home of their friends, John and Carolyn Fairchild, was part of their UFO group activities. Arnie owned the camera and scope they'd use to view and record it. But she giggled to herself.

Steve smiled in response. "Sounds great."

Shelly headed to the bathroom, thinking how lucky she was Steve had never found out about her fling. It would've killed their marriage, plus Steve's friendship with Arnie, though Arnie was used to that. He'd killed a few marriages and friendships by sleeping with a buddy's wife. The guy couldn't seem to keep it in his pants.

In the bathroom, Shelly turned on the water in the tub and let it run over her hand, adjusting the temperature. She let her mind wander and wondered was now the time to start a family? Steve had broached the topic recently, and she'd hedged again. She'd always wanted kids but refused to commit to it.

Maybe she'd take that step now. If she put this fling with Arnie behind her, perhaps she'd settle down at last and be a mother. Steve would be excited, and it would be a sure-fire way to kill the affair with Arnie.

But was she ready to get fat? She tried to imagine her stomach round and heavy, sticking out in front like she'd swallowed a watermelon whole. She thrust her pelvis forward, practicing her pregnant-lady stance. Perhaps she could handle it.

Shelly slid the shower curtain aside and braced her hands on the wall as she stepped into the tub. While she washed her hair, she thought about tonight. They were having more sky watches lately. With Ralph Drummond now in a mental hospital, Arnie insisted on it. She still couldn't believe it. Ralph had seemed so stable the last time she'd seen him.

Arnie maintained Ralph had been coerced, and Ralph's wife, Beth, wasn't talking about it. She'd cut them off from the family and told them not to contact Ralph. It was surreal.

Would the government force someone into the nut house just for talking about UFOs?

The shower curtain parted, and Steve stepped into the bathtub. Shelly smiled at him.

"Welcome aboard, sailor." She lathered him with soap, pleased she'd given him a fun afternoon in bed. She couldn't remember the last time they'd taken a whole afternoon like this.

Fifteen minutes later, Shelly was dressed in denim shorts and a T-shirt that read, "Someone went to Salem, Massachusetts, and all I got was this bewitching T-shirt." A gift from herself.

Shelly checked to see what Steve was wearing. A green polo shirt and khaki golf shorts.

Thank God. Not the shirt with the horizontal stripes. She hated that stupid shirt. Didn't he know how fat he looked in it? Suddenly, she wanted like hell to get out of there.

"Let's go," she said, trying to keep the irritation out of her voice. "Carolyn said to be there for six o'clock and it's already five."

Steve glanced at the time and then gave her a slantwise stare. "Sure."

He was wondering why she sounded on edge, but she noted he

22

wasn't curious enough about it to ask. They left the apartment together, and Shelly locked the door. In the hallway, she felt another twinge of guilt and took his hand.

"I love you," she said, meaning it.

Steve looked down at her, his affection showing in his eyes. "I love you, too."

Shelly thought about seeing Arnie at Carolyn's tonight. Steve was so oblivious.

Or really trusting. He trusts you and you screw around on him. You really are a 'ho'.

She tried to clear those thoughts from her mind. She'd end it soon and tell Steve they could have a baby. Not tonight though. First, she needed to talk to Arnie alone, in person, somewhere no one would overhear the conversation in case it didn't go well.

Shelly wished the affair were behind her so she could get on with her life, doing penance for her transgression. She'd make it up to Steve even if he never knew about it. If only he hadn't gained all that weight, or at least dressed better, maybe she wouldn't have cheated on him.

She dropped his hand when they stepped out into the parking garage. As they walked to the car, Steve took her hand again.

"Is everything all right, Shelly?"

"I'm fine. Sorry. I hate running late, and if we stop to pick up the munchies I promised to bring, we're going to be late," she replied, deflecting.

"Relax. We'll call Carolyn on the road so she'll know we're on our way. We won't be more than fifteen minutes late, tops. It's just a sky watch, not a formal dinner."

"You're right. It'll be nice to have an evening with the group, especially after having the whole day to ourselves. It was good, right?"

"It was great. We should do stuff like that more often. I've been working too many hours and haven't spent much time with you lately. I can change that," he said.

Shelly cringed at the prospect. She'd grown used to having a lot of time to herself. She didn't know what she'd do if he started hanging around.

"Well, your job's pretty important. You got that promotion, and they need you there more. I understand. We'll do what we did today. Take a day off work sometimes and be together? You have

23

tomorrow off too. How rare is that, even for a Saturday? And our vacation's coming up in a few months. That'll be fun." Was she rambling? She thought she was rambling.

They got in the car, both silent, and drove from the parking garage. On the road, she caught him glancing in her direction. She back-pedalled. "I didn't mean I don't want you around. I'm worried it'll affect your career when you're starting to move up. When you're settled, you'll spend more time at home."

"Sure." He fell silent again.

Shelly stared ahead. Her mind was on Arnie. Perhaps she would sleep with him just one more time and then break it off.

CHAPTER 6

Arnie Griffen inspected the open case that held his scope and camera equipment, readying it for his UFO group's sky watch at Carolyn and John Fairchild's. He was sure he had everything, but he double-checked for the power inverter. He'd forgotten it once, and recording the sky watch had been cut short when the battery died. The others were good sports about it, but since then, Arnie obsessed about his equipment.

It hadn't been entirely a wash. He and Shelly Rudolph had stayed up late that night, and it was the first time they'd locked lips and made with the hot and heavy. Arnie had craved her almost from the time they'd met, but she was the wife of one of his friends, so he'd tried to control himself. As usual, that never lasted.

This time, though, he'd been able to hold out for over fifteen years. He was proud of that. But that night, Shelly had flirted with him all evening. When everyone else packed it in and went to their tents, Arnie and Shelly were left alone, sitting by the fire, stargazing. Shelly moved in on him almost from the moment they heard Steve snoring like a hibernating bear in the tent he shared with Shelly.

Shelly sat close to Arnie—almost on top of him. There was no mistaking what she wanted. He no longer remembered what they'd talked about, but he would never forget what they did. She raised her lips up, inviting his kisses. He didn't need to be asked twice. He dropped his mouth over hers, exploring with his tongue. She took his hand and stuck it under her shirt.

Arnie pulled away, grabbed her hand, and led her to the kitchen tent where they'd have privacy. He was naked and holding a condom in his hand by the time she zipped the netting closed. Her clothes hit the dirt right after. She ripped the tablecloth off the picnic table and spread it out on the ground. He pressed her down on it and kneeled between her open thighs.

She clawed at him while he fumbled to put on the condom, and her nails raked his biceps. He bit his lip to stifle a moan, but when he shoved into her, he couldn't hold back, and he groaned, not caring if the whole park heard him. Shelly writhed under him, and her hungry gaze roved over his body.

That his friend, her husband, slept nearby did cross Arnie's mind, but he soon let it go. It's not like he'd had to talk her into it, and what a woman did behind her husband's back was up to her. That platitude had served him well for years, though it had earned him a few black eyes, too. After that, they got together whenever Shelly could get away and Arnie wasn't working. He'd been banging her for almost two years now. She was a sweet ride.

Arnie took out his cell phone and made sure there were no messages. He wasn't on call this evening, but they still sometimes called him anyway. Arnie was a senior developer for a company that created and sold custom software for insurance companies, and he knew more about the product than anyone else.

He loved programming but hated the stress of the long hours. Sometimes, he'd found himself still at the office at two-thirty in the morning. It was during those times he'd had some of his UFO abduction experiences. Most people were abducted from their beds. Arnie was abducted from his office.

Not today, thanks. I gave at the office. Ha, ha, ha.

Arnie checked the time. He should leave soon. The drive to Carolyn and John's was going to take him about half an hour, and he wanted to get there a little early. He closed the camera case and picked it up. It was heavy, but he was used to lugging it around.

The antithesis of the computer nerd, he worked out and bulked up, though not to steroidal extremes. He didn't need glasses. He towered over most men. His blond hair, the light fuzz on his chin and cheeks, straight nose, and perfect teeth made him a woman beacon. Arnie had won the gene pool lottery.

He first realized girls were attracted to him in grade one when twin sisters in his class fought over him. They each claimed him as a "boyfriend," and one grabbed one arm, the other grabbed the other arm, and he was sure he'd be split like a turkey wishbone until the teacher on yard duty intervened.

The girls got a lecture; Arnie got a lesson in charisma. He decided they could both be his girlfriends and added a couple more to his entourage before the year was out. Of course, at that age, when they played doctor, it was with a toy stethoscope and kept their clothes on. He didn't graduate to gynaecology until he was fifteen.

Arnie carried his case to the door of his condo. He then went to check on his mother, who was living in his spare bedroom, and no, she didn't cramp his style. Arnie had found the ladies he brought home were more infatuated with him when they saw he was taking care of his mother. It made him feel like a hero.

His mother didn't comment on anything he did. She simply sat, day after day, in her armchair, with her knitting needles and her television going, and the occasional cognac to cheer her up. Arnie had Beverly, a nurse, come in to tend to Mom's basic needs—he slept with the nurse at the end of her shift most times—and made sure his mother never lacked for anything. If she disapproved of her son's sexploits, she didn't say so.

Mom looked up from her knitting when Arnie stuck his head in her room. She paused, her needles poised mid-clack and hovering expectantly over the sock she was making. The socks-in-progress were lime green and neon, and he'd wear them around the apartment when they were done.

"I'm going," he said.

"Okay, Arnold." Only his mom called him by his full name. He hated his name. It was his one feature that screamed "nerd."

"Do you want me to get you anything before I leave?"

"A tea might be nice. Thank you. And maybe some of those cookies with the chocolate on them?" Mom liked her sweets. Arnie was surprised she wasn't diabetic. She wasn't even pre-diabetic. Her blood sugar consistently tested normal. He counted his blessings. By the time his father had passed away, he'd been on a whole pharmacopoeia of drugs, including insulin. Arnie had no wish to deal with all that again.

Arnie went into the kitchen and got the kettle going. He put some cookies on a plate, setting the plate on a round, red tray with snowmen and children painted on it, a souvenir from his childhood. His mother had bought it when his kindergarten class had a fundraiser. Thirty-five years ago.

A sugar bowl, saucer, teaspoon, and small pitcher of milk went onto the tray, and he carried it to his mother's room. She smiled her thanks when he set it on the table next to her.

He returned to the kitchen as the kettle clicked off. Arnie poured the water directly onto the tea bag in the mug. Tea grannies everywhere would've fainted to see how he made tea, but he couldn't be bothered using a teapot, and he sure as hell wouldn't let his mother try to pour herself a cup of tea from a full, hot pot. He took the mug of tea into his mother's room and set it on the tray.

"I could call the nurse back. She'd come and stay the night."

"I'm fine. You don't need to pay someone to look after me. If I want to use the washroom, I'll go slowly. I got time. It's all I've got left." Mom smiled, but it wasn't bitter.

He made up his mind. He'd never enjoy the sky watch if he left her alone. Arnie picked up his cell phone. His mother's big, brown puppy eyes of reproach watched him while he talked to Beverly, who assured him she'd be right over.

"Don't start. Okay?" Arnie said. "I'd be as irresponsible to leave you here alone as you'd have been to leave me at home alone when I was five." The moment he said it, he could tell it had been the wrong thing to say.

"I'm not five," she said.

The indignant tone brought Arnie another stab of guilt.

"I know, Mom. I'm only saying it would be hard for you to manage all night here alone." He tried not to sound like he was talking to a five year old. He thought it worked. "She's on her way. Be nice."

"When am I not nice?"

Arnie sighed. "If you don't want her to keep you company, tell her to hang out in the living room. Don't worry about the money. I have it to spend."

"You go," she said. "That nurse will sit here doing nothing, and you can pay for it. But if it makes you feel better, then make yourself feel better. Who needs to save money when you have it to throw around? Your father was never so wasteful."

"It's not wasteful. But you're welcome anyway." Sometimes, being a hero was tough. Arnie leaned over, kissed her wrinkled cheek, and gave her bony shoulders a hug. "I'll see you tomorrow."

She nodded.

He left the room, and she called after him, "You're a good boy, Arnold."

Arnie smiled. "Thanks, Mom."

At least one woman thinks so.

He picked up his case, opened the condo door, and stepped into the hallway. He couldn't wait to get to Carolyn's and kick back for a while. A nice, relaxing sky watch was what he needed to get away from it all. He whistled as he walked to the elevator.

CHAPTER 7

Carolyn and John Fairchild lived inside the southeast limits of the town of Newmarket in a two-story century home nestled in a valley on a one-acre chunk of land complete with duck pond and forest. The forest stretched out beyond the boundaries of their property, and it was in the forest that Michael "Mick" Valiant set up his post.

Close to the property line he picked a spot with an ideal view of the backyard and balcony. He'd barely settled in when his cell phone vibrated. It was Gerry "Torque" Muniz. Michael answered it, keeping his voice low.

"Yes?"

"It's Torque. Where are you?"

"Out. What's up?"

"Seriously, Mick, where are you?"

"That UFO group is having a sky watch tonight. They're going to get buzzed, and I want to see it."

"That's against protocol. Cornell is losing patience with you—says you're not much of a team player these days. You're not supposed to spy on these people yourself. That's what we have field grunts for."

"I have some thoughts on that."

"You don't get paid to think. You'll cause trouble for both of us. Spend the weekend with your wife. We're having this conversation too often."

"Relax, Torque. I won't interfere. I'll talk to you tomorrow." He hung up.

Michael considered leaving, but only for a second. He wouldn't let Torque drive him away. He supposed he wasn't being much of a team player, but, lately, he hadn't been feeling much like part of the team. Torque and Cornell were both acting cagey, freezing him out. And what he was seeing made no sense.

When he observed these people, he didn't understand why the Agency watched them, followed their blog posts, tapped their phone lines, and bugged their homes. It seemed ludicrous. They were no different than any other group of UFO enthusiasts, though Ralph Drummond and Patty Richards had definitely known more of the truth than most UFO nuts, and he suspected Arnold Griffen also knew more.

But the group as a whole seemed innocuous enough, particularly the two couples, the Fairchilds and the Rudolphs. They gathered for sky watches, read books about UFOs, attended conventions, searched the Internet for information on UFOs, reported a few incidents to the Mutual UFO Network (or MUFON, as it was more commonly known), and generally played around with the idea that there were extraterrestrials visiting Earth. They also had, as most UFO groups did, a few members who claimed they were abductees, and who, Michael knew, were experiencing what they claimed to experience.

He'd seen his share of spies and terrorists or people whose goal was to expose the Project, and this group didn't fit the profile. Arnie Griffen was the closest to a loose cannon the group had right now. Arnie certainly screamed "conspiracy" like the Internet town crier, but even Arnie didn't seem to have the inside scoop on the Project itself.

The information Michael had stolen from the evidence room was devastating to the Agency and for Michael. If Drummond had gone public with it, they'd have been terminated, of that Michael had no doubt. He agreed with Torque it would've been better to silence Ralph permanently except for one thing: if what he'd found in Ralph's files was true, then Drummond wasn't the enemy—the Agency was. Michael vowed to get to the bottom of it before more people died.

He looked at the balcony through his binoculars. No one was outside yet. He'd packed himself a thermos of coffee, a bottle of water, and some snacks. He'd almost left the coffee at home, considering how hot it was.

The beginning of May was usually still cool, but they'd been having a heat wave—the second one this spring. It reminded him how quickly the end was coming. Michael pulled out the thermos, poured himself some coffee, and settled down to wait.

***

Inside the house, Carolyn Fairchild took a pizza from the oven and set it on the counter.

"John. Pizza's ready. Did you find the laser pointer?"

He appeared at the kitchen door holding up the pointer. "When is everyone supposed to get here?"

Carolyn glanced at the clock on the stove. "Any minute now."

He turned his nose towards the pizza and gave an exaggerated sniff. "If they don't hurry, I'm going to eat it myself."

She smiled, snatched the laser pointer from his hand, and handed him the pizza cutter. "I'll let you cut it up for me, but that's all."

John gave her his best pouty face but set about cutting the pizza into squares. There was a knock on the front door, and she went to answer it. It was Arnie, and he had a large case next to his feet.

She gazed into his eyes. They were his best feature, of many great features, and, like most women, she was drawn to them. Unlike most women, though, she knew better than to keep gazing. Arnie was one of her best friends, probably because she'd been able to resist his charms. Admittedly, it had taken an effort of will and a stubborn commitment to her marriage on her part.

Arnie smiled his magic smile, which always reached his eyes.

"That looks heavy." She nodded at his case.

"It's okay," he replied.

John appeared from the kitchen door and waved. "Hi, guy. Do we need to be up on the balcony, or can we set up on the lawn?"

Carolyn waited, trying to be patient while Arnie pondered. She heard a car drive by on the street, hidden from view by trees and shrubs and their long, winding drive. She scanned the floor to make sure Fox, their cat, wasn't around. Finally, her fear of feline escape got the better of her.

"Arnie, come in so the cat doesn't get out."

He picked up his case and stepped inside, bumping the umbrella stand as he did. Carolyn reached out to steady it as Arnie's hand caught it. When their hands touched, an impression of an owl flashed into her mind, followed by an image of Arnie screaming in terror. Startled, she kept her hand over his, and stared into his eyes. Her mouth went dry and her gut gave a lurch of fear.

"What's that look for?" Arnie said.

"I have a terrible feeling." Carolyn slowly released Arnie's hand. *Angels and guides, please clarify this message for me.*

"What are you up to, Arnie?"

"Nothing." Arnie took her hand again.

Carolyn waited to receive another message. Fear crept through her, lodging in her solar plexus.

Don't let him set up his camera.

"Don't set up your video camera."

"You're joking, right?" Arnie frowned, irritation in his voice.

Over the years, Arnie had acknowledged Carolyn sometimes had accurate hunches, but he preferred to believe they were coincidence.

"I wouldn't joke like that," Carolyn said.

There was a knock on the door. She opened it and Shelly, oblivious to the tension in the air, stepped in, her big voice preceding her.

"Steve is getting the stuff from the car. I hope you don't mind some junk food. I know you rarely eat it, but I had a craving for chips and liquorice. Weird combination, right? Probably PMS—what?" she said, finally taking notice.

No one spoke.

Then John said, "Carolyn thinks we shouldn't use the equipment tonight."

Steve appeared, carrying a box of drinks and food. Everyone shifted to let him in the house, and Shelly closed the door. Carolyn led them into the living room and sat down on the sectional sofa. The others followed, gathering around the coffee table. Shelly sat next to Carolyn.

"What did you see, Carr?" Arnie asked.

She told them and then said, "I'm uneasy about setting up the recording equipment tonight and using it to sky watch." How to explain that sense of impending doom? She had to make them understand.

They all stared at her.

"Maybe you're interpreting it wrong," Shelly suggested.

Carolyn's eyes widened, and her mouth dropped open. Had she heard correctly? Shelly usually backed her up without question, trusting that if Carolyn sensed something, then it was accurate. In some ways, Shelly was too much of a believer, never questioning, always jumping to the paranormal explanation.
Now she decides to become a skeptic?
"I'm not interpreting it incorrectly," Carolyn said. "I know what I feel. It's only one night. Let's skip it."
"I'm sure it'll be fine. What might happen? Arnie, it won't blow up or anything, right? It's only a camera." Steve was using his reasonable voice. It sounded patronizing.
You don't know, Steve.
"It'll be bad," Carolyn insisted.
"What if we set it up on the balcony? It'll be off the grass, close to the house," Arnie said.
"Carr, you think this was a warning, but seriously, where's the harm? We're going to view the sky and record what's there. The laser pointer's more dangerous. If you shine that at a plane, you could bring it down. It's illegal to point it at a plane. We won't use it," John said.
Carolyn was silent. She thought about the pointer. "It's not the pointer."
"We're not harming anyone, the equipment isn't hazardous, and we're not going to play loud music, have a fire, or do anything that could cause trouble. We'll take it easy, and if it looks like there'll be a problem, we'll put everything away. Does that sound reasonable?" John said.
Everyone but Carolyn nodded. All eyes turned to her. Reluctantly, she nodded.
"I don't feel comfortable with this, but if you all want to go ahead anyway, I won't stop you."
"You have our permission to say 'I told you so' if something happens," Arnie replied.
It'll be too late then. At that thought, she almost protested again, but changed her mind. *They're not saying it, but they think I'm being ridiculous.*
She looked over at John. His expression was neutral. She stared at him for a moment and then turned to face Arnie. He was already halfway up the stairs.

CHAPTER 8

While Arnie, John, and Steve went upstairs to get the TV and set up the equipment, Carolyn and Shelly went into the kitchen, Shelly carrying the box of food and drinks.

"Would you like a hand?" Carolyn asked.

"I'll be okay," Shelly said. She set the box on the counter and took out the snacks.

"Doesn't it bother you I had a premonition?" Carolyn couldn't help asking. Of all people, Shelly should know what that meant. They'd been friends since high school, and Shelly had heard Carolyn predict many things. "I thought you'd back me on this, Shelly."

"I'm sorry, Carr, but I don't understand how anything can go wrong." Shelly at least had the decency to look apologetic.

"Others never get how it can go wrong. I'm frustrated no one will listen to me," Carolyn said.

"We're listening. We'll be careful. I'm sure if his equipment gets broken or something, then he'll get it fixed."

"You're assuming. It feels bad. Not just camera-knocked-over-and-smashed bad, but someone-getting-hurt bad, or all of us getting hurt."

Shelly looked away, raised a hand to touch the back of her head, and then scratched her neck. Carolyn could almost hear the debate going on in her head. Then Shelly appeared to firm her resolve.

"It'll be fine. I think you don't realize the times you get it wrong. You only note the times when you're right."

Carolyn was stunned. "Is this how you've always felt?"

"No, I trust you. But I think it's not as bad as you imagine."

"I'm not imagining."

Shelly sighed. "I don't mean to imply you're making this up. But the problem is, it's rarely anything concrete. I can't constantly live in fear of something happening."

Carolyn sighed and gave up. She arranged slices of pizza on a plate.

"Not to change the subject," Shelly said, "but can I ask you something?"

Carolyn looked up. "Sure."

"I'm thinking about telling Steve I'm ready to have a baby."

"Oh, that's wonderful." Carolyn went to her friend and hugged her.

"Don't say anything, especially to Steve. I'm only thinking about it. I keep waiting for the right time, but I've been thinking we should just do it."

"It wasn't perfect for us when we had Samantha, but we managed."

"How long did it take you to get pregnant after you started trying?"

"Almost a year. Some people get pregnant the first time."

"Is that why you only had one child?"

Carolyn was silent for a moment. She'd never talked to anyone about this before, not even Shelly.

"No," she finally replied. "We tried to have another child, but I couldn't get pregnant. The doctors don't know why. There doesn't seem to be a valid reason for it. John tested fine, so it's me."

"I'm sorry," Shelly said.

"It's okay. I'm happy I was able to have Sam. Are you worried? Most women are fine, you know."

"I know. Do you think I'd make a good mom?"

"Of course." She smiled at Shelly. "Steve will make a great dad, too."

Shelly smiled back. "Yeah, he'll spoil the kid rotten."

Carolyn laughed. "Yes, he will. Go ahead and take the drinks upstairs. Don't worry. I won't give away your little secret, but you have to promise to let me know when you start trying."

"Of course." Shelly grabbed the box with the drinks and left the room.

Carolyn poured the chips into a bowl while the knot of worry in her gut became more pronounced. Ignoring it, she pulled out a large tray, loaded snacks, napkins, and plates on it, and left the kitchen. She climbed the stairs, keeping a firm grip on the tray. Their voices reached her when she approached the den. Arnie was talking, which wasn't unusual. She smiled affectionately at his enthusiasm.

"It's so much better with the upgraded scope. That's right above us. We don't need it to be dark, but it has night vision. It picks up things at a greater distance than the other one I had."

Carolyn paused at the screen door. "Could someone get the door for me, please?"

John, closest to the door, opened it for her, and she stepped outside. She glanced around to make sure there was no equipment in the way and wove her way through the chairs and potted plants scattered around the balcony. She set the tray down on the table. Carolyn noted the citronella candles scattered around the balcony, grateful that John had remembered to put them out.

The others already had open drinks on the tables. John opened a cooler and handed it to Carolyn.

"Thanks," she said, and looked at the TV they'd set up. "Is it recording?"

"Everything on the TV screen is being recorded. The picture is so clear you can zoom in on anything that passes overhead," Arnie replied.

Steve said, "I love that you don't have to tilt your head up and get a sore neck."

Everyone was watching her, waiting for her approval. Carolyn let go of her fears.

"It looks amazing."

The others visibly relaxed, and Carolyn silently connected to her angels and guides: *Archangel Michael, Guardian Angels, Spirit Guides, I ask you to surround us with your protection.*

The knot in Carolyn's stomach dissolved. She trusted her angels were there to help her and took a deep breath, sucking in the warm night air. A slight breeze took some of the edge off the stifling heat. She wasn't uncomfortable herself, but she knew the others were suffering from it.

John's T-shirt was wet with perspiration. So was Steve's. Even Arnie looked wilted. Shelly seemed comfortable enough in her shorts and T-shirt. She'd tied her coppery hair back in a ponytail, and Carolyn decided the effect was cute.

Arnie fiddled with his camera, positioning it on the tripod. "That'll let me pan it across the sky with one hand." He let go of the camera. "Whatever footage we get tonight, I'll post on the website. You can all access it from there."

The website was Arnie's baby. He and Ralph had started it three years before, mostly to have an online repository of videos and stories about UFOs. Every sky watch they'd ever had was documented on their website.

A small but involved community of users visited regularly and compared notes on UFO experiences and conspiracy theories. Carolyn was surprised that after coding all day, Arnie would want to do more work on the website, but he insisted it was what he loved to do.

"I don't think you should do that," Carolyn said. The knot was back in her stomach.

"Don't start that again. We've got tons of footage up there, and no one cares." Arnie scowled.

She fell silent, gazing back at him. Nothing she said made a difference. An image of a runaway train hitting a brick wall came into her head. Carolyn picked up her drink and took a sip. She looked out over the balcony railing into the forest beyond and shivered, despite the heat. She felt exposed, watched.

Everything was silent. For a moment, it was as if the forest held its breath. Then she heard the frogs and crickets again, and the moment passed. She turned away from the forest, back to the gentle light of the citronella candles on the balcony.

Her thoughts went to a time when she was in elementary school, grade two it was, and the class was on a field trip to the museum in Toronto. The kids were lined up in twos, holding hands, and waiting to get onto the school bus to return to school. Carolyn was lost within herself, staring into space. Her stomach tingled, and in her mind, Stuart Gibbs stumbled out onto the road, a taxi careening into, and then over, him.

The image snapped her out of her reverie. She must tell Miss Doolittle, the teacher, something bad was going to happen to Stuart Gibbs. She dropped her partner's hand and moved towards the teacher.

Mrs. Garvey, the parent volunteer in charge of Carolyn's group, immediately stopped her. "Sweetie, we stay in our groups. Come back and hold Monica's hand."

Carolyn glanced at her and said, "But I have to tell Miss Doolittle that Stuart is going to get hurt."

Mrs. Garvey looked over at Stuart, who was quietly sucking on a rainbow lollipop he'd bought at the museum gift shop.

"Stuart's fine," she said. "Please get back in line, Carolyn."

Carolyn hesitated, reluctant to do what Mrs. Garvey told her to do. She wanted to stop Stuart from being hit by the car. She trembled and crossed her arms over her chest.

"It's okay, Carolyn. Everything is fine. We'll ask Stuart." Mrs. Garvey called over to Stuart. "Stuart, dear, are you enjoying that lollipop?"

Stuart looked up, puzzled.

"Sure," he said.

Mrs. Garvey turned her gaze back to Carolyn, smiling. "See? No trouble at all."

Carolyn frowned, returned to her place in line, and took Monica's hand. Then everything seemed to slow down. Frankie Darwin snickered, and in a whiny voice, he mimicked Mrs. Garvey while he grabbed at Stuart's sucker.

"Stuart, dear, are you enjoying that lollipop?"

Stuart smacked Frankie's hand away, and Frankie shoved him. Mrs. Garvey, seeing the commotion, walked towards the two boys.

Carolyn's eyes went wide, and she screamed, "Stop! Stop him."

At that moment, Frankie gave Stuart a shove that sent him stumbling backwards, towards the street. Carolyn glimpsed Stuart's startled, scared eyes as he flapped his arms, trying to keep his balance, and then spiralled off the curb.

Carolyn's vision turned into reality when a taxi barrelled into Stuart, knocked him forward, and thudded over him. Horns blared and fell silent. The taxi skidded to a stop and everything became deathly quiet.

Tears cascading down her face, Carolyn fell to her knees, muttering, "I said stop him. I said stop him."

The other kids backed away from her.

After that, the kids at school had treated Carolyn with a mixture of fear and awe. Most of them were afraid to come near her, but they didn't make fun of her, either. Ever after, Carolyn had lived in constant fear and guilt herself: fear of something like that happening again, and guilt that knowing what could happen didn't let her change the outcome.

She often wondered if Stuart would still be alive if she hadn't said anything.

What if this is the same thing?

What if by trying to prevent something from happening, she was actually orchestrating its inevitability?

Enough already. I give up. Whatever happens, happens. That didn't make her feel better, but at least it was a decision.

All was silent, except for the forest sounds beyond the balcony. The temperature dropped as the night deepened. Carolyn stood up to go in the house and get a sweater, but stopped when Steve said, "What's that?"

He pointed to the TV screen. "A light. Arnie, go up a little."

Arnie grabbed the handle on the camera and manoeuvred it around, searching. He quickly found the light and tracked it using the attached scope.

"Satellite?" asked Carolyn.

"So far it could be. It's moving steadily. It's not a shooting star, that's for sure," Arnie said. "Too high up to be a plane. Plus, no flashing lights. It's a steady light. Man-made, no doubt."

Carolyn looked up and watched the light track a path across the sky.

"Ralph insists we can't see satellites from earth, especially not with the naked eye. He says they don't reflect anything and have no lights on them."

"He's wrong. When something is low enough and large enough, you can see it with the naked eye. You can see the Space Station for sure. It even has solar panels that provide reflection," Arnie replied.

The last time Carolyn had seen Ralph Drummond he was convinced the government was after him. He'd talked about men in black and being run off the road after a sky watch. His intensity had been unnerving, and she'd been relieved when he told them he wasn't going to attend any more sky watches.

Two weeks later, he was in a mental hospital in Toronto. Carolyn had asked his wife, Beth, about what had happened and when he was coming home, but all Beth had told her was, "He's not stable, Carr. He thinks he's being stalked by lizard men and by government agents. The doctor thought it would be best if he received full-time care. He was becoming violent."

Then Beth told her never to call again.

Beth hadn't told her much, but Carolyn wanted to respect their privacy. If Ralph wanted her to know what was going on, he'd call her. They'd been friends for years, and he'd confided in her numerous times. Yet when she thought about him, she felt as if she'd deserted him.

The sense of danger returned.

Maybe some of Ralph's paranoia is rubbing off on me. The uneasiness became stronger, and she thought perhaps Ralph wasn't so crazy.

"There's something," Steve said.

A white ball made its way slowly across the screen. Arnie tracked it. It stopped. Then the white light intensified. The ball moved down. Arnie followed it.

"What the hell is that?" asked John. "Arnie, have you seen anything behave like that before?"

"Yeah, a helicopter."

The light became brighter, then sped up, moving erratically across the screen and shooting up. Two smaller lights moved towards it, imitating the pattern of the larger light. Carolyn looked up at the sky but saw nothing. "How high up is that?"

"High," Arnie said. He pulled out a laser pen and shone it up into the sky, angled away from the lights.

The lights moved in the direction of the beam, which was invisible to the group. Arnie clicked it off.

"They're following the laser. Definitely not space junk, and not a station or a satellite. It's got to be a craft of some kind, but that's no helicopter."

They all stared, hypnotized, while the lights moved around on the screen, first separating, then converging, and then moving in formation. The larger ball of light got brighter and larger.

They're coming. Dread filled the pit of Carolyn's stomach.

"Let's go inside. Now," she said. "Something is coming, and it knows we're here."

They all turned and looked at her.

"Now. Please." She walked to the door, but when no one moved to follow, she stopped.

The ball of light on the screen grew, blotting out the stars and filling the screen. Abruptly, it winked out. The stars returned.

"Wild," Arnie said.

Carolyn exhaled. She giggled, self-conscious. The others talked at once.

Steve was saying, "Man, did you see that? What was that? That had to be alien. Nothing on earth moves like that."

Arnie was saying, "That was incredible."

John was saying, "Could the military have craft that does that?"

"Not the Canadian military," Shelly interjected. "Maybe U.S.?"

A creeping brightness grew around them. Carolyn thought something moved out on the grass at the back of the yard and glanced again at the screen but saw only stars and sky.

Arnie and John were high-fiving, but they moved slowly. Then they dropped their arms and stood motionless. Arnie started to rise. His eyes widened and his mouth opened, but he didn't cry out. He rose above her.

Carolyn tried to tilt her head up, but couldn't. Her legs felt like lead.

There was a sound like the clicking of insects and like the hissing of gas leaking from a ruptured tank. Her chest felt as if there was a weight crushing down on it. She tried to speak, but her lips wouldn't move. Her eyelids were heavy, but she forced them to stay open.

Carolyn realized she was rising and looked down. She was at least five metres above the others and continued to rise, shouts accompanying her ascent. Terror built, but then it drained out of her. Her muscles relaxed, and her head fell forward. Everything faded away.

***

Michael saw the bright light overhead and pulled out his binoculars, aiming them above the house. The huge craft floated down towards the roof of the building, hovering over the house and the yard. All the windows in the house went dark. Power outage.

He thought he could hear shouts coming from the yard. But when he focused on it, there was only silence. He glanced towards the road, in the direction of his car.

Nothing moved.

He gazed back up at the spacecraft in time to see a body, probably Arnie—it looked like one of the men—rise towards the craft. The light enveloped Arnie's prone body. He floated, a corpse-like shadow. Shortly after that, a female body drifted up towards the ship.

Carolyn.

Michael checked his watch. It was 12:33 AM. They'd be gone two hours. Michael pulled out his thermos of coffee and poured himself a cup. He settled in to await their return.

It took over two hours.

Michael was pouring his third cup of coffee and wondering if he should have another sandwich when a flood of light engulfed the Fairchild home. He set aside his thermos and snatched up the binoculars. A spacecraft hovered over the house. A vertical cylinder of light shone from it, connecting the house and the craft like an umbilical cord.

Carolyn returned first. Her body floated towards the house, and Michael almost dropped the binoculars when she somehow went through the solid roof like it wasn't there. A few minutes later, Arnie performed the same impossible feat.

Michael wondered what it looked like from inside the house and made a mental note to review the surveillance footage. Motion-activated cameras should have triggered when Carolyn and Arnie were inside. He'd review them in the morning.

When both abductees had disappeared, the light cut off. By the time Michael's eyes adjusted to the darkness, the craft was gone. Light shone in the windows again.

Michael listened for any sound of activity from the house. He stood and made his way to the backyard, but didn't want to get too close. He used the binoculars to scan the back balcony. No one was there.

A light was on in the kitchen window. His heart gave a lurch when he saw movement in the dining room window, then relaxed as he recognized the cat. He was jumping at shadows. Time to call it a night.

Michael returned to the spot where he'd set up his surveillance and packed up his things. He headed to his car and checked the time. Three twenty-five. He hoped Jess was asleep when he got home.

CHAPTER 9

Carolyn opened her eyes. Their cat, Fox, sat on her chest and pawed at her face as he did every morning. John lay sleeping beside her. For a moment, everything felt normal. The alarm clock on the night table said 6:43 AM. She pushed the cat off her chest and rolled over. Then she realized she didn't remember going to bed and sat up in a panic.

"John. Wake up." She shook him.

He opened his eyes. "What?"

"Last night. I remember nothing after we saw that light."

John was silent for a moment. "Me either."

Fear in her voice, she said, "You're still in your clothes." She looked down at herself. "So am I."

Carolyn climbed out of bed and went to their en suite bathroom. When she checked herself in the mirror, she thought she appeared tired but otherwise okay. She twisted her long hair up and ran her fingers along her neck and behind her ears. Nothing unusual. She relaxed a little and used the toilet.

As she pulled up her shorts, she noticed a bruise on her upper right thigh. It was about five centimetres in diameter, an ugly red and bluish-purple mixture of colours. She pressed on it with her index finger—a little sore, but okay.

Carolyn washed her hands and put some toothpaste on her toothbrush. She leaned over the sink, which made her queasy, but she managed to brush her teeth.

I'll feel better if I wash up.

She tied her hair back and splashed some water on her face. Her nose ran and she sniffled. A drop of blood splashed down into the sink. Carolyn tensed. She yanked a tissue from the box next to the sink.

With shaky fingers, she pinched her nose. The tissue saturated, and she grabbed another one, switching them out and throwing the used one into the garbage. She grabbed a towel and blotted her face.

Carolyn returned to the bedroom.

John was still lying in bed. When he saw her, he sat up. "Nosebleed?"

She nodded. "Check yourself out in the bathroom." She told him about the bruise.

John went pale but said nothing. He got up and went to the bathroom.

Carolyn ran to the den and scanned the room. Everything seemed normal, except Arnie was asleep on the couch. She woke him up, told him to check himself over, and went to find Steve and Shelly.

They were in the living room on the sofa. Steve lay on the longer piece of the sectional; Shelly lay curled up on the shorter section. Shelly stirred, loose hair spilling over her face and into her eyes.

Carolyn knelt beside Shelly. "Are you okay?"

Shelly opened her eyes. "Yes. What happened last night?"

"I don't know. But we're all present and accounted for."

Steve mumbled something and sat up.

Carolyn rose and went into the kitchen, Steve and Shelly behind her.

"You look rough," Carolyn said to Steve. She wondered if he'd always had so much grey in his hair. She lifted the bottom of her shorts up a little, uncovering the bruise on her right thigh. The sunlight coming in from the kitchen window deepened the colours, making the bruise a stark contrast to her pale skin.

"Shit. You okay, Carolyn?" Steve asked. He glanced over at Shelly.

"I think so," Carolyn replied. "I think my nose has stopped bleeding." She took the tissue away from her face, holding it close in case it dripped again. Nothing happened.

In childhood, she'd suffered from recurring nosebleeds. The

doctor could find no cause for it. When she joined the UFO group to feed her interest in the paranormal, she learned that nosebleeds with no physical cause were a sign of alien abduction. She hadn't had one of her nosebleeds since moving to Newmarket five years earlier.

Arnie walked into the room. "I found a bruise on my hip. It's covered by my shorts."

Steve and Shelly exchanged glances and left the room.

Carolyn turned to Arnie. "Doesn't that freak you out?"

He shook his head. "I'm used to it."

Carolyn ground beans for coffee, but found it difficult to focus on what she was doing. She turned on the coffee maker as John walked into the room.

"No marks on me," John said.

Steve and Shelly walked into the kitchen as John finished speaking.

Steve said, "Just Carolyn and Arnie, then. That makes sense, doesn't it? You two are the ones with a history."

"Arnie is," Carolyn replied.

"You know you are too, Carr," Arnie said.

"I've seen one, Arnie. I have no recollection of being abducted." Carolyn went to the fridge to get the things they'd need for breakfast, and for a while, everything felt normal as they prepared eggs, toast, and sausages. While they ate, they chatted about the previous night, Arnie exuberant about what they might have caught on film.

Carolyn's appetite diminished when she thought about the possibility of having been abducted by aliens. She shoved congealing eggs around on her plate and nibbled at a piece of toast. She looked across the table at John. He was busy eating and didn't notice her staring.

His hair is getting a little long. I should remind him to make a haircut appointment.

She dropped her fork and stood, picking up her plate and reaching for Shelly's.

"Are you done, Shell?" she asked.

"Yes," Shelly replied, her voice a whisper. "Thanks."

Carolyn stacked some dishes and took them to the kitchen. She could hear the others stirring and getting up. Shelly walked over, carrying a stack of dishes, and set them in the sink. They worked in silence. Carolyn gazed out into the backyard while she rinsed. The plants in her garden drooped towards the ground. Patches of yellow dotted the lawn. No rain in the forecast and the town bylaw demanded she only water her plants on even days. She sighed. At least she'd do the flowers before they died. Something in the grass caught her eye. At first, she thought it was a small, brown animal lying there.

"Shelly, look over there."

"Where?"

Carolyn waved her hand towards the back of the yard. "There. Three indents in the grass."

Shelly peered out the window, craning her neck and squinting her eyes.

"I see them," Shelly said. She turned away from the window and hurried to the living room.

Carolyn added the last few dishes to the dishwasher and followed Shelly. The guys were setting up the camera. Shelly told them about the marks in the grass.

"Can you get your camera, John?" Carolyn said. "It's better than mine."

John nodded and headed for the stairs.

Arnie paused long enough to get his Geiger counter and tape measure from his equipment bag. Grabbing a pen and paper from the kitchen counter, Carolyn went outside and walked in her bare feet across the dew-damp grass. Shelly, Steve, and Arnie followed. They stopped when they reached the first depression.

The three round holes in front of them reminded Carolyn of photos of UFO evidence she'd seen from Rendlesham Forest in England. The encounter involved military personnel and had been nicknamed "The UK's Roswell."

UFOlogists insisted it was a legitimate, verifiable sighting, while debunkers insisted it was an optical illusion from a lighthouse, and that the depressions in the ground were nothing more than rabbit scrapes.

"We should get some plaster casts before they're destroyed and people try to tell us they're rabbit scrapes. If we can prove once and for all aliens are visiting our planet, we can stop focusing on finding proof and deal with the implications of extraterrestrial contact, like we should already be doing," Arnie said.

He bent down to one circle and measured it. "It's twenty-five point four centimetres in diameter."

Carolyn recorded it. Arnie went to the next hole and measured it, then the last one. All the holes were twenty-five point four centimetres. Arnie and Steve measured the distance between the holes. Each length was three metres.

Arnie snapped the tape measure closed and grabbed his Geiger counter.

"Let's see if it's giving off any radiation."

At the mention of radiation, everyone took a step back. The Geiger counter sputtered at them in response. Arnie checked the reading.

"It's not lethal, but it's higher than normal."

The back screen door banged open. John stepped outside and walked towards them, holding his video camera and snapping pictures as he approached. He moved next to Arnie, who bent down and stretched the tape measure over the hole at their feet so John could photograph it.

While John continued to snap pictures, Carolyn walked closer to the trees. She noticed some damage to two trees at the edge of the yard and went to the nearest one.

The forest covering the back acre of their property consisted of mostly maples, beech trees, some birch trees, and a variety of evergreen trees. She found scorch marks on two birch trees.

"John," she called out, "come here and look at this."

John moved to Carolyn's side and examined the trees.

"It's like they've been burned," he said and snapped a few pictures.

"Do you have enough photos?" Carolyn asked.

"I think so."

"Let's go see what's on Arnie's camera," Carolyn said, raising her voice so everyone in the group could hear her.

Nodding acknowledgement, Shelly turned and headed towards the house. Steve, crouched in front of one of the holes in the dirt, stood and followed Shelly. Arnie caught up to Steve. When John started after them, Carolyn grabbed his arm.

"Wait."

John stared at her, puzzled. "What?"

"If there's footage of an alien craft, we have to be careful whom we share it with. You've got to help me convince Arnie not to splatter it all over the Internet. He's going to cause trouble for all of us, especially for himself. Okay? Promise me?"

"Let's see what's on there first before we get hysterical about it."

When she opened her mouth to protest, he held up his hand, forestalling her. "I'm not saying you're wrong. Let's just see what's on it."

Carolyn frowned. "Maybe there's nothing but static anyway," she said without conviction.

They walked into the house together.

CHAPTER 10

When Carolyn and John reached the living room, they found Arnie fiddling with the camera. Carolyn's stomach twisted into an anxious knot. In all the years they'd been hunting UFOs, they'd never found anything concrete. Arnie had stories, but he'd only recovered memories after using a hypnotist.

The hypnotist himself had explained that forensic hypnosis was unreliable at best, and there was no way to verify if the memories were false, imagined, or real. To Arnie, they were real, but there was no proof.

Carolyn had also had some UFO sightings. The most remarkable one was the craft she'd seen hovering over the elementary school her daughter, Sam, had attended in Bradford.

It was six summers ago, and Carolyn had gone for a walk after dinner. The evening was warm, and she walked for about an hour before turning around and heading home down a street that ended at the schoolyard.

When she approached the deserted school, she spotted a huge, metallic craft hovering over the soccer field. She continued her approach, expecting it to disappear like a mirage. Windows covered the outer rim. She looked around for other witnesses and found none.

There wasn't one single soul walking down the street, driving down the road, or out in the yards of the surrounding homes. On a beautiful summer evening, the neighbourhood looked like a ghost town. She considered knocking on doors to get someone to come out and verify it for her, but feared they wouldn't see it, and she'd only get confirmation she was losing her mind. Then she thought of her cell phone. She could get a picture of it, at least.

Carolyn reached down to her hip when she remembered she'd left it at home. She considered walking underneath the craft, though immediately all the science fiction movies and television shows she'd ever seen of aliens using humans for food ran through her head, and she changed her mind.

She decided to run home and get her camera. If it was still there when she returned, she'd get pictures, which would prove to everyone, including herself, that it was real. If it was gone, she wouldn't have proof, but she'd be here to talk about it.

After that, her recollection became hazy. She remembered running down the street, but she didn't remember walking into the house. Her next memory was of folding laundry in her laundry room.

She could never explain why she hadn't returned and couldn't remember what she'd done, or what she was thinking, when she got home. When she told the story to Arnie, he asked her about missing time, a common occurrence with UFO abductions.

Carolyn couldn't tell him. She hadn't checked the time and had noticed no anomalies. She couldn't even tell him if the sun was still setting or completely down by the time she arrived home.

Though he'd bugged her to get hypnosis, she'd refused. She feared the memories would be terrifying. Arnie's retrieved memories included an invasive physical examination by alien beings that made him feel angry and violated. Carolyn recoiled at the prospect of exploring that possibility.

The sound of the television dragged Carolyn back to the present. Arnie started the video. The frame wobbled. That must've been when Arnie was adjusting the tripod. There was sound, and they heard Arnie giving his tech talk, explaining how the camera and scope worked, and what they were looking at. Carolyn's voice chimed in, asking someone to open the patio door. For a time, the sky was light, though the powerful scope was able to pick up stars far up in the sky and display them on the screen.

Carolyn realized she was standing and sat beside Shelly. She kicked off her slippers and pulled her knees up under her chin. She shivered. On the screen, a "satellite" moved steadily while Arnie tracked it. Carolyn cringed inwardly at the sound of her voice.

She checked the clock, trying to remember how long it would be until the strange lights should appear on the screen. She shivered again, stood up, and went to get her shawl.

When she returned, she found the others staring open mouthed at the TV screen, where a white ball made its way slowly across the picture. Carolyn stood behind John and put her hands on his shoulders.

"Your hands are freezing," he said when she touched him.

"Sorry," she whispered and removed them. She watched, barely breathing, while she relived what she remembered from the night before: the appearance of the white ball, Arnie using his laser pointer to attract it, her fear when she realized they were coming for her, and the refusal of the others to go inside. When the light had disappeared, she'd hoped they'd left, but she'd been wrong.

Shelly's voice piped up on the video. "What's that? Look over there."

Arnie's voice answered her. "I see it. Over by the trees."

Her own voice: "The power is out. What's that vibration? Do you feel it?" She sounded like she was shouting. She couldn't recall experiencing any of it.

The picture on the television grew fuzzy. The voices continued. They heard John's voice say, "I can't move. I feel so heavy."

Shelly's voice, fearful, trembling: "It's above us."

The image on the television showed nothing, just bright light getting brighter, and a fuzzy picture. The audio crackled. Then something dark moved across the frame, something unrecognizable, because it was so close to the camera lens. Darkness filled the screen, blotting out the light. The dark blob morphed into the shadow of a man's body as the distance between the camera and the body increased. Carolyn recognized Arnie's silhouette.

Her mouth went dry. She tried to swallow, but found it difficult. Her gut knotted up again. She had a flash of memory, of being lifted, floating up.

"Arnie. It's got Arnie." Shelly was screaming. "I can't move."

Then Steve shouted, "Carolyn."

Carolyn watched in horrified fascination when another dark blob on the screen morphed into her own silhouette. The voices stopped as if cut off. A white flare filled the screen and then burst apart. The sky returned. Stars sparkled overhead. Everything was silent except for the crickets.

Then, Steve's voice: "I'm going to lie down."

"Good idea." Shelly. "I'll go with you."

John, calm, casual: "They'll be okay. We have to go to bed. They'll be here when we wake up."

The patio door gave a whispered swoosh as it opened, followed by the sound of footsteps walking near the camera. Then another swoosh and a click indicated the patio door was closed.

The group in the room watched in silence, and the video quietly played on.

"I don't know what to think," Steve said. "Does anyone remember any of that? It didn't jog my memory at all."

"At least the camera kept rolling," Arnie said. "Even batteries have been known to go dead at times like this. I wonder why they didn't."

"Maybe the craft wasn't close enough," John speculated.

"You guys didn't seem too perturbed we were gone," Arnie said.

"Nothing personal," John replied.

"Smartass."

Steve said, "If I could remember anything, I'd be able to explain that. One minute, it sounds like we're freaking out, and the next, we're calmly going off to bed. I'd say there was some kind of influence there."

"Perhaps the camera caught something when Arnie and I came back," Carolyn suggested.

They continued to watch, but the scene didn't change.

"Arnie," Carolyn said, a realization dawning, "you agreed not to use the laser pointer, and yet you did."

"I'm sorry. I did it without thinking. When those lights appeared, I wanted to see if they'd be attracted to it. There were no planes around. There was no issue with using the pointer."

"I know. But you broke the only concession you'd been willing to make," Carolyn insisted. "I'm glad nothing happened, and we know the problem wasn't with the pointer. It's with the video. Now we need to decide what we're going to do with it."

"I want to post it to the group," Arnie said.

"I knew you'd say that." Carolyn immediately jumped on it. "That's not a good idea."

She was so tired of arguing with Arnie. Why was it always her against him? He'd do something reckless, she'd try to stop him, and he'd go ahead anyway, even if it caused problems for all of them. Yet no one else got into the argument. She supposed they didn't want to take sides, but she wished that, just once, one of them would.

"Do me a favour," she said. "Don't post it until we all agree what to do with it. I know it's your video; I know it's your UFO group. But it's our lives."

"We don't have to say who's on the video or where we filmed it. But people need to know the truth," Arnie argued.

"What about what Ralph says about government threats?" Carolyn was determined to hold firm.

"You don't believe Ralph. You never have. Why are you using him as an excuse now? Because it's convenient?" Arnie asked. "That's how you're going to justify suppressing it? The government doesn't care what we do. Most home videos on the Internet get ignored. But it should be shared. We know people who'd want to see this."

"I don't mind showing it to legitimate UFO investigators. That doesn't mean you should post it online. Please keep it under wraps for now? Until we figure out what we want to do?" Surely, he'd be reasonable now.

"I'll consider it." Arnie frowned.

"How long has the video been running?" Steve interrupted.

Arnie checked the camera. "Over an hour. It looks like it ran for seven hours. We should see Brent and get him to hypnotize us."

An expert hypnotherapist, Brent Morgan worked with several UFO experiencers. Arnie and Carolyn consulted him frequently, and both trusted him. Carolyn had known him for a few years now, the expert she turned to whenever she had questions about hypnosis. She also referred clients to him when she thought they'd benefit from his services. She liked his professional attitude and his kind nature.

"I'll agree to that," said Carolyn. "We need to go before too much time passes."

Arnie took out his phone and went into the other room. Carolyn heard him talk, but not what he said. She gazed back at the television screen though there was nothing to see but stars. Occasionally, a plane flew across the frame or a bird passed overhead. They saw one shooting star and two small lights most people would call satellites, but Ralph would insist were alien spacecraft.

Carolyn felt trickling in her nose and sniffled. She put her hand to her face, and blood seeped through her fingers. She jumped up, grabbed a tissue, and went into the kitchen just as Arnie hung up the phone.

"What did Brent say?" Carolyn asked, her voice nasally. She went to the sink and washed her hands, one at a time, while she squeezed her nose shut using the tissue. Some blood trickled down her throat, making her nauseated.

"He'll see us this afternoon," Arnie replied. He stared at her, but didn't comment on her nosebleed. "I'm surprised you're agreeing to this. I thought you were against regression hypnosis."

"It has its place."

"Come and take a look at this," Steve shouted.

They hurried back into the living room.

On the screen, a greenish glow infused the entire frame. There were no stars. A background hum vibrated from the speakers. This lasted for ten minutes. Then, as if a switch had flipped, the light winked out, the noise disappeared, and the stars and sky returned. All was quiet, except for the natural sounds from the yard.

"That was probably us returning," Carolyn said. "What time was that?"

Arnie checked the camera. "2:53 AM."

"Look," Steve said.

Three red dots appeared. They converged, forming a triangle. Five other red lights appeared, encircling the three. Then the five lights shot away in different directions. The three remaining lights hovered in triangular formation. Then, one by one, they disappeared. They didn't fly away, but simply vanished from sight.

"There are still hours of footage left, but I suspect we've seen everything. Carolyn and I should leave to see Brent soon. Are you coming, John?" Arnie asked.

"Yes," John replied. "What about you two?" John looked over at Steve and Shelly.

"We have to go home. I'm dying for a shower," said Shelly. "We'll catch up to you later."

Steve and Shelly stood up to leave.

"Well, thanks for an interesting evening. I don't think I'll ever remember it," said Shelly.

When Steve and Shelly were gone, Carolyn turned to John and Arnie. "Okay with you guys if I use the shower first?"

When both men agreed, Carolyn headed up the stairs. She hoped a shower would help calm her nerves. She was terrified of what the hypnosis session would pull out of her unconscious mind.

CHAPTER 11

Michael left his house before Jess woke up and arrived at the office by eight. He'd spared himself the guilt of having her watch him dress and leave on a Saturday morning, but he hadn't been able to spare himself the guilt of leaving.

So far, it had been a fruitful morning. Michael had trolled through the video and audio files from the Fairchild residence. Most of the group's conversations were banal chitchat though he found Carolyn's premonition interesting. And he'd been taken aback when she said she'd been unable to conceive after she'd had her daughter. It'd given him another stab of guilt, and he'd chalked that up to guilt by association. Either the Agency or the aliens were responsible.

He'd finally located the recording he'd come to the office to see: Carolyn and Arnie returning to the house after their abduction. It was a short clip, but mind bending. When Carolyn, the first to return, floated into her bedroom, the camera activated, and he watched while she drifted into her bed.

At that point, he made a mental note to check his bedroom for surveillance cameras. Though the purpose of the cameras in the Fairchild home was to pick up footage such as the one he was currently viewing, there would also be footage in the archives of Carolyn and John having sex. Nothing was sacred to the Agency, and considering how things had been going, it wouldn't surprise him to learn they were watching him just as closely.

He moved on to the next file and watched Arnie drift to the

couch in the den. Neither clip caught the abductee coming through the ceiling. That would've been an amazing sight, but the cameras weren't angled to capture anything on the ceiling.

Both clips ended when the abductee set down. When motion ceased, the recording played for thirty seconds more, and then the camera shut down.

Michael turned his attention back to the files he'd stolen from the evidence room. He'd saved them to a memory stick so he could carry them with him. He didn't want to leave them lying around the office in case Torque snooped around.

Indicators he'd set on his desk would tell Michael if anyone had rummaged through it. So far, there was nothing to suggest anyone had violated his privacy. He also regularly checked to see if any suspicious processes were running on his computer. Again, things seemed to be okay. No one was monitoring what he was doing on his computer.

He'd taken similar precautions at his home office. He felt some empathy for Ralph Drummond. Paranoia was time consuming.

His current focus was trying to find anything to tell him why the Rudolphs and Fairchilds were on the list of those who must be silenced. Neither couple was especially vocal or public about their UFO activities. In Carolyn's case, she was actively discouraging it. Why would the Agency want to kidnap someone who sought to keep what little she knew under wraps? It made no sense.

He dug into his briefcase and removed the folders he'd scooped from the evidence room. Whoever had stolen this for Ralph knew exactly what to take. He leafed through it, pausing to read anything that related to himself, Torque, or Cornell. To his relief, there was only minimal information about himself—not much more than a vague description and a reference to his former position when he'd lived in Nevada.

Michael opened the next folder. This looked like it might have something. Reports, describing in detail the results of tests performed on the abductees by the Agency. He scanned for anything on Carolyn, Ralph, and Arnie. Most of the reports centred on Carolyn.

He read with some horror about the tests they'd performed when she was both conscious and unconscious. After each session, they erased her memories of the tests. The tests focused around her psychic abilities. Each round tested a different function.

They seemed particularly interested in her ability to remote view. She could not only accurately view things in a specified location within the same building, but also anywhere on earth, provided she had something on which to focus. Her accuracy was astounding. The two most involved in leading the experiments were Cornell and Torque.

This explained why they wanted her. It could also explain why they'd want John out of the way. Michael blanched and went cold. How could he go along with this? It wasn't only that the aliens wanted to experiment on these people. The Agency did too, and from the look of it, they wanted to use the people with the greatest abilities as weapons.

It reminded him of the MKUltra experiments the U.S. government had conducted on unsuspecting people from the 1950s to the 1970s. They'd experimented with mind control, using drugs, torture, and other means to manipulate their subjects. It also brought to mind the experiments in remote viewing done by the Stanford Research Institute and the CIA's Stargate Project in the 1970s.

Where would he be himself if he'd never been approached to join the Agency? Would he have believed the conspiracy theories, ending up on the receiving end of a death ray?

What if, like Ralph, he'd found out the Agency was accelerating the destruction of life on earth? Would he have acted to intervene? Should he intervene now, or just continue to save himself and his wife and count himself lucky to be among the chosen ones?

They had told him, when he first joined the Agency, it existed to ensure American interests were protected in any dealings with extraterrestrials. The first offer they'd made him was for a job at Area 51, in Nevada, at Groom Lake.

When he accepted, they told him about the existing treaty between extraterrestrials and the United States government, though they didn't tell him the details of the treaty. The Eisenhower Administration had made the original agreement. It had been upheld by every administration since, and other countries, including Canada, had jumped in.

The president himself was kept completely ignorant of it through each administrative change. Conspiracy theorists were fed enough disinformation to make them believe there was something being kept from them while at the same time making them appear crazy for having that belief.

Michael placed the folders back in his briefcase and closed the files on his computer. After placing the memory stick back in his pocket, he checked the time. Eleven o'clock. If he hurried, he could go home before Jess got too mad at him. He shut down his computer. When he stood to leave, the door opened.

Torque stepped into the room. "What are you doing, Mick?"

Michael stopped himself from glancing at his briefcase. He kept his eyes focused on Torque's and his expression neutral.

Torque closed the door behind him. "You might as well tell me. I know what you were up to last night."

CHAPTER 12

Michael sat down, leaned back in his chair, and draped an arm over each armrest. "I came in to review the surveillance footage from the Fairchild house. Is that a problem?"

Torque moved to the chair across from Michael's desk and leaned back, ankles crossed. Playing it cool, Michael supposed. He waited for Torque to break the silence.

"It depends. You shouldn't have been there in the first place. What happened that made you want to snoop around in here on a Saturday morning when your wife is already pissed at you? What's so important that it couldn't wait until Monday?"

"I needed the peace and quiet."

"I've never known you to complain about Jess being too loud. What are you doing here, Mick? The truth."

"You want to know? I can't face Jess. Something's up with her and it's making things at home unbearable." He exaggerated the situation, but not by much. Things were tense between him and Jess. He would play that up, and hopefully, Torque would believe he was hiding from his domestic problems at the office.

"You're lucky it's me Cornell has asked to monitor you. I'm willing to cut you some slack because I know you've been distracted by whatever's going on between you and Jess. But don't you think you ought to man up and talk to her about it? Get a fucking hobby if you want to be away from home. Don't throw yourself into stuff that doesn't concern you."

Michael rose. "Sure. I was just going to leave when you walked in. I found nothing in the surveillance footage anyway. Carolyn and Arnie were abducted, as scheduled, and returned, as scheduled. Nothing unusual happened. But that's what makes me wonder why they suddenly need to be silenced. There's nothing new here. Nothing suspicious."

Torque stood and walked around Michael's desk. The computer had already powered down. Torque stared at Michael, suspicion in his eyes, but some relief too.

Michael met his gaze. "I told you," he said, "I was just leaving." Torque stepped aside.

Michael grabbed his briefcase and walked to the door. He turned back to face Torque.

"Root around my office all you want. I've got nothing to hide."

Torque's face remained neutral though his eyes might have flickered.

Michael left the office without a backward glance. He wasn't worried. Everything he had to hide was on him.

***

Just before one-thirty, Michael arrived home. He went into the house and called to Jessica. Silence greeted him. He checked the kitchen. She wasn't there. Her car was in the driveway. She couldn't be far.

"Jess?"

He moved on to the living room when there was still no response. Fear streaked through him. He reached under his jacket, pulled out his gun, and cocked it. He made his way up the stairs, gaze darting around, watching for an ambush. At the top of the stairs, he stopped and listened. He thought he heard a sound from the bedroom.

The bedroom door yawned open. Michael crept up to it and listened. It sounded like someone was retching in the en suite bathroom.

She's sick. That's all it is.

He exhaled loudly, relieved. Still, he scanned the room before entering, and continued to hold his gun up and ready. After verifying the room was empty, he made his way to the bathroom.

She was there, hunched over the toilet, wiping her lips with a tissue. He slipped his gun back into its holster as she turned to face

62

him. She spoke before he could say anything.

"Where have you been?"

"I had to go to the office." The old standby. But it always came out sounding like "I needed to get the fuck away from you."

Her eyes showed their disappointment.

"I'm back now." It was such a useless thing to say. He hated himself for saying it. What he wanted to do was hug her, but he feared she'd push him away.

"I'm sorry you're not feeling well." That was better.

She acknowledged it with a nod.

He considered what he needed to do.

"Why don't I help you set up outside on the lounge chair? You can relax, read a book. I'll bring you whatever you need."

She continued to stare at him, wary.

Michael kept talking, distracting her. He put his arm around her and guided her out of the bedroom.

"Don't worry about anything. I'll take care of lunch. You relax. I've got some work to do, but I can do it here."

He had to get her out of the house, and he had to make it look natural.

"The sunshine and fresh air will be good for you." He wondered then why she'd said nothing. "Jess? Are you okay?"

To his horror, she burst into tears.

"No. I'm not okay."

"What's wrong?" He couldn't get into it. Not now. He needed to get her out of the house. He wanted to check the place for bugs, for cameras, but he couldn't let her see him do it.

"You're what's wrong." There was pain in her eyes, and he knew the same pain was reflected in his own. It hurt because it was true.

"Come outside. You should get some air." He doubted there'd be listening devices out there.

Get out of the house, damn it. It was all he could do not to give her a shove. He took a breath. She wasn't feeling well. He had to calm down.

They made their way down the stairs and to the back of the house on the main floor, then out to the patio. He closed the sliding doors behind them, knowing it would shut off anything in the house that was motion activated.

He walked her to the lounge chair under the gazebo next to the pool. The filter was running, the sound reassuring. It would help to mask what they said even if there was a bug out here.

"Sit, Jess. I'll get you some water."

"Michael." There was a sound of desperation in her voice.

He did hug her then, and her body felt good against his. He stroked her hair.

"I just have some things I need to do inside, and then we'll talk. It'll be okay." He tried to believe it so that she'd believe it.

She relaxed against him and sighed. It sounded like relief.

He kissed the top of her head.

She looked up at him.

He brushed the tears from her face.

"Come on. Sit."

She looked a little green, like she might throw up again. He hoped it wasn't food poisoning. She let him seat her on the lounge chair.

When she was settled, he went back into the house and got her some water and the book she'd been reading. She didn't protest when he suggested he make her tea and put food together for her. He went inside, closed the doors, and shut the drapes.

Michael began in their bedroom, the memory of Carolyn floating into her bed motivating him. It took him two hours to go through the whole place while at the same time making Jess tea and something to eat so she wouldn't be compelled to come inside. He found nothing.

Done, he went into his closet and pulled out their bug-out bags—bags he'd prepared for them when they first moved to Canada. These packs would allow them to leave at a moment's notice, and they could survive anywhere, provided the environment wasn't toxic.

He hid the files and the memory stick in a safe in the bedroom closet. The map to the alien base in Algonquin Park he put into his bag.

Satisfied that the house wasn't under surveillance and that his secrets were safe, he went outside again to face Jess. It was time to have that talk he'd been putting off.

She was asleep, the book lying open on her lap.

He set the book on the table next to her, gently kissed her lips, and returned to the house.

CHAPTER 13

Carolyn tried to relax. She'd never been hypnotized before and feared nothing would happen. She sat in a reclining leather chair, a shawl over her shoulders to ward off the chill of the air conditioner. John sat on a couch opposite her. Arnie waited in the room outside, and wouldn't be influenced by anything Carolyn might say. Brent Morgan, the hypnotherapist, sat on a chair next to her. A digital recorder and box of tissues sat on the table beside him. Carolyn wondered if he expected her to cry.

Brent had a way of disarming and charming people, making them comfortable and secure. If anyone could make her unselfconscious enough to cry, he could. He was easy on the eyes, too, dark and handsome, but without Arnie's in-your-face sexuality.

What she liked most about him, however, was his integrity and compassion. She'd seen him a few times when she'd been having difficulty coping and confided intimate details to him she hadn't even told her husband in over eighteen years of marriage.

Brent smiled. "Do you have any questions before we begin?"

Carolyn considered and shook her head.

"All right. Let's begin. Keep your eyes open and get comfortable."

Carolyn gazed ahead and tried to relax.

"Take a deep breath. Breathe slow and deep ..." He led her through the induction.

Her eyes drifted shut. She eased into the chair, comfortable and warm. There was a whir when the air conditioner kicked in and cool air wafted through the room. The shawl around her shoulders was a warm hug.

" … Now, we're going to go back in time, to your last birthday. Can you recall your last birthday?"

"Yes."

"How old are you?"

"Thirty-nine."

Brent asked her some more questions about her day and then asked her to talk about what happened after her workday was done. Carolyn described for him her happiness at going out for a birthday dinner with John. She smiled, reliving it.

"Okay, good. Now, I'd like to move forward in time a little. We're going to go to last night. It's around six o'clock. Tell me where you are."

"I'm in the kitchen, standing in front of the oven."

"What are you doing?"

She told him about making pizza, Arnie's arrival, and how that triggered a vision that made her fearful of setting up the camera for the sky watch. Her voice rose in pitch, and her stomach churned. Her hands curled into fists, swatted the air in front of her, and then wrapped around her elbows. She hugged herself, and her body shook.

"You're okay. Just observe. Do you set up the equipment?"

"Yes. I don't like it, but they all want to, so I stop arguing. I don't know what the bad thing will be, so I can't argue. They won't listen. They never listen."

"Okay, Carolyn. We'll leave that for now. Let's skip ahead, to later in the evening. It's around midnight. Where are you?"

"Sitting outside. We're on the balcony."

She recounted seeing the lights, her fear that something was coming, and her nervous relief when the lights disappeared. She giggled, reliving the moment, then frowned.

"What happens next?" Brent prodded.

"There's something at the back of the yard. Right there." Her arm rose, her hand pointing at an object only she could see. "I can't make it out." She dropped her arm.

"How do you feel?" Brent asked.

"Scared. I can't move." She recalled being frozen in place and watching Arnie float away. She clenched her jaw, gritting her teeth. Her hands fisted, nails digging into her palms.

"Go on."

"Arnie's disappeared, and I'm lifting off the ground." Her voice softened, and she gave a slight sigh. Relaxed, her hands unclenched, resting open on her thighs. It was okay. *Nothing to worry about.*

"How are you feeling?" Brent asked.

"Peaceful. I get the message I'll be okay. I don't want to fight."

Over on the couch, John stirred.

"What do you see?"

"A bright light. I'm floating in it. I see darkness in the centre of the light, and I'm moving towards it."

"What happens when you get to the top?"

"I'm moving into a tunnel. I pass out. When I wake up, I'm lying naked on a table. I turn my head and see Arnie unconscious on another table. There's a tube sticking out of his head." Carolyn's hands covered her eyes. She wanted to hide. Her mind rebelled at the sight of the beings standing around the table on which she lay exposed and defenceless.

"I'm scared. Creatures are doing something to Arnie. There's something attached to his leg. Some machine thing presses against my leg." Carolyn screamed when a leathery hand touched her bare flesh. "No, get away. Get the fuck away from me." Her eyes squeezed shut, and tears rolled down her cheeks.

From a distance, she heard Brent's voice, calm, assuring. "It's okay. You're safe. It's like you're watching a movie of what happened. Take a deep breath, Carolyn. You're going to relax and observe. Tell me what you see."

She stopped crying and relaxed. She lowered her hands to her thighs again. It was okay. She could just watch.

"I can't move, and they're doing something inside my nose. It hurts." She grimaced. Her hands twitched, clenched, and unclenched.

"What's happening?" Brent asked.

"I can't lift my arms to stop them. I can only lie here, and they do what they want."

"You're okay. Just relax and observe. Can you tell me what they look like?"

They surrounded her. "Yes."

"Describe them to me."

"There are small grey ones. They have large heads, and they

look like the aliens on the covers of books and in movies. There is another one, bigger. The doctor. He gives the orders. They don't speak aloud. I see people. They look human. They have blond hair, and they're wearing blue uniforms."

"What happens next?"

She sighed and her arms relaxed at her side. "One of them points at me, like he sees that I see them, and suddenly I'm calm, tired. I try not to sleep, but I think I fall asleep. The next thing I know, I'm waking up in bed."

"Okay," Brent said. "I'm going to bring you back now." He paused and continued. "You're relaxed. When you come back, you'll be refreshed, alert—like you've had a lovely nap, and tonight, you'll sleep deeply and well."

He counted her awake. "How do you feel?"

"Good."

"Do you remember everything?" Brent asked.

"Yes," she said. "It all came back to me. I remember how I got the bruise on my thigh, and they stuck something in my nose. Arnie was there, and they did things to him."

"Okay. How do you feel about that?"

"Angry. They have no right to do that."

"We can do more sessions if you like, and see if you can remember other incidents. It'll be easier for you to recall now."

"I'll have to think about it. Is it okay if I stay in here while you talk to Arnie?"

"It's up to Arnie," Brent replied.

Brent went to the waiting room, and called Arnie in. Arnie entered and looked at Carolyn.

"How'd it go?" he asked.

"Good," she said. "Would you be okay with me and John staying and observing your session?"

"Sure. We're all friends here."

Carolyn relinquished the chair to Arnie and went to the couch. She sat close to John and took his hand.

John released her hand and put his arm around her. "Are you sure you want to stay? We can listen to the recording later."

"I'd like to be here for Arnie. It was helpful to have you here," Carolyn said.

Carolyn studied Arnie. He seemed relaxed, unconcerned even. She found it hard to believe he wasn't afraid of what was coming.

She recalled the creatures she'd seen and shuddered. In the past, she'd thought she'd be curious, or amazed, or awed by meeting alien beings, perhaps even humbled by their presence. She hadn't expected the overwhelming surge of rage and hate. Probably she'd doubted they'd victimize her the way they'd done last night.

Brent led Arnie into the hypnosis. Arnie reclined comfortably. His eyes drifted closed, and his hands rested loosely on his thighs. After asking some basic questions about Arnie's past, Brent directed his attention to the events of the previous night.

Carolyn's stomach did a back flip while she listened to Arnie describe setting up the camera on the balcony and turning it on. A rush of heat spread through her body, and her underarms and the back of her neck became moist though the office was cold.

Arnie's description of the beings and the tables was identical to Carolyn's. He described the pressure on his head, verifying her story that there was a tube protruding from it. Everything he said echoed Carolyn's version of events. John's arm around Carolyn tightened. She leaned her head onto his shoulder and put an arm across his chest, hugging him.

Carolyn wanted to leave the room, but she forced herself, for Arnie's sake, to stay and listen. Finally, it was over, and Arnie described waking up on the couch in John and Carolyn's den. Brent's low, quiet voice started the process of bringing Arnie out of the hypnosis.

John's expression was grim. Carolyn couldn't tell if he was more shocked, scared, or worried. Silently, she asked her angels and guides for help.

In front of her, Brent sat back in his chair and shut off the digital recorder. Arnie stretched, now completely awake and alert.

"Thanks, Brent," Arnie said.

"You're welcome. What do you feel about what you remembered?"

"Nothing."

"You were taken aboard a spacecraft against your will. Your friend was forced aboard also, and she suffered trauma. You must have a reaction. What are you experiencing?" Brent asked.

"I used to hate them. I used to want to fight them, to take back my power. But now? I live with it. What matters to me is the government's role in this. The government knows about alien abductions and aren't doing anything to stop them. In fact, they encourage it."

His voice rose, and he leaned forward, hunching up his shoulders. "They pretend they're oblivious because they're a part of it. They're benefiting from it. I don't know how, but they are. We need to expose what's going on. It's not fair that many of us can't sleep in our own beds without thinking we're going to wake up on an alien's operating table, experimented on like some lab animal."

Brent sat back in his chair and crossed his legs. He fiddled with the wedding band on his finger, a habit that triggered when he was trying not to state the obvious.

"What are you feeling, Arnie?"

Arnie smiled and his shoulders relaxed. "Okay. I'm angry and frustrated at the apathy of other people. I'm a monkey in a cage, and no one cares. Well, my friends care, and my family would care if they knew, but I don't want to worry my mother with this."

"Is it possible your mother's also an abductee?"

Arnie started. His expression told Carolyn it was something he'd never considered, even though he knew abductions run in families.

"No," he said, softly. "She can't be. I'd have known."

"Perhaps that's something you might want to broach with her," Brent said. "Or maybe she can tell you if your father had any strange experiences he never shared with you."

"What's the point of that?"

"It'll help you to understand what's happening with your family and to investigate whether they've discovered ways to cope you can use. But mostly, it's because you need to get support from others who've experienced this. Now you and Carolyn share this experience, perhaps you can support each other through the times when this happens."

Arnie considered. "What about getting this out there? Carolyn doesn't want me to post the video. I think we should. The more people know about what's happening, the better." He turned to Carolyn. "It's when victims remain silent that abusers get away with what they do."

Carolyn considered it. "But it's dangerous."

"We have to stick our necks out for something. This is important. We can't just meekly submit. I don't know how else to lodge a protest than to get the proof and put it out there for everyone to see. We have the tools to do it now. People had to suffer in silence before, but not anymore. We can help ourselves by finding others in our situation and getting them on our side."

Carolyn had that sensation again of speeding towards a brick wall on a train.

"Arnie, it'll be bad."

"We'll deal with it together. They can't silence all of us."

"But you don't have any kids to worry about. I do. I don't want that out there. Let's report it to MUFON and then forget about it."

"You should do this to help Sam. What if she's an abductee too?"

"She's not."

"Until yesterday, you insisted you weren't. Sam may have kept it a secret, or she may not remember."

"You mean like your parents? A minute ago, you didn't want to go there. Now you're telling me I should?"

"If my parents were abductees, I'd want to help them by going public and encouraging people to do something about this." He turned to John. "What do you think? Sam is your daughter too."

They all stared at John. He looked only at Carolyn.

"Carr, I think Arnie's right. You don't understand what it's like to be forced to witness this and not be able to do anything about it. The more people we can make aware of this, the more power we have against it."

"Ralph says we're being watched, and they'll come after us if we're not careful."

"Maybe we can get enough people together on this that we can figure out a way to help each other. If many of us say the same thing, they can't continue denying it, and they can't silence all of us. We must create a tipping point."

"Why does it have to be us?"

"It has to start somewhere, why not with us? I can't continue to live like this. Can you? They'll come for you again. Do you want that?"

That stopped her. She thought about going through it again. And again. Would it last a lifetime or did they stop after a while? What if something they did to her had caused her to be infertile? What if they were coming for Sam too? Would Sam be unable to have children too? Somehow, she found herself agreeing.

She nodded her head and said, "Okay."

CHAPTER 14

Monday morning, Michael sat down at his desk and turned on his computer. He picked up the report the receptionist, Helen, had left for him. He skimmed it, barely registering the information—something on the world situation, collated from the other agencies. It looked bad.

He opened his web browser and Drummond's blog loaded. A new posting from Arnie included a video.

Nice going, Arnie. You're going to raise a shitstorm over this, my friend.

Michael was surprised Cornell hadn't called yet and glanced at his phone as if thinking about it would make it ring. He ran the video and watched it in its entirety. It had been condensed down to thirty minutes of footage, showing the lights overhead, the bodies of Arnie and Carolyn sailing up, and the lights returning. What was happening was obvious to anyone familiar with the UFO abduction scenario.

Even more troubling was the transcript from the hypnosis session. Images from physical evidence from the backyard supported their claims. The call to arms to end alien abductions and expose the government's involvement with UFOs ensured Arnie would find himself in the trunk of Torque's car in the next few days.

Michael considered Arnie's position. His life was pretty much over, and he didn't know it. Everyone was expendable, and the closer it got to doomsday, the less concern the Agency bosses had over wiping out or disappearing the troublemakers sooner rather than later. They were all sitting on a powder keg and those asshat UFO nuts were striking matches.

On that cue, Torque tapped on Michael's open door and stepped in, closing the door behind him.

"Cornell wants us to make a couple of house calls. Pay a visit to Arnie and escort him to his new accommodations at the home for wayward UFO experiencers. Also, he wants John silenced. We'll use the TR and make it look like a heart attack."

Michael nodded. The "TR" was the Tesla Ray they'd used on Patty Richards. Physicist Nikola Tesla had created the plans for a death ray, which the FBI confiscated at his death. The American government subsequently developed it into doomsday machines.

The Aurora Project created high-frequency radio transmission dishes around the world, which could affect the weather and otherwise inflict damage and destruction on a large scale, and the Sleep Project developed pocket-sized death rays that could make it appear a person had died of a heart attack or stroke.

Torque continued, "We have to make it look like Arnie committed suicide."

Michael nodded and didn't speak. He wasn't going to argue. He'd expected Arnie was going to pay large for going public.

"Where is he right now?" Michael asked.

"He's at his condo. His mother is there though. We'll have to watch for him to come out."

"What about getting him during the night? We could give his mother a bit of something to keep her asleep and take him out?" Michael suggested.

"That might be an option. Or we might take care of John first. That'd flush out Arnie. He'd want to see Carolyn," Torque replied.

"A small group of people having accidents, incarcerations, heart attacks, and committing suicide looks suspicious, but it'll all be written off as a huge coincidence. It's unbelievable when you consider it," Michael said.

"Let's execute this in an hour." Torque grinned and turned away. "I'll be in my office. I've got some things I need to do before we go out."

Michael returned to his computer, but couldn't focus on anything. He glanced at the clock. Almost fifty minutes. He opened up one of Drummond's files. This one had some interesting notes in it. Drummond's contact had given him information about the alien base in Algonquin.

According to the source, whom Michael had yet to identify by anything other than the code name "Dragonfly," a group of aliens opposed to experimenting on humans had set up a base where they helped people avoid further abductions.

How was that possible, considering the Agency also kept tabs on abductees?

Michael also found evidence that showed Drummond and his family were planning to head to the base. It was too bad for them that Michael and Torque had gotten to Ralph before they could get away. Michael clicked on another file, opened it, and started reading.

When he glanced at the clock again, it was time to head out. He shut down his computer. Michael removed his gun, a 9mm Glock, from his desk and slid it into his shoulder holster. He'd sign out the death ray as they were leaving.

He considered changing, but decided the business attire would be appropriate if they were spotted. They'd be sitting in Torque's car in the plaza next to John's workplace. The building in that plaza was a professional building, and they'd be more conspicuous in jeans and T-shirts.

Michael made his way to Torque's office.

Torque sat at his desk, leaning over his computer, chin on his hand, staring at the screen. He sat up when the door opened.

Michael stepped into the office. "Ready to go?"

"Be right there."

Michael closed the door. "I was thinking about some of the things in those blogs. Maybe silencing these people would martyr them and escalate their cause."

"Did you see the comments after the video went up? And since then, activity on the MUFON site has gone crazy. I swear Griffen has lost his mind. Did he think he could spout off about this stuff without repercussions?"

"Now that you ask, yes, he did. As far as he's concerned, it's a free country."

"Perhaps, but if it continues to escalate, they're going to encourage someone to come to them and give them more information than is good for us."

"You mean Drummond's source?"

Torque stared at him. "Why'd you say that?"

Michael swallowed, realizing he'd let slip something he should have kept to himself. It was hard to think of Torque as someone he couldn't trust. He tried to recover.

"I'm assuming Drummond had some inside information. I read his blog. He talked like he knew things that come close to hitting ETAP."

"Where exactly in his blog did he mention anything about ETAP?"

Michael deflected. "Read between the lines. He alludes to things close to the truth. I'm wondering what else he says that might be correct."

"Where are you going with this, Mick?"

"Do you think there's any truth to what he says about how much of this crisis the government has deliberately created?"

"Of course not, and you'd better be careful whom you talk to about this stuff. If Cornell heard you talking like that, you'd find yourself in the cell next to Arnie."

"We've been partners a long time, right?"

"Yeah."

"I trust you."

"Glad to hear it. I trust you too, partner."

"So if you knew the truth you'd tell me?"

Torque didn't hesitate. "Sure, Mick. Of course."

Michael nodded, but looked away, certain Torque was lying. His stomach felt queasy when he realized Torque had threatened him with a cell next to Arnie rather than with termination—a fate reserved for abductees.

CHAPTER 15

Michael and Torque sat in the parking lot of the office building next to John's workplace in Aurora. John spent a lot of his time in and around the loading dock area at the back of the building. Michael waited and watched. He wanted to time it so John would be lifting something heavy when hit with the death ray.

"What do you want to do for lunch?" Torque asked.

"Chinese food?" Michael suggested.

"We just had that on Friday. How about Thai?"

"I'm not in the mood. How about Italian? That Italian place here in town serves the best veal sandwiches."

"I could do that," Torque replied. "How's it looking? Any activity?"

"It's busy. I want to make sure there aren't too many others around. Wouldn't want to make a mistake," Michael replied. "Gotta hit the target."

Torque nodded. "That'd be a major screw up, my friend. Take your time."

Michael settled back in his seat. The day was sweltering again, and he was glad they could keep the windows rolled up and the air conditioning on. They'd have to be careful though. The town had a law against idling, and if they were tagged here for it, they'd have to call off the hit and think of another plan. Torque kept an eye on the surrounding area in case a police cruiser came into view.

John stepped out of the open loading bay doors and glanced towards the road, probably looking for an overdue truck. Michael's hand twitched. He waited. If there were a truck about to pull in, then perhaps there'd be an opportunity. Most unloading would be done with fork trucks, but if he were lucky, John would have to do some heavy lifting.

Michael took a deep breath and ran his hand through his hair. This time, Torque wasn't oblivious. He grinned at Michael. "It's a wonder you're not bald."

"Very funny, wise guy. It's a habit."

Torque snickered.

They continued to wait. Minutes later, a transport truck pulled into the loading dock. John waved the driver into the berth. Michael continued to watch and wait.

How would Carolyn handle the death of her husband? Best not to think about that. Michael was in no position to second-guess orders right now. But it bothered him that he hadn't found anything to justify eliminating John other than to clear the way for kidnapping his wife.

Michael reminded himself that the ones who died before the shitstorm hit were the lucky ones. It wasn't going to be long before those in on it would head to the underground facilities the government had been working on for the last few decades. Most of those left topside would perish.

He was relieved to be one of the chosen few but didn't have any illusions about why that was so. It was only because he was a scientist, survivalist, and, most of all, a trained killer. His skills would be in great demand when the world turned upside down.

John, his back to them, bent down to lift a box sitting at his feet. Michael aimed the ray, removed the catch, and waited, staring at John. The TR suddenly weighed heavy in Michael's hand. John's only crime was that he'd married a super psychic the Agency wanted to get their hands on.

"What are you waiting for?" Torque said. "You'll never have a better shot."

"What did he do?" Michael asked.

"What do you mean?"

"I mean, what did he do that makes it necessary to kill him?"

"I don't know. I don't need to know. Cornell said to do it, so we're doing it. You're going to lose your chance. He's getting up. Press the fucking button."

John stood, the box in his arms. Michael continued to stare at him, vacillating. He heard Torque swear. Torque's hands covered Michael's, forced his finger down, and triggered the ray. Four seconds later, John collapsed, the box pitching forward to the ground while John went down in a heap behind it.

Torque dropped his hands. Michael released and locked the button and lowered the TR. He turned to Torque and waited for him to say something. Torque's face was red fury. He popped open the glove box.

"Put it in there."

Michael set the weapon inside, and Torque locked it up. He shoved the car into drive and pulled away. They drove in silence out of the parking lot.

When they were clear of the area, Torque said, "You fucked up, Mick. What the hell was that?"

Michael steadied himself. He had to speak convincingly—make Torque believe he was okay with what just happened. "I wanted to know why we had to eliminate him. It didn't make sense, Torque. I was going to do it. I just wanted a reason."

"When the fuck did you turn into Mother Teresa? Listen to me carefully, amigo. I won't tell Cornell how badly you just screwed up. Any more hesitating, though, and you're done. I won't cover for you again. I've never seen you like this before. What the fuck happened back there?"

"We're neutralizing a lot of people. Don't you think I'm entitled to know why?"

"No, you're not. You know you're not. You've been fucking *programmed* not to question orders."

Michael didn't reply, and they drove in silence to the restaurant.

CHAPTER 16

Two veal sandwiches plus an hour-and-a-half later, they were back in Toronto. Torque pulled up in front of their building. "I've got an appointment, Mick, so I'm dropping you here. You go ahead and report to Cornell. Tell him everything went as planned, and I'll back you up. This time. Tell him I'll catch up to him later. I shouldn't be too long."

"Where are you going?"

"I'm following up on a suspect for Cornell."

As Torque expected, Michael didn't ask for details, but stepped out of the car and slammed the door. He started to walk away, but turned back.

Torque lowered the window.

"The TR is in the glove box."

"It's okay. I'll sign it in for you when I get back."

Michael waved acknowledgement and headed into the building.

Torque pulled into traffic, headed down the street a few blocks, and then turned the corner to pull up to a doughnut shop on the main floor of an office building. He found a parking spot not too far from his destination and went inside.

She was already there, sipping a tea and trying to read a book. Torque thought she looked lovely. Sometimes he envied Michael Valiant his wife, and as he approached Jess, he drank in her loveliness—long brown hair, deep blue eyes, though she hid those behind glasses. Some would've called her plain, because she dressed in drab colours, but Torque had always appreciated the beauty of her face, especially her eyes and the shape of her lips. He thought there was nothing plain about her face.

When he stepped in the door, she waved to him, confirming she hadn't been concentrating on the book. Torque waved back. As he reached her table, he said, "Hi Jess. Thanks for meeting me."

"I was surprised to hear from you, Gerry. In all the time you've been Michael's partner, you've never asked to talk to me. I hope it's nothing serious. Why don't you grab yourself a coffee and tell me what's going on?"

"I don't want to worry you, Jess, but I do want to talk to you a little and see how things are going with you two. Putting my nose in your business a bit, but he's my partner. Do you want anything while I'm up there?"

"No, thanks. I'm still enjoying my tea. I sat down about a minute before you got here, so I'm okay."

Torque smiled and nodded. He walked to the counter. It was busy, and he found himself standing in line behind five other people. While he waited, he glanced back at Jessica, who had returned to staring at her book. He hoped what he found out from her today would help him draw Michael back into the fold.

He was afraid they were losing him. After what had happened earlier with John, Torque was glad he'd set up this meeting. Perhaps after talking to Jess, he could figure out a way to regain Michael's trust and return things to the way they were.

The red-faced, muddy-haired boy-man behind the counter brought Torque out of his head. "Can I help you, sir?"

Torque stepped forward and asked for a black coffee. He took the coffee and carried it over to Jessie's table.

"How's the book?" he asked, sitting down across from her.

"It's okay. Let's get to the point, Gerry. What's going on?"

"Okay. I'm worried about Michael. He seems distracted lately, unfocused. Please don't mention to him I met with you. It would probably upset him. But I'm concerned he's losing his motivation. I want to see him get ahead, and if there's anything I can do to help him excel, I'll do it. I hate to see him lose it now when he's so close to success. Have you noticed any changes in his behaviour lately?"

Jessica studied him for a moment without answering. Torque wondered if she was contemplating lying to him or whether she was reflecting on Michael's behaviour. Finally, she spoke. "I guess he's been different. We've been disconnected lately. Michael acts like he's under stress, but he doesn't want to talk about it. He avoids me and spends most of his time at the office. Even when he's home, he locks himself in his office and spends hours there, working, even weekends. He stays up late into the night, and that's if he doesn't go back out. I'd suspect him of having an affair if I didn't know him better. He's always got his briefcase and his netbook with him, and he takes his field kit along all the time."

"How are things between the two of you?"

"Like I said, distant. I've been worried about him. But I think things might be looking up. At least, I hope he'll be happy with what I have to tell him."

"What's that?"

"Well, I'd prefer to tell Michael first, but maybe he won't mind if I confide in you. You're his best friend, and it's sweet you're so concerned about him. A few weeks ago, I suspected I might be pregnant."

Torque's mouth went dry. He waited for her to continue.

"Remember when Michael and I went away for that three-day visit to my sister's cottage? He was upset, because it was forced on him, but I felt he needed to get away. It went well. He was more relaxed than I've seen him in years. We were like newlyweds. Last week, I got confirmation from the doctor that I'm pregnant."

"Congratulations." Torque pasted a smile on his face. "That's great news, Jess."

This was *not* good news. The last thing he wanted was for Michael to have a family to protect. If anything, this would push him further away from the Agency.

"You haven't told him yet?"

"No. He's been so distant and absent, the time never seemed right. I want to surprise him with a nice dinner and a happy announcement. I wanted to give him some time, but I'll have to tell him now that you know."

"Perhaps you should give him the rest of the week, Jess. He'll have completed a couple of major assignments by then. That should ease things for him. Plan that special dinner for Friday. I'll make sure he's there for it."

"Thank you so much, Gerry. That's so sweet. I'll wait. I'm sure it'll make things better for us to be planning our baby's arrival. No doubt, that's all he'll need to snap him out of this melancholy. It's been so hard to keep quiet, but he was so moody I was afraid he'd be angry about it. He always said he didn't want children. He said his work didn't leave room for them. But my work does. I don't mind raising them with little help. I know how hard he works, and I think he'll be happy we did this. Don't you think?"

"I'm sure he'll be happy. How could he not like kids, especially his own? It'll be fine. I'll prime the pump for you a little, feel him out, and encourage him. I bet when he knows there'll be a little Michael Junior around, he'll be over the moon."

That was the problem. Michael *would* be happy. When he got used to the idea, he'd want that child, and that would be bad. Torque hadn't been delighted when Michael had announced his engagement. He'd even tried to talk Michael out of marrying Jessica. People in their line of work shouldn't try to settle down and have families. But Michael had been in love, and nothing was stopping him.

They married, and, Torque thought, the relationship had been in trouble ever since. At one point, it had been on the verge of complete disintegration when Michael came close to having an affair with Althaea Dayton, a colleague. Gerry had done his best to push Michael into the woman's arms, even orchestrating a brief period where Michael and Althaea were partnered on some assignments.

The chick transferred to one of the alien bases, and Michael had snapped out of it, much to Gerry's dismay. This child would make Michael's marriage take an upward spiral and force him to consider everything from the perspective of a new father. It would turn him from the Agency, and Torque would be forced to have him neutralized.

That he couldn't let this child be born was Torque's immediate thought, and he accepted it as a solution. He needed to make sure it happened before Michael even knew Jess was pregnant. Releasing Michael from his troubled marriage at the same time, killing two birds with one death ray, so to speak, was, Torque decided, the most pragmatic way to go.

He smiled at Jess and patted her hand. "Don't worry, Jess. I'll take care of everything."

CHAPTER 17

Carolyn ushered her client to the door. Alis had just received her third Reiki session and seemed much more relaxed and peaceful now. She described herself as chronically tense, a "Type A" personality. Carolyn worked on assisting her to relax enough to at least stop clenching her teeth through a session.

Alis, a cupcake of a woman, hugged Carolyn at the door. "Thanks so much. I think I was able to relax this time. I feel good."

"That's wonderful." Carolyn smiled. "I think you're making real progress. By next time, you'll be sleeping like a baby. Maybe you'll turn into one of those people who fall asleep on the Reiki table."

Alis laughed. "I'd love that. See you next month."

Carolyn stepped outside. Alis walked to her car, a Civic, parked in front of the garage. The Civic crawled backwards out of the driveway and onto the road. Carolyn stood for a moment, breathing in the fresh air. It was hot out, but she found it comforting to stand there in her sundress and soak in the sun.

The moment passed. It was as if a dark cloud had obscured the sun though the brightness of the day itself didn't change. She tensed and held her breath. Something was wrong. She scanned the property to see if anything was amiss.

Plants in the garden below swayed subtly in the slight breeze. A squirrel darted across the grass. Almost lazily, a robin flew by and landed in a tree. She continued to wait, the uneasiness growing, then turned and walked back into the house.

The phone rang. A chill ran through Carolyn. She snatched it up, knowing it was bad news involving John.

"Hello?" She held her breath and waited.

"Is this Carolyn Fairchild?" The voice on the other end was male.

"Speaking."

"This is Paul Reid. I work with John."

"I remember you, Paul. What's wrong?"

"I'm so sorry. John might have suffered a heart attack. He collapsed on the loading dock a short while ago. They took him to the hospital in Aurora."

"Is he … is he okay?"

"I don't know anything. Are you okay to get to the hospital yourself? Do you want me to have someone come and drive you over?"

"I'll drive myself."

"Please call me if there's anything I can do for you."

"Thank you." She ended the call and looked around the room, trying to orient herself.

Arnie. She dialled, praying Arnie would pick up.

"Hello, Carolyn?"

Thank God for call display. "Arnie, something's happened to John." She explained the situation and asked him to meet her at the hospital.

After she hung up the phone, she hurried upstairs to get her keys and purse. Afraid to feel, afraid she'd find out before she got there that it was already too late, Carolyn made herself go numb. She grabbed her purse and fumbled for her car keys, feeling as if she was moving in slow motion.

When she reached the door, she threw it open and slammed it shut behind her. She stopped when she was halfway down the stairs and ran back to lock the door. When that was done, she realized she'd forgotten to open the garage and had to unlock the door to press the button on the garage door opener. Then she slammed the door again, locked it, again, and headed back down the stairs.

She stepped into her car and started it up. Time was racing. She glanced at the clock on the dashboard. Too much time had passed. She had to get to John. Car in reverse, she looked behind her, making sure the driveway was clear. She backed out of the garage, trying to control the trembling in her hands.

Carolyn eased the car down the driveway and had to force herself to stop when she reached the bottom, reminding herself to check for oncoming traffic. She took a deep breath. It wouldn't help John if she got into a car accident trying to get to him. She said a prayer to her angels, asking them to help John and to protect her. Then she pulled onto the road and headed into town.

Twenty minutes later, she was walking through the doors into the hospital's Emergency department. A triage nurse greeted her and directed her to get in line.

Carolyn shook her head. "No, please. My husband. He's here. They said he had a heart attack."

The nurse took her details and directed her to Laura, one of the volunteers, a grey-haired woman in a blue uniform, peering out a window embedded in a set of double doors. Carolyn followed Laura, who said the doctor would see her in the Family Room.

Perhaps Arnie had arrived already. Carolyn searched the Emergency area for him but didn't see him.

Everything was a haze. It occurred to her she should have sent John some Reiki. Never mind. She'd give him Reiki when she found him. She needed to find John and know he was okay. Why did she have to go to this "Family Room?" Why couldn't she just go to John? Was John in the Family Room?

They arrived at the Family Room, and the volunteer ushered her in. Chairs lined the perimeter, and a coffee table, covered in magazines, sat in the centre. A TV, bolted to the wall, silently ran a newsreel. A crate of toys and children's books sat under the TV. There was no hospital bed. No John.

Laura was saying something, but Carolyn couldn't hear her. A buzzing noise drowned out whatever the woman said. Carolyn tried to focus when Laura repeated herself and realized the volunteer was asking her if she'd like a coffee or something to drink. Carolyn shook her head.

Numbness spread through her. A roaring sound in her ears drowned out everything. She watched the volunteer's lips move some more, but didn't hear any sound.

When would things become normal again? There had to be a mistake. She only had to wait, and John would come out and explain. Someone called her name, a man's voice. *John? Thank God.* She turned to face him.

It was Arnie. He'd arrived and stood by her side. How had he found her? It didn't matter. Why was it taking her so long to find John when Arnie found her so easily?

Arnie took Carolyn by the elbow and said something to Laura, who nodded and touched his shoulder.

A man appeared. Nurse? Doctor? Yes, it was a doctor. He gave his name, but the buzzing drowned it out. The doctor's mouth moved. She thought he was saying sorry. Why was he apologizing?

Arnie hugged her. Carolyn put her arms around him. The doctor was saying John didn't make it.

Carolyn frowned, confused. "He didn't make it? You mean he's not in the hospital?"

"Mrs. Fairchild, I'm sorry. I mean he died. We did everything we could to resuscitate him, but he died."

"No. I'd know. I want to see him. Where is he?" Her voice was getting shrill. She couldn't help it.

"He's in a room down the hall. Laura will take you to him, and you can have some time alone."

She wished the buzzing would stop so she could hear what people were saying. She put her hands to her ears. The fog was everywhere. Pain raced through her body. The smells from the hospital were overwhelming.

Floral scents, sweet, pungent, cloying; disinfectant, bleach, soap, medicine, sweat, and grease, mingled, everything at once. Something dripped somewhere, voices mumbled, carts crashed along the hall on rickety wheels, rattling, shaking, and noise from everywhere at once.

A spirit stood in the doorway of the Emergency room. He was confused, just starting to recognize he'd passed. His spirit-wife was trying to get his attention. In another room, a young man wearing a soldier's uniform, also in spirit, waited for his cancer-riddled mother to leave her body. Carolyn knew he had a couple of days waiting ahead of him, but his mother sensed he was there, and it comforted her.

Each life's thread passed into Carolyn's awareness and then out again, to be replaced by the cacophony of visions, smells, and sounds that drowned each other out and made everything a blur of confusion.

She hadn't put up any protection. As if struggling to climb out of a deep well, Carolyn silently called on Archangel Michael to come and clear her body and aura. She visualized a mirror ball of light growing out of and around her.

At once, the buzzing stopped and the pressure in her brain eased. The present, immediate noise and bustle of the hallway outside the room came to her ears. A muted odour of disinfectant replaced the other smells. Fog no longer obscured the doctor, and his voice came to her clear and final.

"If you like, we can call a priest or someone for you. Would you like the hospital chaplain to come over, or do you have a parish priest you'd like to contact?"

Carolyn shook her head. "I just want to see him."

Arnie kept his arm around her, and they followed Laura through the corridors into a room where a single bed stood, machines hovering near the head of the bed. Someone moved out of her way when she walked into the room, and Carolyn only noted that a person had crossed her path. A haze in front of her eyes parted when she blinked, and she realized it was tears. She reached the bed and looked down at John.

His eyes were closed. His hair, the hair she'd thought needed cutting on Saturday morning, framed his face in a sticky mass. A blue blanket covered him up to his chin. He was white and pale, but he still looked like he might open his eyes and speak to her. Carolyn went to him and stood next to his beautiful face. She put her hand on his cheek. She could feel his absence. It was too late to give him Reiki. There was no longer anyone there to send it to.

She looked over to the other side of the bed. That's where he was. He'd waited for her after all. He'd been standing there while they worked on him. She saw the whole thing as if through his eyes. His grandmother stood next to him. She'd come through and would help him cross. Thank God, she'd come right away. John had loved his grandmother and it would be comforting to him to have her take him home.

"Please, John. Why? Not yet. Not now." She didn't want him to go. She didn't want to make him stay. "It's okay," she told the space on the other side of the bed. "I want you to be okay."

The emptiness across the bed struck her, and she hung her head and sobbed.

Beside her, Arnie's body shook. He was crying too, but quietly. She turned and hugged him.

"He's gone," she said.

CHAPTER 18

After saying goodbye to Jess, Torque rushed out to his car before she could get up to leave. He opened the glove box. The TR was there, where Michael had set it after their last job. Torque contemplated whether he should do this now or wait another day or so.

If he waited, he risked Jess telling Michael she was pregnant. If he did it now, there'd be no taking it back. He decided sooner would be better. Even if Michael somehow found out Jess had been pregnant, it was better than having him begin to get used to the idea of fatherhood and worrying about his kid's future.

From where Torque sat, he had an unobstructed view of the entrance to the doughnut shop. Jess wouldn't stay in there long. She had to get back to work too. For a moment, he considered that Michael might close himself off even more if his wife died, but then he dismissed that. Torque would make sure Michael knew his best friend was there for him. Then it would be like it had been before Michael and Jess had married, when Michael could come and go as he pleased, and they only had to worry about themselves.

It was a time of freedom Torque wanted back. Michael should never have tied himself down to one woman. Torque had never gotten involved seriously with any woman. In that regard, he completely understood Arnold Griffen.

Griffen's mistake, in Torque's opinion, was to get involved with married women or women who had boyfriends. It wasn't so much the morality of it Torque objected to as it was the personal repercussions. Torque didn't want to risk attracting attention to himself from an angry boyfriend or spouse.

He checked his watch. It was 2:46 PM. He'd been with Jess for almost an hour. Surely, she'd leave the doughnut shop to head back to work soon. She worked nearby, so she'd be walking, and her route would take her past his car, though on the other side of the street.

There she was now.

How lovely she is. Too bad she has to be put down. If only she hadn't married Mick. Torque's gaze followed her as she walked to the intersection and pressed the button to cross on her side.

He held the TR up and aimed it at her head. The intersection was busy, but it wasn't anything he couldn't get around. He unlocked the TR.

She stepped onto the road.

He panned along with her while she crossed the street.

She neared the centre of the road.

He flicked the button to turn on the weapon. For a second, she looked up and over. Their eyes met, and she smiled when she recognized his face.

Then the second passed, and she staggered, careening into the traffic going the other way. A cab cutting into another lane struck her, and she was flung across the hood.

Torque opened the glove box, dropped the TR into it, and pulled away from the curb. He turned down a side street, away from the commotion at the intersection. He wanted to get back to the office to be there when Michael received the news about Jess. Michael would definitely need his best friend at his side for what was coming.

***

Michael sat on the couch in the living room of his home. He and Torque had returned from the hospital where Michael had identified Jessie's body. He tried to grasp that it was really Jess lying there cold on the hospital bed. She was already dead when he'd arrived. Relieved that Torque had been there to drive him, Michael felt like he'd been cut adrift.

He glanced at the DVD player to check the time. It read 4:43 PM. On a normal day, he'd still be at the office, and Jess would arrive home at six o'clock. She'd make some dinner for them and wait for him to come home. When he didn't show, she'd eat alone. Then she'd wait for him to come home some more, and when he didn't show, she'd go to bed alone.

Michael realized that what had become the norm for Jessie wasn't a happy life, and it was his fault. He never should have married her. Torque had warned him not to tie her to him, but he'd believed—they'd both believed—that all they needed was to be together. For weeks now, he'd told himself each day that he'd come home and at least have dinner with her. But each day, when the time came, he'd stayed at the office.

Half the time, it wasn't because he was too busy to come home. He'd been nervous to face her. He was afraid she was ready to call it quits, and when it came to it, he didn't want her to leave him. But how do you tell someone you love her when you've been showing her day after day that you don't?

"Mick, can I get you anything?"

Michael looked up at Torque and shook his head. "It's so empty here. I planned to make things up to her, you know."

"Yeah. It's rotten luck. She knew you loved her."

"I keep expecting her to call me to ask when I'm leaving work. She'd call me around this time every day. I always told her 'soon,' and I never meant it. She deserved better than that."

"It's not your fault. It's this business we're in. I don't know anyone who made it work whose spouse wasn't in the business too. You want me to stay here tonight and keep you company?"

Michael shook his head. "I'll be okay. But thanks."

"Listen, if during the night you can't cope, you call me. Jess meant a lot to me, too. She was a lovely person. I'm sorry she's gone. Perhaps we should consider, though, that she won't have to go through what's coming. She's safe now, from everything."

"Yeah. I guess that's one good thing. But I'd rather have her with me."

"Of course. But she's been spared a lot, and that's a consolation."

Michael said nothing. He stood up and went to the kitchen. A glass sat on the counter where Jess had left it. She liked to reuse the same glass during the day and would leave it on the counter in the morning when she went to work. Then she'd use it again when she came home, putting it into the dishwasher before going to bed. He picked up the glass.

At the thought he'd have to live without her now, anger and fear surged through him. Tears threatened, and before they could flow, he windmilled his arm over his head and smashed the glass to the floor.

Torque rushed into the room. "You okay? What did you do?"

"I can't do it, Torque. I had no idea how much I depended on her to just be here. She can't be gone. I thought the worst thing in the world would be for her to leave me, to divorce me. But this? I never knew what the worst thing was until this."

"You don't think so right now, and I don't blame you, but it'll be okay. You need some time."

"This is what we're putting Carolyn Fairchild through."

"Don't go there. We can't do anything about that. She'll have to get through it too. They all will. They brought it on themselves. This wouldn't be happening to them if they weren't traitors to their country."

"How are they traitors? I see a bunch of UFO nuts who want the government to acknowledge what's happening to them. How does that make them traitors?"

"You don't have the whole story. They're interfering with the Project. If they destroy what we're doing, then no one will survive what's coming. They'll ruin everything."

"What will they ruin? They won't be protected. They'll have nowhere to hide. How does it help them to protect the Project when the Project isn't in place to protect them?"

"No, it's in place to allow humanity to survive. Mick, there are limited spaces. We're protecting those we can."

"How the hell are these people traitors? You still haven't explained that to me. What have they done? What are the Fairchilds doing?"

"That's classified. You have to trust me. We don't randomly exterminate innocent people. Why are you questioning this?"

"I need to know we're doing the right thing. I joined the Agency because I wanted to serve my country. I left my country to join the Project up here because I wanted to serve the world. This was supposed to be for the good of all mankind. It smells like world domination."

"You're wrong. I'll see you through this and help with the arrangements for Jess. We'll take a couple of days and forget about what else we have to do. Jim understands. The targets are occupied with John's funeral. We'll get past the next couple of days and then go back to it. We'll get Arnie and Carolyn locked up at the Agency by the end of next week. If that doesn't scare Shelly and Steve into silence, then we'll take care of them, too. But only if it's necessary. Right?"

Michael nodded, but couldn't think straight. He let Torque guide him back to the living room and onto the couch.

"I'll clean up the glass. You sit. Do you feel like eating something? I can order a pizza?" Torque said.

The thought of food sickened Michael. He shook his head.

Torque went back to the kitchen, and Michael heard his partner open the closet door beside the stove and take out the broom and dustpan. Michael picked up the remote and turned on the TV. He flipped through the channels without registering what was on the screen. It wasn't until the screen blurred that he realized he was crying.

The phone rang.

***

When the phone rang, Torque paused in his sweeping. "Do you want me to get that for you?"

"No, I'm getting it." Michael walked over to the phone, picked it up, and said, "Hello."

Torque tried to listen while he continued to sweep glass into the dustpan, but Michael's voice was muffled. When Torque dumped the last of the glass from the dustpan into the garbage can, he heard Michael hang up the phone. Torque put the broom and dustpan away and hurried into the living room.

Michael stood by the phone, staring at it. A look of grief worse than any Torque had seen on him yet today contorted his face. Fear surged through Torque at the sight of it.

"Who was that? What happened?"

"God, Torque. She was pregnant."

Torque's bowels tightened. "Who told you that?"

"The doctor—from the hospital. He called to tell me what they believe happened. He said the heat and her pregnancy affected her, and she became disoriented and stepped into traffic. When the cab hit her, it shocked her system into heart failure. She was fucking pregnant. They said she was almost five weeks along. She never told me."

Torque went to Michael, took him by the arm, and walked him over to the couch. "I'm so sorry. She should have told you. Maybe she was waiting for the right time?"

"Yeah, and you know why she never found the right time? Because I wasn't here. She had something on her mind, and I thought it was that she wanted to leave me. She just wanted to tell me she was pregnant, and she was afraid to, because she knew I didn't want to have a baby. I'm a cold son of a bitch, Torque. She didn't deserve to be treated like that. I didn't deserve her."

"We have someone you can talk to. Do you want me to ask Helen to set that up?"

"I don't need grief counselling. I appreciate everything you're doing, but I'd like to be alone now. I have to go to the funeral home tomorrow and make arrangements. Her family will be flying in from California. I can't wait to deal with her mother. She'll find a way to blame it all on me no matter what happened to Jess."

"I'll leave. But if you feel the need to talk or you want anything, call me. It doesn't matter what time it is."

"Okay. Thanks."

***

After Torque left, Michael wandered around the house, trying to figure out what to do. Jess had spent many hours alone in the house. He wondered how she could stand it. Now he was here by himself, all he could do was imagine her wandering around, waiting for him, and knowing he probably wouldn't show up until long after she'd gone to bed.

Michael went into his office and turned on his laptop, but as it booted up, he decided he didn't want to dig anymore. Torque was right. His obsession with the UFO group members was a waste of time. It was an excuse to stay away from home and Jessica, and he didn't need that excuse anymore. He'd focus on quietly burying his beautiful Jessie, and the baby he'd never know, and then put all his energy into his work.

Arnold Griffen would soon find himself at the Agency.

CHAPTER 19

They were at Carolyn and John's—now just Carolyn's. The group alternated between hovering over her and keeping their distance. A pallid shock suffused them. Carolyn sat curled up in the corner of the big couch in her living room.

Flowers had already arrived. A large bouquet from John's workplace sat in the middle of the dining room table. Whenever she got an urge to vomit, she'd focus on the white lilies, roses, and carnations, and the purple delphiniums and irises, and the feeling would go away.

So far, she'd managed not to throw up, though once, she'd run into the bathroom, gagging. She didn't want to picture night after night without John. Carolyn tried to push it from her mind, because if she didn't, she'd go mad. How much time would it take to heal this wound? She was positive eternity wouldn't be long enough.

"He wasn't old enough to have a heart attack," she said. The others looked at her. She wondered if they'd also been thinking that, or if this was news to them. He was too young. He was barely forty.

The uneasiness from earlier returned. Something nagged at the back of her mind. Something was wrong that she couldn't identify. It wasn't just that her husband had suddenly dropped dead.

Arnie cleared his throat, and, his voice even and soft, said, "What happened, then?"

"I don't know," she admitted. "He had a physical recently and checked out fine. His cholesterol levels were okay, his blood pressure was okay ..." She trailed off.

"Sometimes people check out fine and then this happens. It's not fair, but it has happened before," Steve said. "But I'm not sure if that's true in John's case. He wasn't the most physically active guy, but he wasn't out of shape, either."

"Heart attacks don't run in his family," Carolyn said.

"So what happened? You don't think someone at work did something, do you?" Steve asked.

"No. The people at work respected him. No one there would've wanted to hurt him. But I find it a little suspicious he drops dead shortly after we posted that video and wrote those blog posts," said Carolyn. "If you remember, I was opposed to using the video camera Friday night." *I told you so.*

"Do you think someone killed him? There were people all around him. How can you orchestrate something like that? Do you think something was done to him on Friday night, during the abduction?" Shelly asked.

"I don't know. But I asked them to do an autopsy. They resisted, but I pressed them to do it. I don't know how to prove this wasn't just a heart attack. Maybe Ralph's right, and the government is after us," Carolyn replied.

"Ralph is saying some weird shit though. He's talking reptilians. I've never seen reptilians anywhere, not any of the times I've been abducted, and not anywhere that wasn't on video. The videos on the Internet could be fakes," Arnie said.

"The reptilian theory might be too out there, but what if there's truth to some of the other stuff? Perhaps we should take a look at what he's said." Carolyn shuddered and wrapped her arms around herself.

"What do you propose to do?" asked Shelly.

"I want to talk to Ralph, but I won't try to go through Beth. I'll go to the hospital and get his doctor to let me see him."

"Do you want us to go along?" The kindness in Shelly's voice touched Carolyn.

"No. The doctor might let one or two of us in, but not all four. Arnie can come with me." Carolyn looked at Arnie.

"Of course, I will, Carrie," Arnie said.

She nodded, grateful. A lump grew in her throat and she bit her lip to stop the tears. He hadn't called her "Carrie" in years. She'd outgrown the name. But coming from Arnie now, it seemed more poignant than anything else they'd said to comfort her.

"Okay. Thank you," she said. "We'll go tomorrow." She fell silent, her thoughts returning to John. She hadn't felt John's presence since the hospital, but might sense him when she was alone. "You guys don't have to hang around here. I'll be fine."

"I should go spend some time with my mother," Arnie said. "If you need me at all during the night, call me. I don't care what time it is."

"I promise," Carolyn said.

Arnie stood up to leave and Carolyn hugged him, his cheek pressed against hers. Pulling herself away, she smiled at him, reassured.

He returned the smile and walked away. At the door, he waved to them and checked for the cat before he stepped outside.

Carolyn followed to watch him leave.

Arnie hurried down the stairs to his car. While he was getting in, Shelly and Steve stepped out onto the porch. Arnie waved to them one last time and backed out of the driveway.

***

Michael called Torque on his cell when Arnie appeared. When he saw Carolyn, Shelly, and Steve leave the house, he remained crouched behind the trees and spoke softly into the phone. "Don't move. He's not alone. Steve and Shelly are coming out behind him. We'll have to wait for a better opportunity."

"Okay," Torque answered. "He's planning to come back in the morning. We can probably get to him after he drops her off."

Shelly and Steve got in their car and reversed down the drive. Arnie was already gone. They pulled onto the road and drove away. Carolyn remained on the porch for a moment, then went inside and shut the door.

Michael watched the house, imagining Carolyn inside by herself. He wondered if she'd be able to sleep. Michael hadn't slept at all last night. He hadn't eaten much since Jess had died either.

He shook his head and remembered where he was. Torque would be wondering why he wasn't back at the car. He needed to focus on what they had to do. If he could get Arnie and Carolyn to the Agency cells, then he would take some time off. It was Tuesday now. Jessie's funeral was scheduled for Friday. All he needed to do was keep busy until then.

Cornell had suggested he let someone else handle Arnie and Carolyn, but Michael had a compulsive need to do it himself. Besides, if he were left alone at home he might go insane.

At least Carolyn has her daughter.

Michael rose from his hiding place and returned to the car.

CHAPTER 20

Shelly and Steve arrived at their apartment after a mostly silent drive. Steve sat on the couch in front of the TV. Shelly suspected he wasn't seeing what was there since he kept randomly flicking from one channel to another. She'd parked herself on the edge of the loveseat diagonally across from the couch. Shelly couldn't decide whether to continue to sit, or get up and do something.

She tried not to think about what would happen now John was gone. His loss was like a hole in her heart, but she also felt something akin to jealousy. She couldn't get the idea out of her head that something would develop between Carolyn and Arnie. Carolyn was now free and single, and if she wanted to turn to Arnie for comfort, it shouldn't bother Shelly. But it did.

It irritated her that she couldn't stop thinking about him. She'd been planning to break it off with him anyway. This should make it easier for her. It's not like he'd been faithful to her. She hadn't been faithful to him—she was married for God's sake.

When Arnie and Carolyn had hugged, Shelly's stomach had dropped a metre and then bounced up into her heart. She tried to shake it off. Carolyn was her friend. Arnie was, well, Arnie. He owed her nothing, certainly not fidelity.

No doubt, she was just projecting. Carolyn and Arnie had been friends for years, and nothing physical had ever developed between them.

Steve set down the remote. "We shouldn't go to any more sky watches for a while."

Taken aback, Shelly said, "Are you afraid?" It was the only explanation for Steve's pronouncement.

"It would be safer for us to lie low for a while. I don't care what Arnie wants to do. It's his crusade, not ours. We need to look out for ourselves."

"Okay." She wasn't opposed to keeping her distance for a while. "Do you want some tea?"

"Sure," Steve replied.

Shelly went into the kitchen and filled and plugged in the kettle. She set the teapot on the table, opened the fridge, and saw there wasn't any milk. "I'm stepping out to the store. I can't have my tea without milk."

"All right."

She picked up her purse and took twenty dollars out, which she stuffed into the front pocket of her shorts. She'd walk. The sun was down, the heavy heat from the day easing up. She wouldn't be gone long. The store was nearby.

"I'll be back in a moment," she called out. "I'm not taking my keys." She checked that her cell phone was hooked to her waist, and, when she saw it was, she headed for the door.

"Isn't it a little late for you to be going out by yourself?" Steve asked.

"What are you, my mother?" she said. "I'm just going down the street. I'll be back in twenty minutes."

"Okay," Steve replied. "But you'd better hurry. Don't make me come after you."

Shelly stepped into the hall and closed the door. She thought about Arnie again, and how fun it had been to spend time with him. He was a nice guy, attentive, a bit wild. If he were a one-woman man, he'd be perfect. She wondered how many other women had suffered over him, wanting him, but not being able to have him. He was like a drug.

The elevator door opened when she reached it. She stepped in and pressed the 'G' button. She watched the floor numbers count down while the elevator descended. Her thoughts returned to Arnie.

She'd phone him tonight when Steve was asleep and see if he'd meet with her tomorrow afternoon, when Steve was at work, and before she started her shift as a Personal Support Worker at the old folks' home.

The elevator reached the third floor and pinged open. A man stepped in, reached out to push a button, saw the glowing 'G,' and dropped his hand. Shelly didn't recognize him. Probably a visitor. He looked young, twenty or so, but she couldn't be sure. The hood of his sweatshirt covered his hair and shaded his face. *Sweat pants and a sweatshirt? In this weather? He must be roasting.* At first, it confused rather than frightened her when he reached out and pressed the "Stop" button, causing the elevator to halt. But puzzlement turned to fear when he pulled out a knife. He shoved her against the back of the elevator and pressed the knife to her throat. The point stuck into her neck, but didn't break the skin. She heard a whimpering sound and realized it came from her.

"Give me your money, bitch," he grunted.

She looked into his eyes. They were intense, frenetic.

"What are you staring at?"

"N-n-n-nothing." She tried to look away, but her gaze was frozen onto his.

"Give me your fucking money."

"Okay, okay. Please, don't hurt me. I'll give you everything I have." She stuck a hand into her pocket for the twenty dollars. "Here." Her voice trembled. Her mouth was dry. The breath caught in her throat.

The man snatched the money out of her shaking hand. He leaned forward and kissed her on the mouth, forcing his tongue inside.

She wanted to resist, but feared what he'd do, so she kept her mouth still while he rolled his tongue around inside it.

He squeezed her breast, kneaded it.

She gagged, and he dropped his hand.

He glanced down at the bill she'd given him.

"That's not enough." He sliced the knife across her throat.

She gurgled and slid to the floor when her legs gave out. The pain took over. Her head dropped forward. A moan tried to escape her lips and failed.

The man started the elevator again.

By the time the doors opened, Shelly had stopped twitching, and the blood soaked her top and shorts. Everything faded to black.

CHAPTER 21

The room reminds Michael of a hospital room—a private one from the look of it since there's only one bed. He ignores Jessica holding the baby in her arms and zeros in on the absence of a TV. He turns to her and says, "There's no TV."

She smiles. "I'll manage."

He looks around. Three men in brown robes stand in the corner. They remind him of monks. Were they always there?

They say nothing. They observe.

"How did you get here?" Michael asks.

"I escaped."

"Is that our baby?"

"Yes. Don't worry. She won't be gone for long. You'll see her again."

"She? A girl?" He doesn't know what to make of that. His thoughts, ever since he'd found out about the baby, were of a little boy. Mike Jr., perhaps. Seems so silly now.

"Yes. She wants you to call her Christina. Tina."

He doesn't question the logic of that. "Of course. Are you okay? Why are you in the hospital?"

She flashes her beautiful smile, the one he fell in love with. He tries to savour the moment, but she speaks and the smile is interrupted. "They said I need to rest. I wanted to tell you I was okay so they let me see you."

Michael searches for a place to sit. He wants to spend some time with her. There's no chair, so he stands in the doorway.

She came back, his mind screams. Then it goes blank. He should ask the important questions but he can't remember what those might be.

"You have to go. They won't let you stay here," she says.

"No. Jess. Please. I just got here. Please. Stay with me." He realizes she's dead. She's here, but she's dead, and now she says she has to go. No. She'd said he has to go. He won't. He'll stay. They can't make him leave. He just realized he was with her. He doesn't want to let her go again.

"No, Jess, please ..."

Michael awoke, his face moist from sweat and tears, and he regretted he hadn't run to her and held her. Why had he just stood there? It was only a dream, but he ached for her. He'd felt her with him. He rolled over and tried to go back to sleep. If he dreamed it again, he'd put his arms around her and squeeze her tight. The thought that he'd missed an opportunity made him want to scream or punch something.

He lay in bed, but after fifteen minutes of rolling around, he admitted he couldn't sleep. The clock read 1:43 AM. A whole two hours of sleep tonight—a record these days. He sat up and turned on the light, automatically looking over to Jessie's side of the bed.

Still empty.

***

Carolyn awoke in the middle of the night to the ringing of the telephone. Arnie.

"Carolyn, something's happened to Shelly."

"What? Is she okay?" But she knew the answer before he said another word.

"No. Carolyn, she's dead."

"No, no, no, no." It spilled out of her in a screaming flood.

Over the phone, Arnie shouted her name.

The thought came to her that she should tell him to stop before he woke his mother. Through choked sobs, she said, "What happened?"

"I spoke to Steve's brother. Shelly was found stabbed to death in the elevator in their building. It looks like a mugging."

"A mugging? Their building has security. How'd a mugger get in?"

"They think he buzzed apartments until someone let him in. Or he was a guest. It was a crime of opportunity. He took her money. Steve's brother said she didn't have any money when they found her. Maybe she resisted."

Carolyn knew. "She didn't resist. She gave him money. It wasn't enough."

Arnie didn't comment on that. "Carolyn, there's something more." He paused.

"What?" She held her breath.

"Steve said he doesn't want us contacting him again. He's afraid it's because of the UFO group that Shelly was killed. He doesn't believe it was a mugging."

"That's ridiculous. We should go to him."

Arnie sighed. "When I talked to Steve's brother, he told me Steve's a basket case. He can't handle this, especially after what happened to John. We haven't even had John's funeral yet, and this happened to Shelly. Ralph was institutionalized. It's got to be more than a coincidence. Do you want me to come over and stay the rest of the night with you?"

"No, that's okay. I'll manage. I don't want to make you leave your mom and come out here," Carolyn said, though she wished she could ask him to come.

"Are you sure? The nurse will return first thing in the morning. I can leave a note for her," Arnie replied.

"I'm sure. Come over when the nurse arrives. We'll have breakfast together, though I don't know how much I'll feel like eating. Get some sleep."

"Okay. I'll call you when I'm on my way."

Carolyn set down the phone, dazed. Shelly was gone. It couldn't be true. How could this have happened? Friday they were all together, enjoying each other's company and looking forward to an evening of watching the stars.

Then it all fell apart.

Carolyn knew she wouldn't be able to sleep. She got out of bed and went to sit on the back balcony. Everything was quiet, no traffic noises, just crickets.

A deer cried, off in the woods. It sounded like a baby. Tired, but alert, she pulled her feet up onto the chair and hugged her knees to her chest. The air was warm, moist, and fragrant. It felt nice to be outside in only her sleep shirt and panties.

She wished she could go to Steve. Her heart ached for Shelly and John. Shelly was so cute, like a pixie. How could anyone hurt her?

Shelly, where are you? Can you hear me? Are you out there somewhere?

She was able to connect to departed loved ones. It's what she did as a medium. But for some reason, it was harder for her to connect to her own departed loved ones than it was to connect to strangers.

Carolyn found herself crying again and swiped the tears off her face. The prospect of morning and what it would bring scared her. She'd have to deal with the funeral parlour and try to talk to Steve to tell him it wasn't their fault. She'd have to talk to Ralph.

It wasn't their fault. John's death was, but not Shelly's. But there was no proof. The autopsy would be performed on John the following day, but she was sure they wouldn't find anything. They expected he died of a heart attack, and they'd see only evidence of a heart attack.

She sensed a presence.

CHAPTER 22

The balcony was empty though Carolyn felt she wasn't alone. She peered inside through the sliding screen door. Nothing moved. She forced herself to relax, trying to get a feel for who it might be. A figure stood to her left, barely there. She could see one of the chairs through it.

A tall male stood, hands at his sides, staring at her. John?

Before the opportunity slid away, she said, "I love you, John."

A wash of warmth and love spread over her, coming from the figure. Her heart ached to touch him, but it was reassuring just to see him.

"What can I do to help you?" she asked, but the figure disappeared. If he were going to tell her anything about how he died, it wouldn't be tonight. Perhaps he'd come back again. She wished Shelly would also come to her.

Shelly is with Steve tonight. Yes, of course.

Did Steve know Shelly was still with him? Perhaps he sensed it, but he wasn't a believer. He might brush off any intuitive feelings and write them off as manifestations of his grief.

She stood. Her heart was lighter now than at any time since she'd received the news John was dead. What a relief to know he wasn't completely gone. There'd be many days when she'd question whether she'd seen him tonight, but right now, she knew she had.

Carolyn returned to her bedroom. She could probably sleep now. In bed, she closed her eyes and put her hands on her thighs, palms down. Reiki flowed into her body. After a while, she drifted off to sleep.

***

Michael woke to the insistent beeping of his cell phone. He must have slept through the initial call, probably because by the time he'd fallen asleep, it was around 4:00 AM. His alarm clock said 6:11 AM. He checked to see who'd called. Torque. At 5:06 AM. He called Torque back without listening to the message.

"What's up?" Michael said when his partner answered. "You called at five o'clock. No wonder I slept through it."

"Shelly Rudolph is dead."

"What do you mean? Did you do something?"

"Of course not. She was stabbed to death during a mugging. But her friends are speculating that it was wet work by the government. Cornell was furious. He'd jumped to that conclusion too and thought we'd gone ahead without taking care of Griffen and Carolyn Fairchild first."

"So it's a coincidence?" Michael asked. He tried to comprehend what Torque was saying. "What does it mean? I just woke up, so bear with me."

"It means we leave Griffen alone today. We'll see what this does to their little group." After a pause he said, "Then there were three."

"Did Cornell suggest we stay away from Griffen?" Michael asked.

"We both agreed it would be for the best, at least until the dust settles from this Shelly thing."

"Okay. I'll be at the office in an hour." Michael set the phone down on his night table and got out of bed. It was going to be a long day.

***

By 6:30 AM, Arnie was knocking on Carolyn's door. She greeted him wearing a short, light housecoat over what could be a nightshirt. Even under the circumstances, Arnie appreciated the sight of her legs.

"I'm so glad you're here," she said when she opened the door. She threw her arms around his neck and hugged him.

106

He hugged her tightly and kissed her cheek. "Are you okay?"

"Yes." She released him, and he stepped inside. She closed the door. "I managed to get a little sleep. I've put coffee on. Are you hungry? I can make some toast or eggs for you. I'll have a protein shake, if you'd like that instead."

"The shake will be great. I don't have much of an appetite this morning. That will at least keep me going. It'll be a long day," Arnie said.

He felt it weighing on him, making him tired and heavy. Perhaps it was the lack of appetite. He hadn't wanted to eat much lately. His mother nagged him about it, which made him more frustrated and further curbed his appetite. He'd been glad to get away to Carolyn's this morning, and his mother cheered up when he told her he was going for breakfast at a friend's place.

"Yeah, I'm dreading it. Making the arrangements will be difficult," Carolyn said.

They went into the kitchen, and Carolyn pulled out her bullet blender. "Chocolate, berry, or vanilla?" she asked.

"Chocolate," he answered.

Arnie watched while she prepared the shakes and then followed her into the living room. They sat at opposite ends of the sofa. "What time is your daughter arriving from school?" he asked.

"I'm not sure. She's coming with a friend. I suggested to her that she stay at her friend's place while she's here. Sam shouldn't be around here while we're afraid people are being harmed because of our UFO activities. I told her I'd be occupied. Are you okay to hang out while I shower?"

"Yeah, no problem. I'll do some work on my laptop," Arnie said.

She fell silent and then said, "Thanks for being here."

"It's no problem. John was my friend, one of the few I hadn't pissed off."

There was a moment of awkwardness while they both considered why Arnie didn't have many male friends. Carolyn smiled at him, dispelling the awkwardness. "You've got a good heart, Arnie." She turned and headed to the shower.

Arnie took their blender cups to the kitchen and rinsed them. He'd have at least an hour before she was ready. He went out front to the patio and looked around. It was another hot day though better than yesterday. Perhaps the heat wave would ease up. Some rain might be nice, though.

He went to his vehicle, an emerald green sports car. He was proud of it, and loved how it impressed people, men and women. It was amusing to drive his little old mother around in it. She didn't like getting in and out of it, and she chastised him about how frivolous it was, but she seemed pleased he could afford luxuries.

Arnie removed his laptop from the trunk at the front of the car and returned to the house. He booted the laptop up on the dining room table. He'd established a connection to Carolyn's WIFI years ago and connected automatically to the Internet.

Forty minutes later, he posted a blog in honour of John and Shelly. He accused the government of silencing them for wanting to get acknowledgment and help for abductees, and for having too much knowledge about covert government dealings with UFOs. He also stated he was afraid for his own safety and the safety of the other members of his UFO group, though he didn't mention any names.

The sound of a car pulling up the driveway made him get up and look out the living room window. He didn't recognize it. It parked and the occupants stepped out. The driver, an olive-complexioned young man in his early twenties, paused to admire Arnie's car. A young blonde woman appeared next to the young man, and Arnie saw her smile when she recognized his car. She was the spitting image of her mother though she was a much flashier dresser. Samantha Fairchild was home.

Sam bounded up the stairs to Arnie when he stepped outside to meet her. "Oh, Arnie." She threw herself into his arms.

"I'm so sorry, Sam."

She sobbed against Arnie's chest, and he held her for a moment longer. He glanced at the young man and eased Sam away. Arnie held her by the shoulders and looked into her eyes. "I thought you were going to meet us later? How did you get here so fast?"

"We left before dawn. I couldn't sleep and wanted to be with my mom. I can't believe this happened. Dad was fine when I saw him at Easter."

"I know. It was a shock for all of us. How are you holding up? I'm glad you have a friend with you."

Sam smiled. "Arnie, this is Jack. We're in the same program at school. He's been great since I found out about my dad. At least school is finished for the summer. I only had to take time off work to come here."

Jack and Arnie shook hands, and then Arnie turned back to Sam. "Your mom will be happy to see you."

He opened the door and ushered them into the house, Sam swishing in behind him, rattling bracelets and beads as she walked. Jack stepped in last and closed the door.

"Your mom's in the shower," Arnie said. "The funeral will be on Saturday. We're waiting for some of your dad's family to arrive. They'll be staying with your mom's folks in Toronto."

Sam walked into the living room, waving Jack in after her.

"Why did she sound like she didn't want me to come to the house?" she asked, dropping onto the couch.

"She's wanted to make sure you had a friend to lean on in case she was distracted with all the stuff she has to get done."

"She sounded as if she was afraid of something. Is it true her friend Shelly is dead too?"

"Yes. They say it was a mugging. We're not so sure."

"What else would it be?"

"It's complicated. Have you been reading my blog?"

"The UFO thing? Yes. I think you're being a little paranoid. Dad died of a heart attack. He didn't look like he had heart problems, but that's why they call it the silent killer. Shelly's mugging was a coincidence. Mom told me she was taking the elevator down by herself at night."

"They live in a security building in a good part of town."

"It can still happen. Wouldn't the security cameras have picked up something?"

"I'm assuming they did. But I don't know what's happening with the investigation. Steve has cut us off. He's afraid it's connected to our UFO experience the other night and I agree."

"Do you think my mom is in danger?" Sam's voice dropped to a whisper.

"I don't know. We might all be in danger."

"That's crazy," Jack said. "What would the government want to go killing people for? It doesn't make sense. They wouldn't be able to get away with that."

"You're wrong," Arnie said. "They do it and they get away with it."

"Arnie!" Carolyn walked into the room. "Shelly died in a random mugging. She was in the wrong place at the wrong time. I know it. Please don't scare the kids. They have enough to deal with right now."

"I'm sorry, Carr, but I don't agree, and they should know what's going on."

"You've told them. Now let's talk about something else. Please. Sam, honey, I'm so happy to see you." She went to Sam, who rose to let her mother hug her.

"I'm glad to be home, Mom. Are you okay?"

"Yes, I'm fine. I'm glad you're here."

"I dropped off my things at Vanna's. She asked me to spend the night. Jack can drive me over after we go to the funeral parlour. Are you going to be okay here? Do you want me to stay with you instead? I figured I'd come back tomorrow."

"I'll be fine. Don't worry about me. I can call Arnie if I need anything."

"Maybe you shouldn't be alone tonight, Carr. Why don't you have Sam and her friends stay here?" Arnie said. He saw a flash of fear cross Carolyn's face.

She said, "No. I'll be fine." Her tone was abrupt. Then her face softened, and she said, "I'll be getting ready for the funeral all day. Everyone will be coming back here afterward, so I have cleaning and shopping to do, too. It'll keep me busy."

"I can keep you company, if you want," said Arnie.

She hesitated and said, "I don't mind being alone. I feel more connected to John when I'm alone." She looked at Arnie. "Did you get any work done?"

"Yes. Which reminds me, I'd better shut it down and pack it up." Arnie went to the dining room table and began the shutdown of his laptop.

***

In Toronto, Jim Cornell finished reading Arnie's blog post ten minutes after Arnie posted it. Cornell's ulcer gnawed and burned his stomach. He reached for his phone and dialled Torque.

"Muniz here."

"It's time for you to move on Griffen. Enough is enough. If Valiant isn't up to it, grab Carlyle and take him with you. I want this guy gone."

110

CHAPTER 23

Carolyn waited for Arnie to park the car in front of her garage door before she spoke. She'd been stewing in silence since they'd left the funeral parlour. Arnie had either assumed she wanted to be left alone, or didn't realize she was stewing about him.

"Thanks for everything, Arnie."

"You're welcome. Do you want me to come in?"

She paused, considering how to say what she had to say. "I saw what you posted this morning. While we were at the funeral home, I received an email message on my phone from one of my clients who follows your blog. You should've told me you were going to post about John and Shelly."

She decided to be upfront about it. He meant no harm, and he'd been kind and supportive to her ever since John had died. But his actions were continuing to put them at risk, and it was time he stopped.

"I only spoke the truth."

"Shelly was mugged. What you did puts the rest of us in more danger."

"No, it doesn't. The more we publicize it, the safer we'll be."

"I don't agree, and you should've at least warned me you were going to do that. It involves John and me. I should have a say in what goes up on the Internet about us."

"Don't tell a journalist what to print."

"You're not a journalist. You're running a blog site, and I'm your friend. That post shouldn't have gone public. Please take it down. Hopefully, it's not too late. You could cause a lot of trouble for us. Can't we at least get through John's funeral?"

"I love you, Carr. You're one of my best friends. You're my only female friend. I'd do anything for you, but I'm not going to let them get away with this. They have to be stopped."

"What you're doing is making them want to stop us, not the other way around. Take it down. Please."

Arnie changed his strategy. "Shelly didn't deserve to die the way she did."

"No, she didn't. What does that have to do with you putting up the blog?"

"People need to know her death wasn't random. She was executed."

"She wasn't executed—not the way you mean it." Carolyn wanted to shake him.

"It's an awfully big coincidence that she was killed right after John died, right after our UFO incident."

"That you went public with even though I warned you not to."

"Are you saying it's my fault John and Shelly are dead? You agreed to let me post it. Or are you forgetting our conversation at Brent's office?"

"No, it's my fault too. I let you and John talk me into it against my better judgement. But you contributed to getting us all on their radar. They didn't execute Shelly though."

"John and Shelly are martyrs. They were executed for what they believe and for going public about it." Arnie scowled, and his voice rose.

"John and Shelly didn't go public. You did that. If it's a government conspiracy, why haven't they silenced you?"

"They silenced Ralph. If I don't shine a spotlight on myself so the world sees what happens to me, then if I'm next, no one will notice."

"That's an interesting perspective. But I think it makes them want to work harder to silence all of us. Do you think they care if it looks suspicious? There have been many suspicious deaths attributed to the government. No one has ever been able to prove anything."

Carolyn continued, matching him shout for shout. "You're painting a target on our backs. I can't let anything happen to me. Sam is down to one parent."

"It'll be fine. I didn't mention you. What happened to John and Shelly shouldn't be allowed to happen to anyone else. Ralph, too. He didn't go into that hospital on his own."

Carolyn jumped on that. "You're not going to write about Ralph now, are you?"

"I might."

She sighed, and when she spoke again, fatigue filled her voice. "Arnie, please. Leave them alone. Take down this morning's post. I wish I'd seen it earlier. There's no telling who has read it by now. What will Steve say? He's already mad at us. This will make things so much worse between us, especially between you and Steve."

Arnie didn't reply. When Carolyn opened her mouth to speak again, he quietly said, "I'll consider taking down the post. I'm not promising anything. It needs to be said. But there's something else I need to tell you. I don't want to cause Steve any more pain, but I was having an affair with Shelly."

Carolyn recoiled. "How could you? Steve is your friend."

"I know how it sounds, how it looks. She came to me. That time we all went camping, and I forgot the power inverter? Did you notice she'd been flirting with me? When everyone went to bed, she came to me. Before I knew what was happening, we were making out. I never meant for anything to happen with her. We'd been friends for years, and I stayed away the whole time. But *she* came to *me*."

"And you couldn't say 'no'?" Carolyn asked. Then the timing of it dawned on her. "You've been having an affair for almost two years?"

"I'm sorry. I always end up hurting the people I care about. I don't know why I do this. I try, but I can't stop myself," Arnie said. "I didn't want to tell you about Shelly and me, but now she's gone, what should I do? Steve won't talk to us. Ralph won't talk to us. That hurts. Especially after losing two of my close friends in a couple of days. And I'm sure it wasn't a coincidence. If you turn your back on me now, I don't know what I'll do."

Carolyn sighed. "Arnie, I'm upset with you, I'm angry with you—and with Shelly, too, to be honest. It was her responsibility too. She betrayed her husband." Then it occurred to her that Steve was oblivious. "Steve doesn't know, does he?"

"No," Arnie said. "Steve has no idea."

"Keep it that way," Carolyn said. "It'll hurt Steve if you decide to clear your conscience. Let him keep the good memories of his marriage."

Arnie nodded. "Are you and me going to be okay?" He gazed at her, his eyes pleading. Her heart skipped a beat.

"I won't abandon you. It's not like I don't know who you are. But you should talk to a professional since you're willing to admit this behaviour causes problems in your life. What do you think John would've done if Shelly had thrown herself at him? Don't you think he would've turned her down and suggested she work on her marriage? Somehow, you always manage to find a way to justify infidelity."

Arnie shrugged. "If it makes you happy, I'll do whatever you want."

Carolyn sighed again. "Don't do it to make me happy, Arnie. Do it to make your life better. Do it for you."

Arnie stared at her, a woebegone expression on his face.

You'd think I'd just asked him to moon the Pope. "It's okay. I'll help you through it. You need to get counselling. You could see Brent."

He nodded, but didn't speak.

She wasn't sure if his silence meant agreement or disagreement, so she gave him a hug and said, "I have to go now. I'm going to start calling people about the funeral."

"Okay. Maybe I can come and see you later?" he asked.

"Of course. Give me a call to make sure I'm here. I'll be free for the next few days, anyway. I've rescheduled my clients for after the funeral. Most of them plan to come to the visitation, the funeral, or both, anyway."

She leaned over and kissed Arnie on the cheek.

He smiled and took her hand. "I'll come back later, and we'll figure out what to do."

Carolyn got out of the car and walked towards her front porch. Something made her turn back and watch as Arnie backed his car out of the driveway. She had an urge to run after him and keep him here. She tried to shake it off, and when the feeling of fear intensified, she took a few steps after him and called out his name.

Arnie, his head turned away from her, didn't notice. His car backed into the street, and he pulled away without looking at her. Carolyn considered calling him and telling him to come back. She took out her cell phone and stared at it, trying to both talk herself into calling him and into not calling him.

He had to get home to spend some time with his mother. He'd probably say she was being hysterical. She might be worrying for no reason. But he might really be in danger. She dialled his number. His voicemail kicked in. When the beep sounded, she said, "It's Carolyn. Be careful. Don't trust anyone. Call me when you get home."

Feeling better, she turned off her phone and went inside. The cat trotted up and meowed at her. She followed him into the kitchen and dropped some cat treats into his bowl.

"I'm glad you're here, Fox. This place is so empty. Not even a spirit around to keep me company right now." She smiled at the cat, then stood up and went into the living room. She picked up the phone and dialled Steve's number.

"Hello?" It was Ryan, Steve's brother.

"Hi, Ryan. It's Carolyn. I'm so sorry about what happened to Shelly. How are you holding up?"

"I'm managing, but Steve isn't. Did Arnie tell you he doesn't want contact with any of you?"

"He did, but I was hoping that was just the grief talking. We're his friends. I want to talk to him. Shelly was one of my best friends. We need each other right now."

"That's not how Steve feels about it. I'll ask him for you, but don't be offended if he won't talk to you. He's a wreck. Wait a moment, okay?"

"Thanks."

She could hear Ryan speaking to Steve. The conversation was muffled, but Carolyn could tell Steve was arguing with Ryan. Soon, Ryan was back on the line.

"Carolyn?"

"I'm here."

"I'm sorry. He blames the group for her death. It sounds crazy to me. I doubt the government would do something like that, but Steve is sure none of this would've happened if you guys hadn't publicized the footage from Friday's sky watch. Give him some time. Please respect his wishes and don't come to the funeral. He won't be attending John's either, though he says to tell you he's sorry for your loss."

"Ryan, please. He's wrong. It was a mugging. It had nothing to do with the UFO group. Tell him."

"I'm sure you're right, but Steve believes otherwise, and the police haven't arrested anyone. Right now, what he believes is what matters. Please respect that and don't call him anymore. I'm sorry about John. We all hope you're able to heal from it. Goodbye."

The line went dead before she could respond. Carolyn stood in the living room, tears falling. She dialled Arnie again to tell him about it. There was no answer. She hung up without leaving another message.

CHAPTER 24

Michael and Torque sat in Torque's car, watching Arnie's empty parking spot in the underground garage of his condo building. Torque chewed on a chocolate bar and sipped on a takeout coffee. Michael had brought his thermos of coffee and was working his way through it.

"You know, if he doesn't hurry up, I'm going to have to take a piss," Torque commented.

"Maybe he's gone back to Carolyn's? We should have watched for him there," Michael said.

"He'll be back. They only went to the funeral parlour, and he'll have to check on his mother at some point."

"I think it's a bad idea to snatch him. Did Cornell discuss it with you?" Michael asked. "He didn't explain anything to me."

"No. No doubt, it'll scare the shit out of the other two, but we gotta do what we gotta do," Torque replied.

"Sometimes it would be nice to know why we have to do what we do."

"No one is indispensable, Mick, you know that. Do your job, keep your head down, and survive. That's it."

"Interesting. What if I want to thrive and not just survive?" Michael insisted.

"You are thriving, smartass. You get paid very well."

"Maybe money's not everything."

"You should be grateful the Agency values you enough to make sure you survive what's coming. If it can't be prevented, and it's impossible for everyone to survive it, I'd think you'd be happy you're one of the animals making it onto the Ark."

Frowning, Michael turned his face away from Torque and stared at the empty parking space. Arnie had a good job, made a decent living, and was making a crusade out of exposing the UFO conspiracy, probably in the name of justice, perhaps to give meaning to what he was experiencing.

Michael had always thought that what he did at least had a valuable purpose, something that made the body count justifiable. He was starting to see the mould growing on his slice of cheese. Torque was right: he needed to ally himself with the ones who were going to survive the cataclysm if he wanted to survive it himself. But was it worth the price of his soul?

Daylight splashed in when the garage door opened. Both men looked towards the entrance. Arnie's car crept in, gingerly stepping over the speed bumps.

"Ready?" Torque asked.

Michael slipped on a pair of gloves and loosened the revolver in his holster. He patted his jacket pocket, verifying the kit with the hypodermic was there. He nodded.

Arnie pulled his vehicle into its parking spot. Before he finished putting it into park, Michael and Torque were out of the car, and walking towards Arnie. The car's engine shut down and he picked up his cell phone. He fiddled with it and stuck it to his ear, probably picking up his voice mail messages. After listening for a moment, he turned off his phone and opened his car door.

Torque was on him, pulling him out of the car. "Don't move, asshole," Torque said. He shoved a gun into Arnie's ribs.

Reflexively, Arnie cursed. "What the fuck?"

Michael snatched the car keys out of Arnie's hand and glanced around to make sure they were still alone. There was no one in view.

"Keep to the left and walk towards that car over there," Michael told Arnie, indicating Torque's car. If they hugged the wall, they'd avoid appearing on the surveillance cameras. He handcuffed Arnie's hands behind his back, and when they reached the car, Torque opened the trunk.

"Get in."

"Are you serious?" Arnie looked around, perhaps seeking help, perhaps looking for someone he knew to jump out and tell him it was all a joke.

"We're the guys you keep warning people about," Michael said. "Congratulations. You were right. Now get in the trunk. We don't have to kill you, but we can if you don't cooperate." He was lying. They were not allowed to kill him no matter what, but Arnie didn't need to know that.

Michael removed Arnie's cell phone from the clip at his side and shoved it into the pocket of his own pants. "Get in the trunk. Now."

Arnie's gaze darted around again, but he climbed into the trunk and Torque shoved him down. Michael pulled the kit out of his pocket, opened it, and injected Arnie with the hypodermic needle. Arnie's eyes closed, and he sagged into the trunk.

Torque closed the trunk with a gentle slam, then went to the driver's side of his car and opened it. "Follow me. Make sure you keep to the speed limit. Enjoy driving that car."

Michael returned to Arnie's car, climbed in, and adjusted the seat and mirror. He waited for Torque to pull out ahead of him and then shifted into reverse to inch out of the parking spot. Arnie's phone vibrated against his thigh, and he took it out to see who was calling. Carolyn. Michael shut off the phone, turned on the radio, and flipped through the channels until he found the rock station. He settled in for a long drive.

Two hours later, Michael followed Torque down a dirt road on the outskirts of Peterborough. Torque pulled into a wooded area, skirting "Road Closed" and "Detour" signs. They followed the road for a few kilometres to where it dead-ended at a deserted gas station. Construction equipment lay abandoned along the road, indicating recent activity. The gas pumps were off, the buildings dark and lonely.

Torque pulled his car to the side of the road and stepped out. Michael pulled up next to the pumps. He stepped out of the car, giving it a wistful glance. It was going to be a shame to have to destroy such a high-end car. He strolled over to Torque, who was putting on a pair of gloves.

"Sure we can't keep Arnie's car and torch yours?"

"Very funny," Torque said. "Stay here. I'll be right back." He ran to the lone building, used a key to open the padlock hanging on the door, and stepped inside. A few minutes later, he returned, a full body bag slung over one shoulder. He motioned Michael to open Arnie's car. Michael obeyed and stood aside.

Torque set the body down next to the car and unzipped the body bag. He beckoned to Michael to give him a hand, and together they removed the body, which felt like ice from the storage freezer. The dead man was close in height and weight to Arnie though he didn't look much like him. That wouldn't matter when they were finished.

It took about twenty minutes of fiddling, but they set the stage. The body was seated in the driver's side of the car. They'd drenched the body and the interior of the car with gasoline. It would look like Arnie had committed suicide by setting himself on fire and driving his car into the gas pumps.

Dental imprints would be taken from Arnie and given to the coroner to use in his report to positively identify the body as Arnie's. Since the coroner was working for them, he'd list it as a suicide. Michael stepped away from the car. The smell of gas was overpowering.

"Back your car away, and get your netbook connected to the network so we can crack into the car's computer system," Michael said to Torque. "Get ready to peel out when it hits the pump."

Torque nodded and returned to his car. Michael watched while Torque fiddled with the netbook. When it was ready, he waved Michael over and handed it to him.

In less than ten minutes, Michael had control of Arnie's vehicle. He opened the driver's door, holding his breath against the assault from the fumes that wafted out. He put the car in gear, lit a match, and tossed it in. It ignited with a woof, and Michael slammed the door shut. He ran to Torque's car and jumped in.

Flames licked the interior of Arnie's car.

"Back it away. We're still too close," Michael said.

Torque put the car into reverse and drove back another fifteen metres. Michael used the netbook to hurtle Arnie's car backwards.

The crash mangled the back end and shoved the gas pump off its island. The ground shook when the car exploded. Torque drove back to the road, and they watched the flames flare upward and black smoke plume into the sky.

"Okay, let's go," Michael said. "It won't take long for this to attract attention." He ripped off his gloves and threw them in the back seat.

"Yup," Torque agreed and spun the car around. "Arnold

Griffen has ceased to exist." He drove along the dirt road towards the highway at an easy pace. Behind them, they heard an explosion and more black smoke poured into the sky.

"That was a good one," Torque commented, glancing into the rear-view mirror. "Want to hit a fast food joint after we drop Griffen off at the Agency? I'm hungry."

Michael nodded. "Sure."

Torque glanced at Michael and grinned. "And then there were two."

CHAPTER 25

You've reached Arnie Griffen. I am unable to take your call …

Carolyn hung up before the beep. She'd called so many times already that leaving a message was pointless. Why wasn't Arnie picking up? Why wasn't he calling her back?

He might have fallen asleep or put it on silent so he could get some work done. But they'd planned to try to see Ralph, and she still wanted to do that. It was more important to her now than ever to talk to Ralph and find out what had happened to him.

She sat on the couch in her living room, staring at the phone and willing it to ring, to be Arnie on the other end, to have something turn out all right. Unease slicked her skin with sweat that trickled down the small of her back. The phone rang, startling her. She looked at the call display. Arnie's home number flashed on the screen.

Thank God.

She grabbed the phone, pressed the "Talk" button. "Arnie?"

"No," a female voice replied. "It's Beverly—his mom's nurse. I can't reach him. Can you tell me where he is?"

"I'm sorry. I thought he was heading home when he left here earlier. That was hours ago. Has he contacted you at all since this morning?" Carolyn asked.

"No, and I'd like to go home. This isn't like him, and, to be honest, I'm worried. He checks in with me regularly to make sure his mother is okay and to keep me informed of when he'll be back. When he left this morning, he said he'd be gone most of the day, but it's getting on night now, and he should've called."

"Let's give him a little more time," Carolyn said. "It's seven o'clock. If he's not back by nine o'clock, we'll call the police."

"Have you tried calling his office?" Beverly asked.

"Yes," Carolyn replied. "I tried it a couple of times. But I don't want to panic and call the cops if he's out with one of his women."

"But if it were that, he'd at least pick up his messages and then call me back."

"I doubt he's with a woman, anyway. I'll tell him to call you if I hear from him."

"Thanks, Carolyn."

Carolyn set the phone down.

Where was he? She could try remote viewing. She went up the stairs to the den and lay down on the couch. A short while ago, Arnie had lain there, after the extraterrestrials had returned him to the house. She could still feel his energy.

Carolyn closed her eyes, and tried to focus on him, to sense his vibration, to receive information about where he was. She saw only darkness and felt nothing. But the harder she tried, the less likely she'd be to get anything. She deepened her breathing, let thoughts come in, acknowledged them, and let them go.

I should call Sammie ... Ralph, does Ralph know what's been happening? ... Call Beth ... Arnie, focus on Arnie ... tell me about Arnie ...

The darkness, everything was darkness. She breathed deeply and let relaxation spread from the top of her head down to her toes. When her body relaxed, she drifted off to sleep.

Carolyn stokes a woodstove's fire in a three-room log home. She wears a long dress and an apron. There's a knock at the door.

She moves to answer it, but before she can reach it, the door flies open. A little girl bursts into the room, bonnet hanging down her back, dark braids coming apart, and dress dirty and torn. Carolyn recognizes the child from next door. Tears carve a grimy streak down her pale face.

"What is it?" Fear wells up inside Carolyn.

"They took my mama," the little girl says. "They said she's a witch. Please, help me."

Carolyn runs outside. A trail winds away from her house, and she looks across the cornfield to the road. Men in a horse and buggy are heading towards her house. She knows they're coming for her.

"Into the house, quickly," she tells the girl, Jamie. "They're coming for us, too."

She closes the door, desperately looking for a place to hide. She opens a closet door. There are piles of clothes and blankets on the floor of the closet. She pushes them aside. "Get in here. Stay very still. Don't move or make a sound. Maybe they won't find you."

Jamie whimpers, but she does as she's told. Carolyn throws blankets over her and closes the door. She knows the girl will be frightened of the dark, but she can't do anything else. They're already at the door, and she has no time to hide herself. They burst into the room.

The first man through the door approaches her. He looms over her. She stares at him, trying to figure out who he is, why he seems so familiar. He has black hair, an aquiline nose, and full lips.

It isn't until the second man steps through the door that the terror surges through her. This man reeks of hatred. Carolyn realizes he takes pleasure in torturing and killing. The first man grabs her and holds her in a bear hug. She struggles and screams.

He clamps a hand over her mouth. "Silence, witch. You have no power anymore. Time for you to burn."

He drags her to the horse and buggy, which turns out to be a horse pulling a rickety cage on wheels. Arnie is in there. Carolyn knows the prisoners are all similar to her. They all can sense things, but some of them don't know that yet. The men want them for their powers.

Arnie lies on the bottom of the cage, naked. He lies so still, and for an instant, Carolyn fears he's dead. Then she sees the slow rise and fall of his chest. His skin looks raw and red as if burned. A thin, gritty coating of something Carolyn can't recognize covers his body.

"Bring that one here," the other man shouts, pointing at a young woman huddled in the corner of the cage. Carolyn recognizes Liza, Jamie's mother. Liza screams, and then she's outside of the wagon, the man holding her down. He pulls out a jar of what looks like sand and starts rubbing it onto Liza's bare skin.

Liza is completely naked now and where the sand touches her, Carolyn can see it burning her flesh. Her shrieks meld together, like she's no longer taking breaths between the screams. Then there's an unearthly silence. Liza has fainted.

The man turns to Carolyn, points at her. "She's next."

Carolyn struggles, but she's naked now, and he's approaching, the jar of sand in his fist.

"You're to be marked, witch." He tells her this without emotion, without remorse, without regret, or sympathy. It's just something that has to be done. The first man is holding her tight.

She begs. "Please, no. This is wrong."

His arms pinion her to his chest and she's weak, weaker than she'd have thought. Her arms feel like lead weights, and they drop to her sides. The man holding the sand begins to rub it into the skin on her arms, and it burns. Carolyn opens her mouth to scream ...

She woke, drenched in sweat, her mouth open, but the scream stifled. It was dark in the den. She sat up. The dream faded, but the sensation it left behind was still raw and fresh. She marvelled that a simple dream could affect her physically. The ghost of the burning grit prickled on her arms. She glanced at the clock. It was after 9:00 PM. There had been no call from Beverly letting her know she'd heard from Arnie. They should call the police.

CHAPTER 26

Carolyn lay awake the whole night, rising at 5:00 AM when she'd had enough of tossing around in bed. Being up was nominally better, but no matter what she did, the knot in her stomach persisted.

It was worse every time the phone rang. Carolyn jumped on it, hoping it was Arnie. So far, every call, and there were many, had been someone offering condolences about John, or asking if she needed anything, or wanted company. She was grateful, but it made her heart leap into her throat every time the phone rang, and her nerves were frayed.

By now, she was sure something had happened to him. Last night, the last time she'd talked by phone to Beverley, they'd decided Beverly should call the police. The nurse had texted her shortly after, saying she'd filled out a missing person report.

Carolyn tried to sense him in the spirit world and found some consolation in being unable to locate him there. What worried her was the darkness she felt whenever she tried to connect to him. It likely meant he was still alive, but she wasn't getting any kind of reading from him. She'd repeatedly called Arnie's cell, but stopped when the voice mail registered full.

Aimlessly, she wandered around the house with a dust rag and a can of furniture polish. When the whole house was dust free, she pulled out the vacuum. She managed to vacuum the entire house, wash the floors in the bathrooms and kitchens, clean the tubs, and there was still no word. She booted up her computer and checked his blog. The posting they'd argued over was still there. There were no additional posts.

Frustrated, she called Sam.

"Hello?"

"Hi, sweetie, it's me. How did you sleep?"

"Not good. But I did get some sleep. How are you?"

"I'm having trouble sleeping too. Sam, Arnie hasn't been answering his phone since he left here yesterday, and the nurse who works for him hasn't heard from him either. Would you mind coming home? For a little while? I'm afraid something's happened to Arnie, too."

"I'm sure he's fine. But I'll ask Vanna to give me a lift over. I'll be there in about twenty minutes, okay?"

"Thank you. Be careful."

"Okay. Don't worry, Mom."

She disconnected. What should she do now? She had to keep herself busy. Carolyn opened up Arnie's blog again and read posts from the archives, starting with the ones Ralph had written before he went to the hospital. One post in particular caught her attention. Ralph had written about a woman, Patty Richards, who was doing the talk circuit of UFO conventions.

Ralph seemed to hold her in high esteem and worked closely with her, but Carolyn had never seen her before at any of the sky watches. She did a quick search on Patty to see who she was and if she was in other UFO groups. One of the first links that popped up in the search was to Patty's obituary.

A chill ran through Carolyn when she read Patty had died suddenly of what appeared to be a heart attack. This had happened at the end of April, only a short time before their last sky watch and after Ralph had gone into the hospital. The phone rang, and she snatched it up.

"Hello?"

Sobbing greeted her on the other end. Carolyn waited, not breathing, her body tensing. At last, a voice she recognized as Beverly's said, "They found him, Carolyn. He's dead. The police were just here." She started sobbing again.

Carolyn went numb. "What happened?" It was the only thing she could manage to say.

"They said it looks like he committed suicide. They found his body in his burned-out car. He loved that car. He wouldn't have done that."

"What makes them think he killed himself?"

"They said it looked like he set a fire in his car deliberately and then drove it into a gas pump. He's burned up, but they got his dental records. His cell phone was in the car, too. There was no note, but they said it was obviously suicide."

It wasn't suicide. "I don't believe it."

"It's what the police told me. I'm sorry. I have to go. His mother is torn up. I had to give her a sedative."

"Okay. I'm so sorry. Tell his mom I'll come and see her when she's feeling up to it."

They hung up. At the sound of the door opening, Carolyn looked up. Samantha stepped into the house. At the sight of her mother's face, Sam froze. "Did you hear from Arnie?"

Carolyn rushed over to Sam and threw her arms around her. "Oh, God, Sam. They found his body. They said he killed himself."

Sam burst into tears, clinging to Carolyn. They stood that way for a moment and then Carolyn pulled away from her daughter and closed the door.

"It can't be right. I didn't sense him in spirit."

"Maybe you can't know all the time."

"He's one of my best friends. He'd come to me, or I'd at least know he'd passed."

"Do you think they made a mistake?"

"I don't know what to think. I want to talk to Ralph. He might have been right all along. Will you come with me?"

"Of course."

"Let me shut down my computer." Carolyn went to her computer.

Patty's face stared out at her from the screen. Carolyn tried to connect to Patty. She didn't get a response, but knew Patty was in spirit. She tried Arnie again. All she could sense was darkness.

She shut down the laptop and went to get her car keys.

CHAPTER 27

It took some doing, and Carolyn was sure the doctor would call security and have them escorted out. In the end, Carolyn was able to convince him they'd come out of concern for Ralph and wouldn't say anything to cause him distress. In other words, she lied. Not about being concerned for Ralph—that part was true. But she was sure what they had to tell him was going to cause him a great deal of distress.

So, here they sat, in his room. The door was propped open, allowing staff to peek in on them. Ralph sat on his bed while Sam and Carolyn occupied the only two chairs in the room. A table stood between the two women, and Ralph's laptop sat on the table. They'd already dispensed with the small talk, and Carolyn steeled herself for the conversation to come.

"They said you didn't want to see us. Is that true?"

"Yes." Then he qualified it. "But only for your sake."

"What do you mean?"

Ralph glanced at Sam, uncertain.

"It's okay," Carolyn said. "Sam knows I suspect you were forced in here."

"Let's go for a walk," Ralph suggested.

"Are you allowed to leave your room?"

"Yes. Let's go into the yard, where we can get some air."

Carolyn nodded, and they all stood. Ralph ushered the women from the room and led them down the corridor to an exit.

White French doors opened onto a white stone porch. A set of stairs descended to a concrete path. On either side of the path stretched lawns bordered by flowers and trees, abutting barbed wire-topped fences. Carolyn couldn't see a gate.

No one else was outside. Carolyn wondered at that. It was hot for May, but she expected that on such a bright sunny day someone would've been out here getting some sun and air.

"We can talk more freely here," Ralph said. "I don't trust my room isn't bugged."

"Really, Ralph?" asked Carolyn. She didn't wait for him to answer. "How have you been? Did you really ask them to put you in here?"

"I'm feeling okay, but I'd rather be at home. I'm here to keep my family safe. It's safer for all of you, too, if you stay away from me."

"Did you hear what's been happening?"

"I heard Arnie posted a video of an abduction. I talk to Beth once a week. They screen what I can access on my computer, so I can't read the blog. Beth said Arnie has called her several times and no one else has tried to contact her."

"We're respecting your wishes. I did try once to talk to her, but she made it clear she didn't want me to contact her. Your doctor doesn't want me to talk about anyone or anything relating to the group, but I think you have a right to know what's happened."

"What happened?"

"Okay ... Ralph, John died at work of a heart attack on Monday. Then Shelly was stabbed to death in a mugging at her apartment. Now, Arnie was found dead, and they say it was suicide. I doubt Arnie would kill himself. Sorry to lay it on you all at once, but I'm worried about Sam and me. I was hoping you could tell me what to do."

Ralph didn't speak. His face went white, and his hands crept over his stomach in a protective gesture. "Jesus, Carr. John is dead? Shelly? Arnie?"

She nodded as he listed each name.

"I have to sit down." Ralph walked to one of the Adirondack chairs scattered around the lawn and sank into it.

Carolyn gave him a moment to process it. She noticed the grey in his blond hair, the dark circles under his eyes, and the stoop to his shoulders. His round, usually cheerful face was now gaunt and lined and sorrowful. His eyes seemed to sink into his face, making them appear small and squinty.

She reached out and touched his cheek. "I'm sorry."

Ralph gazed up at her. "I'm sorry too, Carolyn—you, too, Sam. I can't imagine what it must be like for you."

Sam nodded her head and then lowered her eyes.

Carolyn continued. "Steve has refused to talk to us since Shelly died. He blames the group. It hurts he won't talk to us, and it hurts you wouldn't talk to us. I'm running out of people I trust or who understand what's going on. I can't tell my family." Carolyn tried to keep the despair and bitterness out of her voice. She wasn't sure she succeeded.

Ralph rose and hugged her. Some of the tension eased out of her. He held her head to his chest and she let her mind clear. Then he dropped his arms, and she stepped away.

"Thank you for seeing us. I don't know what I'd have done if you'd refused." Her voice broke.

"I've missed you, all of you. I don't refuse to see you by choice. They threatened my family. I shouldn't see you again, but I wanted to see you one last time."

"What can we do now?"

"Go away. There's a place in Algonquin Park—a base. There are aliens there who are helping abductees. I heard about it from someone who has been there. I have a map to it at my house. It's in a safe hidden in my basement. Tell Beth I said you could have it. Go to that base and ask them to help you."

"Aliens? A base?" Carolyn was confused. Did he expect her to go to the very beings who kidnapped and experimented on her?

"They're different. They don't kidnap people. They're against it. They help you to avoid getting taken again."

"How?"

"My friend says they do something that makes you untraceable to the others. I don't know how it works. I ended up here before I could verify it."

"Then how do you know this person told you the truth?"

"It was someone with inside information. I can't elaborate."

"Why didn't you mention this before—especially to Arnie? He was your best friend."

"I wanted to investigate it and then tell you. It's important to keep it from the government. They'll destroy it. Something like this goes against what they're trying to do. They're using their own citizens as bargaining chips with the hostiles. Anyone who interferes will be eliminated."

"What makes you think they don't already know about it?"

"I don't. They didn't know about it when I came to the hospital, I believe that much."

"Is it possible your house was searched?"

"It was. They made me commit myself. Then they went through my things and took all my files. Beth had to let them go through everything in my office. But the map isn't in my office."

"What about me?" Sam asked.

"Right now, you're not on their radar. You'll be safer at school," Carolyn replied.

"I don't want to leave you, Mom."

Carolyn put her hand on her daughter's arm. "It'll be okay. I want to make sure you're safe, Sam, and I'll take care of this for good."

"What if something happens to you? I can't let you go by yourself," Sam said.

"She's right, Carolyn," said Ralph.

Carolyn stood her ground. "She can't come. Sam must go back to work and school and carry on as if everything is normal. If we both disappear, it'll look suspicious."

"So how are you planning to disappear, Mom?"

"I'll tell people I'm going camping. I'll leave after the funeral, after you go back to your apartment in Cambridge. The neighbours can check the house for me each day and feed the cat. I wish Arnie were here. I'd have him come along."

Carolyn stopped talking when a white-coated staff member approached them.

"Mr. Drummond, Dr. Randal wants you to come in for your group therapy session."

"Okay, Nick. I'll be right there."

Ralph turned to Carolyn. "I have to go. I'm surprised he gave us this long. Follow me. You have to go through the building to get back to the main entrance."

They turned and headed back into the hospital.

CHAPTER 28

Less than an hour later, Carolyn pulled into the Drummond driveway and parked the car. Sam waited in the car while Carolyn headed to the house alone.

Over the years, Beth had spent a lot of money on landscaping, perfecting the outside. Carolyn noted the overgrowth of weeds, the uncut grass, and the shades pulled down over the windows. She wanted to cry.

A moment after she reached the porch and rang the doorbell, footsteps approached and the door opened.

Beth supported herself with one hand on the door. Her once dark hair, now turning grey, was pulled back into a ponytail, a few errant strands plastered against her sweaty face. Her tired eyes were rimmed with red. The T-shirt and cut-off shorts she wore were faded, and the nail polish on her fingers and toes was chipped. She frowned, making a sound like a wounded raccoon, and took a step back when she recognized Carolyn.

Carolyn tried to speak first, "Beth, I—"

Beth over-rode her, her voice shrill. "What are you doing here? You're not supposed to come here."

"Please, let me explain. I visited Ralph. He told me to come see you."

Beth's eyes narrowed. "He wouldn't do that. We're not supposed to have contact with any of you." She stepped outside and closed the door. "Let's move off the porch."

She's worried about bugs too. Carolyn walked down the steps to the grass. "Have you heard what's been happening?"

"Whatever it is, keep it to yourself and leave. Please."

"Ralph suggested I get something from you. If you give me what I'm looking for, I'll leave and never return. Please. Will you do that?"

Beth hesitated, frowned. "What, exactly?"

"A map. Ralph says it's in a safe in the basement. Please, get it for me?"

"No, I'm sorry."

"Why? We've been friends for years. If you give it to me, I'll leave you alone. I swear."

"It's not that I don't want to help you, Carolyn. I can't give it to you because I gave it to the agents who were here."

"Oh my God. Why?"

"To save my family. They said if I gave them everything, my family would be safe. I gave it to them. My family comes first."

Carolyn wanted to scream at Beth, to hit her. She hugged herself, trying to stop the trembling. Tears threatened, and her voice broke when she spoke. "Do you know what you've done?"

"I had to."

"But they never would've known if you'd kept it."

"They know everything. I couldn't take the chance."

"They'll destroy that base."

"I can't help that. Maybe there are others?"

"How likely is that? If the army or whoever is behind what's going on descends on that base, they'll destroy it. That base was our one hope to escape from this. Ralph is an abductee. Surely, they could've helped him too. Why would you take that away from him?"

"He's locked up. There's no help for him." Beth sounded bitter.

"What about your boys? These abductions run in families. Your boys may already be victims."

Beth shrugged. "Ralph sometimes gave Brent copies of things he had. Go ask Brent for the map. I didn't tell the agents about that. I only did what I had to do to keep my family safe."

"Thank you. I'm sorry for everything you're going through. I hope things get better for all of you." Without waiting for a response, Carolyn left Beth and returned to the car.

"She isn't giving it to you, is she?" Sam asked.

Carolyn shook her head, feeling unsafe talking in the car or using her cell. Was her home bugged? She backed the car out of the driveway and headed towards the nearest coffee shop with a pay phone.

Sam frowned but said nothing. When Carolyn parked the car and got out, Sam followed.

The two women walked to the pay phone, and Carolyn dialled Brent but got his voice mail.

"Hi, Brent, it's Carolyn. I'd like to stop by your office tomorrow morning. Please text my cell with a time." She hung up, and they went to the car. Before they got in, Carolyn said, "You'll stay at Vanna's tonight."

When Sam started to protest, Carolyn held up her hand to stop her. "It's okay. Don't worry about me. I'll ask Erika or another neighbour if I can stay the night there. Erika offered to keep me company, and I'll take her up on that."

Sam's face brightened. "Okay. I'm glad you'll be with someone tonight. If you need me for anything, call."

"I will. Everything will be fine. You'll see."

They got in the car, and Carolyn drove out of the parking lot.

***

Torque and Michael gave Carolyn a head start before pulling out after her.

"Drummond has her jumping at shadows now. She's acting like she thinks her phone is bugged and she's being followed," Torque said.

"Her phone *is* bugged, and she is being followed," Michael replied. "It's not jumping at shadows if it's true."

"Fair enough. It'll be more difficult for us if she makes calls using pay phones unless she's calling someone whose phone we've tapped."

Michael nodded and picked up his cell phone to call the office. If she'd called Steve, Brent, or any of Sam's close friends, they'd know whom she'd called and what she'd said. He pitied Carolyn. She didn't stand a chance against the Agency.

CHAPTER 29

When Carolyn pulled into her driveway, the uneasiness started. She'd felt fine when she'd dropped Sam off at Vanna's. The girls had promised they would stay in all evening, and Vanna's parents were home. Carolyn had kissed Sam goodbye and driven away, confident that her daughter would be safe.

Brent still hadn't called. However, that wasn't the source of Carolyn's uneasiness. When Arnie hadn't contacted her, she'd immediately sensed he was in danger. Her intuition told her Brent was too busy to respond.

Carolyn unlocked her door, anxiety escalating. She had to get out of here. Inside, she picked up her phone and called Erika. Voicemail. When the beep sounded, Carolyn left Erika a message and hung up.

She peered out the living room window. Nothing moved, but she felt watched. Even though the sun would still be up for another hour, she closed the curtains.

Carolyn hurried upstairs to her room and dug around in the clutter of her closet for a duffel bag. She dragged it out and threw some clothes and toiletries into it. She checked her phone again, hoping there had been some response from Erika, even though she'd have heard any incoming texts or calls.

Her bag packed, she considered what to do next. What if Erika was out for the night? Perhaps she should try another neighbour.

I have to get out of here. Carolyn tried to tell herself it was all in her head, she was making it up, but that only increased her angst. She'd call Ginger, another neighbour who lived up the street.

She went into the den to get the landline, keeping the cell phone free in case Erika or Brent called. When she reached out to pick up the phone, she thought she heard a noise from downstairs. Her breath caught in her throat. She listened, hoping it was just the cat, but sensing there was someone in the house.

Carolyn jumped when the cat brushed against her leg, proof it wasn't Fox downstairs. A floorboard creaked, and she was certain there was someone walking around on the main floor. She picked up the phone to call the police.

No dial tone.

She snatched up her cell phone, but her hands shook, and she almost dropped it. She pressed 9-1-1. Phone to her ear, she made her way to the patio doors. If she could get outside, she could get down to the ground and run into the forest.

The distance to the doors seemed to increase with each terrified step she took. When she reached the door, she clicked the lock open, cringing at the sound it made, loud as a backfiring car to her ears. Slowly she eased the inner door open, trying to be silent, but her terror rose at the soft tap of footsteps on the stairs.

She slid the screen door open with less caution, and it made a slight whoosh as it slid. The footsteps sped up. She clicked open the lock on the outer door, sliding it open fast, no longer caring about the noise. When she stepped through the door onto the balcony, a man appeared in the den. He spotted her.

There was no sound from her phone. Why hadn't anyone picked up? She glanced at the screen. Call failed. She whimpered and hit "Retry." There was no time to stop to close the doors. No time to open the gate to get down the stairs.

Her first thought was to jump over the side of the balcony. But the drop was over six metres and she couldn't land without injuring herself.

The man stepped outside.

She backed against the railing.

He pointed a gun at her. "Don't move." He inched towards her.

Carolyn focused on the gun, unable to take her eyes off it. She forced her gaze away and looked over the side of the railing. It was a long way down. Below her sat a woodpile. She wouldn't be going that way.

The intruder snatched the phone from her hand, and glanced at it. He put it to his ear. Satisfied she hadn't been able to place a call, he turned off the phone and threw it over the balcony.

Carolyn's fear overwhelmed her, and she thought she would be sick. She swallowed, but her throat was dry. Taking a deep breath, she tried to clear her head. If she was to survive, she needed to be able to think.

"Who are you?"

She squinted, trying to see his face in the darkness. If she managed to get away, she'd need a description.

He towered over her—at least by four inches, which would make him about six feet tall. He wore jeans and a plain, white T-shirt under a grey suit jacket that, when buttoned, concealed his shoulder holster. His black, slightly wavy hair and tan complexion enhanced the aura of darkness around him. Bangs drooped over his forehead, almost hanging in his brown eyes. His full lips pressed together, and tension oozed from him. He was one of the witch hunters in her dream.

"Who are you?" she demanded.

He didn't reply, but grabbed her by the arm and yanked her back towards the house. She resisted and tried to pull free.

"Stop struggling. I'll only tell you once. Then I'll slug you."

She ceased fighting and walked, trying to think of something to say that would make him let her go. He pushed her inside.

Carolyn called on her guardian angels and spirit guides. *Angels, guides, and departed loved ones, I call upon you now. Please help me. Guide me through this. Help me connect to this man's guides so I can reason with him.*

She tried to get a sense of the man's energy. Pain, anger, and cold flowed into her.

Ask him about Jessica. "Who is Jessica?"

The grip on her arm tightened, and he audibly sucked in a breath.

"You're hurting me," Carolyn said.

The man scanned the room, and then pulled her outside again, closing the patio doors behind them.

"How do you know about Jessica?"

"I just know. My house is bugged, isn't it?"

"I'll ask the questions. Why did you ask about Jessica? Is this some kind of trick?"

"No. I was guided to ask," she replied.

"What do you mean 'guided'? Guided by what?"

"If you've been spying on us, then you know the answer. She means something to you. I can tell by your reaction. She's ..."

Wife. "She's your wife," Carolyn said.

The man pulled her close to him, so her ear was next to his mouth. "How do you know about my wife?" His voice was a low growl.

"The information is coming from my guides. Don't you think you have more explaining to do than I do?" Carolyn said.

He didn't reply, but forced Carolyn inside again. He dragged her to the door of the den, but at that moment, the sound of a key turning in the front door's lock reached Carolyn's ears. The stranger halted and yanked her back into the den. The front door opened, and there were footsteps in the entryway.

Her heart in her mouth, Carolyn froze. The man pinioned her to his chest, his arms around her, keeping her still. He pressed the gun to her temple.

"Quiet," he whispered.

From below, her daughter's voice called out, "Mom? Are you here? Hello?"

CHAPTER 30

At the sound of Sam's voice, Carolyn choked down a moan.

Oh, God, no. Angels, please, tell her to leave. Don't let her come up here.

"Sounds like no one's home. Mom must be at the neighbour's," Sam told whoever was with her. "I'll grab my stuff from my room. Check the kitchen cupboard for munchies. My mom won't mind."

The footsteps faded towards the kitchen.

Carolyn whispered, "Please, don't hurt them. It's my daughter and her friend. I'll do whatever you want, just please, leave them alone."

The stranger whispered in her ear, his breath blowing on her hair, "Stay quiet. If they don't bother us, I won't bother them."

Carolyn froze. An eternity of seconds ticked away. Sam and her friend walked around on the main floor. Then they were rooting around in the cupboards. Carolyn wondered if this was the last moment she'd ever have with her daughter. A sob caught in her throat, and the man tightened his arms around her.

"Shut up. You bring them up here, and I'll shoot them both."

Tears welled up. She closed her eyes, and the tears streamed down her face. There was more movement from the main floor, and the footsteps approached the entryway.

"Ready, Sam?" The voice was male.

Where was Vanna? This sounded like Roger. What happened to Sam's promise to stay at Vanna's and watch videos? Carolyn realized that wasn't important.

Oh, God, Sam, please leave.

"Yeah. Just had to leave a note for my mom," Sam answered.

The front door opened, closed, and then the key turned in the lock. The kids were gone. She let herself breathe again. The man released his grip on her.

"Let's go," he said.

Out of habit, Carolyn locked the patio doors, recognizing the irony as she did so. She turned to walk to her room with a vague notion she should get her purse.

The man grabbed her arm and yanked her back to the stairs. "What do you think you're doing?"

"Getting my purse," she replied, feeling foolish.

He looked at her like she'd lost her mind.

"I've never been kidnapped before," she said, knowing how ludicrous that sounded. At least if her purse was left behind, people would suspect something was wrong.

The stranger guided her down the stairs. When they reached the bottom of the stairs, Carolyn turned to walk through the living room and into the kitchen.

He pulled her backwards.

"Not that way," he said, irritation in his voice.

"I'm going to read my daughter's note," Carolyn said. "If you want to stop me, we're going to have a fight."

He stared at her for a moment, perhaps debating whether to force her out the door, shrugged, and followed her into the kitchen.

She retrieved the note from the counter.

Mom: gone to Nichole's with Roger. Vanna and Jack are already there. Grabbed some snacks. See you tomorrow. Love you, Sam.

Tears running down her face, Carolyn folded the note and put it into her pocket.

The man, his voice strained, said, "Go. Now." He held her upper arm and led her back to the front door. He unlocked the door and opened it.

Carolyn realized she was barefoot. "My shoes are upstairs."

"Then you're going barefoot."

They stepped outside. He closed the door behind them, and she said, "My keys. They're inside."

"Leave them," he said. "Walk. I've had enough of this."

She moved down the stairs, gaze darting from side to side. Maybe she could run into the forest when they reached the bottom.

She could try to outrun him even though she was barefoot. Once he had her in the car, escape would be unlikely.

As if reading her mind, the man said, "Don't try anything. You'll be dead before you reach the trees."

Carolyn nodded, to indicate she'd heard him. The gun pressed into the small of her back. His grip never left her arm. Together they shuffled slowly down the steps. Silently, she asked her guides for help.

She sensed a presence. A spirit. The night was hot, but cold air pressed against her left side, and her left arm tingled. A female presence. She knew who it was.

"Jessica?" she said aloud.

The man halted. They were halfway down the stairs.

"What are you doing?" His tone was angry.

"She's here," Carolyn said. "Michael. Your name is Michael."

Michael spun her around to face him. "What the fuck?" He holstered his gun and gripped her arms. Face thrust into hers and enunciating each word, he said, "How do you know that?"

Carolyn's eyes watered from the pain of his grip. She'd have bruises on her arms where he held her. "You're hurting me."

"Not like I'm going to hurt you if you don't tell me what the fuck you're doing. Are you fucking with me? Where'd you get that information?" Michael kept his voice low, but it sounded loud in her ears. His anger and panic flowed into her. The harsh, vulgar words were like a slap.

"Michael, please. Don't. I'll tell you, but you'll have to have an open mind. Your wife is telling me. Jessie's here," Carolyn said.

"Impossible. She's dead."

"Stop for a second and pay attention. Let me speak. She wants to communicate or she wouldn't be here."

"Sit."

Carolyn crumpled to the steps.

Michael planted himself in front of her. He held the railing on either side in a tight grip. She wouldn't get past him. "Okay. Explain."

"I'm a psychic and a medium. That means I can communicate with spirits. You must be aware of that. Right?"

"I know what you claim to do."

"It's fine if you're a skeptic, but right now, your wife is trying to communicate with you. I can prove it. I'll ask her to tell me more things I wouldn't know, though I've already told you a lot." She opened herself up to receive messages.

Jessica, my name is Carolyn, and I'd like to talk to you. If you have a message for Michael, I can tell him.

She felt dizzy and her whole body hurt. Pain seared her head. She saw a car coming at her. "She was hit by a car," Carolyn said.

Michael's face went white. "Go on."

Carolyn waited. She looked down and to the right—her typical stance when receiving messages.

Pregnant. She saw in her mind an impression of a woman, long brown hair, walking across a busy street. The woman stumbles and staggers into traffic. There's a squeal of brakes, a shriek of tires. Carolyn looked up, away from the sight.

"I'm so sorry," she said to Michael. "She was pregnant. That must have been horrible for you."

Michael's eyes filled with pain, and his breath caught in his throat.

The ray. "Michael, what's 'the ray?'" Carolyn asked. "I just got 'the ray.' I don't understand what it means."

Gerry. The ray. "I got 'Gerry' and 'the ray' and they were repeated. Usually that means it's significant."

Michael gripped her arms again and pulled her to her feet. "What are you saying?" He again enunciated each word precisely.

"I'm telling you what I'm getting. Who's Gerry?" she asked. "He's your partner?" she said, answering her own question.

"Yes," Michael answered. "What's she saying?" He shook her while he asked this.

"Please, stop hurting me," Carolyn said. "Give me a minute." She listened. "He was there." Suddenly, she knew. "He met with her, and then he killed her."

Michael said, his voice a whisper, "Why? That doesn't make sense. What are you trying to do?" He frowned. "You're trying to turn me against my partner. Forget it. Let's go."

"I don't know you or your partner. I'm only telling you the messages I'm receiving as I get them," Carolyn said. "Your wife is trying to help you learn the truth."

"We have to go. He's waiting, and he'll get suspicious if we don't come down to the car. Move." Michael pulled her arm, and she stumbled down another two steps.

"You call him Torque? Jess is the one who calls him Gerry, isn't that right?"

He glanced at her, opened his mouth as if to reply, nodded his head, and said, "Walk." He held her arm, escorting her down one step at a time. The sound of the gun sliding from its holster reached her ears, and he shoved it into the small of her back.

"Must you do that?" she asked.

He didn't reply, and the gun stayed put.

Carolyn picked her way down, watching where she stepped. Would pushing him down the stairs allow her time to get away or just make him angrier? Again, she received sudden knowledge, and her own thought echoed the knowledge.

"They'll get you too," Carolyn said. "She's telling me they'll lock you up."

Michael stopped again. "Who will?"

She listened. "A man named Cornell. He no longer trusts you."

Don't get in the car. "She says we shouldn't get in the car."

By this time, they'd reached the bottom of the stairs. Michael gripped her arm, leading her to the road. The gun was in his right hand. He continued to point it at her.

"We can't get into the car. Please. Jessica says not to," Carolyn insisted.

"What do you expect me to do? Believe you're talking to my dead wife?"

"I *am* talking to your dead wife." Carolyn tried to stop walking, but he tugged on her arm, making her stumble. "Stop. Just listen. Please. Jessica, please tell me what you want Michael to know. Tell me something to help him know it's you."

A woman's voice spoke into her left ear. *Gerry didn't want me to have the baby.*

"She says Gerry killed her because he found out she was pregnant."

Michael stopped again. "Gerry knew about the baby?"

The voice spoke again.

"Gerry knew everything," Carolyn said.

No family. The rest of the knowledge came to her. "Gerry was afraid you'd become concerned about the child's future, and it would cause you to turn against them."

"So just like that he decided the solution was to kill my wife?" Michael asked.

"Yes. Is that what they did with Shelly? Did you kill her? If you think Gerry shouldn't have killed your wife, what does that say about the things you've done in their name?" Carolyn said.

"I didn't kill Shelly. Torque didn't either. It was what it appeared to be: a mugging. You've said it yourself." Michael lowered his head, avoiding her eyes. "They had you all flagged as traitors to your country."

"Is that what they told you? How are we traitors? Arnie and I are abductees. What were we doing that makes us traitors?"

Michael didn't reply. Instead, he pulled her to him, his grip firm. "Quiet," he whispered in her ear. "I can't let Torque know I'm talking to you. We've already taken too long. He knows the second we stepped out the front door, and he's watching for us. Our instructions were to take you in, not kill you."

"Take me in where?" Carolyn asked. "Where Arnie is? You didn't kill him, did you? He didn't kill himself."

"Never mind that," Michael said. "Just do whatever I tell you. If you don't listen to me, then he'll kill me and take you in. Do you understand?"

She stared up at him. His eyes were intense. She could smell sweat on him and his grip on her arm was moist and slippery.

"You believe me? You believe we're communicating with your wife?" she asked.

"Yes," he answered.

"Do you still think I'm a traitor?" she asked.

"I was finding it hard to believe you were a traitor a long time ago," Michael said. "Let's go. He's seen us. He's pulling the car into the driveway. When we get there, do what I tell you."

Carolyn nodded and let him lead her down the rest of the driveway.

CHAPTER 31

Just before they reached the car, Michael waved to Torque, indicating he should pull in closer. The car backed into the driveway, all the way off the road. Michael banged on the trunk and it popped open. He pulled Carolyn behind the car, her body hidden from Torque by the trunk lid.

Michael leaned around the car and gave a low shout. "Grab the cuffs for me. I don't have mine here." To Carolyn, he whispered, "Stay out of my way. I gotta do this fast, so don't make any sudden moves." He shifted his gun to his left hand and waited.

Carolyn heard some shuffling and the sound of the car door opening. A man's voice said, "Not cool. You're supposed to have these things on you all the time. She should already be cuffed."

Torque appeared around the side of the car. Carolyn recognized the other man in her dream and her fear intensified. He held a pair of handcuffs out to Michael. Instead of taking the cuffs, Michael grabbed Torque's wrist, pulled Torque towards him, and swung the hand holding the gun at Torque's head.

Thrown off balance, Torque ducked the blow by a hair's breadth. He shoved Michael away from him, knocking the gun from his hand.

"What the fuck are you doing?" Torque shouted.

"You killed her, you son of a bitch," Michael shouted back.

Torque reached for the gun in the holster under his arm.

Michael lunged at him, and they both went down onto the asphalt, struggling.

Carolyn grabbed the gun Michael had dropped. She pointed it at the two of them and said, "If this fires, I don't know who it'll hit. I've never used one before. So, both of you, stop fighting now." She had a sudden, insane urge to giggle. *I sound like I'm talking to a couple of little kids.* She hoped they didn't see how badly her hands were shaking.

The two men, looking startled, froze.

"Get his gun, Michael," Carolyn said.

Michael snatched the weapon from Torque's holster.

"Now get up and take over. I don't know what I'm doing, and if anyone makes a move my way, I might fire. No one wants to see that happen." She took a couple of steps back to let Michael stand.

Michael levered off the pavement and waved the gun at Torque. "Get up."

Torque rose.

"Put the cuffs on," Michael said.

"What are you doing, Mick? What happened up there? Whatever she told you, it's a lie. She's a traitor. You'd be crazy to trust her," Torque said. "Take the gun out of my face. We're partners, for Christ's sake."

"You killed Jess," Michael said. "You found out she was pregnant, and you killed her without even considering alternatives."

"Is that what she told you?" Torque nodded at Carolyn. "If she did, she's lying."

"I don't think so. You were there. You watched her die," Michael said.

Torque started, and then his face went cold. "I told you, I was following up on a suspect. It was near our office. I was sitting in traffic when she got hit."

"If that's true, then why didn't you tell me? Why keep that from me? Why wouldn't you have tried to help her or call 9-1-1? I'm the 'suspect' you were following up on, aren't I? What's waiting for me at the end of this ride, Torque?"

"She's lying to you. She's a traitor," Torque repeated. "Why would you believe her?"

"Your response tells me all I need to know. Put the cuffs on." Michael raised the gun, aiming it at Torque's face. "I won't tell you again."

Torque cuffed his hands in front, taking his time.

"Take the key from him," Michael ordered Carolyn. "But first, give me my gun, before you hurt yourself."

"I'll get the key," Carolyn said, "but I'm keeping the gun." She walked over to Torque and held out her left hand for the key. She held the gun in her right hand, away from Torque. He fished the key from his pocket and dropped it into Carolyn's outstretched palm.

"Get in the trunk," Michael said to Torque.

"What are you going to do?" Torque asked. "They'll know. Whatever you do to me, they'll find out. You won't get away with this. They'll track you down. You're a traitor now too."

Torque turned to Carolyn. "Did he tell you how he killed your husband? Did you tell her, Mick? He zapped him with the death ray. He killed John, and then we went for lunch, didn't we Mick?"

Carolyn stared at Torque, horror in her eyes. "The ray. That's the same ray you used to kill Jessica?" She turned from Torque to Michael. "You killed John? You did it yourself?" Her voice rose, a shriek of pain.

She pointed her gun at Michael. Her hands shook, but still she held it, aiming at his face. She gritted her teeth and sweat trickled into her eyes, stinging them. She squeezed one eye at a time, and tears and sweat trickled down her cheeks. .

"Don't listen to him, Carolyn," Michael said, "He's only interested in saving his ass right now. Get in the fucking trunk, Torque, or I'll shoot you and put you in there myself."

Put the gun down. Carolyn wasn't sure if that was her own thought, a directive from her guides, or communication from Jessica, but she lowered her gun.

Torque steadied himself on the bumper of the car and climbed into the trunk. "You'll regret this, Mick."

"Shut up. Lie down." Michael's face was livid. "Carolyn, there's a black bag in the back seat of the car. Bring it here."

Carolyn went to the back door of the car and opened it. She picked up the medical bag and took it back to Michael.

"Set it down next to me and open it."

She did.

"Now take out the syringe that's in the top. It's already loaded. It's in a tin in the top pocket of the bag."

Carolyn removed the tin and opened it. Inside rested a syringe with needle. She picked it up. "Was this meant for me?"

"Just give it to me." Michael held out his hand, continuing to watch Torque, and holding the gun on him.

Carolyn surrendered the needle to Michael.

He drew closer to the trunk of the car. "Make one move, Torque, and I'll shoot you." He jabbed the needle into Torque's neck and hit the plunger.

Torque stared at them a moment, and then collapsed into the trunk.

"If it was set up for me, how is it that it would knock him out? He's bigger than I am," Carolyn said.

Michael stared at her, puzzled. "That's your question?" He shook his head.

"You had enough in there to knock him out, even though it was meant for me."

"Get in the car."

Carolyn hesitated.

Michael slammed the trunk closed and picked up the medical bag. "Please. Get in the car. I don't want a Mexican standoff. You'd find it's easier for me to pull the trigger than it is for you. We can't stay here. If you go back into your house, they'll know something went wrong. The whole house is bugged. If I let you go, someone else will hunt you down. We have to get far away from here, now."

Carolyn tamped down the urge to argue. She went to the passenger side of the car and got in, setting the gun down on the floor between her feet.

Michael climbed in on the driver's side and started the car. He leaned over, reached between her feet, and, before she could react, picked up his gun. "I'll take that."

She blushed. "I couldn't use it if I had to."

He smiled, and his face softened.

"Where are we going?" Carolyn asked.

"First, we'll get my bug-out bag from my home in Aurora. Then we'll find a place away from here to hole up for the night."

"Are we going to find Arnie?" she asked.

"I can't help you get Arnie back. They had us stage his death, and he's in, well, let's call it custody." He pulled out of the driveway and headed back towards town and the highway leading to Aurora.

CHAPTER 32

They were on the highway, driving south along the 404 towards Aurora.

"What do you intend to do with me?" Carolyn asked.

He ignored her question.

She tried another one. "Why are the aliens abducting us?"

"Because you're more intuitive than the average person. The aliens are experimenting with it. So is the Agency."

"You work for the Agency?"

"Yes."

They rode in silence, Carolyn trying to think of something to say that wouldn't anger him. She searched for Jessica's presence but felt nothing. She closed her eyes. The inside of the car was chilly. She was barefoot and in shorts and a tank top. She shivered and goose bumps prickled on her arms and legs. Michael must've noticed because she heard him fiddle with the controls on the dash, and the cold air blowing on her diminished.

"Sorry. I should've at least let you get your shoes," he said.

"Yes. I hate walking around in bare feet."

"I thought you tree huggers loved going barefoot?"

"Not me." She opened her eyes. He was staring ahead at the road. She turned and looked out her window. "When can I go home?" She knew the answer but wanted to make him say it.

"You can't. I doubt you'll ever be able to go home. If it's any consolation, I can't either."

"My husband's funeral is on Saturday."

"You'll miss it. My wife's funeral is tomorrow. I'll miss it. We can't do anything about that. If either one of us shows our face now, we're dead. At least, I'm dead and you're locked up. Our best chance is to get you away from the Agency and the aliens so they can't abduct you again. There's an alien base in Algonquin Park that might give us a way to get that done. But either way, we have to disappear."

"How do you know about Algonquin?"

Again, he didn't reply. Carolyn turned away from the window and faced him. "Why won't you answer me? How do you know about the base?"

"I have Drummond's map."

The map Beth had turned over to the government agents. Michael had it. Should she be relieved or frightened?

"I can't do this," she said.

Michael turned his head and met her gaze. "You have to." He returned his focus to the road.

Carolyn fell silent, wondering if she should tell him Sam knew about the base. She decided against it, not wanting Sam on anyone's radar.

Twenty minutes later, they turned into a long driveway that led to a large two-story home on a fair-sized lot. He stopped the car halfway up the drive and lowered the windows. Michael opened the caddy between their seats and handed her a cell phone. "Here's Torque's cell phone. If you hear or see anything suspicious, hit three on the speed dial. That's my cell number. No other calls. Don't try Brent; don't try your daughter. As far as everyone is concerned, you've disappeared. The last thing you need to do is put your daughter in danger. Is that clear?"

She nodded.

He handed her a gun. "If Torque wakes up, shoot him. Point it at him and pull the trigger, but make sure you put direct pressure on the trigger or it won't fire. There's a suppressor on it, which is why the barrel is so long. You don't have to do anything else. It's already cocked."

Her eyes went wide, and she made a choking sound of protest.

"It's okay. I'll get the bag and come right out. The gun's probably unnecessary, but if you need it, it's better to have it than not."

"Michael?" she said, in a small voice. Her heart was beating rapidly, her pulse thudded in her ears. Now he planned to leave her alone, she didn't want to let him go.

Michael looked into her eyes. "I'll help you, I swear. No one will take you again."

She swallowed. All she could do was nod.

Michael stepped out of the car and closed the door. When he neared his front door, a motion sensor detected his presence, and a light flicked on. He unlocked the door and disappeared inside.

Carolyn hunkered down, feeling exposed even though Michael had parked in the shadows. In front of her, light splashed on the ground. She hoped it would turn off soon.

Head tilted towards the back seat, she listened for any sound from the trunk.

If he wakes up and pounds on the trunk while I'm sitting here by myself, I'll have a heart attack without the help of the ray. Carolyn picked up the cell phone and toyed with the idea of turning it on and calling someone. She sighed and put it down. She wasn't going to be that stupid.

That Michael had left her alone, had trusted she'd be waiting for him when he came out, told her a lot. She could run right now and he'd have difficulty finding her, especially if he was exposed as a traitor to his agency. If she ran, the Agency would find her. Her only chance was to stay with Michael and hope he'd protect and not betray her.

Carolyn checked the time on the phone. How long had Michael been gone? It was 7:48 PM. She thought at least ten minutes had passed. How long should she give him before she started to worry? She'd give him another ten minutes before deciding there was a problem. She sank lower in her seat.

***

Inside the house, Michael headed to his bedroom. He grabbed Jessie's pack for Carolyn. Michael's pack contained a two-person tent and his military gear, which made it heavier. He lifted his wife's pack with one arm, wondering if Carolyn could carry it. She was lean but not muscular. The bag weighed about thirty-five pounds. She'd have to manage.

While he was in there, he paused long enough to dig in the back of the closet and remove a plastic storage container that held photo albums. He opened one and peeled a picture of him and Jessie out of it. It had been taken the weekend they went to Jessie's sister's cottage. They'd stopped at a restaurant on the way up north, and Jess had asked the waiter to take their picture. She'd printed it up when they got home.

Michael had thought that was cheesy, but went along with it. She'd probably gotten pregnant that weekend. He was glad they'd had that one last weekend together and she'd suggested taking this photo. It didn't seem so cheesy now. He stuck the picture into his backpack. If he couldn't go to her funeral, he at least wanted something to remind him of her.

He snapped himself out of it. Torque might wake up at any moment. He headed out of the bedroom without a backwards glance. He checked his watch. Time felt like it had sped up. He rushed down the stairs. When he passed the kitchen, he realized they'd want some small bottles of water. He went to the kitchen to get them. It would only take a moment.

CHAPTER 33

Carolyn checked the time again. She'd start worrying in five minutes. It was silly, putting her worry on the clock like that, so she tried to relax by slowing her breathing.

It occurred to her she hadn't investigated what was in the car. She tried to open the glove box, found it locked, and glanced at the ignition. No keys. So, he didn't trust her that much. She lifted the lid of the caddy between the seats. Empty. She looked in the back seat and reached for the medical bag.

This proved more interesting.

It held a variety of drugs, syringes, and first aid paraphernalia. These guys had their own little mini hospital going for them. They even had surgical tools. She shuddered. What kind of surgeries might they want to perform and on whom?

On the edge of perception, she heard a scraping sound. Carolyn dropped the scalpel she was holding back into the bag and snapped it closed. She set the bag down on the floor behind the driver's seat and listened. A glance at the door to the house showed no sign of Michael.

Carolyn turned back around in time to see the back seat fold forward. Torque's feet and legs thrust through the opening. She gave a small shriek and frantically looked for the gun, in her panic forgetting where it was. There, on Michael's seat.

As Torque moved to crawl out of the trunk, she grabbed it and pointed it at him. "Don't move. I'll shoot." The gun wobbled in her shaking hands. She wasn't capable of pulling the trigger.

Torque's forehead was wet with sweat and his hair spiked up. He grimaced. "You dumb bitch. Get that gun off me." He lunged at her and, afraid he'd get the gun, she tossed it out the window. It hit the ground but didn't fire.

Carolyn cried out again and grabbed for the door, but Torque had her by the hair. He yanked her head back, swung his manacled arms around her chest, and pulled her into the back seat. She clawed ineffectually at his hands.

"Where's Mick?" he demanded. "I'll fucking kill you." He wrapped his hands around her throat, squeezing off her air supply.

Carolyn's legs kicked. She tried to brace her feet on the dash and shove herself into him, away from that strangling grip. Her fingers clawed his hands. He was too strong for her. The world spun. Her vision blurred, and her consciousness swam towards darkness.

Before she was completely lost, the hands relaxed. She was thrust aside, and her head hit the window. There was a new struggle behind her, and while she reoriented, the sound of Michael's voice cut through the haze. She gasped for breath, trying to get air flowing normally through her windpipe. Torque gone, she collapsed onto the seat.

A muffled shot reached her ears, then another. Not knowing if Michael had fired the gun or Torque, she dragged herself to the open car door. She tried to focus her eyes. One man stood over the body of another man, and she gratefully noted that the man who was standing was Michael.

Michael bent down to pick up the bags he'd dropped and ran over to her. He pushed her aside while he shoved the seat back up into position and threw the bags into the car. The door slammed in her face when she tried to speak to him.

He hurried back to where Torque lay, grabbed Torque under the arms, and dragged him back to the car. Michael grunted, and the car jostled as he stuffed Torque into the trunk and slammed the lid closed.

Without a word, Michael jumped into the driver's seat, started the car, and threw it into reverse.

Carolyn held herself steady in the seat while Michael backed out of the driveway. "Torque," she said. "Is he ...?"

"Dead? Likely. I didn't verify."

When Michael pulled onto the road, Carolyn climbed into the

front, taking care to stay out of his way. "Shouldn't we check? He'll need medical attention."

Michael frowned, opened his mouth, and then closed it again.

She stared at him, not understanding.

At last he spoke. "We can't help him. He's likely dead, and we have to get out of here. Don't think about it."

Horrified, she dropped her eyes. What kind of person could shoot his partner and not feel anything? He could kill her without remorse too. She tried to make her voice sound normal and keep him talking. "Did you get everything you needed?"

"Yes. I had the bags ready a while ago. I lost my faith in the 'Project' weeks ago. That stuff you said was from Jess? That's how they operate. They tell you enough of the truth to make the lies sound believable. But I never would've thought Torque had it in him to kill my wife." He fell silent.

Carolyn filled the void. "What are you going to do about Torque? If he's not dead, then he's injured."

"If he's not dead, then I'll kill him," Michael replied.

"No. Please, no more killing."

"He'll come after us."

"Then we'll be careful. Please, haven't you killed enough people in your lifetime? Aren't you sorry? Don't you have any regret?"

Michael didn't respond. Carolyn stared at him, waiting for some kind of response. He frowned. "I was trained to do what I was told without question, for the sake of the Agency. No remorse."

"And now?"

"Right now, if I have to kill Torque to protect us, I'll do it."

"I can understand self-defence. I can't conceive of killing someone in cold blood. It's wrong."

"That's what you've been trained to believe."

She fell silent and stared out the window.

After what seemed hours, she looked at the clock. It was 8:51 PM—earlier than she'd expected. There were few cars on the road. They were well away from Aurora. Carolyn gazed out the window as they passed fields, forests, and the occasional house.

When she looked up at the sky, she could see a faint spattering of stars. There were no clouds. The moon was a crescent. She wondered how long they'd drive before they stopped. She was tired, but she'd never be able to sleep with this trained killer sitting next to her, no matter how much he promised to help her.

Interrupting her thoughts, Michael said, "What's your shoe size?"

She looked up, confused, but answered the question. "Nine. Why?"

"My wife's survival bag has a pair of hiking shoes in it. I hoped they'd fit you, but she's a size eight."

She considered whether she should ask him where they were headed and decided she had a right to know. She cleared her throat and timidly asked, "Where are we going?"

"Peterborough. We can get a room there for a few hours and get some rest."

"What about Torque?"

"They'll find him eventually."

"What if he's alive?"

"Carolyn, if he's still alive, it's a miracle. I'm using hollow-point bullets, and I capped him twice in the chest. If I hadn't shot him, he'd have killed me. You'd be with him, and he'd be carrying out our orders to take you in. He'd set it up to make it look like you were dead so no one would ever look for you again. That's what we did with Arnie. His family will believe they're burying him, and that's the end of that."

"And what happens to Arnie?"

"He spends the rest of his life, however long that might be, locked up where no one will find him except the extraterrestrials. The aliens will always bring him back where they found him, so he'll be there until he dies. If, or when, the extraterrestrials have no more use for him, he'll be executed."

"We can't let that happen."

"I can't do anything to stop it. They have him. They'll have you, too, if we don't get where I want to go."

"To Algonquin?"

"Yes." Michael glanced at her and then put his eyes back on the road.

Carolyn stared out the window and thought about Torque in the trunk of the car. The least she could do was help him by sending him some Reiki.

She put her hands together and mentally went through the process of sending distance Reiki to Torque. She caught Michael staring.

"Are you praying?" he asked.

"No. If you must know, I'm sending distance Reiki to Torque."

"Dare I ask?"

"Ask away. Reiki is a universal life force energy. It's intelligent and goes where needed. If Torque isn't dead, it'll send him healing energy. If he's dead, it'll help his spirit."

Michael didn't comment.

"You think that's crazy, don't you?" Carolyn asked.

"I didn't say that."

"But you think so, don't you?"

"I don't buy into this new-age stuff. Sorry, but it doesn't make sense, and there's no scientific evidence it does anything."

"Actually, there is. Studies have been done. I don't care if you approve. It's something I can do."

"Why didn't you use the phone and call me when he started moving around?"

She blushed. "I wasn't paying attention, and when he pushed his way into the back seat, my first thought was to grab the gun. But I couldn't shoot him."

"You might have to learn to do that. If anything happens to me, you're on your own, and they'll keep coming for you. At some point, I want to show you the map. You should know where this base is, in case I don't make it."

Dread speared through her. "What do you mean 'in case you don't make it'?"

"These people are ruthless. When they realize Torque and I are AWOL, they'll be out in full force tracking us down. We have a limited amount of time before they start the hunt."

His words terrified her, and she didn't reply. Carolyn peered out her window at the darkness over Scugog Lake while they passed over it. She looked up at the stars and wondered if the aliens were out there and if they'd come for her.

"Would they come for me while we're driving?" She shuddered.

Michael glanced at her, and his face relaxed. "No," he said. "You're not scheduled to be picked up by the aliens again this soon."

She frowned. "They have a schedule? If I wasn't going to be abducted, and I wasn't doing anything wrong, why did you kidnap me tonight? Why'd you people take me away from my family now? Couldn't you at least let me bury my husband who your agency killed?"

Her voice rose when she remembered what they'd done, what they wanted to do. "I was trying to stop Arnie from posting those entries. If you were eavesdropping on us, you knew that. Why did you need me to disappear?"

Michael didn't answer her. She glared at him. She refused to let him stay silent on this one. The longer the silence dragged on, the more she wanted an answer.

At last, he cleared his throat and spoke, his voice so low she had to strain to hear him. "I don't know. That's the last thing you want to hear, but it's the truth. I understand why they locked up Drummond and Griffen, but I couldn't figure out why they'd want you. That's one reason you're not in the trunk right now, though if you hadn't talked to me about Jess, you would be."

"You'd have gone through with it if I hadn't connected to Jessica?" she asked, her voice shaking. "The way you were at my house, you had a gun to my head. You threatened to shoot my child. I don't know what to do. I'm afraid of you, and you want me to trust you. The worst part is, I don't know what'll happen to me now. I don't know if you're my enemy or not."

"Sorry about what I did at your house. You have no idea ..." He exhaled loudly. "It's important that you trust me, so I want to make sure you're clear on where we stand. Do you understand I won't turn you over to them? If you have any doubts, you'd better tell me now. I don't want to have to constantly wonder whether you'll try to sneak away while I'm not watching you. So, do you understand I won't turn you over to either the Agency or to the aliens?"

His tone was firm, confident. He made her believe what he said was logical and she should trust him. Her uneasiness dissipated while he talked. Alarmed at how easily he was able to placate her, she nodded.

"Don't nod. I want to hear you say it."

"Yes, I understand."

"Do you understand if you leave me, if I lose you, you won't survive for long on your own? They'll come after you, and they'll find you. I want to make sure all this is clear in your head. Do you believe you're safer with me?"

She considered what it felt like to be by herself, without Michael. A shudder went through her. There was a surge of fear and a sensation of drowning. She then considered what it felt like with Michael, having him by her side, trusting him, and depending on him. Warmth flooded her, and in her mind's eye, there was an impression of a shield.

"My head tells me I shouldn't trust you, but my intuition tells me if I don't trust you, something awful will happen to me. I guess until that changes, I'm better off with you," Carolyn said.

"Okay. That's good. Carolyn, I'm trained to deal with this and you're not. I know you don't like it, but some things will be out of your control."

Carolyn sighed. "You're not the first person to tell me that."

CHAPTER 34

They left Highway 115 outside of the Peterborough city limits. Michael drove for ten minutes and then turned onto one of the many dirt roads they saw. This led them to a forested area, where he drove onto a fire route. When he spotted a clearing along the side of the road, he pulled into the small meadow bordered at one end by swamp and on the other sides by forest. He parked close to the swamp.

As soon as the car stopped, Carolyn jumped out and slammed her door shut—a little too quickly, Michael thought. He didn't blame her for being nervous. She was in the middle of nowhere with the man who'd kidnapped her.

Michael opened his door and the interior light flicked on. He glanced out into the field on his left. The ground was damp. That reminded him Carolyn was barefoot and probably uncomfortable. He'd have to do something about that soon. At least the night was warm.

He stepped out of the car. Carolyn waited, her hands balled into fists at her side, her posture tense. When he went behind the car, she joined him, but kept some distance between them and stared pointedly at the trunk.

"I'm going to open the lid. If he's alive, which I doubt, he might try to get up. You let me deal with him. If I have to shoot him, I don't want you to try to stop me. Is that clear?" He stepped close to her.

She nodded, eyes wide.

"Carolyn, answer me. If he makes a move and I pull a gun on him, you can't interfere."

"I won't," she said, her voice barely a whisper.

Michael studied her for a moment. All he saw in her face was fear. "Go sit in the car."

She frowned and chewed her lower lip, but then turned away and got back in the car.

He pulled his gun from its holster, held it ready, and opened the trunk with the other hand. The slight but foul odour that wafted out of the warm trunk told him Torque was indeed dead. Michael stared down at the body of his partner for a moment.

This man had brought him into the Agency. Torque had taken him under his wing from the moment Michael had started his training and had helped to make Michael a killing machine. Michael grimaced, recoiling in pain. For a moment, he wished he'd found Torque alive so he could shoot him again.

Michael went to Carolyn's side of the car and opened the door. She stared at him, face pale and eyes wide. "You didn't shoot him."

"I didn't have to."

She lowered her head.

Michael crouched down next to her.

She didn't look up.

He might as well tell her straight out. "Torque has a tracking chip in his neck. I'm going to remove it, and I want you to watch me do it."

She kept her head down, but shook it. "I can't."

"You have to." He hesitated, charged on. "I have a chip in me, too. You'll have to remove mine. It'll buy us some time if I take out his chip and keep it with mine. And it'll be easier for you to remove my chip if you've seen it done."

Her head remained lowered, and he saw a tear drop onto her thigh, but she nodded. "Okay." She said it so softly he almost missed it.

He reached out, wanting to touch her hair, but caught himself and lowered his arm. She wouldn't want him to touch her.

Michael stood, opened the back door of the car, and picked up the medical bag. He removed a flashlight, a scanner for detecting the chip, a scalpel, and a pair of surgical gloves, and returned to the open trunk.

His partner stared at him, unseeing. Michael tried not to think about how supportive Torque had seemed after Jess's death. He needed to focus on the necessary task and feared what he'd do with that scalpel if he thought too much about the last few days.

"Carolyn." He waited, hoping she wasn't going catatonic on him. When she appeared at his side, he exhaled, relieved.

She stared into the trunk, tried to speak, but made a strangling sound. She closed her mouth and looked away.

Michael set his tools down in the trunk next to the body, and this time, he did touch her. He put a hand under her chin and lifted her face up to his. "Torque was my partner. My friend. This isn't what I want to be doing right now. Do you understand? We have to do this if we want to stay alive."

She was shaking.

He ignored an urge to put his arm around her. Afraid he'd add to her panic if he continued to touch her, he removed his hand from her face. "Can you focus on what I'm doing? I need you to pay attention."

"Yes. I feel sick."

"Anytime you want to pull away, tell me, and I'll stop."

She nodded and wrapped her arms around her body, hugging herself.

The urge to take her in his arms grew stronger. He turned back to the body in the trunk, put the gloves on, and leaned in a little to get a better view. Since Torque was lying on his back, Michael had to haul on the body and yank it into place. It required some effort to position him since rigor had already started to set in.

At least Torque had short hair, so his entire neck was exposed. Michael felt around with his finger to find the spot he needed, explaining to Carolyn everything he was doing. She kept her gaze on his hands. He used the scanner to locate the chip. It hadn't migrated far from its original location.

Michael sliced into Torque and opened up a cut large enough to see the chip. He used the edge of his blade to pop the chip out. Next, he showed her how to stitch up the wound. When he was done, Carolyn turned away and threw up.

"Go sit in the car. There's water in the bags. Help yourself. You don't have to watch anymore," Michael said.

She wiped her mouth with her hand and stumbled back to the car. Her sobs drowned out the cricket sounds around them.

Michael set his tools aside and leaned into the trunk again. He grasped the body under the arms and dragged it out onto the grass. At least they wouldn't have to drive around with a body in the trunk anymore. Michael glanced around and then dragged Torque's body to the swampy area, into the bulrushes and tall grass. He shoved the body into the water amongst the reeds and returned to the car.

After he picked up his tools and slammed the trunk lid down, Michael sat in the back of the car behind Carolyn, his feet on the ground. The open medical bag resting on his lap, he tucked Torque's chip into a plastic bag. He then set about cleaning and sterilizing everything, preparing the things Carolyn would need to remove his chip.

Michael peered over at her. Sweat rolled down her temples and a spot of dampness grew on her tank top under each arm. A fingerprints-shaped bruise decorated the outside of each of her upper arms. He'd been rough with her when he'd dragged her out of her house. He turned away, ashamed.

For a moment, he considered leaving her there, letting her take her chances on her own. He could easily disappear. He'd get her to remove his chip, drug her, and leave. Without Carolyn to slow him down, he'd be far away by the time the Agency found the car.

He looked up at the sky. It was clear, dotted with thousands of stars visible to the naked eye in this remote area. Michael shook his head. He wasn't going anywhere without Carolyn. He looked at her again and had an urge to comfort her. His hand reached out, but he stopped himself.

Confused, he wondered where all this concern for her was coming from. Why should he care what happened to her? A month ago, he'd have death-rayed her without hesitation. Maybe it was her connection to Jessica. He wondered if Jess was around them.

"Jess?" He whispered it.

There was only the silence of the night, broken by cricket song and woodland sounds. Carolyn was no longer sobbing. She was staring at him. She'd heard him. Possibly she sensed the emptiness inside him. A lump grew in his throat, and he scowled. He looked at the time. Almost ten-thirty. He closed the medical bag.

"Carolyn." He sounded brusque.

She glanced at the medical bag in his lap. "You want me to remove your chip now." Her eyes went wide, and she covered her mouth with a fist.

"It has to come out."

"I don't know if I can do this." She snatched up her bottle and swallowed some water, coughing when it went down the wrong way.

He waited for the coughing spell to subside. When she was quiet, he said, "I could try to do it myself but it would take a lot longer. You have to do this for me."

"It was bad enough watching you do it. What if I make a mistake?" Her voice trembled.

"I'll talk you through it. It'll be fine. I've prepared everything."

He saw how pale she was. She didn't feel fine.

"What if I throw up?"

"Lean out of the car and throw up. Sanitize your hands and carry on."

"What if I pass out?"

"I'll wait until you come to and then you'll carry on."

"It's too dark. How am I going to see properly?"

"We'll leave the car light on. I have a flashlight, too. Quit stalling."

"Okay," she whispered. "Let's get this over with."

***

For Carolyn, the next twenty minutes seemed like hours. When the bandage was on Michael's neck at last, she climbed out of the car. She took a few steps away from the car and sank to her knees, shaking. Would she ever find her way out of this nightmare?

She heard footsteps and turned to see Michael holding out a bottle of water. Carolyn accepted it, rinsed her mouth, took another swig, and swallowed it. It was better, but she could feel the water pooling in her stomach.

Michael crouched next to her. "You okay?" He sounded concerned.

She thought, *No, I'm not okay. I'll never be okay.* She said, "Yes. I'll be fine."

He stood and held out his hand. She took it, and he pulled her to her feet. When he let go of her hand, she had to stop herself from grabbing him. His touch had been comforting. She took another swallow of water instead.

Michael held the baggie with the chips in it. She followed him around to the passenger side of the car. He opened the door, sat in Carolyn's seat, and unlocked the glove box. Carolyn noticed a small, plastic folder in the glove box but nothing else. Michael set the baggie on top of the folder, closed the glove box, and locked it.

He turned to Carolyn. "We have to get moving."

CHAPTER 35

They were back on the 115, approaching the Lansdowne exit. Michael left the highway and pulled into a gas station. The parking lot was busy, considering the hour. He parked the car between two transport trucks. Carolyn couldn't see any drivers in the cabs.

Michael turned off the car and removed the baggie with the tracking devices in it from the glove box. He also took out his and Torque's cell phones and dropped them into the bag.

Getting out of the car, he went around to the back and opened the trunk. Carolyn couldn't see what he was doing. In a few seconds, he closed the trunk and disappeared behind one of the trucks. He returned a few minutes later. The bag of tracking chips was gone, and he held a roll of duct tape in one hand.

"Did you just duct tape those chips and cell phones to that truck?" Carolyn asked him.

"Yes. That should confuse them for a bit."

He started the car again and drove out of the gas station. They pulled into a nearby plaza with a twenty-four hour pharmacy. Michael parked on the other side of the parking lot, away from the store.

"Wait here." He stepped out of the car.

Carolyn watched him walk across the parking lot and into the store. A phone booth stood next to the store. The sight of it brought on an urge to run over and call 9-1-1. The police would be here before Michael returned. Her hand reached for the door latch, but she didn't touch it.

If she ran now, would she be risking her life, as Michael insisted? What would happen to Michael? He was a murderer. It was self-defence, but that was only in Torque's case. How many other people had he killed? He'd possibly killed John. Her hand touched the door latch and weakly she tugged at it. The door opened. The interior light flicked on. Startled, she jumped out of the car and shut the door.

She looked over at the phone booth again. She'd promised Michael she wouldn't try to run, but she was here because of him. No, that wasn't quite true. Someone had told him to kidnap her. According to Michael, getting the police involved wouldn't keep her safe—if he was telling the truth.

She'd felt intuitively before that she should stay with him. Despite the great urge to call the police, the thought of going through with it made her feel uneasy. Her intuition suggested there was greater danger in doing that than in staying with Michael.

"Carolyn? What are you doing out of the car?"

She jumped. He'd approached her, and she hadn't noticed he'd left the store. She'd make a lousy spy, agent, whatever Michael was.

"I had to stretch. I couldn't bear sitting in the car anymore," she said.

He glanced at the phone booth and then at her. He held up the bag he was carrying. "I hope you don't mind going brunette. We'll have to colour our hair. Also, they didn't have sneakers. Flip-flops. Better than nothing, for now."

She opened her door and got back in the car.

When Michael was settled in his seat, he turned to her and put his hand on her arm. "You can't call the police. I know it's tempting, and I appreciate you managed to control the urge. But if you call them, you'll get both of us killed. No protective custody anywhere can keep you safe from the Agency. If you feel like running, tell me. Believe me, if calling the cops was an option, I'd call them myself."

She hung her head, avoiding his eyes. He'd known what she was doing. He put his hand under her chin and tilted her head up.

"It's understandable you'd want out of this. But we have to do it my way if we want both the Agency and the aliens off our backs forever. Okay?"

She nodded. "Yes. Okay." She changed the subject. "How's your neck?"

"Fine. It's like you've been doing surgery for years," he replied, while he put the car into drive and headed out of the parking lot.

"Very funny."

"That wasn't sarcasm. I'll heal fine."

"I hope it doesn't get infected."

"It won't. You worry about everything, don't you?"

"Not everything. The important things."

"Let me guess. Everything's important?"

Carolyn smiled. "Okay. I worry too much. Just one more thing?"

"Yes?" Michael glanced at her and raised his eyebrows.

"Why didn't we ditch the car in Aurora?"

"Because they won't be looking for us until the morning. They'd have expected us to get to the base, which is near Peterborough, sometime during the night. If they've checked on us during the night so far, using the tracking devices, they'd have seen we were en route. No one will notice something is wrong until the early morning when we haven't shown up, and my boss finds out we never checked in to say we'd delivered the package."

"You mean me. I'm the 'package.'"

"Yes. Sorry."

"It hurts to be referred to as a 'package' like I'm a thing to be couriered somewhere. I can't believe our own government is able to treat its citizens like this."

"They're not. Our agency doesn't officially exist, but there are some powerful people involved, and they can make things official."

"I don't understand."

"I hope you never have to."

She thought for a moment, then said, "Wouldn't they have suspected something if they saw us stopped for hours?"

"They might. Or they might give us the benefit of the doubt. They likely won't figure it out until later in the morning. But we're running out of time. If they check all tracking simultaneously, they'll know something's wrong."

They drove for another few minutes, and Michael pulled into the parking lot of an inn. He drove around to the back, where there was additional parking, and parked the car.

"We're leaving the car here. Grab everything." Michael stepped from the car and hefted his backpack onto his back. He picked up the medical bag and turned to Carolyn.

She stepped onto the pavement and tried to struggle the backpack onto her shoulders.

Michael chuckled. "Let me help you."

Carolyn flushed. "I guess I'm a bit of a princess. I'm going to slow you down, aren't I?"

He paused for a moment and then said, "We'll manage." He took the pack from her and set it down on the ground. "Put the flip-flops on."

She took the flip-flops from the bag and slipped her feet into them. They fit fine, but she could tell it wouldn't be long before the rubber thong between her toes started to chafe.

He opened her pack and removed Jessie's hiking boots, tossing them into the car. "One less thing to carry," he said. He closed and locked the car and helped her set the straps of her pack more comfortably on her shoulders. "Can you walk with this?"

I doubt it. "Yes."

Michael looked around.

She followed his gaze. There was no one in sight.

"That way," he said, pointing. He started walking, and she followed. They headed for the tree line.

CHAPTER 36

Carolyn sat on the edge of the king-sized bed in their hotel room, alternating between staring at the TV and at her hair in the mirror above the dresser across from the bed. She couldn't get used to seeing herself with short, dark brown hair. Michael had assured her it was "cute." She'd told him he looked cute too, but she was being a smartass. He looked the same even with his black hair dyed light brown. Of course, he hadn't had to cut his hair. Every time she looked in the mirror, she saw a stranger looking back.

It was 1:18 AM, and neither one of them had suggested going to sleep. The TV had been playing since they walked into the room. Michael had tuned into a Toronto news channel, and the reel had looped around three times already, but they left it running. A particularly disturbing development had been the disappearance of a popular horror writer who was also a well-known alien abductee.

When the announcer had said Jason Meacher was missing, a chill went through Carolyn. As the clip about the writer began again, she looked at Michael. He sat at the table cleaning the guns, something Carolyn found unnerving, though she understood it was necessary.

She glanced at the TV again, which continued to display Meacher's picture with "missing" flashing across it in large letters. She turned back to Michael.

"Do you think this is happening all over, to all abductees? You said you kidnapped us to silence us for what we were saying about the government. This guy wasn't saying anything about the government. He was only talking about his abduction experiences."

"I don't know. Perhaps he was becoming too public."

Carolyn scanned their honeymoon suite. The clerk had told Michael it was the only room available. The fireplace, which was reflected in the mirror next to the heart-shaped whirlpool tub, gave off light, but not heat. They'd turned off the blower.

It had been Carolyn's idea to start it up. She found it comforting, but it was too warm to turn on the heat. They'd argued a little about the air conditioner. She'd wanted it off and Michael had wanted it on. They'd set it to twenty-three Celsius.

The tub reminded her of her last anniversary. She and John had rented a room at a bed and breakfast with a similar tub in Niagara-on-the-Lake. They'd spent an hour sitting in the swirling water, enjoying champagne and chocolate-covered strawberries, laughing at themselves for being so cliché.

If she'd known it was to be their final anniversary together, she'd have savoured the time. Now, here she was in a honeymoon suite with a complete stranger. A bottle of sparkling wine and two glasses perched on the edge of the tub, complimentary with the room. Carolyn thought about opening it and drinking it down to smother her memories.

It would be John's funeral morning after next. Sam would have to bury her father without her mother there to comfort her. What if the Agency caught her, and she never saw Sam again? Panic flared up, and she had a wild urge to pick up the phone and call Sam. Instead, she said, "Michael, if something happens to me, promise me you'll find Sam and make sure they don't hurt her."

"I won't let anything happen to you." He'd finished cleaning the guns, and they sat, reassembled, on the table next to him.

"But what if they get me? When Torque jumped me, I didn't stand a chance."

"Let me show you some self-defence moves. I can't teach you anything fancy, but I can show you how to hurt someone enough to allow you to get away."

"Only if it doesn't involve killing."

He grinned. "No problem. I'm just happy you'd be willing to hurt someone."

"I don't want to, but I think I can manage to fight back."

"All right. Stand up."

They both rose.

"First thing I want you to understand is you have to be pre-emptive. It's better to avoid getting too close than it is to have to fight your way out. The second thing is you have to be okay with inflicting pain and injury. When you're attacked, it'll be you or him. Your best bet is to hurt and run. Okay?"

She nodded. "This feels so surreal."

"I know. It's okay. Pay attention to your surroundings. Make note of anywhere someone might hide and avoid walking there. Keep your head up and your eyes moving. Use store windows for reflections to see behind you. If you have a makeup mirror, you can use it to see behind you. If you see an attack coming, try to escape."

He continued. "Use anything to put a barrier between you and the attacker. Grab a chair if there is one nearby. You're using it as a shield. If someone attacks you with a knife, wrap your jacket around your arm to protect yourself, while you use the other arm for more offensive moves. When you're cornered, you have to do whatever you can to protect yourself, fight off the attacker, and get out of there."

Carolyn was uncertain. She envisioned grabbing her end table and confronting Michael in her den. She still thought her best protection was a working phone and enough time to call 9-1-1.

"Be willing to fight for yourself. Get angry if that helps. Action is quicker than reaction when it comes to fighting. It's okay to defend yourself, and it might make the difference between getting away and getting captured. At least it'll buy you time."

"Okay. I feel so weak and helpless."

"You won't if you know the things you can do to protect yourself. Never let anyone closer than two arm lengths. Let me show you how to stand."

He posed, feet hip width apart, one foot back, his body turned at a forty-five degree angle. Elbows close to his body, he held his fists up. "This pose gives you stability. It lets you stand strong. Your hands protect your body." He relaxed his arms. "You try it."

She tried to imitate his stance, feeling self-conscious as she raised her hands into the defensive position he'd demonstrated. Michael reached out and shoved her. She stumbled back a few steps.

"You have to plant your feet. Stay firm. I didn't shove you hard. I can help you with the techniques, but you'll have to work on your confidence."

She nodded and planted her feet more firmly. When he shoved her again, she stayed in place.

"Much better," he said. "Remember, it takes time for a person to react. Do you understand?"

"Yes." Her own reaction time was slow, she knew.

"If an attacker gets closer to you than two arm lengths, don't hesitate. Use your palm to strike. Using a fist can get your hand hurt. If your hand isn't conditioned, punching someone in the skull can break your fingers. The heel of the palm is the best for striking. Smash him right in the nose using the heel of your hand. His eyes will water, and you can use that moment to get out of there."

They spent the next hour practicing a variety of techniques that made Carolyn sick to consider executing. Her movements were at first hesitant and fearful, but Michael made her practice each one repeatedly until the motions became more fluid.

He removed the ammunition from his gun and showed her how to snatch a weapon from an opponent and to run away in a manner that reduced the risk of being shot. When they finished, he said, "I feel better knowing you can defend yourself a bit. Now, I think you should get some sleep. You look beat, and we have to leave early."

She wasn't sure she'd get any sleep with him in the room. "What about you?" she asked.

"I'll nap on the couch in the living room."

"Okay. Take one of these pillows with you. I saw a spare blanket in the closet by the door. I feel bad taking up an entire king-sized bed and making you sleep on the couch."

He smiled. "I've slept on worse." He stood and looked out the window, something he'd done with alarming regularity since they arrived. Carolyn had asked him if there was someone out there, but he'd shaken his head and didn't comment. He went into the other room.

Carolyn peeled off her shorts, leaving on her panties and the T-shirt from Jessie's backpack she'd put on after her shower.

I'm wearing another woman's clothes—a dead woman's clothes. She pushed the thought away. At least they fit, though loosely. Jessie's feet may have been smaller, but she wore approximately the same size in clothes as Carolyn.

The bed welcomed her, and she snuggled into it and pulled the sheets up to her chin. She turned off the TV and lay on her back, staring up at the ceiling. Her mind didn't want to shut off, and she tried to relax and stop the thoughts.

The room was dim, not dark. Michael still had a light on in the living area. Sounds of movement reached her, then there was a click, and the fireplace in the mirror went dark. She heard more shuffling, and saw in the mirror Michael removing his pants. Carolyn turned her head away, prudishly, though part of her was tempted to watch him undress. She shifted onto her side, facing away from the living room.

The clock on the bedside table read 2:16 AM. She closed her eyes. Michael shut the light off in the other room, and everything became dark and quiet. Her thoughts wandered randomly while she drifted off.

***

Jim Cornell stirred, the fragments of a dream dissipating until he had no recollection of it. A ringing he'd thought was part of his dream continued, and he realized it was his phone. He answered with an abrupt "hello," his voice gravelly with sleep. He glanced at the clock. It was 3:47 AM. This couldn't be good.

A voice on the other end acknowledged the early hour and apologized for waking him. "It's Traegar, sir. I'm calling from Peterborough Compound. We've been expecting your delivery since oh-two-hundred, but nothing has arrived. We checked the tracking, and it appears the car is sitting in a hotel parking lot in Peterborough. Both agents are on the highway heading towards Ottawa. The woman appears to be in another hotel in Peterborough."

Cornell shook his head, trying to process what he'd heard. None of it made sense. He didn't respond, trying to think of a way to handle it.

"Sir?" Traegar persisted. "What would you like us to do?"

Cornell suggested the first thing that came to him. "Send a couple of guys to retrieve the car. Monitor Fairchild's movements and the movements of the two agents. I'll contact Muniz and Valiant and figure out what to do when I know what happened. If there was something wrong, they'd have contacted me. Thanks for your call, Agent. I'll get right back to you."

He hung up the phone without saying goodbye. He had a

sinking sensation in his gut. What if Valiant had lost it? Torque had been assuring Cornell he could handle Mick, and Cornell had given Torque free rein with that situation, but Cornell had always had his doubts.

He dialled Torque's number. Voicemail picked up immediately. That meant Torque's phone was either dead or off. He dialled Valiant. It also went into voicemail immediately. He grimaced and called Traegar back at Peterborough Base.

"Traegar."

"Yeah, it's Cornell. Listen, I can't reach Muniz and Valiant. Send two agents after them. Monitor the woman. Don't lose her. We can't have her running around out there. Call me when you have the car and let me know what you find. When you catch up with Muniz and Valiant, call me immediately."

"Yes, sir."

Cornell hung up the phone. He checked the clock again: 3:52 AM. He got out of bed to start his day.

CHAPTER 37

... Carolyn and John are in a cab, driving by the ocean. The cab heads for a pier and drives onto it. John protests, telling the driver to stop the car. They yell at the cab driver, while the car gets closer to the edge of the pier, with no indication the driver is planning to stop.

The cab flies off the end of the pier and into the water. Carolyn finds herself outside of the car, swimming towards the shore. John is with her. There's no sign of the driver. When they drag themselves up onto the beach, Carolyn realizes the agency she works for is trying to kill them. She realizes they're also trying to kill her mother. They'd all become expendable and were to be erased.

They go to the hotel to check out. Carolyn remembers they've left their suitcases in the room and insists they go back for them. When she steps out of the elevator, John is no longer with her. She panics.

She wants to run to her room, but can't remember where it is. The elevator opens and agents step out. They're coming to kill her. Carolyn tries to run, but they grab her. She screams and struggles, grabbing at their hands, trying to get them off her. The terror intensifies. They're smothering her. She can't breathe and opens her mouth to scream again ...

"Shh. It's okay. It's only a dream." The voice was Michael's. He sat on the bed, holding her, his body pressed against hers.

"Don't let me go." She wrapped her arms around him, holding her head against his hard chest. Its solidity reassured her. "I dreamt agents were trying to kill me."

"You're having a nightmare." His hand stroked her hair.

"They were coming after me, off the elevator. I was lost and alone."

"You're not alone."

"Please don't go." Need for him pushed aside everything else, and she didn't care who he was or why they were here. She wanted his body next to hers, on top of hers. She wanted him to take her. Carolyn lifted her face up and kissed his lips. He hesitated, but it was only for a moment. His lips responded, and he returned the kiss. His tongue parted her lips, while his hands went to her hair, to her back, to her breasts, first over her T-shirt, then sliding under it to her bare skin.

She gasped when his hands slid over her nipples. Desire flamed through her from deep in her belly. She ran her hands over his arms and then stroked his back and stomach too. He wore only his underwear, and she wanted that off him, so she tugged at it until he nudged her hand away and removed it himself. She ached to touch every part of him, and her hands roved everywhere at once.

He grasped her T-shirt and pulled it off over her head. Then it was his turn to tug at her panties and her turn to nudge his hand away and strip. When they were both naked, she pressed the length of her body against him, savouring him with every part of her. His skin was soft, but his body was hard, and his perfection drove her towards blissful madness.

She could hear his breathing as short gasps that matched her own. Neither said a word. They made love silently until the moment when they could no longer hold back. Michael's body melded with hers. She fused with him. It was more than physical. She experienced all of him. She received him, and he gave himself to her.

When they were done, they lay together, limbs still entwined. Carolyn laid her head on Michael's shoulder. She ran her hand along his chest, tracing her way down from his heart chakra to his sacral chakra.

He stopped her before she could go any farther. He gently took her hand and lifted it to his mouth to kiss it. When he did, a surge, like an electrical charge, ran through her hand to her core.

"I don't know what happened to me," Carolyn said, self-conscious. "I couldn't stand it if you weren't touching me."

"Are you sorry?"

"No. Are you?"

"No. Surprised, maybe, but not sorry."

She looked into his eyes, seeking. "I felt close to you. It was overwhelming."

"For me, too. It might be a way of off-loading what's happened over the last couple of days."

She didn't reply. She wanted to hang onto the experience for a while longer, and analyzing it would spoil it. But Michael was back to reality, and she caught him checking the clock. She turned her head to see what time it was. The clock read 6:31 AM.

Michael spoke first. "God, I don't want to get up. But we need to get out of here. It's best for you to wear long pants even if it's hot. I expect to go into Algonquin today, and we should dress for it."

Carolyn went into the washroom, going through the routine of using the toilet, washing her face, showering, and brushing her teeth. She hadn't been with anyone other than John for over twenty years, and what had just happened confused her.

Michael was a killer, a kidnapper. She didn't want to feel anything for him. Carolyn gasped. *Is this what they mean by "Stockholm Syndrome?"* Was she experiencing something psychological that had nothing to do with who he was but grew out of the situation she was in?

Carolyn dressed, putting on the pants she'd fished out of the backpack. They were a little loose. Evidently, she was slightly thinner than Jess around the middle. How much longer would she continue to compare herself to Jessica?

She put on her bra—her own—she'd noted with some satisfaction her breasts were larger than Jess's, so Jess's wouldn't fit. As she picked up a clean T-shirt, there was a knock on the bathroom door. She slipped the T-shirt on and said, "Come in."

Michael opened the door and stepped into the bathroom. "I've packed everything."

"Okay. I'm finished in here if you want to take your turn in the shower." She went to walk past him, but when she did, her hip brushed against his and a thrill surged through her gut, making her feel like the wind had been knocked out of her. She tried to ignore it, but Michael put his arms around her and held her.

He pressed his lips to the top of her head. "I wish things weren't this way," he said.

"If things weren't like this, we'd have never met."

He let her go. "It's Jess's funeral today. I don't know if I'm betraying her. When you touch me, all I want to do is grab you."

"I don't know what this means either. Could be the stress from the situation. We've both lost our spouses to it. Perhaps it's natural to turn to each other for comfort. We've got no one else. I can't even call my daughter to tell her I'm alive." Her voice broke.

He put his arm around her waist and pulled her into an embrace. "I'll fix that. You'll see her again, I promise."

"All right." She hugged him back, not wanting to let go, but knowing they should hurry.

Her head was fuzzy from lack of sleep. She couldn't think straight, and being near him made it worse. She extricated herself from his arms and stepped away. He went into the bathroom and closed the door. Water ran in the tub, and then the shower started. She glanced at the clock: 6:44 AM. He'd better hurry.

CHAPTER 38

The phone rang. Jim Cornell snatched it up. It was 6:45 AM, and he'd already heard back from one team. They'd found Muniz's car abandoned in the parking lot of a hotel in Peterborough. Cornell continued to call Valiant's and Muniz's phones, and each time he'd been connected immediately with voicemail. This had better be news about them, or, better yet, one of them calling to explain.

"Cornell speaking."

"Traegar here. We found the chips."

"You mean you found Valiant and Muniz?"

"No, I mean we found their tracking chips. They must have removed them. They were in a plastic baggie, along with their cell phones, duct taped to a transport truck heading to Ottawa."

"Son of a bitch. It's Valiant, I'm sure of it. But why would Muniz go along with him?" Cornell asked.

"Sir?"

"I'm thinking out loud. What about the woman?"

"Her tracking chip indicates she's in a hotel in Peterborough. We've located the room she's in. We've got two agents watching the hotel. Do you want us to move on her?"

"If Muniz and Valiant have removed their chips, they're likely with her. They probably don't realize she's been chipped too. See if you can find an opportunity to get her alone. If you can snatch her when she's away from them, then we can deal with them later. I don't want anything to happen to her."

"Yes sir."

Cornell hung up the phone. One way or another, Carolyn Fairchild would be locked up today.

***

Michael opened the bathroom door and stepped out. He wore jeans and a T-shirt, and his feet were bare. Carolyn's gaze tracked him while he walked to his bag and put on his socks and running shoes.

He went to the window and peered outside. The room overlooked the parking lot at the back of the hotel. Michael spotted a man sitting in a car, watching the exits.

"We can't go downstairs for breakfast."

"They're out there, aren't they?" Carolyn whispered.

"Maybe."

"How will we get out of here if we're being watched?"

"I'll get us out. It might not be Agency. I don't want to take a chance."

"If they know we're here, how will we get a car?"

"We'll figure it out. I don't understand how they found us so quickly. They knew right where to go. There must be another chip on me." Michael opened the medical bag and took out the scanner. "I'm going to strip down and I want you to scan my body. It'll beep if it locates a chip."

Michael stripped and stood in front of her. He turned on the scanner and handed it to her.

She inspected his entire body, starting at his head. After five minutes, she'd finished scanning. "There's nothing on you."

Michael stared at her, thinking. "Maybe it's you."

"I guess it could be. Aliens abduct me regularly. Would they have put a chip in me the government could use as well?"

"The aliens don't need to use chips to track you, which is why I didn't think of it. They have other ways. But there's no telling what arrangements they made with the Agency. Let me check you out."

Michael dressed while Carolyn stripped down. He then picked up the scanner and searched her body. Her eyes went wide and she recoiled when he scanned her nasal area.

"What's wrong?" he asked while the wand swept silently over her face.

"I get nosebleeds sometimes, and I was afraid that's where they stuck it. I don't want to think how we'd have to remove it from inside my nose."

"It's okay. I didn't find a chip, but they might have put something there this wand can't pick up."

He moved around behind her. The wand beeped when he scanned across the back of her right shoulder. "There it is," Michael said. "You understand we'll have to remove it?"

Carolyn's face went pale, but she nodded her head.

"They're probably waiting for you to leave the room. I'll remove the chip and we'll get out of here." Michael opened the medical bag while Carolyn dressed. He watched her, unable to take his gaze off her body.

She glanced up while she pulled on her track pants and caught him staring. She smiled.

Michael blushed. "Sorry."

"It's okay." She left her bra and shirt off. "I'm ready. Where do you want to do this?"

"Lie face down on the bed. Give me a few seconds while I wash my hands and get ready." He went into the bathroom and washed his hands and arms up to the elbows. He returned to the bed.

She lay face down, a pillow under her chest elevating her shoulders.

He sat beside her. "The procedure is exactly the same as when you removed my chip. It'll be okay." Michael put on a clean pair of surgical gloves. He removed some alcohol wipes from the bag and cleaned the area where the chip was located.

She stiffened, tense.

To distract her while he worked, he talked to her. "You'll be fine. Tell me about how you can talk to spirits. Could you always do that?"

"I was a little girl when it first started. I was close to my grandmother. When she died, I saw her in a dream. She came to me when I was sleeping and told me she wasn't sick anymore. She said I shouldn't cry or feel sad because she wasn't going to be too far away. I could always connect with people who passed, but that one really opened me up. Spirits seem to know when you have the gift, and they come around."

She stopped talking and flinched when he slipped the hypodermic into her and pressed the plunger. He touched her shoulder and leaned closer to her. "It's the local. We'll give it a minute." He paused. "I dreamed about my wife after she died. Was that really Jess?"

"Yes. It's common for people to dream about their departed loved ones. It's the easiest way for spirits to communicate with those who can't see spirits when they're awake. You're more open when you sleep, and it's easier for them to get through to you. I saw John, too, but not in my dreams. I was awake. He didn't say anything, but I knew he was okay and he loves me."

"Why can't Jess come to me when I'm awake?" He felt cheated Jess hadn't appeared to him after that single dream. Didn't she know how much he wanted to see her again?

"She might if you worked at being open enough to feel her around you. If you work at raising your vibration, you'll be able to connect with her. You can also ask her to give you signs she's around. One of the things spirits do to show you they're around is leave coins in strange places around the house, or they mess with electronics or with the lights. If the TV suddenly turns on by itself, that could be your departed loved one."

"I'd like to see her again. My dream ended so abruptly. I didn't get to hug her or even go near her."

"That's common too. I think it has to do with their energy and how much it takes out of them to visit you like that."

"There were three men in robes with her. They looked like monks. Who were they? Or was that symbolism in the dream?"

"Some people think they're spirit guides. Others think they help everyone who passes make the transition. Was she in a hospital bed when you saw her?"

"Yes. How did you know?"

"That's common too. It's like they have to rest for a while when they first cross."

His voice changed, becoming lower and gentler. "Stay still. I'm going to get started. Tell me if you have any discomfort and I'll stop."

"Okay."

He noticed she was holding her breath. "You can breathe."

"Sorry." She exhaled. "I'm nervous."

"It's okay. I'm not going to hurt you."

It took Michael ten minutes to remove the chip, stitch her up, and bandage the wound. When he finished dressing the small cut he'd made, he considered what they could do to distract those agents. He assumed there'd be two agents. They couldn't watch all the exits. One was probably the guy in the car at the back of the hotel. The other could be at the front or in the lobby.

"I have an idea," he said. He dropped the chip into the pocket of his jeans. "Don't move from this room and don't open the door unless it's me."

"Where are you going?" Her voice rose with fright.

"I'm going to take care of these guys so they can't follow us."

"Don't kill them."

"We can't debate that right now. Latch the door when I'm gone. Torque's gun is on the table. If you need it, use it." He went to the table and picked up the gun. "Aim and shoot, putting direct pressure on the trigger. Don't hesitate. If you do, you're in trouble."

"Is the safety off?"

He shook his head. "It has internal safeties. That's why you have to put direct pressure on the trigger. Come here. I'll show you how to hold it."

Carolyn stood, picked up her bra and T-shirt, and he helped her put them on. She flinched when the material touched her shoulder.

"Are you okay?" he asked.

"Yeah. It feels weird."

She turned to him and looked at the gun in his hand. He pulled the slide back to cock it and held out the gun. She hesitated and then took it from him.

"Use two hands, one to hold the gun, and the other to steady it. When you fire, it'll recoil a bit, but you should be able to keep it steady. This is an easy gun to use."

He helped her position her hands on it. "When you want to fire, put your finger here, right on the trigger, and then press on it like you mean it. It won't be loud, because the suppressor is on it, but it won't be silent, either."

She nodded, frowning.

"If I'm not here and something happens, then you'd better be prepared to use this. They're here to take you back with them. Understood?"

"Yes."

He let go of her hands, and she set the gun back down on the table. She frowned, her eyes wide, but he turned away. He'd have to trust that if things became critical, she'd use it.

Michael put on his shoulder holster, screwed his suppressor on the gun, cocked it, and placed it in the holster. He put a jacket on to conceal the weapon and pressed his arm against it. When he stepped into the hallway, he put the "Do not disturb" sign on the outside of the doorknob. He pulled the door closed and Carolyn latched it behind him.

CHAPTER 39

Michael went to the stairwell and headed down the stairs, stopping at the second floor. The door at the bottom of the stairwell creaked as someone opened it. Michael slipped into the hallway, pulling the gun from his holster and using his jacket to conceal it.

He pressed his ear to the door. Someone coming up the stairs abruptly stopped. The agent in the car was likely tracking his movements using a receiver and communicating with his partner over a wire. They were expecting Carolyn to be on the other side of the second-floor door.

The door eased open. Michael smashed his body into it. A grunt of pain followed a thud, and the door slammed shut. Michael raised his gun and shoved the door open, jumping onto the landing.

The agent staggered back, raising his gun and aiming at Michael, who fired into the agent's chest blowing him backwards. Michael shot him again, this time in the face, blood and brain matter splattering around him.

Michael removed the chip from his pocket and dropped it in the pocket of the agent's pants. He checked the agent's ID. Robert Cunningham. No one he knew. He removed Cunningham's jacket and wrapped it around the man's head, taking Cunningham's gun and slipping it into his own holster. The gruesome evidence would remain on the wall and stairs, but at least he could move the body. Michael used the fireman's carry to take it down to the ground floor.

He dropped the body at the bottom of the stairs, shoving it

under the stairwell out of sight. Michael opened the door to the main floor, peeked out, and glanced around. Everything seemed quiet. He opened the door wider and looked down the hall to the left. It was empty, the hall stretching down through rooms on either side, with a break on the right where the entrance led to the lobby.

Gun raised and ready to fire, he stepped out, quickly turning right. He could see an exit to the parking lot a short distance away. He waited, expecting the other agent to appear from that direction. Nothing moved.

He walked down to the exit, alert for any sound or movement. When he reached the exit, he stood to the side and scanned the parking lot. The car he'd seen earlier was still there, but the man in it was gone. Why wasn't he coming to find his partner? He should've been tracking both his partner's movements and the movements of Carolyn's chip.

Unless he knew it wasn't Carolyn using the chip.

Michael's gut did a flip-flop. He ran back to the stairs, taking them two at a time. He had to get back to their room.

***

Two minutes after Michael left the room, Carolyn was pacing back and forth through the bedroom and the living area. She was terrified Michael would be killed trying to stop those agents and she'd be on her own. Then she was afraid her fears would manifest what she didn't want, and visualized Michael returning to the room. She said a quick prayer for him and asked the angels to protect him.

She went back to watching the news, but couldn't bear sitting still and started pacing again. At one point, she paused to turn off the TV. The noise was getting on her nerves. She tried to sense any spirits. She hadn't felt anyone around for a while. There was nothing.

Michael had seen someone outside. If she looked out the window, would she be able to spot the agents? She didn't know what to look for, but she went to the window, moved the sheers out of the way, and peered out.

Nothing moved. Then she noticed a car parked at the right side of the parking lot. Someone was sitting in it. She shielded her eyes, squinting for a better view. At that moment, the person in the car gazed up in her direction. Carolyn staggered backwards.

He has binoculars. He'd seen her and knew she hadn't left the room.

Cursing herself for going to the window, Carolyn wondered what to do. She was afraid if she stayed in the room, they'd get to her before Michael realized she'd given herself away. She should at least leave the room and hide somewhere. But then how would Michael find her? The latch was on the door. They couldn't get in through the latched door. Could they?

She opened the door and peeked into the hallway. Empty. She closed the door again and stuck her key card in her back pocket. She peered out into the hallway again. Still empty. She stepped into the hallway and pulled the door closed. She hesitated, trying to decide which way to go.

Carolyn fled down the hall towards the elevators, which were about fifteen metres away. The stairs should be nearby. Or perhaps there was a utility room or closet to hide in. The elevator pinged, and the doors opened. A man stepped out, did a double take when he saw her, and ran at her.

She realized she'd left the gun in the room, and her panic escalated. She spun around and ran back to her room. No choice now. The only place to go was back to her room. She reached the door, yanked the key card out of her pocket, and shoved the card into the slot. After a second, she slid it out. It didn't work. She'd pulled it out too fast. Frantic, she jammed it in again.

The indicator light on the door changed to green. She flung open the door and rushed into the room. She shoved on the door, but the man had reached it and was pushing it open.

Somehow, with an adrenaline rush perhaps, she forced the door closed. She locked the deadbolt, flipped the latch on and jumped back. To her horror, she heard him kick against the door. The latch rattled, and wood splintered. She ran to the phone to call 9-1-1. Instead of picking up the phone, she grabbed the gun from the table. She aimed it at the door with shaking hands.

Point and shoot. Don't hesitate. Her heart thudded, and she thought her knees might buckle. The door shattered away from the jamb and the latch went flying.

The man burst into the room. He was big, shorter than Michael, but not by much, and he was stockier and more brutal looking. He lunged at her.

She pulled the trigger. The shot went wide. She swung her arm down again to take another shot, but he was on her.

He knocked the gun from her hand and punched her in the stomach.

Carolyn dropped to the floor and doubled over, tears leaking from her eyes. She couldn't breathe, and her mouth opened and closed, opened and closed, like a stranded fish. The dream she'd had this morning flashed through her mind. She was alone with this man, and he would kill her or take her away. Michael wasn't there after all.

CHAPTER 40

In a panic, Michael burst into the fourth-floor hallway. He raced around a corner and ran to the room. The door was ajar, the splintered jamb keeping it from closing. His heart in his mouth, he raised his gun and shoved the door open, afraid she was already gone. Relief flooded through him when he saw her.

Carolyn was curled up like a foetus, trying to suck air into her lungs. The agent hovered over her. He didn't even have his gun on her anymore. He went rigid when Michael crashed into the room and lifted his weapon.

Gun already raised, Michael beat him to the punch and fired. There was a muffled report, and the agent dropped when the bullet hit his head. He wouldn't threaten them anymore. Half his head was gone.

Michael ran to her side, pulling her to him. He stroked her hair, held her head to his chest. "We have to get out of here. That door breaking must have alerted someone. Can you get up?"

Carolyn nodded her head. When she tried to stand, she collapsed again, shuddering. Michael stood and went to the door. He repositioned it, lining it up so the hinges and bolt were holding it in place. At least when it was shut, someone walking by wouldn't notice it was broken. Carolyn would need at least a few minutes to recover.

He scanned the room and spotted a bottle of water on the table. He retrieved it, uncapped it, and put it to her lips.

"Sip some water."

Her gasps were slower and quieter. She coughed, tried to take a sip from the bottle, and got some down her throat. As her breath became regular, the shock set in. She shook, and Michael went to the bed and yanked the sheet from it. He took it to her and wrapped her in it.

"You'll be okay."

He couldn't believe no one was pounding on the door. Had no one heard the door being smashed in? Or were they all trying to stay out of what they assumed was a domestic dispute? Whatever the reason, he was grateful for the favour.

Michael sat on the floor, holding Carolyn in his arms, rocking her. She was sobbing now and clinging to him. Fear welled up, and he crushed it. He refused to think about what would've happened to her if he hadn't realized what was going on.

After a time, she stopped sobbing. She looked up at him. He stroked her hair and kissed her forehead.

"Can you stand?"

"Yes." It came out as a croak, and she cleared her throat. "Yes."

He kissed her lips, softly. Then he stood, lifting her to her feet. She walked to the washroom, and he noticed she stumbled a little. When she was in the bathroom, he crouched next to the body of the agent he'd killed and searched his pockets. He opened the agent's wallet. David Mathers. The name meant nothing to Michael.

He rose, picked Torque's gun off the floor, and put it into his pack. At least this time, she'd pulled the trigger. The other agents' guns went into his pack as well. He'd acquired quite an arsenal, but he didn't want to leave the guns lying around. He removed the suppressor from his own weapon, put it away, and put the gun in his holster, closing his jacket over it.

Carolyn reappeared, looking much better. Michael went to her. She stared at the body, her eyes going wide and her face turning green.

"Don't look," he said, and turned her away. "Let's get out of here before the police descend on us."

After Michael helped get her pack on, he hoisted his pack onto his shoulders and picked up the medical bag. He went to the door, and Carolyn stepped through the opening he created. Michael closed the door. It was difficult, but he made it look like a firmly shut door—if you didn't examine it. The "Do not disturb" sign lay on the hallway floor, and he hung it from the doorknob.

Carolyn automatically headed for the closest set of stairs, and Michael gently took her arm and turned her around. Not wanting to use the stairs with the body at the bottom, he led her to another set. He held the door open for Carolyn, and she entered the stairwell.

They made their way down, Michael keeping the pace slow so Carolyn could manage. She followed him without a word. When they reached the bottom, he motioned her to stay quiet. He opened the door a crack. When he saw the housekeeping trolley a few metres down the hall, he closed the door again.

"Housekeeping is nearby. Let me check it out. I'll come back for you when it's safe."

Immediately, her eyes registered fear and panic.

He brushed her cheek lightly with his fingers. "Don't worry. I'll only be gone for a moment."

She didn't reply.

He turned and cracked open the door again. The trolley still stood in the hall. Michael stepped out, closing the door behind him. He strolled past the room with the trolley, glancing in through the open door.

It was a utility room. Someone was inside, but out of his view. He returned to the stairwell and waved Carolyn out. She slipped past him, and he took her hand, feeling her relax at his touch.

When they reached the exit, Michael motioned her to wait while he checked the grounds. No one stirred. He checked his watch. Just after eight o'clock. They'd lost a lot of time. More agents would be coming soon.

"Stay close."

She nodded. The air felt hot already. The afternoon would be scorching. A slight breeze stirred the humidity, and Michael took a deep breath.

"Let's go," he said, and walked with her out into the parking lot. He glanced around to make sure no one was observing them from a distance, and when he was satisfied, he took Carolyn's hand and led her away.

CHAPTER 41

By 7:30 AM, Jim Cornell had reached his office in Toronto. He checked his messages. Nothing from Valiant or Muniz, but Traegar had left him a message letting him know things were moving forward at the hotel.

Cornell called him back, and Traegar told him that the last report from the agents at the hotel said that Fairchild had left her room and was heading down the stairwell. One agent was on his way to intercept her.

Cornell booted up his computer, glancing at the phone every few seconds, expecting it to ring. He didn't know how this job got so screwed up, but when he got his hands on Valiant and Muniz, they were going to have some 'splainin' to do, Lucy. He felt a headache coming on and buzzed Helen.

"Yes, sir?"

"Get me a coffee, would ya?"

"Yes, sir."

He opened his desk drawer and pulled out a chocolate bar. Breakfast. He'd wash it down with coffee whenever Helen showed up with it. The phone rang at seven fifty-eight.

"Cornell."

"It's Traegar."

"Well, what have you got for me?"

"I'm sorry, sir. Muniz is dead. They found his body dumped in a swampy area along the route to Peterborough. According to the GPS data, the car had been stopped there for over an hour."

"Shit. How did he die?"

"Gunshots to the chest, sir."

"Any thoughts on who killed him?"

"It's too early to say, but they speculate it was Valiant."

Cornell paused. Valiant and Muniz had been partners for what? Twenty years? What had made Valiant turn on his partner and mentor like that? The woman?

"Sir? Are you there?"

"Yeah. Anything else?"

"Yes, sir. There seems to be a problem at the hotel." Traegar didn't pause to let Cornell respond. "Looks like Mathers is in the hotel room alone. Cunningham appears to be in the stairwell with the woman. None of them are moving."

"Assume they're dead and the woman is gone. Get agents down there now to clean up the mess. Go to the hotel manager and give him a cover story that it was a domestic dispute and no one else is at risk. Don't let any cops near anything until it's been sanitized."

"Yes, sir. Where do we go from here?"

"Check surveillance cameras in the area. See if you can spot them anywhere. Find out what name he used from the guest registry. If you have anything to report, call me right away. I want them found. And Traegar?"

"Yes, sir?"

"We need Fairchild alive. I'd prefer to have them both alive, but use lethal force on Valiant if necessary."

"Yes, sir."

Cornell hung up the phone. There was a knock on his door, and Helen appeared with his coffee. He nodded, indicating she should set it down on his desk. He grunted his thanks when she placed it on a coaster at the top of his desk.

"Will there be anything else, sir?"

"Yeah. I want the surveillance tapes from the Fairchild residence. Everything they have from last night to now. And have them monitor any calls in or out of the Fairchild place, anything from landlines and cells. Anything significant, they should notify me immediately."

"Yes, sir."

"Thanks, Helen." Cornell watched her leave.

She'd been with them since they'd moved the offices up here five years ago. She was bright, all business. He'd found her to be a good listener, but not nosy. She was somewhat homely. With her short, mousey hair and her business attire, she resembled a librarian. He sometimes had the urge to get her a makeover, but it was none of his business.

Cornell was married, his wife and kids mostly living without his presence. He didn't think they minded too much. They had all the luxuries they wanted to compensate for that.

The phone rang. He snatched up the receiver. "Yeah? Cornell here."

"Traegar again. As you guessed, they located Cunningham in the stairwell. Dead. Fairchild's chip was on him. She wasn't anywhere in the hotel. Mathers was in the hotel room. Also dead. We figure it was Valiant."

"Anything else?"

"No, sir. That's all for now."

Cornell ended the call. Where'd Valiant go with the woman? What were his options? Disappear out of the country? No matter where he took Fairchild, the aliens would find them. Once they did, it would be easy for the Agency to reclaim her from them.

His phone rang again. He picked it up. "Cornell."

"It's Helen, sir. I have the files you requested transferred to your network folder. They're in a folder with today's date."

"Thanks, Helen."

Cornell hung up the phone again. He logged into his computer and went to the network to retrieve the files. There were hours of audio and video files. He transferred them to his external hard drive and opened up the video from the other night. He trolled through the footage and paused when he located a scene that showed Carolyn in the den.

She looked panicked and was trying to call for help on her cell phone. Valiant showed up before she could connect and chased her outside. Cornell couldn't hear their conversation. They stepped back into the house. Cornell heard the woman say, "Who is Jessica?" and he noted Valiant's reaction. Valiant dragged her back outside and closed the sliding doors. The camera stopped filming thirty seconds after Valiant shut the doors to the porch.

It picked up again when Valiant and the woman stepped back in the house. At this point, it appeared as if someone, probably the daughter, entered the house. Valiant held the gun to Carolyn's head and kept her from crying out. So far, it looked like Valiant was still in the game and on board with what he was supposed to be doing.

Cornell continued to examine the footage until he'd reviewed everything. There was nothing in there to explain why Valiant was helping Fairchild instead of delivering her to the Agency as he'd been instructed.

The one odd piece was her question about Jessica, obviously a reference to Valiant's wife. But how did she know about Jessica? Her psychic abilities. She'd picked up the truth about Jessica's death and told Valiant. That had to be it. Cornell felt his ulcer burning a hole in his stomach. He had to get that woman away from Valiant. God knows what else she'd find out just by being around him.

His phone rang again and he snatched it up. "Cornell."

"It's Groser. I'm monitoring the surveillance on the Fairchild residence. I thought you might like to know the daughter is at home. The main phone lines are still out though she's called the phone company for service using her cell. She also called the neighbours and Brent Morgan, looking for her mother. She established no one saw her last night, and they don't know where she is."

"Has she notified the police yet?"

"No, sir. She called a friend of hers. This same friend dropped her off at home this morning. They decided she should wait since they aren't certain she's missing."

"Anything else?"

"Yes, there is one thing. The daughter suggested to the friend her mother might have tried to go to Algonquin Park because of something Drummond told them. Does that mean anything to you?"

"No. But maybe I'll head over there and question the girl myself. Thanks."

Cornell hung up the phone. He dialled Helen. When she picked up, he told her he would be stepping out and to forward any calls from Traegar or Groser to his cell phone. All other calls were to be sent to voicemail. He put his computer in "sleep" mode and made a note to get an unregistered gun on his way out. Cornell wasn't expecting to use it on the daughter, but he wanted to have it ready.

He unlocked a drawer on the bottom left of his desk. There was a small box in it containing various badges and identification cards with his picture on them. Today, he'd be working for the RCMP.

He took out his wallet and slipped the relevant ID card and badge inside.

Cornell nodded to Helen on his way out of the office. He felt optimistic for the first time since he'd been awakened with the news his agents had gone AWOL. By the time he reached his car, he was whistling.

CHAPTER 42

A black Mercedes rolled up to the Fairchild's garage, Sam tracking its progress from the living room window. A man she didn't recognize got out of the car, and she crossed her arms and hugged her chest while he climbed the stairs. When he knocked on the door, she opened it.

"Carolyn Fairchild?"

"No." She hesitated. "That's my mother."

She studied him carefully, but he wasn't familiar. He was overweight, balding, and his large, round eyes reminded her of an owl, but his face seemed kind. He was probably a lot older than her mom.

"My name is Jim Cornell. I work for a branch of the government that investigates UFO sightings." He held out his identification.

"I thought the government denied having anything to do with UFOs?"

"We investigate certain events that come to us through military channels. Many times, it has more to do with investigating the people who report the events than with the possible existence of extraterrestrials. I'd like to talk with your mother. Is she available?"

"I'm sorry. She's not here right now."

"Do you know a man named Ralph Drummond?"

"He's a friend of my mom's. Has something happened to Ralph?" She tensed. If something had happened to Ralph, something terrible might have happened to her mother.

Cornell frowned and then shook his head. "No. Nothing's happened to Ralph. I'm investigating his involvement in a cult. They recruit people who believe UFOs are abducting them and send them to their camp up by Algonquin. I'm tracking down anyone he's had any affiliation with for questioning. It would help me reunite many people with their missing loved ones. Once they get involved with this cult, they cut off all connection with their families. It's heartbreaking the pain this group causes."

"Oh, my God," Sam said. "My mother might be going there. We visited Ralph the other day, and he told my mom to go to Algonquin. He sent her there. Please, come in."

Cornell smiled and stepped inside.

"Can I make you a cup of tea?" Sam asked.

"Yes, that would be nice."

"Please, come into the kitchen, and we can talk while I put the kettle on."

"Thank you, dear." His voice was kind. "Where's your mother now?"

Sam picked up the kettle from the kitchen counter and filled it from the water purifier. Cornell sat on a bar stool at a counter along the side of the kitchen.

"I don't know. Maybe she went to Algonquin." There was panic in her voice. "Ralph said there are aliens helping abductees in Algonquin Park. My mom believed him. He said he had a map."

"Did you see this map?"

"No. We went to Ralph's to get it from his wife, but she said she gave it to the government people. Was that you?"

"Perhaps. I'll investigate. If you didn't get the map, why would she go to Algonquin now?"

The water boiled, and the kettle shut off. Sam went through the motions of preparing the tea, which reminded her of her mother, and she thought she'd go crazy with worry. She was silent for a moment, trying to collect herself so she wouldn't cry in front of this stranger.

When she could speak without her voice breaking, she said, "Ralph's wife said he gave Brent a copy of the map. My mom was trying to get it from him. I can't reach my mom though. She was supposed to spend the night at a neighbour's last night, and the neighbour said she never did. I'm worried. Should I call the police?"

"I'm sure nothing has happened to her. Perhaps I can help you find her. Let me make some calls, and I'll verify for you she's okay. If we haven't located her by tomorrow, I'll contact the authorities myself."

"Her purse and all her things are here. She wouldn't leave without her wallet and everything. I'm afraid something has happened. She even left a duffel bag with her clothes and personal stuff in it sitting on the floor in her bedroom."

"I see. Was there anything in the house to indicate a struggle?"

"No. Everything looked fine. A note I wrote to her was gone. When I came in last night, she wasn't here, and I left her a note telling her where I was going. After I left, she must have come in, picked it up, and then left again. It doesn't make sense. Her car is still here. Unless she left with someone else, I don't know what could have happened. I don't understand why she wouldn't have left me a note to say where she was going, and I don't understand why I can't get her on her cell phone."

"Perhaps she's somewhere where there is no service?"

"I guess. But she wouldn't have gone away when my dad's funeral is tomorrow."

"I'm so sorry. This must be a difficult time for you."

"How will I get through it without my mother? I want my mother." Her voice sounded shrill to her ears.

He took a gulp of his tea and stood up. "Before I go, would you mind giving me this Brent person's contact information? I'll talk to him and see if he can shed some light on what's happened to your mother. Don't worry, dear. We'll find her." He patted her hand.

Thank God, someone would help her. "Thank you so much."

Cornell reached into his shirt pocket and pulled out a card. "Here," he said, handing it to her. "If anything comes up, please call me. If you hear from your mother, or you find out anything else, call me. Anything I learn about your mother, you'll be the first to know."

"Thank you." Sam smiled at him. She turned and headed for her mother's office to get Brent's contact information.

CHAPTER 43

Cornell pulled up in front of Brent Morgan's home in Bradford at 10:15 AM. He strode up the cobblestone walkway to the door of a large, ranch-style bungalow. Brent's practice was obviously doing well. The property was professionally landscaped. Cornell rang the bell and waited. Footsteps approached, and the door swung open.

"Brent Morgan?"

"Yes?"

"I'm Agent Jim Cornell, RCMP." He flashed his badge. "May I come in? I'd like to ask you a few questions about Ralph Drummond."

Brent allowed Cornell to step inside. "Has something happened to Ralph?"

Cornell shook his head. "It's nothing like that. Are you aware Ralph checked himself into a mental hospital?"

"Yes. What's this about?"

"Mind if we sit down? This could take a few minutes."

"Come in." Brent led Cornell into an immaculate living room, painted white and sparsely furnished.

What, no plastic on the couches? Cornell listened for the wife's presence. There seemed to be no one else in the house, but he thought he'd better make sure. He noted Morgan didn't offer him anything to drink. "Is your wife here? She might help."

"No. She's at work."

"I'm not keeping you from a client am I?"

"No one's here. What's going on?"

"We believe Drummond has been working with a cult located near Algonquin Park. They scam UFO abductees, making them believe they can help them."

"I've never heard of this." Brent's voice was guarded. He wouldn't be as easy to convince as Fairchild's daughter.

"Carolyn Fairchild may be involved with this group at Drummond's suggestion. Has she contacted you in the last two days?"

"She left me a phone message yesterday. I didn't get it until last night. I tried to call her back this morning, but when I called her cell, she didn't pick up."

"Can you tell me what she said in her message?"

"She said she needed to talk to me."

"She didn't mention what it was about?"

"No. Has something happened to her?"

"We're not sure. Her daughter fears she's missing, and we suspect she might be headed to Algonquin."

"Why would she do that? Her husband's funeral is tomorrow."

"She was in an agitated state after visiting with Mr. Drummond at the hospital yesterday. A map divulging the cult's location exists. Drummond would've given it to you for safekeeping. Samantha said her mother was looking for it and wanted to get it from you."

Brent's eyes narrowed.

Cornell tensed. If Morgan saw through this, he'd have to be eliminated.

"What branch of the RCMP are you working for exactly?"

"We investigate UFO-related events. Mostly incidents involving people who claim sightings or encounters, or who fall victim to people taking advantage of experiencers."

"May I see your badge?"

Cornell retrieved the badge from inside his wallet and held it out.

Brent still looked dubious. "I'll just call police dispatch and verify this." He reached for the phone.

Cornell was faster. He pulled his gun and pointed it at Brent. "Don't move."

Brent froze.

"Where's the map?"

"I don't know."

"Did you give it to Carolyn?"

"She was never here. I told you that. And I don't know what you're talking about. I don't have any map."

"You do. Drummond's wife said you do. Where is it?"

"I don't know what you're talking about."

"Where are Drummond's backup files?"

"I don't know what you're talking about."

Cornell decided he didn't have time for this. "Have it your way." He shot Brent in the stomach.

Brent collapsed to the floor, hands pressed to his abdomen, blood trickling from between his fingers.

Cornell aimed the gun at Brent's heart and put another bullet in him.

Brent went limp.

Cornell took a pair of gloves from his jacket pocket and went to search the house, starting with Brent's office. He found memory sticks and an external hard drive he took to review later.

He pulled open a filing cabinet. There were some UFO-related documents, but no map. Perhaps the map was hidden in a safety deposit box? If so, it would take a while to get access. Somehow, he didn't think Morgan would've gone to that much trouble.

Cornell used his cell phone to call the office. "Helen, I want you to send two agents to the address I'll give you. They have to do a cleanup. I'll wait here for them and explain everything when they get here."

He gave her the information. When the team got here, they could go over the house a final time and make sure he hadn't missed anything. He'd also instruct them to call local police and tell both the police and Morgan's wife that Brent had been the victim of a robbery, and it was related to his involvement with Ralph Drummond.

Cornell collected the items he'd retrieved from Morgan and went to the door. He'd been careful not to touch anything with his bare hands during his search of the place. Anything he'd left on the door or in the living room was fine. He'd claim to be the one to have found the body. Next, he wiped the unregistered gun free of prints and dropped it in the trashcan in the kitchen.

He took one more look around the house. Satisfied, he went outside. He left the front door closed but unlocked and went back to his car. He was anxious to get to his office to examine the files he'd found. If some of the aliens were interfering with the experiments, they'd have to be stopped.

Cornell pulled out his cell phone and dialled his office again. When Helen picked up, he said, "Can you check for me the next scheduled abduction for Carolyn Fairchild?"

"Yes, sir." There was a pause while she searched her files. "The end of May."

Cornell considered. "Send in a request to change that to tonight and specify we need four agents to be there when it happens. I want two of the agents returned with her to the Peterborough compound. The other two should be left where they pick up Fairchild so they can acquire Valiant."

"I'll do that right away."

"I also want ETAP military personnel ready to go into Algonquin. When we locate that base, they have to be ready to go in and clean it out."

"Yes, sir."

He disconnected. He had a solid action plan now. They could still get to Fairchild. The aliens working with the Agency would find her location and, likely, Valiant as well. If she was picked up in Algonquin, they might even nab her near the rebel alien base. In the meantime, he'd take what he'd found at Morgan's and see if he could find that map.

His optimism from earlier returning, he smiled. Perhaps he'd take Helen out to lunch tomorrow to celebrate when it was confirmed they had Fairchild. A van and a car approached. The team had arrived. Cornell stepped out of the car to greet them.

CHAPTER 44

Carolyn shifted in her seat to better observe Michael. He stared straight ahead, focused on the road. She noticed he glanced often into the mirrors, probably to make sure they weren't being followed.

They'd rented a car and cleared out of Peterborough. Michael had made her wait in a nearby coffee shop while he went to the rental place. The forty-five minutes she'd sat with her head down staring into her coffee and pretending to read a newspaper had felt more like forty-five hours, but at last, she saw him walking up to the door.

He'd come in long enough to tell her everything was fine and order the egg sandwich. She'd only been able to stomach a fruit muffin and coffee, though she questioned if the fruit was real and assumed the muffin was made with genetically modified ingredients.

Michael insisted they'd make only bathroom stops along the way, and she was sure he'd expect her to go into the bush to do it. The rations in the packs and wild edibles he foraged at the park would have to keep them going once they left the coffee shop. At least, the wild edibles would be healthier than the food at the coffee shop.

The one exception to his "no stopping" rule was when they'd halted in the town of Bancroft to get her a pair of hiking shoes. He'd found a shoe store with a decent pair, and he'd allowed her to come into the store to try them on. She'd felt like a kid let out of detention. While she'd enjoyed the little outing, Michael had acted the entire time like a cat in a room full of sleeping dogs. He'd remained tense until they were back in the car and away from the town.

Carolyn softened. When things were most terrifying, he'd come back for her. She ached to hold him, but settled for running her hand through his hair.

He turned to smile at her. "What's up?"

"I'm happy to be with you."

"Are you crazy?"

She laughed. "No. I'm not happy about the circumstances. But I'm happy you came back for me. I was afraid that guy at the hotel would take me away forever."

"I would've hunted him down and taken you back. Don't dwell on it. It didn't happen."

"I'm still happy you came back."

He frowned. "I hope you didn't think I'd leave you."

"No," she said quickly. "I knew you'd want to come back. But you didn't know he was coming after me, and I didn't know what had happened to you." She paused, thinking about it, reviewing the sequence of events in her head. "Was he trying to kill you?"

"He probably was ordered to take me alive. I, however, was under no such restrictions."

Carolyn fell silent again. It was difficult to think of Michael as a killer. Since she'd met him, he'd killed three people, seemingly without remorse. To him, it was simple necessity. She wondered if she could ever become the type of person who'd choose to kill. Perhaps if Sam were in danger. It was different when you were protecting someone you loved. Did that mean she didn't love herself enough to protect herself?

"How many people have you killed?"

"I can't talk about that with you."

"Was it a lot?"

"What do you think is a lot?"

"Well, for me, one would be a lot, and you topped that in the last two days, so I guess I have my answer."

"I won't justify anything to you. You can't possibly begin to understand."

"No, probably not. Was it all just for the money?"

Michael glanced at her. "What do you want me to say? If I

hadn't agreed with what I was doing, I wouldn't have been doing it."

"I'm trying to understand how you could take a life and feel okay with it. I can't comprehend that."

"Would you have preferred I let Torque kill me and take you in?"

"Of course not. Why didn't you just tie him up and leave him? You didn't even flinch."

"I can't afford to flinch. Are you forgetting he had a tracking chip in his neck?"

"No. But you could've removed it. You removed it when he was dead."

"A much easier procedure to do when the person is dead."

"Do you have a license to kill?"

That made him smile. "You've seen too many movies. There's no such thing. It's not like they issue agents a hunting license."

"Not even in the British Secret Service?"

"I doubt it. I'm sure that's just in the movies."

"Do you like to kill?"

"No. I do it because I have to."

"That's debatable. You didn't have to kill John." There it was. Now she'd said it, she couldn't take it back.

He looked at her again, and his expression told her he'd been there. Uncertain if he'd been the one to do it, but he was a part of it.

Michael didn't respond immediately, but drove in silence for about a kilometre. He turned onto a dirt road and pulled over. Agony on his face he took both her hands in his and cleared his throat.

"I was ordered to do it. I started to. My hand was on the button, but I didn't press it. When I hesitated, Torque put his hands over mine and forced my finger down. I'd give anything to change what happened. I go over it in my head. There are things I could've done, and John wouldn't have died that day. John didn't deserve that. I can't expect you to forgive me. But understand, I'll have to live with that for the rest of my life, and I'll regret it for at least that long. I'm truly sorry. I questioned it, but I didn't take a stand, and John died."

She hung her head. Numbness spread through her. She thought she should be crying, or be on the verge of crying, but she was too numb even for that. She pulled her hands out of his. He didn't stop her.

"They said it was a heart attack. How is that possible?"

Michael didn't reply for a long time. He stared at her, frowning. She waited, trying not to interrupt whatever mental gymnastics were going on in his head. She hoped his conscience would win.

Finally, he said, "A weapon referred to as the Tesla Ray. It uses directed energy. It can make someone's heart explode, and it'll look like a heart attack. The coroner won't be able to tell the difference." He paused and then said, "Knowing that, are you still happy to be with me? Do you hate me now?"

She sensed fear in this man who wasn't afraid of anything. But she refused to ease his conscience. Not yet. She was afraid of betraying John. Or was it too late for that? Could she forgive Michael for the role he played in John's death? If not, was it wrong to stay with him and accept his help? Would that make her just as evil?

If she left Michael, they'd hunt her down. He risked his life by helping her. If all he wanted was to get away from the Agency, he'd have a better chance without her slowing him down. She looked up at him. She refused to believe he was evil. Michael's gaze met hers, unwavering.

"I'll do everything to make up for what I've done. Carolyn, I swear to you. I swore before I wouldn't let anyone take you again, and I meant it."

They stared at one another in silence. Carolyn wanted to touch him, to take him in her arms and tell him it was okay. His regret eased her pain, but it didn't eradicate it, and it didn't change that he was still capable of killing. It showed he was capable of remorse, which helped.

"Did you love your wife?"

"Yes, of course, I did."

"Did she know you killed people for a living?"

"No."

"Then she thought you were someone you weren't. You were living a lie."

"I was protecting her."

"It didn't work, and she never knew who you really were. In the end, keeping her ignorant didn't help her."

"Don't talk about my wife. They're burying her today, and I'm not there." It came out an agonized shout. The anger in his voice frightened her. His pain flowed through her.

"Michael."

He waited.

"I don't know what to do," she said at last.

He started the car again. "Then do the practical thing. We have to get to Algonquin. If you don't let me help you, you'll never be free of either the Agency or the aliens. They'll hunt you down and take you. You'll live out your life in their cages. I'll never do anything to hurt you again. I'm not asking you for anything except to let me help you."

"Okay. That much I can do."

She fought the urge to touch him. She wanted to tell him she'd forgive him. They drove in silence, neither looking at the other.

***

Jim Cornell stared at the map on his computer screen. There it was: Drummond's map. It was on Morgan's hard drive and had been scanned in from a hard copy. How had there been no trace of the map amongst the items retrieved from Drummond's home? They'd collected everything. Drummond's wife had said agents had taken everything, and she'd personally given them the map.

So, why wasn't it in the storage room?

Cornell could come to only one conclusion: someone had removed it from the evidence room, and he had a feeling he knew who that was. It couldn't be a coincidence Valiant disappeared with Fairchild headed in the direction of Algonquin. He picked up his phone and had Helen connect him to Folliott down in Evidence.

Folliott was on the line within seconds. "You wanted to speak to me, sir?"

"Yeah. I want you to check the sign-in and sign-out data for the evidence room and review the footage from the cameras. Focus on the evidence brought in from the Drummond house the day our guys searched it. I think there might be some evidence missing. See who went in and out of there and who handled it before it was catalogued. Notify me if you find anything suspicious."

"Yes, sir."

Cornell hung up.

Valiant, you son of a bitch, if you removed evidence, you're fucking dead.

He was sure Valiant had been turning before he'd vanished with Fairchild. All Cornell needed was some evidence, and he'd justify having Valiant terminated. If only he hadn't let Muniz handle it. Muniz had been too close to Valiant. They'd been partners for so long he'd been blind to the signs indicating Valiant had cracked.

Cornell would be blamed if anyone found out he knew an agent was a potential problem and hadn't removed him from the Project. He had to clean it up now. If Valiant caused them to lose Carolyn Fairchild, it would be even worse. Cornell tried to push that thought away and failed.

He realized he should consider the possibility the two would make it to the base before it was cleaned out and get help. Would the aliens accept Sam as a subject in Carolyn's place? They often abducted members of the same family. He hoped he'd be able to work something out if Carolyn escaped. He'd have to keep a close eye on Sam and make sure she didn't disappear as well.

Cornell checked the time. It was 2:00 PM. The aliens wouldn't be coming for Carolyn until tonight. He couldn't wait to get his hands on Valiant. It'd be satisfying to drag him back to the Agency.

Hatred and rage welled up. No one betrayed the Agency. Valiant had been handpicked to survive, and this is how he repaid them for their generosity? Valiant would suffer for it. In the meantime, Cornell would send a copy of this map to Peterborough Compound and get the military unit out to Algonquin. He reached for the phone, wondering how many helicopters he could commandeer.

CHAPTER 45

They rode in tense silence. Carolyn lost herself in her thoughts, and she assumed Michael was doing the same. Perhaps he was as afraid as she was of having another argument. Michael had turned on the radio, and it was a blessed distraction, putting a wall of music, news, and commercials between them.

They were driving along Highway 60, approaching Algonquin Park. Michael had told Carolyn they'd enter the park through the East Gate. To her surprise and puzzlement, though, Michael pulled the car into a secluded area before they reached the gate. He turned to Carolyn, and his expression told her she wouldn't be happy to hear what he had to say.

"Get out of the car." He opened his own door and stepped out.

She stepped from the car, fear rising through her gut.

He didn't waste any time. "I want you to get in the trunk."

Her stomach lurched, and the blood drained from her face. "Michael ..."

He approached her, and she backed away. His hands brushed at the air, the gesture placating. "It'll be okay. I don't want anyone to see us together when we enter the park. Any agents looking for us will ask about a couple. If I go in alone, it'll help keep us off the radar. I'm sorry. I don't know of a better way."

She took a step back, away from him. "Please. No." She whispered it, begging.

Her thoughts went to Torque, locked in the trunk, dead in the trunk, of their abandoned car. The day was hot, and the trunk would be stifling. The fatigue and stress backed up on her. She cried, her body shaking as she pictured herself in the trunk and something preventing Michael from letting her out again.

Michael stepped over to her and put his arms around her. She let him pull her to him. Her arms went around his waist, and she pressed herself tightly against him.

One of his hands cupped the back of her head, and he stroked her hair. His lips pressed the top of her head. The gestures of compassion from this hired killer frightened her more than if he'd tried to force her into the trunk against her will. The sobs came unrestricted. He let her cry, holding her until the weeping subsided.

She took a deep breath to steady her voice. "What if something happens, and you can't get me out?"

"I wouldn't let anything happen. I'll show you how to get yourself out. Would you like to see? The car has a lever in the trunk."

She lifted her face to look up at him. "I'm sorry. I understand what you're saying, but I can't stop thinking about Torque. What if I suffocate?"

"You won't suffocate. It's not airtight. Let me show you how it'll work."

He took her hand and led her around to the back of the car. He popped the trunk using the remote. "There are two ways you can get out. One, you can do what Torque did and kick the back seat down. Then you'd be able to crawl out into the car. Two, use the lever at the bottom of the trunk. Look."

Michael pointed to a handle near the trunk latch. "This handle should glow in the dark. It'll be easy for you to turn it and open the trunk. We can test it out before we get back on the road so you know you can do it."

She nodded, tension easing. "Okay. Yes, I'd like to practice opening it."

Michael helped her get into the trunk, and she held her breath as he closed the lid. Eyes squeezed shut for a moment, she opened them again and saw the handle, a faint firefly glow in the dark. She jiggled it, not knowing which way to turn it. The trunk lid yanked upward, and she lost her grip on the handle, letting it slide out of her sweaty palm.

"It's okay, right?"

She nodded.

He helped her climb out again. Michael retrieved her backpack from the back seat of the car and stuck it in the trunk. He opened her pack, removed a bottle of water, and handed it to her. "You'll need this. Do you want to take your pants, shoes, and socks off? It'll be hot in there for you if you don't."

Carolyn smiled. "You're just trying to get me out of my pants." But she did as he suggested.

Michael returned the smile. "If I'd known it would be that easy, I'd have told you it was hot in the front, too."

She giggled, self-conscious. Tension eased. She placed her things into the trunk and gripped the car. Michael held her arm, steadying her as she climbed in.

When she was settled, he said, "It won't take more than about ten minutes to get there. We're close. When you hear me turn off the radio, you'll know I'm through the entrance. Stay quiet and stay hidden. Don't panic. Once I have the map and the permits, I'll drive to a secluded spot to let you out."

"Okay," she said, resigned. As he moved to close the trunk, she called out, "Michael."

He halted, puzzled.

"Why didn't Torque use the handle to open the trunk and get out? Wouldn't that have been easier for him than crawling out the back seat?"

Michael took a moment to answer her. Finally, he said, "The handle in Torque's car was disconnected. It didn't work."

Before she could respond, he closed the trunk. The car jiggled as he opened the driver's door and got in. The realization sank in that the handle in Torque's car had been deliberately disabled because they used it to transport kidnap victims.

Carolyn rested her head on her arm. The trunk was warm and close. She gripped her bottle of water. What would it have been like to travel from Newmarket to Peterborough in the trunk of Torque's car? Then she remembered she would've been drugged and handcuffed, and unaware of most, or possibly the entire, journey.

Arnie had endured that. The thought of her missing friend brought tears to her eyes again. John, Arnie, and Shelly were all gone. As far as everyone else was concerned, she was gone too. She closed her eyes, trying to sense anyone with her. There was nothing.

Why couldn't she feel anyone?

Guides and angels, please give me a sign you're around. She needed something to help her spiritually connect. The lack of presence made her feel separate and alone. It was as if closing her in here had cut her off from the unseen world as well as the physical world.

She tried to recollect how long it had been since she'd connected with anyone: John, her spirit guides, Jessica. She'd connected with Jessica the night before. It seemed a lifetime ago. Since then, she'd slept with Jessica's husband. Guilt welled up. She hadn't meant to. It had just happened.

Were John and Jessica aware of what had happened between her and Michael? Were they angered by it even though they were now in the spirit world and outside of what happened on the earth plane?

It bothered her she'd compromised her values. She didn't know Michael, and what she knew of him should have made him despicable to her. But when she thought of him, when she looked at him, all she wanted to do was touch him and be with him. She wondered if she was going crazy. She closed her eyes and clung to the bottle of water as if it were an anchor to reality.

CHAPTER 46

Michael approached the East Gate. The sun blazed in a clear sky, the highway stretching ahead through a valley of evergreen trees rich with needles in varying shades of green. Wildflowers lined the edge of the road, filling the culverts. The recent drought left some of the grass scorched and brown, but the beauty of the natural wilderness still shone through.

It wouldn't last much longer. Whatever they did to put a stop to the Agency's plans, this would still all be doomed to disappear. If only he could stop time for a moment, sit with Carolyn in his arms, gaze out over the land and just be. When the end came, this would be a better place than most to face it.

Michael drove up to the arch of the East Gate and veered right, taking the road leading to the information centre. He turned off the radio, signalling to Carolyn they were through the gate.

The Information Centre included the Parks Store and a separate building with washroom facilities. Michael pulled up across from the washrooms, parking the car as far from the buildings and other cars as possible. On one side, a field of grass stretched about fifteen metres to the forest beyond. On the other, about five parking spots away, was an RV.

Michael hurried into the information building and got a permit for the Source Lake access point to the backcountry. He had a tense moment when the grey-haired woman behind the counter insisted he should've made a reservation by phone two days ahead of time, but since the park wasn't booked up, she let it slide.

Once back in the driver's seat, he stuck his permit on the dashboard and drove the car onto the highway. He continued along Highway 60 until he'd left the parking area out of view. Pulling over at the first spot that offered some cover off the side of the road, he got out and looked around.

Nothing moved. It was hot—at least twenty-five Celsius with the humidity. Carolyn must be stifling. He hurried to the trunk and popped it open. Dyed-brown hair plastered to her face with sweat, Carolyn sat up, blinking in the sunlight. Her water bottle was empty.

"Come on out."

She nodded, looking too hot and miserable to reply.

Michael picked up her pants and handed them to her. "Much as I admire the view, you should probably put these back on."

Carolyn gave him a slight smile.

When her pants, socks, and shoes were back on, Michael opened the passenger door for her. "Climb in. It's cool in there."

She started to get into her seat, but paused, startled. She reached down and picked something up. "How did this get here?"

"What have you got?"

"This," she said, holding up a small, white feather.

He shook his head. "I guess it must have floated in from somewhere when I opened the door."

She smiled. "I was looking for a sign. This is it."

"A sign of what?"

"You'll laugh at me."

"Try me."

"White feathers are a sign of angelic presence. When I was in the trunk, I asked for a sign from my guides that I wasn't alone. You might think it's a coincidence, but it's a strange place to find a white feather, and I'm taking it as the sign I asked for."

"I'm not laughing. This time yesterday, I wouldn't have expected to ever hear from my wife again, and you've convinced me she was with us last night. Nothing is too weird for me anymore."

She smiled and climbed into the car.

When she was settled in her seat, he handed her a bottle of water, and she opened it and took a long swallow. He shut her in with the cooler air and got back in the car.

"Are you okay?"

"Yes."

"I'm sorry you had to do that."

"I know."

He pulled onto the highway. "We can drive on for a little while, but then we have to ditch the car and cut across the park towards the north. The base is somewhere beyond Sunny Lake if that map is legitimate. We'll be breaking all kinds of rules and regulations, veering off accepted routes, and we have to keep you out of sight as much as possible."

"How long to get to the base?"

"At least two days of hiking. Maybe more. It depends on how fast we can get through the underbrush. There are no trails where we're going. Also, we can't have any fires. Much of the area is probably dry from lack of rain. Though it would take a longer drought to completely dry up some of the soil here, we have to be careful."

"This weather is frustrating. A few years ago, roads were closed and bridges were flooded out at this same time of year. Now, there's a drought and spring feels like summer. I can't believe there are still people who deny climate change," she said.

Michael didn't respond. He wondered if he should explain to her what was happening. He decided it wasn't the right time. If she knew what was coming, she'd panic and want to get back to her daughter. He couldn't risk that. He'd have to tell her sometime, but not until she was at least safe from the aliens. If they kidnapped her again before he could get help ... At the thought of losing her, he unconsciously reached out his hand and took hers.

She stared at him; her brows furrowed, and then she squeezed his hand.

"I'm sorry. I did that without thinking." He let go of her hand though he didn't want to.

"I don't mind. I find it comforting." She took his hand again.

They drove in silence for a while. Michael wondered where this ache for her was coming from. He hadn't felt anything this strong before, not even when he'd dated Jess. He'd definitely had a physical attraction to Jess, and they were compatible, but with Carolyn, it was as if he'd found something he hadn't known he was looking for. Now, when she wasn't with him, or when she was with him but not touching him, he felt like a piece of him was missing.

He glanced at her. He sneaked peeks at her often. Her slightly greasy hair hung limp around her face. Her sweat-damp shirt clung to her body, and she wore a pair of track pants slightly too big for her. She'd never looked more appealing.

"It's beautiful here," she said, and turned to catch him staring. She smiled. "Eyes on the road, pal."

He laughed and released her hand to put his own back on the steering wheel.

She moved her hand to his thigh. "Does that bother you?"

"No, but we might crash if you keep it there."

Carolyn blushed and laughed softly. She moved her hand away, and he felt a piece of him go with it.

***

Cornell cursed under his breath. Folliott, standing next to Cornell's desk, waited. Cornell paused the video. He'd seen enough. The footage from their surveillance cameras not only showed Michael Valiant breaking into the storage area to steal evidence, but also continuing the theft while the security guard slept on the couch in the reception area.

He couldn't immediately get his hands on Valiant, but he could take care of the security guard. He picked up his phone. "Helen, get the security manager up to my office right away. We have a problem."

"Yes, sir."

Cornell hung up the phone and turned to Folliott. "Good work. You can go on back to what you were doing before I pulled you away."

Folliott nodded and left.

Cornell again called Helen. When she answered, he cut her off before she could speak. "Helen, get me the Peterborough commander. What's his name?"

"Weeks, sir."

"Oh yeah. Weeks. Thanks. Get him on the line for me."

He hung up the phone. He needed to hear back on those choppers. If they beat Valiant to the base, they could clean it out, leaving Valiant and Fairchild trapped with nowhere to go.

The phone rang. He snatched it up. "Cornell here."

"It's Weeks. I know what you're going to ask. It's been done. We sent five choppers out to Algonquin. There are enough personnel on board to clean out a small base with due force."

"Thank you, sir. I look forward to hearing from you when the mission has been accomplished."

"Will do."

Cornell set the phone back onto its cradle. He looked at the clock. It was 4:09 PM.

CHAPTER 47

They'd been hiking since early afternoon. It seemed as if they'd been walking for hours, but Carolyn suspected it hadn't been as long as it felt.

Ahead, coniferous trees grew in clumps. Mushrooms and, where there were gaps in the trees, ferns sprang up from the dark soil. Evergreen needles, leaves, twigs, rocks, pinecones, and a variety of buggy, yucky, mouldy-looking things she didn't want to examine more closely carpeted the ground.

Black flies made walking even more of a frustration. Michael had wanted to spray her with his chemical bug spray, but she'd refused until she thought she'd go insane from the constant buzzing and biting. Then she'd yielded and let him spray whatever he wanted. It helped, a little.

The longer they walked, the more she was ready to snap. The worst part of it was that it all looked the same. They could've been walking back and forth along the same path since they'd left the car.

Michael stopped every once in a while to pick a plant and shove it in a plastic bag he carried. So far, she hadn't had the nerve to ask what was in the bag.

Once, she'd almost stepped in a pile of dung that looked like the world's biggest St. Bernard had deposited it—a vegetarian St. Bernard, from the look of it, as she saw traces of berries in it. Her stomach gave a lurch at the sight, and she almost tossed what little she'd eaten that day. Michael told her it was from a bear. That made her draw closer to him.

Carolyn kept silent, focusing on walking and keeping an eye out for more bear pies. She also didn't want to distract Michael. He was leading them by using the map, a compass, and, apparently, the sun.

At last, he called a rest.

Grateful, Carolyn sat down on a log, checking first to make sure there was nothing too icky on it. Michael checked the map, the compass, and the sun.

She opened her pack and fished out a protein bar, continuing to watch him. Finally, she broke the silence. "Everything okay? Are you lost? I'd say 'we,' but I know I'm lost. I was hoping you weren't, but the amount of times you've checked your bearings concerns me."

He dropped next to her and gave her a look as though he was wondering if he should be insulted or not.

"No, I'm not lost," he said without rancour. "I admit, though, a GPS would be great right now. What are you eating? Protein bar? Not a bad idea." He opened his pack and dug around.

"How much longer must we walk?" she asked.

"Until almost dark. Not sure how long we have. If they send the aliens to track you, we may not make it."

"How can they track me? You removed my chip."

"That was an Agency tracking device. The aliens use a mode of tracking I'm unfamiliar with. You said you've had regular nosebleeds?"

"Yes." She remembered the nosebleed she'd had after her most recent abduction and felt sick.

"They probably inserted a tracking device into your nose. Or it could be anywhere on your body. Do you have any scars you can't explain?"

She nodded. "On my thigh. I had a bruise there after Friday night. There's a scar on my arm, too. I had a small lump under the skin, and the doctor removed it in the office. I asked him what it was, and he said he didn't know and then threw it into the garbage."

"He didn't speculate on it at all?"

"No. He barely looked at it. I expected him to want to send it for testing, but he didn't seem to care. He gave me a couple of stitches and sent me on my way. That was the end of it."

"I doubt that was a tracking device. The alien tracking devices are organic and difficult to locate. They move. If you try to remove them, they burrow deeper into the tissue."

"That didn't happen. It was something close to the surface and looked like it could be organic. It was white." Carolyn popped the last bite of her protein bar into her mouth and stuck the wrapper into her backpack.

She looked up and caught Michael watching her. He appeared on the verge of saying something, but when he didn't, she said, "What? You look like you want to tell me something. I hope you're not going to talk about stuffing me in the trunk of a car again or something like that."

"No." He laughed. "It's nothing like that. I was wondering about this angel stuff."

"I get it. You don't believe, so it must be my imagination or superstition, right? And you're wondering how I could be so gullible?"

"Not quite. You believe you have angels around you, protecting you?"

"Yes."

"Everyone does?"

"Yes."

"Even Jess?"

"You're wondering why Jessie's guardian angels didn't step in and save her from Torque?"

He nodded.

"It might have been her time. Wait," she said, when he opened his mouth, probably to argue. "Let me explain what that means, or what I believe that means, based on my experience and the studying I've done."

"You can study this?"

"Yes. Will you let me explain?"

"Go ahead."

"It's possible she had uneasy feelings that might have helped her to avoid what happened, but most people are oblivious to the guidance they receive. As well, you need to be aware of having angels around you and ask for help. They can't interfere with free will to help you unless you ask them, or unless it's not your time to pass.

"Sometimes, people who have near-death experiences say they

were told it wasn't their time to go and were sent back. Some people believe that we create our life path before we're born, and that major events, particularly death, are predetermined. Perhaps it's true, and I keep an open mind about it, but I haven't seen any evidence to verify it."

"You don't believe in fate?"

"I don't believe the future is set. But you can be directed towards something and possibly arrive there and fulfill an intention. Whether you set that intention prior to your birth or whether some divine force sets it, I don't know."

"Interesting take. How do you explain Hitler? That's a lot of people to have intended to die. Some divine force wanted that?" Sarcasm tinged his voice.

"What happened with Hitler had to do with his vibration. It aligned with enough people who also vibrated at that resonance to cause the Holocaust. But, also, too many people missed the warnings that something was spiralling out of control. It didn't need to happen to propel humanity forward spiritually, and I don't think anyone agreed to be a victim. You can progress more through joy than from sorrow."

"I hope you're right. We'll need all the joy we can get real soon." Michael put his arm around her. "If they find us, if we get separated, no matter what happens, I'll find you again."

"Michael …"

"No, listen to me. The aliens could come, and they'd take you. If they do, I want to make sure you remember that I won't leave you. I won't give up. I'll find you and get you out."

"You mean at the Agency?"

"Yes."

"I don't understand. Isn't the Agency what they call the CIA? That's American, not Canadian. How can they be here?"

"I'm sure they can be wherever they want, but this isn't the CIA."

"Then what is it?"

"I can't tell you. The less you know, the better."

"That's not fair."

"It's safer. Trust me. What's important is, I know where they'll take you, and I'll come for you no matter how long it takes me. Okay?" His eyes became intense, worried.

She frowned. "You said that couldn't be done."

"I'll find a way. Even if they kill me, I'll come for you." He smiled. "Luckily, you can talk to the dead."

"Please don't say that. I've lost John. I can't bear to lose you, too. Don't joke like that."

"I'm not joking. I'm trying to tell you there are no guarantees. If the Agency finds us, they'll want you alive, but I doubt they'll care if they kill me to get to you."

"Then you'll have to let them get me. I'd rather be captured than watch you die. Promise me if it comes to that, you'll let them take me." Then it occurred to her that if she disappeared, Sam would never know what happened to her. On impulse, she removed her engagement ring and wedding band, and reached out to give Michael the wedding band.

"If something happens to me, give this to Sam and tell her what happened."

Michael frowned. "That's not necessary. You can tell her yourself when we're sure the aliens can't get you anymore."

"Michael, please. This is proof you were with me. She might not trust you otherwise."

"Keep it, Carolyn. It'll be okay. I don't want to take your wedding band. Go ahead. Put it back on." He leaned in and touched her forehead with his. It was a gentle touch, but a powerful surge of energy flowed into her from Michael.

She gasped and had to steady herself as a wave of dizziness hit her. Then his lips pressed her lips, and instinctively, she put her arms around him, holding him, running her hands through his hair.

Michael slowly pulled away. His breathing was shallow. "I'm sorry. I don't mean to ..." His voice broke. "God, I want you so much."

Carolyn tried to speak, but he stopped her, pressing his lips to hers again. They kissed, losing themselves for a moment, forgetting everything for a brief, blissful, precious moment. But Michael wouldn't let them forget for long where they were and why. He pulled away and took Carolyn's hands in his.

"We must keep going. If we don't, they'll find us. We only have until nightfall. Then we'll have to stop whether we like it or not. Go ahead. Put the ring back on your finger." He watched her while she did that. Then he pulled her to her feet, hugged her, and released her.

That's when she heard the sound of helicopters.

CHAPTER 48

Michael grabbed their packs and threw them into the underbrush. He pulled Carolyn after him into the cover of some trees.

"Don't move. Military choppers."

Frightened, she clung to him. They huddled, waiting. Through the trees, they could see three helicopters flying in from the south.

"It looks like they're heading in the same direction we're heading. They've discovered the base," he said.

"What'll we do? They'll destroy it, won't they?"

"I'd have to assume so. All we can do is carry on and hope we find something that'll help us, even if they beat us to it."

"Could we go somewhere else? There might be other bases."

"If there are, the only way to find them is through this one."

They continued to stare up at the sky. Carolyn glanced occasionally at Michael, but she couldn't read his expression. Suddenly, Carolyn sensed a presence. Someone was with them. She reached out with her psychic senses to figure out who it was.

Torque.

"Michael," she said.

He looked at her.

"Torque is here."

Michael's body went rigid. He looked around as if trying to see the spirit. "Why do you think that?"

"I feel him. He wants to tell you something."

"What about Jess? Why aren't you connecting to her? Why him?" Hurt permeated his voice.

"You said her funeral was today. She's probably there."

Michael's jaw dropped. "You're joking. That's more important than anything else?"

"In the grand scheme of things? Yes. She has grieving family. You're not the only one who lost her. She'll be there for all her family. She's already connected with you. You've had more communication than anyone else who loved her." Her voice became gentler. "The failing could be mine. I've been under stress. It blocks me. That I can sense Torque at all is a relief. But it means he needs to get through to tell you something important, like Jess did before."

"What does he want?"

She closed her eyes. Pain. There was a flash and an image of Torque's body by the car in Michael's driveway. There was no more pain, only surprise. Michael stood over Torque's body, now a shell. She viewed the scene as if from above.

"You shot him in the chest. There was pain, but that was fleeting. He saw a flash, and he was above the scene, out of his body. You stood over him."

"I know what happened. So do you. You were there." He sounded irritated, impatient.

"Michael, usually a spirit will tell me how it died. I was there, but I didn't see what happened. I heard the shots and then saw you standing over him. For most spirits, their death isn't only the last thing they remember from the physical plane, but also, for obvious reasons, it's one of the most important events in their lives. They start there when they begin communication. At least, that's my experience."

"I'm sorry. It's hard to accept. I had to do it, but it doesn't mean that's how I wanted things to play out."

True. "He knows." She paused, trying to pick up anything else. There was sadness. Regret. She had a flash of a spacecraft. "He's making me feel sad ... He's sorry ... I don't know for what, specifically, and I won't speculate ... He's showing me a spacecraft."

Faster. "Something about going faster. Any idea what that means?"

"Does he want us to move faster?"

Accelerating. "I hear the word 'accelerating.' Does that mean something to you?"

"I don't understand. Can you get him to explain?" Michael sounded frustrated.

"It's difficult. All I can tell you is what I get. He's trying." She got a flash image of a spacecraft again. It grew larger in her mind's eye, as though coming at her. "I see a spacecraft coming towards me."

Michael cursed, his eyes betraying a sudden realization. "They're coming. He's telling us they're coming for you. You're not supposed to be abducted again this soon, but that's changed. I expect they'll come tonight."

Terror overwhelmed her, and it escalated as she pictured herself floating away from Michael, leaving him, maybe forever. Then she received an impression of two men pulling guns on him, shooting him. "They want to take me and shoot you."

When she said that, she no longer felt Torque's presence. "Torque's gone. I think he wanted to tell us that, and then he left."

"Can't he help us?"

"I think spirits do what they can, when they can. But they're still only human. He hasn't been in spirit long, and he had a violent and traumatic death. He probably had difficulty coming through with just this much."

Michael opened up the map and studied it, motioning her to look. "Here's the base." He pointed. "This is where we are." He pointed again to another spot southeast of the base. "We're too far to get to the base today. But there are other places, close to here, where we might shelter amongst the rock. We need to reach something before nightfall."

"Will that help?"

"It might. This whole area is part of the Canadian Shield. If we get underneath, it could help to conceal us. The rock itself may keep them from picking up whatever signal you're giving off."

"What makes you think so?"

"This rebel alien base is underground. Without the map, the Agency never found it. The only thing I can think of is that it's something about the composition of the earth here. They built a base in a provincial park, and no one has ever found it. There has to be a reason they chose this location. That's my best guess."

"How do we find somewhere to hide?"

"Some of the lakes around here likely have rocky nooks or places to hole up in. There's a lake close to us, and we can try that.

We'll stick to the trees in case those helicopters come back. It's okay. We'll find something." He hugged her. "They won't get you, and they sure as hell won't shoot me."

He pointed to a lake on the map. "Here," he said. "That's where we're going. The shore will be all stone. There's a lot of granite and gneiss here. The granite would contain quartz."

Carolyn grabbed his arm. "Quartz is an amplifier."

Michael arched his brows. "It's mostly smoky quartz."

"That's grounding. It can raise your vibration, which will help me. Granite and smoky quartz are protective."

"I don't know about that part of it. It should interfere with their tracking devices."

"Yes, that makes sense energetically."

He smiled. "Then let's go."

He led her in the direction she guessed was northeast. They'd been heading north. At least, that's what Michael had told her when they'd first headed out, though she'd quickly become disoriented. The helicopters were circling in the direction she and Michael had been going. The closest lake, according to Michael's map, was away from their original destination.

In the distance, a loon cried out. The sky was cloudless, the air still and close. Shadows lengthened though the humidity continued unabated.

"What time is it?"

Michael checked his watch. "It's just after six o'clock. We have two hours of daylight left. I don't think they'll come right at nightfall, but it would be dangerous to keep hiking in the dark."

"If all this is Canadian Shield, aren't we walking on it already?"

"Yes, but we need to at least have it around us. Under it would be best."

She nodded, hurrying to keep up to his long strides. He took her hand and pulled her after him. In the distance, they heard explosions. Carolyn threw a terrified gaze at Michael.

"They're blowing it up."

"Possibly," he said.

"Won't that attract park rangers and harm campers?"

"No. They would've radioed park officials and had them block off the area. Hikers and campers aren't supposed to venture into that area anyway. Anywhere near that base is off the accepted routes. We're doing it, but most people play by the rules when they vacation here. Besides, this is a government agency backed by private funding. They can get the cooperation of local law enforcement anywhere without having to explain anything. That's one reason we can't call the police. We're fugitives from the law as far as the police are concerned. If they take us in, we'll be handed over to the Agency. They'll simply follow orders from their superiors and no one will ask questions."

She didn't reply, but tried to walk faster. Michael would've been running if she hadn't been here to slow him down. The pack on her back grew heavier the faster she tried to go, but she didn't complain. Michael's pack was heavier, and he was moving quickly without breaking a sweat. She asked her angels and guides to help them find cover before nightfall. It was the only thing she could think of to do.

CHAPTER 49

Samantha Fairchild stood in Ralph Drummond's room and stared at him in disbelief. Ralph sat on his bed, head down, avoiding her eyes, either from shame or fear.

"What do you mean, 'go away?'" she asked him. "My mother is missing. Brent was found shot to death. Help me. Please. Tell me something I can do. I don't know what to do."

"I can't help you. Get out of here. Stop talking to me." He lurched to his feet and lunged at her. Taking her by the shoulders, he guided her to the door. "Go away." His voice was rough, desperate.

He shoved her into the hallway. "If you don't leave now, I'll call security. Stay away from my family, too."

She spun around to face him and struggled to push the door open as he tried to close it.

"Please. Don't do this. I have no one else. They took your map. They killed Brent before we could get the map from him. Please. Help me."

Ralph's eyes went wide. She couldn't tell if it was fear or horror. "Shut up." It came out as a snarl. "Get out," he bellowed. Ralph gave the door a shove that made her stagger backwards. The door slammed in her face.

Sam stumbled along the hallway in a daze. She noticed a ladies' washroom on her left, went inside, and leaned against the wall, shaking. Ralph had refused to help her—had actually pushed her away. Why had he turned his back on her?

She went to the sink and examined herself in the mirror. Tears stained her cheeks. Sam turned on the water and rinsed her face. She searched for paper towels, but there was only a hand-drying machine. Frustrated, she pressed the button to turn it on and dry her hands. She used the bottom of her blouse to pat her face dry.

A wave of longing and sadness for her lost parents flowed over her. Tears threatened again, and she choked them back. She reached into her purse and took out Jim Cornell's business card. Should she call him and ask for help? He'd tell her what to do. She had no one else she could turn to, and he'd been nice to her. He seemed to care about her mother. So far, he was the only one who'd shown any interest in finding Carolyn.

Sam left the bathroom. Yes, she decided, she'd call him from her car. She stuck the card back in her purse, walked to the elevator, and pressed the "down" button.

A flurry of activity made her look up. Orderlies ran past her. She turned her head and was shocked to see them run to Ralph's room.

Heart in her throat, she followed them. Behind her, the elevator pinged, signalling its arrival, and the doors swished open. She ignored that and walked to Ralph's door, which was wide open. She stared, wide-eyed, into the room.

At first, she didn't comprehend the scene. Ralph was hanging from the light fixture, his body swaying as an orderly struggled to cut it down.

Sam screamed.

Someone said, "Get her out of here now." A man blocked her view and pushed her away from the door. The man handed her over to a nurse, who led her down the hall.

People tried to talk to her, but she ignored them. The nurse led her to an office. The doctor there asked her about Ralph. He seemed to care if she could get herself home. "Do you have someone you can call?"

She nodded, not bothering to explain the "someone" was a stranger. Briefly, she considered calling Vanna or one of her other friends, but she wanted to call Jim Cornell.

How could Ralph be dead? She had to hear it. "Is Ralph dead?"

The doctor looked at her, puzzled. "Yes. I'm sorry."

Then terror overwhelmed her, as the reality sank in, and what if it was her fault? What if the people here had killed Ralph? They might try to kill her, too. She had to get out of here.

Sam jumped up. The doctor stood and tried to grab her arm. Terrified that he wanted to hurt her, she leapt back and screamed, "Don't touch me!"

He dropped his hands, shock crossing his face. As she ran out of the office, she saw him pick up his phone. She ran faster, blindly, her one thought to get to the car, her mother's car, and call Cornell.

She raced past security. The guard stared at her, but didn't try to stop her. Out in the parking lot, she automatically scanned the cars to see if anyone was watching her. Nothing moved, and she didn't see anyone.

Sam hurried to the car, climbed inside, and locked it. She pulled out her cell phone and Cornell's card and dialled his cell number.

"Cornell."

She cleared her throat. "It's Samantha Fairchild."

"What can I do for you?" He sounded delighted to hear from her.

"I didn't know who else to call. Sorry to bother you."

"Not at all. How can I help you?" Genuine concern laced his voice. Sam relaxed a little. He'd help her.

"Some terrible things happened."

"Tell me. I'll help you."

She exhaled her relief. "The news said my mom's friend, Brent, was shot."

"Yes. I'm sorry about that. I can't comment on what might've happened. We're investigating. We'll catch whoever did it. Don't worry. I'm sure you're okay."

"No, I'm not. I went to see Ralph because I was scared and didn't know what else to do. I'm at the hospital now."

"Yes? Have you talked to him?"

She thought she detected a note of alarm. "I tried. He told me to get out. After I left his room, I guess he ... I don't know. He ... Maybe it's my fault for going there. He hanged himself. They said he's dead." She burst into tears.

His voice broke through her sobs. "Sam, listen to me."

She fell silent.

"Are you okay to go home?"

"Yes. Do you think someone will come after me?"

"No. Not at all." His confidence put her at ease. "I'll come over and make sure nothing happens to you. Will you go straight home? Don't call or talk to anyone. Do you understand?"

"Yes. Thank you." She opened the glove box and pulled out a tissue.

"I'm going to hang up now. Go home and wait for me. Is that clear?"

"Yes, Mr. Cornell. Thank you."

"Sam?"

"Yes?"

"Call me Jim," he said, his tone kind and reassuring.

"Okay, Jim."

There was a click, and he was gone. Sam grabbed a tissue from the glove box, wiped her eyes, and blew her nose. She started the car. Everything would be okay now. She had help.

CHAPTER 50

They found refuge along the shore of the lake and were inside, as far away from the entrance as they could go, in what was an opening in the stony shoreline. A rivulet of water flowed up into its bowels, and Michael said it would be safe to have a small fire for warmth, cooking, and light. The energy of the rock, powerful and ancient, surrounded them.

While the air outside was hot and humid, inside their shelter it was cool and damp. They collected enough tinder and pieces of wood to keep a fire going for a while. They sat on Michael's sleeping bag near the flames and ate a salad made up of the plants Michael had collected. Carolyn was surprised at how tasty it turned out to be.

"What's in this?" She scooped another mouthful from her bowl. "It's good."

"Dandelion leaves, garlic mustard flowers, pigweed, some lamb's quarters, a little bergamot, and wild grape vine leaves—whatever I could find in prime condition for eating. Worse comes to worse, you can even eat bulrushes. You can roast them."

"I ate pigweed?"

"You might be more familiar with its other name: Amaranth."

"I've heard of that. It was a nice change from the protein bars. Bulrushes sound kind of gross."

"It's amazing what you can get used to if you have to."

Michael pulled out a stainless steel pot and filled it with water. He went out to the shore, collected some flat-topped rocks, and set them in the fire, which had burned down to coals. He set the pot on top of the stones and threw in some herbs.

The smell of the herbs wafted through the enclosed space as the water heated and then bubbled. Carolyn took deep breaths and let it refresh her. Michael carefully poured some of the herb-infused water into two mugs and handed her one. Carolyn let it cool for a minute, breathing in the delicate aroma. She blew on it, took a small sip, and raised her brows in surprise. "Nice."

Carolyn set the mug next to her to let it cool. She pulled her knees up and rested her chin on them. Michael built up the fire again while she watched him. His face was so serious. His wide mouth and full lips made her think of someone ... She had a revelation.

"Torque called you 'Mick.' That's because of your lips, isn't it? You kind of resemble—"

He cut her off. "I try to ignore that. It started during training. Guys always make up nicknames for each other. That was a long time ago, but it stuck. Even my boss calls me that. My family doesn't use it. They call me 'Mike' or 'Michael.'"

"Why do you call Gerry 'Torque'?"

He grinned. "That didn't start with me. When he first joined the Agency, he got a reputation for being a 'twisted force,' and someone started calling him Torque. I'm not sure what they meant though I think it had to do with his enthusiasm for carrying out his orders."

They both fell silent. Talking about Torque reminded Carolyn of when Michael broke into her house and dragged her out into the night, away from her family and her life. Michael seemed to draw inward as well. He fiddled with the fire though it didn't appear to need tending.

She stared into the flames and sipped her tea. When she finished, she said, "I'm going to wash up in the lake."

"Stay close to the rocks. Don't swim out into the lake. You're not protected out there."

He pulled out a bottle of biodegradable liquid soap from his pack. "Here." He tossed it to her. "This will be fine for your hair and body. Take this pot and use it to rinse yourself away from the lake. Don't go too far up on the shore. I'd rather some soap went into the lake than you risk exposure."

Carolyn stripped off her clothes and made her way to the water, climbing over the stones around the shore of the shelter. She washed the sweat from her body and out of her hair, then moved from the water onto the rocks to lather up and rinse off.

Done, she placed the soap and pot at the cave's entrance and returned to the shallows. She paddled around, enjoying the cool water. She glanced up to catch Michael watching her.

"You look like a mermaid." He grinned.

"Come and join me. It's way warmer than it usually is at this time of year."

Michael removed his clothes and walked towards her.

She picked up the soap and the pot and motioned him over to the shore. She poured some soap into her hands.

"Let me wash you." Her voice came out low and husky. She stepped close to him, offering her soapy hands.

He nodded his head.

She placed her hands on his shoulders, massaging them and rubbing soap onto them, mindful of the bandage on his neck. When she'd finished washing his body, she helped him clean his hair. She could feel and see his desire for her, but he didn't touch her, and it made her want him more.

When she finished helping him rinse out his hair, he clasped her hand in his and led her back into their nest. She hurried to him, unable to endure another moment without his body touching hers. They sank to their knees, lips pressed together.

His hands on her body at last, she in turn stroked him, running her hands over the hard muscles of his arms, belly, and thighs. He released her mouth from his lips and kissed her forehead, then bent his head down to her throat. She moaned. Time seemed to stand still as she let herself be engulfed by him.

After, when Carolyn allowed herself to wonder about mundane matters, she looked towards the entrance to their little cave and realized she couldn't see it. Darkness had fallen outside, and all she saw was velvety blackness and the sparkle of stars.

"It's okay," Michael said.

"I do feel protected in here." She shivered, finding the air chilly though Michael's body next to hers was warm, and the fire beside her lapped heat onto her bare skin.

Michael sat up and grabbed her pack. He removed the other sleeping bag and draped it over them. "Is that better?"

She nodded, breathing shallow as desire for him flooded

through her once again.

His face hovered over hers, and she looked into his eyes. It was like gazing into the eyes of an old friend. "I didn't realize I was missing you when we hadn't met, but I feel like you've returned to me after a long absence."

He stroked her cheek. "Every time I look at you, it's like I recognize you from somewhere. At first, I thought it was because I'd seen surveillance photos. But it's more than that. You always seemed familiar."

She remembered the dream in which Michael, a witch hunter who wanted to burn her, had captured her. She wondered what it meant. He'd come for her but hadn't harmed her.

Then she realized what he'd just said.

At first, I thought it was because I'd seen surveillance photos. And he knew the layout of her home and the things she'd said in private conversations. Michael must also know she was infertile—he wasn't just assuming she was on the pill.

She gasped.

"What's wrong?" He frowned.

"You know I can't get pregnant, don't you?"

"Yes. I'm sorry. It must be hard for you."

"Can you tell me why?"

"I don't know. I didn't know you had a problem until your sky watch last Friday. Then you talked about it with Shelly."

"You were listening?"

"Not then. I listened to the recording after."

She put her head on his shoulder and draped her arm across his chest. Her hand stroked his hair, his cheek.

"Are you okay?" he asked.

"Yes. You know so much about me. I guess that includes how many men I've been with too?"

"Carolyn."

She smiled at his worried tone to show him she wasn't angry. "It's okay. But if you have information about me, then tell me the truth about it. After all we've been through together, be honest with me."

"When I started investigating your group, I looked for everything we had on all of you. The file on you is extensive."

"Why can't I have any more children? Is it something the aliens have done?"

"I didn't find that information. What the aliens do to you and why wasn't in there. There must be files on that somewhere, but it wasn't where I could find it."

"Promise me you won't keep things from me?"

Michael gently nudged her off his chest and propped himself on one elbow, facing her. "I promise. I told you before I don't want to hurt you ever again." He bent down and kissed her forehead.

"What are we going to do now?"

"Well, we have all night." His lips puckered, and he nuzzled her neck.

She laughed. "That's not what I mean, and I hope we have all night, but what if they find us? We can't stay here forever. How are we going to get away from them?"

His face fell.

She regretted breaking the spell, but she was afraid again.

"We'll figure something out by morning. We have to," he said. "But let's forget about everything for a little while longer." He leaned down to kiss her, and she let him.

CHAPTER 51

She's with Ralph. It's so good to see him again. She steps into the room, and there he is. He's not in bed, and he's alone, standing in front of her, waiting. When he sees her, he smiles. She thinks she should give him a hug, but her body won't respond so she sits on the chair she finds next to her.

"Oh, Ralph, I've missed you so much."

"I've missed you, too, Carr." He sounds happy to be with her, but his expression is worried. She knows he has to tell her something important.

"Sam's in trouble."

The words pierce her heart. She's allowed herself to be distracted from her child. "Where is she, Ralph? I'll go to her right away."

"It's not that simple. She's with someone."

"Who?"

"He means you harm. He's looking for you."

"Why are you telling me this? It sounds like a Catch-22."

"It is. But choose."

"Tell me."

"I'm not permitted to give you the answers."

"You're dead," she says, realizing in her heart it's true.

"Yes."

"How did you die?"

She feels it—the noose tightening around his neck. It is quick. Carolyn sees Sam staring in through the open door, face blank with shock.

"No."

Ralph nods. "If you don't go, they'll hand her to the aliens."

"What about Michael?" He's there, sleeping, at peace.

"That's up to you."

"You're telling me I have to leave him and let them take me or they'll take Sam."

"No. You can choose to stay with Michael and tell him."

"Will he believe me?"

"That will be his choice." Ralph looks at her, pity in his eyes. *"I'm sorry. I should have done more for you and Sam, but I was afraid and wanted to save myself."*

"We're all afraid, and we all want to save ourselves," she says.

"They want me to go now."

"No, Ralph. Wait. Tell me what to do ..."

She woke. The fire was out. Everything was black, except the slight glow from the embers and a faint grey space that told her she was looking at the cave entrance. She felt the warmth of Michael's body next to her. God, she'd miss him.

Her heart despaired at the thought of leaving him. He wouldn't know why, but if she woke him and tried to explain, he wouldn't let her go, and her only thought now was to keep Sam safe.

She groped around for some kindling and placed it on the embers. She blew on the twigs to get them to spark up. When it caught, she had enough light to see her pack. She hunted in it for some clean clothes.

Carolyn wanted to leave something of hers for Michael as a message. The only thing she had was her wedding band, so she removed it from her finger. She put the wedding band into a zippered pocket of his backpack. He'd take it to Sam and get her away from whoever had her.

She dressed, making as little sound as possible. When she was ready, she slipped on the shoes he'd bought her. It almost made her cry. She wanted to hug him, kiss him, and touch him before she left, but if she did, she would certainly wake him, so she took one step away from their bed and then another.

Carolyn wished that the last time she'd hugged him she'd done more. She should have caressed him more, kissed him more. Now there was no going back. She could have said the same for the last time she'd hugged John, or Arnie, or Shelly, or Ralph, too. They were all lost to her now.

Sam was still out there. She had to give herself up so they wouldn't start in on Sam.

She reached the mouth of the shelter and stepped out into the moonlight. When the night breeze hit her face, she realized her cheeks were wet. She wiped the tears away and climbed up and away from the cave. She'd have to walk as far away from Michael as possible. If she were near here when the spaceship came, they'd get him, maybe kill him.

Carolyn left the shore and walked into the forest. She wondered if there were bears and then decided she didn't care. She found a stick sturdy enough to use as a walking stick, and she walked. Since the direction didn't matter as long as it was away from the cave where Michael slept, she headed into the trees. Using the stick like a blind person using a cane, she slowly made her way through the forest.

Time passed. She sensed no one around her. If there were spirits with her, she didn't feel them. It seemed she walked for hours, but the moon had moved only a little way through the sky, so perhaps it hadn't been that long. Somewhere, an owl called out. The air smelled fragrant.

Where were they? When would they appear? It would be soon. She didn't need precognition to know they were getting close. Something in her besides her innate abilities was responding to their proximity. It was almost time.

Carolyn halted and waited for them to find her. Tears continued to pour down her face. She'd just found Michael and now she had to give him up. An ache to hold him again overwhelmed her. Why hadn't she told him she'd forgiven him when she'd had the chance? He'd told her how sorry he was, and she hadn't given him absolution.

She'd made him suffer, punishing him. Ashamed, she recalled how she'd told him he'd failed his wife. Now she would never get the chance to tell him how sorry she was that she'd thrown that in his face.

Carolyn wished, too, that she'd told him she loved him, and that she wanted to be with him. It might have made being apart more bearable. Even if he found her now, she wouldn't be able to go with him—not while there was a chance that the aliens would abduct Sam. Regret begat more regret, and she wished she'd told him she knew what a good heart he had.

She covered her face with her hands and cried.

After a while, she could control the sobs, still the tears. The ache became a dull throb. She would always have the memory of their time together. No one could take that away from her. In that way, they'd always be together. It comforted her, a little, and she could face them now. She thought about Michael's strength and courage, and it made her stronger and more courageous. She forced herself to stand tall.

The ship, when it appeared, came suddenly. She looked up at a star-filled sky, and then the stars were obliterated and brilliant light engulfed her. As she rose, she saw two men on the ground where she'd been standing. Agents. They expected Michael, but he wasn't there.

Her heart gave a lurch of fear as she realized that if they had any tracking skills, they'd be able to backtrack her trail and find him. One of them looked up at her, and she met his eyes. It frightened her to know that if she had a gun, she could bring herself to shoot him. Rage surged through her when she realized he'd hunt down Michael, and she knew she would do anything to stop him.

She pushed the violent thoughts away and replaced them with more helpful ones. She silently asked her angels and guides to protect Michael. For a moment, she saw the trees below her, and she thought she felt him waking up. He was such a part of her now she could feel his despair at her absence. Afraid they'd read that from her, she struggled, knowing her struggles would cause them to knock her out. As the blackness came to take her, she smiled.

CHAPTER 52

Michael woke with a start. Even before he opened his eyes, he knew she was gone. He felt the void—a void he'd had all his life though now he knew her absence caused it. Dull dawn light poured in from the direction of the opening of their small cave. In the dimness, he could see the pile that was his clothes and the two lumps that were their packs. She'd left without her pack. He knew then she'd gone to meet them.

He wanted to scream. How could he have slept through that? His life had walked out into the darkness, and he'd slept on, oblivious. He dressed in military gear and strapped on a belt with a sheathed knife. When he put his holster on, he verified his gun was loaded and cocked.

Michael doused the fire and threw his pack onto his shoulders. He went to the mouth of their shelter and looked out onto the lake. A light mist covered everything. He was sure she'd have left an obvious trail. She was a city girl all the way, and he'd track her easily.

He climbed up above the shoreline and headed into the trees, alert to any sounds. When he reached the trees, he searched for the point where she'd entered the forest. Easily found as he'd expected. She'd left a track a blind, scent-deprived dog could follow. He shook his head, loving her for being so careless.

Michael pulled out his gun and screwed on the suppressor. He stepped to the side of the trail. He'd find a place to hide. Two agents likely headed this way. All he had to do was wait for them.

He moved into the underbrush and crouched behind a copse of fir trees. The air wasn't as heavy as it had been the last few nights, and a slight breeze rustled the trees. It occurred to him that he was acting under the assumption that they'd already retrieved her. Without knowing how, he was aware they had.

Why had she left? Something must've triggered it. Had she received a message during the night that made her conclude sneaking away was her only option? Her disappearance had to be a reaction to something. But what? Worry about her daughter? If that was the case, then why didn't she wake him and tell him? He shook his head. It was useless to speculate.

As he stared at the trail, he realized he waited here only to get revenge. Killing these agents wouldn't help him get Carolyn back, and she wouldn't want him to kill them. He could try to get them to tell him where she'd been taken, but they wouldn't know. Their orders would be to either take him in or kill him. Where Carolyn ended up wasn't their concern.

The more Michael considered it, the more he realized he could walk away, continue on to the alien base, and find help. The two agents would find Carolyn's trail. They'd find the cave, which now contained only Carolyn's backpack and sleeping bag. There would be no trace of Michael. They'd report the two hadn't been together.

Michael put away his pistol. He hoisted his pack onto his back. Leaving no trace of his passing, he crossed Carolyn's trail and headed away from it towards the alien base they'd originally sought.

As he walked, the sky brightened. It would be another sunny day.

Were any spirits around if Carolyn wasn't there? He'd found it fascinating to watch her communicate with Jess. The thought of his wife aroused guilt. Carolyn was a stranger to him, but he felt her absence in his core. He missed Jess, he loved Jess, but he didn't feel as if she was a part of him.

Maybe he was going crazy. Perhaps he should ask for a sign from the spirit world as Carolyn had.

Couldn't hurt. Self-conscious, he thought, *If I have guides out there, give me a sign I'm not alone.* He looked around, wondering if something was supposed to happen right away or if this would be a process. He remained still, listening. Nothing.

He removed the pack from his shoulders and set it on the ground. As he did, he noticed the front pouch, the one containing his wallet, was slightly open. He went to close it, then decided to take his wallet out and put it in his pocket. As he pulled it out, something popped out with it and dropped to the ground, landing next to a small white feather. Startled, he picked up both the feather and the item, and examined the item first.

A woman's wedding band. There were no markings, save for a single, tiny diamond in the centre of the band. He recognized it from when she'd tried to give it to him the day before. *Carolyn's.* She'd left it for him, probably so he'd find Sam and give it to her. And it had landed next to a white feather.

Give me a sign I'm not alone. Perhaps this was it. He put the ring in his pocket and released the feather, letting it drift to the ground. He'd keep the ring for her and give it back to her when he found her again.

As he walked, he reached into his pocket to touch the ring, and it reassured him and gave him faith he'd see her again. Confident he'd find what he needed at the base, he quickened his pace.

***

Cornell sat in the Fairchild's living room, his cell phone pressed to his ear, listening to an update from Weeks. Finally, he'd received the message for which he'd waited all night. They had her. They didn't have Valiant, but they had Carolyn Fairchild. Her death had already been staged. All that remained now was to wait here until the cops arrived and then deliver the news to Sam.

He thanked Weeks for the information, hung up, and looked towards Sam's bedroom. She'd gone to bed late, expressing gratitude that he'd stayed to watch over her and guilt that she'd kept him from his family. He'd assured her it was all in the line of duty.

Poor kid. It was going to be hard for her to go through the loss of both her parents so close together. At least he wouldn't have to hand her over to the aliens now in lieu of her mother.

Of course, she wouldn't last long on her own. When the crisis hit, she'd be wiped out along with everyone else, and it might be a protracted death—a slow slide into sickness and starvation, if she wasn't killed in one of the natural disasters.

Should he take her with them? She'd be like a daughter to him and help his wife with the kids when they went underground. It would be one way to make it up to her. He'd have a word with his wife. She was a sweet kid, and she thought the world of him. It might be nice to keep someone like that around, and, of course, he could use her as leverage with Carolyn. Carolyn would do whatever he wanted if she knew her daughter's life was at stake.

Cornell heard a vehicle pull up to the house and looked out the window. A police car. He checked his watch: 8:06 AM. He rose and walked to the door. Show time.

CHAPTER 53

The helicopters' appearance three days before warned Michael he was probably too late. His fears were confirmed as soon as he drew within eyeshot of the point on the map indicating the base. The area surrounding the base, and what was marked on the map as the entrance, were a smouldering ruin.

He'd withdrawn, keeping an eye on any activity for a day, trying to gauge the risk of going in there. Michael wanted to verify the place wasn't radioactive or otherwise contaminated. He'd observed agents entering and exiting the building without protective suits, so he was sure now that wasn't a concern.

Thoughts of Carolyn intruded constantly, making him want to throw caution aside and just get in there. But he forced himself to put her out of his mind. She couldn't afford for him to get reckless.

A man in military gear hovered near the rubble, guarding access to the base, which had been reduced to a gaping hole leading into what resembled a mineshaft in a cave. The man wasn't Canadian or even US military. He was Agency personnel. The FN Herstal assault rifle gave it away.

Thankful the sun was going down, the coming darkness providing extra cover, Michael observed. Silently, he backtracked ten metres to where he'd stored his pack in the shelter of some bushes.

He loosened the knife in the sheath at his side. Besides the Glock he held in his hand, he had another one strapped to his leg. That he'd have to kill to get into the base wasn't an issue. He saw this as his only option. He put on a pair of night-vision goggles and crept closer to the base.

The guard hung out near the entrance. He'd lit a cigarette and stood smoking, his gaze roving the surrounding area. Michael inched nearer, but froze when he heard a shout from his left, and, more disconcertingly, a dog bark. Another Agent, leading a German shepherd on a leash, approached the man guarding the entrance.

"Find anything else?" the smoker asked as man and dog reached him.

"No. They're either dead or gone."

Another man appeared from the cave entrance. The man with the dog shouted to the newcomer, "All clear, Captain Trecartin."

Trecartin gave a nod and strode to the guards. The smoker dropped his cigarette and put it out with his boot. When the captain reached his men, he said, "I'm going to head back to the chopper. You two will be relieved in four hours. No one goes in or out, is that clear?"

"Yes, sir. What about the other entrance?" Smoker asked.

"There are guards posted there as well. Right now, I want this sealed off until Cornell gets here, which ought to be by morning. He doesn't want anyone tampering with anything. Don't get curious. Got it?"

"Got it, Captain."

Trecartin took the dog's leash and walked towards the area to Michael's right, but paused as the dog stopped and sniffed the air.

Michael raised his gun, pointing it at Trecartin. The dog growled, and Michael ducked and watched from the ground as the captain scanned the bushes and trees, panning over Michael's hiding place.

"Something wrong, Captain?" Smoker walked over and stood next to Trecartin. All three men standing by the entrance wore night-vision goggles.

Michael kept still. If they caught the right angle, they'd spot him.

Then the captain shrugged and turned back to Smoker. "Guess it's nothing." He yanked on the dog's chain. The dog continued to pull in Michael's direction, but yelped when the captain tugged roughly on the chain again. The captain stared once more into the trees.

It seemed to Michael Trecartin gazed beyond his hiding spot. He allowed himself to relax.

The captain said something to Smoker that Michael couldn't catch. Smoker nodded, and Trecartin led the dog towards the trees on Michael's right.

Michael continued to wait, listening for the sound of a helicopter taking off. Ten minutes later, he was rewarded and heard the chopper leaving.

If what he'd overheard was correct, there were only four men left to guard the base, which had probably been cleaned out. He'd be lucky to find any survivors.

Smoker and the other agent raised their guns, holding them ready. They were on alert.

Michael tensed. He sighted his gun on the two guards, targeting Smoker first. Before he could pull the trigger, he heard rustling behind him. He started to turn and felt searing pain as something struck the back of his skull. Everything went black.

**

Michael returned from the darkness to a throbbing headache. He was lying on his back, pressure on the back of his head causing him to feel sick as the pain lanced through him. He kept his eyes closed, reaching out with his other senses to get an idea of where he was.

Straps held his body in place—across his chest, his lower belly, and above his knees. It was cold. He was naked. He panicked when he realized they had Carolyn's ring. Anger followed panic. If it killed him, he'd get it back.

The chill struck him then, and his body shook, his teeth rattling together.

"Cap? He's awake." It was a woman's voice.

Michael opened his eyes.

A woman in army fatigues pointed an assault rifle at his head.

He winced. "I'm flattered you think you need that."

She didn't reply, but the gun barrel moved away from his face. However, she kept it levelled at him.

Michael sensed the approach of another person and tried to move his head in that direction. Another wave of nausea swooped through him.

Captain Trecartin appeared, and they stared at each other.

Trecartin spoke first. "Glad to see you're awake. I was afraid I'd killed you. That would've been a shame. Cornell wants you alive though I don't know why."

"You gave me a fucking concussion," Michael said.

"You'll wish I'd killed you."

"Where am I?"

"In the alien base in Algonquin. You made it. But abductees will get no more help from this quarter, especially that little bitch you were trying to save."

Michael grimaced and took a deep breath to calm down. Trecartin was baiting him. If he were going to get out of here and help Carolyn, he'd have to stay in control. "You killed them all? I find that hard to believe."

"Oh, no. Not all. Some we saved for experiments of our own as you'd see if you weren't restrained so well. The aliens working with us don't care. The ones who built this base were rebels. They were interfering, sabotaging the experiments, and helping the abductees escape. We were given carte blanche to use any prisoners as we see fit. They're traitors to their race as you are to yours." He leaned in close to Michael as though searching for something in his face.

"They say you're special," he said. "I don't see it. Doesn't matter. You'll be part of the experiments now, too."

Michael averted his eyes, hiding his hope. If they turned him over to the aliens in league with the Agency, maybe he'd be transferred to the same holding cells where they kept Carolyn. They'd take him right to her.

As if reading his mind, Trecartin shook his head. "No, you're not going anywhere near Peterborough Compound. You're going up." He pointed at the ceiling, meaning into the ships. "And you ain't coming back down."

Footsteps approached, and the captain straightened and turned. "Welcome, sir."

"Thank you, Captain Trecartin."

Michael slowly turned his head and faced Cornell. Cornell stopped about a metre away. Trecartin and the other agent disappeared.

"Why?" Cornell uttered the one word.

Michael stared at him, amazed. "Why do you think?"

"You had it made, Mick."

"How did I have it made?" He almost said "Jim." He stopped

himself. Fuck him. "You fucking killed my wife—you and Torque."

"What are you talking about? What do you mean we killed your wife?" His arms opened, palms out, a gesture of innocence.

"Don't play the fucking innocent with me. I know the truth. She became a threat to the status quo, didn't she? You couldn't let us be happy, have a family."

"She had an accident in the street, Mick. There were witnesses."

"Torque used the ray on her. Don't try to deny it. The two of you were huddled together, talking about how to get me back on side. He killed her, and when that made things worse, you planned to take me in. So don't look so surprised that I defended myself." The accusation that Cornell knew Torque had killed Jess was a wild guess.

"Very well. I won't deny it. I'm not here to 'get you back on side' anyway. It's too late for that. It was too late for that the moment you ran off with the Fairchild woman." He paused, smiled.

Michael's intestines turned to stone.

"I have her." The smile became a grin. "The daughter, too. Neither one of them knows where the other is." His voice had filled with glee.

Michael tested the restraints, pressing on them with the side of his leg. He couldn't move. They'd strapped him in tight.

Where are they?" Michael forced his voice to stay even, confident. He had to make himself sound neutral.

"The daughter is living in my family's guest house. I've convinced her to rent out her family home and stay with us as a live-in nanny. All the better to keep her safe, you see." He grinned again, baring his teeth this time.

"And Carolyn?"

"You know where she is. Safely locked up." Cornell took a step towards him, an eager glint in his eyes. "She's got a cell next to Arnie. Don't worry. I'll take very good care of her." He tilted his head to the side. "What's she like in bed?"

Michael's heart thudded against his chest. He couldn't speak.

Cornell licked his lips, leering. "I know you fucked her. They tested her. How was it? Anything I should know before I take my turn?"

"Keep your fucking hands off her. I'll kill you." He struggled against the restraints. They held him tightly in place.

Cornell chuckled. "Sorry, Mick. You'll never see her again, and if by chance you do, she won't even recognize you."

"What do you mean?"

"You know what's nice about revenge?"

Michael opened his mouth, but Cornell waved him down. "Don't bother. It was a rhetorical question. Everything is nice about revenge. In your case, I get to control what happens to you for the rest of your life, and I get to make you pay for what you did to the agency and to me."

Cornell's voice rose. He was almost screaming. "You betrayed the Agency, and that was bad enough. But you almost destroyed everything I'd built. You tried to steal one of our subjects. Fairchild was ours. You had no right to take her from us. Worse than that, I trusted you. Anyone else would've had you terminated when you started to crack, but I didn't. If they'd discovered I was giving you that kind of slack, I'd have been ruined."

He reached out a hand and stroked Michael's hair, a father, forced to chastise a prodigal son, desiring to forgive, but unable to do so. "Well, I guess it can't be helped now. You brought it on yourself. She'll never be yours. I'll make sure of that. We have ways to manipulate her mind. She'll think you're the enemy. She'll think I'm her lover. Whatever I want her to believe, she'll believe."

Michael remembered the reports he'd found in the evidence room. MKUltra. He was talking about the mind control experiments. Had they succeeded? Was it possible to tamper with Carolyn's mind to the extent that she'd believe her abductor was her lover? Cornell had to be bluffing.

"The aliens won't let you. They're experimenting on her. They won't let you tamper with her." That had to be true.

"When they're done with her, they'll turn her over to me. I can terminate her if I want, or I can keep her for myself."

"You sick fuck. What about her daughter?"

"Sam thinks I'm a hero. I won't have to do anything to her. She thinks her mother is dead. The police gave her the sad news a few days ago. I was there to guide her through that tragic event. The funeral is tomorrow. Sorry you'll have to miss it, but you'll be participating in some experiments yourself."

Horror swept over Michael.

Cornell smiled that big-bad-wolf smile again. He tapped

Michael on the forehead with his index finger. "Don't worry about your mind. I want your mind intact. They'll just experiment on your body. I want you to be aware of everything that happens to you—and everything that happens to Carolyn—or what's the point? No. I need you of sound mind, but not sound body."

He leaned close to Michael's ear. "I'll let you in on a little secret. You're one of them."

Michael grew colder. "What do you mean?"

"The aliens. You have their DNA."

"You're lying. That's impossible."

"Not really. Your mother was part of the experiments. They allowed her to carry you to full term and keep you, but you have their DNA. Why do you think we cared so much about what happened to you? Why do you think we recruited you?"

Michael heard a door open, then footsteps, and a woman in a lab coat appeared next to Cornell. She carried a clipboard. More footsteps. A man appeared—Smoker.

"Ah. I see they're ready to start work. We want to run a few tests on you before the aliens take you. Nice chatting with you, Mick. I'm heading to the Peterborough compound now. Shall I give Carolyn your regards?" Cornell flashed his teeth once more.

He turned and walked away, Michael's curses following him out.

CHAPTER 54

While struggling against the restraints, Michael lifted his head and peered into the dim light. The table on which he lay and the straps that held him down were all he could see. He slowed his breathing and relaxed his muscles. A vision of Carolyn in bed with Cornell popped into his head, but he pushed it away.

Never. Not on my watch.

The woman in the lab coat drew close. She looked him over, made some notes on the clipboard.

"You a doctor?" Maybe if he got her talking, he could convince her to remove the straps.

She ignored him. The guard didn't. He punched Michael in the jaw, snapping his head back onto the table, smacking the bump Trecartin had gifted him with.

Michael gritted his teeth against the pain, refusing to give the fucker the satisfaction of hearing him cry out.

"You'd be wise to keep your mouth shut and cooperate," the guard said.

Michael resisted an urge to struggle again. He was worse off than an animal in a leg trap—at least trapped animals had the option to chew off the leg and escape.

"I'll need the cart." The doctor pointed in the direction from which they'd come, and the guard walked away.

Michael heard the squeak of wheels, and the guard reappeared, pushing a medical cart with various implements on it. Michael eyed the hypodermics and scalpels. In seconds, he scanned the entire tray, determining the best weapon. All he needed was an opportunity.

The doctor picked up a tourniquet. She paused, staring at Michael and then turned to the guard. "Remove the top strap. I have to take blood, and I need his arm free."

"Not a good idea," the guard replied.

"He's not going anywhere. I have to take a blood sample. You can hold him down or do whatever you want to restrain him. But I need his arm free."

The guard pointed a pistol at Michael and then unfastened the strap holding his chest and arms down. The doctor tied a tourniquet onto Michael's arm. She slipped on a pair of latex gloves and searched for a vein. She swabbed the inside of his arm and looked Michael in the eyes for the first time since she'd arrived.

"Make a fist."

Michael did. He used it to punch the guard. Before either could react, Michael snatched the scalpel from the tray and slit the guard's throat. Blood spurted and Michael shoved the man to the floor.

The doctor shrieked and tried to back away, but Michael grabbed her upper arm, pulling her to him. He held her in a chokehold. Her legs kicked out, knocking the cart over. Michael tightened his grip, holding her until she was unconscious. He released her, and she slumped to the floor.

Michael removed the other two straps and lowered himself from the table. He was covered in blood. A glance at the guard verified blood drenched his clothing. Michael bent down and picked up the pistol. A Glock. Perfect.

He went around the table, removed the doctor's lab coat, and used it to wipe the blood from his body. Michael turned to look around and swayed a little on unsteady feet. The room tilted, and he grabbed the edge of the table. When the wave passed, he scanned the room.

Emergency lights near the ceiling gave off a faint glow. He estimated the room was large, twenty metres by thirty metres. The walls were solid rock. He spied a vent close to the floor on one of the walls. It was too small for him to climb into. There were other tables in the room, ten or twelve of them. Most were empty, but five of them looked like they contained an occupant. Each was covered with a sheet, head exposed. Aliens.

There was a closet next to the door, and he hurried to it, listening for any sound of approach. The closet door was unlocked. His clothes. Thank God. He dressed, checked his pocket for Carolyn's ring. It was still there, and so was his wallet. His weapons and ammo were gone, but at least, he had clothes and boots.

He cracked the door open, listened. Nothing. He was about to step out of the door when something made him turn back. He had to go look at the beings on the other tables. Even as he argued with himself against it, told himself how stupid he was and that he had to get the hell out of here, he closed the door again, locking it. He went to the closest table and lifted the sheet.

A Grey. He'd seen many of them during the years he'd spent with the Agency. They were always around when people were abducted, mostly assisting the other beings in charge of the experiments.

The creature was strapped down. Did that mean they were still alive? He touched the alien's shoulder. Nothing happened. Had it died on the table? Another wave of vertigo hit him then, and he lurched into the table. The table rattled, and he gripped it, dropping the gun to the floor. He closed his eyes, hoping that would ease the dizziness. When he did, images poured into his mind's eye, then out again, like a slide show.

He tried to follow it. A giant crystal, clear as quartz, glowed with an orange light. That was replaced by an identical crystal, but smaller. Opaque eggs suspended from a ceiling. Growing foetuses. A cave.

Images rushed by. He felt nauseated again. The pictures flashed by so quickly he couldn't see them. It was like watching a fan start up. The faster it went, the more the blades blurred together until it looked like one solid plane.

The aliens weren't dead. They were dormant. He didn't know how he knew that, but it was true. He touched the alien again. More images poured in, but slower. Carolyn lying on a cot in a cell. Other people in other cells. The crystals again. They were showing him there was a connection between the crystals and the people.

He saw the base he was in as it had been before the Agency arrived to destroy it. Abductees arrived. The beings used the crystal to sever the connection the aliens had to the abductees.

The images stopped. Michael looked down. The alien opened its eyes.

CHAPTER 55

Michael backed away from the thing, regretting coming back. He should have left. He should leave now. When he tried to turn away, his body refused to cooperate. Instead, he reached out and, one by one, removed the straps holding the alien down. It sat up. Michael stood, unable to move. It reached out and touched Michael's head. He was repelled, but his arms hung useless at his sides.

He didn't move, but simply watched it and allowed it to do whatever it wanted. He had no urge to resist. Is this how Carolyn felt when they took her? It cupped its hand around the back of Michael's head, and all the pain disappeared. His headache was gone. The lump, too, was gone, though he couldn't lift a hand to check.

The alien placed its hands on either side of Michael's head, adjusted, and then pressed a finger on the space just above and between his eyes. Holding the finger there, the being traced a line from that point to the back of Michael's head, along the left side of his head. Next, it traced another path along the other side of Michael's head, again to the back of his skull. Finally, it removed its hand from Michael's forehead and gripped his face between its palms. It leaned its own head into Michael's so their foreheads touched.

Michael felt queasy, but he also noticed a heightened sense of awareness. He wanted to leave, to get out of here and rescue Carolyn. But he needed to find a way to sever her connection to the aliens, or they'd just capture her again. The large crystal

258

appeared in his mind's eye again. He felt a sense of urgency. The thing was in his head, in his mind. He tried to move and couldn't.

It wanted him to go to Nahanni, in the Northwest Territories, to a place known as "The Valley of the Headless Men," after the bodies of some prospectors were found there with their heads missing. Legend also had it that an entire tribe of Aboriginals had disappeared from that same area.

Michael thought again about Carolyn. He wanted to go to her, get her away from Cornell. When he turned his thoughts in that direction, pain and fear stabbed him.

"No." It came out of his mouth as a croak. Through gritted teeth he said, "I'm going to get her."

An image came to him. He saw himself in Nahanni, in a cavern with the large crystal. The image expanded, and he watched himself as if in a dream.

He creates a physical, mental, and spiritual connection to the crystal with his hands and then severs the connection between the aliens and the abductees. They are all freed.

"Why didn't *you* do that?" he asked.

The image flashed to a view of Algonquin Park. His vision flew to the entrance of the alien base within the park, then down, through tunnels, rooms, elevators, down through circular levels, into the depths of the base, where a smaller crystal, the mirror image of the large one in Nahanni, sat. He watched as Agents broke into the cavern. The next image showed the crystal in fragments, its glow extinguished.

His new awareness gave him comprehension. He realized this was how things worked for Carolyn. She just knew things. Information burst into her mind, and she recognized it as the truth. He knew now, for instance, that the base in Nahanni wasn't a rebel base as this one in Algonquin was. It belonged to the hostile aliens in league with the Agency. The crystals were interconnected, like a communication link, but so much more than that. Nahanni's crystal was the master. The others, you could say, were the slaves.

Only, the rebel group had managed to somehow hide that they were using this particular slave to free the abductees. He looked down at the alien again and went cold. The pupils in the alien's eyes were gone, the eyes milky and clouded. He looked closer and exhaled in relief. The alien had a nictitating membrane—another eyelid that slid closed horizontally.

Afraid the alien was going dormant again, or, worse, dying, Michael touched its shoulder. He swayed again as his own vision blurred. Urgency flowed through him. Get to Nahanni. *What about Sam? I can at least get Sam away from Cornell.* A searing flash roared through his brain. *Notimenotimenotimenotime.* At first, he couldn't make out anything in that slur of words, and then it slowed, and he heard it, *no time, no time, no time,* while the images in his head showed spacecraft sucking up people in droves.

So this was his choice: rescue Sam or help the abductees, Carolyn included. If he went after Sam, the abductees would be pulled onto the ships by the time he got to Nahanni to free them, and, if the images were correct, they wouldn't be coming down again. He remembered what Trecartin had said when Michael was strapped down on the table. *You're going up. And you ain't coming back down.*

They were planning to take them all. What would happen to them then, Michael didn't want to know. He'd have to go to Nahanni. Then he'd go straight to Carolyn and get her away from Cornell.

He left the alien sitting on the table and quickly released the one on the next table, not stopping to see if it regained consciousness. He released them all. As he freed the last one, he heard someone unlocking, and then opening, the door. He grabbed the pistol and ran for the door. The door swung open. Captain Trecartin stepped through.

Michael was ready for him. Trecartin's shocked face exploded when the bullet hit it. His body collapsed, the door hitting it on the backswing. Michael ran to the door, aiming his gun at the gap. Trecartin had been alone. Michael dragged him into the room, letting the door close.

He glanced back at the aliens. Three of the five were still lying on their table, but the one he'd communicated with and another were standing.

"I'll go where you want," Michael said. "Then I'm going to find her."

He didn't wait for a response but took Trecartin's holster, which had ammo and a knife. He stuck the Glock in the holster, shouldered the assault rifle, and picked up the night-vision goggles. Thankfully, the man hadn't been wearing them when Michael blew his face off. Michael put them on.

He listened at the door. All was silent. He opened it and stepped into the deserted corridor, swinging the rifle around. Nothing moved.

Which way? He had to get out without being detected.

Go down. He wasn't sure where that directive came from. His intuition? The aliens? He didn't care. He may as well see where it led him. It was better than blindly running around the base.

Which way was down? The corridor dead-ended on one side and led to a T-junction on the other. He headed for the junction, pausing before he reached it. The passageway on the left sloped down. He checked the tunnels. All were empty. He suspected there were minimal Agency personnel here. Cornell was confident they had the place secured. He followed the passageway on the left.

Up ahead, the light grew brighter. The tunnel opened again, and this time, the opening terminated in a deep pit. There was a rim around the pit, about a metre wide. Every five metres vertical rows of metal rungs, used as ladders, led into the pit. More alien bodies were scattered below.

This pit appeared to be some kind of storage area and the entryway into the rest of the base. There were three doors at the bottom of the pit, about ten metres apart, probably elevators to the levels beneath. All were blown open, and the shafts were dark.

Michael walked to one of the rungs and began to climb down. It was a deep pit and descending the ladder was a slow process. He wasn't afraid of the height, but he still didn't trust there was no one waiting to ambush him when he reached the bottom.

At last, he reached the bottom and put his back to the wall while he looked around. There were desks here, computers, and lockers. It reminded him of a military installation. He wondered what the aliens were doing with this stuff. There must have been humans here.

Michael walked the perimeter of the pit, noticed a hatchway in the centre, and went to it. He spun the wheel, opened the hatch, and peered into the opening.

Rungs led down and he faintly made out the bottom. Everything looked empty. No sound from below, but sounds of activity from beyond the outer rim of the pit reached his ears. They must have found the Agents and doctor he'd killed.

He stepped into the hole and climbed down the rungs, pulling the hatch closed behind him. It wouldn't take them long to find the hatch, but if he was lucky, he could be well away before they did.

When Michael reached the bottom, he found a circular room. Corridors led in different directions. Which way? He waited, hoping whatever thought had been guiding him would voice an opinion again. When he started to think he wasn't going to get any help on this, it came.

Straight ahead.

He ran. The sense of urgency was unbearable. The walls glowed a soft green. After half an hour, he was still running, but he'd slowed his pace. The corridor seemed to have no end. There had been no openings along the route, and no forks to give him pause. There was only the long, green glow of the corridor and the hard rock floor.

As he walked, his thoughts turned to Carolyn. If she was with the hostiles, they were doing tests, possibly hurting her. Arnie, and who knows how many others, were likely held where she was. There'd be no way to get them out without help. He was a wanted man, and if they found him, they wouldn't hesitate to kill him.

His only hope would be to get to Nahanni and remove the hold the aliens had on them. Carolyn would have to wait though it tore him apart to leave her with the Agency.

He was going to have a hell of a time getting out of this place with agents hunting for him. He didn't think he could do this.

You're going to have to. Michael paused. Whose thought was that? He'd said the same thing to Carolyn once, what seemed like eons ago. Yes, he'd have to.

Michael ran on.

The End

A RING OF TRUTH

The Valiant Chronicles: Book II

by

Val Tobin

ACKNOWLEDGMENTS

Editing by Alan Annand (Sextile) sextile.com and Kelly Hartigan (XterraWeb) editing.xterraweb.com. Thank you, Alan and Kelly.

Thanks to Patti Roberts of Paradox (paradoxbooktrailerproductions.blogspot.com.au/) for the amazing cover.

Dr. Alis Kennedy, Miigwech for help with the Aboriginal details and reading my manuscript multiple times.

Judy Flinn, thank you for consulting on story, reading it through more than once, and for all your help and support.

Thanks, also, Bob Tobin, Michelle Legere, Kathy Rinaldo, Val Cseh, Andrea Holmes, Chris Brown, John Erwin, Susan Barbour, and Chris Jenkins for support, advice, or beta reading.

All of you helped make this a better novel.

For Bob, Jenn, Mark, Chanelle, Savannah, and Jack. Always.

CHAPTER 1

Carolyn Fairchild lay on a cot in a cell, a thin blanket draped over her waist. She shivered and sat up to pull the blanket over her feet. Even with socks on, she felt chilly. She reached under her pillow but found no more crackers. She'd eaten them all during the night.

Whenever crackers appeared with her meals lately, she squirrelled them away. They helped combat the all-day nausea. She was positive now it was morning sickness.

At first, she'd thought it was a stomach flu. But when she'd thrown up after even just smelling any kind of meat, she'd realized she was pregnant. She told her captors she was vegetarian. When they continued to give her meat, she hurled it at them.

She kept at it, even after the female guard, Tasha, took a meat patty in the face and blackened Carolyn's eye in revenge. Then, last night's dinner had appeared minus the meat. But the substituted food wasn't the complete nourishment a pregnant woman needed. Carolyn worried the baby wasn't getting enough, leaving her with even less.

By her calculations, she'd been imprisoned for a month, making it early June. The morning sickness had started a few days ago, although without a window, marking the passage of time was a challenge.

Carolyn swung her legs onto the floor and leaned back against the cold brick of the wall. After a few deep breaths, she stood slowly. No sudden moves. She shuffled to the sink near her bed. Was it morning yet? If it were close to breakfast time, the guard would bring food soon. She'd better pee now or be caught with her pants down.

The Agency didn't allow her much privacy. If the guards wanted to watch her use the toilet, they could stand at the cell bars and get an eyeful. Most of the time, they ignored her. Occasionally someone was mean enough to try to catch her in the act.

So far, she'd seen only guards who monitored her, took her to the showers, or brought meals, and they rarely spoke to prisoners. The other day, she'd grasped Deuce, a bearded, burly guard, by the arm. His reaction had been swift and brutal.

He'd flung Carolyn's hand away as if it burned, opened her cell door, and slugged her in the face, all without a word. That had blackened her other eye. If any of them had a conscience, they hid it well.

Carolyn swallowed, and her stomach gurgled. She needed water to calm her queasiness. In her former affluent life, she wouldn't have dreamed of sipping water from the tap. It still revolted her, but it was the lesser evil between that and whole-body nausea. She cupped her hands and slurped the water.

The attempt to control the nausea made her break into a sweat. Carolyn ran hot water to rinse her face. A wave of dizziness hit her as she leaned over the sink. Her stomach lurched. Tears welled up at the thought of being trapped throughout her pregnancy. She didn't dare think beyond that.

Carolyn gripped the sink and inhaled deeply. She suppressed the tears and pivoted to glance through the bars to check for guards. All was quiet.

She slipped her pants and underwear down and sat on the toilet, stretching her T-shirt to cover herself as much as possible. Even without guards present, she hid her body. The cameras always watched.

After washing her hands, Carolyn baby-stepped to the bars and stood by the main door. A smaller trapdoor at floor level allowed the guards to deliver meals without entering the cell. Once, eating from a tray that had sat on the floor would've disgusted her. Now it was just another thing she did to survive.

Arnie Griffen, her friend and fellow alien abductee, was in the cell next door. The guards had warned them not to talk, and so far, he and Carolyn had risked only surreptitious whispers at night. They'd learned that if they both stretched their hands through the bars, they could touch fingers.

Until her morning sickness put an end to it, they'd reached out to one another each night. Now, she couldn't lie on the floor, arm stretched out, without making herself ill. It'd been two nights since they'd touched.

Carolyn pressed her face to the bars and looked in both directions. Nothing moved. She could see part of each cell kitty-corner from hers. One was empty. In the other, a woman spent most of her time huddled, weeping, on her cot.

When Carolyn had tried to talk to her, Weeper had threatened to tell the guards. Fear had washed out of the woman and into Carolyn, and she'd had to clear and shield herself. Since then, she spoke only to Arnie.

She hoped he was awake now.

"Arnie?" A loud whisper. No response. Voice raised to normal speaking level, she tried again, and thought she heard him shift on his cot.

"Carr?" His cot creaked.

Thank God. "I need you." Carolyn lay on the floor and reached her arm through the bars. A swell of nausea hit her—she'd pay for this stunt in a few minutes.

His fingers touched hers. "I've got you."

Relief flooded through her. "Can you hear me okay?"

"It's difficult, but yes."

She took a deep breath. "I'm pregnant." Telling him was risky, but she didn't want to be alone with it anymore.

Silence. But the grip on her fingers tightened.

"I'm scared. What'll happen if they find out? I won't be able to hide it for long."

"How far along?"

"A month. Since early May."

"Right before John died," Arnie said.

Here it was—the moment of truth. Carolyn was positive she'd gotten pregnant after her husband John had died. Which meant her unborn baby's father was Michael Valiant, the man who'd kidnapped her to turn her over to the Agency.

Instead of surrendering her, he'd helped her escape. Along the way, they'd turned to each other for physical solace. Carolyn had believed she was infertile after her daughter Samantha was born and hadn't considered birth control. Michael knew her secrets and hadn't worried about birth control either. Now she was pregnant.

But she couldn't let Arnie know who her baby's father was. Michael, along with his partner Gerry "Torque" Muniz, had kidnapped Arnie and handed him over to the Agency. Carolyn kept silent.

"We have to escape," he said.

"I can't leave."

"What do you mean? Chances are slim we can manage it, but we should at least try."

"If I leave, they'll give Sam to the aliens."

"One of your hunches again?" Arnie was skeptical of her premonitions.

"No. They told me." Carolyn sighed. Better he believed the news came from Agency personnel than from the spirit world.

"Bastards. I'm here for you, no matter what."

"Thank you."

The steel doors clanked and rattled.

Her fingers slipped away from Arnie's. Bile rising, Carolyn rushed to the toilet. Her effort to stifle it only brought it up. She retched into the bowl as the guard appeared, pushing a food trolley. Breakfast was served.

CHAPTER 2

The dungeon door rattles. Two guards drag a woman into the cell and chain her to the wall across from Carolyn and Arnie. The woman is missing a hand, the stump wrapped in filthy, blood-soaked rags.

All prisoners are naked, all chained to the wall. The guards grab Carolyn and unchain her, catching her when she falls forward with a whimper. They half-drag, half-carry her to another section of the dungeon. The sight of the iron maiden, the rack, and other instruments of torture fills her with terror. She struggles, but their grips are firm.

As the guards lay her on the rack, Carolyn sobs and pleads, denying she's a witch, insisting they've made a terrible mistake. They remain impassive and when she's bound, leave.

A man Carolyn recognizes as Michael's former partner Torque enters the room. Another man, shorter, balding, with owl eyes steps up and strokes her body. She trembles and pleads with him to release her, but the man's touch becomes more invasive. Carolyn closes her eyes and screams, a high, wailing shriek of despair.

The door bursts open. Michael. He tells the men someone has broken into the dungeon and is releasing the prisoners. The man molesting Carolyn hurries from the room. Michael pulls out a knife and attacks Torque.

Taken by surprise, Torque is no match for Michael, who kills Torque. Michael removes the restraints and lifts her into his arms. He races from the room towards the outside world and freedom. Carolyn tries to put her arms around his neck, but doesn't have the strength. Her head flops against Michael's shoulder.

Shouts and footfalls follow in their wake. Guards.

"Leave me." *Voice hoarse from screaming, it comes out a croak. Michael must escape. She loves him more than life.*

Carolyn awakens in chains, wrists and ankles manacled. Trapped in the owl-eyed man's bedchamber, she's his possession.

Did Michael escape? Did they kill him? Loss overwhelms her, and she bursts into wracking sobs. The man whose name she still doesn't know drags her into bed.

Tears streaming down her face, Carolyn wrenched awake. She leapt up and launched herself at the toilet, letting her breakfast fly when she reached the bowl. Stomach muscles ached from the unrelenting spasms. Drained, she slid onto the floor.

She lay there until she mustered the strength to drag herself to the sink. The void that was a placeholder for Michael had increased after that dream, and she'd give anything to hold him again. Carolyn rinsed her face and returned to bed. She flipped her tear-drenched pillow over to the dry side and waited for the guards to bring lunch.

***

Lunch was over: vegetable soup, which meant crackers. Score. Although still hungry, Carolyn tucked the packet under her pillow. While she used the toilet, she listened for footsteps and moved quickly. Most of her privates stayed private, even from camera eyes, by stretching her T-shirt to cover her crotch. But the awareness of being on display remained constant.

Still, it wasn't as degrading as a trip to the showers. That didn't happen often enough to feel clean, but too often to get over the humiliation of undressing in front of an audience. Usually a woman accompanied her, but not always. While most of her male escorts at least pretended to look away, others leered. So far, none had tried to touch her.

When guards came to take her for questioning, she lay curled up on the bed, blanket clutched to her chest, trying to sleep. For a moment, she thought they'd come to take her for a shower.

Why would that require two men?

The taller man pulled the blanket off her. "Stand." His tone was neutral, as if he didn't care whether she obeyed him, but he'd slug her if she refused, so she stood.

When the other guard cuffed her hands, Carolyn considered

protesting. Did they seriously think she'd fight? But she stayed quiet and shuffled between them down the corridor.

***

Carolyn gazed at the floor so Jim Cornell wouldn't see her reaction to whatever he said. Brown hair hung like a curtain over her face, though it wasn't much of a curtain. Michael had made her cut and dye her hair when they were trying to elude the Agency, and her blonde roots showed. Perhaps Cornell would let her fix it as it grew out. The thought bubbled hysteria up to the surface, and Carolyn choked back a sob of laughter.

She sat in a chair facing Cornell, who side-saddled the front of his desk, looming over her. Intimidation tactic, she thought, and it worked. Cuffs still bound her hands. The guards had left the key, so Cornell could remove them if he wanted, but she refused to ask him.

"Look at me, Carolyn."

What would he do if she disobeyed? Afraid of getting hit, she raised her head, and they locked gazes. A whimper escaped her when she recognized the owl-eyed man from her dream.

"Tsk. Both eyes blackened." He sounded contrite. "You were mistreated." Cornell said it as if it shocked him, as if it might be news to her. He reached out and touched her cheek with his index finger.

Carolyn recoiled and sucked in her breath with a terrified hiss.

"Don't be afraid." Gentle. "I won't hurt you. It's necessary for you to stay here, but we can try to get along."

Carolyn lowered her face again, the sting of tears in her eyes. She wouldn't cry in front of this monster.

Not. Going. To. Trust. Him. She had to hang on to that.

"I don't know what Valiant told you, but maybe you should hear my side of it before you decide I'm the enemy. Have an early dinner with me, and we can talk. I'll remove those cuffs. The restraints weren't necessary, but it's protocol." Cornell leaned towards her.

She flinched when he cupped a warm hand around her cheek. Her body inclined away from the touch. Tenderly, Cornell smoothed the hair from her face. "I said I wouldn't hurt you. Hold up your wrists."

Carolyn raised her arms. He removed the cuffs and set them on the desk while she studied him.

He was shorter than Michael—five foot seven to Michael's six feet, which made Cornell an inch shorter than Carolyn. His belly rounded over his belt. Bald on top, he had a monk's fringe of grey-flecked black hair. Round, thick-rimmed glasses cemented his resemblance to an owl.

She broke her silence. "You're Michael's boss? The one who ordered him to kill my husband and to kidnap Arnie and me?"

Cornell frowned, disappointed. "Is that what he told you?"

"Are you going to deny it? You know I'm psychic. If you lie, I'll know." She lied herself in this—she couldn't always see the falsehood. But in this case, she knew she'd guessed correctly.

"My dear lady ..." He rose and walked across the room to a table set for dinner for two. Beside it, a sideboard displayed a buffet feast, most of it vegetarian. A large vegetable platter loaded with carrots, broccoli, celery, cauliflower, and other fresh, crunchy vegetables formed the centrepiece. In the middle of the platter sat a bowl containing a creamy white dressing. There was an antipasto platter with olives, pickles, melon balls, bruschetta, sun-dried tomatoes, and crisp crackers.

A cheese platter held a variety of cubed and sliced cheeses, most of which she couldn't identify. There was meat: various cold cuts, a mound of tuna salad, and one of salmon salad. An assortment of breads and buns overflowed a wicker basket. A bottle of wine chilled in a bucket on the table, along with a bottle of spring water.

They hadn't forgotten dessert. Petit fours, mini cheesecakes, éclairs, brownies, cookies, chocolate truffles, and other tasty treats sat next to the savoury platters. A coffee urn and teapot stood beside pitchers of milk and cream, and a bowl of raw sugar. It made her hungry and nauseated at the same time.

Her fear increased. She could hate them if they tortured her or were cruel, but how long could she fight them if they were nice to her? She swallowed and realized she salivated. When her stomach growled, Carolyn burst into tears.

CHAPTER 3

Arnie paced the width of the cell. Carolyn still wasn't back, and it made him crazy. Steel rattled, and Arnie glanced up in time to see a dinner tray slide through the small door. He checked out the guard who'd brought it. Tasha. She flashed him a grin.

When Arnie had first arrived here, he'd tried to stay aloof, no matter how hot Tasha was. But she'd been the only guard to pay any attention to him, and before long, he fantasized about seducing her and convincing her to help him and Carolyn escape. The fantasy grew more spectacular the longer Arnie remained trapped in this human zoo.

Tasha was gorgeous: long brown hair worn braided and twisted around her crown, and doe eyes the colour of mahogany. A petite five-foot-three powerhouse, fit and muscular, but not in an unfeminine bodybuilder way, she looked as if she'd be great in bed. The woman oozed sexy even in fatigues, and most of the time, she wore a tank top, no bra. Oh, Lord.

Arnie forced his thoughts back to Carolyn, and when he saw Tasha wasn't leaving, called to her, his voice worried and distracted.

She raised her brows. "Easy, sweetie. We're not supposed to talk, remember? Want them to think I've been a bad girl?"

Arnie swallowed and sweat broke out on his neck. She'd aroused him with that one simple question. He tried to reorient.

"I'm worried about Carolyn. Is she okay?"

Tasha frowned and clenched her jaw.

He gulped. "Where is she?"

"Oh, Arnie." When Tasha said his name, it was like a caress.

He shivered. "Can you tell me?"

"Why?"

"Please? Are they bringing her back soon?"

"When they're finished with her."

Arnie's mouth went dry, and his stomach knotted.

She held out her hand. "Come here, sweetie."

He went to the door and gripped the bars. Tasha stroked his face, fingers gentle, caressing.

Arnie's eyes closed, and he sighed, relishing the contact. An ache spread through his loins, and his breathing became shallow and rapid. It'd been a long time since he'd had sex. Celibacy wasn't the norm for him.

When he opened his eyes, Tasha smiled, and it was spectacular. "Relax. Carolyn's getting acquainted with my boss. You'll get to meet him soon enough."

The blood drained from Arnie's face.

Her hand wandered to his crotch and rubbed the growing bulge. "Want to go to the showers?" The words carried a seductive undertone.

Arnie nodded, speechless. Tasha grabbed his hand and slid it under her top, and he explored her breasts, relishing the soft skin. When his fingers found a nipple, he pinched it and rolled it between his thumb and index finger.

She gasped, grabbed his hand, and pressed it between her legs. "Want that?"

He nodded, fearing he might come in his pants.

Tasha snickered, unlocked the cell door, and held out the handcuffs. Arnie stuck his hands out and she cuffed him.

The shower room had two shower stalls, both without doors, but Arnie had never seen anyone else in there. Tasha ordered him to the other side of the room and locked the door.

She crossed the floor like a predator creeping towards her prey and stood before him. Dropping the cuffs on a nearby table, she said, "Take off your clothes."

Arnie removed each article of clothing and set it on the table, the cold air making his skin prickle. Her eyes grew wide when he hooked his thumbs into the waistband of his briefs and slid them off. The briefs joined the pile of clothes on the table.

They stood together in silence while her gaze wandered over his naked body. Arnie flushed. Tasha chuckled and ordered him into the shower. When the water was flowing, she pulled off her tank top. She removed her holster and set it on the table.

The sight of the gun triggered thoughts of escape, and he couldn't stop staring at it. Then their gazes locked, and Arnie tensed. She'd caught him ogling the weapon.

Tasha laughed and wagged a finger in his direction. "Uh-uh. Don't even think about it. I don't want to shoot you, lover boy. Do what I say, and we'll have fun."

He looked away. Tasha terrified him, a new experience for Arnie, who'd never feared any woman. However, that didn't dampen his ardour. Another glance at her naked body aroused lust and desire. He decided to behave. She strode across the room and stepped into the shower stall.

"What if someone comes to the door?" he asked. Would discovery be worse for him or her?

"No one's coming. Just you. And me." A snicker. She did that often, as though everything was contemptuous. It was part of what made him fear her. She was gorgeous, sexy, and scarier than anyone he'd met.

He forgot everything, including Carolyn, when Tasha eased to her knees and took him in her mouth. He groaned. It'd been so long since he'd experienced this kind of pleasure. He panted and moaned, Tasha's busy mouth making his testicles pulse and shooting sensation through him. She pulled away when he grew thick and ready to burst.

"Not yet. Me first." Tasha stood and kissed him, rolling her tongue around his mouth. Arnie touched her breasts, and a pulse zapped from his mouth and hands to his loins.

"Yes, that's good," she whispered. "Now on your knees."

Arnie slid to the floor. Tasha leaned against the wall and gripped his head with her hands while he put his mouth where she directed. Hers to command, he got lost in the hedonistic moment, drowning under the water pouring from the shower and the demanding woman to whose thighs he clung.

Tasha screamed a climax and pulled him up, and he gasped for air, surprised to be alive. Stifled, claustrophobic, he pulled back, but she jumped into his arms, wrapping her legs around him and impaling herself on him. A moment later, Arnie let go with a loud moan that sounded more like pain than pleasure. His legs shook, knees on the verge of buckling.

She leapt to the ground and retreated. "Better?"

No, worse. Oh, God, I want to go home. Arnie nodded and tried to collect himself, but confusion set in. What was this? Where was his confident, carefree self? Why did he hate what just happened? Why did he feel violated, obliterated? The real Arnie had disappeared, and the doppelganger that replaced him was a snivelling coward, used and abused by a woman the size of a pixie.

In the past, he'd been the one to choreograph sex, to take control, even with the women who'd initiated it. He'd enjoyed women, giving them pleasure while using them for his own needs. Now he felt dirty and used. This place had turned him into a non-entity, a shell. What repulsed him most was how grateful he felt that Tasha had condescended to fuck him. Arnie burst into tears.

CHAPTER 4

Carolyn sobbed quietly, hands resting limp on her thighs. Too drained to muster the energy to wipe the tears, she let them fall. She wondered what Michael would do.

Not cry. Thinking of Michael helped.

Cornell rushed to Carolyn's side and knelt beside her chair but didn't try to touch her. He handed her a tissue from the box on the desk, and moved back, giving her space. She accepted the tissue but held it crumpled in her fist while the tears continued to fall.

"Stop, Carolyn." Cornell's voice was stern, but gentle.

Carolyn took a deep breath and calmed. She dabbed her eyes with the tissue and wiped her nose.

Cornell gripped her shoulder. "I want to help you. Things can be different, better."

"Why am I imprisoned here? What did I do to deserve this?"

"It's not what you did. It's what others want to do to you. You're here for protection. Let's have dinner together. You're hungry. You've been rejecting food, and haven't been eating enough calories to sustain yourself, never mind the baby you're carrying."

She froze. *Oh God, he knows.*

"Don't worry. Together we'll handle this. Allow the Agency to help."

"Trust the people who murdered John, kidnapped me and Arnie, and institutionalized Ralph Drummond? That's the solution? The Agency pushed Ralph until he committed suicide."

The shocked look on Cornell's face told Carolyn he hadn't expected her to know Ralph was dead.

"That's right. I know what happened to Ralph."

"Drummond had mental problems. That's why he checked into the hospital. The Agency didn't put him there." Cornell sounded hurt, offended.

"Sorry, but your every utterance is suspect. Ralph didn't voluntarily commit himself to a mental hospital. The Agency forced him there. Agents stalked everyone in Ralph's UFO group, me included. The Agency bugged my home and phones. Why should I trust them?"

"Are those Michael Valiant's words? Valiant misled you so you'd follow him."

"No. I wanted Michael to forget about kidnapping me, which he did as soon as I proved to him that Torque murdered Jessica."

Michael's wife, Jessica, had died the same day John did, and Torque had killed them both. Carolyn stared Cornell down and waited for him to respond to this latest charge.

"Let's not hurl accusations. Sit and eat, and we'll have a civil discussion. Take care of yourself, for the sake of John's unborn child."

Carolyn fought the urge to look away, afraid to arouse his suspicions, struggling to hide that the baby was Michael's. She walked to the table, pulled out the chair nearest the door, and sat.

Cornell sat across from her, setting the napkin from his plate on his lap. Carolyn did the same with her napkin, keeping her movements slow and deliberate. Her stomach growled again, and she picked up the bottle of spring water. She filled her glass, trying to mask the sound.

He glanced at her and smiled. "It'll be okay. I promise."

Carolyn set the bottle back in the bucket. "Your promise is worthless."

"Eat. We'll talk when your blood sugar and hormones aren't muddling your thinking."

She ate. At first, she nibbled delicately on an apple, testing her stomach, and followed that with a few crackers and carrot sticks. When the food stayed down, she dared a piece of bread. After eating the processed white bread served in her cell, the fresh, whole-grain bread felt nourishing and alive. She gave a blissful sigh.

Cornell raised his head. "Good? Eat all you want. There's

plenty."

Reluctant to admit how wonderful it was, she nodded, unable to deny it was delicious. She sipped the water, grateful it didn't come from a bathroom sink.

Cornell poured wine into his goblet and held up the bottle. Red wine, Cabernet Franc, from an estate in Niagara-on-the-Lake.

"I assume you won't be having alcohol for a while?"

She shook her head. Cornell replaced the bottle in the bucket and sipped from his glass. When he set the wine glass back on the table, he said, "Want an update on your daughter?"

Carolyn leapt from her chair and lunged at him. "What have you done with Sam?"

Startled, he jumped up, faster than she would've expected a man of his girth to move. He pinned her against the wall, his face near hers. Carolyn smelled meat on his breath and her stomach roiled. She turned her face away and closed her eyes, a sob escaping her throat.

"Listen," he said. "Sam is fine. She's safer than anyone else on the planet right now except us. Understand?"

Carolyn nodded once, and Cornell eased the pressure on her arms. "Can I let you go? Or would I be risking another attack with that butter knife?"

She looked at her hand and almost laughed out loud. Her fist held a butter knife. She hadn't been aware she'd grabbed it.

"Prove Sam is safe and she'll stay safe."

Cornell took the knife from Carolyn and set it on the table. He towed her to his desk and set her in the chair at the computer. A few mouse clicks brought up a view of the kitchen inside a home Carolyn didn't recognize.

"That's my house." Cornell changed the view. The living room. No one in sight. Backyard. There they were: Samantha and two boys. Sam wore a two-piece bathing suit and looked stunning. The two boys swam in the pool, and Sam reclined on a lounge chair in the shade, reading a book. She seemed content.

"Why is Sam at your house?" Carolyn put acid in her voice and Cornell tensed. *Good.*

"For protection." His voice was even. No trace of tension.

"I'm supposed to believe that?" She scowled. "Why did you steal my engagement ring?"

Carolyn had left her wedding band with Michael, but had kept her engagement ring. When the aliens brought her to the Agency, the guards had confiscated the engagement ring. Attempts to get it back had failed.

"We didn't steal the ring. Sam has it."

"Sam? Why?" She gasped, struck with a realization. "Sam was with you." She leapt up from the chair, and Cornell grabbed her again. This time, she remembered a self-defence technique Michael had taught her, and spun away from him. She grabbed the chair, used it as a shield.

"Let go of the chair." Cornell waved his hand, directing her. "No one will harm Sam. Let's discuss this rationally."

"Are you insane? You've kidnapped Sam. I'm your prisoner. You murdered John. And you ask me to be *rational?*"

"I didn't kidnap Sam. I hired her as a nanny. To keep her safe."

"Safe from what? You and the Agency are the biggest threats to our safety."

"There's more. Please release the chair. What are you planning to do? You can't leave here." Cornell pressed a button on the phone. When the receptionist answered, he said, "Helen, send in a guard, please."

The guard opened the door and peered into the room. "Yes, sir?"

"Just letting the lady here know you're right outside. That's all for now."

The guard closed the door.

"Let go of the chair."

"Or what? You'll beat me?"

"I told you I won't hurt you."

"You'll get a lackey to beat me?"

"No one'll hit you. Drop the chair and listen."

Carolyn hesitated. Michael had convinced her he'd protect her, but this was different. Silently she asked her angels and guides for help and pushed the chair away.

"The climate is changing. The environment's deteriorating. Bees are disappearing, and without the bees, no one will survive. Quakes, floods, and tsunamis will cause more devastation."

Carolyn swallowed and nodded.

Cornell continued. "We built underground facilities where communities of people can live when the environment won't support life anymore."

"I don't understand. If you can create an underground habitation, why can't you fix what's happening above ground?"

"That's why we've partnered with the aliens. They'll take over the ruins and heal the earth. It's beyond our capacity to fix things."

The conversation was getting surreal. Then she remembered. "You planned to turn Sam over to the aliens in my place. You say she'll be safe, but you're lying."

"That was then. You're here now. What makes you believe I considered that?"

Carolyn smiled, coldly. "Ralph told me. I talk to the dead, and they know the truth."

Cornell didn't reply.

"No comment?" she said, unable to resist a smirk.

"I'm protecting Sam. Even with the aliens, she would've been safe. She's living at my house, so they'd have returned her there. She'd have no recollection of the abductions, as you didn't."

"But they would've been abducting her, experimenting on her, making her infertile the way they did me."

"Clearly you're not infertile."

"I couldn't have another baby for nineteen years. The doctors said I couldn't conceive."

"Then how do you explain your current condition?"

"I can't. No doubt the aliens and the Agency are involved."

"I can protect Sam and bring her along when the time comes to go underground. But I'll only guarantee her safety if you cooperate."

"Cooperate how? What do you expect me to do? I doubt it's something I'll want to do. If I don't, will you tell me you'll kill her? Hurt her? Turn her over to the aliens?"

His face darkened. "Get something straight. You're here, and you're staying. I have Sam, and if forced, I'll give her to the aliens. Cooperate, or I'll leave her on the surface. Do you want her to die of starvation, disease, or flood? Those things will happen up here."

"What happens to me and Arnie and the other prisoners when you go underground?"

"Depends on how useful you are. Become indispensable, and you can survive, join the rest of us underground. Be a nuisance, and you're as dead as everyone else."

"What do you want?"

"Right now? Tell me where to find Michael Valiant."

CHAPTER 5

Arnie believed he'd experienced more degradation than was tolerable when Michael Valiant had forced him into the trunk of Torque's car and brought him to this monkey house. But that didn't compare to the humiliation of sobbing in Tasha's arms now. Too embarrassed to meet Tasha's gaze, Arnie kept his head lowered. But if she thought him weak, she gave no sign.

She stroked Arnie's bare back and pressed his head to her shoulder. "Relax. Talk to me. Perhaps I can help you get clear of this, huh?"

He stopped crying. "What do you mean?" Was Tasha implying she'd help him escape? It didn't make sense. A short time ago, she'd threatened to kill him.

"Help me and I'll help you. Play nice, and your stay here can be comfortable. But you need to give me something."

Arnie tried to pull away, but she pressed him tight to her body. Tasha's naked flesh rubbed against his, and he felt himself stiffen.

"Yes," she said. "That's better."

Lust surged through Arnie, followed at once by rage. He gritted his teeth, remembering Carolyn. The Agency had her somewhere, and he had no idea where. It worked. The hard-on ebbed away along with his lust.

"Baby," Tasha purred, both hands stroking, caressing. "Don't do that. Come on now."

He struggled.

"No, darling. You go when I release you. Be nice. Let's talk."

Speaking out against Tasha felt like the most difficult thing Arnie ever had to do. But if he didn't take back his power, he'd fold and do whatever the Agency wanted.

"Then let me go." A simple statement, but to Arnie, it meant everything, and when Tasha released him, it seemed a victory.

The room echoed with Tasha's laughter, and he deflated. Arnie waited for her to speak, but she remained silent, watchful. He shivered and gooseflesh prickled his arms and legs.

She picked up her clothes and got dressed.

Hands shaking with nerves and chills, Arnie reached for his T-shirt. Instantly, Tasha pulled her gun from its holster and pointed it at him.

"No, sweetie. Not without my permission."

Arnie pulled his hand back. "I'm cold."

"Let's talk first."

"About what?"

"Who tipped Ralph Drummond off about the Agency?"

"An interrogation? That's why we had sex? Are you kidding?"

"Better than torture, sweetie. What's that saying? The way to a man's heart is through his stomach? But that's not the way to your heart, is it?" Tasha's hand snaked between his legs and gave his scrotum a squeeze.

Arnie gasped.

She chuckled, eyes sparkling. "Each correct response earns you one piece of clothing. The opposite of strip poker."

"Did you question Drummond?" A sinking sensation pelted him in the gut.

"No, honey. Drummond's dead."

Arnie's stomach clenched, and his knees wobbled. Dizzy, he pressed his hands onto the table and leaned forward, head drooping. Eyes closed, he let the tears flush out until the vertigo and nausea passed. "How?"

"I'm asking the questions. But I'll give you that one. Ralphie boy hanged himself."

"That can't be true. Ralph wouldn't hurt his family like that."

"What he did and why don't concern me. But now we can't question Drummond, tag, you're it."

Tears welled up again. This time, he stifled them. "Fuck you."

***

283

Carolyn cheered silently. *They can't find Michael.* She hoped her face didn't show her joy.

"Why would I know where Michael is? I left him to surrender to the aliens."

"Valiant went to the alien base in Algonquin Park. What were his plans after that?"

"I don't know. That was the point of going to the base."

Anger flickered for an instant on Cornell's face, but when he spoke, his tone was neutral. "What did Valiant tell you about the base?"

Carolyn considered what to say. The truth would suffice because nothing she said could direct him to Michael. She truly had no idea where he was.

"Michael said the aliens in Algonquin might help me avoid abduction by the hostiles."

That Michael had found the base and escaped the Agency delighted Carolyn. Relieved he was safe, she tried to sense any spirits around Cornell.

She'd been at the Agency for a month, and no spirits had made contact. Was she blocked? Had the aliens done something during the last abduction? She didn't feel any different. Perhaps it was stress and the pregnancy.

Cornell stared at her.

She returned the stare and shrugged. "Sorry. Can't help you."

"Not an option. Cause and effect, Carolyn. I can reunite you with Sam, or I can have you executed. The choice is yours."

"I think the choice is yours."

"How hard do you want to make this? Consider, but not too long. We'll talk again. Give any of my people trouble, and I'll make sure you're uncomfortable. Work with us, and you'll earn rewards. How would you like decent clothes to wear? A private shower?"

Appalled, curses about to spill out, she stifled them, and instead asked her angels and guides for help.

"Keep your bribes."

His face became a mask, and he buzzed the receptionist. "Send in the guards."

When the guards entered, Cornell sat behind the desk, staring at the computer. Without looking up, he said, "Get this woman out of here. The cuffs won't be necessary. She won't give you any trouble. If she does, don't hit her." He looked at Carolyn one last time. "But report it to me."

***

Carolyn braced herself as she and the guards neared her cell. She'd walked sedately between them all the way from Cornell's office, pretending to be docile and cowed. Her stomach fluttered in anticipation.

One guard pulled ahead and opened the door, while the other stood next to Carolyn, looking bored. This was it. Act now or miss the opportunity. Carolyn lunged for Arnie's cage and grabbed the bars, holding them in a firm grip.

She screamed his name, willing him to run to her. She wanted to hug him, ached to at least touch him. Carolyn stared at his empty room in disbelief. A guard pried her fingers off the bars. Head bowed, she returned to her cell.

***

Tasha stood over Arnie. She'd forced him to sit in the only chair in the room. Made of metal, the chair intensified the chill spreading through his body.

"Drummond's source," Tasha said. "Talk."

"Fuck you."

Tasha laughed. "You just did, sweetie. Now talk, and I'll give you something to wear."

"There's not much to tell. I don't know his source."

"Oh, Arnie. You're so full of shit. It's a woman, and you fucked her. Your dick will be the death of you."

The blood drained from Arnie's face. "She never told me her name, and I didn't ask."

"Describe her."

"What will you do to her?"

"Nothing."

"What will the Agency do to her?"

"Not your concern."

"I disagree. The Agency thugs will hurt her, and it'll be my fault."

"Consider what'll happen to you if you don't talk." She leaned forward.

Arnie swallowed, his mouth dry. How could this be happening? He couldn't betray the contact. He hoped Dragonfly was trying to find others to blow the whistle to, or whatever the Agency did to him would be even more tragic.

He steeled himself. "Fuck you."

Tasha was quick. She handcuffed Arnie's hands to the chair and produced a knife from a hidden sheath at her waist.

"What's your biggest asset, Arnie?" His name still sounded like a caress when she said it. Tasha held the knife to his right eye. "Your beautiful blue eyes?"

Arnie slammed his eyelids shut.

She laughed. "Perhaps not." Tasha moved the knife down his cheek.

The knife scraped along his skin, and he felt blood trickle down his face. He suppressed a sob.

"Maybe your handsome face?"

He gritted his teeth, waiting for the sting to become excruciating pain.

"Guess where I'm headed."

Arnie groaned, anticipating the knife's descent. "Please, no." Finally reduced to begging.

"It would be a shame to turn you into a eunuch, wouldn't it, stud? Talk."

Ashamed, he gave her something. "She went by the name Dragonfly."

Tasha slapped him across the face. "Tell me something I don't know."

Arnie let out a gasp that was part sob. "What do you want? If you know already, why don't you find her?"

She punched him in the face, and he groaned as his head snapped back. She had a better right hook than most men. His stomach churned, and bile rose in his throat. "I'll be sick."

"I don't care."

He gagged on the vomit and swallowed it, eyes watering from the effort to hold it in.

Tasha slid the knife down his belly.

Arnie's breath became shallow. "Please." His voice pitched higher.

"Dragonfly."

"She's five-six. Muscular. Brown hair. Wore it short. Green eyes." The words spilled out, and once he'd started, he couldn't stop. He tried to clamp his lips together, but they kept going. "Said she worked at a base outside Toronto. Didn't say where."

"Good. You can put on something." She picked up Arnie's socks and slid them onto his feet.

Her touch revolted him now, and he flinched when her hand brushed his skin.

"Now, now." She'd noticed the flinch. "Just a bit more, sweetie. Remember, I can give you pleasure, too. Cooperate."

Arnie closed his eyes, ashamed at the betrayal. He should be man enough to bear anything Tasha did to him without giving Dragonfly away, but he couldn't. The terror of the pain was too intense.

Tasha flicked the knifepoint across his thigh, and Arnie felt the trickle of blood again.

"If I cut you, the aliens can heal you, and I can do it again. As many times as I want. It's marvellous. They can create living tissue, and it'll have your DNA. They'll reconnect nerves, so you'll experience it intensely every time. Want me to ask them to give you a bigger dick?"

"Stop. Please. I'll talk."

"Distinguishing marks?"

"A tattoo ... Small dragonfly on her right shoulder ... Details too vague ... Green and black ... Other colours. What more do you want?"

"Where did she live?"

"She didn't tell me anything personal. She never told me her name, for Chrissake. Please. Stop."

"Where was she getting her info?"

"She never told us that."

"Did she say why?"

"No."

It was silent for so long that Arnie opened his eyes. Tasha perched on the table watching, face serene. She smiled and held up the knife, his blood speckling the blade. She locked eyes with him and licked the blade, then her lips. "You taste delicious, sweetie."

Crazy fucking bitch. He fainted.

CHAPTER 6

Michael Valiant heard the roar of the South Nahanni River and ran towards it. Pursuit was close behind, and he was afraid they'd soon be near enough to score a hit if they fired. His lungs screamed for relief. He had to do something to speed his getaway.

Three agents tailed Michael, and she was one. Althaea Dayton—the biggest mistake and closest near miss of his life. Althaea and Michael had almost had an affair once. But that wouldn't stop her from pulling the trigger if she managed to get close enough to put a bullet in his brain. She'd have more reason than anyone else. The relationship hadn't ended well.

So Michael ran, telling himself that talking to Althaea would be fatal, because if he stopped running, it would be over for him. It was early June. Michael had been on the run for the last month— ever since he'd left Algonquin Park.

Undetected, he'd made his way north, a tribute to his skills and the ineptitude of the Agency's bureaucrats. After six hours in the air, not including a stopover in Calgary, Michael arrived in Yellowknife from Ottawa. Then he'd gone to Fort Simpson and chartered a floatplane to Nahanni National Park's Virginia Falls.

The end of May was a chilly and buggy time of year to be out in the wild above the sixtieth parallel. For once, he was grateful for climate warming.

Michael had made a possibly fatal mistake two nights ago.

He'd spotted an agent standing outside a log cabin. Althaea. He'd have recognized her anywhere. She oozed raw sexuality, a sensuous beauty he'd found almost irresistible during the brief time they were partners.

Althaea looked like a princess warrior—her long blonde hair tied back in a single braid, wearing army fatigues, and an assault rifle slung over her shoulder. A tank top showed off her muscled arms. She still gave off that feral energy Michael had wanted to tame years ago. That he'd turned her away from his bed—rejected her—might get him killed now. She wasn't the forgiving type.

Michael had already taken a few steps towards her before he realized she'd kill him without question. So he'd melted back into the trees. The mistake was that he didn't leave. Althaea wasn't alone, and one of the men with her spotted Michael.

Easy to blame her, but his own carelessness had exposed him. She still had the power to unnerve him, and he hated himself for it. How many people would pay for that mistake?

Briefly, Michael had lost the agents, but they'd found him again when he'd stopped for a rest. Two days of running had brought him to exhaustion and close to delirium. He'd lost his pack and hadn't eaten much. A canteen of water kept him from dehydrating, but it was almost empty. The sound of the river was like music for many reasons.

He burst through the trees a short sprint from the river. Water smashed over stones jutting up like worn teeth.

Only an idiot would enter the river here.

Michael jumped, the water sweeping him under, and he hit a rock that tore his shirt and sliced open his left shoulder. Water surged over his head, but he resurfaced and grabbed a boulder.

Without thinking, he hauled himself up, but dropped back into the river when something smacked into his left shoulder. A bullet. He looked back. Three people approached the water. Two held back the third, keeping her from jumping in after him. The crazy bitch wanted to risk it.

Michael kicked off his shoes and swam with the current, but the injured arm threatened to sink him. The current would sweep him out of reach if Althaea didn't jump into the water. He might drown escaping, but at least he'd get away. When his head went under again, he kicked and focused on staying alive.

The shore sped past. The water's chill seeped into his bones, and he shivered, nauseated. He'd have to get to shore—soon or never. With an effort, he aimed himself at the opposite side and kicked.

Michael moved towards the far shore at glacial speed, though the current swept him farther from his pursuers. Eyes blurring, a wave of dizziness sank him. He kicked harder and got his head above water. Michael swallowed the bile rising in his throat. If he vomited here, he'd go under and die.

At least he was below Virginia Falls and wouldn't have to contend with a ninety-metre plunge. His efforts became increasingly feeble, and for a moment, he viewed his struggle from a vantage point above his body. Was he dying?

The shore approached. Inhospitable as the jagged rocks looked, they'd be a place to lay his head.

Just for a moment, God. Just let me rest for a moment.

Although it brought heartache, he let his thoughts go to Carolyn. He missed her. Every day. She was so beautiful, so unusual. A skeptic, Michael hadn't known what to make of her psychic abilities. He'd scoffed at her claim that she was a medium until she'd connected with Jessica, then Torque.

That she'd abandoned him in Algonquin puzzled and hurt Michael, though he assumed her reasons were altruistic. The wedding band she'd left behind hung around his neck on a chain, where it would stay until he found her again.

Michael's feet hit ground. His lungs ached, and he'd swallowed river water, but at least it was fresh. He'd stopped shaking only because he'd gone numb.

When the water was shallow enough, he stood, but his legs wouldn't support him. He crawled to shore and lay with his head on the stones, eyes closed.

For a moment.

Michael's body shivered; his arms and legs prickled; his left shoulder burned. He clutched Carolyn's gold wedding band in his hand, squeezing so tight it dug into his palm.

Okay. He could still feel but drifted towards unconsciousness.

No. Not now. If he lost consciousness, he'd die.

Blackness came.

Michael stood. He felt good. The pain was gone. He swung his arms and did a few jumping jacks, marvelling at his energy. When he looked down, he saw the body lying in the mud and the stones and the wet.

The body belonged to a tall man. Close-cropped, dark hair

spiked up, dishevelled from the water. Detached, Michael saw the body was his. He stared at the pallid skin, the closed eyes. The right hand still clutched the ring. Whoever found him would have a hard time prying his fingers open.

Yes. They won't get it until they pry it out of my cold, dead hand.

He found that funny.

Ghosts have a sense of humour. Who knew? Michael thought of Carolyn again. He'd failed her, his mission to sever her connection to the hostile aliens not completed. Now he wouldn't be able to find her, rescue her from the Agency, and have a life with her.

Who'd shot him? Althaea? Probably. She was a good shot. He hadn't died instantly, and that was enough for him to get away. Would humans find his body before the animals? The thought didn't upset him—he was simply curious.

If only he could see Carolyn one last time.

At that thought, Nahanni faded away, and Michael found himself in an Agency cell. Carolyn lay on a cot. He thought of approaching her and found himself beside her bed.

She'd been trying to sleep, but sensed the presence. Her eyes peered into the dim light of the cell. Carolyn herself glowed with a light that attracted Michael. She'd be able to see him, and he wanted that more than anything else.

When her gaze landed on him, fear and dismay crossed her face. "No, Michael, no. Please. Don't be dead."

Her agony cut into him.

Tell her it'll be all right.

He didn't know where that came from, but it was a good idea. "Carolyn, it'll be all right." When he spoke, it came out as a buzzing sound. Had she heard him?

Face contorted in agony, she shook her head and said, "How can it be all right? You're dead."

He supposed he was dead, but he denied it. "No."

She frowned, confused. "How did you die?"

"No." He said it again because it seemed right.

Her eyes widened, as if something had occurred to her. "Michael, I'm pregnant. It's your baby. Please. Help us. Help me save our baby."

Pregnant. How? She couldn't have any more kids.

Someone appeared next to Carolyn. The young girl stood before him, more solid than was Carolyn, who seemed to be behind a curtain of haze. This girl, about eighteen, was clear and distinct. She had black hair, but Carolyn's eyes.

"Dad." The girl's voice was musical, comforting.

"I don't understand," Michael said.

"I'm your daughter. We'll be together soon."

At that, Carolyn screamed. "No, no. You can't both die."

The girl turned to Carolyn and smiled. "It's okay. I'll see you soon too. I'm Christina. You'll call me Tina. We'll all be together soon." Tina vanished.

Something tugged at Michael. A roar filled his head, like a jet taking off next to his ear. He turned back to Carolyn, to reassure her, to look at her one more time, but he found himself in a long, dark tunnel. His surroundings a blur, he moved rapidly.

When his pace slowed, he yearned for company. He hadn't met anyone in the tunnel, and he'd lost Carolyn and his daughter. The emptiness made his heart hurt.

Light surrounded him, and Michael sensed someone near him. Jessica.

She smiled, looking radiant in a flowing gown, and extended a hand. Michael clasped the hand and marvelled at its solidity. She spoke though her lips didn't move.

"You can't stay here, but you're allowed to come with me for a time."

"I love you, Jess." He had to say it now. He'd missed his opportunity once before when she'd come to him in a dream.

"I know." She smiled, and his heart overflowed.

Michael stepped into a sunlit meadow.

"Go on ahead. To the light." She pointed, and his gaze followed her arm.

A brilliant light. If he'd seen it with his physical eyes, he'd have gone blind. He walked towards it, but ran when he absorbed the love and joy spilling from it. Home. He wanted to go into the light now, yearned for it.

But he paused and looked back. Jess waved, encouraging. As if from behind a waterfall, Michael saw Carolyn sobbing on her cot in the cell. He hesitated, not wanting to abandon her. But he had to leave right now. Carolyn would have to handle it. Michael turned back towards the brilliance, and a smile broke out on his face. That's where he belonged. Happy, he ran into the light.

CHAPTER 7

When Michael disappeared into the light, Carolyn screamed in despair. Arnie shouted her name, but she was too dazed to respond. Deuce and another male guard entered the cell and yanked her upright.

She struggled, not caring if they hit her or reported it to Cornell. They didn't strike her, but dragged her through the corridors to Cornell's office.

He stood in the doorway and pointed to a couch along the left wall. The guards dropped Carolyn onto the sofa, drained and limp, chin on chest. Sunlight from the window made her blink and squint.

She dragged her head up. The Agency boss sat in an armchair before her, wearing an eager expression. Her heart sank. He knew everything she'd said to Michael.

"Any news to share?" Cornell talked as if they were chatting over coffee.

"Go to hell."

"You must be upset. That's the closest you've come to swearing, angel girl."

She pulled her legs up and hugged them, resting her forehead on her knees.

"No, Carolyn. I want to see your face."

"Go to hell."

He sat on the couch and shifted closer to her.

"Don't touch me." Her voice held a warning note.

"The baby isn't John's." A statement. "You told Valiant it was his."

Carolyn remained silent. Cornell invaded her space, but made no physical contact. She closed her eyes, keeping her face buried.

"No wonder you didn't want to make that common knowledge. You slept with the man who killed your husband. Before John was even in the ground. Did Valiant rape you, or did you throw yourself at him?"

"Go to hell."

"This is boring. I'm trying to be patient, but if you won't talk, I'll give you to Tasha. She's my best interrogator."

Carolyn swallowed her fear, certain Cornell was truthful in the boast about Tasha's skills. "You said you wouldn't hurt me."

"If you don't cooperate, I'll renege. I don't have time to fuck around. You want to see Sam suffer? Or stay oblivious to all this, go back to school, finish her degree, and never know her life hinges on your playing nice?"

Carolyn raised her head, chin on knee, and glared at him. "How do you sleep at night? Be so cruel and live with yourself?"

"All for the greater good, angel. You don't understand because you don't have all the information. We're trying to save humanity. I can't let anyone interfere."

Her stomach knotted. *Lying.* She sighed. "You don't even believe that."

He pressed his lips together and frowned.

"Did that piss you off? You can't lie to me." What did he want? *Power.* "You're driven by power. It's a need stronger than greed in you. Greed is there, but it's all about power for you."

Cornell didn't reply, but stood and walked to the desk. He buzzed Helen. "Send the guards in, please."

The door opened, and the two guards entered.

"Chain her to the ceiling, standing." Cornell waved a hand, the sweep encompassing Carolyn and a spot in front of the desk.

Carolyn jumped to her feet. The guards grabbed her before she could take a step.

"No. Let go." She wrenched an arm free. Deuce recaptured it.

"Shut up." Cornell's voice was even, conversational. He motioned for the guards to continue.

They dragged Carolyn to the centre of the room. She shook, more from fear than from cold. Afraid the guards would hit her, she stopped struggling and sent a silent request for help to her angels and guides.

Deuce snapped cuffs on her wrists, and the other guard ran a chain through a ceiling hook. They looped the chain through the cuffs and hauled on it, yanking her up onto her tiptoes. Deuce clipped the chain in place. A nod from Cornell dismissed the guards.

Carolyn tried to move, but the chain held her in place. Cornell went behind her, put his arms around her waist, and squeezed tight. Cheek to cheek he held her as she thrashed and kicked.

"Stay still," Cornell whispered in her ear. "This'll go smoother if you behave."

Carolyn froze, but sobs quivered her body. "Please take off the chain."

"Too late. I asked you nicely. Now we'll do this my way."

Angels and guides, please help.

He pressed his body against hers and stroked her abdomen. Terrified, she feared he would rape her and moaned through clenched teeth. Tears streamed down her face. She focused on her breathing, calming herself enough to connect to any spirits or guides in the room.

Her left side grew cold, and her left arm tingled. Someone was here.

Torque. Michael's former partner. *Torque, please help me. Tell me something I can give to Cornell that'll help me.*

Cornell whispered in her ear. "What did Valiant tell you about us?"

"Michael said you veil the lies with truth."

"What did he tell you about what's happening?"

"That the aliens were abducting me for my psychic abilities, but he didn't trust the Agency. Michael said it could all be lies. Please let me go."

Cornell's hands moved under Carolyn's shirt and stroked her belly. One hand slid under her waistband and threatened to slide lower.

She whimpered.

He released her and came around to stand in front of her. "You know rape is a weapon in wartime interrogations? No one admits it, but it works." He stroked her cheek.

She didn't reply, but the fear must have shown in her eyes,

because he said, "It wouldn't be my first weapon of choice. But you need to work with me. I'd hate for Sam to experience anything like that."

"Please. I'll answer whatever questions you want. Please don't hurt her."

"I knew you'd be reasonable. I don't enjoy this, angel. I'd rather reward you than punish you, but you aren't giving me much choice." Cornell wiped her tears away with gentle fingers. "Where's Valiant?"

"Dead. Michael's spirit came to my cell." When she said it out loud, the loss overwhelmed her again, and she sobbed, closing her eyes so she wouldn't have to look at Cornell.

"Open your eyes, angel."

She did, but refused to meet his gaze.

Cornell put his hands on her shoulders. "How did Valiant die?"

"He didn't say."

"That's the first thing they tell you. Don't lie."

"I'm not. Michael said he wasn't dead, but I saw his spirit."

"What does that mean?"

"Michael appeared before me. I asked him how he died. He said 'no.' Maybe he was in denial or hadn't realized it yet."

Not dead.

She listened for more, not daring to hope Torque was trying to tell her Michael was alive. If it were true, she wouldn't tell Cornell.

Torque, please, give me something I can tell Cornell. She waited, listened, and looked down and to the right.

Cornell's grip on her shoulders tightened, and he shook her. "What? Is Valiant here?"

"No. Torque."

"What's he saying?"

"Nothing. I feel him here."

Nahanni.

Carolyn didn't understand.

What is Nahanni, Torque? As soon as Carolyn asked, she realized that's where Michael was. But she couldn't tell Cornell. He'd send agents there. Again, she silently asked Torque to give her something she could tell Cornell that would help her without hurting Michael.

Ionosphere.

Carolyn didn't understand that either, but didn't think it would hurt Michael. "Torque's saying something about the ionosphere."

"What about it?"

Carolyn waited.

Too much heat.

"Too much heat?" Carolyn repeated it as a question, not comprehending.

It meant something to Cornell because he went to his computer. He clicked his mouse and typed furiously. She watched him work. Her wrists and shoulders burned with the weight of her body hanging on the cuffs.

"Jim." Carolyn used his first name, trying to make it more personal.

He looked up in shock. Terror washed over her. Was he reacting to his name or to something on the computer screen?

"What is it?" There was fear in his voice, and her terror escalated.

"Please. Take the cuffs off," she whispered.

Cornell went to her and unlocked the cuffs. "How did you know?" His voice held panic.

Carolyn sank into a chair and swallowed, trying to clear the fear lodged in her solar plexus. Weary, she said, "What?"

"The ionosphere's heating up."

"What does that mean?"

"Trouble. Things might happen faster than we thought."

Carolyn's gasp seemed to snap Cornell back to himself. "You're going back. I've got work to do."

"Are we in danger?"

"Not your concern." He picked up the phone and called for the guards. He turned to her. "Say nothing to anyone. If you do, I'll be angry. Clear?"

Carolyn nodded.

"Say it." Cornell's voice was low, menacing.

"I understand."

The guards arrived and Cornell waved his hand at her. "Back to her cell."

They each grabbed an arm and dragged her away.

CHAPTER 8

Robert "Soaring Eagle" Holden guided the motorboat through the roiling waters of the South Nahanni River. The rapids weren't so bad here, and he could manoeuvre the boat with relative ease. His son, Daniel, sat in the front of the boat.

"We'll go ashore around that bend," Robert said. "We camped here last year, and I found some good herbs." Robert wild-crafted his own herbs and edible wild foods. He foraged most of it from Nahanni, leaving plenty for others, and never picked anything on the park's restricted list. That still left him plenty of plants to add to his stores, so he visited the park throughout the spring, summer, and fall.

Robert and Danny lived in Tryst, a small town near Nahanni National Park, populated by people descended from Nahanni's original inhabitants. Robert was the closest the town had to a medical doctor, using mostly plants to treat any afflictions that came his way. Forays into the park helped replenish his supply of natural medicines.

For the last four years, he'd been able to forage earlier each year, something he attributed to climate change. Spring started earlier; fall started later. In the north, it meant a longer growing season, a larger variety of vegetation. The warming trend benefited life above the sixtieth parallel, though Robert knew in his heart it was wrong. Any disruption to the delicate natural balance was likely to end in disaster.

But this trip involved more than gathering plants. An urgency to get into the park this week had overwhelmed him, even though, as far as the plants went, next week would've been better. Robert had been having premonitions, then dreams.

Last night, they'd camped in the Third Canyon, downstream of The Gate, a 460-metre-high limestone wall across from Pulpit Rock, which loomed like a sentinel. Anxious as they settled down for the night, Robert worried he was wasting time.

He slept fitfully and dreamed of a man who exposed the beings who'd abducted Robert. In the ensuing confrontation, Robert fought at his side. Aliens surrounded them, one tall, skinny alien grasping Robert by the throat and suffocating him.

He'd awakened to Danny shaking him, and though he'd told Danny it was just a dream, Robert had remained agitated. It was important for them to continue their journey along the river.

Danny pointed towards the rocky bank ahead. "Dad, there on the shore. It looks like a person."

Robert squinted against the sun and discerned a dark lump close to the water's edge. He would've mistaken it for driftwood if Danny hadn't said something. Robert's old eyes weren't what they used to be.

He considered himself in good shape, but his eyesight had always been poor. Since turning fifty-six, he could feel age catching up to the rest of his body. He was grateful Danny still had good eyes and the agility of a twenty-five-year-old.

Robert aimed the prow at the mass on the shore, easing the boat as close to the riverbank as was safe for the motor. They dragged the boat onto the rocks, anchored it, and then waded to the man lying there.

Through the torn shirt, Robert saw a bloody shoulder and recognized a gunshot wound and lacerations. He knelt. Two fingers on the man's neck established a faint pulse.

"Take the gear up the bank where it's dry," Robert said. "We'll need a fire. He's in shock and suffering from hypothermia. Lucky we came along. He wouldn't have lasted much longer without help."

The man clutched something in his fist. When Robert pried the fingers apart, he found a wedding band on a chain around the man's neck. Robert removed the chain. When the ring touched his palm, a shock went through him, and a slideshow of images flickered before him. He stuffed the ring in his pocket, snuffing out the glimpses into the man's life and that of the woman who'd owned the ring.

Robert glanced up to see Danny returning.

"Fire's ready, Dad. I've laid a sleeping bag out. We can put him there while we pitch the tent."

"Help me lift him. Good thing he's not conscious; otherwise, he'd be in pain."

They rolled the man onto his back, mindful of his wounded shoulder. Shock speared through Robert as he recognized the man from his dream.

Danny grabbed the man's arms, Robert his legs, and they hauled the stranger to the sleeping bag, setting him down gently. Robert peeled off the man's wet clothes and covered him with a blanket. To warm him with body heat, Robert climbed under the blanket.

While the stranger's body warmed up, Robert examined the wound. No exit wound, so the bullet was still inside the shoulder. The slug had hit no internal organs, fractured no bones, and the cold water had minimized blood loss. Robert opened a medical kit and prepared to remove the bullet.

He'd had no formal medical training but what necessity had taught him about medicine and first aid. More knowledgeable about herbs and plants than about surgery, in an emergency, he could stitch up a wound. Although the wounded man was fortunate they'd found him, there was no guarantee he'd survive. But the odds had just improved.

"I have to treat his wound, and he'll need food and water when he wakes up," Robert said. *If he wakes up.*

Father and son stared at the man and then exchanged glances.

Danny said, "You think whoever shot him might still be around?"

Robert shrugged. "I hope not. When he comes to, we'll ask him."

Danny nodded. For a moment, Robert considered leaving the man here. Strong premonitions spoke of danger, but the urgency to continue on the river had disappeared. Now he'd found the man, Robert had nowhere else he needed to be. They turned to their gear and prepared to set up camp.

CHAPTER 9

Crouched at the corner of his cage, Arnie reached his hand through the bars and called to Carolyn.

"Arnie." Carolyn's hushed voice sounded close.

"Are you okay? Are you hurt?" He kept his voice low. No telling what the guards would do if they caught them talking. This chat was necessary though. Arnie wanted to ensure she was okay, but had more on his mind than her physical condition.

"Cornell questioned me, but he didn't hurt me."

"Give me your hand, Carr."

When Carolyn's fingers touched his, Arnie grasped them and held tight. If he wanted to ask her anything, he'd better hurry. Prisoners were always on borrowed time when they talked to each other, and this conversation was riskier than most.

"Who's Michael?"

A sharp intake of breath.

"You talked to someone named Michael this morning. Who is he?"

"We were together for a few days before the aliens caught me."

"You slept together? You're carrying his baby?"

"It's complicated, Arnie. The Agency killed Michael's wife and wanted to capture both of us. It just happened."

"I'm not one to judge. It's a shock, that's all. How do you know him?"

Her fingers tensed.

"What's wrong? Who is he?"

"Michael tried to kidnap me. I convinced him to help me instead."

"Did he have a partner?"

Another long pause.

"Carr?"

"Gerry Muniz. Michael called him 'Torque.' I'm sorry, Arnie. Michael and Torque are the guys who kidnapped you."

Arnie released Carolyn's fingers, snapped his hand away. "You slept with the guy who kidnapped me?" Spoken too loud. This could bring the guards in here, and if he saw Tasha, he'd shit his pants.

He dropped to a loud whisper. "How could you do that to me? To John?" Arnie had an epiphany. "Michael killed John. You slept with the guy who killed John." This hurt. He'd never believed Carolyn could be that cold.

"Arnie, please. Don't do this. You don't understand."

"Did Michael kill John?" She fucking owed him an answer.

"No. They'd ordered Michael to do it, but he hesitated, so Torque killed John."

"You traitorous bitch. I can't talk to you anymore. John loved you and that's how you repay him? You fuck his killer?" He gripped the bars, tried to shake them, but they had no give.

"No. Arnie, please. We need each other right now."

"Do we? Or does the Agency need you to spy on me? What did they offer you? Sam? Sam's safety for what?" Arnie went to his cot and dropped onto it. He wanted to hit something. Leaping up, he stalked to the bars.

Unbelievable. Carolyn had let herself be seduced by that psycho who'd kidnapped him. All these years, Arnie had stayed away from her because she'd made it clear she'd never betray John. John dies, and before he's even buried, she's banging not just any guy, but John's would-be assassin? It was that easy for Carolyn to turn her back on John? Fuck.

She was probably on their side now, doing their dirty work. They'd stolen Carolyn from him. Arnie wished Michael were here right now. He'd tear that fucker apart.

Unable to control himself, he continued to spew venom. "Assholes. Miserable rat bastards." Arnie planted himself in front of the camera, fists flailing. "I won't talk to her. Hear me? Take this spy away."

"Arnie!"

"Shut up, Carolyn. I'm not talking to you." Arnie paced, uncertain what to do, trying not to think, unable to stop thinking.

Carolyn cried out again. "Please! You'll get hurt. The guards will come."

"I don't care. Tasha, you psycho bitch. Where the fuck are you?"

"Oh, God." Terror infused Carolyn's voice.

He stopped pacing. Footsteps approached. Arnie peered through the bars and staggered backwards when Tasha and Deuce appeared. His heart palpitated, anger evaporating and replaced by dread at what he'd brought on them.

"What do you want, Arnie? A little more Tasha time?" Tasha asked. "Did you enjoy our chat the other day? I can arrange another. Or should I show your friend here a good time?"

"No. I'm sorry. I lost my temper." Arnie poured contrition into the words.

"We heard. It's all on tape, so no need to repeat it. Thanks for bringing it to our attention. I'll make sure you have extra food with your next meal as a reward. Now behave." She winked at him. "You kids don't make me come back here, or I'll knock your heads together."

Deuce laughed and smacked Tasha on the ass.

She turned on him. "You want to lose that hand?"

Fear flashed across the face of the brawny guard.

Tasha's fucking crazy. Even the guys who work with her know it. Arnie backed away from the bars and slunk to his cot.

After the guards left, Arnie tried to calm himself. The thought of Carolyn sleeping with someone other than John made him crazy.

Someone other than you, you mean? So that's how a jealous rage feels.

Arnie had never felt that way about a woman. He'd desired Carolyn for years, but kept it under wraps because she'd made it clear she considered him just a friend. Yet he'd always had it in the back of his mind that someday things might be different. When John had died, Arnie had thought perhaps he'd get his chance. Maybe he'd be able to settle down with her, monogamous at last.

That she wouldn't reciprocate hadn't occurred to him. He'd assumed they'd never hooked up because she wouldn't cheat on John. It was a shock to realize the attraction wasn't mutual.

"Arnie." She sounded sad, frightened.

His heart skipped a beat. His outburst might cause her hardship. He didn't know what Tasha could do to Carolyn and didn't want to find out.

Face against the bars, he said, "I'm here."

"Arnie, I'm sorry this hurt you."

"Me too, Carr. I had no right to talk to you that way. We've only got each other here." It dawned on Arnie that when Carolyn had communicated with Michael this morning, it was with his spirit. If true, then the guy was dead. This outburst had been over nothing. Arnie still had a chance. If he could get her out of here, they might go to Mexico and disappear.

Arnie crouched on the floor and stretched out his arm. "Take my hand." A moment later, Carolyn's fingers brushed against Arnie's, and he grasped them. "I've got you," he said.

CHAPTER 10

Michael regained consciousness. Eyes closed, he listened, trying to determine if he was in Agency hands or with someone else. A fire crackled nearby, warmth on the back of his head. His shoulder hurt, but he could tell someone had dressed the wound.

A sleeping bag piled with blankets insulated Michael from the brisk air. When he opened his eyes, he saw a tent and gear. A few metres away, a young man hovered over a camp stove, his back turned. Not Agency. Michael tried to rise. Nausea and pain overwhelmed him. His eyes misted, and he groaned. Someone shuffled nearby and pressed Michael back onto the sleeping bag.

"Don't move. You almost died."

The man who spoke came into Michael's field of vision, an older man with obvious native origins. The man had long black hair streaked with white and grey, his face lined and wrinkled. A smoker, Michael suspected. Nicotine stained the man's teeth and fingers.

Michael said, "Who are you? How'd I get here?"

The man smiled. "One thing at a time. Drink some water."

A canteen appeared in the man's fist, and he helped Michael shift onto his side and gulp the water.

"Slow down," the man said.

Michael eased up. "Thank you." He drank more water and sagged back onto the sleeping bag. "Did you dress my wound?"

"First I removed a bullet."

Michael nodded. "I'm grateful."

"I'm Robert Holden." He pointed to the other man. "My son, Danny, over there cooking stew. And you are?"

"Michael Valiant." Agency personnel called him "Mick," but if he never heard that name again, he'd be happy, so he kept it to himself.

"Hunting's restricted in the park. How'd you get shot? This wasn't a rifle, and I doubt it was an accident."

Michael hesitated and went with half-truths. "I'm with a government agency. Someone tried to stop me from doing what I'm supposed to do."

"RCMP?" Robert asked, referring to the Royal Canadian Mounted Police.

"No."

"Whom are you working for and why are you here?"

"The less you know, the better."

Robert frowned. "I'll need more than that. You're in no condition to go anywhere at the moment. Rest for at least the night. How good are they at tracking you?"

"Highly competent and determined." Michael thought of Althaea. "I'm glad you found me first. Do you have any weapons?"

"Two rifles."

"Is that it?"

"Yes."

"Where's my weapon?"

"With our gear, cleaned and ready to use. It should work fine."

"Thanks. I owe you."

Robert stood. "Dinner's almost ready. You should eat something. I applied herbs on your wound. That'll help you heal, but you need to build up your strength. You lost blood, and I assume you haven't eaten in a while."

Michael nodded.

"These people must want you bad."

"You could say that."

Robert's gaze held Michael's. "I looked through your wallet, Mr. Valiant. You have multiple identity cards. While you don't appear to pose a threat, I'm concerned about what you're not telling me. I didn't see an ID badge tying you to a government agency."

Michael kept his gaze locked on Robert's. "I'm covert ops. I don't want to attract trouble, and I don't want to cause any. Let me stay tonight, and I'll leave in the morning."

"Stay longer. That's a serious wound."

Michael nodded, relieved he'd get a night to recover. "Would you get my gun? If my pursuers show up, you'll be glad you did."

Robert went to the tent and returned with Michael's clothes, Glock, and holster. "Everything's dry. Danny's closer to your build. His shirt should fit, and here's a pair of shoes. Your watch and ring are in your jeans' pocket."

Michael sighed. "Thanks. Sorry to be trouble."

"No worries." Robert turned to Danny. "How's the stew coming?"

"Ready anytime you are."

Michael sat this time without wanting to pass out. Robert helped him put on a denim shirt. Danny was shorter than Michael, with a stocky build, so the sleeves stopped shy of Michael's wrists. The shirt fit otherwise and didn't put pressure on his wound when he moved his arms.

He finished dressing and washed. Danny ladled stew into bowls, and the three men sat by the fire to eat. Michael's hand went to the ring dangling from the chain around his neck. Carolyn. The sight of her in that Agency cell had enraged him. He had to get her out.

Danny indicated the ring. "Does that belong to your wife?"

"No. A woman I promised to help. I'm keeping it for her."

"You're wearing a wedding band. You're married?"

Michael lowered his eyes for a moment. "My wife, Jessica, died a month ago." It hurt to say it. "Jess was pregnant when she died."

"Sorry," Danny said.

"Thanks. What about you, Mr. Holden? Where's Mrs. Holden?"

"Margaret and I divorced years ago. She raised Danny, and I helped as much as possible. She's remarried with another family now."

"You never remarried?"

"Too many community responsibilities. I run a healing centre that keeps me busy."

"A remote place for a healing centre, isn't it?"

"Doctors up here are scarce. I learned what I could about healing, though I'm not a medical doctor. I follow the old traditions, use alternative therapies."

"What traditions?"

"Aside from healing with herbs and plants, I run sweat lodges, do soul retrieval, journeying, that type of thing. You were on a journey while you were unconscious, Mr. Valiant. I'd be interested to hear your experience."

Michael watched the flames, remembering. Danny threw another log into the fire pan. Smoke curled up in grey fingers. Michael turned back to them. "How'd you know?"

"I can tell when a man's soul has wandered. You fragmented under trauma. You left your body and travelled to the spirit world."

"I remember parts of it," Michael said. "They sent me back for a reason I don't remember."

"Then it's not for you to see. Sometimes we get glimpses of what might happen, but a lot must unfold with no prior knowing."

Michael ate more stew. "Not to change the subject, but great stew. What's the meat?"

"Bison," Danny replied.

Michael nodded in appreciation.

"If you don't want to talk about it, Michael, that's okay," Robert said. "But if you don't mind sharing, we won't find it strange."

Michael noticed the change from "Mr. Valiant" to "Michael." A positive sign. He set down his now empty bowl and told them about dragging himself out of the river and collapsing, then finding himself standing over his body.

They listened, rapt, while he described how thinking about Carolyn had drawn him to her. Michael didn't mention her imprisonment in an Agency cell, but talked about seeing Tina and Jessica, the dark tunnel, and the light.

"The light was incredible. I experienced intense joy and love. Like I'd returned home after a long trip." Michael fell silent, and they watched him collect his thoughts.

"In the light, I saw everything I've ever done in my life and how it affected other people. The light showed me what it was like to be another person, because I experienced what they experienced, what they thought and felt. When I hurt them, or sometimes, brought them joy or happiness. The light knew everything I'd done. I was embarrassed, but it didn't judge. It left that to me."

Michael lowered his eyes, recalling how it'd happened so quickly. Given a second chance, he wanted to do better. Next time, he wanted a more positive review. He looked up again. "I realize we're all connected. That sounds like new-age bullshit, but it's what I learned. What I do affects me and everyone else. It wasn't easy to endure. I've done horrible things. I can't forgive myself, even if others do."

He looked to Robert. "Do you teach that in your shamanic work?"

"I help them figure it out for themselves, like you did. You describe a typical near-death experience, or NDE. Many people who've returned from the dead give similar reports."

"I wanted to stay, but they said I had something to finish. They showed me what it was, so I'd agree to come back, but they said I'd forget it when I returned here."

"That's not unusual," Robert said. "My guides sent me here to find you."

"What makes you think that?"

"We weren't planning to come to the park until next week. Intuition told me to come early. Obviously, it was to help you."

"You sound like Carolyn."

"Do you believe in aliens, Michael?"

Michael felt as if he'd stuck his finger in a light socket. He tried to make his voice sound normal. "Why do you ask?"

"This area has frequent UFO activity. I've had experiences myself. The extraterrestrial activity is the only thing here that might attract a covert ops agent. What's going on?"

Michael was honest. "Their base is here in the park. I've been getting guidance on which direction to take. Deadmen Valley."

"We can take you. It's down river."

"Too risky."

Robert had finished eating, and his bowl sat on the ground before him. He stared at it as if it were a rare gem. Then he looked up at Michael. "I had a dream someone was in my house. Something woke me, and a red light like from a laser shone on the bedroom wall. At first, I thought it was coming from outside. Then I realized that was impossible, because blinds covered the window. Afraid, I got up to investigate and found nothing. But I felt the alien presence. I don't remember getting back into bed. Next thing I know, I'm floating out through the ceiling. These aliens abducted me and performed experiments. If you're looking to make them stop, I want to help."

"Robert, you're an experiencer." Michael was incredulous.

"I'm an abductee. Call it what it is. 'Experiencer' makes it sound like tourism. The aliens kidnap us. We don't volunteer, and they don't ask permission. I've been waiting for you, Michael. I'm supposed to help you with this."

Michael hesitated. He didn't want to take Robert to the alien base. He might be a good tracker in the wilderness, but could he be invisible? Could he fight? Could he shoot someone? "Better we go our own ways. I'm not making a social call. I might need to use lethal force."

"Understood. But I'm familiar with this area. If I don't go, intuition tells me you'll fail."

Michael glanced at Danny, then back to Robert. "He can't come."

"Agreed," Robert said.

"You're not going without me," Danny said.

"No, Danny," Robert said. "In my visions, you weren't there."

"Just because you didn't see me doesn't mean I'll be hurt if I go. I can help."

Michael said, "Sorry, Danny. Your father can come, but I can't be responsible for you."

Danny's face darkened. "I'm responsible for myself."

"Nothing personal. Come as far as Deadmen Valley. Robert should return in a day or two."

"What if he doesn't?"

"Get the hell out of here."

Robert placed a hand on Danny's shoulder. "I'll be back. Your mother would kill me if I took you."

"I'm an adult, Dad. I can make my own decisions."

"Not in this. You'll stay and watch the gear."

Danny, sulking, collected their bowls and went to the bucket to wash the dishes.

CHAPTER 11

Michael gazed at the river. Staying here made him uneasy, but he was too weak to help Danny and Robert pack up and move. They'd use the river tomorrow to get down to Deadmen Valley. He picked up his gun and pulled back the slide.

"Where's your rifle, Robert? Keep it close. You too, Danny."

Robert went to get the rifle, and Danny finished the dishes and did the same. They sat around the fire again, and Robert lit a cigarette. "Hope you don't mind if I smoke. It's my one vice."

Michael shrugged. "As long as I'm upwind, it doesn't matter. I'm surprised you smoke, considering the alternative therapies you do."

"When I was a kid, no one realized how addictive cigarettes were." Robert leaned back against a log. "You want to set watches?"

Michael nodded. "I'll take the first. I've slept enough."

Robert exhaled a cloud of smoke. "I'll take the second."

Michael stared at the river, wondering where Althaea was. He'd escaped her and her partners almost a full twenty-four hours ago. She wouldn't give up, knowing her, and she just needed to follow the river to find him. Something didn't feel right. Michael rose, gun in hand.

"I want to look down the river."

"Want company?" Danny asked.

"No thanks. Stay alert." Michael made his way to the water's edge and sat among the rocks. From there, he'd spot a boat if one

311

showed up, and he'd definitely want to see Althaea before she spotted him.

Last time he'd seen her, she was transferring back to Nevada, and he was on his way to Canada, all triggered by the fiasco in France. They'd followed a spy to Paris, had neutralized the target, and Althaea had suggested they go back to her room to celebrate. Michael went, knowing she wanted to sleep with him. They'd been heading in that direction for a while.

When Cornell had first assigned Michael to be her partner, he'd tried to keep it a working relationship. That she was beautiful and sexy made it difficult, not impossible. But she was also smart and wild, and when he was with her, he wanted to take her, possess her.

She was aloof at first, making him want her even more. When he found that her reputation for being unattainable was true, a weight lifted. She was all business, and he hoped to keep it that way. But the more they worked together, the more respect they gained for each other, and the more comfortable they were with one another, the harder it was to remain detached.

That night in her hotel room, everything came crashing together. On the sofa beside the bed, they shared drinks from the mini bar. Neither wanted to say good night. Exhausted from the gruelling assignment, they both had a restless energy, after-effects of the hunt and kill.

Althaea touched Michael's arm when she said his name and laughed at his dry wit. He eased closer to her, drinking in her scent, while he tipped little bottles of rum into his mouth. She smiled, and his resolve melted under desire for her.

Without thinking, he leaned in and kissed her, tasting her. She responded instantly. He pulled her muscular body into the circle of his arms. His lips wandered from her mouth to the hollow of her throat, to the space between her breasts. When he reached down to rip her blouse open, he flashed on a memory of Jessica, head thrown back just so. He froze and released Althaea, almost dropping her on the floor.

"Mick? What is it?"

"You know what."

"I don't care if you're married."

"I do. Jess doesn't deserve this."

At first, she'd argued instead of pleaded, as if an affair could be made logical. "You want me. Don't deny it."

"I do want you, Ally. All I want is to rip off your clothes, throw you on the bed, and do things I've never done with anyone else. But I love Jess. It'd be just sex, and I don't operate that way."

"It's not just sex and you know it. I *get* you. You're unhappy. Jess doesn't understand you. She doesn't even know what you do for a living. I don't care if you stay married. I want to be with you. We're great together. The sex would be incredible. Jess won't know. It'd be just one more secret you keep from her. We can do this without hurting anyone."

She sounded so reasonable, his stomach turned. When he'd realized he'd thawed the ice queen, he'd puffed up with pride and virtually patted himself on the back. But after the triumph, came the shame.

If he did this, he'd lose Jess. Even if she never found out, he'd lose her, and the thought of life without her killed it for him. He stood, shook his head, told Althaea it couldn't happen, and left.

That's when the thawed ice queen turned into the abominable snow bitch. She threatened to tell Jess, threatened to kill Michael, to kill herself. Finally, she calmed down and got herself transferred to Nevada.

He'd always thought of Althaea as logical and pragmatic, and seeing her lose it had scared the shit out of him. He'd kept his gun handy twenty-four seven until she'd left for Nevada, and he and Jess had moved to Ontario.

Now here he was, gun in hand again, waiting for her to come after him, and this time, she had the Agency's blessing to kill him.

He searched the water in both directions, scanning the tree line on each side of the river, wishing he had binoculars. He relaxed a little after verifying nothing was coming towards him. But the camp was fifteen metres from the shore and visible. Anyone who came down the river would spot the boat and then the campsite.

Michael returned to camp, explaining his concerns to Robert and Danny. They helped him set up a lookout from which to keep an eye on the water. Robert had binoculars, and Michael scanned the far shore. He sat on a blanket sipping cedar tea and waited for Althaea to come back into his life.

CHAPTER 12

In darkness, Carolyn Fairchild's daughter, Samantha, tiptoed into the Cornell's kitchen. She crept to the fridge and opened the freezer door, determined to find the ice cream. It was late—almost midnight—but sleep eluded her, and she needed comfort food. Unable to get the ice cream out of her head, she'd snuck out of the guesthouse and into the main house to get it.

Ever since her mom had turned up dead in Algonquin Park last month, Sam barely ate or slept. During the day, stomach in knots, she couldn't choke down anything. But at night, when sleep became the problem, she found that eating something rich and fatty helped her quell her stress and get a few hours rest.

Sam weighed herself every morning and found she'd lost five pounds in the last month. *I've invented the pie-cake-ice cream diet. No food during the day, but pastries and ice cream at night.*

The freezer light illuminated the tub of ice cream behind bags of frozen veggies. *Come to mama.*

As Sam reached for the ice cream, the kitchen lights flicked on. She jumped back, almost tripping over her own feet. She slammed the freezer door closed and turned.

Jim Cornell's wife, Virginia, stood glaring in the doorway, hands on hips. "What are you doing, Samantha?"

To Ginny—*excuse me*—Mrs. Cornell, she was always Samantha. Cornell called her Sam, as did the boys, and even the hired help. But with the Missus, it was always "Samantha," as if she were in permanent trouble. Sam's mother had only called her by her full name when angry. God, how she missed her mom.

"Just getting ice cream. There's none in the guesthouse. I can't sleep and thought it might help."

"No food after seven o'clock."

"Sorry, Mrs. Cornell."

"Samantha, you know we have this rule. What if the boys saw you? You're in a nightgown. At least have the decency to wear a robe."

"Sorry. I didn't expect to see anyone."

"Go back to bed. Buy ice cream tomorrow. Then you'll have it in the guesthouse."

"Okay." Sam turned to leave.

"Samantha."

"Yes?" She turned back.

"When you enter this house, I expect you to be properly attired. Don't come in here half-dressed."

"Okay." Sam returned to the guesthouse and locked the door. She flopped onto the sofa, turned on the TV, and channel surfed, not registering what was there.

Her stomach growled. She hadn't eaten today, but after that encounter with Ginny, she couldn't stomach any food. She went to the kitchen and opened the fridge. White wine. Alcohol helped her sleep, too, though she worried about making a habit of it. She poured a glass, took a sip, and warmth spread through her body. She set the glass on the coffee table and flicked through more channels.

Don't think. Damn. Oh, Mommy, Daddy. Why did you leave me? Sam picked up the wine again and sipped. Flick. Next channel. She was wide-awake. She wished Jim were home. He never minded when she slipped into the kitchen for a late-night snack. Sometimes he'd even join her. Ginny never bothered her when Jim was home.

Sam sipped the wine. Flick. Sip. Flick. Before she knew it, the glass was empty. Her legs tingled. Her head felt swoopy. She giggled. Was swoopy a word? She put her head on a sofa pillow and stared at the TV until her eyes closed.

When Sam awoke, she stretched and basked in the glow of the good night's sleep she'd had. She checked the time. Eight o'clock. Wow. She hadn't had more than a few hours' sleep in over a month. The boys would already be dressed and waiting for breakfast. She'd better get moving.

By the time she dressed and made her way to the house, it was almost eight-thirty. She unlocked the kitchen door and hurried inside. The boys, George and Wade, were finishing breakfast. Sam shot a look of gratitude at Marnie, the housekeeper. It was Sam's responsibility to get them their breakfast.

"Thanks, Marnie," Sam said. "I owe you."

"No problem, honey," Marnie said.

"Where is she?" Sam asked. No need to elaborate. Marnie knew whom Sam meant.

"Upstairs. I told her you'd set the table and put the food out. Don't worry. I know you've had trouble sleeping. Set an alarm clock so it doesn't happen again."

Sam peeked at the boys. They were staring at her. She smiled at them. Six-year-old George smiled back, his grin exposing a missing front tooth. Wade, twelve, tilted his head and said, "I won't tell my mom, Sam."

"Thanks, Wade." Sometimes she found Wade a little unsettling, like he was filing things away to use later.

Sam rushed them through breakfast. She got them to school on time, driving them in her mother's car, which the Cornells let her keep in their garage. When she arrived at the house, she returned to the kitchen, looking for Marnie.

She heard voices and paused, staying out of sight. If Ginny were there, she'd talk to Marnie later. Sam had no desire to face Ginny this morning and get nattered at about something stupid.

"I haven't had a moment's peace since she moved here," Ginny said. "What do you think of her, Marnie?"

"Seems nice. I'm sorry for her. It must be difficult to lose both parents so close together."

"I suppose. But she's rude and disruptive. She doesn't follow house rules. The boys see that, they'll act up themselves. They're so impressionable."

"It'll be fine. Maybe she needs time to adjust?"

"You're too kind, Marnie. Like it or not, Jim wants her here, for whatever reason." A mug thudded on the counter.

Sam had heard enough. She slipped out of the house, heading to the guesthouse through the back gate. Once inside, she locked the door and poured herself a glass of water from the purifier on the counter. That was all she could stomach. Her hands shook as she raised the glass to her lips.

She sat on the couch in the living room and turned on the TV. A sob caught in her throat. School wouldn't begin again until September. How would she manage that long? She was lonely.

Sure, she had Fox, her mother's cat, and she could invite a friend or two over, though Ginny didn't approve of them. But this aura of disdain where she lived hurt and confused Sam. She wished Jim were home. He made her feel safe and welcome. She picked up the phone and called him.

CHAPTER 13

Jim Cornell hung up the phone. He'd spent the last fifteen minutes assuring Samantha that his wife didn't have a problem with her. He buzzed Helen on speaker. "Get Tasha in here."

"Yes, sir."

Thank God, he'd moved Helen up here from Toronto. He didn't want to break in another receptionist. It was hard enough being away from his family. Cornell wished he could go home more often, for Sam's sake as much as anything else.

This last phone call worried him—the girl almost sounded depressed. She'd talked about returning to school in the fall, and he'd pretended to go along with the idea. Soon he'd talk her into changing her plans, get her to transfer to the university in Peterborough. He preferred to keep her close.

After investigating the information Carolyn had shared about the heating ionosphere, Cornell had grown concerned. It could cause more catastrophic storms. Hurricanes, tornadoes, and typhoons had already gotten stronger and more violent over the last few years, each storm worse than the last. Amp it up ten-fold by heating the ionosphere and it would be Armageddon.

A knock on the door, and Tasha poked her head in. She flashed him a smile, swaggered into the room, and dropped into a chair, legs stretched out, hands clasped behind her head.

"Congratulations," Cornell said. "I don't know how you got what you did from Arnie, but we've identified Dragonfly."

Tasha gave him another huge grin. "Who is she, sir? Do I get to interrogate her?"

"Julie Helliwell. I'm having her transferred here. She suspects nothing. We'll let her think we trust her, see what she does with it. Let her hang herself."

"Anytime you want her taken down, just say the word."

"Of course."

"When do you expect her to start?"

"Tomorrow morning. I'll assign her to Arnie's block. We'll see what happens when she realizes she's guarding the person she's leaked information to."

Tasha smiled. "Okay. Thanks for the heads up. I can't wait to see the look on Arnie's face."

Cornell cringed. He had an aversion to Tasha's sadistic nature even though he made use of it. He didn't do what he did for pleasure, but for himself and his family.

"We're done here," he said, voice clipped.

"Yes, sir." Tasha chilled him with a stare. Jesus, she was creepy. She left the room without another word.

Cornell called his wife. The housekeeper answered, and he waited while Ginny came to the phone.

"Hello?" Ginny said.

"It's me. Checking in."

"Will you be home this weekend?"

"Doubtful." Richmond Hill was too far to commute from when he had to spend so much time in Peterborough. "I might get back for two days during the week. Everyone okay? How's Sam?"

"Fine." Ginny's tone sounded anything but fine.

"What's wrong?"

"Why do we need this stranger in our guesthouse? I can't even invite friends over for a girls' weekend."

"Sure you can. There's room in the house. So they share the guest room. I have to keep her safe, which is easier to do if she's living with us. If it doesn't work out, she'll need to move here, but I don't have time to monitor her activities."

"Why can't she go to someone else's home?"

"Because I can't divulge to anyone where she is. Trust me on this. Okay?"

A sigh floated up through the phone. For someone who had everything, Virginia complained a lot. Cornell waited for her reply.

"Yes. Okay." She said it grudgingly.

"Sam's not staying inside the house, and she's watching over the boys. What's the problem?"

"Do you watch her? Over the monitors? Do you?"

"Oh for the love of—I'm too busy to spy on the girl. You're supposed to be monitoring her. Do you know her whereabouts at all times? Because it's important. When you're keeping an eye on her, I don't have to check the monitors as often."

"Yes. She goes nowhere without my permission. After what happened to her parents, she's okay with it."

"Make her welcome. She feels like an intruder."

"Did she call you?"

"I check in with her regularly," he said.

"Samantha entered the house during the night. I thought someone had broken in, and it terrified me. She wanted ice cream. After seven."

"Sam's a scared young woman, Ginny. If she wants ice cream in the middle of the night, get her a bowl and spoon. Understand?"

"I'm supposed to cater to her?" Ginny's voice turned shrill.

Cornell leaned back in his chair. "Be nice. Promise me you'll do that."

Another sigh. "All right."

He changed the subject. "Are the boys okay?"

"You mean do they like having a gorgeous blonde in a bikini around? Yes, the boys are okay."

"I wasn't asking that. How are they doing? School okay?"

"No different than usual. They spend more time at home and bring their friends over to gawk. The girl has her friends over, too. I can't say no. They stick to the guesthouse or by the pool. I try to minimize the times she has friends here, but she'd go out more if I didn't let them come over."

"You're doing the right thing. It's better if she sticks close to home. I need to go, but I'll call you tonight after dinner." Cornell hung up the phone. He'd check in with Sam later and make sure Ginny had eased up.

Cornell had known it'd be difficult for his wife to have an attractive young girl living in the house. Not that Ginny was unattractive—she had a classy, mature style. Maybe a little on the heavy side, but she carried her weight well and still got him hard. But her insecurity made her a wild card.

The phone rang, and he snatched it up. "Yes?"

"Althaea Dayton on two-thirty-two."

Althaea? Wasn't she out in Nevada? What did she want from him? "Thanks, Helen." He pressed the extension. "Cornell here."

"Hi, Jim. Long time."

"Althaea. How are you?"

"I've seen him."

Valiant. She had to be talking about Valiant. He exhaled slowly. "Where?"

"Nahanni. They transferred me here last year. Can't say I was pleased, but things happen for a reason. We use a cabin in the park when we're off duty. I was there with Stephenson and Moser. Valiant showed up. I'd seen he was wanted, of course."

Nahanni? What's in Nahanni? Cornell pulled up a map of the Northwest Territories on his computer, zooming in on the park. *An alien base.*

"What happened?" He expected bad news. If Althaea had Valiant in custody, he would've heard about it already.

"We almost caught him. I shot him when he jumped into the river, but he escaped. The current was strong, and the guys wouldn't let me go after him."

"You shot Valiant?"

"Mick and I didn't part on good terms, and the details on this manhunt said we could use lethal force if necessary. I deemed it necessary."

"Did you try to find him?"

"We followed the river a ways but didn't have a boat. We get choppered to the cabin, and there's a canoe, not a motor boat. No one would be crazy enough to shoot those rapids. But I have a plan."

"Spill."

Althaea told Cornell what she intended, and his smile grew wider while she talked. "I like it. Good work, Dayton. Keep me posted."

"Yes, sir."

He hung up. Valiant wasn't dead. Was Fairchild deliberately misleading him? One way to find out. He buzzed Helen.

"Yes, sir?"

"Have the guards bring Carolyn Fairchild to my office." Anger boiled up. If she'd lied, she'd regret it, and she was damn well going to pitch in and help them locate Valiant now.

CHAPTER 14

Do you watch her? Over the monitors? Do you? The words rang in Sam's ears. She'd returned to the house again to find Marnie, but as she'd passed the library, she'd overheard Ginny on the phone. Sam hadn't intended to eavesdrop until she'd heard her name. She pressed against the wall and listened.

From the gist of it, she realized Ginny was talking to Cornell. When Ginny ask him if he watched Sam over the monitors, Sam's guts froze. He could watch her? The Cornells had cameras in the guesthouse? Sam hugged herself, body trembling. Was there a camera in her bedroom?

She ran down the hall, opened the front door, and slipped outside. On her way back to the guesthouse, the thought of cameras changed her mind. She sat on a lawn chair by the pool instead, head in her hands.

The patio door rolled open, catching her attention. Ginny. Sam's mouth went dry.

Ginny took a chair across from Sam. "I'm sorry about last night, Samantha." Her voice was warmer than it had been, but Sam didn't buy it. Cornell had probably told Ginny to make nice.

Sam wondered why he wanted her around so much. Maybe it wasn't just compassion. "I'm sorry too."

"I'm stressed lately."

What could be so stressful in Ginny's life? They were rich, and Ginny didn't have to work. She didn't even look after her own kids. Sam nodded as if she understood.

"If you need a midnight snack, help yourself. Just wear appropriate attire, please."

"Okay. I'm sorry I never considered the boys walking in on me. I guess I'm distracted."

"With what?"

Sam stared at her. Did she really want to know? "I miss my parents. It's hard."

Sorrow flickered across Ginny's face. She patted Sam's hand. "I forget what it must be like for you. I don't mean to be harsh."

Sam fought the urge to pull away and looked Ginny in the eyes. "Why am I here?"

"What do you mean?"

"Why does Mr. Cornell want me living here?"

"To help us with the kids. We need a nanny."

"Marnie was taking care of them just fine before I came here. Why me?"

"What are you implying? You think there's an ulterior motive for having you stay here?"

"Am I in danger?"

Ginny glanced away.

Sam's heart skipped a beat. That was it: Cornell thought she might be in danger.

"Jim's in a difficult position, with a great deal of responsibility. He can't talk about what he does, but when he says something is for the best, I trust him. You should, too."

"What's he afraid of?"

"I don't know. Perhaps nothing, but better to be safe, right?"

Sam nodded. But she still worried about cameras in her bedroom. What if Cornell was a perv, getting off watching her undress? Sam considered what to say. "I thought I saw a camera in the guesthouse, Mrs. Cornell. Am I being monitored?"

Ginny sucked in her breath. She hesitated, but only for a second. "Those are security cameras, Samantha. They're for your protection."

"I don't understand. Are they recording me? Is there one in my room? In my bathroom?"

"Of course not. They monitor the entryways, the windows. Are you accusing us of something? We don't deserve that." Ginny frowned, and her face grew dark.

Sam looked away, guilty. "I'm not accusing you. I felt weird about it. Wouldn't you?"

"No. I'd be happy the place is secure. Do you activate the alarm when you go to bed?"

Sam nodded, though it was a lie. She'd activate it if she ever went to bed. Since she hadn't been sleeping, just passing out on the sofa, she hadn't turned on the alarm.

"Are we okay?" Ginny asked.

"Yes. I'm sorry to be any trouble. I don't want to intrude on your family."

Ginny smiled, but there was no warmth in it. "You're not intruding. The boys enjoy your company, and it helps Marnie. So we're okay?"

Sam forced a smile. "Yes." But she wondered if anything would ever be okay again.

CHAPTER 15

Carolyn looked up when doors clanked in the corridor and two pairs of footsteps approached. The guards had already cleaned up today's last meal, so this visit had nothing to do with food for prisoners.

Heart freezing as always when the guards appeared at odd times, Carolyn huddled under a blanket. Terrified they were coming for her, but not wanting them to come for Arnie either, she choked back frightened sobs. Whenever the guards went to someone else, relief paired with a stab of guilt. But it didn't stop her from praying they'd pass by both her and Arnie.

The guards stopped at her cell. Deuce and a woman Carolyn hadn't seen before. The shorthaired woman was muscular, but not as scary as Tasha. Deuce unlocked the door. Carolyn watched without moving as the two entered her cell.

"Get up." Deuce wrenched the blanket off Carolyn. "Let's go."

She stood before he could touch her, but he gave her a push towards the door anyway. "Grab her, Julie."

The woman grasped Carolyn's arm and steadied her when she stumbled. Carolyn tried to shake her arm loose, but Julie's grip was steel. The guards liked to show they could touch her whenever they wanted. They were never gentle, and she had the bruises to prove it.

They took her to Cornell's office. Increasingly uneasy, Carolyn crossed the threshold. Cornell was angry with her, but she didn't know why.

He looked up from his computer and motioned for the guards to plant her on the chair before his desk. A good sign—at least she wouldn't be chained to the ceiling this time.

The guards performed their duties silently. Carolyn assumed they wanted to heighten her sense of fear. It worked. Once she was in her seat, they left. She stared at the floor. Whatever Cornell said, she'd keep her reaction to herself. As usual, he didn't let her.

"Look at me, Carolyn."

She raised her head. He came around to perch on the front of his desk, looming over her. She swallowed, trying to suppress nervousness. Always cold in here, she shivered. He glared at her. Carolyn vowed to keep her face blank no matter what he said.

"He's alive."

She held her breath. Michael was alive. She tried not to flinch, but her eyes reacted.

Cornell didn't miss it. "You knew, didn't you?"

"I wasn't sure."

"You suspected, but kept it to yourself to protect him." Not asking, telling.

"I wasn't sure because Michael hadn't shown me how he died."

"But Torque told you Valiant lived, didn't he?"

Without thinking, she looked away, and it told Cornell he was right.

"This isn't a game, Carolyn. You must tell me what you know when you know it. Otherwise, there'll be repercussions for Sam and Arnie. This little oversight will cost your friend."

"No. Please." Carolyn regretted she hadn't realized the depth of their cruelty. "Leave Arnie alone. I'll do what you ask."

"You need to understand I'm not making empty threats." Cornell buzzed Helen. "Have Arnie taken to the interrogation room." He clicked off.

"No. Don't. I'll tell you whatever I can. Please don't hurt Arnie."

Cornell ignored her and buzzed Helen again. "Send in Julie and Deuce."

"Yes, sir."

The guards returned. Cornell waved his hand in Carolyn's direction. "Take her to interrogation."

"No!" she screamed. "You sick bastards. There's no reason."

The guards ignored her screams and hauled her from the room.

Carolyn looked at Helen, who sat at her desk, staring as though Carolyn were a curiosity. She struggled to break away, but the guards were too strong for her. She screamed at Helen. "You work here? How can you go along with this?"

Helen's expression remained impassive.

The guards dragged Carolyn down the hall to a room she'd never seen. They'd chained Arnie shirtless to the ceiling. His eyes grew wide when he saw her. "What's happening, Carr? The guards said you'd explain what we're doing here."

Deuce shook her. "Tell him."

She sobbed, terrified. "Cornell said he thinks I'm not cooperating. He said ..."

Deuce twisted her arm and pushed her up against the wall, yanking her from Julie's grasp. He shoved his face into hers. "Every time you refuse to obey, you increase his punishment."

Carolyn turned to Arnie, sobbing. "I told Cornell I'd tell them anything he wanted, but he wouldn't listen."

"Tell him what you kept to yourself."

Although she knew he'd take it as a stab in the back, she talked to protect Arnie. "Torque told me Michael was still alive."

Arnie grimaced at her words.

Deuce grabbed a whip Carolyn hadn't noticed hooked to the wall.

"No!" she screamed.

Julie pinned Carolyn and kept her turned towards Arnie. Deuce glared at her. "Here are the rules: every time you look away, he gets another; every time you speak, he gets extra."

Carolyn sobbed quietly. She thought she'd choke on her tears.

Deuce positioned himself behind Arnie and struck hard. Arnie screamed in agony. Deuce didn't pause. He hit Arnie again, the whip cutting into his back. Blood sprayed up and Carolyn gagged. When the whip cracked again and more blood flew from Arnie's back, she crumpled over and vomited on the floor. Julie pulled her up by the hair, forcing her to watch.

His screams were getting hoarse. Carolyn lost count of how many times Deuce struck Arnie until he lost consciousness. His spirit detached from his body. At first, it was a vague mist, and she thought she was hallucinating. The mist coalesced into a form, and Arnie's spirit stood next to his body.

"I can't feel it from here," he told her.

Afraid he was dead, Carolyn wanted to tell them to stop. But she feared that if she spoke, Deuce would continue beating Arnie, and she wasn't sure if he was dead or just out of body. She tried to communicate with him.

I love you, Arnie. Please don't die. Oh, God, I'm so sorry.

Deuce dropped the whip, rubbed his hands together, and moved over to Carolyn. "We're done here."

"You killed him," Carolyn said.

Deuce checked for a pulse. "Nah. Just unconscious. Now move."

"You can't leave him like that."

"Someone will come for him. You're going back to Cornell."

"No."

Irritation crossed his face.

Terror engulfed Carolyn. Was that uncooperative? He might pick up the whip again. "Sorry. I didn't mean that. I'm coming."

They grabbed her arms and frog-marched her out again. She had one final glimpse of Arnie, hanging unconscious by his wrists, blood dripping onto the floor. Would he ever forgive her? She tried to stifle fresh sobs and gagged. She barely registered being dragged through reception to Cornell's office. The guards dumped her in the chair again.

Cornell leaned against his desk and smiled as if happy to welcome back a long-absent friend. "Give you a clearer picture of what'll happen if you hide anything else from me? This time, Arnie; next time, maybe Sam."

Carolyn clapped a hand to her mouth and jumped up. Cornell sprang clear of his desk. She dashed to the garbage can behind his desk and threw up in it. She knelt over it, gagging. When she raised her head from the trashcan, Cornell offered a box of tissues.

She wiped her mouth and blew her nose. He helped her up, led her to his en suite bathroom, and stood in the doorway while she rinsed her face. When she finished, he led her back to the chair. Her stomach rumbled, ravenous—the baby wanting to be fed. If she didn't eat soon, she'd be sick again.

"I didn't want this," Cornell said.

She suppressed a sarcastic reply, afraid to speak. Who knew what they'd consider uncooperative behaviour? She kept her head lowered. If he wanted her to talk, he'd ask a direct question.

Cornell sat behind his desk, having satisfied his need to loom over her. "We have an idea where Valiant went. I need you to verify his location. We've set up a lab where you can do remote viewing. I don't care how long it takes or what's involved. Locate and track him. Help us set a trap for Valiant. You'll start today. If you don't, Arnie returns to the interrogation room, and you'll observe again."

"If you keep it up, you'll kill him. The aliens need him."

"The aliens can heal physical injuries. We can do this indefinitely, and Arnie won't die."

When the implications of that sank in, bile rose again in Carolyn's throat. Shaking, she bowed her head and prepared to betray the father of her unborn child.

CHAPTER 16

Julie Helliwell studied the guardroom monitors, flicking from one cell to another. She was only interested in Arnie's cell but played as if she were viewing each prisoner. Her heart broke every time he appeared on screen, lying face down on his cot, back covered in bandages.

At least they'd given him first aid after beating him unconscious. It had killed her to hold Carolyn still and watch Deuce whip Arnie. If Julie'd had her way, she'd have beaten the shit out of Deuce. But it was her first day at the Peterborough compound, and she had to be careful, or they'd discover she was the Agency leak.

When Ralph Drummond had first introduced her to his friend and fellow abductee Arnie Griffen, Julie found herself attracted to him. It thrilled her when he showed it was mutual. Julie looked forward to meeting with Ralph and Arnie, and spilled more information to Ralph than she otherwise would have, wanting to impress Arnie.

Worried that Cornell might have had her transferred here because he suspected her, she'd kept her distance from Arnie. So far, no one treated her any differently, so she relaxed. Perhaps she was just paranoid.

She'd covered her tracks, never using her real name with Ralph and Arnie, but if their paths crossed, Arnie could betray her by accident. That had been foremost in Julie's mind when she'd brought Carolyn into the room to witness the whipping. Arnie's terror had been so great then, he hadn't given Julie a second glance. But she wouldn't be able to avoid him forever.

She saw an opportunity when Cornell summoned the guards to take Carolyn to the lab. Julie pulled a pad of sticky notes from the desk drawer and jotted "don't let on you know me" on it. She went to the infirmary and asked the nurse for a bottle of pain meds.

"Are these for you?" the nurse asked.

"No. Griffen's in pain. He's making too much noise and disturbing the others on the cellblock. I figured I'd give him something to shut him up."

The nurse handed over the pills.

Julie hurried to Arnie's cell, where he lay on the cot, eyes closed. She unlocked the door and hurried to his side, shielding his face from the camera with her body. "I brought you pain medication."

He nodded feebly and showed no sign he knew her. Had he forgotten her? Had she meant nothing to him? She pushed those thoughts aside. He'd recognize her sooner or later, and when he did, she didn't want it to be with witnesses or on camera.

She held the bottle out, the note stuck to it. "I'll get water. The nurse wrote the dosage on that paper."

Julie went to the sink and filled a paper cup with water. She turned back to him. He stared at her, dull eyed, unseeing. She wanted to cry.

"Sit." She said it roughly though it hurt to do it.

He made a half-hearted attempt to sit and groaned. She grasped his arm and helped him up, again blocking his face from the camera. Arnie looked at the bottle, plucked the paper off and read. He looked puzzled and then did a double take as he recognized Dragonfly. He closed his eyes a moment. When he opened them, his face was blank, his gaze glued to hers.

"Open the bottle and take two pills." Her voice warned discretion.

He exhaled in a hiss. His eyes continued to stare into hers. She watched while he put two pills in his mouth. Julie handed him the cup of water and he drank it. She took the pill bottle and the note back.

"Okay?" she asked.

He nodded. "I am now."

***

In the lab, Carolyn sat in an armchair beside a table. The lights were dim. She had a notebook in her lap and a pencil in her hand. A digital recorder lay on the table. She leaned back, trying to get comfortable.

Cornell observed her from across the table. "Tell me everything you get even if you think it's irrelevant. Make notes and sketches. Discover where he is and with whom. Determine his intentions."

"What if I get nothing?" They wanted results, but what would they do if she failed? If they thought she was misleading them, they'd hurt Arnie or Sam.

"I trust your abilities. You know what'll happen if you lie. Failure isn't an option. Arnie's depending on you."

She closed her eyes and concentrated on Michael. She asked her angels and guides to help her connect. One thing she could do without alerting Cornell was warn Michael she was tracking him for the Agency.

Carolyn allowed her body to relax, letting it loosen from her toes through her body. She inhaled, engaging her abdomen, and took three deep breaths, easing herself into a meditative state. When her mind wandered, she brought it back to Michael. Open, she waited for information.

The impressions flowed, and she said aloud whatever she saw. "Mountains … Trees, mostly evergreens … A river … Wide, with white caps and rapids … Rocky shoreline." She fell silent, letting more information flow to her.

She continued. "Daylight … Two men with him … Natives … Father and son." She described Robert and Danny, lingering on their features so she'd have more time to connect to Michael.

Help me talk to Michael, angels, please. Help him realize he has to beware. They're coming for him.

What image could she send him to make clear he was hunted? No guarantee it would work, but she had to try. She formed an image of Michael with guns pointed at him and raised a sense of urgency, of close pursuit. She beamed it at him with all she had.

Afraid her silence would tip off Cornell she was trying to send Michael a warning, Carolyn returned to receiving images. "Boat … Aluminium … Anchored at the riverbank."

A boat with landscape markers formed on the paper, a rough sketch, but passable. Carolyn stuck to major items, leaving out details, keeping Cornell ignorant of the full extent of her abilities. "Can't see a name on it. Might start with 'M.'"

She lied about not seeing the name of the boat. It said "Misty River" on the side. The 'M' would make them think she was trying, but couldn't quite get it. "They're camped ... One on watch, two sleeping."

She fell silent again. Michael was awake. If he were asleep, it would've been easier to communicate with him. She'd try later in her cell. "Camp stove ... A tent, near trees." She felt pain in her shoulder. "Injured ... Michael ... Wound's healing." She sent him Reiki. "It's going blank. I'm losing it." She opened her eyes.

Cornell stared at her, slack-jawed. He closed his mouth and leaned forward, beckoning for the notebook. She gave it to him.

"The pencil too. I'm not leaving you with a potential weapon."

She set it on the table. He stuck it in his shirt pocket. She hoped he'd let her return to her cell now so she could find out how Arnie was and send him Reiki too.

"You've earned a reward," Cornell said, sounding so pleased it made her stomach turn. "I'll see you get pyjamas to wear at night. And tomorrow morning, a private shower while the guard stays in the hall. I trust you won't cause any trouble."

"Thank you. That's kind." She hated herself for sounding like a sycophant.

Cornell motioned for her to stand. "We're done for today."

He ushered her out of the room, and the guards took her back to her cell.

***

Julie turned to leave Arnie and found Tasha and Deuce blocking the cell door.

"What are you doing?" Deuce asked.

"Just giving him pain meds."

"On whose authority?"

"I checked with the nurse. It was four hours since he'd had any. She said it was okay." Julie kept her voice steady, ready to fight. She'd take Arnie with her, but he was in no condition to help her fight their way out.

Tasha stared at her with amusement, and Julie's stomach sank. She'd seen that look before. Tasha expected a fight. Did they know her connection to Arnie? Had Cornell transferred her here to expose her? If so, she'd played right into it.

"Hand over the bottle." Deuce held out his hand.

Julie slipped the note from it, hid it in her fist. She gave him the bottle.

Deuce grasped her wrist. "The note, too."

Julie dropped the note and kicked Deuce in the knee. She heard a snap, and he howled in pain. Tasha pulled her gun, but Julie grabbed Tasha's wrist and twisted. The weapon fired, a bullet drilling into the wall opposite the cell. The gun fell to the floor.

Deuce rose on his bum leg. He drew his pistol and aimed it at Arnie, still catatonic on his cot, oblivious to everything.

"Stop, Julie, or I'll fucking blow his head off."

Julie ceased fighting. Tasha punched her in the face, and Julie dropped to the floor. Deuce kicked her in the stomach, causing her to curl up like a foetus.

Tasha retrieved her gun and held it over the wounded woman. "Good night, bitch." Tasha slammed the gun into Julie's head.

Everything went black.

CHAPTER 17

Michael glanced at his watch. Close to ten o'clock. The sun would set at 10:40 PM and rise again at 3:28 AM. His wounded shoulder stabbed him when he yawned and stretched, making him wince. He'd caught himself dozing off a few times.

At one point, he'd imagined Carolyn was with him. It made him uneasy. Ever since she'd come up, a sense of danger pressed on him. Had she put images in his head? He'd seen guns pointed at him.

He'd trust the message and head out earlier than planned. Sleep now, wake Danny instead of Robert, and leave with Robert after Danny's watch. Michael scanned the area one more time. Nothing moved. He scoured the river. All clear. He half-expected to see Althaea roaring along the river in a motorboat, guns blazing. She was out there, and waiting for her to pop up any minute made him crazy. Only action would release his tension.

He went to the tent and jostled Danny, who rolled over and opened his eyes. Michael motioned for him to get up and then waited outside. Moments later, Danny joined him.

"I thought my dad was taking the next watch."

"Change of plan. We've got to get moving. Wake us at dawn."

Michael crawled into the sleeping bag Danny had vacated. Robert snored lightly. Michael lay on his right side to spare his throbbing left shoulder, closed his eyes, and tried to relax.

Was Carolyn okay? The desire to go to her made focusing on his current goal difficult. Forced to be here while the Agency held her tormented him.

Michael pushed the distracting thoughts away and concentrated on what had to be done. The alien base pulled him, the being he'd met in Algonquin Park a constant presence. He'd lost the connection for a while after Althaea had shot him. The more pain he felt, the weaker the connection to the aliens.

He gripped Carolyn's ring and his tension eased. Fatigue wrestled him to the mat, and he fell asleep.

***

Michael stands at the edge of the crowd, heart thudding against his chest as if trying to punch its way out. The gallows is too far away. He's too late. Carolyn and seven others are lined up behind the row of nooses. Five women and three men to be hanged, their bodies burned.

Excitement fuels the crowd as people shout, "Hang the witches!"

Michael would happily take a cudgel to their brains if it'd help save Carolyn.

Jim Cornell appears next to the hangman.

Michael draws a knife and works his way through the crowd. If nothing else, he'll send Cornell to hell. Scaffold looming, his gaze fixes on Carolyn. She lifts her head and spots him, eyes growing wide. She shakes her head, warning him away.

He draws nearer to his target.

Cornell whispers in Carolyn's ear. She turns and spits in his face. He grabs her arm and drags her to the nearest noose. His voice rings out over the crowd. "This one first."

The hangman covers Carolyn's head with a hood and slides the noose around her neck. Panicked, Michael rushes forward, but the faster he moves, the more distant she seems. Hands grab him, and he slashes blindly at them, screaming at Cornell to stop.

He arrives on the scaffold as the trapdoor opens and Carolyn drops into space.

"No!" rips from his throat ...

Michael awoke, the word on his lips, but not vocalized. What a fucked-up dream. Sweat drenched his body. The dream prodded him with a sense of urgency, and he wanted to leave. Dawn hadn't yet arrived. Might as well rest while he could. Michael lay back on the sleeping bag, clutched Carolyn's ring, and closed his eyes, hoping this time sleep would be dreamless.

CHAPTER 18

When the guards brought Carolyn back from the lab, Tasha and Deuce were dragging Julie out of Arnie's cell. Deuce limped, and Julie was unconscious, her face bloody. Carolyn slumped on her cot, waiting until the guards left the cellblock before trying to get Arnie's attention.

The doors slammed behind the departing guards, and Carolyn pressed herself against the bars by Arnie's cell. She didn't know if he was conscious. What if they'd hurt him in the scuffle that got Julie banged up? She doubted Arnie had caused that damage.

Her first attempts to get his attention failed. Carolyn's voice stayed low and even, but after calling him for at least ten minutes, there'd been no response. "Arnie, even if you don't want to speak to me, please, tell me you're okay."

No sound, not even the cot's creak. If he was awake, he wasn't moving. Or he wasn't on the cot. Carolyn returned to her bed. They'd had their evening meal, so it was night, but she didn't know how late. Was he asleep? Surely, he couldn't have slept through Julie's beating.

Carolyn paced back and forth. Every pass she made, she paused and listened, hoping to hear evidence that he was awake and aware. While she walked, she sent Reiki to Arnie and Michael. When she scanned Michael's shoulder, the pain from his wound shocked her, and she sent him extra energy.

A cot creaked. *Arnie.*

She stopped pacing and listened. The cot creaked again, and she dashed to the bars of the cell. "Arnie?" She held her breath, listening.

"Carr?"

Oh, thank God. "How badly are you hurt? I'm so sorry. I swear I'll do whatever they want so they won't hurt you again."

"Hold my hand?" His voice was weak, tired. Arnie was always so energized, so strong and confident. Now he sounded beaten, and not just physically.

She sank to the floor and stretched out her hand. "Arnie, I'm here." Her fingers wiggled.

He groaned, and his fingers caught hers.

Carolyn gave a squeeze, savouring the touch. "I've got you."

"Ralph's dead, Carr."

"I know."

"You do? Why didn't you tell me?"

"I communicated with him in a dream and was afraid you wouldn't believe me. I'm sorry Arnie."

"It's not your fault. You try to be strong, but these assholes break you. The Agency found Dragonfly because of me."

"Who's Dragonfly?"

"Julie. The new guard. Ralph's contact. Tasha made me tell everything I knew about her. They brought her here and beat the shit out of her. It's my fault. I couldn't take the pain and told them everything. Now they'll torture her, kill her."

Tears rolled down Carolyn's face. "You have to get away. They'll kill us when they're done with us."

"I'm not leaving without you. Not that I'd know how to escape even if you'd come with me."

"Cornell has Sam. I can't leave."

"Then we're not leaving."

"But if you got away, you could find Sam and take her somewhere safe." Hope surged.

"Are you forgetting the aliens can track us? They'd find me."

"There has to be a way. I'll meditate on it."

"All right." He squeezed her hand.

Affection fluttered in her heart, and she longed to hug him. She snatched her hand away when the doors to the cellblock opened and footsteps approached.

She climbed into bed, and Arnie's cot creaked as he did the same. She gripped her blanket like a child and waited to see whom the guards were coming for. Carolyn prayed they'd pass her and Arnie by, but suspected one of them was at risk.

She was right. Deuce and Tasha unlocked Arnie's cell door. Deuce still limped, and it looked like he had a tensor bandage at his knee.

"Get up." Tasha's harsh voice echoed through the cellblock.

The guards led Arnie past Carolyn's cell. When she saw his shirtless torso, back swathed in bandages, she burst into tears. Their footsteps faded. The cellblock doors slammed closed. Carolyn hugged her blanket and began the long vigil of waiting for Arnie's return. When she realized she was sucking her thumb, her sobs grew louder.

***

Arnie walked between Tasha and Deuce, not registering where they were going. When he realized they headed to the interrogation room, the terror failed to cut through the numbness.

Tasha opened the door, and Arnie preceded the guards into the room. This time, Julie hung by chained hands, her torso bare.

A table against the wall held a water jug and paper cups, along with an open black duffel bag. Arnie couldn't see what was in the bag, but was sure it wasn't party favours. A chair sat at the table. On the wall, the whip hung, waiting. Arnie shook and his extremities grew cold—so much for numb and impassive.

Tasha pushed Arnie in front of Julie. His gaze met hers though it was difficult. One of her eyes had swollen shut. She looked unafraid and gave Arnie a half smile.

"Don't give them anything."

Tasha laughed. "By the time we're done, you'll be begging to tell us everything. Griffen's here to help you along. His back's a write-off, but he can sacrifice other body parts to your cause." Tasha spun Arnie around to face her and gave him a chilling smile. "Thanks for helping us find the bitch. We haven't forgotten who provided the information to identify Dragonfly."

Before anyone could stop him, Arnie whirled away from Tasha and threw his arms around Julie. "I'm sorry," he whispered as he kissed her cheek.

Tasha wrenched him away. "Do that again and I'll string you up next to her. Screw orders. I'll fucking flay the skin off you if you make another move without my say-so."

Arnie hung his head but knew he'd won something. Not much, and it wouldn't last, but he'd defied them in a small way. He still felt Dragonfly's cheek against his lips.

Tasha motioned for Deuce to get the whip. The festivities were about to begin. Arnie braced himself. Before the end, he'd want to kill them. Could he get Tasha's gun and shoot them both? Anger and frustration bubbled up in him as he realized he'd never make it. At home, he used to work out, and even here, he did sit-ups, push-ups, and whatever he could manage in the confines of his cell. But he'd be no match for trained fighters.

Helpless, he looked into Julie's eyes. She gazed back, unflinching, conditioned to endure torture. She'd braced for the impending ordeal, but these psychos would compensate, and he'd be forced to watch. He wished he were back in his cell and felt a surge of guilt. It was his fault she was here; the least he could do was bear witness.

Deuce cracked the whip, cutting into Julie's back. She clenched her teeth and didn't cry out. He swung harder. Still she kept silent.

Arnie broke. "Tell them what they want. They'll get it eventually."

Julie met his gaze and shook her head. "They haven't asked me anything."

Tasha laughed. "Yeah, we're just warming up."

"Deuce," Julie said.

Deuce grunted. "What?"

"My back's itchy. Scratch it for me?"

Arnie screamed. "No! What are you doing?"

Julie laughed, but the whiplash cut it short. A small cry escaped her as blood erupted from her back. Tasha stroked Arnie's chest. "This is turning me on."

Arnie wanted to vomit. "Don't touch me, you psycho."

Tasha blew into his ear. "Relax, cowboy. There's a chance you'll get out of here without a scratch." She gave his chest one last stroke, but removed her hands. Another point for Arnie.

Deuce paused, whip hanging limp in his hand, flushed face dripping with sweat. "Ask the bitch something, Tasha. If she passes out, we'll get nothing."

Tasha snaked her arms around Arnie's waist and squeezed. "Where'd you two meet to fuck?"

Arnie opened his mouth to answer, but Tasha stifled him with her hand. "No. She'll tell me."

"Fuck you," Julie said. "I won't tell you shit."

"You can take a lot, Julie, but Griffen can't. Are you ready to sacrifice him?"

"You can't kill him. The aliens need him."

"The aliens will repair whatever we do. Pull out finger nails, for instance."

Sweat broke on Arnie's neck. He trembled and his knees threatened to buckle.

Tasha said, "See what you've done? He's quaking with fear, and I haven't even started. Shall I hog-tie him and pull a few nails? I thought you preferred real men. This weenie caved as soon as I started interrogating him, and I barely scratched him."

"I'm sorry, Julie," Arnie said, voice breaking. "Tell them. What difference does it make? It was a random place." Unless it wasn't. Arnie tried to remember. Did he pick the place or Julie? Julie did. *Shit.*

What was she hiding? Or rather, *whom* was she hiding? If she were trying to protect someone she valued more than Arnie, they'd torture him. Tasha was out to break Julie even if she mutilated Arnie in the process.

Julie glared at Tasha. "I'll kill you for this."

"You're in no position to make threats. Die under interrogation or survive to be hanged, you're not leaving here alive."

Arnie tried to break out of Tasha's arms. "No!"

"Hold still. Don't make me tell you again. That's how the Agency penalizes traitors."

Arnie's mouth went dry. That was true for all prisoners, himself and Carolyn included. Carolyn had said it before, but he'd refused to believe it. He finally gave up thinking their captors might let them go back to their lives. One day, the aliens would no longer need them, and they'd be executed.

"Enough bullshit. Julie, where'd you two meet? Jog her memory, Deuce."

Deuce brought the whip down on Julie's back again. She gave a low moan, her head flopping forward. In the ensuing silence, she struggled to meet Tasha's gaze, but the effort seemed too great.

"Where did you meet?" Tasha screamed. "Tell me or Griffen loses a nail."

Julie tried to speak, but gagged, and her chin swayed on her chest.

"Lift her head, asshole. You're not supposed to kill her."

"I'm not. You're the one making me hit her," Deuce grumbled.

"A hotel on Yonge Street," Julie croaked. "The Traveller's Den in Thornhill."

Arnie prayed he wouldn't betray the lie. Tasha grabbed his hair and yanked his head back, putting her mouth to his ear. "Is that true?"

Pain brought tears to his eyes. His reply was shaky and weak. "I-I-I ... Y-yes."

"Fuck it. The bitch is lying. Hit her again, Deuce."

Deuce struck again with the whip.

Tasha shoved Arnie towards Deuce. "This fucker's backing her lies. Tie him to the chair. You two will not do this. This'll cost him."

Arnie screamed and struggled as Deuce dragged him to the chair. After they'd bound him, Tasha secured his arm to the table. Deuce reached into the duffel bag. When Arnie saw the pliers, he hollered and thrashed, but Tasha held him fast.

His terror escalated as the pliers got a purchase on the nail of his pinkie finger. Unbearable pain shot like an electric current into his brain. Arnie screamed long and loud, flinging tears and sweat from his face. He blacked out.

CHAPTER 19

They left the boat hidden among bushes on the riverbank. Danny camped amongst the trees, keeping watch over the area. If anyone appeared, he'd text Robert. Michael and Robert left Danny with the promise that Robert wouldn't enter the base though Michael suspected it was a promise they wouldn't be able to keep.

The two men walked for ten hours. Robert carried a backpack loaded with gear, and Michael focused on not collapsing. He carried a small duffel bag over his right shoulder—all he could manage though it frustrated him. They foraged most of the food they ate, and so didn't have to haul too much with them.

Michael was getting careless, his mind wandering, and the pain in his shoulder distracting him. He was grateful for Robert, who'd more than once spotted edible wild food Michael had overlooked.

Sometimes Michael sensed he'd veered off course and corrected. He recognized the path they followed even though he didn't know how he knew it. Most of the time, the alien intelligence from Algonquin guided him, while other times, he thought it was someone else.

Once, he caught a glimpse of Jessica as a light, translucent presence. His heart perceived her, and he hurried ahead so fast Robert almost lost sight of him, calling out for him to slow his pace. Afraid he was hallucinating, Michael stopped to let Robert catch up. The mist that was Jessica slipped away and left his heart aching.

They continued hiking. Up ahead, the trees thinned and patches of sky peeked through the foliage. Michael blundered into a clearing and sensed danger. Behind him, Robert's footsteps stopped.

Michael turned. Robert stood alert, a finger to his lips. Michael nodded. He felt like a deer surrounded by hunters. Silently, they slipped back into the forest.

"What is it?" Michael whispered.

"In the forest," Robert said so low Michael strained to hear it.

A butterfly fluttered across the clearing, the only movement.

He scanned the woods but saw nothing. Birds twittered, and a crow called out. The breeze stirred the leaves, and he caught a whiff of pine and cedar. A woodpecker tapped on a tree. Something rustled in the underbrush, charging towards the glade.

Michael drew his gun, prepared to shoot. A chipmunk darted out of the trees, across the grass, and into the underbrush. Michael laughed.

"That little guy sounded like an elephant." He stepped out of the trees, gun still ready, but relaxed.

"Wait. No," Robert called out.

Michael continued cautiously. When he reached the centre of the clearing, the brush rustled again, and a caribou stepped from the trees. Tall and brown, antlers majestic, it strode towards Michael.

Antlers tilting at Michael, it swung its head and knocked him onto his back. The animal loomed over the man and their gazes locked. It planted a hoofed foot on either side of him and snorted, but didn't appear to want to hurt him.

He glanced at the gun in his hand and holstered it, hoping he wasn't making a mistake. His gaze fell onto the antlers. The beast raised a hoof, let it hover over Michael's chest, and planted it again near his injured shoulder. Abruptly, as if frightened by something, the caribou turned and ran back into the forest.

Michael lay on the ground, staring up at a cloudless patch of sky. How blue and magnificent it looked. Clouds scudded overhead, sailing swiftly on their way.

Robert stepped out of the bushes. "You hurt?" He leaned forward, cutting off Michael's view.

"Just stunned. That was strange."

"That was your power animal."

"What do you mean?"

"An animal sent to give you guidance. Caribou tells you to keep moving, take action."

"Did he have to knock me down to tell me?" Michael regained his feet with Robert's help, while his left shoulder screamed in protest.

"Examine my shoulder? It feels damp, and it's on fire. Is the bandage leaking?"

Robert opened Michael's shirt and inspected the bandage. "Not leaking. It'll be fine until we camp. Okay?"

"Yeah." Michael took a swig of water and weighed the direction to take. No surprise when he realized they'd follow the caribou's path. The two men stepped into the forest and continued their journey.

***

By the time they made camp, they'd left the river and foothills behind. They built no fire and ate what they'd foraged, supplemented with trail mix and jerky.

"I'll take the first watch," Michael said.

"Works for me." Robert climbed into his sleeping bag.

Michael sat wrapped in a blanket, his back against a log. The remaining daylight filtered through the trees. He reached inside his shirt and caught Carolyn's ring in his fist.

"You do that often," Robert said.

Michael met Robert's gaze. "It gives me faith we'll be together again."

"Her spirit's strong. When I held the ring, I got images of her."

"What did you see?"

Robert raised himself on one elbow. "Visions, but they scrolled through too quickly."

"Was it bad?" Michael's voice betrayed concern.

Robert shrugged. "I didn't want to intrude, so I didn't pay attention."

"If I let you hold it, can you tell me if she's okay?"

"Maybe. I can't control the images I receive." Robert held out his hand. "Want me to try?"

"Please." Michael removed the ring from the chain and handed it over.

Robert held it in his left hand and closed his eyes. "You have a deep connection to this woman." He opened his eyes.

Michael shook his head, denying it. "I haven't known her long."

"She carries your child."

Michael sighed. "I'm aware of how it sounds. I met Carolyn right after my wife died. Her husband died around the same time."

"But you were watching her before then, and you were there when her husband died."

Michael noticed Robert was telling, not asking and had a sudden urge to take back the ring.

Might as well go all the way. I need to verify Carolyn's okay. "My agency ordered me to kill John. When I hesitated, my partner did it."

Robert closed his eyes. "You've been together in other lifetimes, acting out the same drama in each lifetime. You fail every time."

Michael's mouth went dry. "What do you mean?"

Robert opened his eyes again. "I saw you—both—in other incarnations. There's a pattern. Others are involved, including the man who holds her captive now. Your partner too. You're with these men, then you meet her, you fall in love, and try to escape with her."

Michael shivered and pulled his blanket tighter. Sensing what Robert would say next, he held his breath. He recalled the dream in which Cornell hanged Carolyn.

Robert continued, "You kill your partner, but the other man gets her back. You try to rescue her, but fail. They kill her, or kill you. Either way, you lose each other, so you come back and do it all over."

"How can I stop this?"

"You'll figure it out. Each life, you bring what you learned from the previous one. Each life has a lesson and you evolve over lifetimes. When you don't resolve something in one life, you continue the lesson in the next."

"I could've died on the river the other day, and it would've ended it in this life."

"You hadn't fulfilled your purpose—which is something different than the lesson you're supposed to learn."

"Who decides that?"

"Some say we decide before we're born."

"What do you believe?"

"Creator decides."

Michael fell silent. What could he say to that? Was his dream a glimpse into a past lifetime? It'd explain why Carolyn felt so familiar to him, why they'd drawn together. "Can you tell me what's happening to her right now?"

Robert closed his eyes again. Fear clouded his face, and his eyes opened. He handed the ring back. "I'm sorry."

Michael scarcely dared breathe. "Where is she?"

Robert looked up at the darkening sky and pointed.

CHAPTER 20

Naked and shivering, Carolyn lay on the operating table. Why was she here less than a month since the last abduction? The aliens didn't even bother erasing her memory anymore, as if keeping Carolyn oblivious no longer mattered. During certain procedures, however, they still anaesthetised her.

Once the aliens brought her here, she spent long periods alone, except for the blond humanoids who came and went. Even they ignored her when she tried to communicate with them. They didn't understand, or they didn't care?

Footsteps approached and Cornell appeared at her side. Carolyn had seen him here during an earlier abduction and assumed he often visited. She wished she could force him to trade places with her. Trying to release her swelling anger, she exhaled, but the tension remained.

"Why am I here?" Maybe she'd at least get answers.

"The aliens verified Valiant's the father. You'll carry the baby to term for them."

Carolyn tried to struggle, but paralysis was total.

"The aliens have been taking your babies for twenty years. Do you really think you were never pregnant since Sam?"

Horror overwhelmed her. "That can't be. I would've known."

"Consider it your contribution to science." Cornell sounded smug. "This'll be an interesting child, considering your psychic powers and that Valiant is part alien." Cornell grinned.

The bastard's enjoying this. He was trying to break her. Tears welled

348

up, and Carolyn held her breath for a moment. "Michael?" she whispered. Invoking him brought a moment of relief, as if he were there.

"Right. When Valiant's mother conceived him, the aliens mixed their DNA with his."

"No one is taking my baby."

Cornell chuckled. "Not your call. It'll be safe, don't worry. They'll raise the kid as one of them."

Carolyn thought of the blond humans she saw on the ship. "It'll never be one of them." She noted Cornell referred to the baby as "it." He didn't know it was a girl. Carolyn calmed herself and focused on getting information while he was in a sharing mood.

"Why would they want John's babies? He was neither psychic nor part alien. Was he?" Now Carolyn doubted everything.

Cornell shook his head. "In your case, the father's identity was mostly irrelevant. The aliens allowed you one pregnancy, to make sure everything functioned. After that, they harvested ova and any growing foetuses. You've had a few alien kids. Most of them were used in experiments. You've had babies with Arnie, and once he even fertilized you in the conventional way."

Carolyn gasped. "That's not true."

"Neither of you remember, but you were both willing enough."

"That's sick. How many people are they abducting for experimentation?"

"Lots. It's unavoidable—the cost of doing business with them."

A wave of fear engulfed her. Cornell admitted this because there was no need to hide it, just as the aliens no longer cared if she remembered the abductions.

"Why tell me this now?"

Cornell leaned down to whisper in her ear. "It's almost over. Your blissful ignorance doesn't matter anymore."

Michael. Part alien. Was that possible? Carolyn supposed so. The aliens were capable of anything. Loss and grief swamped her as she looked back on twenty years. She and John had been so full of hope trying for another child. At first, it'd been a game. She'd tracked the days she was fertile, and they got creative finding time alone while Sam was little.

How many attempts had succeeded? How many babies had the aliens plundered from her womb? The urge to struggle became overwhelming. Carolyn shot Cornell a look of hatred. His hand rested on her shoulder, and she fumed, frustrated she couldn't shake it off.

"We didn't have a say in whom the aliens chose," Cornell said. "They have their own method of selection. Feel good, angel, knowing you helped save some of us. Our species will survive."

"A colony of psychos."

"Sam will be there. I'll keep her safe for you. Soon she'll be an orphan. Sorry." Cornell sounded genuinely regretful.

Carolyn tried to gather saliva in her mouth to spit at him, but her mouth was dry. She grunted with the effort and frustration of struggling against the paralysis. "Get away from me!" she screamed, hoping an alien would intervene if she got too agitated. None came.

Cornell put a hand on her thigh, a gentle touch that sent chills through her body. She remembered her dream, lying on the rack, and what he'd done to her. Heart racing, she pleaded. "Please don't touch me."

"Such a beautiful body." He said it absently, talking to himself more than her. Fingers brushed her skin like feathers. His hand drifted to her belly, ran a finger lightly over a stretch mark, one of the few souvenirs of her first pregnancy. "It doesn't have to happen this way. I can save you." He touched her cheek, cupped her face in his hand.

She wanted to turn away, but couldn't escape his eyes. It became difficult to breathe, and she fought for air.

Cornell stroked her cheek, brushed a wisp of hair from her forehead. "I tried to be good to you, but you wouldn't let me. We could've had a better relationship. Still can. We'll talk when you get back." For a moment, he looked as if he would kiss her. He leaned forward, but then straightened up and walked away.

Carolyn shuddered. After he'd left, she screamed and cried, and there was no stopping her tears now.

CHAPTER 21

Arnie awoke on his stomach, his back still a mess. Eyes closed, he listened. Silence. He tried to orient and realized he was on a cot. They'd returned him to his cell? His throbbing right hand reminded him what had happened.

He shivered with both fear and cold under the thin blanket. A quick inventory found him naked from the waist up. Gauze wrapped his little finger. Tasha had ripped the nail off, but someone had bandaged it.

The Agency taketh away and the Agency giveth. Fucktards. What had they done to Dragonfly? *Julie. Her name is Julie.*

They might have already killed her. Did she tell them what they wanted? He hoped not. He hoped she'd confounded and obfuscated. Arnie wasn't sure what "obfuscate" meant, but he'd heard Carolyn use it once, and it sounded appropriate.

Arnie's mind rambled. Whoever had treated his hand must have drugged him too. It'd be so easy to go back to sleep. Locked up in a cell he had few options and nothing useful to do. He couldn't even help himself let alone Carolyn or Julie.

Worry for his mother consumed him then. She probably still suffered over his "death." According to Carolyn, Valiant and his partner had faked Arnie's death when they'd abducted him. Everyone Arnie knew thought he was dead.

Fury overwhelmed him whenever he pictured his frail mother struggling to cope with a death that hadn't happened. He wished he could make someone pay for it. But he was so tired. Sleep would be a welcome escape.

Arnie rose and went to the cell bars. "Carolyn." No response. "Carolyn?" *Please answer.* "Carolyn." Now Arnie used a normal speaking voice. Stomach knotted, he feared he'd attract attention if a guard was nearby.

"Arnie, I'm here."

Relieved, Arnie sank to the floor and reached out his good hand. Thankfully, Carolyn was on his right, and he always reached out to her with his left hand.

"Here's my hand," Carolyn said, and their fingers met.

Arnie heard sobbing. What had they done to her while they were torturing him? How much shit did the fucking Agency expect them to take? This place was sucking the life out of them. That it led to their execution was just the blood on the bowel movement.

"What happened?" he said.

"They took me again."

No need to specify. Alien bastards.

"Cornell said the aliens verified Michael is the baby's father."

Arnie wanted to pull his hand away but squeezed her hand tighter. She needed him. He needed her.

"Cornell told me something you should know."

"What?" Fear churned in Arnie's gut. Cornell never shared good news.

"He said I've been pregnant many times since Sam and ovulating regularly."

"What's that mean?"

"The aliens have been harvesting my eggs and conceived foetuses. They kept my babies."

"Son of a bitch."

"There's more."

Arnie fought the urge to hit something. What could be worse than that?

"A few of the babies were yours."

Arnie went numb. There was a sound in his head like ocean surf.

"Artificial insemination?" *I have children with Carolyn?*

"Not always artificial." Carolyn fell silent.

Arnie shook his head at what that implied. Naked sex. That was just crazy. Relief washed over him. "I'd remember that. Cornell lied to mess with your head."

"The aliens would've erased that memory along with the others. But maybe we recognize it at an unconscious level. Perhaps that's why we're so close."

"I don't believe it." But he did. With all his heart. "Oh God," he whispered.

To his horror, she said, "There's more."

"What else?" Arnie gritted his teeth.

"The aliens will take this baby when it's born." She sobbed out loud, in great gasps.

Arnie's arm was numb, but his grip tightened on her hand. "Why would they let you carry this baby just to take it?"

"For their own purposes. It doesn't matter how I feel."

"We have to escape."

"If I do, they'll hurt Sam."

"We'll find Sam and rescue her too. Isn't she at Cornell's house? We'll find it and take her away."

"How will we rescue her?"

The despair in her voice chilled him. Usually Carolyn gave warnings or vetoed ideas based on premonitions. Now she'd discarded this idea without checking. He realized she'd been using her intuition less often.

"What do your guides say?" He had to help her recover from whatever hell Cornell had put her through.

"I don't know."

"Ask."

"You don't believe. Why are you saying that?"

"You believe, and you've always asked for help from your guides. What happened?"

"I'm tired. Everything's heavy. I can't meditate. What if the aliens or the Agency disconnected me from my guides?"

"If so, they wouldn't make you do remote viewing."

"Okay. But do me a favour."

"Anything."

"You ask too. We need all the help we can get."

"Okay. I will," Arnie promised. It couldn't hurt.

CHAPTER 22

Danny set the frying pan with the fresh three-pound lake trout on the camp stove. He'd taken a risk coming out of hiding to catch and cook the fish, but it'd be worth it. He sipped a mug of cedar tea while he watched it fry.

How much longer should he wait? It'd been almost twenty hours since his dad had gone off with the stranger who'd ruined their trip. He built a small fire in the fire pan. Michael had told him not to, but the air was cold, and Danny reasoned that whoever had been chasing Michael was long gone. It'd been over two days since they'd found Michael, and they'd seen no one else. Valiant was paranoid.

Danny checked the fish. Trout done, he turned off the stove. He carried the frying pan to the fire using a towel and set down the pan. The fish's flesh flaked away when he picked at it with a fork, and it was delicious.

Something in the sky caught his attention. A helicopter passed soundlessly overhead. Not one of the tour copters that frequented the park, but a military chopper. Should he put out the fire? No. Military was government, and they weren't interested in him. He thought of whoever hunted Michael as the bad guys, whatever that meant.

The bad guys weren't the government—especially not the military. They were the good guys, protecting Canada. Still, Danny felt uneasy, and when the chopper disappeared over the mountains, he was relieved.

He finished the trout and his tea and then cleaned up. As afternoon became evening, the sun still high in the sky, the chopper came around a few more times. After the third pass, Danny extinguished the fire, probably too late. Even though Danny had used dry wood and had stripped the bark to minimize smoke, they would've seen it if they had binoculars or heat sensors.

Danny went to the tent and took out his rifle. Should he text his father about the choppers? Had he and Michael seen them from where they were? Danny checked his cell and found no messages. He'd wait and see. If anyone found him, he'd say he was in the park by himself, wild crafting—what he and his dad had started out doing anyway. He had the picked herbs to prove it.

Tension eased, Danny returned the rifle to the tent and picked up a digital reader. He settled down to read while he waited for his dad to show up or darkness to fall.

***

Althaea Dayton stepped from the helicopter and motioned for Stephenson and Moser to move towards the camp. They'd have to hurry before it dawned on the young man camped nearby that they were coming for him. The helicopter ran silent, the blades making use of stealth technology, but he'd likely seen it circling overhead.

Althaea indicated to Stephenson and Moser to come at the campsite from the other side. She approached the tent and waited for the others to get in position. After five minutes, she stepped into the clearing. All was quiet.

It was past midnight. The man might be asleep, but she couldn't take any chances. If armed and ready, he might panic and fire. Her partners converged from opposite directions, signalling all clear. Althaea peered into the tent.

The man was armed, but not ready. A rifle lay beyond his reach as he sat on his sleeping bag reading by the soft glow of a digital reader. Althaea sliced open the tent with her knife and grabbed the man before he could move. She dragged him outside. He grunted and struggled, his efforts feeble and futile.

When he saw the three agents, his eyes widened, but he showed no fear. He stopped struggling and relaxed.

"Are you military?" he asked.

So that's why he wasn't afraid. The guy assumed he was in

355

secure hands. She continued the charade. "Yes. We're looking for someone."

The young man's eyes grew wider and now she saw fear. Without saying anything, he'd told her he'd seen Michael, and he knew who they were. She couldn't let him live. But first, he'd tell them everything he knew about Valiant and what he was up to in Nahanni.

"Hold him," she said, and her partners complied.

Althaea took a deep breath. This wasn't something she enjoyed, but it had to be done. She crouched before the young man and held her knife to his throat. "Let's talk about Michael Valiant."

CHAPTER 23

Michael checked his gun. The suppressor was on, the weapon cocked and ready. He watched the guards patrolling behind them. He and Robert had managed to slip past the Agency patrols and now huddled between dense brush and the side of a cliff.

The journey had taken them southwest of the South Nahanni River, into the heart of Deadmen Valley. Trees and scrub had given way to grass, the loss of cover forcing them to wait until twilight to cross the open. The rocks and sparse vegetation provided scant protection, and Michael was anxious to get inside the mountain.

The path to the base entrance was here; they just couldn't see it. They'd seen a helicopter come and go from this direction, and Michael's intuitive guide had led to this spot. His left hand drifted up to grab Carolyn's ring. It dawned on him that he didn't compulsively run a hand through his hair anymore—he grabbed at the ring.

Wonder what Torque would think?

Michael closed his eyes, trying to sense where the entrance was. Where was the inner voice that had taken him thousands of miles out of his Goddamn way? *Where are you when I need you, boys? Hello? Can you hear me now?*

Robert stared at Michael, no doubt wondering what they'd do next. Michael wondered the same thing. Suddenly, a desire to walk the perimeter of the cliff washed over him, and he was back in the game. He waited for the guards to pass.

The sentries went by every fifteen minutes. Five minutes after the guards walked past, they'd move. They'd have to be careful not to expose themselves to the cameras. Michael checked his watch. Time.

He motioned for Robert to follow, and they crept forward, moving from cover to cover. Michael kept tabs on the urge to follow the perimeter of the rock wall. After a hundred metres, Michael lost the compulsion to keep walking. He stopped short and Robert almost collided with him.

"Sorry," Michael muttered under his breath. He scanned the area. The entrance had to be near, or he'd want to continue walking. Above them, a trail cut through the rocks. They'd have to climb the almost vertical slope. Michael's shoulder throbbed at the prospect, but he ignored it.

He nudged Robert and pointed upwards. Michael picked his way through the rocks and stones, found footholds where he could, and grasped whatever looked strong enough to hold his weight. They'd have to hurry. If they got past the twenty-five-metre mark, the rocks below would conceal them. Until then, they were like bugs on a windshield. Michael quickened the pace.

The next time he stopped, Michael looked at the ground far below. Perhaps they'd make it after all.

***

Carolyn pulled out of a trance. "That's everything."

Once again, Cornell had her in the lab, notebook and pencil in hand, connected to Michael. He and another man climbed the side of a mountain. She told Cornell, hoping he wouldn't be able to narrow it down to any specific location.

Mountain ranges were huge, and he could be anywhere. But Carolyn sensed Cornell knew more than he let on, and she'd just told him where Michael was.

Whenever she connected to Michael, Carolyn tried to warn him of the Agency pursuit. So far, she didn't think she'd succeeded. There'd been no inner knowing she'd reached him. She begged the angels to protect him, and sent telepathic messages to his guides and angels, asking them to warn Michael.

Carolyn still felt bogged down as if a fog surrounded her and blocked her from reaching out. She'd experienced it the night before when she'd agreed to call on her angels and guides to help her and Arnie escape.

"Try again." Cornell sounded angry, impatient.

The irritation in his voice was a good sign, indicating the clues she'd provided weren't enough. Carolyn tried not to betray her spasm of happiness, but closed her eyes and connected to Michael.

She saw a caribou.

Something in her expression must have changed because Cornell shifted in his chair. "What?" A demand.

"It's probably nothing," Carolyn replied, opening her eyes. It probably *was* nothing. What would that give him?

"I don't care. Tell me."

"I saw a caribou."

"A real caribou?"

"I guess." *No, a figurative one.* She didn't say it aloud, fear censoring everything she said here. Maybe it wasn't real. Then she realized it was Michael's spirit animal guide and remained silent. Let the Agency grunts search for a herd of caribou.

"Try again." Cornell didn't sound irritated this time.

She relaxed, eyes closed, and reconnected to Michael. Two men with guns appeared below him, but were unaware of his presence. This would pinpoint Michael's location, so Carolyn kept her face a blank mask. She needed something less significant, less specific.

"There's a faint trail. I'm losing it. The images are fading. It's gone."

"Draw it."

"I suck at drawing."

"I don't care."

Carolyn opened her eyes and sketched a narrow trail along the edge of a mountain. The fugitives were getting to higher elevations. Scrub brush. Boulders. Rocks. Powdery snow coating everything. She sketched the rough shape of what she saw through Michael's eyes and tossed the finished drawing on the table.

"That's everything."

Cornell picked up the sketch, glanced at it, and pocketed it. "We're done here."

The guards entered, and Carolyn prepared to return to her cell.

***

Cornell rushed back to his office, shouting to Helen to get Althaea on the phone. The phone rang as he reached his desk. "Ally?"

"What's up, Jim? Sounds as if there's news."

"Valiant is climbing the mountain. I'm emailing you a sketch of the trail. No doubt, he's found one of the access routes to the base. Figure out which path he's using and get him. The son of a bitch has been free too long."

"I'll call you when we have him."

Cornell hung up the phone and gave Helen the sketches, instructing her to scan them in and email them to Althaea. He returned to his office, optimistic that by day's end, they'd have Valiant in custody.

He fought an urge to book a flight to the Northwest Territories. Valiant would be transferred here—drugged, so the bastard couldn't escape. Cornell wasn't going to trust anyone to get Valiant here without chains and sedatives. No way would he risk having to do another manhunt.

It'd be a pleasure to tell Valiant they'd give his baby to the aliens. Cornell thought back to when he'd held Valiant captive in Algonquin. He'd told Michael the Agency would brainwash Carolyn, making her believe Valiant was her enemy and Cornell was her lover.

Cornell had been bluffing—what an expensive endeavour that would be. But it might be worth attempting. He'd have to commandeer resources, but no one would question it when he proved how useful Fairchild could be as one of them. Perhaps she'd even pull the trigger on Valiant.

CHAPTER 24

Michael and Robert climbed for hours. The air was chilly, and a thin coating of snow blanketed everything. If the cold became extreme, it'd penetrate the layers Michael wore. He'd lost his winter jacket escaping Althaea, and while Danny had provided turtlenecks and sweaters, Michael had refused to take the young man's parka.

Helicopters came and went. Once, Michael thought he heard Carolyn calling, but attributed it to fatigue. It felt nice to be reminded of her voice even though she sounded alarmed. Michael took it as a sign to be more cautious and slowed their pace. He constantly checked for an ambush or pursuit.

Robert expressed concern that Danny was in danger. Michael tried to reassure him but had his doubts. Worry nagged him whenever he thought about Danny.

They approached another bend in the trail, and Michael raised his gun. So far, they hadn't encountered even a bird, but he didn't trust the silence. He motioned for Robert to halt and peered around the curve.

The trail grew wider here. Wind picked up, blowing through the surrounding scrub brush. The air smelled fresh and clean, and the view was spectacular. Across the tree-covered mountain, in the valley far below, the river sparkled in sunshine.

Michael inhaled, refreshed, and stepped out from behind the shelter of the cliff face. Robert followed. Five metres from the bend, six men and one woman appeared, surrounding Michael and Robert.

"We've been expecting you," Althaea said. "Cornell has been forcing your little 'ho' to track you, Mick." She smiled.

Michael's stomach twisted. Maybe he *had* sensed Carolyn earlier. He didn't react. Althaea stared, licked her lips—a habit. Michael remembered kissing those lips.

"Let Robert go." Michael figured he'd start with the obvious. "This doesn't concern him."

"He's involved more than you know. Daniel is on his way to becoming part of the Nahanni legends. You're going back to Cornell."

Robert took a step towards Althaea, and the agents raised their weapons.

"What do you mean? What happened to Danny?" Robert's voice shook.

"We found him where you left him, though he didn't want to admit he'd seen you, Mick." Althaea looked at Michael as if she wanted everyone to know this was his fault. "We persuaded him to talk, but couldn't let him go, so he's now one of the headless men."

Robert screamed in rage and ran at Althaea.

Michael grabbed him, held him back. "They'll shoot you."

"I don't care."

"You'll join him soon enough," Althaea said. "Bring them."

They handcuffed Michael and Robert, and Althaea led them up the trail. Before long, she dropped back to walk with Michael. "You'll die and it won't be quick. Was she worth it?"

When he didn't reply, Althaea's pretty face clouded over. Michael turned away, scouring the surrounding area, trying to sense Carolyn. If she'd connected with him, perhaps he could hear her voice again. It'd be preferable to listening to Althaea prattle on about the terrible things they'd do to them.

The trail continued though the grade wasn't steep. The group approached an opening in the mountain, like the mouth of a cave, which a moment before hadn't been visible. They stepped into a dim tunnel, lights spaced three metres apart. Robert walked as though in a daze, grief etched on his face. Michael wished he could help Robert and regretted bringing him.

Althaea took Michael's arm as though they were on an afternoon stroll. He tried to shake her off, but she held firm.

"Stop it, or I'll slug you." She said it low, so the others couldn't overhear.

"Try it," Michael replied, not so low.

She grinned at him. "Come on, Mick. I meant something to you once. We were soul mates."

Michael tried to detect mockery but heard none. "You don't know what that means, Ally." The nickname slipped out.

Once, he used to love the familiarity of calling her that. They'd had many intimate dinners together, times when Jess had been far away and out of mind. His heart stabbed with longing for his wife.

Althaea drew closer to Michael. She stuck her gun back in its holster and brought her other hand up to squeeze his arm. "I've missed you."

"You have a funny way of reconnecting."

"How did you expect me to react when you rejected me?"

"I expected you to understand that I love my wife."

"You no longer have a wife. It didn't take you long to get over her death."

Michael fought the urge to push Althaea away. If she thought he was cooperating, he'd find the opening he needed. "I still love Jessica, and the Agency murdered her."

"There's no proof of that."

"I have all the proof I need."

The tunnel forked and two agents split away, leaving four guards. Althaea's group followed the tunnel leading to the left.

After walking for fifteen minutes, they halted at a double row of empty cells. Althaea stopped at the first one and removed Robert's handcuffs. She opened the door and motioned for him to step inside.

Like an automaton, Robert stepped into the cage, and she slammed the door shut behind him. He moved to the single cot in the room and sat, dropping his head in his hands.

Althaea dismissed Robert's guards and tugged on Michael's arm. "Next one's yours."

After Althaea removed the cuffs, Michael entered the cell, Althaea once again clinging to his arm.

"Wait outside," she told the two remaining guards. Althaea released Michael's arm and motioned him to sit.

"I'll stand, thanks."

"I can force you."

Michael sat.

"The abductions are ending," she said.

"Why tell me?"

"I want to see your face when I tell you that the bitch you impregnated is scheduled to be terminated as soon as the baby is born. The others will be executed—the ones the aliens don't keep permanently. They might keep your girlfriend, and you'll never see her again."

Michael kept his face blank. "Old news. If you've nothing else to offer, leave."

"No reaction? I guess she meant little to you. That makes me feel better. You just wanted to fuck her. Did you rape her?"

"I love her."

She grimaced. "You can't. After your wife, there's me."

"Althaea, what do you expect to happen here? There's nothing between us. We had something. *Had.* It's long gone. You didn't respect me or my marriage. Whatever I felt for you died when you reacted like a crazy, jealous stalker."

Althaea flinched. Michael stood. She took a step backwards. *Good.*

"Sit, Mick."

Michael made a move as though to comply, but lunged for her gun. Althaea had braced herself and beat him to it. She snatched the gun from its holster and hit Michael on the side of the head with it. Dazed, he grasped her wrist and twisted her hand, but the gun remained firm in her grasp. When the two guards pulled him off her, Michael knew he'd failed.

Althaea snarled. "Hold him for me."

They braced Michael between them. She stared into his eyes. "I'll enjoy what Cornell does to you, but frankly, I can't wait that long."

Fluid as a dancer when she moved, Althaea swung her fist and smashed it into his face. Michael's nose spurted blood, and she backed up. She wasn't done. Her fist connected with his stomach, and he'd have doubled over if the guards hadn't been holding him. Althaea used him as her punching bag, avoiding blows that would knock him unconscious.

His breathing became ragged and laboured. By tomorrow, he'd have two black eyes. When she'd had enough, Althaea wound up for the last strike. She raised the gun and hit Michael in the head. At last, everything went dark.

CHAPTER 25

"We have him."

The words, coming at him over his speakerphone and said by Althaea Dayton, energized Cornell. It gave him the infusion of hope he'd needed ever since Valiant had escaped from the Algonquin base. Cornell wished Althaea were here so he could hug her.

"Good work, Ally. Are plans underway to get Valiant here ASAP?"

"Yes, sir. I'll deliver him myself. What do you want us to do with Robert Holden?"

"Keep him locked up. The aliens need him for a while. When they're through with him, terminate him."

"Yes, sir."

"We'll celebrate when you get here." He hung up.

Things were looking positive. If only he could get Carolyn Fairchild on side. Despite her desire to help Valiant escape, she'd been invaluable in helping the Agency locate and capture him. If Cornell could get her on board with what they were doing, she'd be more useful. He called Helen again.

"I want to take Fairchild underground with us. Once the baby's born, we'll put her through the training programme. But I want nothing to interfere with the baby's development. Schedule it for two months after the baby's due date."

"Yes, sir."

He disconnected. Yes, that'd work out well. They'd manipulate her mind, and Carolyn would view him as a benefactor—perhaps more—and Valiant as an enemy. Cornell recalled her beautiful, naked body and felt himself grow hard.

***

When Michael regained consciousness, every part of his body throbbed, his head most of all. He sat, but it made him woozy. To control the dizziness and nausea, he closed his eyes. He probably had a concussion and would have to force himself to stay awake.

An idea formed. He waited a few minutes, listening for guards, and then called out to Robert. A cot creaked.

"Michael? How badly are you hurt?"

"I'll manage. You okay?"

"We never should have left Danny alone."

"I'm sorry. We should have sent him back to town."

"I've connected with him in spirit."

"Did it help you?"

"Yes." Robert lowered his voice. "Danny explained what you need done."

"That makes things easier."

Michael kept Robert chatting for another fifteen minutes, mostly about family. Halfway through a statement he was making, Michael dropped to the floor and shook as though convulsing, eyes rolling back in his head. Robert screamed for the guards.

At the sound of footsteps, Michael feigned unconsciousness. Robert shouted to the guards that Michael was in trouble. The cell door rattled and clanged. Eyes shut, body limp, and breath deep and slow. He sensed the guards nearby. Someone checked Michael's pulse with a finger at the throat. He itched to leap up, but forced himself to lie still.

"Pulse is fine," the guard said. "Should we take him to the infirmary?"

"No. Just put him on the cot. It'll be safer to bring the doc here. Grab him. I'll cover you in case he's faking."

The guard's hands slid under Michael's armpits and dragged him along the floor. The scenario he wanted to play out scrolled through his mind, and he estimated the other guard's location by his breathing.

Now.

He leapt up, turned, and grabbed the guard holding him. Michael shoved the guard towards the wall. The guard holding the gun tried to get a clear shot and failed when his partner slammed him into the wall. A fight for the gun had the three men grabbing and struggling. The gun fired, and one guard dropped to the floor.

The remaining guard jumped on Michael, and they struggled for control of the weapon. A wave of dizziness hit Michael, but he held on, though his eyes blurred. Time was running out. Any moment, Althaea or more guards would appear. Michael dug down deep and mustered a burst of energy. He punched his opponent in the gut, shoved a knee between them, and wrested the gun from the guard's hands.

He hit the guard on the side of the face, making him pitch backwards. Michael fired, hitting the guard in the chest and then fired again, this time hitting the face. It was over.

"Michael?"

"Wait, Robert." Michael snatched the keys and another gun from a guard. He hurried to Robert's cell, handed him a weapon. As Michael struggled to free Robert, the cellblock door crashed open.

"Company," Michael said. "Get ready."

Two guards appeared. Michael shot one guard and pushed Robert back into the cell as the other guard fired her weapon. Michael dropped to the ground, returning fire, and the woman fell. But she wasn't out. Her gun aimed at Michael, her gaze locked on his, finger poised to squeeze the trigger. Robert's weapon discharged first. The guard slumped to the ground and didn't move.

"Thanks. You saved my life." Michael jumped up. The guard's lifeless eyes stared up at him.

"This way." Without waiting to see if Robert followed, Michael ran down the corridor.

The route took them past the guardroom. Michael motioned for Robert to get down and crouched by the open door.

"You wait here. Boyd, come with me." Althaea.

Michael heard the sound of guns drawing from holsters. He snatched the weapon from Althaea as she stepped out the door. Her body a human shield, he shot Boyd in the head. Robert stepped into the breach and fired at the remaining guard. He missed and had to jump back as the man raised his gun and fired.

The fight lasted five minutes. Michael coldcocked Althaea and focused on putting the last guard down. When it was done, he picked Althaea up and slung her over his shoulder. "She'll help me get into where I need to go," he said, in answer to Robert's puzzled look.

They continued down the corridor, but still hadn't found the room Michael was looking for when Althaea stirred. He set her down, handcuffing her with her own cuffs before she was fully awake.

Her eyes opened, focused, and then widened in shock. She struggled to back away, but he grabbed her arm and hauled her to her feet. "You're coming along for the ride, Althaea."

"You won't escape."

"I'm not trying to." He gave her a shove, and she stumbled forward. "Walk. Follow the corridor. No turns."

"Whatever you've got planned won't work. They'll find the bodies and come after you."

He ignored her. Instead, he said, "You know, I always wondered why aliens would need us—the Agency, I mean, not the people they abduct—that one's obvious. You know what I figured out?"

"What?" She sounded genuinely curious.

"They physically can't fight and need soldiers. They're incapable of doing their own dirty work."

She remained silent, lips pressed together, eyes narrowed. He'd nailed it.

They continued to walk, Michael leading the way. Somewhere, the benevolent alien he'd met in Algonquin guided him. Althaea stopped short, and fear flashed across her face. "Where are we going?"

"If you recognize the route, you know the answer."

"How can you possibly know the way?"

"I don't."

"You can't do this. You'll blow us up."

"Michael?" Robert sounded concerned.

"Trust me, Robert. This isn't a suicide mission. Carolyn's waiting for me, and I intend to get to her."

Althaea laughed. "You'll fail and we'll die."

"Move it." Michael quickened the pace and pushed Althaea ahead. He pressed the gun to her back, making sure she could feel it. The closer they got to Michael's target, the greater grew his sense of urgency. They were almost running by the time they reached the door he wanted. When they stood before it, he said, "Open it" and pushed Althaea to the keypad.

"I don't have access."

"Bullshit. Quit stalling, or I'll blow your head off and get in anyway."

She punched the code into the keypad and pressed her thumb to the scanner. The door slid open.

They entered a rocky chamber, the door whisking shut behind them. Carved from the bowels of the mountain, it was a rough, cold cavern. Water sweated on the walls and glowing crystals carpeted the floor.

A low henge of stones in the shape of a Vesica Piscis—two intersecting circles, the centre of one circle hitting the perimeter of the other—lay before them. A large crystal stood within the intersection. Michael didn't recognize the composition. The crystal wasn't anything formed of this earth.

Bubbles of what looked like acrylic hung from the ceiling, suspended by thick tubes. Something floated in a clear liquid inside them. Horrified, Michael realized each bubble held a foetus in it, all at varying stages of development.

"Jesus." Had they taken babies from Carolyn and brought them here? He shivered and looked away, the whole idea unbearable.

"Mick, why are you here?" Althaea sounded terrified.

Terror surged through Michael as well, but he brushed it aside. This was Carolyn's only hope. "Cover her. If she moves, shoot her. Think you can do that?" Michael said, without looking at Robert.

"Yes," Robert replied, grief and anger in that one word.

Michael believed him. "I'm breaking the hold these bastards have on all abductees. If anyone else shows up and tries to interfere, shoot them."

He made his way to the edge of the Vesica Piscis while Robert led Althaea away from the door. Michael had a sudden urge to walk the sacred symbol before he entered it. He began at the nearest intersecting point, walked clockwise around first one circle, then counter clockwise around the other. He repeated the walk around the circles again, completing seven laps in total.

Michael stepped into the centre and placed his hands on the crystal.

CHAPTER 26

Althaea watched in horrified fascination while Michael walked the Vesica Piscis and ran his hands over the crystal. He then sat, lotus position, eyes closed. The door slid open. Three guards ran into the room, guns raised.

Robert dragged Althaea in front of him. Afraid the guards would damage the crystals and the incubators if they fired, she held up her hands, halting them. They paused, uncertain.

"Don't shoot. You're too far away."

"Come any closer and I'll kill her," Robert said.

Althaea opened her mouth to tell the guards to approach, let Holden shoot her if he wanted, when a vibration filled the room. It amplified, and humming filled her ears. She didn't recognize a specific chord—she knew nothing about music—but the sound was beautiful. Tears streamed down her face. She looked at the guards, and they were also crying.

Robert released her, but she didn't move. She sensed Robert on the ground behind her and turned to him. He'd dropped her gun and writhed, screams tearing from his throat. His eyes rolled back in his head, and his back arched. Blood gushed from his nose— more than she thought possible.

When the blood from Robert's nose slowed to a trickle, a lump crawled from his left nostril. The blob of goo slithered down his face, leaving a gory trail of blood, snot, and bits of flesh.

One of the guards also ejected the thing from his nasal cavity. So even some of the Agency's own were abductees. But not her.

Althaea looked at Michael, who continued to sit, meditating. Not Michael either.

The sound eased. She had to act before he snapped out of his trance. Robert lay unconscious. He wouldn't be any trouble.

She shouted to the two guards, who stood dazed by the door. "Get these fucking cuffs off me."

***

Cornell hadn't called Carolyn to the lab in over a day. Did that mean the Agency had caught Michael? A constant knot of worry twisted her gut.

She and Arnie tried to figure a way out, but nothing came to mind. Neither Carolyn nor Arnie was a fighter, and every plan they came up with involved over-powering the guards and grabbing their guns. They'd never succeed.

Carolyn spent most of her time lying on the cot in her cell, alternating between tears and numbness. Despair blanketed her. She called on her angels and guides but nothing happened. It was difficult to trust they were helping without evidence of it, and her faith faltered.

Part of Carolyn felt relieved when she resigned herself to captivity. If the decision to leave was out of her hands, then it wasn't her fault if the aliens took her baby. But Sam would be safe.

Guilt overtook her then. She couldn't let this baby be sacrificed to the aliens to protect Sam, whose safety wasn't exactly guaranteed. Whatever Cornell told her should be considered a lie. He'd tell her whatever he needed to so she'd cooperate.

Carolyn made a move to stand and get water from the sink when she felt a dull ache in her head. The pain increased, became unbearable. She moaned, cried, and screamed. In the next cell, Arnie also screamed. The whole cellblock became a symphony of agony as the other inmates joined in.

Her head. Carolyn pressed her hands to her head.

Stop it. Stop it. I can't take it. She screamed, screamed, screamed, but it wouldn't end. Carolyn's back arched, and she thrashed on the cot, writhing in agony. The pain burned, ripped her apart.

Red fluid spewed from her face, and her mind registered that blood flowed from her nose. Something crawled out of her nostril and slid along her face. The last thing Carolyn heard before she fainted was the wet smack the fleshy blob made when it hit the floor.

***

When Carolyn came to, she lay strapped to a bed in the infirmary. No one else was in the room. She looked for a call button, but didn't see one.

"Hello?" Surely, someone was monitoring her.

The door opened and a hook-nosed man with a scar on his cheek entered the room. He wore scrubs, so Carolyn assumed he was a nurse.

"What happened?" But she already knew. She'd lost her tracking device. The aliens couldn't home in on her anymore—unless they captured her again and shoved another tracker up her nose. Carolyn blanched when she realized it'd been a living creature.

The nurse checked the monitor hooked up to her.

"Is my baby okay?"

He glanced at her. "The baby's fine."

"Why am I the only one here? Are the others okay?"

"Yes." The nurse pressed a button and two guards entered. "Doc says she can go back to her cell." He turned and left the room.

The guards—one of them was Deuce, and he walked much better—removed her restraints. "Get up," Deuce ordered.

Back in her cell, guards gone, she talked to Arnie, who made it clear he was more determined than ever to escape. Certain that Michael had done this, Carolyn wanted to scream the news out to the other abductees, but kept it to herself. No doubt, the others had figured out they were no longer traceable—they just wouldn't know who'd liberated them.

Maybe Michael would come for her now. Perhaps he'd get here before the baby's birth and help them escape. If anyone could do it, Michael could. Carolyn said nothing to Arnie—she wouldn't say anything to anyone. She didn't want to risk tipping off Cornell or anyone else in the Agency.

Where was Michael now? Had he escaped? Carolyn lay on her cot, eyes closed, trying to connect to him. She breathed deeply, trying to relax. Impressions came to her in dribbles. She saw large crystals in a cavern. Shapes. Something about a fish? Everything was too vague. Large stones. Intersecting circles.

Carolyn experienced a moment of frustration and breathed through it. In a clear flash, she saw Michael place his hands on a large crystal, and she knew the end had come.

CHAPTER 27

Grabbing the gun from the ground, Althaea stepped over the still unconscious Robert. She'd almost reached the interlocking circles when Michael's eyes opened. She froze. Radiant and beautiful, he stung her eyes, and she forgot what she was doing.

She forced her gaze away and searched for the guards. One lay on the floor, unconscious. Another stood transfixed. The last one, still holding the cuffs he'd removed from Althaea's wrists, hunched next to Robert, eyes glazed.

The gun. She looked at the gun in her hand. So archaic—a primitive weapon for a primitive people. The thought surprised her, the source unknown. Never mind. It would do the job.

She closed her eyes and took three deep breaths. When Althaea opened her eyes again, she fixed her gaze on the floor and strode towards Michael. Slow and steady.

A sunny day's stroll in the park.

One step at a time, she drew closer to the target, forcing her mind away from what she intended to do. Michael moved behind the stone on which the giant crystal sat. Still she kept her head tilted towards the floor.

The closer she got to the circles, the greater was the energy. It was thick, like walking through water. The energy opened for her and snapped shut behind her when she stepped into the circles.

A glance at Michael showed him glowing, filled with light. His arms embraced the crystal. Beams of light linked the crystal to the stones, to the crystals, to any living beings. A vortex of energy fed her knowledge of what he was doing.

She lunged forward—as much as she could, considering the liquid feel of the surrounding energy—and fought her way to Michael. When she reached his side, Althaea dropped her gun, and tried to push him away from the crystal.

"Stop!" Although she screamed, her voice came out muffled.

Eyes gleaming, Michael held firm, either ignoring Althaea or unable to hear her. Wind whipped around them in shrieking gusts. The cavern became translucent. Red light glowed outside their circle. One of the guards dropped to his knees and clasped his palms together. Was he *praying?*

The ground shook. Part of the ceiling caved in, burying the unconscious guard and the one who'd been praying.

Althaea put her arms around Michael's waist, hands clasped across his abdomen, feet braced. She pulled. The man was a rock. Desperate now, she squeezed herself between Michael and the stone, then pushed against him as hard as she could. She couldn't fucking do it. She screamed at him, pounded on him.

The floor rocked. Althaea watched, mouth hanging open, as her gun slid past them.

The gun. She dropped to her knees and reached for it, but it slipped from her grasp. She pounced and grabbed it. Legs shaking, she stood and faced Michael.

Fuck you, Mick. I don't want to shoot you.

Althaea raised her hand to hit Michael on the head when the floor shifted again. She lost her footing, crashing into him. A jolt went through her, and she screamed, this time in agony. The room dimmed.

No. Can't pass out.

Michael shoved the crystal off the stone, and it crashed to the ground, shattering. Like dominoes falling, the rest of the crystals in the room split and cracked. The incubators shattered, spraying their contents everywhere. Something dripped down her face, soaking her hair. Althaea brushed it with her hand. Amniotic fluid. She gagged, trying not to think of what might be stuck in her hair.

She braced herself against Michael, pulled her arm back, and clocked him. He dropped, yanking her on top of him when he fell. She lay quiet, his warm body under hers. God how she'd missed him. She checked his pulse. It was strong.

Althaea looked around. She'd failed.

CHAPTER 28

Cornell hung up his phone. Something had happened at all the alien bases, but the Nahanni base was the epicentre. Near as he could tell, based on the garbled reports flooding in from around the world, the aliens and their ships were gone.

Valiant. It had to be. He called Helen and told her to have Carolyn Fairchild escorted to the lab. He had to sort this out. Without the alien technology, Earth would never be repaired. They'd be stuck underground forever, and the facilities weren't designed to last that long—two or three generations, maybe, but not indefinitely.

Next, Cornell called his wife. "Pack up, Ginny. We're heading underground."

"What happened, Jim?"

"Something no one expected. I'm mobilizing everyone. We need to evacuate before everything goes to hell."

"What about Sam?"

"Sam's coming with us. Trust me. Okay?"

"Yes." Ginny sounded reluctant.

Cornell couldn't waste time explaining it again. They'd have a long talk when they were safe underground. Sam had to trust them both. If Ginny screwed this up with her petty jealousy, he'd never forgive her.

"I have to go. Tell me you'll watch over Sam. We can't lose her, or I'm screwed—we're all screwed. Understand?"

"Yes." Ginny's tone was now resigned.

"I'll call you later." He disconnected.

One last call to make. He contacted Helen.

"Send a memo out to the Agency heads. Tell them it's time to go underground. They must do a thorough clean up before heading out. No non-Agency personnel are to remain."

"Yes, sir."

Call ended, he rose from his desk. Time to chat with Carolyn. She'd be the exception to his non-Agency personnel rule. They needed her special abilities underground, but the others would be eliminated. At least he'd spare them the coming hell.

***

"You know what happened." Cornell leaned towards Carolyn, who sat in the recliner in the lab. She'd tried to deny it, but he refused to believe her.

"What did Valiant do?" He asked.

Carolyn closed her eyes though she didn't bother to connect. She opened her eyes. "Michael's out of reach."

Cornell's face turned red, and he frowned. "What happened?" he asked through gritted teeth

Carolyn sighed. "I don't know. Why won't you believe me? I saw strange images—crystals, stones, fish shapes. Weird stuff. Michael was there. Then he wasn't." Carolyn refused to say Michael wasn't dead. She wouldn't give Cornell that.

An energy field surrounded Michael, but she wouldn't tell Cornell. The truth was, she couldn't connect to Michael.

The lights flickered. They'd flickered periodically for at least the last hour, Cornell growing increasingly agitated. When Carolyn had told him she wasn't getting anything, he'd left the room for a while. She'd feared at first he'd forgotten her, then she'd hoped he had. But he'd returned and now sat haranguing her.

His chair crashed to the floor when he abruptly stood. Carolyn recoiled as he rushed around the table and yanked her from the chair. "Let's go."

Why wasn't he calling the guards to come and get her?

Cornell pulled out his gun and pointed it at her. "Move." He motioned towards the door.

She went.

"You don't have to do that." It reminded her of Michael. She'd said that to Michael when he'd kidnaped her. She tried to clear her head. Best not to think about Michael now.

Carolyn stepped out into the observation area where a guard waited. He looked young—barely older than Sam. His red and freckled face looked innocent. But he was an agent, so Carolyn knew that was deceptive. The young man would be as cold and hard as the others.

"Take her to my office and keep her there until everyone else has evacuated. If anyone but me tries to get in, shoot to kill. You have your cell?"

"Yes, sir."

Carolyn's mouth went dry.

He wants to take me underground with him.

The thought sent shivers down her spine. What about Arnie? Carolyn was afraid to ask, afraid to remind Cornell of Arnie. Instinct told her to stay quiet, so she did.

Without sparing her another glance, Cornell left.

The guard grabbed Carolyn by the arm and walked her out the door.

When they entered the reception area of Cornell's office, Carolyn noted Helen wasn't there, her belongings gone. The guard released Carolyn's arm and ushered her into the office. He opened the door, scanned the room, and waved her in. Carolyn entered, the guard right behind her.

"Sit." He didn't sound mean, just brusque.

She took a seat on the couch. The guard shut the door and joined her. How long would they have to wait here? Carolyn considered asking him, but feared he'd hit her. At least he'd holstered his gun.

The silence was creepy. Beside her, the guard shifted and pulled out a cell phone. She watched while he flipped through some images. Suddenly she felt sick, and it wasn't morning sickness this time. Something was wrong.

Oh, God. They're killing everyone. Without thinking, Carolyn jumped up.

The guard leapt to his feet and forced her back onto the couch. "What do you think you're doing?"

"They're killing the prisoners. Why?" Tears rolled down her face. *Arnie. Oh, Arnie. No.* Carolyn shook, sobs wracking her body.

He loomed over her, his face impassive. "Don't move. If you

get up again, I'll hit you."

Carolyn put her head in her hands and fell into grief.

The lights went out.

***

When the lights flickered, Arnie had the first hint that something big was happening. Tasha and Deuce ran into the cellblock amidst shouting and clanking doors.

"You do one side, I'll do the other." Tasha's voice held panic. "Don't open the doors. Just do it. We've got to go."

Arnie had never heard her sound like that, and it chilled him. Then the meaning of the words sank in, and his stomach knotted. His fears were confirmed when the begging, screaming, and shooting started.

Carolyn wasn't in her cell. What would happen to Carolyn? Did Cornell take her out to spare her this last indignity? Was he keeping her for his own uses? Arnie wished he'd had the chance to say goodbye.

Moments dwindled as Tasha and Deuce worked their way through the rows of cells, and Arnie's turn loomed. He decided not to beg. He'd done enough begging, and it hadn't helped him. These people were psychotic. At least he'd be free.

He lay on his cot, eyes closed. He'd never believed in God or the angels Carolyn always turned to, but a little superstition couldn't hurt. Arnie asked any angels around to help him through this.

Sounds of death grew louder. He sensed Tasha's presence and waited for the bullet to hit him. A sudden urge to put the pillow over his face came over him, and he covered his head.

"Move the pillow, Arnie."

He slid the pillow off his face, but kept his head concealed from her view.

"Very funny, asshole. Remove it."

"Not if you begged me, Tasha."

"I don't have time for this shit. You'll suffer for this."

He heard her carry on the shooting rampage down the row of cells. He'd received a stay of execution, but she'd be back. Arnie closed his eyes and prayed that when she returned, he would have the nerve to fight.

Ten minutes later, he heard the rattle of keys and clink of the cell door as she entered. Everything after that became a haze of anger, instinct, and adrenaline. Tasha snatched the pillow from his face, and Arnie grabbed for the gun. She swore when he pulled her on top of him. Her knee thudded into his thigh, narrowly missing his groin.

He arched his back, trying to escape the pain from her pressing him into the cot. The gun fired, a bullet ricocheting off the wall. They both grunted and struggled. She was stronger. His hand gave, the gun pointing at his face.

Her thighs pressed into him and she loomed above him. In a burst of strength fuelled by terror, he twisted her wrist as she squeezed the trigger, and the bullet hit the wall next to the cot. Arnie felt the ping in his side when the bullet hit him.

A scream tore from his throat. "Fuck you."

He twisted the gun again. This time it pointed at her face, and his finger rested on the trigger. "Fuck you."

Her face blew apart, and he thrust her away, her body slamming against the wall. "Fuck you." He bellowed it again and again, punctuating each curse with a pull of the trigger. When the anger and terror receded, and the gun clicked uselessly, he dropped it to the floor.

The cries of the other prisoners had dwindled into silence. Blood trickled down Arnie's side, but he remained immobile, standing and staring at Tasha's body. He shook himself and focused on taking deep breaths. The lights continued to flicker.

He hoped Carolyn still lived, but didn't expect Julie did. They'd probably killed her days ago. Was it days ago he'd last seen Julie? He didn't know. Time had no meaning here.

Silence became his world. Too tired and nauseated to walk, he sank to the cot. How long before he bled to death? The lights flickered and died. Arnie clutched the gun and closed his eyes.

***

Julie Helliwell was not dead, but she was close to it. Deuce and Tasha had tortured her, wrung what information they could from her, and thrown her into a cell. She'd spent most of her time since then surviving minute by minute, aware it'd end with her execution.

When the gunshots, screams, and pleading reached Julie's ears, she knew something had gone wrong. Instead of a formal execution, they likely planned to shoot her with the abductees.

Julie smiled. Finally, she'd caught a break.

She'd have to act fast, and with her broken ribs and toes, and her missing fingernails, "acting fast" was a relative term. She steeled herself, ignored the agony, and stood. She attempted to simulate a body on the cot using her blanket and pillow and went to the cell bars.

With luck, whomever they'd assigned to her little corner of hell wouldn't expect her to be ready and waiting. She'd be last, which was a shame. If she succeeded, she could save others, perhaps even Arnie.

Julie squashed herself into the wall and waited.

Before long, Deuce arrived. He swept to the cell door, focused on the cot where he expected her to be. In one fluid motion, Julie reached through the bars, twisted the pistol from Deuce's hands, grabbed him by the shirt, and shot him in his surprised face.

She gritted her teeth against the searing pain and yanked Deuce's body to the cell. Blood sprayed from Julie's hands when the makeshift bandages slid off her fingers, exposing raw, meaty fingertips. She focused on the hallway. Tasha would come soon.

Julie swiped the keys from Deuce, unlocked her door, and dragged him into the cell. Sweat poured from her body, dripped from her forehead into her eyes. She hauled Deuce's body to her cot.

She set the guard down for a moment, dizzy. When the vertigo passed, she ripped the blanket off her bed. The pillow fell onto the floor, but she ignored it. She hauled Deuce onto the cot and draped the blanket over him. The cell looked like a Roman arena after a gladiator-lion fight, most of it her blood, but at least it looked as if Deuce had done his job.

Julie drew a raspy breath, returned to the cell door, and closed it. She listened. Where was Tasha? The silence continued for so long, Julie suspected she was alone in the cell block. She left the cell silently. Nothing moved along the corridor. Tasha was gone? Or she was hiding, ready to ambush. Only one way to find out. Julie hugged the wall and crept along, one cell at a time.

CHAPTER 29

After the lights had died and the shattering had ceased, Michael came back to consciousness from a warm and cozy place. He thought it was a dream. No images, only floating in peace and darkness. He awoke, however, to Althaea slapping his face.

Michael sat and slapped her back, then instantly regretted it—not hitting her—that had been self-defence, but the sudden move. He rolled over, pressed his hot face to the cool floor, and willed the room to stop spinning.

"Why'd you hit me?" Althaea asked.

"Why were *you* hitting *me*?"

"To wake you."

"I'm awake." Michael remembered everything and jumped to his feet—another regrettable move. Bile rose in his throat and he couldn't stop it. Michael fell to his knees and vomited. "You gave me a concussion."

"Get over it. You've just killed us."

Michael ignored her. "Robert?"

"I'm here." Robert's voice seemed to come from a distance.

The room spun and Michael sat. He second-guessed the move and lay on his back, Althaea standing over him.

"This is all your fault," she said.

"Really? I had to stop you maniacs."

Robert moved into Michael's line of sight and looked at him. "What happened?"

"He phased the aliens and their ships off of Earth," Althaea said.

"I don't understand," Robert replied.

The guard joined them, looking puzzled and confused. Michael figured he was trying to decide whether to draw his gun or hang out and chat. Lying in this huddle of people turned Michael's stomach again and made him claustrophobic.

"Back up or I'll puke. Althaea, explain what happened."

"Mick phased the aliens and their ships back to their world, then destroyed the portal. That'll start a chain reaction of destruction here. Parts of our technology depended on the energy supplied by the alien crystals set up around the world." Althaea turned to Michael. "It'll look like Pompeii out there soon."

"How?" asked Robert.

"The main portal was here. It makes use of zero point energy, combining with the energy of the crystal in the Vesica Piscis." Althaea turned to Michael. "How did you know what to do?"

"The aliens helped me."

Althaea stood, hands fisted on hips, accusing. "That's insane. Why would they help you? Back in their world, they're as good as dead. They need to be here to survive."

"Perhaps the ones that helped me didn't like sacrificing humans to save themselves. Some of them have a conscience." Michael rubbed his head. They'd told him what to do, but not what would happen when he succeeded. Head aching, mouth dry, he turned his attention to immediate concerns. "Does anyone have water?"

"I should shoot you instead," Althaea said. But she pointed to the guard and asked him to give Michael a swig of water from the canteen on his belt. The water settled Michael's stomach, and he risked sitting, but put his head in his hands when the world threatened to spin again.

As the fog in his brain cleared, he said, "The aliens were experimenting on humans, my family included. They stole foetuses from pregnant women and ova from fertile women. It had to stop."

"They'd have reconstructed the Earth. It'll never recover now, and you've triggered the Aurora machines. That'll decimate whatever remained. Congratulations. You're the man who unleashed Armageddon, and you knew that when you did it," Althaea replied.

"You think they'd rebuild the world for us? Cornell thinks he can rule over the new world, but he's deluded. And I didn't realize sending them back to their world would trigger the Aurora machines." He'd expected the aliens to return to their world, understood their sacrifice, and expected upheaval at this end. But he hadn't realized until the moment he'd done it the extent of the damage and systems failures.

Yet this was what he'd been sent back from death to accomplish. The knowledge of it came in a burst, although he didn't remember why he'd had to do it. He turned to Althaea. "You know a lot too."

She looked puzzled. "I don't know how."

It hit him. "You're like me." He stood and approached her.

She backed away, and the guard raised his gun.

"Relax, fella." Michael waved a hand, the gesture placating. "Althaea, I won't hurt you." In fact, Michael didn't want to do what he felt compelled to do, but that wouldn't be the first time today.

She stood, rigid, and he held her face between his palms. When they drew close together, she closed her eyes, as though waiting for his kiss. His forehead touched hers, and images flowed into him.

He viewed Althaea's past. The traumas: her family's friend molesting her when she was five; her parents' denial; her angry adolescence; the drug overdose; then the self-mutilations and eating disorder at seventeen; the physical altercations—she became a violent, uncontrollable whirling dervish, in prison by the age of nineteen.

The Agency approached her during her incarceration, and she went to them gladly. Michael sensed something beneath the images pouring into his mind—a sense of corruption. But when he tried to focus on what it was, pain pierced his skull and his mind retreated.

The images continued to flow, and Michael saw Althaea's life at the Agency. Focused on work, she kept most men at arm's length, except for Michael. She let him in, and the decision ended up hurting them both. He experienced déjà vu as he relived the time they'd spent together. Her heart broke when he rejected her, and she expressed her anger inappropriately, as always. It drove him further away.

Michael pushed deeper, to her origins. He'd been right when he said she was like him. The aliens had tampered with the Althaea foetus. They spliced in alien DNA as they had with him. She hadn't

384

fully activated yet, but her psi abilities were awakening. She knew things intuitively, especially when they pertained to the aliens and their world.

He felt her trying to pull information from his own mind and blocked her.

Althaea pulled away and slapped him across the face. "You invade my mind but won't let me see yours?" Her voice shrilled with agony.

Horrified, Michael realized he'd violated her. Without thinking, he tried to take her in his arms, but Althaea pushed him away.

"I'm sorry. I wasn't in control of it," Michael said.

Her eyes watered. "That was mind rape. Fuck you."

"I'm sorry. I didn't realize until you intruded in my head." The sense that something was wrong in Althaea's mind lingered. Unable to understand it, he let it go.

She looked as if she'd retort, but the guard who'd given Michael the water spoke. "What happens now?"

"I find Carolyn," Michael replied, his gaze meeting Althaea's.

"I can't let you do that, Mick. Cornell wants you." Althaea nodded at the guard, and he raised his gun.

"Do you plan to walk to Peterborough from Nahanni, Althaea?" Michael said.

"Were *you* planning to walk to Peterborough?"

"If necessary."

"There's your answer. But we won't have to walk. The choppers will work as long as the storms hold off. They'll be evacuating all the compounds now, and we need to get to the underground community." Althaea turned to Robert. "I'm sorry."

Michael moved over to Robert. "Let him go. What's he going to do? Robert will be lucky to survive out here, but he deserves the chance to try."

Althaea shook her head. "You know the drill, Mick."

"Let him go, Ally." This time, he deliberately used the nickname. "I'll allow you to take me in."

"I won't bargain. I'm taking you in."

"Have it your way." Michael lunged at her.

The guard raised his gun, but Robert jumped on him, and they grappled. Michael and Althaea wrestled, each trying to reach her gun. She grabbed it and swung around to aim it at him.

Michael forced her to the ground, and they struggled. He

applied pressure to her hand, and the gun slipped to the ground. He leaped for it, but she grabbed him and dragged him back. Althaea punched Michael in the face, and he saw stars. He grabbed her in a chokehold, almost losing his grip when she slammed backwards into him. It threw him off balance, but he held on. Soon the thrashing subsided.

He checked for, and found, a pulse. Relieved, he pushed the unconscious Althaea off, rolled over, and picked up the gun. On his knees, he aimed at the guard, who straddled Robert, hands around Robert's throat.

Michael fired twice in rapid succession, rushed over, and knocked the guard's body away. Robert's eyes stared vacantly.

"No!" It was a useless gesture, but Michael checked for a pulse anyway. It wasn't there. He bowed his head. "I'm so sorry, Robert."

It was some consolation that Robert and Danny were together. How could it have ended like this? Robert had said he was supposed to come with Michael to the base. Did it mean he'd been fated to die here? Before he could think more on that, he heard Althaea stirring. He held the gun on her.

She rose on one elbow. "Are you going to kill me?"

"I'm taking you with me."

Althaea looked surprised. She stared at Robert's body. "It was nothing personal."

"Murder is always personal," Michael said. "Even when you think you're just doing a job."

"You've become quite the philosopher."

Michael didn't reply, but looked around the cavern. The door through which they'd entered lay shattered, and the ceiling had crumbled. Smoky, burnt-orange sky stretched out above, and rubble surrounded them. Michael was grateful they could breathe the air though it was thinner and blanketed with smog. They'd acclimate.

He tried to gauge the best way out. It was a miracle they'd survived. Althaea sported cuts and bruises. Michael's shoulder burned, and his head ached.

"To the right," Althaea said.

Michael turned towards the direction she indicated. The walls had crumbled more at that end, which was adjacent to the centre stone and the greatest force of outward-directed energy. He went to the pile of debris that had been the west wall.

"I think we can climb this." He estimated the best route to take without bringing the whole thing down on them. Michael motioned for Althaea to lead. She picked her way up through the ruins, and he followed.

CHAPTER 30

When the lights went out, Carolyn raised her head. The guard remained motionless. A pale light shone through the windows, illuminating his face. His expression told her nothing. Carolyn asked her angels and guides to help her connect to his guides, then risked speaking.

"What's happening?"

The guard's eyes darkened; he frowned and made no reply.

"Please." A whisper, afraid to push, but more afraid of not knowing.

The guard shook his head.

"Why are they killing everyone in the cells? The guards are shooting the prisoners."

Startled, he turned his face away. Carolyn tried to sense anyone around him. She asked for his departed loved ones to come through and help her talk to him.

Erik. A female presence.

Carolyn cast a sideways glance at the man and said, "Your name is Erik."

Erik jumped up and yanked her off the couch.

"How do you know my name? They'll think I talked to you. I didn't tell you." His voice sounded panicked, and his grip hurt.

"I'm connected to one of your loved ones in the spirit world, and she told me."

"What are you saying?"

Silently Carolyn asked the spirit's name.

Lisabet.

"Who do you know named 'Lisabet?'"

"How did you get that name?"

"I'm connected to her."

Fear crossed his face. "What are you trying to do?" He pulled out his gun, pointed it at Carolyn, his other hand still gripping her arm.

Lisabet, please help me talk to him. Who are you?

Mother.

"Lisabet's your mother. She's here. Talk to her."

"It's a trick. Stay away from me. Stop talking." Erik shook her while he spoke, and Carolyn stumbled, tripped, and would have fallen if he hadn't been supporting her. The gun in his hand oriented on her temple, and her stomach twisted.

"Please. Jim doesn't want you to shoot me. Put down the gun. I won't try anything. I want to help you connect with your mother."

"She's dead."

"Why do you think the Agency locked me up here? I can communicate with spirits. The Agency wants to use it. That's why Jim needs me alive." Carolyn used Cornell's first name, making it more personal, though it disgusted her to talk about him as though he were a friend.

Doubt showed on Erik's face, but he lowered the gun. Carolyn focused on Lisabet, trying to establish a stronger connection.

A young mother, fair-haired, pretty. Walks with two young kids: Erik and a little sister. Erik looks to be eight, his sister six. Mom and children walk into a convenience store.

The man behind the counter shouts at them, confusing them. They turn to see a man holding a gun. Lisabet pushes the children aside as the gun fires. The bullet strikes her, hitting her heart. She goes quickly, the children screaming and crying while she passes in front of them.

Carolyn spoke again, whispering. "I'm so sorry. She died in front of you and your sister."

Erik raised the gun. "Stop that. One more word out of you and I'll beat the shit out of you."

Lisabet, please, help him listen. Carolyn fell silent, giving it time, though she couldn't wait too long. She needed someone on her side. If Erik carried out Cornell's orders, she'd be lost forever. Her terror escalated at the thought of going underground. Fear she'd never see Sam again overwhelmed her.

Silently Carolyn thanked Lisabet for coming through and asked her to stay close. The room darkened. A storm approached. Lightning speared across the sky and seconds later, thunder rumbled. Outside the office door, everything was quiet. In her head, Carolyn reviewed the self-defence techniques Michael had taught her when they were in Peterborough. Doubtful she could pull off an escape, but she had to try, even at the risk of a beating.

Erik checked his watch. "Let's go." He waved the gun.

Carolyn considered her options. She'd have to be quick and sure when she tried to disarm him. Erik was a trained fighter, but Michael had shown her how to grab a gun from someone's hands even if they'd had training.

Don't over-think it, Michael had told her.

Okay, Michael, this one's for you.

When they approached the door, Carolyn slowed her pace, letting Erik get near her. She reached for the doorknob. Instead of opening the door, she whirled, twisted the gun out of his hands, and smashed him in the face. Erik's nose spurted blood, and his eyes watered.

Carolyn ran, slamming the door shut behind her, and sped through the office. The doorknob rattled, and the door swung open. A glance back showed Erik rushing from the office. She stumbled into the hall, straight into Jim Cornell's arms.

He grabbed the gun from her hand and punched her in the face. Blood and tears smearing her face, Carolyn dropped to the floor.

Erik caught up to them. "I'm sorry, sir."

Carolyn looked up in time to see Cornell level the gun at Erik and shoot him in the gut. He doubled over, dropping to the floor. Cornell shot him again, this time in the head, and Erik went still. Cornell snatched a pair of handcuffs from the body.

"That was your fault. I have no use for anyone who can't keep you under control." Cornell grabbed Carolyn's arm and dragged her to her feet. "Turn around, hands behind your back."

She complied, knees wobbling and hands shaking. She wanted to wipe the blood from her cut lip, but he bound her hands behind her. Carolyn watched a drop of her blood land on the carpet.

"Kneel."

"What are you going—" Carolyn choked on a sob as she had a sudden thought he wanted to execute her.

"Don't make me tell you anything twice." Cornell forced her to her knees.

Out of the corner of her eye, she watched him fish the key to the cuffs off Erik's body. When Cornell returned, he lifted her up and spun her around.

"I have Sam. If you escape, she'll still be with me, and you'll never know if I killed her until you talk to her ghost. Let's go."

He led her away.

CHAPTER 31

The sound of the cell door unlocking shocked Arnie. He realized a moment of terror before he yanked the pillow off his face to confront the torn wreck that was Julie. His heart broke with grief and relief.

"Julie. Oh, God. How are you here?" Arnie tried to keep his voice low, but it still seemed loud to his ears.

She crouched at his side. His T-shirt lay on the floor next to the cot, and she picked it up and tore it into strips. While she talked, she bandaged his wound.

"We need to hurry," she whispered. "If they find us alive, they'll finish what they started."

Arnie wrapped his arm around Julie's shoulder, and leaning on each other, they hobbled to the cell door. Shadows filled the cell, but the hallway glowed from emergency lights located every few metres along the wall near the ceiling. He listened, but heard nothing.

"Did anyone else survive?" he asked.

"I haven't checked every cell yet. Help me do it, but hurry. If anyone's monitoring the cameras, we're dead."

"Wouldn't they have spotted us by now?"

"Maybe not. It's likely chaos up there. Deuce and Tasha were careless, or neither of us would've survived. But it means something terrible happened."

They slipped into the hallway. Julie closed the cell door, a slight sound of metal meeting metal. In silence, the pair limped from cell to cell. In all cases, it was obvious the person was dead. Most of the bodies lay on the floor, or draped half on the cot. Blood spatters marked their final moments.

Tears rolled down Arnie's face. What a waste.

These corpses would rot. But it told him no one planned to return to this death camp. At least Carolyn's cell had been empty. Thank God, he didn't have to see her lying discarded on her cot. He could hope she'd survived, and he'd find her though he didn't know where to look.

They reached the end of the cellblock finding no one alive. Arnie couldn't believe he'd survived. His furtive prayer to the angels came to mind. Unbelievable. But he sent a quick thank you and a request to help him find Carolyn.

Julie led him to the infirmary. "I need pills and bandages."

We both need pills and bandages, Arnie thought.

They found the supply cabinet and grabbed whatever would be useful. Julie pulled out a bottle of painkillers, opened it, and gulped two.

She tipped two into Arnie's hand, and he swallowed them with water from the tap. He hoped they worked fast. The pain had become unbearable.

Julie located a black medical bag and they packed it. "I need to remove that bullet from your side soon, Arnie."

He nodded, afraid to speak. Expecting it to burst open at any moment, he glanced at the door often.

When they left the infirmary, Arnie carried the bag and led the way through the corridor. Julie limped, and Arnie hoped she'd be able to run if they encountered any Agency personnel. At least she had a gun. If only he could find Carolyn.

* * *

Arnie and Julie hid behind a pillar near a set of stairs, the main exit to the compound up ahead. In front of the double doors and their avenue to freedom stood Carolyn Fairchild and Jim Cornell. Carolyn had blood on her cheek, chin, and shirt. Cornell gripped her arm, her hands cuffed behind her.

Outside, rain poured, and trees whipped violently in the wind. Cornell pulled out his cell phone and released Carolyn's arm.

"What's your ETA? It's getting worse out there."

Carolyn stood, passive, staring at the floor. A lump grew in Arnie's throat. He'd lose her if he didn't do something fast.

Cornell hung up the phone and put his arm around Carolyn, who remained mute, immobile. He said something to her that Arnie couldn't catch. She shook her head, and Arnie saw the glint of tears on her cheeks.

"Consider it an adventure." Cornell sounded jovial, excited, his words echoing across the deserted reception area. "Wait until you see what we've done. It's a miracle. Took us thirty years to build it right." He reached out and stroked her cheek. "We'll get you a shower and clean clothes."

Carolyn wrenched her arm, but his grip on it was firm. "Behave, angel."

Arnie looked into Julie's eyes and set the medical bag at his feet. He motioned for her to give him the gun. She shook her head and pointed at herself, then at Cornell. Arnie nodded. Even with her mutilated fingers, she'd be the better shot.

If they didn't stop Cornell, he'd walk out those doors with Carolyn, and Arnie would lose her forever. He couldn't let that happen. He had to at least try. *Try or die.* Not inspiring words, but they'd have to do.

He edged his way around the pillar. Julie touched his arm and motioned for him to stay put. She slipped closer to the side of the pillar away from Cornell and Carolyn, Arnie following close behind her. They were halfway around it when Cornell spun around and pointed his gun in their direction.

"Did you think I didn't know you were there, Griffen? Helliwell?"

They froze. Carolyn gasped and came to life then, moving her body in front of Cornell's gun. He wrapped an arm around her and yanked her tight against him.

A Humvee pulled up at the entrance. Cornell's ride. His head inclined towards the door, but he didn't glance at it.

"Let them go. Please," Carolyn said. "If you do, I'll leave with you. I won't fight you."

"I have Sam. You'll do what I want regardless."

"No. I won't. If you kill Arnie, you'll have to kill me, and if you kill me, I'll protect Sam from the other side."

Cornell paused, uncertain.

Carolyn pressed her point. "I won't let you kill Arnie."

"I'd be doing him a favour. He's as good as dead if I leave him here."

"Then what difference does it make?"

Two agents with assault rifles stepped from the Humvee and headed for the doors. Arnie stood frozen, watching them. The agents entered the building.

Carolyn screamed, "Run!"

Cornell shoved Carolyn at the two agents. "Take her to the car."

Arnie grabbed Julie by the arm and ran. A bullet pinged off the pillar behind which they'd hid. Julie took two shots, the bullets hitting the wall. Arnie ran blindly through the doors and into the corridor, his wound burning agony.

Silence behind them told Arnie no one pursued them, but he kept moving, dragging Julie with him. A set of double doors blocked their path and Arnie pushed through them. The pair hobbled along the hallway, listening for Cornell's footsteps.

They'd made it almost to the cell block when Arnie finally stopped running and turned. No one followed. Cornell was gone, and he'd taken Carolyn away. Arnie and Julie were alone, with only the dead to keep them company.

CHAPTER 32

Michael hovered the helicopter over the Peterborough compound's deserted parking lot. Wind and rain battered them, and he struggled for control, but he landed it without killing anyone.

His heart told him Carolyn was gone even before he saw the vacant parking lot and dark building. But he needed to verify Cornell hadn't killed her and left her body behind. He shut the engine off and turned to Althaea. "I'm going in."

"No one's left. We have to get underground."

"I'm not going anywhere until I know what happened."

Althaea scowled, but kept silent.

Michael waved the gun in her face. "You first."

She rose from her seat with difficulty. "Can't you at least take the cuffs off?"

Ignoring her, he hoisted a backpack onto his shoulder and waved the gun at the door. The raging wind forced them to cling to one another as they climbed from the chopper. They fought their way to the main entrance and found the place locked.

He used C4 to blow the doors, dragging Althaea around with him as he set up everything. The storm lashed at them while they huddled outside the blast radius and Michael detonated it.

Gun held ready, he guided Althaea into the building. Shell casings littered the floor, but he saw no bodies. A trail of dried blood, maybe two days old, led away from a pillar in the lobby.

He dragged Althaea to the reception desk. The wind blew rain into the hole he'd made, and Michael had to raise his voice to shout over the noise. "I'm not carting you around this place. You're too much of a distraction."

"You can't leave me here."

Michael didn't reply, but forced her to sit and cuffed her to the chair.

Althaea's face darkened, and she struggled against the cuffs. "You asshole. What if someone's in here?"

"Charm them with your sunny personality."

Michael jumped out of the way as Althaea's booted foot swung at him. He hurried away, following the trail of blood.

The trail ended at the infirmary. He tried the door. Locked. He kicked it open, using the wall as cover. His heart skipped a beat when he found the room occupied. When he realized the man and woman occupying the two beds were either asleep or dead, he lowered his weapon.

He recognized Arnie, but not the woman. Both looked wounded and beaten, especially the woman. Arnie's eyes popped opened, and he groped for the gun on the nightstand, his motions groggy and feeble. Michael snatched it up.

"Arnie." Michael kept his voice low.

Arnie jerked up when recognition flashed in his eyes. He screamed in pain, and Michael grabbed his flailing fist.

"Easy. I'm not here to hurt you."

Arnie's eyes bugged out, and his lips contorted in rage. "You fucking kidnapped me. You killed John."

Michael stepped back, out of fist-flailing range, and aimed the gun at Arnie. "Calm the fuck down. I'm here to help you. Where's Carolyn? Is she okay?"

Arnie collapsed back on the bed. "Last I saw her, two of your psycho buddies were dragging her into a Humvee. Her mouth was bloody, and she was in handcuffs."

Michael winced. "Let me help you. Blood's seeping through that bandage around your abdomen."

"Help Julie. She's dying. I haven't been able to wake her for the last day." Arnie's voice broke. "Please. Do something."

Michael turned to Julie. He set Arnie's gun on her bed and shoved his into its holster. A blanket covered her to the neck, and Michael eased it down to her waist. Bandages swathed her torso, and her hands and feet were beehives of more bandages. Dark bruises decorated the skin around her eyes, a stark contrast to her pale face.

"If I check her back, will I find it covered in welts?"

Arnie nodded.

"Was she Drummond's source?"

"Yes." Arnie averted his gaze.

"She's lucky to be alive. You must tell me one day how you two survived. I've seen the cellblock."

"Can you help her?"

"I'll try. She probably has an infection. I'll give her antibiotics and painkillers intravenously. Her breathing is regular, but her colour looks terrible. What happened to you?" Michael nodded at the bandage around Arnie's abdomen.

"A guard shot me when they executed everyone. The bullet's still in there."

"Shit. Why didn't you remove it?"

Arnie looked at Michael as if he were crazy.

"All right. I'll take it out." Michael found what he needed, talking to Arnie while he did. Arnie spoke grudgingly at first, but then told Michael everything that had happened since Carolyn had arrived in the cell next to his.

"I overheard Carolyn talking to you that day," Arnie said.

Michael glanced up from Julie's arm, where he was removing the needle after inserting the catheter.

"You heard everything?" Michael asked.

Arnie nodded.

He knows the baby is mine.

"Turns out we've both given her babies," Arnie said.

Michael froze, heart pounding against his chest. "What does that mean?"

Arnie smiled as though enjoying Michael's reaction. "Cornell told her the aliens had me impregnate her—in the traditional manner."

"Then I'm sorry for you both," Michael said.

Arnie's face fell.

"Don't look so disappointed. Nothing they do surprises me, and what Carolyn has done in the past isn't my business— especially when she has no memory of it. My business is leaving here and going after her before Cornell hurts her any more than he already has."

"Do you know how to find her?" Arnie's voice rose, hopeful.

"I know where they headed. I would've been going with them had I not taken a permanent detour to help Carolyn escape." He checked Julie's temperature—too high. He went to the sink, wet a washcloth, and handed it to Arnie. "Wipe her down with this, then rinse it again with cool water and apply it to her forehead. I have to get something from the lobby."

"What about my bullet?"

"I'll take care of it when I get back."

Arnie rose, taking his time, wincing with every movement.

"When did you last take a painkiller?"

"A few hours ago, I took four of whatever Julie found in the cupboard the other day. I can't handle the pain."

"No more painkillers while I'm gone," Michael said. "I'll give you more when I return and find out what you took." He handed the gun back to Arnie. "Keep this handy. Make it a habit."

Arnie nodded and turned his attention to Julie.

Michael hurried from the room and down the hall. Hopefully, Althaea was still where he'd left her. He pulled the gun from its holster though he was sure no one remained in the building. In the reception area, water pooled on the foyer floor. A fine mist covered Althaea's hair.

She looked up when she heard him and cursed when she saw him. Michael rushed to her side. She held a pin in her hand and had been trying to pick the lock on the cuffs. Michael pulled out his key, freed her hands from the chair, and then handcuffed her again, hands front. "I don't have time to screw around with you, Althaea. Get up." The gun aimed at her head reinforced the statement, and she complied.

While they walked, Michael told Althaea about the two survivors. He contemplated his next move. Until the weather cleared, he was stuck here. Althaea would try to interfere at every turn. The underground facility was locked down tight—getting in would be near impossible. But if he didn't find a way, he'd lose Carolyn and his baby daughter.

He refused to abandon them. He'd told Carolyn he'd find her no matter what it took, and he'd keep that promise. Death hadn't kept him from her, so he sure as hell wouldn't let the Agency stop him. Michael's hand strayed to Carolyn's wedding band, and it gave him hope.

CHAPTER 33

Julie slipped into the spirit world during the night. Michael dozed on a chair in front of the door, but snapped awake to the sensation that something touched his cheek. He grabbed the gun from his holster. A glance around the room showed everything was normal.

Arnie slept, eyeballs rolling under the lids while he dreamed. He'd kicked off his blanket, exposing the bandages around his ribs where Michael had patched him up after removing the bullet. Althaea remained handcuffed to a bed Michael had dragged in from another room. Eyes still, she slept dreamlessly now, though she'd been restless most of the night.

Michael looked at Julie and noticed she wasn't breathing. He holstered his gun, crept to her side, and checked for a pulse. Too late, and he'd known it was even before he touched her. Was Julie's spirit still here, watching them?

I'm sorry, Julie. I wish I had Carolyn's ability.

Arnie stirred and opened his eyes.

Michael released Julie's hand. "I'm sorry." He glanced at Althaea to make sure she still slept.

Arnie sat, grief etched on his face. He clasped Julie's other hand in both his own, gaze riveted on her face. "I dreamed I talked to her."

"What did she say?"

Tears slid down Arnie's face. "She said it wasn't my fault."

"It's not."

"It is. The Agency wouldn't have found her if I hadn't told

them what I knew. It didn't take much for Tasha to make me spill my guts. I couldn't keep my mouth shut." Arnie kept his gaze on Julie's face.

"How could you have kept your mouth shut while they tortured you? It's not your fault."

"I never should have slept with Julie. If I hadn't gone along when Ralph met with her, they wouldn't have had anyone to interrogate. Ralph's dead, so they couldn't get anything from him."

Michael started. "Drummond's dead? What happened?"

"You don't know?" Arnie's head snapped up.

"No."

Arnie returned his gaze to Julie. A wisp of hair on Julie's cheek caught his attention, and he brushed it to the side and then stroked her head. He talked to Michael in a quiet voice. "Tasha told me Ralph hanged himself, and Carolyn said she'd seen Ralph in a dream." He told Michael what Carolyn had revealed.

Michael went numb. "That's why she left me in Algonquin." Michael clutched Carolyn's ring in his fist. "Why didn't she wake me and tell me?"

"She knew you'd stop her, and she wanted to keep Cornell from giving Sam to the aliens."

"I would've helped her get Sam back."

Althaea stirred. "Maybe Carolyn didn't trust you."

He whirled on her, but couldn't bring himself to reply. She returned the stare and then looked over at Arnie. "I'm sorry about Julie. Michael's right. It's not your fault. The Agency can break anyone." She paused. "It was pointless, too, if you consider it. Whatever they wanted Julie to tell them doesn't matter anymore."

"That's not helpful, Althaea," Michael said.

"Mick—"

"Don't call me that." It came out a snarl. He grimaced.

She gave him a puzzled look, but that was all.

"What do we do now? Can we get to Carolyn?" Arnie asked.

"I'm not leaving her there," Michael replied. "I'll do whatever it takes to get her back."

Althaea interrupted. "Do you feel that?"

She tried to get up, but the cuffs wouldn't let her. Michael's chair shook, the beds squeaked, and bottles rattled in the cupboards.

Arnie set Julie's hand down and stood. "An earthquake?"

"Stay here." Michael pulled out his gun and rushed into the hallway. Everything was dim. Emergency lights gave off a feeble glow. He raced to the lobby. The wind howled outside, the storm still raging. They'd have to patch up the hole where the doors used to be. The ground continued to tremble.

The wind roared louder and trees on the other side of the parking lot bent to the ground. One large tree snapped in half and flew onto the pavement. Michael watched, horrified, while the helicopter he and Althaea had arrived in fell on its side and slid across the cement. The ground stopped shaking, but the wind and rain continued.

Lightning speared from the sky, thunder crashing seconds later. He could forget about going after Carolyn anytime soon. Michael turned his back on the storm and walked away.

Back in the infirmary, he propped the door open and adjusted Julie's bed. Without a word, Arnie got up and helped Michael wheel it out into the hallway. From the room next door, they brought another hospital bed in for Michael.

"I hate to sound like a chicken shit, but I'm glad I don't have to sleep in a room alone," Arnie said.

"I'm sure there's no one else roaming around here, but we'll stick together for now. It'll get old fast, though," Michael replied.

Arnie shook his head. "I'm not worried about that. The Agency murdered people here. It's not the living that scare me."

They froze, staring at each other, while the building shook again.

CHAPTER 34

The next time Michael opened his eyes, it was morning. Arnie's bed was empty. Michael glanced at Althaea's bed and was relieved to see her still securely handcuffed. She was also glaring at him.

"I'm sick of this, Mick. Take these fucking cuffs off me."

"I can't, even though you've asked me so nicely."

"What do you think I'll do? Those tremors we experienced are the least of our worries. We're stuck here, and wandering around this place by myself doesn't sound enticing. Killing you wouldn't improve my situation. I can help you, but not handcuffed to the bed."

Michael shook his head. "Sorry. Can't risk it."

Arnie walked in carrying a tray of food and drinks. "I found a lot of food in the cafeteria, but if we don't find a generator, we'll lose everything in the freezers. Some of the refrigerated stuff has already gone bad."

Michael glanced at the gun tucked into Arnie's belt. "Scavenge a holster for that gun. Glad to see you're carrying it. Thanks for the food."

Arnie set the tray on the counter next to the sink and passed around Danishes, bagels, fruit, and muffins. "The stove runs on gas, so I made tea. The drinking boxes and water are room temperature, but I guess we're lucky they left it." Arnie turned to Michael. "Doesn't this place have a generator?"

"Yes. They cut the power deliberately and didn't engage the generator when they evacuated. They weren't expecting anyone to stay here."

"We have to do something about those bodies in the cellblock. Should we call someone? The cops? The fire department? I need to contact my mother, too," Arnie said.

Michael and Althaea exchanged glances.

"What?"

"You can't call anyone," Michael said.

"Why not? I have to get in touch with my mother."

"She thinks you're dead." Michael didn't want to be blunt, but he knew no other way.

"Because of you," Arnie snarled. He made a move as though to attack Michael, but pulled back when Michael stood.

"I was under orders. Besides, the phones aren't working."

"When the storm lets up, they'll fix the phones. And we've got landlines in here. They should work."

"Do you realize that storm has been raging for three days now?"

"So?"

Michael looked at Althaea again and she stared back, impassive. He'd get no help from that corner. "I don't know how long it'll last or what'll remain standing when it's over. This isn't a natural storm. It's man-made."

"Why would anyone purposely trigger something like this? *How* could anyone do this?"

Michael told Arnie about the Aurora machines, how they could manipulate the weather and cause large-scale destruction. "The machines triggered when I phased the aliens back to their world."

"You did this?" Arnie's hands balled into fists, and he took a step towards Michael again.

Althaea laughed out loud.

"What's so funny," Arnie snapped.

"You two. Ever since we got here, Michael's been on his guard, and Arnie's looked as if he wants to pounce. Arnie, you're just dying to find an excuse to slug Michael. Why?" She looked from one to the other.

Michael grasped Carolyn's ring, and Althaea noticed.

"It's Carolyn, isn't it? Both of you want her, and this'll devolve into a pissing contest, because neither of you know who she'll pick if you ever find her."

"Enough, Althaea," Michael said and looked at Arnie. "We'll

404

find your mother and see if she's okay."

"Mick—"

"I told you not to use that name, Althaea." Michael scowled.

"Jesus Christ, Mick—excuse me—Michael. I've called you 'Mick' for years. What's your problem?"

"Just don't use that name."

Althaea sighed. "Well, isn't this nice? What shall we do now? Shall I sit here handcuffed to the bed while you two punch each other out, or can we eat and do something productive?"

Michael stepped around Arnie, poured himself a cup of tea, grabbed a muffin, and headed to the door. "Don't leave the room. Arnie, watch Althaea. Don't go near her. If she needs to pee, throw her a cup to use."

Michael left the room, the door thudding shut behind him.

***

"What an asshole." Arnie stared at the closed door.

"He can be."

Arnie grinned. "Did you give him those black eyes he's sporting?"

Althaea grinned back. "Yes."

"Kudos." Arnie's gaze returned to the closed door. "What did Carolyn see in him?"

"I guess the same thing I saw in him."

He spun around, shock on his face. "You and Valiant?"

Althaea flushed, shook her head. "Almost. Mick was married at the time."

"What happened?"

"I'd rather not get into it. He has it in for me, though. That's why the cuffs. I'm not a threat, Arnie. Take these handcuffs off me. I promise, you won't be sorry." She licked her lips.

He looked her up and down. Did she mean what he thought she meant? Arnie took a step towards her before he realized what he was doing. He stopped, shook his head. "I don't think so. Michael said to stay away from you. Besides, I don't have the key."

"I'm sure we could use something here to spring the lock. Please? I have to go, and I don't want to pee in a cup."

He shook his head again, but not forcefully. She arched her back, her breasts pressing up, nipples outlined against the tight shirt she wore. He pictured himself on the bed, suckling those breasts. A drop of sweat ran down his back, and he grew hard.

Althaea's gaze locked on Arnie's. "Please. This is killing my back. I can't move."

Arnie stepped closer.

"Help me?" She beamed a smile at him.

For the first time, he noticed her deep blue, almost violet, eyes. Long blonde hair haloed her face. Arnie imagined raking his fingers through it, wrapping a fist in it to tilt her head back and ravish her throat.

He gulped and almost took another step towards her, but stopped. She continued to stare at him, lips parted. What would it be like to kiss those lips, to nibble on them?

Arnie looked away, remembering Tasha, the humiliation and pain. "I can't." *Son of a bitch, I want to, but I won't think with my dick ever again.* It could be a trick. He walked away and stepped out into the hall. When the door swung shut, Arnie leaned against the wall and covered his face with his hands.

"Well done." It was Michael.

Arnie looked up, confused.

"I heard the siren trying to lure you to your destruction. Congratulations on pushing through the pain. She was after your gun."

Arnie looked at the gun in his belt and then back at Michael. "You're an asshole." Before Michael could respond, Arnie said, "Why do you have Althaea handcuffed? What's she going to do?"

"Althaea's Agency. No matter what she says, she's programmed to follow their agenda."

"Carolyn trusted you, and you're Agency trained. Why aren't you following their agenda?"

"I decided to think for myself. Althaea has had no epiphany."

Arnie opened his mouth to speak when a crash inside the room rattled the door. Michael tried to open it, found it blocked, and forced it.

Still cuffed to the bed, Althaea had used both feet to shove Michael's bed into Arnie's, sending Arnie's bed into the door.

"You could've called us. We were right here," Michael said.

"I need to use the washroom."

Michael dug in his pocket and fished out the key, but he also drew his gun. He went to Althaea and handed her the key.

"Go ahead. Take off the cuffs."

She did, rubbing the liberated wrist. The other end of the bracelet dangled from the bedrail. She stood, massaging her lower back.

"Give me the cuffs and the key," Michael said.

Althaea handed both to Michael, and he waved his gun at the door. "Pull your gun, Arnie. She's getting an armed escort. If she tries anything, shoot her in the leg."

Arnie hesitated, studying Althaea's face. She stared back at him, neutral. What the hell. If she was anything like Tasha, Michael wasn't the asshole Arnie thought. He pulled the gun from his belt and stepped into the hallway.

"Where are we going, Mi—Michael?"

"Down to the cellblock. Arnie, do you have the keys to the cells?"

"Yeah." He located the key ring Julie had taken from Deuce and handed it to Michael.

When Althaea opened her mouth, Michael cut her off. "Let's go."

***

The smell drifted out to them as they drew near the cellblock.

"You won't lock me in here with them, will you?" Althaea spoke softly.

"No," Arnie said and turned to Michael. "I won't let you. I don't care what she's done or was thinking of doing."

Michael scowled. "No. What do you take me for?"

Althaea exhaled loudly.

"Then why are we here?" Arnie asked.

"We have to remove these bodies before the stink gets any worse." Michael turned to Althaea. "You're going into one of the empty cells. Use the toilet. Arnie and I will remove the bodies. I'll get the generator going and we'll burn them."

"I can help you," Althaea said. "It doesn't make sense to decommission me."

"Given the chance, you'll kill Arnie and try to take me in or kill me. Tell me that's not true."

"What I say doesn't matter, does it?" she replied.

"I'm afraid not." He grabbed her by the arm.

Althaea kicked out, but he was ready for it and wrenched her arm behind her back. He shoved the arm upward, making her scream. "You're so predictable." He whirled her around. She lunged forward and head-butted him, their foreheads colliding.

Michael saw stars and a flash of an image. As they grappled, the nagging feeling he'd had in Nahanni that something was wrong with Althaea's mind returned. This time, he wasn't going to overlook it. He put her in a headlock, bending her over almost double.

"Stop it." He shook his head to clear it. "For fuck's sake, Althaea, did you feel that?"

"You're hurting her!" Arnie approached the struggling pair. "She's crying, Valiant."

Afraid Althaea would grab Arnie's gun if he got close, Michael shouted, "Stay back, Griffen." The sobs reached him then and he almost released her.

No way. Althaea Dayton doesn't cry.

He held her against his body, immobilizing her. Her pulse raced, and her breath came in hoarse gasps.

"Ally, listen to me."

"Okay."

He barely heard it, but she went limp against him. Michael sank to the ground with her in his arms.

She leaned into his chest, eyes closed. "What was that?" She shivered, and Michael knew it wasn't from cold.

"It's as if there's something in your head."

"When we connected, it felt like my brain was shredding. I saw an animal. Am I going crazy?"

"It's not you. There's something there. I felt it in Nahanni. They did something to you. It sounds crazy, but I can feel it." Michael put a hand on her forehead.

She groaned. "That head-butt should have hurt you, not me."

"Trust me, it did. But there's something else going on. If you'll let me, I'll help you find out what."

"No. You're not doing that to me again."

"Do you know another way?"

"Fuck it. Lock me up."

Michael hauled her up by the arm as he stood and turned towards an empty cell. "Fine. Open the door, Arnie."

Arnie unlocked the cell, but when Michael tried to push Althaea inside, she collapsed. He lifted her in his arms, carried her to the cot, and covered her with a blanket. He left the cell and made Arnie lock the door behind them. When he glanced at her again, she was asleep.

***

Althaea awoke, alone in the cell. The racket from the corridor told her Arnie and Michael were still working. A dull throb in her skull reminded her of what had happened. She'd head-butted Michael and in that instant saw a vision of a large animal that might have been a jackal.

Michael seemed to think there was something wrong with her. Uneasiness made her stomach tighten. She had a feeling he was right. Ever since he'd connected to her in the cave, she'd felt off, like she wasn't herself. Dreams plagued her—terrifying scenes that made her wake up in a cold sweat with an unshakeable feeling of doom.

What had the Agency done to her? It had to be the Agency. She hadn't had an alien tracker in her, so that meant she wasn't an abductee. But something had been done to her. Michael had knocked it loose when he'd invaded her mind, and now she couldn't function. The son of a bitch would have to fix what he broke.

But the only way to do that would be to let him access her mind again. Did she really want to let him in? She'd have to trust him, because there was no one else who could do it. Pain swelled behind her eyes, forcing her to close them. Instantly, a parade of images scrolled through her head and nausea churned in her gut.

She used the toilet and washed her face, hoping that would help, but she continued to feel queasy.

Please, no. Was this hideous sensation the new normal? She couldn't keep going like this. She made up her mind.

"Valiant!"

He appeared at the cell door faster than she'd expected, and Arnie was right behind him.

"You okay?" Michael sounded genuinely concerned.

"I want you to do it."

He didn't seem surprised. "If you're willing, I'm willing. But I won't let you in, Ally. It'll be me probing you. If that doesn't seem fair, then I'll be back when we're done for the day."

Althaea gritted her teeth, but nodded her head. "Fine. I just want my brain to stop killing me."

Arnie watched the exchange, puzzled. "What are you talking about?"

"I can probe her mind," Michael replied.

"Like some kind of Vulcan mind meld?"

"Just open the cell door and cover her while I do this."

Arnie unlocked and opened the door. Michael holstered his gun and approached Althaea, drawing in close to her. He helped her stand and steadied her when she swayed. She closed her eyes while Michael reached out his hands and drew her into the circle of his arms. He leaned forward and touched her forehead with his.

CHAPTER 35

Carolyn stopped pacing and sat at the table in the open kitchen of a small apartment where she'd spent the last two days. The apartment in the underground community was an improvement over the cell in the Peterborough compound, but she remained a prisoner. The unit had no windows, and the exit door locked from the outside.

She had new clothes; a fridge stocked with healthy food; clean, filtered water; toiletries; and actual sheets, pillows, and a comforter on her bed. But she had no books, no TV with DVDs—nothing to do but pace or eat. And no human company other than Cornell.

In the cell, Carolyn could at least talk to Arnie, even if it was surreptitiously at night. Where once grasping his fingers wasn't enough physical contact, now it would be everything to her.

She didn't know where the community was located, only that it was near the city of Peterborough. They'd headed south on Highway 115 after leaving the compound, but she'd lost her bearings after that. They'd entered farm country, mostly fields and forests along secondary roads, and then a dirt road with forest on either side.

Above ground, the facility looked like a cement fortress with a barbwire moat. Electrified fences, security cameras, and manned guard towers ensured no one approached undetected. She despaired that Michael could ever rescue her, and even if it managed it, they'd still need to find Sam.

Carolyn stood again and returned to pacing. Worry knotted her

411

gut. Her hands settled on her belly, a protective gesture she made instinctively whenever she thought about her baby.

The deadbolt in the door clicked. She stepped backwards and bumped into the table. Heart in her throat, breathing rapid and shallow, she watched the door swing open. Cornell. The devil she knew.

He frowned when he glimpsed her face. "What's wrong?"

"Are you kidding?"

"No. You look frightened. Did something happen?"

"You can't be serious."

"Carolyn, you're safe here."

"You killed everyone at the Peterborough compound. You expect me to believe you when you tell me I'm safe?"

"I didn't bring you here to kill you."

"Why am I here then? The aliens are gone. I spent all day yesterday establishing that for you." Carolyn stopped talking and tried to collect herself. Tears threatened. When she could speak without her voice breaking, she said, "Where's Sam? I want to see her."

"That's impossible. She believes you're dead. She's happy here and doing well. I don't want to do anything to traumatize her."

"You mean like tell her you're a lying psycho responsible for her father's death and her mother's disappearance?"

Straight faced, he said, "Yes."

"What do you want?" Carolyn's hands moved to her pelvis.

He set his briefcase down and walked towards her. She backed away, bumping into the table again. He smiled as he approached her—a friendly smile that made her insides churn. Hands pressed on the table, Carolyn leaned back, bracing herself. When Cornell reached her, he gripped her shoulders, steadied her, and brushed a strand of hair off her face.

Panic rose, filled her. Carolyn's mind raced. She contemplated kneeing him in the groin, but feared reprisal. Tears sprang to her eyes.

"Still so afraid," Cornell whispered. "Work with me, and we'll be able to accomplish so much. I don't want to use force on you, angel. This is a new world we're creating, and you can be a vital part of it." Cornell's breath, reeking of stale coffee, puffed in her face when he spoke.

Carolyn's stomach turned, morning sickness always close to the surface, and she averted her face. "I'll never willingly work with you. You destroyed my life, tore apart my family. How can you expect me to accept this?"

"You're smart, a survivor. On the surface, the world is in its death throes. Michael Valiant triggered that. If Sam were up there, she'd be killed along with everyone else. Do you still think Valiant's a hero?"

"Michael's doing what he has to do, and I trust nothing you tell me."

Cornell put an arm around her and drew her to him. She tried to push him away, but he held firm.

"Let me go. What are you doing?"

Cornell's other arm came up, tightening the embrace. "I'm proving a point, angel. I can do whatever I want to you or Sam, and no one will interfere." He released her and stepped back. "But I'd rather not."

"What do you want?" Carolyn's voice shook.

"A helicopter disappeared from the Nahanni base. We've located it at the Peterborough compound. I want you to remote view the place and tell me who's there."

Carolyn's heart leapt. Remote viewing wasn't necessary to know who it was. *Michael. It's Michael.* He'd find Arnie, and they'd come for her. Hope swelled.

Cornell must have seen something in her expression, because he smiled, but this time, it wasn't friendly. "It's Valiant?"

Carolyn stared at the floor, avoiding his eyes.

"Answer me."

She nodded. Cornell's finger lifted her chin so her gaze met his. "When I ask you a question, I expect you to answer me. It's Valiant, isn't it?"

"Yes." A whisper.

He took her hand in his and led her to the recliner in the living room. "Sit."

She sat, leaned back.

Cornell set his briefcase on the coffee table in front of her and opened it. He handed her a pad of paper and a pencil. "Go ahead. Write or draw whatever you get. Be thorough." He took a seat on the couch opposite her.

Carolyn closed her eyes and focused on the Peterborough compound. Three souls' energies touched her: Arnie; Michael; a woman she didn't know. She wrote down everything. The connection to Michael strengthened, his familiar energy easing her tension.

Something diverted his attention, and he didn't sense her. Michael focused on the woman. Images flowed past Carolyn, faster than she could see them, making her dizzy. Something snapped near her ears and she found herself in a hallway as real as the most vivid dream she'd ever had.

Carolyn barely oriented when the floor trembled, and a deep growl echoed through the corridor. Something large moved in her direction.

She turned, quickened her pace, running away from that feral sound. She sensed Michael somewhere in the vicinity. The snarling grew louder, paws padded and claws clicked on the floor behind her. Terrified, she glanced back.

A huge jackal closed the distance between them at an alarming rate. Carolyn screamed and ran. The jackal snorted, and a paw swiped at her bare ankle, a claw tearing into the skin. She screamed again and ran faster, her ankle stinging and burning.

The jackal overtook her, threw her onto the floor. She tried to roll over, but the animal pressed on her back, trapping her. Strong jaws closed on her arm and dragged her backwards. Carolyn twisted and shoved a finger in its eye.

The mouth opened just enough for her to slide her arm out. Blood streamed down the arm, but Carolyn hardly noticed. She jumped up and ran towards the sound of human voices.

Her heart skipped a beat when she recognized Michael's voice. She ran forward, rounded a corner, and there he was.

Michael looked up, eyes widening when he recognized her. He grinned and ran to her. "Carolyn?" His look changed to panic when he noticed the blood on her arm.

"Michael!" She collapsed into his arms. Pain lanced through her when the beast gripped her again, and she slid from Michael's arms.

She snapped back to the room with Cornell. Carolyn opened her eyes and gasped for breath, the room spinning around her. She couldn't breathe. The pencil fell to the floor, the notepad following it. Her back arched, and she bucked in the chair.

Cornell called to her, but she couldn't answer him. Blood spurted as she flailed her arms. Carolyn managed a wheezing gasp, but continued to struggle for air. His hands pressed her into the chair.

She stood next to the chair, watching, while Cornell leaned over her now limp body. Carolyn thought about Sam, tried to go to her, but she was yanked back into her body. She landed with a thud, sucking in air, grateful to breathe. Her eyes snapped open, gaze meeting Cornell's.

Carolyn said, "He's seen what you've done." She fainted.

CHAPTER 36

Footsteps approach and Althaea turns to see Michael heading towards her. He takes her hand and leads her to a room. The door stands wide open, a mess of toys on the floor. Five-year-old Ally is there, sitting on the floor playing with toy cars. Dave, her father's friend, peeks into the room and steps inside. Uncle Dave lifts her into his arms.

When he throws her high in the air, she laughs. She's flying. The air whooshes around her, dress fluttering, legs kicking out. Uncle Dave catches her—Ally didn't doubt he would—and cradles the child in his arms. He moves over to the couch, and fear hits her.

Althaea turns to Michael and shakes her head. No, she can't watch this. She knows what happened in that room. This man molested her, one of the many times he did.

"Please, stop this," she begs and thinks, I'm always begging Michael for something. Anger bubbles up.

Michael shakes his head.

No? Can he be that cruel? Althaea looks over at the scene where the child struggles and cries, trapped, helpless in the man's arms. The scene wavers, shatters, and reforms.

Little Ally's on the floor, playing with her cars. Uncle Dave enters the room, lifts her up, and she laughs, joyful. He sets her down and watches while she scurries over to the toys.

"Play with me?" She smiles, hopeful.

He laughs and sits in the midst of the mess, picks up a car. "I only have a moment," he says.

Her face falls. Uncle Dave is her favourite "uncle," always kind, always making time for her. He's never hurt her, will never hurt her.

Althaea gapes at Michael, shocked. Unbelievable. A more authentic memory has replaced the foul one.

"Did you do that?" Has Michael done something to her?

"The Agency took your memories, Ally. We're retrieving the real ones." Michael has used her nickname. It's reassuring.

He takes her hand, and they move on to the next room.

Ally is fifteen and cowering in an alley—Ally in an alley. She remembers this one too. She'd run away from home to escape her parents' denials, her schoolmates' taunts, her own self-loathing. Razor cuts cover her arms, a physical expression of her anger. She's thin, emaciated.

After she's lived on the streets for a week, a pimp finds her. He forces himself on her, but she escapes. He finds her, beats her, and drags her away. Ally's life on the streets begins in earnest.

Again the scene shatters, melts, and reforms.

Ally is fifteen and playing basketball in the high school gym. She's the captain of the girls' basketball team, tall, powerful, and agile.

Althaea smiles. How she loved playing basketball. Where had that memory gone? She hadn't left home, hadn't left school, and did have friends, even a boyfriend, though not serious.

She looks at Michael. "The Agency took that too, didn't they? Everything I thought I remembered was something they wanted me to believe. None of my memories are real? Who am I?"

"Do you want to see more?" Michael's voice is gentle, soothing.

"Yes."

He leads her to another room, and she has to ask: "Whose house is this?" Michael smiles. "Don't you know?"

Althaea shakes her head, but even while she does, she knows the answer. "My house," she says, a look of amazement crossing her face. "It's me."

Michael nods and smiles, encouraging her. "You don't need me to show you anymore. You can go through it yourself. But I need to know: what about the Agency?"

She places her hand on Michael's shoulder. "Destroy them."

Growls from somewhere down the corridor reach their ears, and the hallway trembles. Footsteps. Michael shouts, half in excitement, half in fear, and pushes past Althaea.

"Carolyn."

The woman screams in terror. "Michael."

He reaches Carolyn, embraces her. Blood drips from her arm.

The thing chasing her appears. A roar, and a hairy, monstrous jackal paw

reaches out and snatches her from Michael. He cries out. "Help me, Ally."
Althaea runs, the desperation in Michael's voice spurring her on.
Carolyn's screams are cut short when the beast wraps its paws around her
throat, squeezing. Michael has a sword.

How is that possible? *Althaea catches up to him and tries to pull*
Carolyn away from the jackal, but its grip on her is strong. Michael's sword
whistles through the air and slices into one paw. The beast howls in agony.

The jackal releases Carolyn, and she disappears. Michael lifts the sword
and skewers the beast through the chest.

***

Michael released Althaea and stepped away from her. Hands gripped his shoulders, and he shrugged them off. He spun around to find Arnie there, concern and fear on his face. "What happened?"

Michael ignored Arnie for the moment and looked at Althaea. "You okay?"

She trembled, eyes moist, and exhaled a tattered breath. "The Agency brainwashed me to kill for them." Her pale face had a green tinge.

Michael nodded, understanding what she felt. He'd had the same revelations once. Althaea moaned. "Robert. Danny."

"I know." Michael held Althaea's face in his palms. He looked into her eyes, consoling. One repentant killer to another. "I know."

Althaea placed her hands over his. "Okay." She looked stricken, but calmer.

Michael released her.

"What was that thing?" she asked.

"I think it was a guard."

"I don't get it."

"They inserted something into your mind that would trigger if you poked around in the memories they built for you. When we dismantled their illusions, we triggered it. We wouldn't have gotten as far as we did, but Carolyn distracted it."

"How did she get there? Where did she go?" Althaea asked.

"Back to where she left her body, I assume. Maybe she tried to connect to me. When Carolyn arrived, your mind would've recognized her immediately as an intrusion."

"Was it real?"

"It was to us. I have to find her."

Arnie grabbed Michael's arm. "What about Carolyn? What happened?"

Michael recounted their experience, leaving out the details of Althaea's past, but telling Arnie everything else.

Arnie's eyes bugged out. "Could it have hurt her?"

"We weren't dreaming. It was fortunate she came along, because it gave us enough time to shatter the illusions they'd planted in Ally's mind. Carolyn is strong enough to get back, but I'm worried they made her do this to track me. Arnie, you said Cornell left you here?"

"Yeah. They had to clear out before the weather trapped them. It was already storming when they left. I guess chasing Julie and me down was too much trouble."

"Now he knows I'm here too."

CHAPTER 37

Carolyn woke from a dreamless sleep to the throbbing of her arm and ankle and opened her eyes. She was in her bedroom, Cornell seated on a chair beside the bed. Her arm, swathed in bandages, lay atop the comforter. A slight brownish stain on the bandage showed where blood had seeped through and dried.

When Cornell realized she was awake, relief flashed in his eyes. He smiled, friendly again. "Glad you're okay. I feared we'd lost you."

"The baby?"

"The baby's fine. What happened?"

"I connected to Michael and a woman in a house with many rooms. A jackal attacked me." Carolyn looked at her arm. "It clawed my arm and my ankle."

"How?"

"What I experienced in my mind manifested in my body."

"Are you saying Valiant isn't in Peterborough?"

"I don't know." Carolyn lied in that, but jumped on every opportunity to fudge the truth. The longer she could keep Cornell ignorant, the more time she bought for Michael.

"Why did you say he knows what I've done?"

"What do you mean?" Carolyn didn't remember saying that.

"You said 'he knows what you've done.' Did you mean Michael? What does he know?"

"I don't know. The last thing I remember is strangling and fighting for my life, a huge jackal clawing at me. I'm unaware of

420

anything I said."

Cornell frowned. "Can you make a guess?"

"I guess it means Michael knows what you did. I don't know everything you've done. It could be any number of awful things. Pick one."

He stood. "You're obviously feeling better. I'll bring the doctor in to talk to you, but he said it doesn't look as if there's any nerve damage. You'll have scarring, but the lacerations aren't deep."

Cornell left the room, and she heard him leave the apartment.

***

Cornell went straight to the lab. Thomas Scielo, a psychiatrist and former CIA director, and the man in charge of the research department, rose from in front of his computer. "Still intent on doing this, Jim?"

"More than ever. The aliens don't need the baby. If Carolyn loses it, we'll erase the entire pregnancy from her memory. Having said that, do everything to protect it. This child could become an asset." He went to the cooler and poured water into a disposable cup.

Scielo paused, staring at Cornell as though uncertain of what he wanted to say. "This will take a huge toll on Fairchild physically. I can't guarantee she'll retain her psychic abilities."

"What do you mean?"

"How will you prevent her from learning the truth if she can communicate with spirits? All she has to do is talk to her husband once, or Valiant's former partner or late wife, and the jig is up. If you erase Fairchild's memories and replace them with new ones, you must block her mediumship abilities."

"Can you make her believe she's hallucinating? Or schizophrenic?"

"Yes. We could give her an antipsychotic. There's a new one available that should block the mediumship, but won't interfere with her ability to remote view. That's what worries you, right?"

"Yeah. What are the side effects?"

Scielo hesitated. "Low white blood cells. The subject would need regular blood tests. This drug is only used when nothing else works. It can cause seizures, heart problems, or low blood pressure. Most of the time, it's fine, but you plan to manipulate her mind.

That involves physical intervention, and I don't just mean the meds."

Uneasy at this hint of what else they'd put Carolyn through—hypnosis, verbal and sexual abuse, torture, and sensory deprivation—Cornell turned away from Scielo.

"Jim? Second thoughts?"

He shook his head and forced his mind back to the conversation. "What about one of the other antipsychotics? Something without the extreme side effects?"

"Not powerful enough. You want to stop the voices, so to speak? We need something that'll completely block her. Nothing gentle will do."

"Do what you have to do. She's wounded now. Get working on her. I want her greeting me after work with a kiss, a martini in her hand, and ready to shoot Valiant by September."

"A Stepford wife and an assassin? Really, Jim?" Scielo laughed. "That's quite the combination. What will you tell Virginia?"

"That's classified." Cornell smiled, considering it. Time with Carolyn would be like a mini-vacation, a spa visit, and not the ordeal he currently experienced.

"You look as if you're salivating."

He grinned, showing teeth. "If this works, consider the potential. What if I wanted her to connect to a spirit? Can it be done?"

"Well, she'd have to stop the meds, which would take preparation. You can't stop it cold turkey. To control it, you'd need to put her under using hypnosis, so you could guide it. But yeah, it would be feasible. Did you have someone specific in mind?"

"No. Just trying to understand the limitations. I don't like reducing Carolyn's abilities, but it helps if we can tap into them if the need arises."

"There's one problem with the timing though."

"What's that?"

"The pregnancy. We can't give her the drugs until she has the baby. She'll lose it, or it'll be born defective. How far along is she?"

Jim frowned. "The first trimester."

"No good. But it's possible to make the subject think she doesn't believe in that stuff. We can hold her in a cell that is so strongly shielded she can't connect to anyone or anything and keep her in there until the baby is born. The mind control stuff will affect her, but not the child. When her time's up, we can induce labour and begin the drugs."

"Okay, get it implemented. I want her so far out of Valiant's reach that even if he gets her back, she'll want to kill him."

"Yes, sir. I'll have them set up her new quarters immediately, and we'll go get her. We can start this afternoon."

"I want daily updates on her progress, but I don't need the details. Your methods are disturbing, Tom. Ensure you don't kill her or the baby. Carolyn has grown on me. I don't want to lose her."

Cornell crushed the empty paper cup in his fist, dropped it into the recycling bin, and left the lab. He'd see Carolyn once more before the doctors came for her. He rather liked her the way she was. Too bad she wouldn't cooperate and they had to re-educate her. There was no telling who she'd be when they finished.

CHAPTER 38

Holed up in the Peterborough compound for three months now, for Michael, the waiting had become intolerable. August had come in like a *Tyrannosaurus* and had gone out the same way. Two funnel clouds passed through in that one month, along with two hurricanes, four earthquakes, and many storms with wind gusts strong enough to rip trees out of the ground.

Michael was grateful they were in a building designed to withstand almost everything. But if either of the funnel clouds had hit them, he didn't think the building would still be standing. The helicopter he'd brought from Nahanni was nothing but wreckage now.

He'd hoped August would be better, but there'd been no break in the violent weather. Now it was September, and they still hadn't been able to head out. How did others cope with the storms? The environmental upheaval would've caught most people unprepared. At least the compound contained ample stores of food, water, medical supplies, and a generator.

The group had cleaned up the bodies using an incinerator designed for such a purpose though Arnie had fallen apart when the time had come to put in Julie's body. They'd had no choice, however, and in the end, he'd let them do it.

Determined to go after Carolyn, but with the helicopter no longer an option, Michael hoped he'd find a vehicle in an outbuilding. But until the storm subsided, stepping outside would be suicide.

The three stared out into the parking lot, something they did at least once a day, hoping for a break. Arnie broke the silence. "I don't know how much longer I can stand waiting."

Michael agreed. They'd spent most of their time preparing to leave, and by now were beyond ready. Frustration permeated everyone, but at least the delays had given them time to teach Arnie how to shoot and fight. Althaea made Arnie train for hours every morning. The activity kept them fit and gave them something to do.

That the two hadn't slept together yet astounded Michael, and even more astonishing, the holdout was Arnie. Althaea and Arnie had grown close, but he'd kept his hands to himself.

Though it was the middle of the day, the black clouds made everything dim and brooding, and inside, emergency lights provided the only illumination. Michael powered off the generator at regular intervals. While a substantial reserve of fuel for it existed, without knowing how long they'd be trapped here, they used the generator sparingly.

Michael turned away from the window, disgusted, and reached for the ring on the chain around his neck. He'd had no communication from Carolyn since that day they'd connected in Althaea's memories. Every moment of delay cut into his heart like a dagger. He was afraid they were already too late.

***

Michael passed the time by scouring the information on the hard drives he found rooting around in Cornell's office and in the storage room. Cornell and his people must have been in quite a hurry to have left these drives intact. The units had been erased, but not destroyed, and some weren't even reformatted. That had allowed Arnie, a former software developer and computer expert, to recover the data on them.

Cornell likely hadn't known the drives were left in storage intact. Protocol would've demanded they be destroyed, and he'd have ordered it. No doubt, the escalating storm had caused the grunt charged with securing the data to just delete and run.

One folder contained documents outlining agreements with the aliens. Michael clicked on a file in the folder. Sections of the document were redacted. He accessed another file, leaving the first one open. Perhaps if he opened all the files, he could piece together the information. He created a new file and got to work.

He was still working on it when Althaea stuck her head in to see if he wanted dinner. When he grunted at her that he wasn't hungry, she left, returning fifteen minutes later with a tray of food.

She set the tray on the desk and put a hand on Michael's shoulder. "I won't bother you, but please eat your dinner."

Michael gave her a distracted nod, and her goodbye went unacknowledged, the door closing behind her unheard. After a few minutes of staring at the screen, though, the smell of fresh bread and beef stew distracted him. He dipped a piece of bread into the hot broth of the stew and nibbled on it. Whatever else you could say about Arnie, the guy was a great cook.

The open document on the screen in front of him caught his attention again, and he leaned back in the chair. Dinner might be a good excuse to stop and pick it up again in the morning. Michael leaned forward, hand on the mouse, hovering the cursor over the close button.

It was then that all the pieces fell into place, and suddenly Michael found it hard to breathe. He was looking at a contract. Those Agency assholes had sold Earth to the fucking aliens. Michael's hands curled into fists.

The agreement stipulated that the people in the underground colonies would remain free. Any other survivors on the planet would be the property of the aliens, who could use them any way they wanted.

Michael closed the file and set password protection on it. He'd let Althaea know it was here and add it to the documentation they were creating. One day, the aliens might return, and whoever was here should prepare for that eventuality.

Desperation to retrieve Carolyn hit him, and he considered the options as he closed everything and powered down the computer. They had to go after her soon, and Sam, too, of course.

I'll have to teach Sam, and the baby when she gets older, to watch the skies.

Michael looked over at the plate of food Althaea had left him and his stomach clenched, his appetite gone.

***

Subject's re-education complete. Please review the attached document for instructions on proceeding.

Cornell read the message from Scielo and almost cheered. He looked up, afraid Ginny might suspect something. She sat on the sofa, watching a movie, Wade seated next to her. Upstairs, Sam read George a bedtime story.

A glance at the clock showed eight o'clock. Cornell hadn't had any contact with Carolyn for three months and was eager to see her. Not wanting to witness what Scielo and his team did to her, he'd stayed away during her re-education. Now it was done, he couldn't wait until morning to visit her.

The baby had survived the ordeal, to his relief. Scielo had reprogrammed Carolyn to believe the child was Cornell's, making it easier for her to accept him as her lover.

He stood. "I have to return to work, Ginny. Tom Scielo sent me an urgent message. He's completed a complicated project I assigned him, and I need to go inspect the results."

Ginny looked at him, puzzled. He'd explained too much. He'd have to be careful not to get talkative. Typically, Cornell told Ginny he was returning to work and that was that.

"I'll be late. Don't wait up."

He said good night to Sam and George, waved to Wade and Ginny on the way out, and walked to Carolyn's house. They'd set her up in a nicer, two-bedroom townhouse with all the amenities, and Scielo's team had ensured the unit was shielded.

Cornell stopped at a greenhouse and picked up a bouquet on his way. The greenhouses were spectacular accomplishments in the underground community. Constructed to simulate daylight, the vast structures grew plants sprouted from heirloom seeds collected over the last thirty years.

Birds, insects, and small animals lived in the bio dome, and if you didn't look up and see the enclosure, you'd think you were outside. Even the circulating air simulated a summer breeze.

When he reached Carolyn's door, he waited, listening. The drone of the TV filtered through the door. Cornell tapped on the door and used his key to open it.

Carolyn sat on the couch, legs tucked under her, a shawl around her shoulders. She was always chilly, even though the temperature in the house was regulated, the humidity controlled.

When the door opened, she gave him a shy smile and paused the movie she watched. His mouth went dry, and he felt a flutter in his gut. She'd never smiled at him. It made her even more beautiful and desirable.

"Hi, Jim." She sounded happy to see him. "I didn't think you'd come see me today. It's getting late, so I assumed you were working or went home."

"I couldn't stay away." He held out the flowers and caught a faint whiff of carnation.

She beamed. "Thank you. They're gorgeous." She went to him and accepted the package, taking it to the kitchen. A large vase appeared from a cupboard, and she unwrapped the paper.

Cornell watched her while she trimmed the stems and put the flowers in water. She moved fluidly, no trace of any injuries. When she set the arrangement on the table, he went to her, and gently grabbed her wrists.

He turned her hands over, examined the nails, the palms. He looked into her eyes, ran his hands through her hair, checking for lumps, checking for cuts and bruises.

Worry crossed her face. "What is it? Something wrong?"

Before he could speak, he cleared his throat. "No, nothing." He exhaled in relief. "I haven't seen you in a while, and I got worried."

"What do you mean? We saw each other yesterday at lunch. Everything was fine."

His heart thudded against his chest. Carolyn had memories of spending time together from as recently as yesterday. He'd have to read through Scielo's notes carefully, make sure he knew every lie they'd fed her.

"Yes, of course. It feels like an eternity when I don't see you." Cornell smiled.

"Why did you think something was wrong? Did something happen?" Carolyn's voice rose, and panic flashed across her face. "Is it Michael Valiant? Is he coming after me?"

He pulled her into his arms. "Shh. No, don't worry. You're safe here. It wasn't anything like that. How's the baby?"

Carolyn nuzzled her head against his neck, and then pulled back, smiling. "I think she kicked today—just a flutter—but I'm sure it was baby and not gas." Her excitement lit up her eyes.

"She? Did the doctor tell you the baby is a girl?" He felt unease though he couldn't have said what troubled him.

"Just a feeling." Carolyn leaned over and kissed his lips.

Cornell responded, desire flooding through him, but restrained himself. He wanted to take her to the bedroom, but needed to make sure she belonged to him. He couldn't afford to shatter the illusion with haste.

Carolyn broke the kiss and giggled. "Are we going to stand here all night? Let's go sit. Watch *Casablanca* with me. I love that old movie." She grabbed his hand and pulled him to the couch.

Cornell settled himself in the corner and put his arm around her shoulder. She restarted the movie, leaned into him, and curled her legs up. He ran a hand through her short hair, enjoying the softness. He'd had them cut the brown dye out of it, and it was a natural golden blonde again. Contented, he kissed the top of her head and sighed. He could get used to this.

CHAPTER 39

Once Ginny had been in bed for an hour, Sam slipped from her room and crept to Cornell's office. Compared to the home they'd left behind in Richmond Hill, this one was small, though still larger than the house Sam had lived in with her parents.

When the Cornells and Sam had first arrived at the underground community, everything had had a dream-like quality. She'd marvelled at the backyard, almost a replica of the Cornells' previous yard. It even had the swimming pool, though, like the house, everything in the yard was smaller. Cornell had even told Sam she must wear sunscreen if she wanted to sit "outside" for any length of time.

At first, things had seemed better here than in Richmond Hill. Virginia was nicer to her—even encouraging Sam to call her "Ginny." Cornell spent more time at home and tension between Cornell and Ginny eased.

Sam missed her friends and regretted leaving them without saying where she'd gone. Cornell had explained they'd come to the underground community because they were in danger from cult members responsible for her mother's death. He'd assured Sam that her friends were safe—she was the one in danger and why she lived with the Cornells.

The underground community, originally built for scientific research, provided a safe place for the family to hide. Sam could even continue her studies here. But then this project came up, and Cornell worked long hours, sometimes spending the entire night at the office. Ginny became moody, the boys restless, and Sam herself grew suspicious.

She guessed it was an effort for Cornell to act as if everything were normal. He seemed excited at the prospect of leaving for work in the morning. Often absent at dinner, when he did show up, he went out again after the kids went to bed. He'd lost weight, too and took extra care when he got dressed in the morning.

Yesterday, Sam had overheard Cornell arguing with Ginny, assuring her there was no one else, that he was working on an important, time-consuming project. Sam didn't believe him, agreeing with Ginny that he behaved like a man having an affair. As a favour to Ginny, Sam had decided to snoop around, though she was unsure what she'd do if she discovered Cornell was cheating. But it angered her to think he'd do that to his family.

A nail file popped the lock on the office door, and Sam slipped inside. She didn't turn on her flashlight until she'd shut and locked the door. She went straight to Cornell's desk and sat in the chair. Without touching anything, she scanned the desk: laptop; a picture of Ginny and the boys; a stress ball; phone; pens and pencils in a stainless steel holder; and a two-tiered paper tray with papers in both tiers.

Sam shone the light on the papers, which were face down in the tray, a paperweight resting on the top stack. She tried the top stack first. Sam riffled through the pages until an email message caught her interest. It was dated two weeks ago, September 18, which was when Cornell had started acting weird.

Re: Subject 4382CF.

The body of the message was brief:

To answer your questions, 4382CF believes you rescued her from Valiant. The subject believes Valiant killed her husband and daughter and kidnapped and raped her. She does not pose a threat to you or your family. Memories can "bleed through," as you put it, but that's rare, and typically limited to minor flashes of inconsequential events.

Regarding training: start with self-defence and weapons training. It should be safe to issue the subject a firearm to keep on hand for protection. Let me know if you have any questions or comments.

Tom

Below this was Cornell's original message:

Tom, what does 4382CF believe is my connection to Michael Valiant? Is there a chance of a relapse? In other words, is it possible for old memories to bleed through and make her a threat to me or my family? Can the subject begin training, and if yes, what do you recommend? Can I issue her a Beretta to keep on hand in case Valiant makes it here when I'm not with her?

Jim

A lump grew in Sam's throat and her stomach fluttered. The new project Cornell had mentioned was a *person*. A woman. When he left here after dinner or didn't come home until early morning, he was probably with her.

Based on the messages she'd just read, the woman believed things that weren't true. But how could she believe she'd been raped if it hadn't happened? Was the purpose of the project to make her think that? Why would Cornell do that to someone?

Sam put the paper back where she'd found it and replaced the paperweight. She'd seen enough. The next time Cornell went out, she'd follow him and find out who this 4382CF person was. Then she'd figure out what to do about it.

***

Cornell awoke and checked the clock next to Carolyn's side of the bed. Just after one o'clock. A glance at Carolyn verified she was sound asleep. He slipped out of bed and reached for his pants. This routine had become tedious, but he had to go home. It was bad enough he kept falling asleep here and getting home after midnight.

After the argument he'd had with Ginny the other day, he'd sworn to go home earlier, but he'd been reluctant to tear himself away. The time spent with Carolyn was more than pleasant. She made no demands on him, had no expectations. Aware he was married, she accepted he'd never leave his family. She greeted him with enthusiasm whenever he showed up, and when he didn't, she occupied herself and didn't complain.

But he'd made sure she had plenty to occupy herself with: DVDs, including exercise videos, books, and a computer— whatever she wanted. Cornell had even gotten a few good old-fashioned games, like backgammon and chess, which they could play when he visited.

He'd set up a mini gym in the back of her bedroom, large enough to accommodate an elliptical trainer, a bench, free weights, and a rowing machine. Carolyn wasn't doing anything too hard core through her pregnancy, but she exercised each day.

She had enough freedom to leave her house, which could be unlocked from inside, though her section remained segregated from most areas. Cornell granted her access to the greenhouse, library, market, park, and cafés frequented by Agency personnel.

A patio and garden in the back of the house provided the illusion of a natural setting. The yard didn't have a pool, but it had a small pond. The gratitude Carolyn expressed for everything he'd done brought with it the occasional stab of guilt, but he told himself she was happy and shrugged it off.

Dressed, Cornell tiptoed from the room. He disliked leaving without saying goodbye, but hated disturbing her sleep even more. She'd told him she understood. He stood for a moment, listening. The fridge hummed in the background; otherwise, the house was quiet. He unlocked the front door and stepped out into the soft summery night.

When he arrived home, he silently let himself in, took off his shoes, and headed towards the kitchen. On the way past the bar, he grabbed a rocks glass and the bottle of scotch. Cornell sat at the table, using the nightlight by the stove to guide him, and poured himself three fingers. With Carolyn, he rarely drank. But when he arrived home, he'd grab one regardless of the time.

The next day's schedule scrolled through his head as he sat sipping the scotch. Carolyn had self-defence lessons in the morning and weapons training in the afternoon. After that, he'd join her at her house and ask her to do remote viewing—the first since her re-education.

The thought of the first remote-viewing session made him nervous, afraid it would trigger a real memory. Scielo had assured him that wouldn't happen. Cornell certainly hoped not. He had to get her back into tracking Valiant. Too much time had gone by, and Valiant might be on his way, storms or not.

A sound in the hallway caught his attention, and he searched for the source. Sam stood in the kitchen entrance, staring at him. She didn't appear sleepy and wore a robe over pyjamas. The bunny slippers on her feet made her look like a kid.

She is a kid. "What's up, Sam? Why aren't you in bed?"

"I couldn't sleep. When I heard you come in, I came out to talk to you."

"Something wrong?"

"Not with me."

Cornell sipped his scotch, anticipating what she'd say next. "Then with whom?"

"You."

"Sit. Tell me."

Sam moved to the chair across from him and sat.

"Drink?" He held up the bottle of scotch.

She shook her head.

"Okay, what's so urgent that you had to confront me at this time of the ni—morning? Already." Cornell sighed. He might not get to bed after all.

"I overheard you arguing with Ginny."

"No doubt. She wasn't quiet."

"I think she has a point."

"What's her point?"

Sam stared at Cornell as if he'd said something incomprehensible. She hesitated, and when she finally spoke, she whispered. "That you're seeing someone else."

"Sam, I have many responsibilities. I don't answer to Ginny. I certainly don't answer to you." He held up his hand. "No, wait. I appreciate your concern. But you should know Ginny often accuses me of this. When you first came to live with us, she was jealous and suspicious of my relationship with you. Were you aware of that?"

Sam nodded once and sighed. "This is different. You act different than when we were back in Richmond Hill."

"I don't know what you mean, but I can tell you I'm under more stress here. I have to keep this place running smoothly." Cornell reached out and patted her hand. "Your concern is touching. I'm not seeing anyone. I'm wrapped up with my responsibilities here. Please, help Ginny understand. She makes it tough for the rest of us when she has one of her jealous fits." He withdrew his hand.

Sam stared at the table. When she looked up, her eyes were guarded, but she gave him a weak smile. "Okay. I'm sorry I jumped to conclusions. You're away too much, and when you leave in the morning, you dress as if you're seeing someone special."

He smiled. "I'm not doing anything different than I've always done."

"Yes, you do. You lost weight. You dress nicer."

"That's kind of you. But I've lost weight because the diet we

434

have here isn't as processed and unhealthy. Ginny lost weight too. You don't think she's having an affair, do you?"

Sam shook her head and smiled. "Okay." She pressed a palm to her mouth, stifling a yawn. "I'm going back to bed. The boys and I have a big day tomorrow—an outing to the library and the public pool."

"What's wrong with the pool in the backyard?"

"The public pool has activities for kids. We're meeting up with their friends, and I'll hang out with the other nannies while the boys have swimming lessons."

He nodded. "Okay. Good night."

After she left, Cornell took another swig of his scotch. He'd have to be more careful. The last thing he needed was Sam snooping into his business. He fought an urge to go back to Carolyn's and never return. If it were just Ginny, he'd do it, but he couldn't leave his boys. He chugged the rest of his scotch and went to bed.

CHAPTER 40

Carolyn slips on her long, white gown and cinches it at the waist with a gold cord. Natalia, her handmaiden, braids Carolyn's hair and wraps it around her head, then leads her by the hand into the temple where the priests wait. The high priest, whom Carolyn recognizes as Jim Cornell, takes her hand from the attendant's and guides her to a chair on the podium.

Once she is seated, Cornell stands behind her, hands gripping her shoulders. The other priests encircle her, and she closes her eyes. Motion ceases, and she hears a rustle of paper. A scribe will record everything. She clears her throat, nervous.

The incense's spicy scent fills her nose, making her nauseated. Cornell's hands stroke the back of her neck, tickling her. She shivers, and his hands slide to her bare arms. The touch repulses her, and she wants to shake him off, but forces herself to keep still. The punishment for rebelling would be brutal.

An image of the moon pops into her head, and she speaks: "I see the moon."

The scratch of a reed brush on papyrus reaches her ears as the scribe writes that down.

"A blue moon, heralding upheaval. Beware."

Screams from outside interrupt. She startles at a crash from the front of the temple. Footsteps running up the aisle close in on where she sits. Curiosity overcomes fear, and Carolyn opens her eyes to see Michael Valiant, a soldier, racing towards her. Blood seeps through the front of his uniform.

Cornell pulls her up from the chair and pushes her behind him while motioning for two priests to remove her from the room. A stream of guards run in behind Valiant, swords drawn. He makes a sound that's part growl, part wail, and runs at Cornell. Carolyn struggles against the priests who hold her. She wants to break free, to help Michael. If she doesn't, they'll kill him. A guard reaches Valiant and runs him through with a sword. She screams in agony and despair.

Carolyn awoke, tears on her face, and touched the space next to her, looking for Cornell. Gone. She flicked on the light and pulled a notebook and pen from the night table to record the details of the dream.

The frequency of the dreams had increased, and they'd become more vivid and strange. Each one involved Michael Valiant, herself, Cornell, and a man she'd never met, who in the dreams was Valiant's partner until Valiant betrayed him.

The pattern was always the same: Michael and his partner capture her. In one series of dreams, it was during a witch hunt. In another, she was an oracle in ancient Greece. Carolyn thought she was in Atlantis in yet another.

Regardless of the dream's setting, she and Michael would fall in love and one or both of them would end up dead. She'd considered telling Cornell about the dreams, but something always prevented her. Perhaps it was because in the dreams, Cornell was always the villain.

Carolyn closed the notebook and put it away. She lay back again and thought about Cornell and what he meant to her. He was kind and generous to her, and she appreciated that, but she didn't love him. She missed John and Sam. The loss of her husband and daughter was more than she could bear.

Thoughts of her family brought her around to thinking of their killer: Michael Valiant. He'd killed her husband, and before she'd even buried John, had broken into her house, kidnapped her, and killed Sam. Carolyn had lived in a constant state of terror when she was with Valiant.

First, he'd taken her to a hotel in Peterborough, where he'd raped her. Then he'd taken her to Algonquin Park, where he'd turned her over to the aliens, but not before raping her again.

Panic and fear escalated as she relived those moments. She calmed herself by remembering how Cornell had rescued her from the aliens. He'd taken her to the safety of the compound in Peterborough and gotten her the help she needed to recover. He protected her now. Yet whenever she had one of these dreams, she'd wake up longing to be reunited with Valiant, her heart breaking at the thought of losing him.

It was obviously residual effects of the dream, but it disoriented and confused her. This man had destroyed her, and she was having dreams of being in love with him and despising Cornell. It'd be a bad idea to tell Jim about the dreams.

She checked the time. Almost five o'clock. She'd have to get up soon anyway. They'd begin her self-defence training today. It unnerved her to think Cornell believed it was necessary, implying the possibility Valiant could get to her here.

Carolyn climbed out of bed and headed to the washroom, a flutter of anticipation making her hurry. She'd train hard. If Michael Valiant ever found her, he'd discover she wasn't the same woman he'd abused and then handed over to the aliens. She'd make him pay for what he'd done to her.

***

Sam waited in her room while Cornell prepared to go out again. He'd come home for dinner at least, but insisted he had to return to work. She'd said good night and excused herself, claiming she had studying. Door closed, she removed her T-shirt and jeans and put on a skirt and blouse. A pair of low-heeled pumps replaced the sneakers she wore. She brushed her hair and twisted it into a bun.

When she heard the outer door close, she tucked an ID badge she'd stolen from Cornell's desk into her shoulder bag. She returned to the kitchen, where Marnie scraped leftover food from dinner plates into the garbage disposal. Ginny sat at the table with a cocktail and watched.

Sam told Ginny she was going to the library, and Ginny gave her a distracted nod. Getting away from Wade and George proved more difficult. They begged to go along with her. She argued that she needed to study, and Ginny withdrew from her haze long enough to yell at the kids to leave Sam alone. Sam hurried outside into the tunnel, a replica of a street, and searched for Cornell.

She spotted him walking along the sidewalk, headed in the direction he took when he went to work. Sam followed him, keeping her distance. Trees lined the street, and if she didn't know they were underground, she'd never have believed the twilight sky above her was an illusion. She could see what looked like the setting sun in the distance. A slight breeze rippled her hair.

Sam pulled the ID badge from her bag and clipped it onto her blouse. Finally, a practical use for the graphics degree she'd been working on for the last year. She'd doctored the ID badge to display her picture. Anyone examining it closely might spot the forgery, but she figured dropping Cornell's name would prevent most people from asking too many questions.

Earlier in the day, she'd taken a test run from the residential section where the Cornell residence was to the restricted Agency section where Cornell worked. No one had stopped her. She'd gone into their library, hung out at a café, and picked up fruit at the market.

She shouldn't have any problems getting back in now. Sam kept Cornell in her sights, but hung back in case he stopped and turned around. When he reached the gatepost entrance to the Agency quarter, she slowed even more. After he was through, she quickened her pace.

Sam got through security again with no issues and fell in behind Cornell through the commercial section. Residential buildings dominated the other side. Sam noted with some smugness that he didn't head to his office building, but instead continued on through the core towards the residences.

She slowed her pace again, and when he turned into a walkway leading up to a townhouse complex, she crossed the street. He never looked back. She waited until he was inside, then stood across the street from the house and memorized the distinguishing features.

Roses grew on a trellis in front of the small porch. Fairy wind chimes hung from the porch roof. The wooden porch was painted a dusty blue with white accents. Lights in the living room and open curtains showed the home's interior.

A movie played on the TV. The movie paused, and Cornell moved into view. He opened his arms, and a blonde woman appeared. She went to him and they hugged. Sam's heart skipped a beat. The woman's movements were familiar.

Sam watched, entranced. The couple kissed. Ginny and Sam had been right: he was having an affair. Anger bubbled up. She had an urge to rush over and bang on the door. At that moment, the lovers parted, and Sam saw the woman's face for the first time. She staggered backwards and gave a wounded cry as she recognized her mother.

CHAPTER 41

"Why isn't Michael joining us?" Althaea called out to Arnie, who was in the kitchen cooking dinner.

"Couldn't drag him away from the windows. The wind's dying down, and he wants to get out and hunt for a vehicle. I said we'd help him after dinner, but he snarled at me, so I walked away." Arnie's voice floated out through the open kitchen doors and into the cafeteria where Althaea sat at a table.

"The wind *is* dying down, but he should eat something. I hope he doesn't go out alone. But he gets obsessive and needs his space. Good call."

Arnie appeared, a plate of food in each hand. He set one on the table in front of Althaea and the other across from her.

"My specialty."

"Scrambled eggs and sausages." Althaea grinned. "Breakfast for dinner. I've always enjoyed that. And not a veggie in sight."

"Now, wait. Veggies coming right up, Madame."

He returned to the kitchen and dishes clattered. A moment later, he reappeared, carrying two bowls, which he set in the middle of the table.

"Asparagus and biscuits." Hands fisted on waist, Arnie puffed out his chest, grinned, and executed a bow. "Don't forget to tip your waiter."

Althaea laughed. She laughed more often these days, and Arnie was usually the cause. "I can't deny this meal is fabulous—not when you're so proud."

The grin grew wider, and when it reached his eyes, her heart gave a thud. This time, she jumped to her feet, threw her arms around him, and kissed him forcefully on the mouth. Arnie's arms enfolded her, and his mouth opened in response before he pulled away.

"What's wrong?" Her voice sounded petulant. Hurt replaced surprise as the rejection sliced through her gut like a sickle. She'd believed the attraction was mutual, and considering Arnie's single status, she'd expected him to make a move on her sooner or later.

Michael had warned her weeks ago that Arnie was a womanizer. When the expected move hadn't come, Ally assumed he'd held back while healing from his bullet wound. But now she wondered if she was a man repellent.

When Michael had rejected her, it was bad enough, though in the end, she understood why. This was different. What about her was so repulsive that even a guy who couldn't keep it in his pants could keep it in his pants?

Arnie directed his gaze at the floor. "Ally," he said.

"Don't. Please. You have a reputation for nailing anything that moves. Yet when I'm like the last woman on Earth, on the pill, ready and willing, you don't want me." Her voice broke. *Damn it. Don't cry like a girl.* She sat and picked up her fork.

"Althaea, it's not—"

She cut him off. "Don't feed me the 'it's not you it's me' bullshit. Okay?"

Gentle, Arnie took the fork from her hand, set it on the plate, and covered her hand with his. "Listen."

The kindness in his voice made the breath catch in her throat. She looked up at Arnie, mesmerized by his eyes. With difficulty, she pulled her gaze away and stared at the uneaten eggs.

"It's not that I don't want to. You've no idea how much I want to. But I don't want to hurt you, which means taking things slow."

"That's not what I heard about you."

"You mean from Valiant?"

Althaea nodded.

"A great one to talk. He was with Carolyn for a nanosecond and slept with her. You were involved with him too, right? You told me so yourself."

She shook her head, finding it difficult to answer that question. "Sit. Eat your dinner. It looks delicious."

"You want to eat?" Disbelief and an edge of irritation laced his voice.

"I don't want to waste good food."

His shoulders dropped, and he laughed softly. "You're so practical it drives me crazy." But he sat and picked up his fork. "Shall we talk while we eat?"

Althaea speared a stalk of asparagus, shattered pride soothed while she focused on the vegetable and nibbled. "Excellent."

"Thanks. But you're not going to distract me."

"I jumped you, and you rejected me. What's to discuss? Just tell me what's wrong with me."

The fork in Arnie's hand clattered to his plate. "There's nothing wrong with you. This isn't a rejection. I want to make sure it's what you want. I've never considered the woman's perspective before, but I want to now. In this fucking hellhole, I found out what it's like to be used and abused. It made me reconsider how I treat other people, Ally, especially women."

Suddenly she felt ravenous. She shovelled eggs into her mouth, grabbed a biscuit, and wolfed it down. "I need a drink. Want one?"

Before he could reply, she stood and hurried to the kitchen, returning with two bottles of water. Arnie took one from her, and, still seated, pulled her to him. He hugged her tight around the thighs. She gripped his shoulders, trying not to fall on him.

"Did you love Valiant?"

After taking a deep breath to squelch her frustration, Althaea pulled away from him. "Is that why you've kept me at arm's length? I didn't sleep with him. Does it matter?"

"Were you in love with him?"

"Yes." It was true. She'd been in love with Michael, or, at least, she'd loved him in the limited capacity she'd had for loving anyone back then.

Arnie's steel-blue gaze locked onto hers. "Are you still in love with him?"

"No. If I was, I wouldn't be throwing myself at you."

"I'd like to think that's true. You guys are awfully buddy-buddy."

Althaea sat in her chair again, but this time didn't pick up the fork. "I understand Michael—we're a lot alike, shared similar experiences. Yes, I was attracted to him once. He's strong, intelligent, and passionate. Qualities that appeal to me. But I'm over him. I got him out of my system, and yeah, most of that was done after we got here, but I'm over him. Why are we analyzing it?"

"I want to make sure you want me, and I'm not just a—a substitute or something." Arnie gazed at his plate of food, dejected.

Althaea sighed. "I'm attracted to you, Arnie. But I don't know if I'm looking for anything more than sex. I assumed you'd be okay with that."

"You mean because Valiant told you I'd nail anything that moved?"

"Yes."

"I'm not looking for that anymore. I'm tired of that."

"What about Carolyn?"

"What about her?"

"Are you in love with her? I see how you get when you talk about her. I can tell you hate it when Michael mentions their time together, or when he grabs for her ring, which he thinks we don't notice."

Arnie leaned forward. "I thought I was. Don't get me wrong: I still love Carolyn, but I'm not in love with her. I think I wanted Carolyn because she didn't want me. It was juvenile. But I had a lot of time to reflect since there wasn't anything else to do but navel gaze and take abuse. I want to rescue Carolyn from that asshole Cornell, but not for me. I just want her to be safe."

Althaea nodded. "Okay. So now what? Are we going to be okay?"

Arnie took her hand, put it to his cheek, and closed his eyes. "We'll be great."

***

Michael stared out into the storm. The wind had quieted at least enough for him to make the run to the garage. Too restless and agitated to wait for Althaea and Arnie, he'd skipped dinner and hovered at the side exit watching for a break.

Backpack loaded with C4, blasting caps, and a radio-frequency detonator, Michael planned to blow the garage bay doors open if necessary. If there were a vehicle in there, he'd get it and finally get the hell out of this place.

Rain battered the door, and Michael estimated sixty kilometres per hour winds. It would make getting to the outbuildings difficult, but not impossible. It was much better than the strong gale-force winds they had until now.

A waterproof windbreaker covered his clothes, and the backpack hung from his shoulders. The sky still showed the puke-green colour that had become the norm, but he was sure there'd be no funnel clouds.

Michael pushed his way out onto the pavement. The wind caught the door, almost wrenching it from his grasp. He wrestled nature for control and forced the door closed.

The garage, fifty metres away, loomed like a barrow mound in the murk. The hood blew off his head, and within seconds, his hair and face were drenched. He ignored the discomfort and pressed on, leaning into the wind.

Michael fought his way to the entrance and tried the insulated steel overhead door first. It refused to budge. He moved to the next door and jiggled the handle. Also locked, but he could pick that no problem—no need for C4. He set his pack down and took out a lock-picking case.

Inside, the bays before him stood empty. Worried, he jogged along the corridor. To his relief, three vehicles, two of them SUVs, sat abandoned. He reached into his pack for the car keys he'd taken from Deuce and Tasha. When he pressed the remote, the lights flashed on the vehicle in front of him.

Michael yanked open the car door and jumped into the driver's seat. The engine started, and he checked the gas gauge. Half full. He turned the vehicle off and inspected the other car, which had over a quarter tank of gas. They'd siphon the gas from this one and add it to the other SUV.

Now they had the means to leave, he was anxious to get moving. But when he returned to the exit and opened the door, his heart sank. The wind had picked up again. Michael stepped out into the storm. Lightning flashed overhead, followed seconds later by thunder. Pushed along by the wind, he ran back to the building.

As he neared the building, Althaea poked her head out the door and screamed something at him. Michael thought it involved the f-bomb. He tumbled inside, Arnie grabbing an arm to keep him from falling.

"What the fuck were you thinking? You should have let us know you were going out." Althaea's face held red fury.

"Forget it. I'm here now. Two SUVs in the garage. We can leave."

Arnie and Althaea exchanged glances.

"Don't tell me no. The wind isn't that bad."

"It's picking up again. Try the radio and find a weather report," Arnie said.

"They don't know what they're talking about. I'm not waiting. We have to get Carolyn."

From outside came a sound like an approaching freight train. Michael cursed and looked out into the storm. In the distance, a funnel cloud reached towards the earth from the roiling green ceiling headed in their direction. He froze. If the tornado hit the garage, it would turn it into rubble and destroy the cars.

Althaea touched his arm. "We'd better get to the basement."

CHAPTER 42

Rooted to the sidewalk, Sam watched while her mother and Cornell canoodled in the window of the townhouse across the street. Carolyn turned her back to Cornell, and he moved to stand behind her. His arms curled around her, and he nuzzled her neck. Sam's legs shook and breathing became difficult.

It occurred to her to move away from the direct view of the house. She walked two metres back the way she'd come, then stopped. Should she confront them? What would Cornell do if she appeared at the door?

She recalled the message she'd seen on his desk. Her mother was the "subject" referred to in the email and thought someone named Michael Valiant had killed her family. Sam gulped at a lump in her throat.

Mom thinks I'm dead—like I thought she was dead.

Cornell had done this.

Afraid the two would see her, Sam continued to walk back towards the gatehouse. It was best to return to the Cornells and figure out what to do next. Knees wobbling the moment she sighted the gate, Sam stopped to breathe out nervous tension.

The guards checked everyone leaving, too. If she looked too flustered, they'd stop her. She grabbed a spot at the end of the line, took a few deep gulps of air, and did another breath check. Steady, even, inhale, exhale.

People ahead passed through the gate, flashing ID badges at the guards. No one stopped or even paused. The process should be easy enough: hold up the badge, walk by the guard without hesitation, go through the gate, and head home. Sam unclipped the phony badge from her lapel and held it ready between numbed fingers.

Afraid the badge would slip through her fingers and attract attention, Sam tightened her grip. Thoughts raced, her brain trying to reconcile seeing her mother with Cornell's assertion Carolyn had died in Algonquin.

Mom is alive.

Sam inhaled, steadied herself, and stepped up to the gate. The guard, who looked about the same age as Sam, smiled. She forced a brief return smile, flashed the badge, and continued walking, careful not to appear anxious or hurried.

"Hey, Blondie. Wait a minute."

She froze and turned to face the guard, trying to look puzzled and bored at the same time.

"Are you new here?" The guard walked over to her, peered into her face. He slipped the badge from her icy fingers and glanced at the name and photo. "Samantha Cornell. Are you related to Jim Cornell?"

Sorry now she'd used the Cornell name on the badge, Sam had assumed it would get her past checkpoints more easily. "Yes. I'm his niece. Is there a problem? I can call him." She looked into his eyes. He blushed, and her tension eased. All she had to do was bluff her way past him.

Face still tinged with red, the young man shook his head. "No problem. I wanted to meet you."

Sam flashed another smile, hoping she looked friendly and inviting. "You've met me." She glanced at his badge. "Trevor. Now we know each other."

She reached for her badge, letting her fingers brush against his hand when she retrieved it. "Is this your regular post?" Sam hoped so. If she got to know him, he'd let her come and go as she pleased. This might work to her advantage.

"Sure. Every afternoon shift—for the next month, anyway. Then my shift changes back to days."

"What time does the afternoon shift start?"

"Two o'clock."

"I'm holding up the line. I'll see you again soon?"

"Can we meet for coffee before my shift?" Trevor blushed.

Sam beamed at him. "Sure. Meet me tomorrow at one o'clock at the cafe."

When he agreed, she fluttered her fingers at him and walked away. A safe distance from the gate, she exhaled loudly, relieved she'd pulled it off. The blouse she wore had soaked through under the arms though she hadn't even noticed she'd been sweating. Sam hurried home.

***

Carolyn sat on the recliner, eyes closed. The pad of paper in her lap already held sketches: a garage door, an SUV, a funnel cloud, and a mangled helicopter. Cornell was particularly interested in the SUV.

"Are they in the vehicle?" he asked for the second time.

"No. It was something Valiant saw, standing in front of it, not looking over the hood from behind the steering wheel."

She tried to sense Valiant again though the thought of connecting to the man who'd murdered her family repulsed her. "Jim, it's too difficult. They went to the basement, which blocked me. That's all I can get."

Carolyn opened her eyes, and Cornell took the paper and pencil from her. A smile played across his lips, and he grasped her hands and pulled her from the chair. He held her, kissing her lips and her neck. When he spoke, his lips moved against her skin. "You don't have to worry about Valiant anymore today, okay?"

She sighed, relieved. "Okay. Thank you. I hate thinking about him. It brings it all back as though it happened yesterday."

Cornell slid his hand up her shirt, under her bra. "Then forget him for now." His voice was thick with desire. He pressed against her, and she let him. Having Cornell with her felt comforting though not exciting. When he wasn't with her, emptiness and longing closed in, and his presence eased her loneliness.

He took Carolyn by the hand and led her into the bedroom. They stayed there the rest of the evening.

***

He's cute.

Sam accepted the coffee Trevor handed her, and he sat opposite her at the table. She'd chosen a booth at the back of the café with a direct view of the door. Even though she was positive Cornell was at the office, she had to be careful.

No longer terrified of Trevor, Sam studied him and decided she liked what she saw. His dark hair was too army cut, but that wasn't his choice. He had a nice face and kind eyes that reminded her of a puppy her friend Vanna had.

"Are you here visiting your uncle?" he asked.

For an awful moment, Sam didn't understand. Then she remembered she'd told Trevor the day before that Cornell was her uncle. "No. I came here to visit you. Uncle Jim would be mad if he knew I was here. He doesn't want me coming here unless it's to see him, and he doesn't want me to date. Don't mention you saw me if you talk to him. Okay?" Trevor might run into Cornell and mention seeing his "niece." She'd better plaster over that hole right now.

"Why does he have a say in who you date?"

"The Cornells are my guardians. I live with them, and I play nanny to their kids. The boys have school now, though, so I slipped away."

"I won't say anything."

"Thanks." Sam fell silent and sipped her coffee. She'd been without a friend for a long time, and she'd better be careful. Trevor could never be a confidant.

God, I miss Jack and Vanna.

"Why are you living with your uncle? Where are your parents?"

Sam stared at her coffee. *Half full.* She glanced at Trevor.

He waited, patient.

"They're dead. Dad died of a heart attack. Mom killed herself when she got involved with a UFO cult." Safest to perpetuate the lie, she decided.

"I'm sorry." He sounded sincere.

She wondered if he knew what was happening. Perhaps she could get information from Trevor. That would mean less snooping in Cornell's office. "How did you get hired?"

"Recruited out of university." Trevor sat straighter, puffed out his chest.

Wide-eyed, Sam said, "Wow. They noticed you? What were you studying?"

"I majored in math at the University of Waterloo, but had more than a minor in astronomy. They also liked that I'm a black belt in

Judo."

"That's impressive. Are your parents here?"

"No. They died in a car accident when I was in my second year at university."

"I'm sorry. So you understand what it's like for me. How old are you?"

"Twenty-four. You?"

Sam smiled. "Twenty."

Trevor checked his watch. "I have to go. Can we meet again?"

"I'd like that. What time do you finish work?"

Trevor raised his brows. "Ten-thirty. Would the Cornells have a fit if I called on you then?"

"Yes, that's too late." Sam let him hear her disappointment. "Let's meet tomorrow before you start work."

"Sure. Same time?"

Sam nodded and beamed a smile at him. Trevor grinned back, and Sam thought she could happily spend the rest of the day sitting here watching him smile. She tossed back the rest of her coffee and stood when he did.

Butterflies fluttered in Sam's stomach when he touched her hand as they said their goodbyes. A woman in army fatigues bumped into Trevor as he headed towards the door. Jealousy pinched Sam for a second when he held the woman to steady her.

She shook it off. He was nice, but she couldn't trust him, and a crush on him might make her careless. But it would be nice to have someone.

Sam left the booth and stood inside the café entrance, which was open to the sidewalk. Before stepping out, she searched for any sign of Trevor or Cornell. She caught sight of Trevor's back as he headed towards the gate.

Only a handful of people wandered about, and no sign of Cornell. Sam left the café and walked to her mother's house.

CHAPTER 43

Michael stood at the exit and tried to determine how severe the damage was to the outbuildings. The tornado had munched the right side of the garage, but the left side containing the SUVs remained intact. When the funnel cloud had passed, it took the gale-force winds with it, and the rain fell in a straight sheet. If the SUVs had survived the damage, they could leave today.

"Grab the bags we packed while I get the vehicle," Michael said.

Arnie and Althaea headed down the hall while Michael pushed the door open and stepped into the rain. Hair and clothes already soaked, the downpour wouldn't add much to his discomfort. He didn't bother to put his hood back up.

The building groaned as if on the verge of collapse. Ignoring the ominous sounds, he heaved open the bay door. He jumped into the SUV and started it. At the sound of the engine turning over, his heart soared.

Michael estimated an hour drive to the underground community. He'd outlined a plan with Althaea for getting them in. If all went as planned, they'd have Carolyn before day's end. He drove up to the main building, pulled over, and jumped out to help the others load the bags into the car.

Everything stowed, they hopped into the vehicle, Michael behind the wheel. Althaea, wearing Agency-issue military-style gear, rode shotgun, and Arnie sat in the back. Michael grasped Carolyn's ring for a moment before putting the car into drive. He manoeuvred around the damaged helicopter and the downed trees.

The road was an obstacle course, and they frequently stopped to move trees and other debris out of the way. He tried the radio. Most of it was static, but a military station broadcast on one of the AM channels. A recorded message played:

"Stay in your homes until further notice. The storm is expected to end soon. Power will be restored in your area in order of priority. A state of emergency has been declared. Those requiring evacuation will relocate to government-run shelters. Stay in your homes until further notice ..."

Michael turned off the radio. So they'd declared a state of emergency. The Agency had abandoned the Aurora Project equipment. Considering the ferocity of the storms since they'd gone underground, Michael guessed it'd taken this long for the military to discover what triggered the cataclysms and deactivate the machines. The drop in wind force told him they'd finally managed it.

"We taking back roads?" Althaea asked.

"Yes. It'll double the time we take to get there, but if they stop us, they'll never let us go."

Arnie leaned forward between the two front seats. "Why would anyone stop us?"

Michael remained silent. After a moment, Althaea responded. "Both cops and military will stop anyone on the roads. Once they identify Michael and me as agents, they'll ask questions we won't want to answer. You're supposed to be dead. When they figure out who you are, they'll lock us up."

Arnie slid back in his seat. "How long until we get to where we're going?"

"About two hours. I want to arrive by dusk," Michael said.

"Will you tell me what you plan to do once we get there?"

"No."

"Did you tell Althaea?" Arnie sounded annoyed.

"It's 'need-to-know,' Arnie."

"Who do you think you are? James Bond?"

"If I don't tell you, you can't blab if you're interrogated. I won't risk Carolyn's life just to let you feel included. You do your part. Leave the rest to Ally and me."

Arnie fell silent. Althaea threw him a glance over her shoulder. "Don't worry. It'll be fine."

Michael stopped the car. Another tree blocked their path. "I'll get this one." He jumped from the vehicle.

A birch tree lay strewn across the road, and Michael dragged it to the ditch. His feet slid through the mud at the side of the road, and he almost fell. The air smelled of dirt, swamp, and cedars. Rain hitting the roof of the car, a constant rat-a-tat that was louder inside the vehicle, drowned out any other sounds.

Arnie stared out the side window. Guilt bolted through Michael. Maybe he should tell Arnie the truth about what they'd planned. But that would be like telling the dog you were taking him to the vet for neutering—it'd freak him out and not change the outcome. Michael shook his head, wiped his hands on his jeans, and returned to the car.

***

Carolyn poured tea from an insulated, stainless steel pot. The aroma of chai and vanilla wafted up from her mug. It was late afternoon, and Cornell wouldn't be coming over until after dinner. He spent more time at home since the argument with Ginny. He'd told Carolyn about the fight, confiding much of his personal life to her, but little of his work life.

She didn't mind the former, but sometimes resented the latter, especially since she contributed to that work with her remote viewing. Perhaps that's why she still refused to tell him about her dreams.

She'd had another one last night—the witch dream again. She'd stood on a scaffold, about to be hanged. Cornell had whispered in her ear that if she gave herself to him, he could save her. She'd spit in his face, and he'd dragged her to the noose. Michael Valiant had pushed his way towards the scaffold.

The sight of him had raised both hope and fear in her. The hope had been that he'd reach her in time, and the fear had been that he'd be captured and they'd both die. In her dream, she'd wanted to die rather than have harm come to him. She always woke from these dreams confused, missing Michael's touch, and loathing Jim Cornell.

She pushed the distressing thoughts and feelings aside and reminded herself Cornell was taking care of her. Without his help, the aliens would've held her captive for the rest of her life. He'd rescued her.

As always when she got reflective, the images bubbled to the surface. Carolyn tried to push them away and failed. John dead in the hospital. Michael shooting Sam. Michael raping Carolyn in a hotel in Peterborough. She'd fought him, but he'd beaten and raped her. The terror escalated and tears welled up. Would she ever rid herself of these cursed memories?

Carolyn jumped when she heard a knock at the door. She grabbed a tissue and dabbed at her eyes while she walked to the door. Hand out to open the door, she stopped, fear making her cautious. Cornell wasn't due yet. Her martial arts trainer came over in the mornings.

Her stomach fluttered. She rushed to the bedroom and got the gun Jim had given her. Another knock, louder this time. She ran to the door and stuck her eye to the peephole. A young woman stood on the other side of the door, and Carolyn's heart skipped a beat. The young woman looked like Sam. Impossible, but what if? Cornell's cautions forgotten, she threw open the door.

"Mom." Sam's voice broke, and she rushed inside, throwing herself into Carolyn's arms.

It was Sam. How could it be? The gun slipped from Carolyn's grasp and landed on the foyer floor. She hugged her daughter, sobbing, hands sifting through the golden-blonde curls, verifying they were real and solid and not part of a glorious dream. Carolyn inhaled, caught the scent of lavender and roses. Sam was real.

Carolyn pulled herself away. "I thought you were dead. How are you here?"

"I thought *you* were dead, Mom. I *buried* you."

"Michael Valiant shot you. I saw it. Your heart wasn't beating. I tried to give you mouth-to-mouth but Valiant dragged me away."

"Wait," Sam said and closed the door. "I don't want anyone to see me here. Jim Cornell can't know about this."

"How do you know Jim?" Carolyn asked. Something fluttered in the back of her mind, like a moth against a window screen.

"I'm living at his house."

Carolyn stumbled backwards, bumping into the back of the loveseat at the edge of the foyer. "Sam, how did you get here? How did you survive?"

"Sit, Mom. There are things you should know about Jim Cornell."

CHAPTER 44

They were close. Michael saw a tall, grey structure sticking out above the trees ahead.

Wouldn't they have wanted to hide it? No, in their arrogance, the Agency didn't care who saw it. What would people do, anyway? They'd assume it was a government building, and they'd be partly right. But if they tried to gain access, they'd be shot.

Michael had already ignored the "Danger," "No Trespassing," and "Keep out" signs and driven around sawhorse barricades. Those were the weakest deterrents. The warnings and threats might keep out Mr. John Q. Public, but not Michael Valiant.

He dropped a hand to his holster and then touched the ring lying against his chest.

Bring it.

A "Trespassers will be shot" sign loomed up, and Michael drove past it without slowing. When he saw the fence in the distance, he turned off the dirt road into the trees. The SUV wove around elms, maples, beeches, and varieties of evergreens, some lying on the ground, others standing only because they'd snagged on another tree when they toppled. When the trees became too dense, he backed up, turned the SUV around to face the road, and cut the engine.

"End of the road." He glanced at Althaea, whose face was stone. She relaxed when her gaze met his. Michael turned to Arnie, whose face was less grim than Althaea's, but white with fear. His eyes had glazed over, and he looked as if he wandered somewhere in the nine circles of hell.

"Arnie," Michael said. "Come back."

Arnie blinked, focused his eyes, and gaped at Michael, jaw slack. Althaea shifted in her seat and reached a hand out to stroke Arnie's cheek.

"Don't worry. We'll get through this." She turned back to Michael. "Better to blow it when we have Carolyn."

Michael frowned, irritated that Althaea was reviving an argument they'd had earlier. "It makes little sense to destroy the one place where there's hope of survival. I want payback too, but we can't kill innocent people, and we don't want to destroy the only place that offers a chance to rebuild."

She shook her head, mouth curling up in a sneer, disgusted. "You should've thought of that when you destroyed the crystals."

"The crystals were Trojan horses with aliens, and you know it. Enough. We can't keep debating this." Michael looked at Arnie. "We're far enough off the road you shouldn't be noticed. This rain will give good cover. Stay alert. Keep your gun handy, and remember, the fence is electric."

Arnie nodded.

"Don't nod. I need to hear you're with me."

"Yeah. I'm fine," Arnie said.

"Understand what you're supposed to do, how to time it?"

"Yeah. I said I'm fine."

"Great. Get out of the car. Give us at least two hours. Got the night-vision goggles?"

Arnie held up the pair he'd kept next to him on the seat, and Michael gave a thumbs up. Arnie grabbed his backpack and stepped out of the vehicle.

Althaea lowered her window. "Arnie."

He went to her.

"Good luck."

"You too." He started to turn away but stopped as though reconsidering. He leaned through Ally's window, pulled her towards him, and kissed her on the lips.

Michael stared into the forest, allowing them their moment. Arnie muttered something to Althaea, and she leaned out and kissed him again. When she pulled away, her eyes were moist. Head bowed, she raised her window.

Michael threw the vehicle into drive and left Arnie behind.

***

Carolyn sat on the couch next to Sam, holding her hand, and still not daring to believe her girl was here. Eyes wide, Carolyn listened while Sam told her everything that had happened since the last time they'd seen each other. When Sam finished speaking, a haze enveloped Carolyn, numbness spreading up from her solar plexus.

Sam lives at Jim's house, and he told me she was dead. Oh, God, why would he do that?

"I have your engagement ring, Mom. They said it was on your body, but they didn't find the wedding band."

Carolyn stared at her bare fingers. "I thought I'd lost them in Algonquin. I fell into a ravine and later noticed they'd disappeared. Valiant wouldn't let me go back to find them." She stopped, frowned. "Why am I remembering things that contradict everything you're telling me?"

Hope sprang into her eyes. "Sam, maybe your dad is still alive. I remember going to the hospital and seeing him there, dead, but perhaps that's a lie too." What if John were alive?

Oh, please let John be alive.

But Sam shook her head, sadness and grief etched on her face. "No, Mom. The funeral was open casket. No mistake. You told me after Dad died that you'd seen his spirit. Dad's dead." Sam put a hand to her mouth as if to hold in the heartache.

Something fluttered again in Carolyn's mind.

"Seen his spirit." Carolyn tested the words, repeating them slowly. The concept seemed at once strange and familiar.

Sam reached into her purse and removed a piece of paper. "This might help. I found it on Jim's desk and stole it before I came here so you'd have evidence."

Horror rose as Carolyn read the email communications between Cornell and someone named Tom Scielo. She stared at Sam, a lump in her throat.

"Brainwashing?" Disbelief oozed from the word.

Her pulse thudded in her ears and she felt numb. Everything was a lie, every memory untrustworthy. Disoriented, she took a deep breath and attempted to focus. Carolyn squeezed Sam's hand, and it helped ground her.

"What about Michael Valiant? Have I even met the man? Sam,

they've been training me to kill Valiant if he shows up here. I remember him as—" Carolyn's dreams popped into her head and she felt sick. Perhaps her unconscious held the truth.

"As what, Mom?"

"Your killer. Your father's killer. My kidnapper. He gave me to the aliens." It was a litany repeated often while she prepared to face him someday.

"I know nothing about Michael Valiant."

Carolyn jumped off the couch. "Jim will come back."

"When?" Sam's voice held panic, and she too leapt to her feet.

"Not for another two hours, but we should leave now. How long before the Cornells notice you're gone?"

"I have time. I told Ginny I was going to the library to study. The kids are at school."

Carolyn considered their options. "I can't leave this area. My ID badge only allows me access to a few places in this section and nothing else. For my own protection." She spat it out, tasting the lie.

I'm a prisoner here.

The loathing she'd felt for Cornell in her dream surged through her. She'd let him touch her, make love to her. *Not make love. He fucked you. He used you.* Grief competed with pain, and she put her hands over her belly, cradling it.

"I can't pretend everything's normal when he comes back." The panic she'd heard in Sam's voice now reflected in her own.

Cornell would know. He'd walk in, look at her face, and know. Her gaze darted to Sam, then landed on the gun lying on the floor. She looked again at Sam.

"I know what we can do."

CHAPTER 45

Infrared cameras picked up their approach. Althaea pulled up near the gate and stepped from the SUV. Through the open window, she glanced into the back seat where Michael slumped as though unconscious. He leaned against the door, hands cuffed in front.

A guard tower thrust out from the front of the building, and she saw movement there. She waited. It didn't take long. A vehicle approached—she didn't see from where it came.

"Humvee." Althaea muttered. "Two occupants."

The Hummer pulled up to the gate, and the agents stepped out. Both wore military gear and carried automatic rifles. Althaea turned off the engine and took the keys from the ignition. She stuffed them in her pocket as she approached the gate.

Both agents levelled guns at her.

"Althaea Dayton, fellas. I'm bringing in a prisoner."

The guards kept the guns raised and waited.

"Radio it in to Jim Cornell. I've got Michael Valiant here, drugged and unconscious."

The guard on the right, who appeared older than his partner, inclined his head towards the SUV. The partner lowered his rifle and returned to the Humvee. Althaea couldn't see what he did but assumed he used the radio.

The guard stepped from the Humvee and waved the older man over. After a moment spent conferring in hushed tones, the older guy returned to Althaea. "Cornell says to let you through to the east entrance. I'll ride with you."

His partner climbed into the driver's seat of the Humvee while Althaea returned to her vehicle. The older guard signaled to the tower, and the gate slid open. Althea drove through the entrance, and the gate rattled closed.

She pulled up beside the guard, who jumped into the SUV's passenger seat. He was tall, but not as tall as Michael, and fit and muscular, though he looked at least ten years older than Althaea. A faded scar ran along the left side of his face and hooked under his chin.

He nodded his head in Michael's direction and said, "I'd heard he'd escaped. How'd you find him?"

"He took me hostage. I turned the tables. It wasn't easy. You don't know what I've been through these past few months."

The guard looked her up and down. "Impressive. You don't look as though you could take him."

"Maybe I'll show you my moves sometime." Ally licked her lips.

The guard flashed a shark-like grin. In her imagination, she slammed her gun butt into his face. Instead, she steeled herself and leered back.

Typical fucking man. If she kept acting as if he were God's gift, she could keep the blood concentrated away from his brain. Then it'd be easy to take him out.

"What's your name, soldier?"

"Call me Pistol. I'll show you why later." Wink.

"Pistol. Okay." She ignored the wink. *If he makes a crack about me getting pistol whipped, I'm knocking out those goddamn teeth.*

Althaea glanced at Michael using the rear view mirror. To his credit, he continued to appear unconscious and kept a straight face. They were around the building's east side now. The vehicle ahead pulled up by a steel door. Althaea parked the SUV behind the Humvee and looked over at Pistol.

Fuck, what a stupid nickname.

"What's your buddy's name?" Althaea asked.

"We call him Shift, 'cause the guy loves the overtime." Pistol jumped from the car and motioned for Althaea to do the same.

She stepped out into the rain and mud, leaving the keys in the ignition, and moved to the passenger side. She stood beside Michael's door. Something felt off, and she tensed, loosened the gun in her holster.

"Cornell coming out here?"

Pistol smiled. "Later." He raised his gun and swung it at her face.

She ducked under it and hurled herself at his chest. The SUV's passenger door opened, and she felt, rather than saw, Michael hit the dirt. The handcuffs rattled when they dropped to the ground.

A pistol fired—the weapon, not the guy—and Michael had fired it. Beneath Althaea, Pistol pushed his fingers into her face, trying to stick them in her eyes. She hauled off and punched him in the head. When the fingers slipped from her face, she kneed him in the groin. He howled.

Althaea slugged him with her gun and pulled back for another blow.

Michael leaned over and waved his hand in her face. "He's down, Dayton."

She paused to look.

Pistol's nose and mouth gushed blood. He remained conscious though he'd stopped fighting. She dragged him to his feet. He spat and a tooth went flying.

Shift lay on the ground, holding his gut, which oozed blood. Michael moved to stand over him and raised his gun.

"Don't move, Valiant. We've got you both covered."

Althaea recognized Cornell's voice coming over a loudspeaker and scanned the area.

"The towers, Michael. Sharpshooters."

The steel door opened and six agents trotted out. Two went to Althaea, each grabbing an arm, and another two went to Michael and did the same.

Pistol staggered to his feet, moved to Althaea, and punched her in the face. "Cornell said not to trust you."

She rubbed a hand across her mouth. "I told you I'd show you my moves."

"And I told you I'd show you why I'm called Pistol. We've got a date later, bitch." Pistol punched her in the stomach.

He turned to Michael, who struggled to shake the two guards holding him back. "Perhaps I'll let you watch."

Michael kicked out, but Pistol had turned and limped to the door. "Take these traitors to interrogation."

***

Carolyn retrieved the gun from the floor and set it on the coffee table. Sam's gaze met Carolyn's. "No, Mom. You can't shoot him."

"I can make him help us escape."

"That's a bad idea. We can't let him know I found you. Let's just leave. We're on the right side of the gate."

"What do you mean?"

Sam sighed and took Carolyn's hand. "Did you see the gate separating the family housing from the Agency sector?"

"Yes. I can't go through. Jim told me it was to protect me. I know now it was to keep me contained." She hugged Sam, relieved at having her close.

"The exit to the surface lies on this side of the gate."

"Okay. Good. I have to tell you something else."

Sam pulled away, concern on her face. "What?"

"I'm pregnant."

Eyes wide, Sam looked at the slight mound under the baggy T-shirt.

Carolyn took Sam's hand and pressed it to her pelvic area. "I know it doesn't look like much, but soon it will."

"Mom. Who?"

Carolyn went into the living room and sank to the couch, tears falling. "I think it's Jim Cornell's. At least, that's what I remember. I hope it's not true, but what if it is?"

"We'll live with it. I thought Jim was nice, too, and I trusted him. He pretended to help me."

"I don't know who I am. I'm missing pieces of myself." Carolyn put her head in her hands. She wiped away the tears as Sam put an arm around her, but jumped at the loud tap on the door. "Get in my bedroom. Hide."

Sam ran for the bedroom.

"On the left."

Sam disappeared into the bedroom as the front door swung open. Heart thudding, Carolyn turned and faced Cornell.

CHAPTER 46

When Cornell's gaze landed on the gun, Carolyn froze.

"Why do you have the gun out? Did something happen?"

She licked her lips. "No. I set it there when I returned from target practice earlier. What are you doing here? I didn't expect you until after dinner." She kept the tremor from her voice and the guilt from her eyes.

"I have something to tell you." He strode to her side, breathless, eyes shining.

Carolyn strove not to flinch when he put his arms around her. Reluctantly, she returned the embrace, struggling to suppress the fear that she broadcasted her distrust, and focused on acting normal.

"What is it?"

"Good news, darling." Cornell pulled back and studied her face. "Michael Valiant is in custody. I want you to confront him in the interrogation room. It's good you've got the gun here. Valiant will be executed. Maybe you'd do the honours? Payback, for what he did to you."

The blood drained from her face. At first, she experienced a surge of excitement and anticipation at the thought of confronting, and even killing, Valiant. It's what she'd trained for. But the realization they'd manipulated her followed, and she tried to squelch her hatred. She was certain of one thing: Michael Valiant hadn't killed Sam, despite what Carolyn remembered.

"You can do this, honey. I'll help you."

463

She tried not to recoil from the endearments. "I can't kill anyone."

Cornell went rigid. "What do you mean? We've discussed this, prepared for this. You've been looking forward to it. Valiant is a menace. He shot your daughter in cold blood. Valiant killed your husband, raped you. He turned you over to the aliens."

As he reviewed the list, Carolyn shuddered, and her hatred swelled. Without conscious thought, she picked up the gun. Blackness filled her, and she wanted to smash something.

Cornell put an arm around her. "Come on. I'm here for you. We'll face him together."

She tucked the gun into her belt and allowed him to lead her from the house. It wasn't until they were almost to the sidewalk she remembered Sam was still in the bedroom.

***

After her mother and Cornell left, Sam crept into the living room. What should she do? She couldn't stay here. What if he returned to the house with her mom? Sam found a pen and paper and wrote a note to her mother: *Be back tomorrow, same time. S.*

Afraid to write more, she scanned the room, searching for somewhere only her mother would look. Sam went into the bathroom and opened the medicine cabinet. She closed it again when she saw the men's razor and toiletries, confirming the intimacy between her mother and Cornell.

She returned to the bedroom and opened drawers in the dresser until she found where Carolyn kept her underwear. Relieved to find no boxers or men's briefs in there, she set the note on top of the panties and slammed the drawer closed. Sam hurried to the front door and peeked out. Coast clear, she stepped outside and headed for the gate.

***

Carolyn followed Cornell past the guard and into the interrogation room. Her heart skipped a beat when she saw the man and woman tied to chairs, gagged, faces swollen, eyes bruised. She waited for a surge of hate at the sight of Michael Valiant. It trickled up while she stared at him.

Images of their past flowed into her mind and passed in a flash: Valiant shooting Sam and dragging Carolyn away while Sam bled out on the carpet; Valiant pinning Carolyn to the bed in the hotel room, punching her, ripping her clothes off, ramming painfully into her; and doing it again in Algonquin; Valiant dragging her, broken and bleeding, to the clearing in the forest, to hand her over to the aliens.

Her pulse quickened and tears sprang to her eyes. She cried out in pain when he looked up and locked his gaze on hers. Hand trembling, she raised the gun and would've shot him, but in the moment's hesitation, Carolyn saw her pain mirrored in his eyes, and she remembered her daughter lived.

Cornell placed a hand on her shoulder. "Do it. No one would blame you."

Jim Cornell, her lover, moved behind her, embraced her. His hands slid around to her belly and stroked it. Warm breath whispered in her ear and soft lips kissed her cheek. "Do it for us, darling. Do it for the baby."

Michael growled through the gag, his palpable rage flowing over and past her, its target Cornell. The agony in Michael's eyes found Carolyn and stabbed at her. She shuddered and choked on a sob.

Valiant strained to speak, groans of despair leaking through the gag. Tears flowed down his face.

Other images flashed into Carolyn's mind: standing on a scaffold, wanting to die rather than allow harm to come to Michael; lying naked, stretched out on a rack, Cornell molesting her, forcing his fingers into her, until Michael burst into the room and interrupted; Michael dying in her arms in a temple, an attempt to rescue her failing. These were her dreams, but they felt closer to the truth than her memories.

Cornell raised his voice now, telling not only Carolyn, but also Michael. "Michael Valiant killed John. Valiant killed Sam. He raped you and gave you to the aliens."

Valiant killed Sam. It echoed in her skull. Carolyn had a flash memory of a man standing over her, repeating this to her.

Valiant killed Sam.

Rage at Cornell's lie overpowered the rage programmed into the lie. She raised the gun, stepped towards Michael. Turned. Faced Cornell.

"Sam is alive, you bastard." Carolyn pulled the trigger.

465

CHAPTER 47

Cornell's face contorted in horror, and he fell to the floor, shouting for the guard. Carolyn fired again and silenced him forever. The door swung open, and the guard swept into the room. He had enough time to glance at the two prisoners, still restrained in the chairs, before she shot him as well. Staggering back, he pushed the door shut, and she shot him again. He dropped, leaving a smear of blood on the door.

Carolyn shoved the gun into her belt and crouched next to Michael. Fingers shaking, she pulled the gag from his mouth, letting it fall loose around his neck.

"Oh, God, Carolyn. What have they done to you? Please, untie me."

Brown eyes. A funny thing on which to focus, under the circumstances. Carolyn didn't move, but simply stared into those brown eyes and waited for something, a feeling, to tell her what to do.

The woman next to Valiant struggled and made angry noises. Carolyn ignored her. She turned her head, and her gaze landed on the bodies.

"I killed Jim." Her voice sounded like a little girl's.

"Untie me." He sounded calm but firm.

Carolyn studied Michael again. Maybe she should leave. She'd run home and get Sam, and they'd leave as planned. But he knew what she'd done. Should she kill him, too, before he hurt her again? What about the woman? She gripped the back of Michael's chair and searched his eyes.

"Carolyn, please. Hurry. There's no time." More urgency this time.

The bruised face brought to mind another dream, and an echo of love for him pressed on her. "I don't know what's real," she said. What if this was a dream? The woman's frustrated grunts and struggles intruded, but Carolyn kept her gaze on Michael.

"Carolyn, listen. I can help you. We were together. Don't you remember? Cornell lied when he said I killed your husband. I didn't kill anyone you love. I didn't rape you. Remember, please. When I died, I came to you, and you saw me. Cornell had you in a prison cell."

Michael's eyes lit up then, and his voice rose with excitement. "Reach into my shirt and get the chain around my neck. Your wedding band is on it. You gave it to me, because you wanted me to find Sam and give it to her."

"My ring?" It came out thick, slow. She shook her head, trying to clear the fog and confusion, but couldn't think. Nothing he said made sense.

"You put your wedding ring in my backpack when you left me in Algonquin Park. Sam's still alive. I'll help you find her, and then you can give it to her yourself. Please. We have to hurry before someone finds us here. Get the ring."

Carolyn touched the collar of his shirt and gently felt for the chain. Michael closed his eyes, as if savouring her touch, though she tried not to make contact and recoiled whenever a finger brushed his skin. She lifted the chain over his shirt, and the ring appeared.

Her wedding band. She recognized it: a plain gold band, not too thick, with a single, tiny diamond in the centre. She gaped at Michael. "Can I take it?"

He smiled. "Of course. I've been waiting so long to return it to you. But Carr, we have to go."

The use of her nickname jarred something loose in her memories. Carolyn started untying Michael, and when his hands were free, he nudged her away and finished the job. The last bit of rope fell to the ground.

Michael moved towards Carolyn, and she scurried backwards.

He winced. "I'd never hurt you. Please believe me. I didn't do what that bastard said." His voice broke.

"Sam showed up at my house. They did something to make me believe you ..." She trailed off, unable to say the horrible accusations aloud. "But now you're a stranger. Cornell said you came here to kill me. Why did you come here?"

"To get you away from Cornell and the Agency. Now we're together, we can get out of here."

"Sam. I left her at my home. Oh, God, I hope she's still there."

"We'll get her. Don't worry." Michael turned to the woman next to him and slid the gag from her mouth.

"About fucking time. Get these ropes off me. Hurry."

Michael shook his head, flashed a half-smile. "I shouldn't have started with the gag. Carolyn, meet Althaea."

Carolyn recognized the woman she'd seen with Michael when she'd done remote viewing. Freed, Althaea jumped up and went to Cornell's body. She grabbed his gun and tucked it into her waistband.

Michael took a pistol from the guard and turned back to Carolyn. "I know the layout of this place. Arnie's outside waiting, and we have to get back."

"Arnie." Carolyn hadn't thought about Arnie for ages. Confusion made her frown. Arnie was alive, too, but she didn't know how that was possible. He should've been dead. She'd thought he was dead. Carolyn glanced at the guard's body, nauseated she'd been the one to kill him. "How will we get away?"

"Leave that to us," Althaea replied. "Ready?"

Michael shoved the guard's body to the side and peeked into the hallway. Carolyn looked over his shoulder into the empty corridor. They headed out, guns raised, Michael leading, Carolyn second, and Althaea bringing up the rear.

Carolyn's heart raced. If Sam wasn't at the house, what would they do? When she found Sam, she'd never let her out of her sight again.

***

Wrapped in a thermal blanket, Arnie huddled under the trees. He put the night-vision goggles on when the sun set and checked his watch. More than ninety minutes since the others had left. Arnie put away the blanket, shouldered his pack and assault rifle, and headed towards the road.

When he sighted the road, he veered to the left, keeping to the shelter of the trees. Michael had coached him on how to spot booby traps, and Arnie maintained a slow pace. The thought of the traps Michael described sent chills up Arnie's spine.

The sick fucks running this place didn't mess around. Risks included pits full of spikes, land mines, and beer cans resting on grenades that would explode if kicked. He gulped, fear escalating. Sweat melded with the rain running down his face.

He stopped walking twenty metres from the gate and hunkered down in the brush to watch the road and the gate. Nothing moved. So far, no alarm had triggered. Arnie settled down to wait.

***

As soon as Sam reached the Cornell house, she ran to her room and threw herself on the bed. George stuck his head in through her doorway, and she smiled. "Hi, George. What are you doing?" She'd miss George, though she wouldn't miss Wade so much.

"I'm bored. Play a game with me?"

"Where's Wade?"

"Joey's. They didn't let me go." George's face fell.

"It's okay, Georgie. I'll play." It would be a good distraction.

He perked up and ran to the living room. She followed at a more leisurely pace. By the time she reached the couch in front of the TV, he'd already set up the game. Sam picked up a paddle and let George take the lead.

She peeked at him out of the corner of her eye. "Where's your mom?"

"In her room."

Ginny spent a lot of time in her room these days. Sam was sure Ginny had started cocktail hour early. That was good news, as far as Sam was concerned. It meant Ginny would stay out of sight, and Sam wouldn't have to act as though everything were okay.

She repeatedly checked the time, worrying about her mother. What if her mother was in danger? What if Mom came back to the house to find Sam gone?

George laughed, a loud, raucous bleat that made Sam jump.

"Ha, I'm winning," George squealed. "I'm beating you, Sam. I never beat you."

She smiled. "I guess you're getting better. Soon you'll be beating

Wade, too." Part of her wished she could stick around and see that happen.

The two played for twenty minutes. Sam was about to suggest they take a break and get a snack when the doorbell rang. She checked the clock. Just after seven. She waited, anticipating Ginny to come rushing from the bedroom.

When she didn't appear, and the doorbell chimed again, Sam dropped her paddle and went to the door. Two men stood outside, both wearing short-sleeved, white T-shirts, khaki caps, and military pants, rifles slung over their shoulders. The shorter one sported a tattoo of a bulldog on his upper arm. The taller one suffered from a raging case of acne and was skinnier than bulldog guy.

Sam paled, took a step backwards, and gulped air. Her thoughts flew to her mother, and she shivered.

"Is Mrs. Cornell here, ma'am?" Bulldog asked, and the two men stepped into the house.

Sam gaped at them in wide-eyed silence, not daring to breathe.

"Ma'am?" He frowned. "Can you get Mrs. Cornell, please?"

Sam nodded. Someone approached, and she turned to face George. She gripped him by the shoulders and bent her face to his. "Get your mom. Quick." She gave him a small shove towards the stairs.

He ran.

She faced the two men. "Is something wrong?"

"We're here to speak with Mrs. Cornell."

They waited. Sweat trickled down Sam's back, and her underarms dampened. She lowered her head and stared at the floor. A strand of hair slipped over her right eye, and she raised a shaking hand to tuck it behind her ear.

At last, she heard footsteps and turned to see Ginny walking towards them. She stumbled a little, confirming Sam's suspicion Ginny had been in her room drinking. George loped along behind her. When the two reached the little group at the door, Sam caught a whiff of alcohol.

The older woman's expression tightened. An attempt at a smile failed, and her mouth formed a combination sneer and grimace. "Gentlemen," she said, a slight slur in her voice. "What can I do for you? If you're looking for my husband, he's not here."

"Mrs. Cornell?" Bulldog asked.

"Yes. What is it?" Fear crept into her eyes.

"I'm sorry. There's been an accident. Your husband is dead."

Ginny gasped. "What happened? Are you sure?"

"Mr. Cornell was shot trying to prevent an escape."

"No. Jim's supposed to come home for dinner." She raised fisted hands to her mouth and shook her head. "He has to come home for dinner."

The two men stared at her, uncomfortable. Bulldog spoke. "I'm sorry, Mrs. Cornell."

Sam's heart almost stopped beating. "Was anyone else hurt?" *Mom. Oh, God, please. I can't lose Mom again.*

The agent glanced at Sam and shook his head. "I'm not at liberty to say."

"Does that mean someone else was hurt?" Sam's voice rose to a near shriek.

"Mama?" George wrapped his arms around his mother's legs and burst into tears.

She looked at her son as if she didn't recognize him. "Sam, take George to his room and stay with him."

"Okay." Sam led the boy towards the bedrooms, but slowly, trying to hear what the man had to say.

"I want to see Jim," Ginny said.

"Yes, ma'am." Bulldog sounded detached, and Sam hated him for being so cold.

"Sam," Ginny called out.

Sam stopped and turned.

"Stay with George while I go?"

Sam heard the pleading behind the words and hesitated. She couldn't stay here when she didn't know what had happened to her mother. "Please, can we come?"

"I need you here with George. He can't come and I have to hurry." Ginny's voice broke. Sam forced herself to hold back her own tears and nodded.

Ginny didn't waste another moment. She rushed outside, the two agents following her, leaving Sam staring at the closed door.

CHAPTER 48

Sam hurried to George's room. He lay on his bed, staring at the ceiling, and didn't look up when she entered.

"My daddy isn't coming home anymore." His voice was steady.

"Wade will like that."

"Of course, he won't."

"Yes, he will. Wade said if Daddy wasn't around, he'd be the man of the house." George's hands lay clasped on his chest.

She sat on the bed beside him. "Wade was teasing, bragging about being the oldest. He loves your daddy." Sam didn't believe everything she told George—Wade could be a dick, sometimes even making her wonder if he was a budding sociopath.

"Sorry about your daddy, George. I know what it's like. My daddy died, too."

George's face contorted, and he bawled. "I want Daddy. I want him now."

Way to comfort the kid. What could she say? *It's okay, George. Your dad was just as big a dick as Wade?* She stroked his arm.

George's crying intensified.

"It's okay to cry," Sam said. *Useless. What do you say to a six-year-old kid whose dad just died?* "Can I get you something? Maybe a chocolate milk?" *Sure. A sugary drink should fix him right up.* She winced. "Or water."

Who could she call? Sam had to get back to her mother's. Carolyn would go home eventually—unless something had happened to her, too. Sam stood. "I'll be right back."

Without waiting for a reply, Sam left the room. It was Marnie's afternoon off, but perhaps the housekeeper was in her room. Sam pounded on Marnie's door. Nothing.

As she raised her fist to knock again, the door swung open. Marnie stood there, cream coating her face. Sam arched her brows, and Marnie, through clenched teeth and tight lips said, "Facial. Can't talk." She waved her arm, inviting Sam inside.

"I can't. Marnie, I need a favour."

"Afternoon off."

"It's an emergency. Something terrible happened." She told Marnie about Cornell's death and asked her to stay with George.

"Wade's not home and I have to find him." She forced herself to look Marnie in the eye while she told the lie. "He's at the market with friends. Ginny went with the soldiers, so she told me to find Wade. George is too upset to go."

Marnie agreed to watch George and told Sam to bring him over. Sam bolted to get George and tried to be patient while she coaxed him off his bed and over to Marnie's.

When he was safely ensconced in the housekeeper's quarters, Sam rushed outside and ran all the way to the gate. A longer line than usual greeted her. She pushed her way through the crowd, ignoring the glares of those she jostled in her haste. At the front, she saw the line had stopped moving.

Sam turned to a woman standing near her. "What's going on?"

"The guards aren't letting anyone through who doesn't have high-level clearance. Someone said two prisoners escaped, so we're stuck here. Some of us have to get to work." The woman raised her voice while she said the last piece, and a guard glanced in their direction.

Sam's hopes rose when she recognized the guard, and she rushed to him. "Trevor."

He gave a distracted smile. But when he recognized Sam, he stepped away from the man whose badge he inspected and waved her over.

"What are you doing here? I heard about your uncle. So sorry for your loss. Are you okay?"

"No, I'm not okay. The boys are devastated. I left them home with the housekeeper to find Mrs. Cornell. They brought her here, and I have to go to her. Please, Trevor. Let me go through." Sam worked to inject grief into her voice but had no trouble getting her panic across. Terrified they wouldn't let her through, it took an effort of will not to sound hysterical.

"I'm not supposed to let anyone through, but you're a logical exception. Come into the guardhouse. Keep walking and act as though you belong here." Trevor took her arm and guided her through the gate. "You're lucky I'm still here. Most of the guards will join the search, so a few more minutes, and I wouldn't have been here to help you."

"Thank you." The flutters in her stomach calmed as he led her into the guardhouse.

Once inside, Sam glanced around. They were alone. She threw her arms around Trevor and hugged him tight, fighting a sudden fear she might never see him again.

"Okay. Okay." He stammered it. His arms went around her, and he pressed his lips to the top of her head. After a moment, he released her. "You have to go. If the supervisor walks in here, he'll send you home. Just go. When this mess clears, we'll talk."

He opened the door to the Agency sector, and Sam hurried through it. Without looking back, she ran towards her mother's house.

***

Carolyn knew the second she stepped into the house that Sam was gone, but she shouted Sam's name anyway. Michael and Althaea appeared at the patio door, making Carolyn jump, even though she'd expected them. She let them inside.

"Sam's not here," Carolyn said, an edge to her voice.

"They'll search for us here, and they've probably found the bodies," Althaea said.

Michael went to Carolyn and looked at her belly. "Is everything okay with the baby?"

Fear prickled through Carolyn. "Why do you care about my baby?"

He stepped closer to her.

She retreated.

"Our baby," Michael whispered, his face pale.

Carolyn took another step back. She tried to speak, but only managed a strangled cry. *The baby is Michael's?*

"Carolyn." Michael made as if to step towards her again, but stopped mid stride, face contorted into a mask of agony. "Whose baby do you think it is?"

"Jim Cornell's."

Michael's hands tightened into fists, and he gritted his teeth. "No, Carolyn. The baby is ours. Try to remember our time together. That memory has kept me going—helped me survive."

"I remember you raped me." Carolyn's voice was low, challenging.

"My God! I didn't rape you. Don't you remember how amazing it was?"

Althaea touched Michael's arm. "Not now. There's no time for this."

Michael rounded on her. "I have to. She has to remember. It's killing me, Ally."

Vertigo made the room spin, and Carolyn thought she might faint. She stumbled to the couch. Her head fell into her hands, and she sobbed. The memories Michael insisted were there wouldn't come. When she thought of Michael, only images of pain and brutality came to mind.

"Michael." Althaea's voice held a warning.

Carolyn raised her head. Michael stood before her. "Althaea's right, Carr. We have to go. Regardless of who you believe is the father, please tell me the baby's okay."

"The baby's fine."

Michael held out a hand to her.

Carolyn stared at it. Reluctantly, she put her hand in his. A vision of Michael punching her in the face popped into her head, and Carolyn wrenched her hand back as if his touch burned.

"I regret that that son of a bitch had but one life to give for the Agency." Michael grimaced.

Carolyn stood. "I can't leave without Sam. She's staying at the Cornell house, but that's not in this sector. I assume when I left with Jim, she went there."

Michael looked to Althaea. "Any thoughts on how to get across to the residential sector without walking through the gate?"

"Let me think on it." Althaea went to the patio door and stared outside. "The main walls have—"

A knock on the door stopped her.

"Into the bedroom, quick." Carolyn waited until the two were hidden, then rushed to the door and peered out the peephole. Sam!

Carolyn threw open the door and yanked the girl inside. "Oh my God, I'm so happy to see you." She hugged Sam tight, flooded her face with kisses.

Sam gave a return squeeze, then extricated herself. "Two men came to the Cornells' and said Jim was dead. What happened?"

"No time to explain. We have to go."

The bedroom door opened, and Michael and Althaea stepped out.

"Sam, Michael and Althaea will help us."

Sam gaped. "Michael Valiant?"

A flush crept up his face, and he nodded.

Sam put a protective arm around Carolyn, pulling her close. "You okay, Mom?"

Carolyn kissed Sam's cheek. "Yes."

"Through the back." Michael opened the patio doors and waved to them to follow.

When they were all outside, he slid the door closed and joined them. "We'll go through the backyards. That whole back part is foliage, no fence. Althaea, you lead." He turned to Carolyn. "Keep your gun ready. I'm happy you know how to use it now. When we were together, I could barely convince you to pick one up."

She nodded, just to agree with him. Her memories didn't include Michael offering to give her a gun to use. She also didn't want to tell him Cornell had trained her specifically to use it to kill Michael. Carolyn touched the wedding band now back on her finger. She looked up and caught Michael watching her.

He smiled. "Shall we ask the angels and guides to help us find our way out?"

Carolyn frowned, confused. "I don't understand."

Michael's face fell and his hand rose as if to touch her cheek, but he stopped himself. "It's okay. I'll explain later." He closed his eyes for a moment. When he opened them again, he glanced around and nodded his head at Althaea.

The group headed to the back of the yard where a row of bushes camouflaged the wall of stucco that rose and disappeared into the fake sky above. Althaea pushed between the leaves and branches and held the opening for them. Carolyn gripped Sam's hand, and they stepped into the breach.

CHAPTER 49

The group reached the elevators that would take them to the upper world and crouched behind bushes fronting the Agency offices. Two guards blocked the doors. A siren wailed, shrieking like a deranged harpy.

Michael motioned for Althaea to take the guard on the left. She nodded. He raised his hand and counted down on his fingers. They fired on one and both guards dropped. Sam and Carolyn remained hidden while Michael and Althaea raced to the elevator.

He pressed the button to summon the lift, and when the doors slid open, they fired, killing two soldiers inside. Althaea held the doors open while Michael dragged the bodies out.

A wave from Althaea brought Carolyn and Sam running. Michael pushed Carolyn to one side, Sam to the other, and then motioned for them to lie on the floor. As the doors closed, Michael and Althaea raised their weapons.

The moment the doors opened, they fired, knocking down two guards, while two more shot at the group from the hallway. Michael aimed and picked one off, but the other continued to shoot.

"Cover me, Ally. Let the doors close, but hold the elevator. Give me thirty seconds and open the doors again." Michael's voice was almost inaudible over the gunshots, but Althaea nodded.

She rapid-fired her gun while Michael ducked under her arm and launched himself into the hallway, rolling behind a wall. The elevator doors whisked shut. The guard who'd been firing at them peeked around the corner.

Michael fired and winged her when the bullet ricocheted. She ducked back behind the wall. He peered into the hallway. If they didn't get her soon, more soldiers would arrive. He gauged where to strike.

When the thirty seconds were almost up, he fired. A pain-filled cry told him he'd made a hit, but the guard held her ground. The elevator doors slid open. The guard leaned out to shoot, and Michael fired again, multiple times. Chips flew off the wall, but when the dust settled, she lay on the floor, arm stuck out into the hallway. A gun lay on the floor next to her hand.

Althaea jumped into the corridor and relieved the guard of an automatic rifle, scanned the hallway, and waved Carolyn and Sam out. Michael ran to them. "This way," he said, urging them to take the corridor leading right.

He led the group to the exit, Althaea bringing up the rear, and again guards confronted them. Michael hung back with Sam and Carolyn, letting Althaea lead the attack with her rifle. She reduced the number of guards from six to three, and Michael joined her, using the more accurate pistol to target each guard. Two guards remained.

Sam shrieked. "Trevor!"

"No, Sam!" Carolyn screamed in response.

From his periphery, Michael saw Carolyn throw restraining arms around Sam as she tried to break cover.

"No, Michael. Don't shoot. Trevor. Stop." Sam struggled against Carolyn.

Althaea and Michael pulled back. He didn't take his eyes off the corner where the guards hid though they'd ceased firing.

"Sam, explain," Michael said.

"One of the guards is my friend. Please, don't kill him."

A male voice called out. "Sam? Are you okay?"

"Answer him," Michael said. "Tell him you're okay and we only want to leave."

"Trevor, I'm okay. We just want to leave. Please, let us go."

"I'm sorry, but I can't do that. I know you're being held against your will. We'll get the prisoners back, dead or alive."

"You don't understand. Jim Cornell was holding me, and he had my mother. Mom wasn't dead. I found her. She's with me. Please. Let us go."

Trevor paused, spoke again. "Drop your weapons, and we'll take you in. Sam, these people killed Jim Cornell. They'll answer for it. We won't negotiate. Drop your weapons."

"You drop 'em. We're leaving. If you don't stand down, we'll fire." Michael shouted back. He lowered his voice, and, keeping his eyes on the targets, said, "I'm sorry, Sam. If it comes to a choice between us or them, I choose us."

Sam sobbed and made another effort to break Carolyn's hold.

"Hold her," Michael said.

Carolyn shifted behind him, likely trying to comfort Sam. He heard heated whispers, Sam's protests.

"We've been standing here too long," Michael said. "Watch the rear, Carolyn. We might have company soon. If you hear or see anything, alert Althaea. Have your gun ready. We might need your help."

Michael had deduced which guard was Sam's friend when Trevor had spoken. He'd take out Trevor's partner. Maybe then, Trevor would step aside though Michael doubted it. He assumed this wouldn't end well. "Drop your weapons. You have ten seconds," Michael said.

"No!" Sam cried.

Michael ignored her and fired, ricocheting the bullet off the wall and into the back of Trevor's partner's arm. When the man cried out and lurched forward, Michael fired again, shooting the man in the head.

Sam screamed, "Trevor!"

"He's still standing, Sam," Michael answered, voice calm. He felt the struggle behind him.

"No, Sam! Michael, I can't hold her."

"Althaea, cover him," Michael yelled. He turned and grabbed at Sam, who'd slipped from Carolyn's arms and ran at Trevor. Michael caught her arm and yanked her back. "Do you want to get us killed? Your boyfriend will do his job. He's programmed to." The words came out gruffer and colder than he'd intended, but he was getting sick of this standoff. He pulled Sam into his arms and held her while she sobbed.

Carolyn wrapped her arms around Michael's, burying her face in Sam's back. "Please, Sam," she said. "We have to get moving."

Sam lifted her head. "Just let me talk to Trevor."

"I'm not letting you go near him," Michael said. "He'd use you as a hostage."

"No, he cares about me."

Michael looked over Sam's head at Carolyn. She met his eyes and shook her head. At least Carolyn understood.

"Drop your weapon, Trevor." One more chance. "You're out numbered and we've got more experience. I don't want to shoot you, but I will if I have to."

"Trevor, please. Don't let him kill you."

Michael hoped Sam's interjection would help but thought it could go either way. Trevor might take what she'd said as a challenge.

"Let Sam come over here."

"I'm not that stupid, son," Michael replied. How long had they lingered here? He'd have to go at Trevor. Michael raised his gun.

Sam screamed.

Trevor fired at them, and Althaea and Michael fired back. Trevor went down in their hail of bullets. Sam broke away from them and threw herself at Trevor's body.

"No, Sam. He might not be dead," Michael shouted. He lunged after her, but was a few seconds too late. Trevor lurched to a sitting position, wrapped his arms around Sam, and stuck a pistol to her head.

Tears streamed down Sam's face. She tried to pull away, but he tightened his grip. "You're not going anywhere. One move and I'll shoot her." Trevor's voice was hoarse, his breathing laboured.

"Then what, Trevor? You'll only get one shot."

"That's all I need."

Sam leaned her head against Trevor and sobbed. "What are you doing? Let me go. I cared about you. How can you do this?"

"Sorry, I can't. Not if it means letting prisoners escape."

In a flash, Michael raised his gun and shot Trevor in the head. Blood splattered onto Sam, and she screamed. She pushed the body away from her, fell forward on her knees, and threw up.

Michael grabbed her by the arm and hauled her to her feet. "No time for that. Move." He dragged her, ignoring her choked sobs.

Carolyn caught up to them. "Michael, let me."

He handed Sam off to Carolyn, who put an arm around her daughter and guided her forward.

"I thought he liked me," Sam said, sobbing.

"Forget him, Sam," Michael replied. "The job comes first for these guys. I know. I was one of them."

The group stopped in front of the exit doors. Michael peered through the window and saw more men and women with automatic rifles. The SUV still sat along the side of the building. He hoped the keys were still in it.

CHAPTER 50

Arnie heard the commotion, saw the armed agents running to the east side of the building, and understood Michael and Althaea were on their way back. He snatched up his pack, tucked the gun into his belt, and grabbed the rifle. He'd have seconds to blow the gate when they were out and in the vehicles. But if he acted too soon, he'd be spotted, and then he'd never be able to help his friends.

Shots fired without pause and guards fell. Other guards returned fire. Arnie could only watch and hope the Agency bullets didn't hit their mark. More shots. The group at the east door thinned, Michael and Ally picking them off. Arnie held his breath. Maybe soon he'd see Carolyn again.

The frenzy at the door continued unabated, and Arnie wished he had a grenade. Michael hadn't trusted Arnie with one—had been reluctant to leave Arnie with the C4 and the blasting caps, but there was no one else. Althaea had to go in with Michael.

Arnie would've felt offended, except that deep down, he knew Michael was right: Arnie didn't have enough training to be left with grenades. They'd practiced the hell out of using the C4 though. Arnie no longer feared handling it, even with the unwieldy rubberized gloves he'd have to wear to protect him from the electric fence. While he wasn't the commando Michael was, he'd come a long way.

A whirring sound reached his ears. Helicopters. *The Agency's choppering in more guys? From where?*

Arnie removed the C4 from his pack and stuck the blasting caps inside each wrapped piece. Should he blow the gate now and join the fray? He thought better of it when an explosion rattled the copter and half the guards flew into the air in little pieces. Michael, apparently, had a grenade.

There they were. He'd recognize Althaea's style anywhere. That woman even made kicking ass look beautiful. Arnie rose into a standing crouch, ready to run to the fence. He cried out in horror when more men rounded the opposite corner of the building.

One newcomer fired off a quick round. Althaea cried out, dropped her gun, and then fell on it. Terrified they'd killed her, Arnie broke cover and raced to the gate. He focused on planting C4 on the hinges and handle of the gate, except for one quick glance in Althaea's direction when it was all in place.

To his relief, she was on her feet again, though one hand dripped blood. She used her left hand now, but still picked agents off with deadly accuracy. Two blonde heads appeared. Carolyn and Sam. His heart leapt.

He backed away, giving himself the distance Michael told him he'd need. *Ready or not, guys, here we go.*

A hit to the detonator emitted a radio signal, triggering the blasting caps. The blast put Arnie on his ass and made his ears ring though he wasn't hurt. The gate ripped open. Shrapnel and debris flew everywhere, but he was far enough away.

He jumped into a crouch and tried to get his bearings. The Agency goons would come for him now they were alerted to his presence. He hoped to Christ Michael and the others were on their way.

***

The blast alerted Michael. They'd better get to Arnie before the Agency soldiers found him. The helicopter veered close again, teetering in the air, the pilot struggling to keep it steady. Michael raised the rifle he'd swiped from a guard and fired at it.

Something pinged. The helicopter plummeted and veered in their direction.

Michael screamed "Duck!" at Althaea and pulled Carolyn and Sam down with him. The 'copter landed in a fireball, killing the agents who were attacking them. Heat washed over Michael, and he covered Carolyn and Sam with his body.

Debris rained down around them, a piece of flaming metal landing close enough to feel its heat. He jumped to his feet, snatching the women up, dragging them to the SUV. He yanked on the door. To his relief it opened, and the keys dangled from the ignition.

"Get in!" he screamed over the noise.

Althaea jumped in on the passenger side. Carolyn opened the back, shoved Sam in, and then climbed in after her. Michael threw the vehicle into drive while the women slammed closed the doors.

"When we reach Arnie, get him into the back," Michael yelled.

They neared the open gate. Arnie crouched, rifle raised. Michael glanced in the rear-view mirror.

A Humvee closed in.

He braked when he pulled up next to Arnie. Sam threw open the door, and Arnie scrambled in as the vehicle rolled forward. Althaea lowered her window, turned around in her seat, and leaned out. She fired at the Humvee. Michael wove along the road, flooring it, determined to outmanoeuvre them.

"Keep your heads down," Althaea yelled.

Michael glanced into the rear-view mirror, and fear raced through his gut when he saw Carolyn, Sam, and Arnie all sitting.

"Get the fuck down," he shouted. The heads in the mirror disappeared, and Michael breathed again. He glanced at Althaea. *Fuck.* She was bleeding. "Ally, get in here. You're bleeding."

She ignored him and kept firing. "It's nothing."

"It's not nothing. You're leaking blood from your arm."

"A bullet grazed me. I'm fine. I can't stop now. They'll close the gap."

"I'll fire at them." Arnie popped up in the rear-view mirror again, worry etched on his face. He leaned forward and touched Althaea's hand. "Get in, Ally. I'll do this. Please, God, just don't—" He stopped talking when she slid back into her seat.

"Okay," she said, "but if you get shot, I'll kill you."

While Althaea took off her shirt, tore it into strips, and stanched her wound, Arnie lowered his window and leaned out, firing at the vehicles behind them.

They reached the end of the road, and Michael barrelled onto the highway without slowing. "Get in," he yelled at Arnie. "Hold on tight. The roads are slick."

Back in his seat, Arnie closed the window.

Michael pressed on the gas pedal, and they sped along the road at a hundred and twenty clicks. He headed west, taking the road towards Toronto. Downed trees blocked the road, and Michael swerved around them without slowing. No oncoming cars to worry about.

Night fell. What streetlights there were along town roads they crossed didn't come on.

Michael checked the rear-view mirror: only darkness behind them. They were okay. No one would risk driving without headlights with all those trees down. Still, he wouldn't feel safe until they'd put a great deal of distance between themselves and the underground community.

"Arnie, thank God, you're okay." Carolyn.

"Yeah, Cornell never came after us when he dragged you away from the compound."

"What do you mean? I thought they found your body in your car. They said you committed suicide."

"What the fuck? I'm sorry, but the Agency locked us up together for weeks at the compound. Last time we saw each other, Cornell was dragging you away and shooting at me and Julie. What happened to her, Michael?" Arnie asked.

"They took her memory." Michael's heart ached to say it.

Carolyn burst into tears, and Arnie hugged her. His gaze met Michael's in the mirror. "Can we help her get it back?"

Michael opened his mouth to reply when Althaea spoke. "Yes," she said, "we can."

CHAPTER 51

Carolyn awoke from a fitful doze, an arm around a peacefully sleeping Sam's shoulders. Arnie held Carolyn's other hand. She'd clutched his hand while Althaea had outlined the idea for triggering Carolyn's memories and hadn't let go after Althaea stopped talking.

Arnie's warm, comforting grip helped Carolyn stay anchored. Terrified to think she couldn't trust anything she remembered from before Sam showed up at her door, Carolyn struggled to control her racing mind. How could the Agency have not only erased memories, but also have substituted them with false ones?

Both the engagement ring and the wedding band were back where they belonged. Michael hadn't forced her to abandon them in a ravine in Algonquin Park. With the pad of her thumb, Carolyn rubbed the rings on her left hand, and tension eased at their familiar feel.

Yet the disturbing thoughts continued. Sam had gone through a funeral for first her father and then her mother, which sickened Carolyn. What nauseated her most was that one of those deaths had been faked so Cornell could keep the two of them for his own uses. It brought her close to breaking.

Opening her eyes, she studied the back of Michael's head. They'd been driving for over an hour now, heading to the homes they'd left behind. Michael had remained neutral from the moment they'd lost the Agency vehicles. He hadn't tried to talk to Carolyn, or convince her of anything, and she appreciated he'd let her be.

She'd tried to dredge up recollections of her time with Michael that didn't involve beatings, rapes, or betrayal. At least now when she thought of him, she found favourable memories. During the escape from the underground community, he'd risked his life for her and Sam. No trace existed of the sadistic psycho she remembered from the trip to, and through, Algonquin.

An urge to hear his voice, to talk to him, made her break the silence that'd hung over the group since they'd left the Agency behind.

"Michael?"

His gaze met hers in the rear-view mirror, and he smiled. "Yes?"

The warmth he exuded brought a surge of affection Carolyn found encouraging. "Back there, you said something about angels and told me you'd explain later. Will you tell me now?"

So he did. She listened, rapt, while Michael explained who she used to be, what she used to do. How she'd talk with people's departed loved ones, their spirit guides, their guardian angels. How she'd always called on her own angels and guides to help and protect her and connected to her own departed loved ones. And how the Agency had blocked it to manipulate and control her.

Story told, Michael fell silent. A squeeze on her right hand made Carolyn glance at Arnie. She squeezed back and listened to the drone of the engine, the swipe of the wiper blades, and the patter of rain on the roof. The shock at hearing of Arnie's death came back to her then. But she couldn't remember any of the details, like what she'd done or how she'd reacted.

She took a deep breath and calmed. She had to stop dwelling on this. No sooner did Carolyn tell herself that than the image of her shooting Cornell popped into her head. That bullet had been meant for Michael. What if Cornell's plan had worked? What if Sam wouldn't have found Carolyn and put doubts in her mind? Michael would be dead, and Carolyn back at the Agency, sleeping with the real enemy.

Breath shallow again, stomach tense and knotted, Carolyn went rigid, her arm sliding from Sam's shoulders, her hand releasing its hold on Arnie's. This had to stop. Frantic, she could almost feel Cornell's hands on her body.

"When can we fix this? Please. I need to get my real memories back—get myself back. I don't know who I am anymore, and I think I'd like who I was better than I like who I am now."

Michael cleared his throat, then spoke. "We can pull over in Port Perry." His eyes fluttered to the mirror and met hers again. "We're almost there."

She settled down to wait.

***

Port Perry nestled at the bottom of the hill through which 7A led. The highway sliced through Lake Scugog, a man-made lake that had barely recovered from massive fish deaths in 2007 when the Aurora machines triggered. Michael had already been doing less than the eighty-kilometre speed limit, but when they approached town and the speed limit dropped to fifty, he slowed to forty.

No cars approached. No cars followed.

He slowed again and then stopped when he saw water from the swampy lake covering the highway. The streetlights were dead. The darkness and teeming rain made it impossible for Michael to determine how deep the water on the road was. He unhooked his seatbelt.

"I'll check it out."

"Want me to go with you?" Althaea reached for her gun.

"No. Stay with them."

Michael checked his gun. Cocked and ready. He stepped from the car and walked the few metres to the water's edge, then placed a foot into the water and found it didn't cover his shoes. Michael went to the guard rail and peered into the lake.

Bulrushes and grasses rose from the depths. Nothing moved. It smelled like raw sewage, the surface dotted with dead fish. Michael wrinkled his nose in distaste and gazed across the strip of roadway into the town. Everything was still. What cars he saw were empty. Stores and restaurants were dark. Somewhere across the lake, he saw a soft glow of light, perhaps from a flashlight, lantern, or candles.

The place looked deserted. Until they'd hit Port Perry, they hadn't gone through any large towns. They'd stayed on dirt roads or secondary highways surrounded by farmers' fields, forests, and blink-and-you-miss-'em towns, where it wasn't unusual for everything to be dark and quiet even in the early evening. But the ambience here gave him the willies. For a moment, he was glad Carolyn had lost her ability to talk to the dead.

Michael returned to the car. "We're going in. There's a restaurant on Queen Street where Torque and I used to go. I know the owner. We can stop there."

***

Arms crossed over her chest, Carolyn faced Althaea in the banquet room upstairs at the King's Castle Restaurant. Arnie and Sam sat at a nearby table. The establishment's owner absent, Michael had jimmied the lock. They'd entered to find the place deserted, but unmolested.

Warmth wafted from the gas fireplace, but Michael had just lit it, and the air in the room was still icy. Carolyn shivered and rubbed her hands up and down her arms, trying to warm herself. Goose bumps prickled her arms and legs. She wished she had warmer clothes, but she'd run away wearing only shorts and a T-shirt.

Michael stepped close to her and put his jacket around her shoulders. She smiled her thanks.

Arms now bare, Michael wore a khaki-green T-shirt tucked into military pants. He'd found another shoulder holster in the SUV and wore that and a gun. When he smiled at her, warmth and kindness replaced the air of tough-guy seriousness under which he usually operated

Carolyn suppressed an urge to fold herself into his embrace.

"Ally and I will both do this with you," Michael said. "I guess you don't remember what happened when I helped Ally, but you were there."

She shook her head, and Michael told her about the creature set to guard Althaea's memories, a trap that had triggered when they'd accessed Althaea's mind.

"We might face something similar when recovering your memories. Ally's coming along to help hold off anything planted in there. That should give us enough time to retrieve some of what's buried, and then you can recover the rest on your own."

Carolyn clutched the jacket tight around her and trembled, feeling exposed. She watched his mouth move while he spoke, appreciating the shape of his lips. She shook her head. Being this near him awakened something in her.

His voice faltered, and he stopped talking.

"Carr." He tried to speak again, but his voice cracked. His eyes grew bright in the dim glow of the candles scattered around the room. He stepped closer to her, their bodies almost touching. Michael raised a hand and touched her cheek, stroking it with the outer edge of his fingers.

The touch brought with it that moth-wing flutter in the back of her mind as though of something familiar. She closed her eyes and inhaled the scent of melting wax from the candles, of Michael, of oiled wood from the dark beams of the rafters above. Gentle fingers brushed her lips and without thinking, she kissed them.

Carolyn opened her eyes, now damp with tears.

"Ready?" Michael's voice was husky.

"Yes," she said, her own voice thick. The others forgotten, she was alone with him.

Michael explained what he'd have to do, and Carolyn agreed. She removed his jacket and set it aside. He placed his hands on either side of her head, leaned his forehead in to touch hers, and called out to Althaea.

Carolyn sensed Althaea step up and join their connection. Althaea placed one arm around Carolyn, and the other, Carolyn knew, was around Michael. The triangle completed when Althaea leaned in.

Pulses fired into Carolyn's forehead, into the space between her brows. *The* Ajna *centre.* That thought popped into her head, but she didn't know what it meant or from where it came.

Carolyn stands in a hallway. Michael takes her hand and leads her to a large, wooden door. It opens, and she recognizes the room she and Michael had rented in Peterborough when Michael had kidnapped her—the room in which he'd raped her.

She glances at the bed and sees herself there, handcuffed. Michael stands next to the bed, removing his clothes while Carolyn sobs, pleads. He's ignoring her, a fierce, predatory light in his eyes. When he's naked, he climbs into the bed and rips at her clothes, one hand stifling her screams.

Her anger and hate well up, and she turns away from the scene. When Michael puts his arms around her, she struggles, fights him.

"Shh. It's okay. Look."

She doesn't want to, but something in his voice makes her lift her head. The scene shatters. Melts away. Changes. Another forms.

Carolyn sees herself in the room, in the bed again, but she's sleeping, undisturbed. No cuffs restrain her. Michael sleeps on the couch in the living area. Light snoring reaches her ears, and she feels a surge of affection. The Carolyn in the bed stirs, eyes darting frantically under their closed lids. She moans and cries out. Michael leaps from the couch, naked except for a pair of briefs. He runs to the bed and cradles her in his arms, reassuring, telling her it's just a dream.

Her eyes open, and she melts into his embrace. The words tumble out, and she tells him how afraid and alone she felt in her dream. Michael soothes and comforts her. She raises her face from his chest, hugs him, and her lips seek his. He hesitates, but only for a moment, and then returns her kiss.

Carolyn watches the couple on the bed for a moment longer, knowing everything about to happen, drawing it from her memory. "I remember. Oh, God. I remember. You. Us." She looks at Michael, her smile radiant, Michael's smile reflecting hers.

He tries to speak, chokes, and takes her in his arms. "Oh, thank God." He hugs her tight, and his lips brush hers. "I was so afraid I'd lost what we had together."

She kisses him, and her hands stray to his hair. She wants to touch him, wants him to touch her.

Althaea's harsh cries break through their joy. "A hydra, Michael. Get out here."

He releases Carolyn and runs towards Althaea's voice. Carolyn follows him out of the room and into the hallway. Althaea holds a sword and slashes at a three-headed beast in front of her. "When you pull out your gun, it turns into a fucking sword. What the hell, Valiant?"

Frozen in horror, Carolyn stares while Althaea hacks at the beast.

Michael catches up to his former partner as one of the hydra's heads tumbles to the ground. When two heads pop out of the stump of neck, he steps back.

"No good," he says. "We can't kill it by cutting off the heads."

Something about that sounds familiar to Carolyn. It's a story or a myth. "You have to stab it in the heart," she shouts. Carolyn pulls out her gun and finds a sword in her hand.

A scream from Althaea jolts Carolyn and she runs to the other woman, whose shoulder and arm ooze blood and ragged flesh. She pulls Althaea away from the creature and steps forward.

"Carolyn, no." Michael, afraid for her.

Eyes fixed on the monster, she stands her ground. "It's mine, Michael. Back off." She knows she can do it. Carolyn raises the heavy sword with ease and swipes the air with it.

The monster's heads orient on her.

She pulls herself up to her full height, standing tall. The beast seems to diminish before her strength and power. Is that a glimmer of fear in its eyes? The hydra bares four sets of teeth, four throats growl, four mouths slaver, and flecks of spittle hit her exposed arms.

Carolyn chokes down the rising bile and scans the hydra's chest. Where's its heart? She'll take a stab at it. The joke makes her smile a little, but grimly. She hopes she'll get the chance. In her periphery, she sees a blur, Michael's arms, waving, distracting the monster for her.

The tactic succeeds, and now she's afraid for Michael as all the heads turn to face him. A lunge forward, and Carolyn's sword drives into the tender flesh where all the necks converge at the top of the body. A roar bursts from the heads.

She draws the sword back out of the monster. It takes more effort to remove the sword than it did to shove it in. When the last of the blade clears the body, she hears a sucking sound and blood spurts from the wound, splattering both her and Michael. Instead of rolling clear of the monster, Michael draws closer to it and stabs the sword upward into its belly.

The heads howl and thrash, the clawed feet stomping around Michael. One foot makes contact, tearing at Michael's stomach. Carolyn screams when blood flows from Michael's abdomen. She lunges forward again and shoves her blade back into the monster, lower down the body this time.

Its thrashes weaken, and it staggers.

Terrified the beast will collapse on Michael, Carolyn drops the sword and grabs Michael under the arms. She hauls him away, and the monster falls, missing Michael by a hair's breadth.

Althaea crawls to Michael and presses both hands onto his wound, attempting to stop the blood. "Finish the fucker and let's go."

Carolyn picks up her sword again. The monster lies dying before her. She raises her sword and plunges it into its body up to the hilt.

Carolyn opened her eyes. She lay on the floor, head cradled in Sam's arms.

CHAPTER 52

Shaking off vertigo, Carolyn jumped up and ran to Michael, who lay on the floor as if unconscious. Arnie had his balled-up shirt stuffed against the wound in Michael's abdomen. Althaea rummaged in the packs, pulling out gauze and first aid supplies. Blood trickled down her arm, seeping through the towel she'd wrapped around her own injured shoulder.

"No. Oh, God, please, no." Carolyn knelt by Michael's side.

Michael's eyes opened, and he flashed a weak smile. "Hi. Good to have you back." He winced and closed his eyes again.

Carolyn clutched his hand and put it to her cheek. "Don't you dare leave me."

Althaea leaned over him. "He'll be okay. The wound is not as bad as it looks. It's not deep, just long, and hit no internal organs. It was close though. Arnie, I'll need your help. You two," she said, indicating Sam and Carolyn, "step away."

Carolyn hesitated. Althaea stared at her, refusing to budge. Reluctantly, Carolyn stood and went to Sam, hugged her.

"Almost everything came back to me," Carolyn said. "I remember Michael breaking into the house to kidnap me, and you came home and left that note. Michael helped me escape, and we grew close during our time together."

She studied Sam's face, trying to gauge her reaction. Sam's eyes were wet, but the tears had stopped flowing.

"You know now the baby you're carrying is Michael's, don't you?"

Carolyn nodded. "It doesn't mean I forgot about your father. I love your dad, and I always will. Michael and I have a connection that goes deeper than anything I've experienced. It was as if we'd picked up the thread of something started a long time ago. We both thought I couldn't get pregnant."

"I guess it was meant to be, then, right? Isn't that what you used to say?"

She smiled. "It's what I still say."

***

Carolyn sat next to Michael, who'd stretched out on the bench seats along the back wall of the banquet room. A blanket covered his torso. Althaea rested on another makeshift bed across the room. Sam and Arnie sat at a table, heads together, absorbed in low conversation.

The night deepened, but Carolyn couldn't sleep now that Michael was awake. He'd slept for four hours while she'd dozed in the chair at his side, holding his hand, longing to talk to him. Every once-in-a-while, Carolyn raised Michael's hand to her lips and kissed it. The last time she'd done that, he'd opened his eyes and smiled at her. Carolyn's heart almost burst at the sight.

"I can't believe we're together," he said. "Do you have any idea what you've put me through?"

He teased, but she frowned. "Althaea told me most of it. Arnie told me more. I remember seeing you in my cell. Michael, you'd died. What if you hadn't come back?"

"But I did. Don't think about the 'what ifs.' That's pointless."

"Yes. But the thought of losing you—"

Michael cut her off. "Stop. We won't do this."

The front door creaked and Carolyn tensed. "Didn't we lock the door?"

He sat up, wincing when he moved, and grabbed his gun from the nearby table. Arnie and Ally both stood, guns ready.

They walked towards the stairs, Michael taking the lead. The floor creaked when they hit the landing.

Carolyn held her breath.

From below, a man's voice called. "Someone up there?"

"Dylan?" Michael lowered his gun. "It's okay. It's the owner." He moved down the stairs and called out again. "It's Mick Valiant."

"Valiant, you old fuck. What are you doing trespassing on my property?" Dylan appeared in the mirror above the landing where the staircase curved up to the second floor. A flashlight reflected off the mirror and shone onto the suit of armour that stood in the corner. His rubber boots squished and squeaked on the polished wood stairs.

It surprised Carolyn to see how young he looked—thirty, maybe. The gravelly voice had made her expect someone older. He wore his long hair tied back in a ponytail, but it was sleek and black, with no touch of grey.

He removed his raincoat while he walked, revealing a red flannel shirt and jeans. Carolyn couldn't decide whether he looked more like a hippy or a farmer. She settled on hippy farmer. The closer he got to them, the more energized she felt. She decided she liked him.

"What happened here?" Michael jumped to the heart of it as soon as Dylan reached them.

A red satin cloth appeared from the pocket of Dylan's jeans. He removed his glasses and wiped the rain off the lenses. "It started a few months ago. Storms. Earthquakes. The power's been out for months. At first, people holed up in their houses. The news reports told us to stay inside, so we did. But then the lake flooded. Scugog just rose up and swallowed most of the beach, blocked the 7A."

"We came in from the east, over Lake Scugog. There's about a centimetre of water covering the highway," Michael said.

Dylan nodded. "Yeah. Now. If you'd been a week earlier we wouldn't be standin' here talkin'. After the rains started, the fish died, floatin' so thick you couldn't see the water. Looked like 2007 all over again when all them carp died. 'Course, when the rain was heavier, you couldn't see nothin'. Then the waves got big and tossed stuff around."

He sat at one of the tables and waved them over. They grabbed chairs and grouped around him.

"People started dyin' after that. Somethin' in the water, might be?" He studied them, frowning. "Haven't been drinkin' the tap water, have you?"

"No," Michael said. "We have bottled water."

Dylan looked around for the first time. "So who's 'we'?"

Michael made the introductions. Dylan rose and went to the back room, returning with a bottle of bourbon and glasses on a tray. "Speakin' of drinks: nightcap? Might help."

Arnie and Althaea exchanged glances. The two sat next to each other, Arnie's arm encircling Althaea's waist. Odd seeing Arnie show affection to a woman other than herself or his mother, Carolyn thought, and smiled at the sight. She pointed to her belly, shook her head, and held up a water bottle when Dylan offered her bourbon.

Drinks distributed, he raised his glass. "Cheers, friends."

The little group clinked glasses, but it wasn't celebratory.

Dylan continued the story. "When folks first got sick, they went to the hospital. Docs couldn't figure out what was wrong with 'em. A flu-like thing. Fever. Stomach cramps. The squirts. Pukin'."

He paused, looked around. "Ella, my wife, caught it. She still feels tired all the time and has bad moments—sometimes so bad I'm afraid I'll be on my own. We've prepared for the worst, but she's hangin' in."

Dylan took a long draw on his drink, draining it. He set the empty glass on the wood table, the sound echoing through the room. Another couple of fingers of bourbon splashed into his glass.

Carolyn peeked at Sam and noted Sam's glass was almost empty. The urge to tell her to slow down hit Carolyn, but she decided it didn't matter. They were lucky to still be alive and together.

Dylan's eyes met Carolyn's, and he nodded as though reading her mind. "Most people who had somewhere else to go left town. We weren't hearin' about shit like this anywhere else—not at first, anyway. Might be we're ground zero for this thing.

"I have the restaurant here. A house. I drop by and check this place every day, make sure no one's broke in. Don't matter much, I guess. What can they do here? You can walk into the liquor store and help yourself to booze if that's what you want. Food's spoiled. I salvaged what I could and figured I'd get a rebate or something on the rest. But there's no one left to get the rebate from, see? They're all gone."

Dylan stopped talking. Michael egged him on. "Who's all gone? What do you mean?"

"Everyone. You go through town, no one's left. Many died, sure, others fled, but they would've had to have flown somewhere, yes? I drove to Newmarket one day. Went through Uxbridge.

Know what I found?" He looked at each of them. They gaped back.

"Nothin' and no one. It's as if they dropped off the earth. Sure, there's the odd person. It's not deserted. But close to it. And lots of bodies. It'll be a hell of a cleanup one day. But they're not all dead. I didn't even get sick. It's weird, Mick. Some of us are fine, never got sick. Others are just gone. That's all I know." Dylan took another gulp of bourbon.

After a pause, he looked at Michael. "So what do *you* know? That's what I'm wonderin'. 'Cause you ain't told me everythin'. Give." Dylan leaned forward and frowned at Michael. "What the fuck happened to our lives, Mick?"

CHAPTER 53

Without flinching, Michael met Dylan's gaze. "We came from the northeast. I sheltered in a military compound during the storms. We're heading home."

Dylan ignored that. "What do you *know*, Mick? I know it's more than you're sayin'." He pointed at Althaea. "You and your gal pal here have nasty wounds. You didn't get those drivin' from the northeast." Dylan's eyes glinted black, shiny from bourbon and candlelight. "Where's your buddy? Torque? That motherfucker was up to no good. I don't care how polite he was or how much money he spent at my restaurant. Butter wouldn't melt in his mouth, and he was a dangerous S-O-B. I always liked you, Mick. But that buddy of yours? Wouldn't turn my back on him."

Michael sighed. "Torque's dead. What do I know? I doubt you'd believe me if I told you. It's safest just to say we're on our own. The government can't help anyone anymore. We should consider banding together, because if we don't, we might not make it."

"That sounds mighty ominous, dude."

"It's the truth. We're heading to Aurora in the morning. But we need to find a central place to hole up and organize ourselves. The compound from which we came is the best prospect for shelter through the winter. We'll be returning in a day or two. I'll catch up to you and Ella then, and we'll talk. Fair?"

"Yeah, man. I'll head home now. Ella hates bein' left alone, and I don't blame her. By now, she'll be worried, I expect. Can't call the house and tell her I'm okay, so I have to git. Lock the door when you leave. You know where I live. If you don't find me here when you return, you'll find me there. Help yourself to whatever you need."

After Dylan left, the group settled down to sleep. Arnie and Althaea pushed two benches together and were asleep within minutes. Carolyn told Sam to do the same and then went to Michael, who was back on the bench on which he'd slept.

"Does it hurt much?" Carolyn sat on the chair next to him, cupped his face with her palm, and sent him a Reiki boost.

Michael nuzzled into her hand for a moment, eyes closed. The bristles on his unshaven face tickled her.

"I'll be fine, Carr. Go sleep. Stay close though. Don't go anywhere without telling me. Sam too."

Carolyn lowered her voice. "What do you think made people sick?"

"Not sure, but I'd bet money Dylan is an abductee."

"What about his wife?"

"Good question. Maybe Ella's lucky she survived. Just promise you'll stay inside the restaurant. No telling who's out there. At the least, there might be scared people with itchy trigger fingers."

"Are you afraid the Agency will find us?"

"I don't assume they've let us go. Promise me you won't even go downstairs without telling me."

"I promise." Carolyn stood and went to where Sam had pushed two benches together. She'd already snuggled under a blanket and yawned when Carolyn climbed in beside her.

"Thanks, Mom."

"For what?"

"Staying with me even though you want to be with Michael. I'm twenty, but I don't want to be alone. This place is creepy."

Carolyn looked around as if for the first time. A dark-haired woman in a long, blue dress stood near the women's restroom. Carolyn could vaguely see the door through the woman's body.

Eyes closed, Carolyn connected to the woman. *Do you mind our presence? We don't want to impose, just sleep.* When she opened her eyes, the woman had disappeared, but her voice echoed: *sleep well.*

The return of Carolyn's memories had unblocked her mediumship abilities, and she found it reassuring. She asked the spirits in the restaurant to alert her if anyone tried to enter the building.

Light flashed at the corner of Carolyn's eye, and when she looked, a young girl appeared at the top of the stairs. She held up a hand, placing her index finger to her thumb, forming a circle. *Okay.* A man on the main floor positioned an ethereal chair by the door and sat. Carolyn sent thanks to him, but told the man she didn't want to put him to any trouble. His wheezy laugh reached Carolyn's psychic hearing, and she caught a whiff of pipe smoke as he settled in for the night's vigil. *My pleasure, ma'am. No trouble.*

Carolyn lay her head on a rolled up jacket she used as a pillow, sent her thanks out to the spirits around them one more time, and closed her eyes. A few minutes later, she slept.

***

Carolyn's eyes open to find Jim Cornell lying next to her in bed. Cornell's mouth forms a toothy grin when he notices she's awake. She struggles to stand, wanting to get away from him, but can't move. Head whipping from side to side, she tries to find the others.

Cornell snickers. The sound reminds Carolyn of a wheezing dog in a cartoon she can't quite remember. He puts a hand over her mouth, stifling a shout. "Think I'd let you call Valiant?" Cornell leans in to her ear. "Keep your mouth shut. One word, and I'll butcher Sam like a hog. Understand?"

She whimpers, nods her head. The hand retreats from her mouth, and she stares at him. He's dead. What's he doing here if he's dead?

Cornell grins again and gags her mouth. "I need you quiet, still." A hand slides up under her clothes, touches her breasts.

Locked in place, she's unable to fight him off.

"You used to like this. Remember?" Cornell waits for a response.

A tear slides from Carolyn's eye, and the hand travels to her belly, stroking, caressing. "I would've cared for the child as if she were mine. Now I'll make it difficult for you. She's trying to come through, and I can keep her from getting to you. Perhaps she'll be stillborn."

Carolyn tries to scream, but the gag stifles it.

"Did you forget Sam? I told you to be quiet." Fingers pinch her nipples.

She tries to pull away. Can't.

He makes a sudden move, sliding a hand inside her pants, between her legs. Carolyn attempts to pull her thighs together, fighting the paralysis, but fails. He plays, touches, probes. "I've missed this. Can't let that fucker have all the fun."

She tries to clear her head, to think. Carolyn hears the sound of a zipper and Cornell shifts and fidgets next to her. The gag drenches with saliva and stifled screams, and she shakes her head, the only movement she can make.

At last she remembers and says silently, Archangel Michael, I call upon you now. Please come and remove any entity attachments from me, any lower vibrating energies, any toxic energies.

In a vision, light fills the room, and she senses the angelic presence.

Cornell rages. "You bitch. You can't win. I'm not done with you."

She screams against the gag, tries to claw with her still paralyzed hands, tears streaming down her face. The bright light behind Cornell silhouettes his body. When he disappears, Carolyn finds her voice and screams.

"You're okay, Carr. You're dreaming." Michael.

Thank God. Carolyn opened her eyes, clutched at him. "Sam. Where's Sam?" She sat. Finding Sam's bench empty, Carolyn leapt up. "Where's Sam?" She said it louder, raced towards the women's washroom.

"What's wrong?" Michael asked. "Sam went to look around downstairs. I made her promise not to venture outside. She's fine."

Carolyn calmed when he said that but wanted to verify. Though her bladder felt ready to burst, she hurried past the women's washroom and rushed down the stairs.

"Sam? Where are you?"

"Here, Mom. What's wrong?"

Carolyn landed at the bottom of the stairs and raced into the dining area, almost knocking over her daughter, who gripped Carolyn's shoulders and peered into her eyes.

"Why are you freaking out? I'm only checking the place out. I was bored and didn't want to wake you."

Carolyn sighed. "Nothing. A bad dream."

Footsteps on the stairs made her look up. Michael hurried towards them, face troubled. "What happened? What did you dream?"

"Later. I have to hit the washroom." She turned to Sam. "Stay inside. Promise?"

"Yes. I already promised Michael." Sam clenched her jaw and put her hands on her hips.

Carolyn hurried to the washroom on the main floor, the mundane motions of using the toilet and washing up helping to calm her. Refreshed, she went upstairs with Michael and told him about her dream.

"Was it Cornell or a nightmare from your unconscious?" Michael asked. The two sat at a table and picked at the food Arnie and Althaea had scrounged from the packs they'd brought and stores Dylan had on hand.

"It was Cornell," Carolyn said. "He's angry and vengeful."

"I don't get it," Michael said. "Torque wasn't like that. He wanted to help us. Why doesn't Cornell? When I had my near-death experience, I regretted everything I'd done that hurt anyone, no matter how small my mistake, and I wanted to atone for it. Why wouldn't Cornell want the same?"

"He hasn't gone into the light. He's earthbound, full of resentment and hate, and he wants to hurt us, so he refuses to cross."

Michael chewed a handful of trail mix and considered what she'd said. "What about when you called on Archangel Michael? Did that force Cornell into the light?"

"There's a chance. I got him away from me for now, but the angels can't go against free will. If someone refuses to go into the light, that person may stay earthbound."

Michael shifted closer to Carolyn, put an arm around her, and kissed her cheek.

"May I touch the baby?" Michael hovered his free hand above her belly and waited. When she nodded consent, he put his hand on the bulge below the waistband of Carolyn's track pants.

"Can you feel her move?" Michael asked.

"Sometimes—more often in the last week. At first it felt like little flutters. Now it's a definite kick."

"Can Cornell hurt the baby?"

"I won't let him."

"But can he prevent her from coming through? Will she be all right?"

"I've got protection around her. I'll always protect her. Cornell can threaten all he wants, but I'm not helpless." She thought about how he'd bound her in the dream. She'd never drop her guard like that again. Carolyn pressed a hand over Michael's and kissed his mouth, gently parting his lips, pouring her love into him.

After a moment, she released him, and he kissed her forehead. The arm around Carolyn's shoulders drew her into a tight hug. "The thought of him harming you or our baby terrifies me. How do I fight a ghost?"

"Ghosts aren't in the physical plane. They can play on our fears, give us nightmares, annoy us, but they can't hurt us unless we let them. Now I'm aware he's around, I'll always have protection around us."

Something occurred to her. "Don't let Cornell suck you into anything on his turf. If you have a dream with him in it, ignore him and call in Archangel Michael. Cornell can harm you in your dreams, but we don't have to play his game."

When Michael promised, Carolyn taught him the words to call in Archangel Michael for help and the steps to put up energetic protection. He smiled while repeating the words and gestures she taught.

"I feel silly," he admitted.

She returned the smile. "I understand. But you'll want to have this protective energy around you. An entity can harm you by clinging to you and muddling your thinking. His anger can infect you and make you angry. Keep him away."

Michael nodded. Both looked up when Sam appeared at the top of the stairs. "The car's packed. No one wanted to interrupt you, but Arnie's eager to find his mom."

"We'll be right down," Michael said.

Sam left, and Carolyn stuffed the few belongings still lying around into a bag. Michael helped her put her backpack on her shoulders. Once again, she wore another woman's clothes. Althaea had lent her a pair of camouflage pants and a black tank top. It reminded her of the days they'd spent running from the Agency. Remembering Arnie's mom, she shuddered.

"It won't be good, Michael."

"Is that your intuition talking?"

Carolyn nodded. "I don't want to tell Arnie because I can't say what's wrong. When I try to sense her in spirit, I fail, but I doubt we'll like what we find."

"All we can do is be there for him." Michael took Carolyn's hand, and they walked down the stairs.

CHAPTER 54

They arrived at the southeast section of Aurora, where Arnie's condo was located in a complex built less than five years before. It was a mix of apartments, offices, and retail spaces. Locals opposed to having the zoning bylaws changed to allow high-rise buildings in what until that point had been single-family dwellings had almost blocked the new development. But when the permits had gone through and units went up for sale, Arnie had lined up to purchase.

The developers had promised a design that would blend buildings into the landscape, and Michael thought they'd succeeded. All the structures sported rooftop gardens, and they'd generously dotted the surroundings with green space. Michael remembered the protests, but hadn't been a part of them. He hadn't cared what they did, knowing it would all end anyway.

When he recalled his former attitude, he felt ashamed. Standing in the drizzle in front of the demolished building and seeing the stricken look on Arnie's face increased the shame tenfold and added guilt.

"Are you getting anything, Carolyn?" Arnie asked for the third time.

Carolyn leaned on a cement block, eyes closed. She took a deep breath and winced. Michael wanted to touch her but feared distracting her. When Arnie reached a hand towards her, Michael intercepted and shook his head.

"She was inside, with her nurse. I can feel them both in spirit, Arnie. I'm so sorry." Tears spilled down Carolyn's face, and she opened her eyes.

Arnie fell to the ground. Michael waved Althaea over and indicated he'd take over for her as lookout. He moved away from the rubble and took up a position near the road.

Althaea dropped next to Arnie and hugged him. He wrapped his arms around his knees and buried his head. His muffled voice drifted up to them. "My home is her tomb. We can't even retrieve her body for burial." Arnie looked up at Carolyn, his face a mask of fear. "Is she earthbound?"

Carolyn shook her head. "She crossed. So did her nurse. Your mom visited you, Arnie, and she's here now. She says you've seen her in your dreams."

"Yes. She looked young. I thought it was just a dream."

Carolyn sat on the ground beside Arnie. "No, that was your mom. She wants you to know she's with your dad, and she's never been happier. Both watch over you."

They sat for a while and let Arnie come to terms with his loss. The earthquakes had been strong in Toronto, the aftershocks so great that buildings as far north as Bradford were destroyed. Millions of people in Toronto and the GTA had died.

Carolyn went to Michael and put her arms around him. She looked up at him, so full of sorrow his heart lurched at the sight.

"I feel Steve in spirit." She whispered it, so the others wouldn't overhear.

When Carolyn's husband had died, their friend, Steve, had lost his wife, Shelly. Losing Shelly had scared Steve into terminating his friendship with Arnie and Carolyn.

Michael put a hand on Carolyn's head and pressed her face into his chest. "I'm so sorry."

"I don't want to check on anyone else right now. What if Sam's friends are dead too? She won't be able to cope with that."

"They might have survived if they were in houses and not apartments."

"I hope they're okay. She'll ask me sooner or later."

Sam walked away from the demolished building and climbed into the car. Perhaps she was thinking about her friends and was as afraid as Carolyn of learning what had happened. He thought about his own house and decided he didn't need anything there. All he needed was Carolyn, the baby, and Sam.

He called over to Althaea. "We have to get moving."

She nodded. One of her hands stroked Arnie's hair, and she leaned forward and whispered something to him. He kept his head lowered. She talked to him some more, and he allowed her to lead him towards the SUV.

Michael stopped him. "I'm sorry. For whatever part I played in this."

"You shouldn't have let them take me away."

A vision of being Arnie, forced into the trunk of Torque's car, fearing for his life, Carolyn's life, and his mother's life flashed into Michael's head. He swallowed, tried to control the sense of being two people at once, a remnant of his near-death experience.

Not knowing what would come out, Michael started to speak. Arnie turned his back and left Michael standing there, mouth hanging open.

"Give him time. I'll talk to him later."

Michael jumped. He'd forgotten Carolyn was there though her hand still held his.

"He's right, Carr. There's a lot on my conscience."

"Forgive yourself, then, before you expect Arnie to." She tugged on his hand, and he followed her to the car.

***

This time, Arnie stayed in the car while Michael, Sam, and Carolyn went up to the wreckage left of Carolyn's house. Most of the charming century home had burned to the ground. Althaea stood next to the car, rifle slung across a shoulder, on lookout once more.

Michael kept an arm around Carolyn while she made her way to the front steps. He remembered forcing her down those stairs, rejecting her attempts to convince him Jessica, as a spirit, was with them. A glance at Carolyn told him she relived it too. Sam went to the bottom of the stairs, looked up towards the front porch, and turned away.

"Mom, where's Vanna? And Jack? Are they okay?"

Carolyn's body went rigid against Michael's side.

"Do you know?" he asked.

She nodded. "They're alive, Sam."

"Is that true, Mom?"

"They haven't passed. I can't tell you where they are without focused remote viewing, and I can't do that here."

"That's all I need to know," Sam said. "Let's go. I hope the people renting this place got away." She turned and headed back down the driveway.

Carolyn and Michael watched her until she climbed into the car. Michael gazed up at the sky. The drizzle had stopped. Fat, grey clouds threatened more rain, but for now, it had stopped. "We'll pass through Port Perry—let Dylan know where we're heading."

"I'm glad we came here. I had to see. Maybe we can come back someday and rebuild."

Michael didn't answer her, just kissed her on the forehead.

"You don't think that'll be possible."

Damn her abilities. Sometimes it made life with her difficult. "Not for a long time. Things will get worse as people discover the infrastructure they took for granted is gone." He sighed. Some things she couldn't see, and it was just as well. They returned to the car holding hands. Michael wondered if there would ever come a time when he wouldn't need her touch reassuring him she was still there.

**

Michael didn't need psychic abilities to tell him something was wrong when they pulled up in front of the King's Castle Restaurant in Port Perry. The door leaned open, and two of the windows on the main floor were smashed. He grabbed his gun from its holster. "Ally, with me. The rest of you stay here."

"Michael, no." Carolyn's voice registered fear.

"I have to check it out. Wait here. Have your gun ready. You too, Arnie. Lock the doors when I get out and don't leave the car for any reason."

Sam whimpered, but Michael ignored it. Carolyn would have to deal with it. He hoped Dylan was okay. Althaea stepped from the car, gun ready, and they made their way to the patio together. Michael motioned for Althaea to stand to the left of the front door. He pushed the door open wider. It made a slight creaking sound, but everything else was still and quiet. He waited. Nothing.

Inside the restaurant, shards of reflective glass stuck to the wall behind the bar, remnants of a mirror. The rest of the mirror lay strewn on the floor and the counter in crunchy, glittering fragments. Barstools marinated in a pool of what smelled like beer and wine.

Althaea indicated she'd take the main floor. Michael nodded and moved up the stairs, pausing on the landing. The suit of armour lay in pieces on the stairs, the shield and sword missing. The floor creaked when he took another step. He froze. Still nothing.

He continued the journey up the stairs. When he reached the top, he scanned the banquet room. Michael's group had cleaned everything up when they'd left, but now food wrappers and broken glass littered everything, the floor sticky with more booze.

A sound behind Michael made him spin around, gun ready.

"Don't shoot." Althaea gazed up at him from the landing. "Main floor's secure, and I peeked into the cellar. It's creepy down there—locked from this side, but I went down anyway. No one's here."

Michael suggested they move on to Dylan's house and the two returned to the car. Relief showed in Carolyn's eyes when they appeared.

Dylan lived nearby. The businesses and homes along the way appeared deserted, the streets empty. Michael thought he glimpsed movement in the window of one house, but couldn't be sure. The SUV pulled up in front of a two-story century home, one of a dozen on the short crescent. Michael jumped out of the car, and the others followed.

The house appeared vacant, curtains closed over the windows. Michael climbed the steps to the wrap-around porch and knocked on the wooden screen door. It opened as the others joined him on the porch.

"Dylan, what happened?" Michael recoiled at his friend's appearance.

Dylan's hair, usually tied back in a neat ponytail, hung loose and greasy. Sweat beaded along his hairline. He wore the same clothes he'd had on when they last saw him. He pointed a shotgun at them, but lowered it when he recognized Michael. Eyes dark rimmed and hollow, Dylan waved them in.

The odour hit Michael as soon as he stepped inside. Somewhere in the house lay a dead body. He stopped the others and asked everyone except Carolyn to wait on the porch. She gave Michael a puzzled look and entered.

Sorrow replaced puzzlement as soon as she stepped through the door. They followed Dylan into the living room. The heavy curtains in the picture window gave the room a stifling, stagnant aura. The cloth-covered couch held a blanket and pillow. Dylan had been sleeping here.

"When did Ella die, Dylan?" Carolyn said, voice cracking.

Dylan dropped his rifle and sank to the couch. Michael and Carolyn took places on the matching loveseat.

Head bowed, Dylan said, "Ella was dead when I got home from the restaurant. I shouldn't have dawdled." He looked up. "It was good to see you, Mick. I enjoyed our visit. But while I was away, Ella took a turn. That disease got her. I know no one who survived it once they got it. I shouldn't have left her alone. My Ella died alone." Dylan broke into wracking sobs.

Carolyn went to him, put an arm around him. She glanced at Michael and he nodded. "Dylan," she said, "Ella's here. She wants to tell you she's okay."

"What are you talkin' 'bout?"

"Carolyn can communicate with spirits," Michael said. "She helped me connect with Jessie. I didn't believe it at first, but it was Jess all right. She can help you get closure."

"Ella came to you after she passed. To see you before she went into the light. She crossed just fine. Her parents were both there to meet her. There was also a dog—a black lab." Carolyn tilted her head, listening. "Spike? Was that your dog?"

Dylan gaped at her and nodded. "Spike died three years ago. It crushed Ella. She loved that dog." He paused a moment, said, "Tell her I'm sorry I wasn't here. Tell her I love her."

"She knows. She can hear you," Carolyn said. "Have you found pennies around the house in weird places?"

"Yeah. I thought I was goin' crazy. After the government stopped makin' pennies, we got rid of the ones we'd had. I'd rolled 'em up and took 'em to the bank. But I must've found ten in the last two days in crazy places."

"That's Ella, letting you know she's around." Carolyn smiled, and Dylan beamed back.

"Will she always be near me?"

"Not always. But she'll pop in and visit sometimes."

Michael hated like hell to break this up, but they needed to get moving. "Dylan, come with us. We're returning to the Peterborough compound. It's a safe place to hole up and winter's

509

coming."

"You're askin' me to walk away from my home? The restaurant?"

"For now. The place was prepared for a shutdown of the grid. We can survive the winter there. If we have numbers, we'll be safer, too. After a while we'll return and rebuild. But you need to be somewhere safe where there's clean water and food."

"What about Ella's body?"

"We'll help you bury her. Then we'll go. You can join us or not."

Dylan remained silent for a moment and then gave Michael a single nod. "Okay," he said.

CHAPTER 55

Ella's final resting place was in the garden behind Dylan's house. After the burial, they helped Dylan pack and returned to the Peterborough compound the following day. The moment Carolyn saw the vast structure looming ahead in the grey light of afternoon, her breathing shallowed and sweat bloomed on her palms. Lips pressed together, she tried not to let the fear show.

When Michael pulled up in front of the garage, Sam jumped out, but Carolyn remained sitting in the SUV. Eyes wide, Sam stood transfixed by the wreckage of the helicopter. Dylan pulled up behind Michael in a Matrix, and Althaea and Arnie climbed out. The others unloaded bags, while Carolyn watched, fighting to quell her anxiety.

"You okay?" Michael touched her arm, gave it a rub.

She nodded, but he wasn't buying it. "Don't worry, Carr. We secured the place, but we'll go through and verify no one's waiting to surprise us. I see no vehicles around, so I'm sure we're alone. Everything looks the way it did the day we left."

Carolyn shifted her gaze to her knees. "It's not that. Memories are flooding back, and it's difficult to enter that prison."

Concern flashed across his face. "I'm sorry. Arnie lived here for months after everyone else evacuated. I didn't consider returning here might trigger you." He took her hand. "We have to make sure you'll be able to give birth safely when the time comes. Ally and I can help deliver the baby in the infirmary. It's well stocked, and you'll have a better chance here than at a hospital."

The group had visited the Aurora hospital after leaving Arnie's condo. It was standing, but had been vandalized, the only people in evidence squatters, the staff dead or gone.

"I'll be fine." Carolyn climbed from the car, giving Michael a half-smile before slamming the door closed.

Arnie and Althaea opened the garage-bay doors, and Michael and Dylan parked the vehicles. The front entrance was boarded up, so they'd go inside through the side doors. Carolyn was glad the main entrance was unrecognizable. It helped push from her head the vision of Cornell dragging her away while Arnie and the woman with him ran for their lives.

The padlock and chain Michael had left on the side entrance door were still intact. He removed them and held the door open to let everyone file into the building. Michael and Althaea had weapons drawn, but neither one seemed concerned.

The moment Carolyn stepped inside, the heaviness pressed in. Not all the souls who'd died here had departed. The farther the group went into the building, the closer they got to the cellblocks, the thicker became the air. Feet dragging, energy draining, and head pounding, Carolyn halted, stumbled, and sank to the floor.

"Mom," Sam cried out and crouched next to her mother.

"Carr?" Michael said.

She pressed her hands to her forehead, pain stabbing through her eyes. "Too much spirit activity in here. Headache."

"Sam, sit with her while Ally and I scope the place out. Arnie, draw your weapon. Dylan, keep that rifle handy. It'll take us a while to check the place out," Michael said.

Carolyn relaxed and leaned back against Sam. "Need to clear myself and put up protection. There are so many." Her breath hitched. "I'll cleanse the whole place when I'm feeling better."

She followed the steps to rid her body of entity attachments and put protection around the group though none of the others were affected. Slowly the pressure eased and her energy returned. She took deep breaths, and though the air she sucked into her lungs was stale, her head unclogged.

Sam helped Carolyn stand, and they waited for Michael and Althaea to return. When almost an hour had passed, Carolyn became worried. They'd heard no shots, which was reassuring, but the two should have returned by now. She opened her mouth to suggest searching for them when Althaea burst through the doors.

Carolyn's heart skipped a beat, but Althaea didn't appear worried. In fact, she smiled.

"Everything's great. Michael's getting the generator up and running. We'll have light and we can cook something."

"I thought this place had solar power?" Dylan said.

"Enough to keep the freezers and a few other things operating. We still need the generator for lights and heat. But we'll have a home-cooked meal tonight." Althaea took a bag from Arnie and led the way back to where they'd set up the sleeping quarters. Carolyn sent a silent message ahead to the spirits waiting in the cellblocks. *I'll visit you as soon as I settle in. You're not alone. I'm here to help.*

***

The compound contained a dormitory. The four sections, each with five bedrooms and a shared bathroom and shower, would be their sleeping quarters for the foreseeable future. Michael had claimed one section for himself, Carolyn, and Sam.

Dylan settled into another section alone, in a room farthest from the others. "Nothin' personal," he explained. "Want my space while I can get it."

Althaea threw her bags into a bedroom in a third section and removed her weapons, dropping them on a desk next to the door. Her movements were stiff, her shoulders sore, the wound throbbing.

The door slamming shut behind her didn't get her attention, but the lock sliding into place did. She turned and stared at Arnie without speaking.

He got to the point. "I want to share your room, Ally."

She sucked in her breath. "Arnie—"

He didn't let her finish. "When you drove away with Valiant and left me in the forest at the underground community, I was afraid I'd never see you again. That was bad enough. But when I did see you, I didn't know if you'd get through that battle alive. I watched you get shot and fall, and the time it took for you to get up was the longest moment of my life. It's as though we've been given another chance, and I want to grab it."

He licked his lips and continued. "I hope you want me, too. Valiant warned you about me, but if it takes the rest of my life, I want to show you I'm not that person anymore. Move in with me, Ally. I want to go to bed with you every night and wake up with you every morning for as long as we live. If we had a priest here, I'd want to get married."

Althaea sank to her bed, not sure how to respond. They hadn't even slept together yet, but that could be rectified right now. Arnie waited. Butterflies flitted in Althaea's stomach.

"Remember I told you I wasn't interested in a relationship? That I was okay with just sex?"

Arnie nodded.

"Before Michael and I left you behind, you said 'come back to me. I love you.' Those words, for all I knew, were the last words I'd ever hear you say." Ally's voice broke, but she continued. "Then the whole time we were on the road, we took care of one another. I've never experienced that kind of caring and affection—neither giving it nor receiving it. When you're not with me, I miss you. No. I ache for you. Being without you hurts and being with you makes me happy. Yes, I'd like it if we could live together, and someday, if we can find a way, we'll talk about marriage." Now it was out, Althaea relaxed.

Arnie exhaled loudly. "Christ, Ally, you scared me. You do over-think things." He sat next to her. "But don't ever change." Arnie smiled, put an arm around her, and when Althaea lifted her face to him, he kissed her.

She parted her lips, and he thrust his tongue between them, exploring. Nervous, she pulled back. "Are we going to sleep together now?"

Arnie smiled. "No sleep involved in what we're about to do."

She laughed, a full, throaty laugh and joy spilled from her.

The smile on Arnie's lips grew wider, and without a word, he helped her out of her tank top. She noticed how careful and protective he was of her injured shoulder. Next, he helped remove her bra and, her torso bared, he kissed first one breast then the other. When she reached out to embrace him, he stopped her with a whisper. "Not yet."

Self-conscious, she fidgeted. "I'll turn off the light."

"No. Please? I want to look at you."

She hesitated, not wanting him to see the ugly scars on her body, though she told herself he wouldn't care. A wisp of hair fell into her face, and he brushed it aside with fingers soft and gentle.

"You're so gorgeous. I want to see all of you. Let me?"

When she gave an uncertain nod, he smiled, reassuring. "You're the most beautiful woman in the world."

Althaea parted her lips, but didn't speak. He took her face between his palms and kissed her again, then broke the kiss, and removed his shirt. His eyelids drifted closed while her hands stroked his soft skin. He undid her cargo pants and shoved them to the floor.

Naked, except for a thong, she shivered. He slid the thong down in a swift motion and it joined the pants on the floor. Her arms wanted to cover her nakedness, and when he saw them rising, he reached out and captured them in his.

His gaze roamed over her body, taking in the muscles, the curves, the long, lean look of her. Goose bumps prickled her skin though more from nerves than from chills.

"It's okay," Arnie said. "Relax. I'll warm you up."

What was wrong with her? She wasn't usually this nervous. Then again, usually it was just sex. She tilted her face forward to gaze into Arnie's eyes, those blue eyes she could get lost in.

He removed his clothes, revealing a strong, muscular body. She gently touched his bullet wound, now healed, and then kissed it. Warm hands stroked her skin, travelled down her back to cup her ass.

Arnie parted her legs so he could kiss her thighs, and she dropped her head back and moaned. Her whole body ached for him. She craved his touch and whimpered, the sound thick with lust. Her hands grasped his shoulders, massaged them, and then sifted through his hair.

He pressed her onto her back and lay next to her. Turned onto her side, she faced him. Her hands wandered over his body. When she stroked the rough terrain of his back, the spell broke for a moment, and sadness overwhelmed her at the reminder of what he'd suffered in this place.

But then she looked into his eyes, and the love and desire in them brought her back to the moment. Her fingers continued to explore, and he lay back and let her touch him. She watched his face, delighting in his changes in expression, which flitted through varying degrees of ecstasy.

Arnie groaned, pulled her into his arms, and rolled on top of her, gentle, watching out for her shoulder. She opened her legs to him, and when she felt him nudging at her entrance, she thrust her pelvis forward to help him.

His eyes mesmerized her as he guided himself inside, watching her face intently while he did. Althaea tried to keep her gaze locked on his eyes, but when he thrust into her, she closed her eyes and cried out. He leaned forward and kissed her, greedy, demanding. He pumped into her faster, harder, as if he owned her.

She cried out, and he paused, lips releasing her mouth, expression a question. She cried out again, in protest. "Don't stop. Please."

Mouth pressed to Althaea's once more, Arnie thrust into her again, his rhythm quick and full of need. Her legs wrapped around his hips. Whimpers escaped her and spilled into his mouth, and she gasped and thrashed under him. "Oh, God, Arnie."

Her muscles contracted around him, taking her over the edge, and she felt his release within her. When the tsunami receded, Arnie collapsed on her. After a moment, he rolled off, but pulled Althaea to him and held her tight.

Heart pounding in his chest so hard she could feel it, he panted, catching his breath.

"Arnie?"

A squeeze. "Yes?"

"We'll need a bigger bed."

CHAPTER 56

All their efforts centred on making the place home. Carolyn cleared out the trapped spirits, and Michael set up the infirmary to be ready for the coming birth. The baby's estimated due date was mid-February.

Each member of the group took a turn monitoring the radio, which played nothing more than static as time went on—even the pre-recorded messages disappeared into limbo. Once a week, Michael and Althaea went out to find people who were good candidates for joining the group. Already, four men, three women, and one child had joined them.

When Carolyn asked Michael why he wanted to bring strangers here, he told her they'd need the safety of numbers while things continued to deteriorate. The new people brought with them a variety of skills and knowledge.

Karen was an expert in edible wild foods, with knowledge that went deeper than even Michael's. John, his wife Mary, and their young son Alexander were farmers. Troy was a mechanic.

"But how will we feed them?" Carolyn said. The greenhouses grew fresh herbs and vegetables, but they'd need to find a source of fresh meat and fruit when frozen stores ran out.

"There are enough supplies to get through this winter, and we pick up more non-perishables on every run to a town. In the spring, we'll farm. The sun will return by then. Have you noticed? We're getting fewer days of darkness, fewer wild storms and earthquakes."

She hadn't noticed. But she'd noticed a lightening of everyone's mood. Carolyn was well into the second trimester of her pregnancy and was as comfortable as she'd ever be while pregnant. She'd passed the morning sickness and weakness of the first trimester, and had the heavy, unwieldy final trimester yet to come.

Most of her days she spent snooping around in the offices, wanting to learn as much as possible about the underground community. One day, she worried, the Agency might come after them, or things would get so bad on the surface they'd need to find shelter underground themselves. When she mentioned this to Michael, he shrugged off her concerns, though he first asked her if she acted from a premonition or from anxiety.

She admitted she'd had no premonitions, but simply worried. She also told Michael about Torque's warning, months ago, that the ionosphere was heating. Michael seemed more interested in that information than anything she'd found in Cornell's files, but he didn't explain what it meant. He was in the midst of preparing for another outing with Althaea.

"I'm glad you're digging around in the offices. If you find hard drives or memory sticks, get Arnie to help you hack into them. If you see anything that mentions the ionosphere or the aliens, give it to me immediately. But I don't want you stressing yourself about stuff that probably won't happen. Are we clear?" Michael leaned over and kissed her forehead.

She pushed the rifle he'd slung over his shoulder out of the way so she could kiss him back without the thing bumping her. She wasn't afraid of guns anymore, but she still didn't like them. Everyone in the group spent part of each day doing target practice, and even Sam was learning martial arts.

Carolyn sat at a table in the cafeteria leafing through the latest pile of file folders she'd brought from Cornell's office. "What if the Agency finds us here? Don't you think that's a possibility?"

Michael shook his head. "If they venture out, we'll be ready."

"Please be careful." Carolyn said this to him every day, at least once.

Michael cupped her face in his hands. "I will. I love you, Carr." He kissed her, making her heart flutter.

The fear rose again, and she asked the angels to protect him and Althaea. She removed her wedding band, and Michael held out his palm. The ring dropped into his hand, and he pulled the chain from his pocket.

She insisted that anytime they were apart, he take the ring with him, and give it back to her when he returned. He pretended to indulge her superstition, but Carolyn knew he liked carrying it with him. The gesture made them both feel better.

"Ready?" Althaea appeared in the doorway.

Michael gave Carolyn's cheek one last stroke before he turned and walked away. Her heart went with him as it always did. She lowered her head, opened a folder, and busied herself.

***

Michael hopped into the SUV's passenger side. Althaea waited for him to shut the door and buckle up before she pulled out.

"The ionosphere's heating." Michael said as Althaea drove out of the parking lot.

The rain pelted down, but the wind had stopped blowing. She flicked on the wiper blades and their rhythmic clicking made the only sound. He waited, let her process the information.

"How?"

Michael shrugged. "Nothing related to what I did in Nahanni. Carolyn said Torque told her about the ionosphere before I destroyed the crystal. Cornell understood what it meant, and she said it panicked him, but he never told her why."

"Of course, he didn't." Althaea frowned. "If that's true, we'll need to go underground. No one could survive that without help from the aliens."

Michael flinched. Was she accusing him of killing everyone above ground by sending the aliens away?

Without looking at him, she said, "I'm not blaming you for anything. It is what it is."

Michael smiled. She always seemed to know what he was thinking. It'd made them a lethal combination when they'd worked together at the Agency. He was glad to have her by his side again.

"I've asked Arnie to see if he can get satellite hookup. I can monitor the ionosphere myself if I can access the correct satellite. When we figure out what's going on, we can decide what to do."

"Okay. What'll we do if the aliens return? Have you considered that possibility?"

Michael waited while Althaea manoeuvred the SUV around a

downed tree. "I try not to, but yes, I've considered it. The threat will always exist. The aliens wanted Earth for themselves. They're not likely to give it up that easily."

Althaea nodded. "I agree. We should tell the others."

"No. Don't even tell Arnie."

"They deserve to be informed. We need to warn them the danger exists. What if something happens to us? Besides, they can help us figure out a contingency plan."

"I don't want them worrying over nothing."

Althaea thumped a hand against the steering wheel. "You're assuming they won't be able to recreate the technology to phase back, but you don't know. They've done it once, they can do it again."

Michael tried to catch her eye, but she didn't glance at him. He sighed. "They took years to figure it out the first time. It won't be easy to rebuild."

"Stop making assumptions. I get you don't want to deal with this, especially with Carolyn's pregnancy distracting you, but you'd better face reality, Michael. The others think they're safe and free, but that could change."

"What do you expect they'll do if we tell them about this?" He didn't let her reply. "They'll worry and they'll panic. But if we keep this to ourselves, we can figure out a way to handle it. We'll document everything we do. If anything happens to us, they'll have the information."

Althaea slammed on the brakes. Inertia threw him forward, and the seatbelt pulled tight against his chest. "Ally, what the fuck?"

"Why are we going to Port Hope?"

Michael didn't reply.

"It's the CFS, isn't it?"

"Yes." Michael had wanted to check out the Canadian Forces Station in Port Hope for months now, but this was the first opportunity to do so. He hoped they could use the Signals Intelligence, or SIGNIT, capabilities there to set up a way to detect changes in existing electromagnetic or light signals. They'd use it as an early warning system to alert them to alien presence on Earth.

"Drive, Ally. We need to do this."

She put her foot back on the gas and continued heading towards the highway. "Okay. I'll keep it to myself for now. But if we ever find evidence they've returned, we tell the others immediately."

"Deal," Michael relaxed into his seat, confident it would never happen.

***

Arnie sat in the cafeteria and watched Carolyn and Sam chatting while they munched on cookies and drank hot chocolate. An empty mug sat in front of him, but his cookie lay untouched on the plate.

"Arnie, they're okay," Carolyn said for the third time.

Distracted, Arnie nodded. "I know." But he didn't. He wished he had Carolyn's confidence in his intuition. All he felt was unease. Arnie had allowed Carolyn to help him practice using his intuitive abilities—he refused to call them psychic abilities—but he still couldn't distinguish between a premonition and needless worry.

Restless, he had to do something and decided to go tinker with the satellite feed. It hadn't taken him long to get the satellite hookup Michael had asked him to do three days ago—three days. That's what bugged him. Valiant and Ally had been gone for three solid days. Arnie's chair screeched across the floor as he pushed it back and stood.

"Arnie." Carolyn's voice was firm.

"I said 'I know.' I'll check the satellite."

"Don't worry."

"I know!" He hadn't meant to snap at her. "I'm sorry. I wish they'd return."

"They're on their way. I checked in with them again."

Arnie's jaw dropped. "While you were talking to Sam?"

Carolyn nodded.

"Teach me how to do that?"

She smiled. "Baby steps, Arnie. But yes, I'll teach you."

He relaxed. Hearing her say Michael and Althaea were on their way eased the worry. He sat again and scarfed the cookie.

Two hours later, Ally was back in his arms where she belonged. They lay in bed, Arnie dragging her there as soon as she'd stepped out of the shower. Her head rested on his chest, and the scent of fruit wafted up from her hair. How long before he could get it up again and go for round two? He couldn't get enough of her.

When he thought about the last three days, he frowned. "What took you so long? I went crazy with worry." He'd sat on the question for as long as he could. "Port Hope's not even an hour away." He hoped he didn't sound angry or accusing.

She nuzzled his neck, kissed his cheek. "I hate we can't keep in touch when we're on the road. We had to set up surveillance at a military station."

"Surveillance of what?"

Ally didn't reply for a moment. "Nothing specific. Just monitoring the airwaves. We'll have to go back to check up on it. Eventually, we'll settle people there to monitor full time."

Tension eased from him. Tech stuff. Arnie could understand that. "I recovered data from the drives Carolyn found in storage. I also got data flowing from the satellites while you were gone. Valiant can get whatever info he wants now."

Ally's hand went to Arnie's chest and stroked his skin, sending shivers down his body. "He'll be happy to hear it. Did you collect data on the ionosphere?"

"Yeah. The numbers were a little higher than Valiant said they should be."

Ally exhaled loudly and her hand froze on Arnie's chest. A prickle of fear traced its way up his spine. "Is that bad?"

She didn't reply, but sat and grabbed her clothes.

"Ally?"

"I don't know. We'd better go talk to Michael."

Arnie got out of bed and reached for his clothes.

CHAPTER 57

Michael reviewed the printout for the second time. Arnie and Althaea perched on the edge of Cornell's desk and waited.

"How bad is it?" Althaea asked.

"Not as bad as you first thought," Michael replied. "It's not great, but it's not lethal. We have to monitor it. As long as the numbers don't trend up, we'll be okay."

Althaea and Arnie both looked relieved.

"So we don't need to worry?" Arnie asked.

"Worry wouldn't help," Michael replied.

"Now you sound like Carolyn." Arnie smiled.

"We need to keep an eye on it, not freak out about it. The industries causing this to happen have shut down. We're no longer contributing to environmental destruction, though there are still risks. But it'll take time to reverse what we've done. If you're in a car doing 120 kilometres per hour and you slam on the brakes, you'll still get forward momentum before you stop." Michael plugged another hard drive into a port and waited for the computer to recognize it.

Arnie nodded. "Okay. I'll make sure the data continues to download." He took Althaea's hand. "I've missed my training while you were away. Shall we go to the gym?"

Michael caught Althaea's glance and waved her away.

"You sure?" she said.

"Yeah. I want to review these drives. We'll talk later." Michael stuck his face back to the monitor and clicked through the folders displayed on the screen.

Althaea smiled and slid off the desk. "Okay, Arnie. I'll enjoy kicking your butt again."

Michael's gaze followed them out the door, enjoying their camaraderie. Althaea had never been so happy before, amazing, considering the circumstances. She'd become a brand new person the day they'd recovered her true memories. Michael even approved of this relationship she had with Arnie.

Folder structure open in front of him, Michael navigated to where he'd left off the day before. So far, he hadn't found anything as staggering as the contract with the aliens, but he continued to troll. No telling what secrets Cornell had tried to obliterate here.

***

Carolyn opens her eyes when she realizes her tormentors are no longer in the room. She's naked, lying on the cold, stone floor in the foetal position. They'd raped her again and had left her broken and humiliated on the floor. After the rapes, and before they'd left her, they'd asked her who'd raped her. As always, if she were to say anything other than "Michael Valiant," they'd beat her. This time they hadn't had to beat her. She'd answered correctly and without hesitation.

Carolyn rolled over and sat up, sweat drenching her naked body, memories of the brainwashing keeping her up again. She'd been getting clusters of memories returning ever since Michael and Althaea had helped her recover what the Agency had stolen. But along with the beautiful memories, the ones of making love with Michael, were the foul ones of the brutal treatment at the Agency.

Michael slept peacefully next to her. She touched his hair, still marvelling they were together after so much.

The group had been living at the compound now for two months. So far, no Agency personnel had shown up to reclaim Carolyn, no aliens had tried to abduct her, and she'd gotten comfortable. She worried less that someone would snatch her away again. There were more nights where she didn't wake up screaming than nights where she did. She was grateful.

The little group had grown to twenty. Michael and Ally no longer went on their forays, Michael saying they had enough people to look after for the winter. Carolyn noticed he'd stopped the scavenging trips as soon as he'd found a doctor to join their group.

She was in the third trimester of her pregnancy. The baby kicked wildly, especially at night, making sleep even more difficult. Sometimes Tina came to Carolyn in dreams though most of the time, she couldn't remember what they'd discussed.

Jim Cornell's spirit no longer intruded on her dreams, and Carolyn made sure she cleared and protected herself every day. She drew her legs up and rested her chin on her knees. Perhaps she should get up so she wouldn't disturb Michael.

"Carr?"

Too late. She was sorry she'd woken him, but not sorry he was awake. The sound of his soft voice brought a tingle to her core. She let her hand stray to his shoulder.

"You okay?" Michael whispered.

Michael and Carolyn had a room to themselves, but Sam's room was right next door. It was both a curse and a blessing that the walls were thin. If something happened in the night, a shout would bring everyone running. But it made lovemaking and late night conversations a challenge.

"I can't sleep. It's nothing." The memories still threatened, but she could push them away more easily when he was talking to her.

"Come here." Michael pulled her into his arms, and she rested her head on his chest.

Carolyn raised a hand to his face and stroked it, fingers sliding over the smooth, soft skin. She kissed his cheek. "I can't stop touching you."

"Fine by me."

Carolyn smiled and pinched his arm.

"Ouch. What was that for?"

Carolyn giggled quietly. "I wanted to make sure this wasn't a dream."

"I think the protocol for that is pinching yourself." A wry smile appeared, making him look young in the moody dimness.

She touched his lips with a finger, returned the smile, but then grew serious. "When I was locked in my cell here, I'd sometimes dream about you. Then I'd wake up and you weren't there after all. Do you think we did it this time? Will we be able to stay together?"

Carolyn raised herself on one arm and watched his eyes. A faint glow came from a clock radio on the bedside table. It was enough to see shadows and outlines and the dark pools of his eyes.

Michael took her hand and kissed it. "I think we did. No more

Torque. No more Cornell. They were always the ones who kept us apart—at least they were in the dreams I had. When you killed Cornell instead of me, you broke the pattern."

The thought that she'd come close to killing Michael brought anxiety shooting up and she frowned. Another memory she had to keep at bay, though it was the memory of only what might have been, so she felt relief in it.

Carolyn leaned down and kissed the softness of his lips. "I think so too," she mumbled into his mouth.

Against her lips, Michael's curled back in a smile. "No talking." He kissed her back, gently at first, then more insistent. Aroused, she ran her hand down his naked body.

When they'd first arrived at the compound, their lovemaking had been fast, frantic, with an aura of desperation and fear, as if bracing themselves against losing it all again. Now it was different, more slow and languid, the undercurrent of fear gone.

Carolyn felt now as though they had all the time in the world and their only concern was pleasuring each other. A nip at his bottom lip, and then she turned her attention to his ear lobe. She nuzzled his neck, and a hiss of air escaped his lips.

All she wanted was to please Michael, make him happy. She peeked at him. Michael had relaxed into the pillows, eyes closed. They clasped hands, and Carolyn continued her journey down his body. She liberated her hands from his, and used her mouth. Michael groaned, and she giggled again, self-conscious of the thin walls.

When he was close to release, Carolyn straddled him, wanting to see Michael's face, to look in his eyes. They clasped hands again while she moved on him, her rhythm picking up speed. She squeezed him with her thighs, mindful of the depth of his penetration. They gazed into each other's eyes while first she climaxed, then he followed suit. She dropped onto his chest, not letting him withdraw from her.

It didn't last long. Her unwieldy belly quickly became uncomfortable. "I have to move," she said.

Michael helped her shift onto her back, and she looked up at him, his face hovering over hers. He opened his mouth to speak, but she beat him to it. "You're beautiful."

He smiled. "Hey, that's what I wanted to say about you."

"Well, you are. You're so beautiful." Carolyn didn't know how else to say it. She stiffened when the baby kicked and grabbed Michael's hand, placing it on her belly. "Feel that?"

Her belly jumped again when the baby punted it. Michael started, but his hand stayed pressed to her abdomen.

"So strong." Michael kept his voice to a whisper, but Carolyn heard the excitement in it. When they finally fell asleep again, their hands rested, fingers entwined, on her rounded belly.

CHAPTER 58

Ready, Mother? It's time.

Carolyn opened her eyes. The voice, Tina's, echoed in her head. Ripe with baby and more than ready to deliver, she hoped it wasn't a dream and today was the day. Movements slow and awkward, she eased into a sitting position and swung her legs over the side of the bed. Carolyn shoved her feet into a pair of slippers and glanced at Michael. His soft snoring continued uninterrupted. She smiled, though some nights he'd get an elbow in the ribs for doing just that.

The building was difficult to heat, and Carolyn shivered in the chill air. To conserve energy, they lowered the thermostats at night, so she'd worn a nightgown to bed, much to Michael's dismay. The pressure in Carolyn's lower back motivated her to get moving and grab her robe. She'd walk to the washroom first, then the cafeteria. No more sleep for her now.

She took three steps and then her abdomen clenched. Carolyn slipped out the door into the hall. Let Michael sleep for a while longer—labour could take all day.

The realization that things were moving faster than expected hit her when she used the toilet and lost her mucous plug.

Still not an emergency. That can happen days before the birth. But her stomach felt queasy, and she considered waking the doc. She checked the time: just after four in the morning. Too early.

Nerves and excitement made her jumpy, and she wished she could talk to someone. The thought she'd be holding her baby soon filled her with anticipation, and she longed to share the news. Michael could have another hour, and then they'd wake the doc together.

Dr. Randy Waters was military, and at first, that had made Carolyn suspicious. But when she'd accepted that he wasn't a spy for the Agency, she'd found she enjoyed his company and trusted him with the welfare of her unborn baby. The last checkup with him had gone well. Three days ago, he'd told her the baby was in position, and she could go into labour any time.

In the cafeteria, she got a drink of water from the cooler. Though her stomach growled for food, she figured she shouldn't eat. Her belly tightened again, a long, forceful spasm. Carolyn gasped and doubled over. She should get Michael.

She turned to leave, but froze when liquid trickled down her legs. Between her feet, a puddle grew. Her water had broken. Definitely time to get the doc. She'd have to ask Sam to come and clean up the water.

Carolyn groaned when the next contraction hit and gripped a nearby table until it passed. The door seemed farther away than she remembered. She took two steps in its direction and stopped when another contraction hit. The pains were coming faster than she remembered it with Sam. *Every baby is different.*

Yes, but she'd been in labour with Sam for *two days*. This was happening too fast. She shouldn't have walked to the cafeteria by herself. Carolyn cursed herself for not waking Michael. She'd assumed there'd be more time and had wanted to let him sleep before the coming ordeal.

The room spun, and she pulled out a chair to sit for a moment. She lowered her head onto her arms and closed her eyes, but speared up again when the next contraction hit. The pain wrenched a whimper from her. Michael. She needed to get to Michael.

Carolyn stood, and something warm trickled down her legs again. Expecting more water, she looked and was shocked to see blood. She cried out, staggered to the door, and braced herself on it. She'd have to use the wall to support herself while she walked through the hall. She lurched away from the door into the hallway, colliding with the wall, leaning on it, the exertion forcing grunts from her.

The double doors leading to the dormitory seemed far away. A glance behind showed a trail of blood following her. *No.*

Carolyn took a deep breath and called on Archangel Raphael, the healing angel, to help her and to keep the baby safe and healthy. *A few more steps. Stop.*

Why had she come here? If she could do it again, she'd wake up Michael and tell him it was time. Carolyn tried to focus on getting back to their room. Michael would help her. He'd get Dr. Randy, and together they'd deliver the baby, and everything would be fine.

Another contraction made her take three hurried steps. Teeth gritted against the pain, she took four more steps. Carolyn looked towards the doors. Still so far away.

***

Michael awoke and his hand drifted to Carolyn's side of the bed. When he didn't feel her there, his eyes popped open. "Carr?" He sat.

Carolyn wasn't in the room. He checked the clock—not even five yet. Maybe she was in the washroom. Michael turned over to go back to sleep, but couldn't do it without her in the bed. It was silly, but she was so pregnant, the thought of her wandering the halls alone bothered him. When ten minutes passed, and she still wasn't back, he went to find her.

Not in the bathroom. He'd check the caff. Surely she wasn't wandering around the building. A glow of lights came from the hallway leading to the cafeteria, and he rushed to the double doors. Relief washed over him when he spotted the lights and realized she was there, but it was short lived. When he pushed open the doors, he found her lying on the floor.

He cried out and ran to her, his pulse thudding in his ears. A trail of blood led up to her and pooled under her. He scooped her up in his arms and ran for the infirmary.

"Michael?"

Her voice startled him. He hugged her tighter to his body. "You'll be fine, honey. I won't let anything happen. We'll get you to bed."

"The baby's coming."

"Okay. It'll be fine." Michael looked at her white face. His throat constricted and worry knotted his stomach.

They reached the infirmary where Dr. Randy had set up everything they'd need for the delivery. Michael laid her gently on the bed. "I'll go get Randy now. Please hang on. I'll be right back."

Carolyn nodded her head, eyes closed. Michael banged through the doors and burst into Randy's room without knocking. Randy took one groggy look at Michael's face and was up and following without question.

When they reached the infirmary, Michael ran to the opposite side of Carolyn's bed and took her hand. "Carr." He kept to a whisper, afraid to disturb her. But when she didn't answer, he called out loudly, fear amplifying his words. "Carolyn, baby, please. Wake up."

Randy shook his head. "She's unconscious, Michael. You can hold her hand while I examine her. Relax. She'll be fine." But Randy's brows furrowed when he opened Carolyn's robe and lifted her nightgown.

"Mamma."

Sam stood in the doorway, Arnie behind her, hugging her. Michael glimpsed Althaea in the background.

"Carolyn?" Arnie asked everything with that one word.

Randy didn't look at them, but when he spoke, the doctor's voice was kind. "Take Sam to the cafeteria, Arnie. Wait there while I examine Carolyn. Ally, come in here and scrub up." He turned to the sink behind him, scrubbed his hands, and slipped on a pair of latex gloves.

Althaea pushed past Sam and Arnie and rushed to the sink.

"Arnie." Randy's voice was sharper. "Close the door. We need privacy."

Arnie led Sam away, the door slamming shut behind them.

Michael's eyes grew moist. He closed his eyes and suppressed his emotions. He'd make sure she was all right. She had to be. They'd come through so much. He couldn't lose her now.

***

"Placenta abruption," Randy said. "The placenta detached when she went into labour. She should be okay. The baby is full term, growing on schedule, and Carolyn's healthy, though she tells me she's been through abuse. She insists any checkups she's had during her pregnancy showed everything was fine."

Her eyes were open, but drowsy. Michael held a wet cloth to her forehead.

Randy continued. "You'll be able to deliver vaginally, Carolyn. You lost blood, but the abruption seems minimal."

Michael frowned. "The baby?"

"Is fine. If the baby's in any distress, the monitor will show us. So far, everything looks all right." Randy looked at Althaea. "Take a break. Carolyn is only five centimetres dilated. Tell Sam and Arnie to stop worrying."

Althaea nodded. "Call me if you need me. Otherwise, I'll be back in half an hour to check in. Can I bring Sam and Arnie back with me? They wouldn't want to miss the birth."

"If Carolyn and Michael are okay with that, sure," Randy replied.

Carolyn looked up at Michael, and he smiled at her. "Whatever Mom here says is okay with me."

"Please, Ally, bring them back with you, if they want to come." Carolyn clutched Michael's hand, and he leaned to kiss her.

***

Carolyn looked at the baby in her arms, suckling at her breast, and then at the baby's father snuggled up next to them on the bed. Michael's eyes were closed, and he breathed deep and slow. One arm curled around Carolyn, protecting her and the baby, even as he dozed.

The baby gripped Michael's index finger in her little hand. Sam beamed at them from her perch on the end of the bed. Althaea and Arnie stood beside the bed, their arms around each other. It was good to see Arnie in a monogamous relationship.

Carolyn smiled at them. "You guys were great. Thank you."

"We're happy for you," Arnie said.

Althaea nodded, glanced at Arnie. "We should go. Give them time." She yawned. "I could sleep for a week now. I'll eat something and go back to bed."

Arnie and Althaea said their goodbyes and left.

Sam reached out and stroked the baby's cheek. "I can't believe I watched a baby being born, and I didn't faint," she said.

"Same here," Michael said, grinning, though his eyes remained closed.

Carolyn glanced from one to the other, happier than she could remember being for a long time.

Sam stood. "If you don't mind, I'll grab something to eat. When I return, I'll bring you breakfast."

"Okay, sweetie,"

Sam left and Carolyn turned her attention back to the miracle in her arms.

Michael sighed and pressed his lips to the top of Carolyn's head. Melancholy swept over Carolyn then, followed by fear. She hitched a sob from her throat. "Michael, into what kind of world did we bring this baby?"

"I don't know. But during my near-death experience, I saw her. Tina was a young woman, beautiful. We were with you in that cell. Do you remember?"

"Yes," she whispered. "She was beautiful, wasn't she?"

"Do you remember I told you Jess appeared in a dream after she died? I saw the baby, too. Jess told me to name her 'Christina.' She said the baby wanted to be called 'Tina,' and she'd see me soon. I didn't know what that meant—just thought it was part of a crazy dream."

Carolyn suspected she knew where he was going with this.

"When she appeared in your cell, I knew we were bringing back my baby with Jessica. Tina belongs to the three of us, Carr. Do you think that's possible?"

She leaned into him, relishing the warmth from his body, and drew in a deep breath, catching his scent mingled with the baby's. "I know it is. She worked so hard to get here. She's supposed to be here now. We have to trust things will improve and she's got a role in that." Something else came to mind. "We survived it all and we're together. We broke the pattern."

Michael studied her for a moment and gave her a slight nod. "I think we did. But what about Tina? What pattern does she have to break?"

Carolyn gazed at baby Tina, who'd fallen asleep on her nipple, Michael's finger still hostage to her tiny fist. "That's her journey. We can't walk it for her."

Michael used his free hand to tilt up Carolyn's chin. He kissed her lips, and she let his warmth and love flow into her. After a moment, he released her, eyes shining. "I love you, Carolyn."

She rested her head on his shoulder, tired, but happy. "I love you, too, Michael."

Carolyn closed her eyes, unafraid of going to sleep. There'd be no more dreams to disturb her peace. It'd be tough, but she thought they could carve out a life for themselves, despite the threats continuing to hover over them. Whatever confronted them, they'd handle, she was sure of it. Sam and Tina had hope for a future, and it would be in a world of their making. It felt right.

Exhausted, she dozed off, but as she tumbled into dreams, she muttered a word she didn't know and would forget by morning: SIGNIT.

The End

EARTHBOUND

A Valiant Chronicles Prequel

by

Val Tobin

ACKNOWLEDGMENTS

Thank you to Andrea Holmes; Val Cseh; Michelle Legere; John Erwin; Alis Kennedy; Wendy Quirion; Diane King, owner of The Hedge Witch in Sharon, Ontario; Mark Watson of AngelEarth Studios; my editor, Sephera Giron at Scarlett Editing; and my cover designer, Patti Roberts of Paradox Book Cover Designs.

"Find That Place," the song referenced in the story, is used with permission, courtesy of Mark Watson of AngelEarth Studios and is found on the CD *Reflections* by Mark Watson.

Concepts explored in the story draw on a variety of teachings, including those of Doreen Virtue, Ph.D., whose courses I attended in Kona, Hawaii in 2008 and 2010, and my education in parapsychology through The American Institute of Holistic Theology

DEDICATION

To all the earthbound spirits. May they find their way home. And, as always, to Bob, Jenn, Mark, Chanelle, Savannah, and Jack

CHAPTER 1

The first thing I noticed about being out of my body was that everyone in the hospital room appeared brighter. They glowed. The second thing I noticed was that I was still shaped like me. I wasn't a ball of light floating around the room.

My spirit body, when I examined it, shimmered with an aura like everyone else's, but it was transparent. I held up my hand and could see through it—not to bones or anything internal, but to the blue coverlet on the bed where my physical body lay.

Tubes snaked from my arms, and my chest rose and fell, so it appeared I wasn't dead. However, I looked hideous: greasy, dull brown hair clumped in thick strings on my pillow or plastered against my face; dark circles under my eyes that made them look as if I'd been in a rumble; and lips that could have used ten applications of lip balm.

Which made me realize the third thing: Inside, I was still me. If I was dead—which was possible, since the machines might have been forcing my body to mimic life—then I hadn't elevated to a more saintly version of me. Judgment and cynicism still came easily.

Damn.

Shouldn't death have made me more evolved?

And where was the tunnel? The light? My dearly departed loved ones? Shouldn't someone who could tell me it wasn't my time be here?

More importantly, where was my family?

Medical personnel were the room's only other occupants, and they were leaving. All looked as if they'd fought a valiant battle, and perhaps they had. They'd tried to save me, and, while the results were nothing to high-five about, they hadn't declared me dead.

No sooner did thoughts of my family wink out of my head than I found myself in a waiting room. Two men and two women I didn't recognize sat on a couch along the west wall of the room, staring at the floor.

My eighteen-year-old daughter, Silver, sat on a padded metal chair, elbows on her knees, face in her palms. Her long, brown hair veiled her hands. She wore the same jeans and long-sleeved, green T-shirt she'd had on when I'd last seen her.

Rory, my ex-husband, perched on the edge of another chair next to her. Also in jeans and a T-shirt, he stroked Silver's back with one hand while he held his girlfriend's hand with the other.

Clara Spencer. A classy lady. Even in what I assumed was the middle of the night, she had on what I can only refer to as an ensemble: blouse, blazer, skirt. Her short brown hair was smooth and glossy.

I liked her. She was pleasant, and she hadn't been boinking Rory while we were married, so all was good on that front.

At least my ex had found a decent replacement for me when our marriage broke apart. Clara would help him get through this as long as he didn't screw it up.

He should've already married her, though I wouldn't wish that on any woman. He's not a jerk or abusive, but life with him can be silent and lonely. Strong and silent may sound sexy, but living with it had been depressing.

The doctor who'd been at my bedside entered the room, and everyone looked up with fatalistic hope in their eyes. When he said "Rory McQueen?" the four strangers in the room resumed staring at the floor.

Rory and Silver leapt up. Clara began to rise and then sat again, back rigid against the chair.

"Doctor, is she …?" Rory choked.

"She's alive, but her heart is weak. I'm sorry. She might last the night, but it doesn't look good." The doc hesitated. His name tag read "Dr. Richler." The bags under his eyes looked almost as bad as mine.

Thanks for knocking yourself out to save me, Doc. I hoped to thank him in person one day.

Richler continued. "You can go in and see her. Take as long as you need. If there's anyone else who might want to say goodbye, you should call them."

"What do you mean? My mother doesn't have heart problems. She's only forty-six," Silver said.

"She had a catastrophic coronary." Richler checked his chart. "The paramedics revived her once already. Her heart won't take another episode and there's a ninety percent likelihood she'll have another one."

"No." Silver waved her hands at him, shooing his words away. Tears streamed down her face.

Rory hooked an arm through hers. "Take us to her, please."

They followed Richler from the room, Clara lagging a few steps behind.

I tried to walk along with them, but, apparently, when you're disembodied, you simply think your way places. No sooner had I decided to go back to my room than poof! There I was.

My body hadn't changed since the last time I'd seen it, but I inspected it anyway.

Having one foot in the grave hadn't made me more intuitive. I couldn't tell if I was about to have another heart attack.

Death has never frightened me. I'm a risk taker, a live-in-the-now kind of gal. The idea of exploring a new dimension excited me, but I didn't want to leave my kids. If an opportunity to avoid dying arose, I'd take it.

Rory's voice approached. He doesn't talk much, but when he does, he's loud. I heard him assuring Silver that everything would be okay. Nice of him to do that, but not practical. Her mother was dying. You can't pretend that falls under the everything-will-be-okay umbrella.

I closed my eyes and tried to feel something. Love for my children flooded through me. The expected sadness didn't follow. Was it because I was still with them?

My son, Marc, was probably on his way from university. He attended the University of Toronto, so it wouldn't be a long drive to the hospital in Aurora, where I assumed I was. It's the closest hospital to my home in Newmarket.

How I'd gotten here remained a mystery.

Richler had said I'd had a heart attack, but I didn't remember what I'd been doing when it happened. The last thing I remembered was …

Oh, damn. Damn.

I'd been arguing with Silver. We'd been loud. Yelling at each other.

Oh, not that. Anything but that.

I opened my eyes.

Silver stood in the doorway, her face pale and tear stained, her eyes red. She held her hands clasped so tight in front of her the knuckles were white. The aura of light around her was white with blue and orange patches. No understanding of its meaning came to me.

The light around Rory was also white but streaked with yellow and green. Clara's light was white, red, and violet.

For once, I regretted not studying any of that new age crap people believe. Sure, I'd picked up the odd article, and when I was in university, I took a couple of philosophy courses. But I'd never cared about anything I couldn't observe with my senses.

"Dad?" Silver whispered. She crept to her father, her gaze never leaving my body.

"Yeah, honey?" Rory hugged her tight.

"Mommy's going to die and it's all my fault." She broke into quiet sobs. The sweet kid. She was trying not to disturb my rest.

"No, sweetie. You saved her when you called 911 and gave her CPR." He spoke with confidence but one look at my body in the bed belied the words.

I yearned to go to Silver and found myself standing beside her. Assuming my hand would go through her if I touched her, I gently set it on her shoulder. It hovered there. I couldn't feel anything from the contact.

She shivered. "I'm so cold, Daddy."

"It's okay, sweetie. I'm here." His arms wrapped around her shoulders, cutting through my forearm.

I winced and stepped away from them. The touch hadn't affected me—I'd felt nothing—however, the visual was creepy.

From behind us, Clara spoke. "Would you like to wear my jacket?"

"No, thank you." Her voice was muffled against Rory's chest. "It went away."

My touch had made her shiver.

Excellent. It meant there was something there for her to feel.

I moved to the machines monitoring my vitals, breathing for me, and pumping fluids into me. I touched the heart monitor.

It beeped.

"Oh, God. Oh, Daddy. Mom! The machine."

The fear and despair in Silver's voice forced me away. No time to experiment—not if it made them think there was a problem.

Rory leaned over my bed and put two fingers on my neck.

"Her pulse is steady. Maybe it's a problem with the machine."

My invisible touch had affected the heart monitor. I filed the information away for later.

Later. Hah.

Who knew what later would bring? When my body died, would I disappear? Or would that be when the famous tunnel appeared and my dead relatives came to collect me? Where the hell were they, anyway?

At the very least, my grandmother should have shown up to guide me through this. I'm certain I was her favourite—my sisters always told me so. I didn't want to think about my sisters yet, though, so I pushed them from my mind.

Another frantic cry from Silver yanked me out of my head. Any of the machines that could make noise were doing so, and my body flopped and twitched like a landed fish.

Richler shot into the room, other medical personnel right behind him. He rushed to the bed and yanked the blanket off me.

"Get these people out of here," he snapped at a nurse, though she was already ushering my family out.

I can't say why, but I followed them. The logical thing to do would have been to stay there to see if they succeeded in keeping me alive. But I was conditioned to listen to authority, and when he said get out, I left.

The last thing I heard was Richler shouting, "Clear!"

CHAPTER 2

My death day was officially September 29, 2016.

We weren't in the waiting room ten minutes before Richler returned with the tragic news. Drops of blood decorated the front of his shirt.

Jesus, Doc, what did you do to me to make me spray blood?

Hot on the heels of that thought came the realization that I hadn't disappeared. Neither had any dead relatives or a tunnel to the light appeared. Was I supposed to wander Earth for eternity? I didn't like the sound of that. No wonder ghosts have a reputation for crankiness. Life sucks and then you die, and then death sucks?

On the bright side, I wouldn't have to go to work ever again—unless I wanted to haunt the place. That thought brought a smile to my face. I had some coworkers I wouldn't mind waking in the middle of the night with moans and rattling chains.

Richler gave my family the "I'm-sorry-for-your-loss" spiel. To be fair, he did look regretful. And exhausted. He'd worked hard to save my life. I was sorrier for his failure than I was for losing my life. There must be something about bodilessness that makes you complacent about your death. Or maybe I was in shock.

What did it mean that I experienced feelings without a body and its chemical reactions?

As I contemplated all this, my gaze fell on the four strangers still sitting in the room. One of the men and both the women watched the scene, grief and relief it wasn't their loved one evident in their eyes. The other man, however, kept his gaze focused on the magazine he'd been reading, his expression relieved, but not in the dodged-a-bullet way the others displayed. While I watched, he calmly closed his magazine, set it on the end table next to his chair, and exited the room. I popped into the hallway after him.

He headed towards the elevators, his stride long and purposeful. It was as if he'd been waiting for this news, and now he could leave. Why? Who was he? I didn't recognize him, so perhaps his departure at that moment was a coincidence.

But if he was waiting for news of a loved one, why would he leave?

Sounds of grief from the waiting room drew me back in, and I shrugged off the mystery man. I had enough to contend with without waxing paranoid. He could've been heading to the cafeteria—probably couldn't handle watching another family face what he might face soon.

My biggest regret at the moment was that my family didn't know I was still with them. I wasn't worried. Silver had sensed me before, and I'd affected the heart machine when I'd touched it. That meant I could make them notice me. I'd find a way.

But ghosts who'd gone before me had probably thought the same thing and had failed. Sure, psychics had always insisted spirits were around us, but I'd never seen physical proof.

I'd promised my mother I'd come back with proof if I died first.

When I was in my twenties, my mom, my two sisters, and I had a girls' night at my mother's place. We'd pulled out the blender and over margaritas had a slurred and somewhat confused discussion about the afterlife.

My mother is a firm believer, and so is my sister Lois. Sarah and I are more scientific minded. We want peer-reviewed studies.

At some point, my mother made us agree that whoever died first would return to the others with evidence of the afterlife. Sarah was sure that was impossible. For once, I was more open-minded about something than she was. I agreed.

Now, I was on deck to haunt my siblings and my sixty-five-year-old mother.

I hope none of them have a heart condition.

***

We all grouped around my bed. Richler told Rory, Silver, and Clara they could stay in the room with my body for as long as they wanted. When he asked them if they wanted the hospital chaplain to come and pray with them, they agreed.

After Richler left, Marc appeared. He was a mess. I could tell he'd been crying, though he'd composed himself by the time he reached my room. At the sight of my corpse, he fell apart and threw himself into Rory's arms. Silver put her arms around Marc as well, and they huddled together until the chaplain walked into the room.

Reverend Elizabeth Parsons brought with her a calming energy that soothed my grieving family. They gathered around my bed, holding hands, and she said the "Lord is My Shepherd" prayer. I was an atheist, though my beliefs were evolving by the second. I hadn't seen proof of God yet, but I'd left my body and hadn't died. Anything was possible.

Prayer certainly couldn't hurt though I wouldn't relate to most of it. The words made the kids cry, which bothered me. I detest seeing my kids cry, even if it's out of love for me. An ache to hold them became unbearable. Without thinking, I touched each child's shoulder with my hands, which sank through to the wrists before I pulled away.

Both kids shuddered and Marc said, "Mom?"

Oh, my babies, I'm here with you. I'd give anything to hold you both one more time.

I had to make them hear me.

"Yes, it's me." My voice sounded mechanical and strange, but I heard it.

No one else did. The reverend finished her prayers, and Rory, Clara, and Silver all stared at Marc with expressions of worry.

They'd dealt with the reality of my death, but Marc was still a newbie to it. No doubt, the others feared he was losing his mind from grief. A flattering thought, but Marc was stronger than that. Silver was the fragile one, and she had guilt to contend with. I worried more about her.

The room grew brighter. It glowed. A pull, strong as a riptide, dragged me backwards.

No. Not now.

I fought it, but with no ability to grasp anything, it sucked me in. The last thing I glimpsed before darkness engulfed me was my son's bewildered face.

***

Everything was dark, but I was conscious and aware. Other spirits swirled around me, and I sensed their panic. A roaring in my ears irritated me, but when it cut off, the silence grew eerie.

A light up ahead was my target. The light at the end of the tunnel is a real thing.

I popped out of the darkness like a pinball out of the shoot and found myself in a wheat field. Children played in the distance and adults wandered around wearing blissful expressions. Crows circled overhead. When I glanced down at my body, I discovered I wore a white nightgown with pale-pink trim and dotted with tiny flowers.

Above me, the sky was yellow-tinged and grey clouds puffed out of the tunnel I'd exited. In the distance, where the people were, the sun shone down in all its glory.

I tried to inhale but discovered I couldn't breathe. A craving for fresh air and the meadow scent that should have permeated the air overtook me, and I struggled to suck it in through my mouth. The attempt, while it didn't hurt, failed, leaving me forlorn.

A shadow loomed over me, and I looked up. Before me stood an exquisite woman, young and golden. Instead of the long, flowing gown I'd have expected from someone in—wherever we were—she wore a sundress and big, floppy sunhat.

"Welcome, Jayden." She grinned as if she couldn't help herself and held out her hand.

I automatically reached out to clasp it and was stunned to find her grip substantial.

Awed, I said, "I can feel you."

Her warm grip almost made me swoon. How I'd longed to touch my children when I was out of body. You don't realize how profound another's touch is until you lose it.

"Yes. Come with me. I'll get you oriented." She turned and took three steps away from me. When she realized I wasn't following her, she faced me again.

"Who are you?" I asked.

What if this was a dream? Or a trick? Maybe I was in Hell, not Heaven, and if I followed her, it would be to eternal agony.

"Suzanne. We've never met, but I watched you grow up. I'm Natalie's niece." Natalie was my mother.

"Your cousin," she added, needlessly, as I'd understood the implication.

Suzanne had died of pneumonia as a child.

"Why isn't Gramma meeting me? And you died when you were ten. You look at least twenty."

She chuckled.

As I struggled to grasp what I was seeing, her body shrank, her hair grew long and twisted into two braids, and her clothes changed. Before me stood a little girl with white-blonde hair and a mischievous grin.

"Is that better?"

"Even if you grew up here, you'd be ..." I did a rough calculation. "Fifty-three?"

She smiled and nodded.

"How did you shift appearance like that?"

"All in good time. Come along. We have lots to do before you return for your funeral." She waved her hand, and this time, I followed her.

CHAPTER 3

Suzanne showed me the way to the Light but wouldn't take me into it. I was still connected to the earth plane. Unless I was completely ready to leave my family, she advised me not to cross yet.

"Once you enter, you lose the desire to return," she explained.

"So, once you're gone, you're gone? Don't you hear your loved ones when they talk to you?"

"Sure you do. We can hear them on the other side and can even visit if we have free time."

"What if—"

"No. There's no what if."

"I don't understand."

"You will. That's part of your job now."

"My job?" I gazed out into the field where I'd first met her and understood that the spirits milling about were waiting for newly departed loved ones. God's arrivals gate.

"Your spiritual work. Don't worry about that right now. Let's go inside."

A small bungalow stood at the edge of the meadow. Cute and cozy, it reminded me of the cabin my grandfather had built in Thornton, Ontario. My grandparents had bought acreage in that tiny, rural community to keep bees, grow fruit trees, and get away from the bustle of downtown Toronto.

Suzanne led me into the kitchen area, a duplicate of my grandmother's kitchen right down to the sunflower wallpaper and bench seats around the dining table. Out of habit, I searched for the box of cookies my grandmother always kept on the counter by the sink.

There it was, a covered tin with green and red flowers. I dove at it, afraid it would disappear or that my hands would go right through it.

Relief flooded through me as I hefted its reassuring weight. I pried it open and picked up a pinwheel cookie. It had no flavour when I licked it. My disappointment must have shown, because Suzanne shook her head.

"We're not here to indulge in physical pleasures."

"There's beauty," I replied. "Sure, I'm thrilled I can see, but sight—"

"Isn't an indulgence. With time, you'll get taste and scent, too."

Suzanne's habit of interrupting me irritated me. She'd been here for decades. Shouldn't she have learned some manners by now?

Her hearty laugh filled my head, and I realized nothing had been physical. I heard without ears and saw without sight. And she'd read my mind.

"I'm sorry," I said.

"No harm done, dear. Patience was never one of my virtues. I'm excited to finally meet you after watching you for so many years. We'll visit a bit before we check in with your family."

My family. They'd slipped my mind. Horrified and ashamed, I dropped the cookie on the counter.

"Don't beat yourself up. This is all new and strange. You have every right to feel disoriented."

"Thank you. I'm glad you're here with me. What happens now?"

We sat at the kitchen table, the way I used to do with my grandparents. Suzanne produced a teapot and we drank tea and ate cookies.

After a while, I could taste them.

"Suzanne?"

"I know, dear. The longer you linger here, the more you acclimate. We must hurry."

I picked up my cup of tea and sniffed. Nothing. I set the cup back on the saucer and rested a hand on either side of it.

"It'll come, but don't get too comfortable. Do you want to attend your funeral?"

"I don't have to?"

She placed her hand over one of mine.

"No. You keep your free will when you pass into spirit. Understand this, though: the more time you spend here, the less desire you have to return. Often, attending their funeral helps people learn some final lessons before they cross to this side and leave their old life behind. We encourage new spirits to go back one last time." She paused. "But you must return here within a few days. The tunnel will open again, and you'll be expected to come home and enter the Light."

"Okay, I can do that." Of course, I could do that. It was pleasant here. No troubles, no worries, no job. I had no physical needs.

I held up my right hand, wiggled the fingers and then made snapping sounds with them, two fast clicks. No twinge of arthritis. Thrilled, I snapped the fingers on both hands, working up a rhythm.

"Jayden, play later." She sounded amused, so she wasn't chastising me.

A revelation struck me. *Oh, man.* I bounced in my seat. *Yeehaw. No hemorrhoids.* I could certainly get used to this. Ever since I'd turned forty, my body continuously reminded me it was aging. Now all the nuisances were gone.

"What about sleep?" I'd had trouble sleeping for years. Sometimes it was worry about my kids, but other times, who knows? I'd toss and turn, counting down the hours to dawn.

"We don't sleep." When she saw my expression, she amended her response. "We don't need to sleep."

I nodded, contemplating.

"Can we read?" Let's face it, if I had all the free time in the world and an eternity to spend it, I'd want to start setting up a To Be Read list."

"If that's what you want. Studying is encouraged on the other side."

She hadn't exactly answered my question.

"What about fiction?"

"Yes, you can read fiction. You can write fiction if you want. Where do you think books originate?"

"Authors create them."

"Yes. They do." Her broad smile told me I had a lot to learn, but she wasn't going to explain it now. "Let's see how things are going with your family.

She waved her hand at the wall, and it shimmered and swirled. When it cleared, it was like looking at a television screen, but three-dimensional. On it, my kids and Rory sat around a table in what was obviously an office at Stevens and Jones Funeral Home. They were planning my funeral.

CHAPTER 4

Rory had gone to high school with Gregory Stevens, and they'd played hockey together, so I wasn't surprised to find my family at Stevens and Jones.

When their parents had retired to Florida, Greg, his sister, and his brother had inherited the family business. They seemed to love their work, which benefited their clients.

As the scene unfolded, Rory leaned back in his chair and asked, "Embalming isn't required?"

Greg shook his head. "Not unless you want an open casket for visitation."

"Daddy." Silver's voice held a warning.

I had a sudden flashback to my argument with Silver. We'd nicknamed my daughter "Quicksilver" when she was five. She was the tantrum queen, able to flare up in a second, going from calm and sweet to hellion.

Right before my death, she'd been more hair-trigger than usual. Palpable stress rolled off Silver now, unrelated to coping with my loss.

"Something is worrying her," I said. "She was on edge before, and my death will make it much worse."

I stuck a finger in my mouth and then removed it when I realized biting my nails was physically impossible.

Suzanne interrupted my thoughts. "Go to your family."

"I'd like that." Then I could uncover what was bugging Silver.

The fight we'd had when I died had been about something

stupid, as many fights are. I'd been tired from working long hours over fourteen days straight. On my way to bed, I noticed she'd left a dirty cup on the counter. I asked her to rinse it and put it into the dishwasher. You'd think I'd asked her to clean the entire house.

She stomped into the kitchen, and amidst sighs and eye-rolling, suggested I should have done it myself. When I protested, she screamed about being picked on. Tired, frustrated, craving bed, I screamed right back at her. Next thing I knew, I was standing by my body in the hospital.

Nevertheless, while Silver has a temper, she's not a crazy bitch. That was out of character. I should have realized something serious nagged at her—much like the way her guilt over what had happened now nagged at me.

My heart attack wasn't her fault. If I had a faulty ticker, it would have happened anyway.

I glanced at Suzanne. At some point, she'd returned to the twenty-year-old version of herself. That gave me an idea.

"Can I make myself look younger before I return?"

She giggled. "Yes. Everyone wants that eventually. You can morph to any age you like. Focus on it."

When I was twenty-four, I was in the best shape of my life. Slim, great hair—this was before I got pregnant with Marc and lost it all. I focused on my appearance from that time.

The video screen changed to a full-length mirror, and Suzanne waved her hand at it.

"Take a look. You're lovely."

I shifted from side to side, trying to see every angle. My nightgown had transformed to a tank top that revealed sculpted arms and a denim mini skirt that displayed my long, sexy legs. My shoulder-length, tousled hair framed my face, which showed a hint of makeup. The cutest flat sandals had appeared on my bare feet. Their base was black leather, and the straps were gold and silver studded with jewels.

I'd never looked this hot when I was alive.

Delighted, I grinned at Suzanne.

"I'm ready to go plan my funeral now. How do I get there?"

***

Once again, the desire to do something or go somewhere was all I needed to accomplish it. My family still sat at the table talking with Greg Stevens as if no time had passed. Silver scowled at Rory, who faced her with a patient expression.

"I want to understand what's required and why, sweetie."

Silver drew in an audible breath and exhaled it in a rush. "You want to cheap out. I won't let you. You're discussing my mother. I want to see her. Everyone will want to see her. We need an open casket."

Rory put a hand on her arm, but she shrugged it off.

"Did I say we wouldn't have her embalmed?"

Greg watched the back and forth silently. As the argument wound down, he cleared his throat and spoke. "We're old friends, Rory. I loved Jayden. You'll get a good deal for the funeral."

"Thank you, Greg. We appreciate that. What do we do now?"

"We've filled out the required forms for the coroner, registered the death, and took care of the burial permit. Jayden's body will be picked up from the hospital today." Greg checked his watch. "We can select a coffin from the casket room now, if you like."

They'd be picking up my body already? I searched for the date. Greg's laptop displayed October 2nd. For a moment, I was disoriented. How much time had I spent on the other side? It hadn't seemed to me as if three days had passed. Not that time mattered to me, but I regretted being away from the kids.

Silver and Marc both looked like they hadn't slept since I'd died. Rory seemed to be holding it together well enough. He was always solid that way, so I didn't take offence. I'm not the type to think people should fall apart over me. I prefer balls on a man, and, quite frankly, on a woman too.

They rose, and Greg led them down the hall to a large room with photos of caskets on the wall and samples of wood below each picture. The real things stood on display throughout the room.

I gravitated to a lovely oak coffin, the lid propped open to show off the cream crepe interior. Not bad. Tasteful, understated. Just my style. I imagined my body lying in it, arms folded over my chest. Yes, it would suit me.

This would be interesting. Rory had terrible taste—or, I guess it would be more mature to say Rory had taste that differed from mine. Thank God, Silver had a better eye for the aesthetically pleasing. If it were up to Rory, I'd end up resting for eternity in a plaid coffin with a pink polka dot lining.

"What do you think of this one, Marc, Silver?" Rory crouched in front of a picture on the west wall. I blinked over and peered past his shoulder.

Mother of God, it was worse than I'd feared.

The picture showed a shiny pink coffin, the interior white with pink roses. What appeared to be plastic red roses decorated the lid.

Rory, if you put me in that thing, at least have the decency to cremate me.

"Oh, Dad, gross." Silver's hand slid through my shoulder and grasped her father's arm.

That's my girl.

Marc shuffled over and studied the image.

"No, Dad." He didn't say anything else, just turned away and meandered over to the east wall.

"Here's a nice oak one. What about this?" Marc touched a fingertip to the specs list below the picture. "Cream crepe interior. She'd like this, Dad."

Rory walked over, stood next to Marc, and glanced at the sticker price. "Nah, that's not her style."

Greg joined them.

"We have this one on display right over there." He waved his hand to indicate the coffin I'd checked out before.

"Twenty-five hundred." Rory contemplated, the fingers of one hand rubbing his chin while his other hand supported his elbow.

"I can let you have it for twenty-two," Greg said. "That's a deal, Rory. It's a mid-priced model. Very tasteful. Good, solid construction."

"I like it, Dad," Silver chimed in. "That's the one."

I popped over to sit inside the coffin. The lining was probably soft and comfortable, but I couldn't tell. It might appear that I was sitting in the coffin, physically supported by it, but I couldn't feel it. Only my will kept me from sinking through it.

Behind me, a man spoke. "You have good taste. That's a nice one."

I waited for Rory or one of the kids to acknowledge him. When they didn't, I turned around. He winked when our gazes met and tipped his fedora. If I hadn't already had a heart attack and died, I would have then.

He was talking to me.

CHAPTER 5

The man looked young, but that didn't mean anything. He could be ninety years old and make himself appear twenty-five. His translucence told me he wasn't alive.

Logically, I should have wondered where all the dead people were before this. Odds were, I wasn't the only one who'd died recently and wanted a peek at funeral arrangements. However, I sensed this guy wasn't new to the death game.

A throwback to the sixties, he wore a tie-dye shirt, flared jeans, hair longer than mine, and that fedora. I couldn't peg the year he was trying to pull off, but the overall effect said "sixties."

"Who are you?"

He disappeared for a second and reappeared next to the casket, his face leaning into mine. "You're not twenty-four. How old were you when you died?"

"Tell me who you are first." I could pop in and out of anywhere, so I wasn't threatened by him. However, he'd intruded on my casket purchase, and I'd asked him a fair question. He owed me an answer.

"Daniel Bowes. Your first guess was right—I'm twenty-five. At least, that's how old I was when I died. Now you."

He'd been reading my mind. Why couldn't I read his?

"Jayden McQueen. I was forty-six when I died three days ago. When did you pass away?"

"Nineteen-sixty-four."

I gasped. "All that time. What are you doing here?"

Maybe he'd been sent here to help me through this, like a tour guide or mentor.

He chuckled. "I can help you if you need it."

Not sure what to make of Daniel but way too preoccupied to worry about it, I said, "No, thanks."

Behind Daniel, Rory made his decision about the casket. Silver and Marc had both insisted on the one I liked, so Rory bought it. My kids are awesome.

As I observed them, Marc glanced repeatedly at the casket, his expression puzzled. He squinted as though trying to see more clearly, and I swear he glimpsed me.

"Can the living see us? My son—" I couldn't continue. I'd give anything for even one of my kids to see me, to know I hadn't left them.

Daniel studied the group and focused his gaze on Marc.

"Yup. Sometimes. Psychics can sense us, sometimes with sight, other times with a gut feeling or another psychic sense. I think your kid is psychic and doesn't know it."

"He senses me? Does he know it's me?" I figuratively held my breath.

"He probably gets 'corner of the eye' flashes and can't understand what's causing them. Don't worry—he'll get better as time passes. Your death likely triggered the ability."

"Fascinating. No one in my family is psychic."

Daniel laughed. "Bet you a hundred dollars you were psychic and never developed it."

"Nonsense. I would've been happy to have evidence of psychic ability, but it doesn't exist."

"Honey, that's what blocked you." He studied me. "You dress like one of the cool kids now, but you went the science route in university. You wouldn't have recognized proof of the paranormal if it jumped on your back and asked for a ride. I'm surprised you don't think this is all a dream."

"You're full of assumptions, aren't you? Computer science. I was a software developer. That doesn't make me closed-minded. It makes me logical. I tested the dream theory, smartass."

In my periphery, the kids and Rory were leaving the room with Greg. Why was I sitting here arguing with a strange dead guy when my family was planning my funeral?

"I gotta go. Nice meeting you."

I focused on Silver and popped up next to her. The group had returned to Greg's office and were seated once more around the table across from his desk. He had his laptop out and was opening a file.

"You've expressed an interest in the basic funeral package. I'll need to ask you some questions to ensure you have everything you need." Greg put a hand on Rory's arm. "Don't worry about cost. Let's get a quote together, and then I'll play with the figures to get you the best deal. Okay?"

Rory agreed, and Greg led them through the options. He was nice to offer the discount, but Rory isn't as destitute as he makes everyone believe—he's a cheapskate, like Silver said.

I'd been touched to hear what Greg had said about me. He and Rory had spent a lot of time together, but Greg and I were never close. I never saw him after my divorce. I was flattered he even remembered me.

They hashed out the schedule for the visitation, the service, and the burial, which would be at the Newmarket Cemetery. Greg helped Rory determine whom to contact about my death, such as the insurance company and my workplace, and what parts of the process S & J would handle for him.

At first, I interpreted the comments about contacting my office as evidence they hadn't received news of my death yet, but it turned out Greg referred to filling out the human resources-related forms. S & J would take care of quite a bit of legwork. I was impressed. They'd even contact my bank.

Mention of the bank pricked up my ears. My death would mean the mortgage on the house would be paid out, and Marc and Silver would own it. Thank God, I'd updated my will two years ago.

When the form was completed and Rory signed off on the final total, Greg helped them complete my obituary. This is what it said:

McQueen, Jayden Anne passed away at South River Health Centre in Aurora on September 29th, 2016 surrounded by her family. Former wife of Rory McQueen. Mother to Marc and Silver.

Jayden was born October 6th, 1969. While building her career in software development, Jayden volunteered at the foundation for unwed mothers in Newmarket. She loved walking the trails, gymnastics, and music.

Family and friends can join us at Stevens & Jones Funeral Home 27 Dauphin Street West, Newmarket on Monday, October 3rd from 1:30 to 2:30 for visitation with service starting at 2:30 PM followed by refreshments.

Interment to follow at 5:30 PM at the Newmarket Cemetery.

If desired, donations can be made to the Heart and Stroke Foundation. Online condolences may be made under www.stevensandjones.com

As obits go, it wasn't bad. At least Rory hadn't tried to add that I was friend to Clara. No offence intended, but I wouldn't have been surprised.

They didn't mention my cousins and nieces and nephews, nor did they mention anyone from Rory's family. But where do you draw the line on these things?

I'd have liked them to mention my parents and sisters, though. They'd been with me throughout my life, loving me. I doubted they'd feel slighted or hold a grudge, but I wanted them acknowledged.

As soon as I finished my silent diatribe, Marc spoke up.

"You forgot to mention Gramma, Grampa, and the Aunties, Dad. I think she'd like it if you mention her immediate family in the obituary."

My son. Bless his soul. The kid sensed my thoughts. God, how I wanted to hug him—Silver, too—but this guy made my ghostly eyes want to water.

"I'd never have pegged you as an athlete."

Daniel.

"I wasn't."

While Greg added the extra names to the obituary, I confronted Daniel. "Are you lost?"

"Just wanted to see how you were doing."

He perched on Greg's desk. The fedora was gone, and his thick, dark hair was tied back with a leather thong. What a freakin' hippie.

"Let me guess, you attended Woodstock in that getup."

"That was 1969, babe. I was dead by then." He smiled. "But hell, yeah. Wouldn't have missed it. What a party."

"Why are you following me?"

"I want to help you. Look, I've been where you are. It's not easy. Sure, it's cool to watch your family buy the casket, order the flowers, and say nice things about you. But you've got some tough stuff ahead."

"And you're going to help me through that?"

"Yes."

"Why?" I gave him the hairy eyeball.

People don't do things for no reason. This guy had to have an angle. Wouldn't be money. The dead don't need money, from what I'd seen so far.

"What's in it for you?"

"A warm feeling from helping another soul." He popped over to stand next to me, grief in his eyes. "I do this, Jayden, because I can't go home."

CHAPTER 6

Daniel's sad eyes broke my no-longer-existent heart.

"Home?"

"To the other side. Our real home."

Before I could ask another question, Greg rose from his seat and offered Rory his hand. When Rory clasped it, Greg said, "I'll see you all here tomorrow at one o'clock. If there's anything you need in the meantime, don't hesitate to call."

He shook hands with the kids, too, and patted Rory on the back as he stepped into the hallway.

"I'm so sorry, Rory. Anyone at Stevens and Jones is here for you, but feel free to call me direct for anything, no matter how small."

"Thanks, Greg."

After my family left, Greg moved his laptop back to the desk and sat. He powered it up and focused on the screen.

"I missed them ordering my flowers. Now I don't know what they got," I said.

Behind me, Daniel spoke. "I'm sorry."

I met his gaze.

"It's not important." It wasn't. "What will you do now?"

"Are you going to your house?"

"I'm going wherever Silver's going."

His eyes went distant for a moment, and then he said, "They're running errands. The bank first. They'll be home later to go through the photos and select the ones they want for the collage."

My chest thudded as if it had a heart in it.

"You can tap into them?"

"Sure. Focus on the thoughts of the person you want to locate instead of their body. It locates them without going there. Sometimes, you just want a bead on a person. This'll give it to you."

I tried it and caught Silver's thoughts. They were preoccupied with the errands they needed to run, the people they needed to contact. I tuned out again, and my eyes misted over. Where were these physical reactions coming from? How could they happen?

"Let me take you somewhere, Jayden. Away from grief and funerals for a while. Get some space. They don't need you hovering over them. Tomorrow will be difficult enough. Let them sort through the red tape at the bank. We'll catch up to them after."

I hesitated. Time with my family was slipping away.

"You'll get quality time later." Daniel had read my thoughts again. "I'll show you wonders."

"Wonders? Are we going to the circus?" A giggle slipped out of me, and I felt a lightness that had nothing to do with being a spirit.

He smiled. "Take my hand."

He reached out, and I slipped my fingers into his.

***

Hawaii in early October was as beautiful as Hawaii was at any time of the year. Daniel took me to The Big Island, to the summit of Mauna Kea, where different countries had built observatories. Canada had an interest in two of the telescopes there.

At the top of the dormant volcano, the terrain of Mauna Kea resembled a lunar landscape. The ground appeared dark brown and grey in moonlight and starlight, and the blanket of snow told me it was cold. At 13,000 feet up, a light snow dusted the boulders and ground even, sometimes, in the summer. It would have been desolate if the view weren't so spectacular.

The sun hadn't yet risen, and we gazed up at the riot of stars in the cloudless sky. When I looked over the precipice, I realized the sky wasn't cloudless at all—we were above the clouds.

"It's gorgeous." If only my kids could see this.

"I'm sorry we missed sunset, but we'll catch the sunrise. Hawaii has spectacular sunsets and sunrises. The VOG—volcanic smog—makes them colourful. Probably not good for your lungs, but," he shrugged a shoulder, "we don't have lungs anymore."

He stood beside me, his face turned towards the heavens. We emitted a gentle aura of light, and I wondered what the scientists in the observatories saw.

Daniel answered my unspoken thoughts.

"They can't see us, but we shouldn't go anywhere near the observatories. It would interfere with their equipment. The scientists aren't even up here—they're monitoring on computers at the bottom of the mountain."

"Convenient for them, I guess. We lose something when we distance ourselves from nature with technology."

He didn't reply to that but said, "Check this out."

Grabbing my hand, he stepped over the edge of the mountain, dragging me with him. I screamed—an interesting sound when you don't have vocal chords.

So that's what a banshee wail sounds like.

If the scientists had microphones picking up audio, they were likely pissing themselves.

Daniel howled too, but with laughter.

"What are you afraid of? We won't fall unless you want to. We sure as hell can't die."

"I know." The response was automatic and a lie—I did not know it at all. I'd assumed it, sure, but hadn't wanted to test the theory.

Unable to help myself, I looked down. We stood on the clouds.

"This is incredible." Mist coated our feet up to the ankles. What a shame we couldn't feel the wind on our faces or smell the fresh air. It would've been invigorating.

We played.

I can't remember the last time I'd had that much fun. We chased each other, popping around the clouds, laughing like children. I wondered again what the scientists saw. Probably nothing. Their telescopes were trained up into the heavens, not down on the clouds.

After, we stopped and fell silent, and Daniel pointed to the constellations above us. Neither of us recognized any of them, so he concocted names for them.

"There's the wild boar." He pointed at a cluster of five stars.

"They don't look anything like a boar." I laughed.

"Does Leo look like a lion?"

"The dippers look like dippers."

"You have to admit, most of them look nothing like what they call them."

"They're beautiful even if we don't recognize them. Thank you for bringing me here." Though my gaze fixed mostly on the stars above, I couldn't help glancing at Daniel.

He had a handsome face with a strong jawline that gave him a rugged look. He must have had his pick of the girls when he was alive.

"Did you have a girlfriend when you died?"

He snapped his head around and stared at me in silence for so long I was sorry I'd asked.

"No, not technically. She'd broken up with me the day I died. I'm still sensitive about it."

We returned to the mountaintop, and I sat on a snow-capped boulder.

"Will you tell me?" I gave him a weak smile.

He leaned against the rock next to me. I'd come to realize that we didn't tire, and so we didn't need to sit or lie down, but it was a habit I couldn't break. You sit down to chat. The act of reclining makes the discussion more intimate.

"I don't mind telling you about my life. And death."

When he started talking, I closed my eyes, which turned out to be a surreal experience. With the physical world blocked out, his words projected a movie into my consciousness.

He'd been born in 1939. Hitler held power in Germany, and World War II started. So much horror perpetrated against so many. Also in 1939, Gandhi began his fast in protest against the caste system in India; Steinbeck published *The Grapes of Wrath*; *The Wizard of Oz* movie was released, as was *Gone with the Wind*; Mackenzie King was Prime Minister of Canada.

How much does what happens in the world influence a child's development? There'd been no Internet then, but world events must have shaped him. His family would have been affected by the war.

Again, he replied to my unspoken thoughts.

"We lost some family to the war when Canada joined the fight. My uncle, some older cousins. I heard stories, and I was terrified my dad would go."

As Daniel got older and went to school, cars became his passion.

"By the time I was fifteen, I could've taken apart a car and put it together again by myself. Physics and mechanics interested me, but I didn't care about going to university. I dropped out at sixteen to apprentice as a mechanic in a garage in Toronto. My family lived in Toronto then. We moved to Newmarket when I was eighteen. That's where I met my girlfriend."

Daniel gave me a regretful look. "We didn't start dating until I was twenty-two. I was sure we'd get married, especially since we were together for almost three years."

He fell silent, and when it dragged on, I prompted him. "What happened?"

"She couldn't tolerate my drinking. I had an alcohol problem but refused to admit it. Back in sixty-four, cars didn't have seatbelts in the back seats, there were no seatbelt laws, and if you were too drunk to walk, you drove." His voice was low but audible, since we communicated without making actual sound. Daniel even heard my private thoughts, a trick I'd have to convince him to teach me sometime.

"You died in a car accident. I'm so sorry."

He'd had a Chevy Impala. I knew nothing about cars, but Daniel gave me an excellent visual. The turquoise colour wasn't bad, but the shape and size of it screamed tank. The back had fins on it, and it was so big I wouldn't have wanted to try parking it in a crowded lot. I drove a little Mazda 3. Rory referred to it as my go-kart, but I loved it. It would fit into any parking space and was amazing on gas.

Daniel's face etched with grief. "That would have been bad enough, but I crippled my best friend. He lived, Jayden, and I died. I was the lucky one. Kirk was paralyzed from the neck down. I ruined his life. He lived a long and depressing life, and when he died in nineteen-eighty, it was a relief."

"But then you saw him again?" My tone vibrated hope.

He shook his head. "He never forgave me. Neither did my girlfriend. I waited for them, and by waiting, by refusing to cross over when it was my time, I got stuck here."

Daniel put his arm around me then, and I leaned into him. He was more solid than I was—I'd noticed that before. He could also walk and run, whereas I had to pop from place to place. Was it because he hadn't crossed?

"That's right," he said. "If you stay here, your vibration lowers, you become more material, and you get stuck here."

CHAPTER 7

The words "stuck here" hovered in the air.

"Forever?" I pictured Suzanne and some of my other departed loved ones waiting for me to reappear on the other side. Wouldn't they miss me and search for me when I didn't show? Didn't Daniel have anyone who cared enough to track him down?

"It's not like that."

Shame flooded through me at his annoyed tone. He'd read my thoughts again.

I faced him, but he avoided my gaze.

"I'm sorry. I didn't mean it to sound the way it did."

"I know. And I don't mean to eavesdrop. After you've been here a while, you have to force yourself not to listen in on other people's thoughts. Hearing them becomes the norm; tuning them out becomes the challenge."

"You mean you always hear the thoughts of the living?"

"Yes. You can, too, like when you tracked Silver's location by picking up on what she was thinking."

"Why can't I hear what you're thinking?"

He gave me a rueful stare. "I'm blocking you."

Before I could say anything, he continued. "Don't be mad. I planned to explain it to you and show you how to block me."

"But you didn't get around to it?" My hands fisted on my hips, and I glared at him.

"I'm sorry." He took my hands in his and placed them on his heart. "I wasn't snooping, and I didn't do it to invade your privacy." He paused. "The connection to you felt good. Intimate. I've missed intimacy."

Our gazes locked, and affection for him swept through me. Perhaps it came from him, and I was picking up how he felt about me. Anger evaporated, and I moved closer to him. An urge to throw my arms around him overwhelmed me. When he didn't move, I knew he was no longer reading my thoughts.

I draped an arm around him and rested my head on his shoulder. For the first time, I felt his touch. His hand stroked my back.

"Do you feel me?" I asked.

"Yes," he whispered.

"Is this weird? Can you touch other things and feel them?"

"Yes. You get all your senses back after a while."

"What does that mean?"

His hand moved to the back of my head and caressed my hair. "It means your vibration is lowering, and you're acclimating to the earth plane." His voice broke then, but he continued. "You don't have much time left before you have to leave."

I nodded without replying.

"Time to go to the visitation. Are you ready?"

"Okay." I'd hear what people thought now. This could get interesting.

***

We stood beside my open coffin in the Roses Visitation Room at Stevens and Jones. My skin looked plastic and fake. The rouge on my cheeks and lips didn't help—it made me think of waxy apples and too much plastic surgery. Even with lipstick, my lips appeared too thin and tight.

Was it vain of me to wish they'd enhanced my appearance?

Was that really me lying in the casket?

At least the casket looked comfortable, and they'd selected my favourite jeans and sweater to bury me in. Silver and Marc had probably battled to get that accomplished. Rory would've wanted something formal. My kids knew me well, though. Why should I decay in uncomfortable clothes? I'd always hated formal wear.

People had sent flowers—gorgeous bouquets of lilies and roses and giant wreaths with ribbons, carnations, hydrangeas, and more roses. My casket floated in a sea of red, pink, purple, and white, and the sweet scent of future rot.

The room itself exuded peace and serenity with neutral colours on the walls and mahogany furniture and trim. In reflection of its name, vases filled with bouquets of roses graced the end tables and coffee tables. A coffee, tea, water, and juice service had been laid out on the wet bar. Guests would be able to soothe their grief with a caffeine kick if they wanted.

How nice.

If that sounded a touch bitter, it was because I wanted coffee. I used to practically mainline it at work. A hit right then would've been welcome. Maybe it would help me get over the sight of my death face. No one would say I looked as if only sleeping and could wake up at any moment. They'd probably say I looked undead and as if I'd leap up and go for their brains.

Daniel put a hand on my shoulder.

"Corpses never look as good as the living person."

When I raised my brows and quirked my mouth, he laughed.

"Sorry. I never know what to say when someone sees their embalmed body for the first time. It's always a disappointment."

"Have you seen many?" How many people had he done this with?

"Yeah. Dozens. I've been here a lot."

"Why?"

He didn't reply, just met my gaze as though contemplating the question. Probably he didn't know the answer.

I sighed, and then almost jumped on him in my excitement. You have no idea how awesome sighing is until you can't do it.

"Don't get sucked into the physical," Daniel snapped.

I answered him quickly, placating both of us. "I won't."

Suzanne, Grandma, Grandpa, and so many others I'd missed after they'd died were waiting for me. I wanted to go back and see them. Still, I appreciated the restored ability.

A male and a female staff member popped the doors open and propped them against the wall. I caught a glimpse of the same burgundy carpeting in the hallway as they had in the visitation room. Subdued voices floated in.

Silver and Marc entered first, holding hands, followed by Rory, and then Clara. Silver's eyes were red-rimmed and shadowed. Marc was dry-eyed but pale and drawn. Rory's hair was tousled, as if he'd forgotten to comb it. Of all of them, Clara was the most pulled together, her hair professionally coiffed in an updo, her mourning dress draping to perfectly accentuate her curves. She clutched a dry tissue in her hand and seemed nowhere near needing to use it.

"Jealous?" Daniel's question yanked me out of my judgmental thoughts.

"Of what?" I cocked my head in Clara's direction. "Her?" I snorted. "Absolutely not."

"Are you sorry you divorced Rory?"

I shook my head. "Believe me, it was for the best. He's better off with Clara."

"But?"

"No buts. They work well together."

Daniel stroked my back, and, to my astonishment, it soothed me. I realized how automatic my judgments of Clara had been. Even when I approved of her, I criticized.

"I guess I hate that she looks so good when I look so hideous. Too much to expect the corpse to be the sexiest body in the room, but it would have been nice if just once I could outshine her."

"Jayden, I have a difficult time believing you never outshone her. You're gorgeous."

I laughed. "Sure, when I was in my twenties I could rock an outfit like this, but look at me." I flung my arm out in the direction of my casket.

Maybe the kids should have let them dress me up. Maybe I should care more about my kids' suffering than about how I look dead.

My family now stood before my casket, staring into it. Silver and Marc were at my head, Clara and Rory at my middle. The lower half of the casket lid was closed.

"They don't put shoes on the body," Daniel said. "That's why the bottom is always closed."

"That's not true." I tried to recall any visitation I'd attended where I could see the dead person's feet.

"Maybe they don't," I admitted.

Why did she have to come with Daddy? She should have come alone, later. She's not part of our family. She won't be my mother.

It took me a moment to realize I'd caught Silver's thoughts. My head whipped around so I could stare at her. Her face angled down towards the casket, and her eyes were closed as if she were praying. But I knew better.

Marc's thoughts cascaded in. *How will I get through exams? I won't think about it. Mom wouldn't want me to louse up my year over her death. But God, it hurts.*

And then Rory's: *She expects me to propose now. I'll have to. No—not have to—I want to. I don't want to rush it. You can't expect a guy to jump into marriage when his ex just died, right?*

Then, unbelievably, Clara's thoughts seeped in: *I can't believe that's Jayden lying there. It's not possible. She used to be so vibrant. What have they done to her?*

I popped over to stand behind Marc and Silver and put a hand on each of their shoulders. Marc's head snapped up, and Silver shivered.

"Mom?" Marc whispered.

Silver grabbed his arm.

"Stop it," she hissed. "Don't you dare start that creepy stuff again."

So, he'd mentioned sensing me to Silver, probably last night. Their thoughts pushed into my head in a jumble, and I popped back to the other side of the room where it was quieter.

"Daniel, how do you block it out?"

He appeared beside me. "Imagine a mirror around you, reflecting everything away from you."

"Visualization? Really?"

"Yeah, really. Do you want to block it or not?"

I focused, mentally building a mirrored wall around me, and the barrage of thoughts faded away.

"It worked. Thanks."

Murmurs from the hallway intruded; one shrill voice bulldozed over the rest. The owner tried to keep it down and succeeded to the extent that she spoke more quietly than she normally did, but there was no mistaking who headed towards us.

"I'm still in shock. She was fine when I saw her at work the other day." Laurel Kincaid caught up to her voice and burst through the entryway into the room.

She rushed to Silver's side and threw her arms around my daughter.

I visualized a chink in my mirror allowing Silver's thoughts in.

Oh, God, who is this? Did my mother like her, or is she one of the backstabbers?

Then for the fun of it, I tapped into Laurel.

The girl is even lovelier than her photos. Oh, Jayden, your poor girl.

Yeah, my poor girl. What was I going to do? Marc had his turn at hugging Laurel, and he guided her to the coffee. I followed them.

"You knew my mother well? I'm sorry; I don't know your name."

"Laurel. Kincaid. Your mother and I worked together. We were close. I'm sorry, I never had a chance to meet you and your sister. She talked about you all the time."

"I think I remember her mentioning you …" His voice trailed off as he tried to recall what I'd said.

It wouldn't have been much. Laurel and I were friends, but I always kept my work life separate from my personal life. I never brought work friends home. Part of me regretted that now. Laurel had always made me laugh, and she'd helped me stay one step ahead of Thomas Devereaux and his boys' club.

Since Laurel and I were the only women in the IT department, we naturally bonded over the typical sexist bullshit we had to put up with. Not all of the men were misogynists, but Thomas and his little band hated us for being able to hold our own against them. If it weren't for us, they'd be able to openly make sexist jokes and deride women.

Thomas and crew also had a small female following in the marketing department. I swear those women wanted to be abused and exploited. For some reason, they believed his pompous boasts and thought he was some kind of computer God.

The sound of his voice chilled my ghostly blood, and when I turned towards it, there he stood in the doorway. To my horror, he bee-lined for Silver, his expression pure fake compassion.

CHAPTER 8

After your death is the worst time to contemplate the guest list for your funeral, but there I was. Ideally, people who will miss you show up to send you off on your final journey. The reality is, those who disliked and resented you will show up to get humanity points for their public show of grief or to gloat.

Tom likely wanted to do both.

He swept over to my daughter and drew her into his arms, his dark bangs feathering across his forehead as he tilted down his face. Tall, he had to slouch a little to give the impression of offering comfort.

While his movie-star face and muscular body had most of the women in the office swooning, he'd never fooled me. I recognized a player when I saw one. Hopefully, Silver would, too.

"Sweet angel," he crooned. "I'm so sorry for your loss."

He halted Silver's instinctive recoil by putting a hand on each of her shoulders and easing her away from his body as though the disconnection were his idea.

At her stunned expression, he chucked her under the chin with a finger and smiled indulgently. "I'm Tom Devereaux. Your mother and I worked together. She'll be sorely missed at the office."

"Nice to meet you." Silver stammered the words out and backed away. *I'm positive Mom thought this guy hated her. Was she wrong, or is this a con?*

"That's my girl. Don't trust him." I shouted it. If only she had

Marc's intuition.

I scanned the room for Daniel and spotted him on the opposite side, checking out a group of Silver's friends. "Daniel!"

He glanced my way and popped over, shaking his head. "It's a funeral, and they're dressed like—"

"Don't finish that sentence. Besides, sixties fashions weren't anything to brag about."

"They were groovy."

I laughed. "So are these—at least the kids think so."

Truthfully, the girls were chic in their form-fitting outfits. When I was their age, I didn't have the money to wear the latest fashions. I'd worked hard to be able to contribute to Silver's wardrobe so she didn't feel left behind the way I had when I was in high school.

"You want to be buried in jeans, but your daughter has the latest fashions?"

"So what? I like that she can wear what her friends wear."

"Does she want them? Or were you satisfying your own unmet needs?"

I stared at him like he'd sprouted an extra nose.

"Yes, she wants them. She's a normal teenage girl." With a sigh, I turned the discussion back to where I wanted it to go. "That jerk from my office is bugging Silver. Can I spook him?"

"What?"

"You know. Scare him. Show me how."

"What do you think we are?" He tilted his head, and gave me a questioning stare.

"Ghosts, Daniel. We're ghosts. When is that going to work in my favour? This guy is a creep." I glanced back at Thomas. He leaned in towards Silver, his expression animated, his hands gesturing in emphasis.

I popped over in time to hear him say, "No, we weren't supposed to take files home, but would you know if your mother did anyway? Did she ever do any work at home?"

Silver considered. "Not to my knowledge. That's why she spent so much time at the office."

He glanced around and abruptly dropped the subject. "Okay, thank you."

I followed his gaze and spotted Bernie, my boss, entering the room, his wife on his arm.

Thomas gave Silver's arm a stroke and, thank God, moved away from her. But now he was staring into my coffin.

"This oughta be good." I popped behind him and grasped his head with both hands.

Nothing—not even a shiver—and I was *touching* him. *Yuck.* I released him.

Jayden, why did you push me away? We could have been so good together ...

As his thoughts drifted off, I threw a desperate glance at Daniel. "What the—"

"Office romance?"

"Never. We competed over projects—and we still are, apparently. The S-O-B just pumped Silver for information on my files. He's a pest. We fought constantly, and he flirted outrageously with every woman he met. Well, except me."

"You felt left out?" He batted his eyelashes at me and puckered his lips. "Did you want kisses from Tommy?"

"Stop it." I swatted my hand in his direction, but he stepped out of my way and continued to wiggle fish lips at me.

I laughed, and if I had a body, it would have gotten to the bellyache and tears in my eyes point. "You're insane. Quit it. You're making me laugh at my funeral."

"Technically, this is the visitation. And I think you have unresolved Tom issues."

"Yes, I do. We dislike each other."

"Oh, honey, that's not what his thoughts implied. You denied your love because you thought you couldn't have him."

I glared at Daniel.

More people arrived—crowds of them. Had I known that many people?

Cousins, aunts, uncles, my sisters, my parents, more coworkers, neighbours, friends, my boss all trudged across the room to behold me in my waxen glory. Unashamedly, I eavesdropped on their thoughts.

Invasion of privacy or not, if the good Lord hadn't wanted me to listen, he wouldn't have given me the power.

"Way to justify it."

I rounded on him. "Pot. Kettle. Black."

"Yeah, and how do you like it?"

"I'm fine with it, or I'd block you."

He waved his hand at the crowd around us. "They don't know

you're listening, and they don't know how to block you."

I shrugged. "What are you, my conscience? Isn't this why I'm here? To say goodbye and to hear what they have to say about me? Why else would we be invisible? It's like having a super power. I intend to make full use of it."

Before she even stepped into the room, I sensed her: Erin Joanne Tremaine—EJ to her friends, and I used to be one. I'd stopped speaking to her when she joined some idiotic network marketing scam thing and tried to suck me into it. Worse still, she never supported my one-and-only attempt at running my own consulting business.

What was she doing here? She should know I wouldn't want to see her.

EJ entered the room, and all heads swiveled in her direction.

I had to admit, she looked youthful, stunning. Her black, tailored suit accentuated her slim figure. The purse she carried displayed a designer logo. Shiny, slim-heeled pumps showed off her shapely, muscular legs.

Behind me, Silver gasped.

Marc rushed to EJ's side. "Auntie EJ, I'm so glad you made it."

"Thank you for calling me, Marc. I appreciate it." Her voice broke when she said his name. They hugged, and then she turned to Silver, who had reached EJ's side.

"I'm so sorry, Silver. I've missed her so much, but I thought we had time to work things out."

Silver hugged my old friend and they exchanged a kiss on the cheek.

"Thank you for coming, Auntie EJ."

Hearing my kids calling her "auntie" choked me up. Had EJ really missed me? She'd seemed too busy with her new friends to bother with me after I'd told her I had no interest in her business.

"You missed her, too, didn't you?"

Damn that Daniel. Did he have to comment on everything?

"Yes," he replied to my unspoken question, "on everything that upsets you. It's too late for us to lie to ourselves. We're dead. Nothing petty matters anymore."

"How long did it take you to figure that out?" I asked, my tone sulky.

"Longer than I'd care to admit. That's why I'm not letting you do it. Don't make the mistakes I made." *It'll hold you here.*

I stared at him, eyes wide. I'd heard his thoughts.

He smiled. "I don't mind."

EJ made her way through the mourners milling around the room, nodding a greeting or exchanging condolences as she did. When she reached my coffin, she placed her hands lightly on the edge.

Oh, Jayden, I'm so sorry. I shouldn't have tried so hard to force my choices on you. Tears rolled down her cheeks, and she dug in her purse for a tissue.

"Here, EJ, let me help." Rory put a hand on her shoulder and held a tissue out to her with his other hand.

She accepted it, smiling thanks through her tears. "I can't believe she's gone, Rory. You and the kids must be devastated."

"I'm sure she's happy you came."

Hah! A lot he knew.

"You're lying to yourself again, Jayden."

"I'm not," I said, but it lacked conviction. He was right. *Oh, God, EJ, your absence was a cavernous hole in my life. What was wrong with me?*

As I reflected on all the time we'd wasted, EJ and I sobbed side-by-side. We were together again, but she'd never know it.

***

At two-twenty, staff directed everyone to the chapel. A song played over the audio system—a new age song called "Find that Place." Lois, my spiritual-minded sister must have selected it. She'd played it at one of our girls' weekends, saying Mark Watson, the artist, had channeled Archangel Michael when writing it. The melody and the words moved me more than I would've expected.

From behind the priest, Daniel and I watched my now closed casket float down the aisle on the shoulders of Marc, Rory, two of Marc's friends, Silver, and Silver's boyfriend Harrison Knight.

Why hadn't Harrison shown up at the hospital, and why hadn't he arrived early to the visitation? Silver and Harrison had been dating since they were both fifteen. They'd attended elementary and high school together. In a year, they'd head to college or university—not necessarily together, so maybe that was the problem.

Was it possible they'd already broken up? Oh, God, that would explain her anger the other night. And what did I do? Screamed at her to rinse her stupid cup.

Harrison, too, seemed anxious and sad—and it wasn't entirely due to my untimely demise. Without hesitation, I tapped into his thoughts.

How long am I supposed to give her? She has to talk to me. This can't go on.

After more of that kind of uninformative rambling, I switched to Silver.

I'm so scared. I want my mom. Why did she have to leave me now?

A hand on my shoulder had me turning to Daniel.

"Something's terribly wrong with Silver, Daniel. I should have known."

"A spat with her boyfriend?"

"No." I had a horrible, sinking feeling in what used to be the pit of my stomach. "She's in trouble. I have to find out what happened."

"Better be quick, then, because you shouldn't stay after tomorrow."

"I'm not—"

The priest interrupted me.

The casket had been set on its stand in front of the altar. The service was about to begin.

CHAPTER 9

Imagine you're at your funeral, people crying, everyone saying wonderful things about you. Your children break down as they begin to speak but then pull themselves together and tell story after story that shines you in a glorious light. You're their hero, their role model. You've made them the wonderful people they are.

Then imagine you had no idea about all this before you died, and you'll understand how I felt observing my funeral service.

The priest didn't get me all choked up—he didn't know me. Me and mine weren't church-going people. I hadn't believed in God. Last I checked, the Earth was still a cold, cruel place. People still tortured one another. No loving being would allow that on his or her watch. Nothing the priest said moved me, though his words offered comfort to many who listened.

But when my children spoke, my heart absorbed their words, imprinting them into my soul for eternity.

Silver talked about her childhood and then her adolescence.

"Mommy," she said, searing me with the word. "I love you. If you can hear me, I want you to know that I want to be the kind of mother to my children that you were to me: generous, caring, loving, beautiful. You made us feel loved, cherished. Because of you, I'm strong enough to carry on no matter what. Thank you."

Marc promised to take care of his sister no matter what.

Rory spoke and also promised to give extra love and support to Silver no matter what.

I understood then that whatever had happened to Silver, her

brother and her father knew.

"Oh, God, Daniel," I said. "What has she done?"

***

After the service, Daniel and I popped over to the cemetery to await the mourners who would attend the burial. I'd be buried in the Newmarket Cemetery in a family plot. The hole in the ground, already dug, waited for my casket. Artificial grass dressing and coco matting surrounded the hole, and the lowering device was in place. Staff from the funeral parlor had transported the wreaths and bouquets from the funeral home and placed them around the site.

As the funeral *cortège* arrived and the pallbearers carried my casket to its place above the hole, I scanned the cemetery to distract myself.

I'd always loved this cemetery, a restful oasis in the middle of Newmarket. Some of the trees were over a hundred years old, and many of the headstones identified citizens who had lived in the town from as far back as the early 1800s.

My breath caught when I spotted a couple watching me, both dressed in 19th century garb. The guy's suit included a waistcoat and the woman's dress had a bustle. They gave me a friendly wave and vanished.

With a little concentration, I adapted my outfit to match the woman's. Because I had no idea what I was doing, her version of the skirt part was poofier than mine.

Must be the undergarments. I'd stuck with a bra and panties. It was all I knew.

Daniel jogged my arm, which I felt as a weird sense of pressure. "What are you doing?"

"Testing something out." I flipped back to my original attire and then changed my mind. I probably should have worn something more modest at the start of the visitation, but I wasn't thinking about my clothes back then.

This time, I selected a navy sleeveless dress that stopped above the knee. I envisioned it as linen without the wrinkles. A loop of pearls appeared around my throat. Pearl earrings dangled from my ears. Navy high-heel pumps rounded out the ensemble.

In life, I'd always worn flats. In the spirit world, where shoes don't pinch, I could wear the highest heels with impunity. Death has its perks.

People filed slowly from their cars and shuffled towards my cemetery plot. Judging by the line of cars streaming up the small roadway, this would take a while.

"Show me your gravesite?" I asked Daniel.

He slanted a look in my direction, and I couldn't read it.

"What?" I asked.

"Why do you want to see that?"

"Why don't you want to show me? You're buried here, aren't you?"

Daniel nodded.

"And anyone can go see it, right?"

He nodded again.

"Please, take me there?"

After a brief hesitation, he hooked his arm through mine. "All right."

We popped out near the front of the cemetery. A large, grey headstone loomed before us. It reminded me of a bishop from a chess game standing on a stone box. *Bowes* was carved into the base on each of the four sides.

Daniel's name, birthdate, and death date were carved into the west-facing side. A wreath of flowers with a ribbon on it, "loving son" stenciled in gold across the front, graced the plot.

When I gasped at the size of it, Daniel shook his head.

"See? Ostentatious. They spent a fortune on it."

"Your family was wealthy?"

"Still is. My nephew owns the business now. It's a multi-national corporation."

I considered for a moment. "Bowes and Sons. You're *that* Bowes?"

"Yes. An extra room on every home. My dad tried to do for home renovations what Bill Gates did for personal computers." He smiled. "Damn near succeeded. It almost killed him when I told him I wanted to be a mechanic instead."

"Why wouldn't you want to be part of the family business?"

"I hated the corporate grind. Cars were my passion—working on them, tinkering with them. Maybe I wouldn't have minded working in the business in the beginning when he still worked with his hands and built things. But he wanted me to go to business school and work at corporate headquarters in Toronto. That's not me."

"Were you into drugs?"

He put an arm around me. "I smoked dope with my buddies. Mostly, I drank."

When he didn't say anything else, I put an arm around him. "We'd better get back. They're about to bury me."

He chuckled. You don't get to say that every day.

***

We returned to my grave. The casket was on the metal and strap supports over the hole in the ground. Everyone had assembled around it.

Out of the corner of my eye, I spotted a man in jeans and a light jacket walking amongst the rows of headstones. He carried a watering can and sprinkled water over a grave. Something about him seemed familiar, and, with fear punching through my gut, I recognized the man from the hospital waiting room.

I tapped into his thoughts. He was watching Bernie, Laurel, and Thomas. His main interest was Thomas, and when the service here ended, that's who he'd follow out of the cemetery grounds.

What the hell was going on at work? What did it have to do with me? I'd had a heart attack. Hadn't I? The paranoia returned full force, and I wondered if somehow I'd been murdered.

But how could that be? I had no enemies, hadn't done anything wrong. Could it have been poison?

The priest was speaking, praying over the coffin, and, struggling to shake off the horror of my thoughts, I tuned into his words.

My mother must have insisted on the priest. If it made her feel better and believe I wasn't roasting in hell because of it, then so what? It couldn't hurt.

Silver's thoughts cut through my musings.

Oh, God, he'll want to talk when this is over. Mom, how can I tell Harry I'm having his baby? How can I wreck his future?

"She's pregnant!"

Daniel whirled around at my shriek, and Marc's bowed head snapped up as if he'd heard me, but no one else moved. The priest continued to talk, oblivious.

I went to Silver's side and tried to hold her in my arms. My attempt failed, and I fell through her, landing with my body engulfed up to the waist by the coffin. I thought my way out to stand next to Daniel.

"She can't hear you, Jayden."

"I know!" Again, it came out a shriek. "But I want to hold my baby. She's my baby, and she's going to have a baby."

My grandchild. Silver carried my grandchild, a child I'd never meet, never hold in my arms. Icy fingers of fear traced a path up my spine. How would she cope without me? What if something went wrong? I wouldn't be around to help her.

Daniel put his arm around my shoulder. "Don't even think about staying. You have to leave. The more you involve yourself with mortal life, the lower your vibration, and then you'll be stuck here."

"Like you."

He nodded. "Like me."

"You seem to enjoy it."

A sigh puffed out of him. "Seem being the operative word."

"Don't you?"

"I do ..."

When he trailed off, I rested my head on his shoulder. "Are you tired of it?"

"No," he said. "I'm not ready to leave yet. But that's not the point. You shouldn't stay."

Around us, people talked about me and wept, but it barely registered. All I could think about was Silver and her baby and how they'd have to live without me.

"You're saying there's no way for you to leave?"

"I'm saying, I can't leave without help."

I contemplated that for a moment. "You can get help to cross?"

He averted his eyes. "I don't want it."

"Why? Why is it okay for you to stay but not for me? You're not so special."

"Neither are you." He grasped my arms. "Everyone goes. Do you want to watch Silver grow old and die and cross over where you can't follow? Her baby, too?"

"I'd rather they had me with them through this hell they call life." I was angry now. How was this fair? Why couldn't I see my grandbaby born? Why couldn't I watch him or her grow up? The baby would never know Grandma Jayden. How was that fair to the baby?

"You're not thinking straight."

"No? Because in my opinion, I'm thinking clearly for the first time since I kicked the bucket. Why can't I stay here and then raise my vibration again when I want to leave?"

"Okay. How would you do that?"

I didn't reply. Instead, I watched Rory step up to my coffin and stroke the shiny wood.

"Goodbye, Jayden. I love you. I'll take good care of our kids." He stepped away, and Silver took his place.

She touched the coffin. "Bye, Mommy. I'll miss you. I love you." Tears poured down her cheeks.

"I can't leave them. Don't you see?" I pleaded with him—a pointless gesture, considering he couldn't force me to leave. For some reason, I wanted his approval.

Marc stood in Silver's place.

"I love you, Mom. I know you can hear us. Don't worry. We'll be fine. Rest in peace."

"No." I shook my head. "No, Daniel, don't make me go." With pleading eyes and hands clasped together under my chin, my body language mimicked my tone.

He refused to meet my gaze.

Slowly, my friends, my family, my coworkers all milled past my coffin. Each had a message for me; some said a few words out loud, others talked to me in their thoughts. All said goodbye.

"No, please. It's not goodbye. I'm here." But I wouldn't be for much longer.

Suzanne had warned me not to stay more than three days after the funeral. Daniel insisted the same. Why did I have to leave if I could still return to visit?

"Right." He'd read my thoughts again, and I felt a prickle of annoyance. "You'll be able to return and visit. People do that."

"But?" There had to be a catch, otherwise, Daniel would have left when he'd had the chance.

He frowned. "You can pop in to visit a loved one, but you can't hang around them. The dead aren't meant to stay in the world of the living."

"I'm not leaving until I know Silver and her baby will be okay."

"Marc and Rory both said they'd take care of her. Silver told you she'd be fine."

"What does she know? She's eighteen. Kids that age think

they're invincible. Anything can happen." But it wasn't just Silver that had me considering staying. What if I'd been murdered?

I glanced at Daniel. He hadn't reacted to my thoughts. My shielding had worked.

Everyone was leaving, saying goodbye, giving their final condolences to my children, my parents. My mother had looked stricken from the moment she'd arrived at the viewing; my father looked hollow-eyed and shell-shocked.

How would it feel to bury my child? They were living every parent's nightmare, and I hadn't spent any time with them. I had more to do, damn it.

"My point," Daniel said, dragging me back to the conversation, "is that Silver is confident she can manage. She's okay. She's letting you go."

I rounded on him. "I'll decide when to leave. Silver doesn't know I'm still with her. She thinks I've disappeared to some etheric place where everything is unicorns and rainbows or nothingness."

"Oh, I don't know. Maybe she thinks you're in hell," he said with a grin.

Tears rolled down my cheeks. Awareness of them dried my eyes. I swiped at the wet trail with my hand, but it had already disappeared without a trace simply at my wish.

"Was that supposed to be a joke?"

He lost his grin. "I'm sorry. I wanted to lighten things up. Everything will be okay. Silver will be fine. Trust me."

When I didn't reply, he said, with hope in his voice, "I'll be here."

"What?" I didn't understand. Was he saying he'd keep an eye on my family? Why? We were nothing to him.

"Not nothing, Jayden. Never that." He put an arm around me.

A change in the air pressure signaled the opening of the tunnel. I shook off Daniel's arm and backed away from the swirling mist forming near me.

"No," I screamed, "not now."

CHAPTER 10

The tunnel entrance yawned before me, a hazy, black shadow—a portal to another plane.

"You see the tunnel, don't you?" Daniel scanned the area around me, but if his gaze found the portal, he gave no sign of it.

"Can't you see it?" I replied.

He shook his head. "It's lost to me. That's why you have to go. It's not forever." His gaze met mine, and he had tears in his eyes as well. "Just for a while. Then you can visit."

"I don't have to leave yet."

"The sooner the better. Go." He clasped my hand.

"I can't. Not yet." I pulled away from him. Focusing on Silver, I followed her thoughts to our home, leaving Daniel at the cemetery.

***

Silver was in her room with Harrison. They sat on the edge of her bed, both wearing agonized expressions.

"What is it, Silver? Tell me. What's on your mind? Whatever it is, I can help."

She kissed his cheek. "I wish you didn't know me so well."

He laughed softly. "Honey, we were friends first, remember? I can always read you." He put his arm around her, pulled her close, and stroked her hair. "You've been pushing me away, and I've tried to be patient. It's not because your mom died. You've been moody for days. I love you. What's wrong?"

Her body shook as the tears burst from her in wracking sobs.

"It's bad, Harry. I don't know how to tell you."

Fear washed over his face, and he tightened his grip on her. When he spoke, his voice was filled with anxiety, though he tried to keep it light. "How bad can it be?"

"I'm pregnant. That's how bad it can be."

Harry kissed the top of her head before he spoke again. "Are you sure?"

"Yes. Do you think I wouldn't verify?" Her words came out clipped with anger. "The doctor confirmed it. I'm eight weeks along."

"How is that possible?" Before she could respond, he said, "You're on the pill. Right?"

She averted her gaze to study the floor. "Remember when I had that chest infection and took antibiotics?"

"Yes."

"I didn't read the warnings. Apparently, it can cause the pill to be ineffective if you take them together." She moaned. "It's my stupidity, Harry. I messed up."

Harrison rose and paced the room, silently. After three back-and-forths, he planted himself in front of her. "Why didn't you tell me when you first suspected?"

Silver lifted her gaze to him, her eyes wide and her lips quivering. "I didn't want to worry you.'

With a strangled oath, Harrison snatched her off the bed into his arms. "Don't you trust me? We made this baby together. We'll deal with it together." He released her and turned away, anger clouding his handsome face.

His hands balled into fists, and when he stalked to the wall next to Silver's dresser, I thought he intended to punch it. All he did was collapse against it, as if he needed it to hold him up.

"God, Silver. What am I supposed to think? News this huge—a burden this huge—and you didn't share it with me."

My sweet girl took two hesitant steps towards him.

The urge to take her in my arms and comfort her had me going to her, but my stupid, incorporeal arms shot right through hers. Wailing in frustration, helpless to do more than watch the drama unfold, I faced them.

She'd reached out her hand but had stopped short of touching Harrison.

VAL TOBIN

"I'm sorry." She choked on a sob. "I was so scared. And then I had a fight with my mom. Harrison, I killed her."

Oh, God, how her words seared my soul.

"No, baby," I said. "No. You can't believe that."

Harrison did what I couldn't. He scooped her into his arms, raining kisses on her hair, her cheeks. "Baby, no. Of course you didn't. Why would you say that?"

She nodded emphatically. "I did. You weren't there. She only wanted me to rinse my stupid cup, and I yelled at her. I was horrible to her. If I hadn't picked a fight with her, she'd still be alive."

"Your dad said the doctor told him it would have happened sooner or later."

Silver pulled away from him, screaming out her agony. "I want later. Not sooner. Later! She can't be gone. I need my mama." She crumpled to the bed.

Harrison rushed to her, pulling her to him once again. "Shh. We'll be okay. I promise."

"How? The baby will be born before I can finish high school. You have to go to university."

"First things first, Silver. We have to tell our families."

"Dad and Marc already know."

Harrison stiffened. "You told them before you told me?" His tone held reserved rage and hurt.

"I had to. Marc saw me throwing up and Dad, well, I needed my dad. My mom had just died, Harry. I only told them yesterday." She raised pleading eyes to him. "I can only say I'm sorry."

The fight went out of his eyes then, and he slumped against her. They sat, shoulder to shoulder, not speaking.

Finally, Harrison broke the silence. "We have to tell my parents, too."

"I know. We'll do it together."

"I should have been with you when you told your family." The words were accusatory, but his tone was mild. He tucked a strand of her hair behind her ear. "What did they say when you told them?"

Yes, what had they said? I pictured Rory wanting to go for a shotgun, which we don't own, thank God. Marc would have been sympathetic but slightly detached. He was studying engineering. Logic, to him, was everything. He'd have been practical, offering

586

advice.

"You know Marc. He's full of wisdom. I had to ask him to stop dishing out advice, but I promised we'd talk to him together when we figured things out. My dad looked so disappointed in me it broke my heart. On top of Mom dying, now he has to deal with a pregnant teenage daughter. I've ruined his life." She pressed in close against Harrison, and he tucked her under his arm.

"You haven't ruined his life. It's a baby. His grandchild."

"You're talking like you think we'll have the baby and keep it."

Harrison and I both gasped. Surely, she wasn't suggesting …

"Silver, what do you want to do?" He held his breath and waited for her to answer.

"I …" she closed her eyes. "We … could have it. Raise it." She opened her eyes, and they were pleading. "You don't have to feel obligated to—"

He cut her off. "To what? Have anything to do with it? It's my baby, too, isn't it?"

That last was said spitefully. When she jerked away from him, he grabbed her arm.

"I'm sorry. That was unfair." He released her. "I'm hurt, Silver. I've loved you for as long as I can remember. There's been no one else."

The term "childhood sweethearts" didn't do Silver and Harrison's relationship justice. From the moment they'd met, it was as if they continued a relationship from a previous life. Maybe that was the truth of it.

But to bring a child into the world and raise it together at eighteen? Someone needed to talk sense into them. Silver wouldn't even have me there to help her. She'd be alone.

When Marc was born, Rory and I had been married for a year. It had still been one of the most difficult experiences of my life. Marc and Silver were both planned. What would an unexpected baby do to Silver's life? She'd be affected the most.

While I'd always loved Harrison and was thrilled he was so supportive, his body wouldn't be the one to change. He wasn't the one who'd have to interrupt his education and give birth and breastfeed.

Oh, Silver, what have you two done?

Behind me, the portal hovered, waiting for me to step through. How could I possibly leave now?

CHAPTER 11

"Jayden." Daniel's voice intruded into my thoughts.

Unable to hide my annoyance, I snapped at him. "Why did you follow me?"

"Because I won't let you trap yourself here. Yell at me, hate me, but cross over."

I thrust my face into his. "What's it to you? You've been following me, interfering in my life—death—whatever. Why are you doing this?"

His gaze remained steady. "What difference does it make? Appreciate that I care and take my advice: leave."

"I'm staying with her." I tilted my head and smiled coyly. "You could use the company, couldn't you? You've been alone for decades."

He sighed, though when you're dead, everything sounds like it's riding on a sigh.

"What I could use isn't the priority here. If you don't go, you'll regret it. I'm trying to spare you that."

"Thanks, but I lost the need to be rescued when I was still alive. She's my daughter, and she's in trouble." I glanced at him. "If you had a daughter, you'd understand."

Up until this point, he'd held my gaze with a solid, confident glare. Now, he looked away.

"What is it?" But I knew. "You had a daughter." My voice held wonder. "Didn't you?"

"Yes," Daniel whispered. "My girlfriend was pregnant when I

died."

"You stayed to be near your girlfriend and your child."

His eyes betrayed his agony. "That's why I can tell you it's not worth it. They die. Everyone dies. Which side of the curtain do you want to be on when they cross over? Here?" he scoffed. "Great. You see them for two, maybe three days. Then they move on, and you lose them all over again."

"Daniel," I said, my voice low, "when they're dead, they'll be okay. It's when they're alive that they need me." I offered him my hand, and he accepted it, linking us together.

He was shaking his head, but whatever more he wanted to say would have to wait. I turned away from him to attend to Silver once more.

She and Harrison lay on her bed, arms around each other. Silver's head rested on his shoulder, her hair obscuring her face. Harrison swept the lock to the side with gentle fingers and tucked it behind her ear.

"We could get a family unit at university. You'll have the baby by then."

"I won't be able to finish high school."

"Of course you can. We can do it." Excitement tinged his voice. "Your dad said your mom left you an inheritance. Use it to fund your education."

"I can't go to school if I have an infant."

"We'll make it work. Even if you did some classes part-time or online. I'll be there to help you."

"You're jumping ahead, Harry. I have to get through the pregnancy first. What do you think will happen at school when they find out I'm knocked up?"

"This isn't the 1950s. No one will condemn you."

She sat up, and when he tried to tug her back, she rose and strode across the room to her dresser. A square, white jewelry box sat on top of a crocheted doily. Silver picked it up and opened it. The ballerina popped up and twirled while "Lara's Song" played. Silver poked it with her finger.

Her gaze fixed on the spinning doll, Silver said, "I know, Harry. But it'll be difficult. I'll be a curiosity at best. At worst, I'll be judged. As my belly gets bigger, I'll feel exposed."

"Who cares?"

She snapped the lid of the box closed, cutting off the music and smushing the dancing figure back down. "I do. It's not even the other students I'm worried about. The teachers will judge me."

"They're adults. If they can't understand your situation, they shouldn't be teachers."

"They might not even let me continue to attend school."

"Now you're jumping ahead. We can speculate all we want, but we need to talk to someone about this. Come on." He stood. "Let's go tell my parents. They can help us." He paused as if a thought occurred to him. "What was your dad's advice?"

I moved to stand beside her, itching to hold her. Rory wasn't known for his tact. If he hurt her, damn it, I'd haunt him.

"He tried to be helpful, but he was in shock." She gave Harrison that pleading look again. "I blurted it out, and he said I should have an abortion."

Nice, I thought. Great advice to give a confused, scared young woman.

"How did you react?"

"Well, I'd considered it. Hearing my dad say it made me realize I can't. Besides, you didn't know yet. I wanted to hear what you thought."

"What if I told you to do it?"

"Do you want me to?"

"No." He pried the jewelry box from her fingers and set it back down on the dresser. "Never."

"Then we're okay," she said with amazement.

He smiled, and, holding hands, they left.

***

The harassing started as soon as Silver and Harrison stepped out the door.

"You have to go now. She's going to be fine."

I snarled—an eerie sound. It was a shame no one I disliked was around to get a fright from it. "She's not fine yet. We'll see what happens with Harry's parents. If they upset her, I'm going to rattle chains in the night and spook them."

He laughed, and it actually sounded like a real laugh. "You talk a big game."

I laughed along with him.

"I'm not bluffing." My expression sobered. "If they hurt her, I'll make them sorry."

"Were you always this vengeful?"

I shrugged. "No one has the right to hurt my kids. If they do, they pay."

"Your friend EJ didn't hurt your kids. They looked happy to see her."

"So?"

"Seems like you were punishing her for something, too."

A lump grew in my throat as I remembered all that had cost me. "None of your business."

"When you go out of your way to hurt someone else, you only cause yourself pain."

"Too late for that, isn't it?" Bitterness permeated every word.

"That proves you need to leave. They heal you on the other side." He waved in the direction of the portal.

I ignored his claim about healing. "You can see it?"

He shook his head. "I know where it appears in relation to you."

The doorbell interrupted our conversation. I popped outside the front door to see who was there.

Thomas. He held a sealed cardboard box in his arms. What in the blue blazes did he want?

Marc opened the door, and a look of puzzlement crossed his face. "Hello?"

Thomas balanced the box on one arm and held out his other hand. "Thomas Devereaux. I worked with your mother."

"I remember you from the funeral, Mister Devereaux."

"Tom, please."

Marc nodded. "Okay. What can I do for you, Tom?"

"Sorry to show up without calling. I was on my way home from work and thought I'd drop off your mother's personal belongings."

He'd rooted through my desk. Why would Laurel let him paw through my stuff when she knew I didn't trust him and couldn't stand him?

"Is your sister here?"

Marc shook his head. "She just left."

"Mind if I come in for a moment?"

"Okay." Marc accepted the box from Thomas. "Can I offer you a drink or a coffee?"

My polite boy. "You don't have to offer him squat, Marc."

For a moment, Marc's expression showed surprise. My heart skipped a beat. Had he heard me?

The moment passed, and Marc stepped away from the entrance to let Thomas in the house.

"Coffee, if you're having a cup," Thomas replied.

The two went into the kitchen. After setting the box on the kitchen table, Marc went through the motions of preparing the coffee.

When had he learned how to do that? Did he even like coffee? There were so many tidbits I didn't know about my children.

"You know the important things."

"Why are you still here, Daniel?"

"To help you."

I let that comment slide as Thomas, sitting at the kitchen table, spoke to Marc. "Your mom will be missed at the office."

He'd said that at the visitation. Was the one and only Thomas Devereaux nervous? If so, it made me edgy. The man was pompous and arrogant. Nothing and no one made him nervous. What was he up to?

"Thank you." Marc leaned against the marble countertop by the coffee maker and crossed his arms, waiting.

"All her personal things are in that box."

Another pointless statement. Something was definitely up.

"Thank you for bringing them."

"Did your mom ever talk about me?"

I glanced at Daniel, who showed no reaction. Of course, he wouldn't react. He didn't suspect Thomas could be after something.

Marc shrugged. "Not that I recall. Should she have?" He squinted at Thomas, frowning. "Was there a problem with her work?"

Behind Marc, the coffee maker rumbled to completion. My son hunted in the cupboard for mugs as Thomas rose from his chair. Sunlight spilled in from the window above the sink, haloing around Thomas.

The glow around him that I'd seen around everyone since I'd died darkened to black.

"What the hell is that around Thomas?"

Daniel's reply sent a chill through me. "His aura turned black. He's going to die."

CHAPTER 12

"What do you mean Thomas will die? He can't." My head spun as I tried to grasp what I'd heard.

"Everyone dies."

That sounded callous. Sure, Thomas annoyed me, but I didn't want him to die—and not just because he was too young. For the love of God, would I have to put up with him in the afterlife now?

"You probably don't have to worry about it. He'll no doubt cross when he's supposed to."

"When will he die?" I tried to focus on the truly horrible part of it—Thomas's imminent death.

"Soon, or his aura wouldn't be black."

"Is there a way to find out how?"

Daniel shook his head. "No. We're dead not psychic."

Marc and Thomas had fixed their coffees and moved into the living room. Daniel and I followed. Marc sat on the couch, while Thomas reclined on the chaise, his feet up.

"He's in my seat, and he never took off his shoes when he came in the house." I gave a low growl. "I know how he dies—I kill him myself."

"You secretly have the hots for him, don't you?" Daniel swiped a hand through the hair at the back of my neck.

"Cut it out." I swatted him away. To think that yesterday I'd been unable to touch anything. To think that four days ago, I'd been alive …

Thomas cut into my thoughts. "Did your mother talk about her work at all? Anything that went on at the office?"

"Not really," Marc replied. "Sometimes she mentioned if she had a difficult project. She avoided talking about work—legally couldn't anyway. You never answered my question before. Did something happen with her work?"

"No, but I'm supposed to take over the project she hadn't completed. I can't find her notes."

"They're on my external drive at work where they're supposed to be." I shouted it at Marc, who flinched.

"He hears me."

Daniel didn't have a chance to reply as Marc spoke. "She never brought anything home. She only has her personal files here."

"Are you sure?"

"Yes. Did you check her hard drive at work?"

Thomas gave Marc a frustrated look. "That was the first place I checked. Has anyone else been here asking about her files?"

"No."

"I'm sorry, Marc. This is important, or I wouldn't ask, but would you let me search her computer?"

"Don't let him." I whirled from Marc to Thomas. "Keep your greedy mitts off my computer."

"There's no point. They don't let employees take sensitive files out of the office."

"No, they don't. But I thought perhaps—"

Marc cut him off. "She wouldn't have disobeyed company policy."

"No." Thomas sounded doubtful. "I'm sorry to have bothered you." His eyes betrayed disappointment as he set his mug down and stood. "Thank you for the coffee."

Marc rose as well. "I'm sorry I couldn't help you."

Thomas considered for a moment. "Would you search her computer for a file if I give you the name?"

"Sure." Marc retrieved a pen and paper from the drawer in the coffee table, and Thomas scribbled down the file name.

I peeked over their shoulders. *Prj211*.

"It's on my computer at work."

So why hadn't Thomas found it?

***

Since Marc didn't have my password, he had to assure Thomas he'd figure out a way to access the computer. After some polite discussion, Thomas left.

Frustrated at having lost the ability to pace—popping in and out of locations is fun, but there's nothing like walking off a problem—I trained my thoughts on Thomas. I traced him to his car and settled beside him in the passenger seat.

He looked good—healthy. How close to death was he? Would a physical issue kill him? He wasn't much older than I was when I dropped dead. How could two of us so young and from the same office suddenly die?

This wasn't a coincidence.

I'd signed a confidentiality agreement for the project and hadn't breathed a word about it to anyone not directly involved with it. Interesting that Thomas was searching for it at my home. Uneasiness fluttered in my gut, but disappeared when Daniel distracted me.

He materialized, a transparent figure already talking, in the backseat. "You planning to follow him around? It's getting late."

"Yes." Maybe we could prevent Thomas's death somehow.

"We can try, but if it's his time, he's going to cross."

"Have you tried to stop a death?" He'd been here long enough, maybe he'd had some success.

"Sure. My daughter, for one." His voice cracked, and he took a long pause. "I failed."

I swiveled in my seat so I could meet his gaze. "I'm sorry. How old was she when she passed?"

"Ten."

"Oh, Daniel. I'm very sorry. How did she die?"

He averted his gaze. "Pneumonia."

"My cousin Suzanne died of pneumonia." A coincidence? "Who are you? Tell me the truth."

"Suzanne's biological father. I'm your uncle—or would have been if I'd married Grace."

"Aunt Gracie was your girlfriend?" Stunned, I tried to recall everything I knew about Gracie and Suzanne. And Charles, Suzanne's father—or the man she'd always called "Dad."

"Did Gracie ever tell Suzanne who her real father was?"

"No. I waited for her to—I even tried to communicate with Grace through a psychic. Nothing worked. She refused to reveal her guilty secret."

"Why?"

"Shame, probably. It was the sixties. They weren't forgiving then to young women who were pregnant and unmarried. She did a great job of raising Suzanne alone until meeting Charles when Suzanne was two. They married shortly after. Charles is the only father Suzanne ever knew."

"Oh, Daniel." My heart broke for this sweet man. My uncle. "So now you're looking after everyone in the family?" I frowned. "That's why you'd be willing to watch over Silver."

He nodded without looking up. When he raised his head, he gave me a sheepish grin. "She's my grand-niece, or something like that. I'll watch over her. You can cross."

I shook my head, making up my mind. "No, especially not now. We both stay or we both go. I'm not crossing without you."

He argued, of course, but I refused to cave. "You've been stuck here by yourself long enough, and if anyone will watch over my child, it'll be me."

"Were you always this stubborn?"

"Were you?"

He laughed that hearty laugh I'd heard before, and it eased the tension.

I faced front again and checked our surroundings. The car was pulling into a driveway in the Stonehaven subdivision. Thomas lived in one of the more ostentatious homes in this prestigious section of town.

A fountain stood in the middle of the circular driveway, a naked cherub peeing into a fish's mouth. Lights illuminated the water, the walkway, and the front of the house. Hedge animals watched any visitor's progress up the white marble walkway. Round, white steps led up to the black, double front doors. Gargoyles perched on stone pedestals on either side of the entrance. All of it looked hideously expensive.

"How much does he get paid?" There's no way he should've been able to afford a place here on one salary.

"You can't rule out inheritance," Daniel said.

"No. But you also can't rule out unequal pay. Or shady dealings." For the first time, I examined the vehicle we were riding in. A Volkswagen Jetta, fairly new, but not indicative of an affluent lifestyle.

"He never flashed money around. Yeah, he dressed well, but never flaunted wealth." I glanced at his suit. If it was designer, I wouldn't have recognized it. Menswear had never interested me.

"Ready?" I asked as Thomas eased the car into a bay in the four-car garage. "We're going in."

CHAPTER 13

By the time Thomas unlocked his front door and let himself into the house, Daniel and I were waiting for him. The inside of the house was as gaudy as the outside. The carpet in the main foyer, hallway, and leading up the stairs was red plush. The paintings displayed on the walls swirled with abstract patterns of colour.

"He should have hired a decorator. He's obviously got the money for it." I stuck my tongue out to show my distaste.

"Oh, I don't know." Daniel ran a hand down the black enamel bannister. "It's kind of ..." He cocked his head at me, raising his brows as he trailed off.

"Yeah, it kind of is." I grinned. "Can you imagine him bringing women back here? They'd probably think he was a serial killer."

"Or that he was loaded, had bad taste, and they could redecorate as soon as they had a ring on their finger."

I laughed. "You'd have been a fun uncle. I wish I'd known you."

He sobered at that. "Thank you. I'm sorry I didn't look in on you more often."

That piqued my curiosity. "Did you? Sometimes?"

"Sure. I attended your wedding. You had a pretty good life. No big problems." He put a hand on my arm. "I was with you through your divorce. I tried to get you to see a psychic then, maybe give you some reassurance from the spirit world. But you're so damn stubborn and so skeptical, you refused to acknowledge any of the signs I tried to send you."

"You were there?" I tried to think back to that time in my life. It had been difficult, but I'd survived by focusing on my children and my work. "Thank you. I'm sorry I refused to see. I didn't know." That last had a defensive sound to it. How could I have known? My beliefs limited me to the physical plane.

"Suzanne popped in on you then, too. So did your grandparents."

"Did they …" The words were difficult to say, but I had to ask. "Did they know you? Is Suzanne aware you're here?"

"Yes."

"Then why doesn't she help you?" Anger made me shout the words. What was wrong with all those dead people? Couldn't they rescue him?

"They would if they could. Don't blame them for the consequences of a decision I made."

Our quarry had disappeared into the kitchen, so we followed him. While Thomas fixed himself some dinner, Daniel and I continued our conversation.

"I'm not blaming them," I said. "But there has to be a way. You can't be stuck here forever. That's not fair."

He smiled. "I got to meet you, so it's worth it."

"I'm glad we met, too, but I'd have been willing to give that up if you could've crossed years ago."

Daniel shrugged. "Maybe things were meant to happen this way."

I snorted. "I've always hated when people said that. Meant to be? Are murders, tortures, rapes—all brutality—meant to be?"

"I don't know. We're dead, not—"

"Psychic. So you said."

Thomas's cell phone juddered, interrupting us. He retrieved it from the holster on his belt. "Tom Devereaux … Oh, hi, Marc … Okay, thanks for trying. It was a longshot. At least this proves she didn't take files home … Yeah, I appreciate it. Goodnight." He disconnected and clipped the phone back on his belt.

The microwave sounded, and he removed from it a plate piled high with some vegetarian pasta dish. He set the dish of food on the table and retrieved a wrapped salad and a bottle of wine from the fridge.

The wine was a pinot grigio, and the sight of it made my mouth water—an exciting sensation under the circumstances. After pouring some into a crystal goblet, Thomas tested the clarity against the white tablecloth and sipped. He smacked his lips and sipped again.

"Here." Daniel held out a glass of wine.

"What?" I asked, astonishment dripping from the single word.

He laughed. "You're drooling. Here's a glass of your own."

I accepted it without another word and sipped. The cool liquid slid down my throat, refreshing it. What a marvel. We could eat and drink? How was that possible? Which of the dozens of questions springing to mind should I ask first?

"Daniel …"

"Here's the bottom line: Yes, we can eat and drink. No, we can't get drunk, won't gain weight, or any of the physical things that happen when you're alive. I manifested this out of energy, but it's as incorporeal as we are." He held up his hand and a lit cigarette appeared between his fingers. "Smoking won't harm me, either. We can't get sick. We can't die—we're already dead."

The smoke from his cigarette wafted under my nose. It smelled heavenly. I'd always liked the smell of cigarette smoke though I'd never smoked and avoided inhaling it second hand.

I glanced from Daniel to Thomas and back again.

"Will he smell that?"

"He might if he's sensitive or if his brain waves are in the right state. If he has a departed loved one who smoked this brand, he might think it's a visit from that person."

Thomas continued to eat his meal and sip his drink without any outward indication he sensed us. I enjoyed my own glass of wine as he ate.

"Why didn't you show me this sooner?" I asked with narrowed eyes.

"I didn't want to give you any incentive to stay."

"Drinking wasn't important to me when I was alive. I used to enjoy a glass of wine with dinner after a long day at work. This is nice."

"What are we doing here? We're watching a guy eat. He doesn't look in any danger."

"I didn't look in any danger either. Then I dropped dead." I contemplated what Thomas had said on the phone to my son. "I assumed Tom was taking over the project, but that doesn't make sense. If he'd taken over, he'd have been given the file."

"You think he's snooping?"

"Maybe. He used to snoop into my work. It drove me crazy. He'd find excuses to look over my shoulder. Or he'd volunteer to partner with me when projects were assigned, especially the ones with huge bonus potential—like my last one. That would explain why he and Laurel seem to be fighting over it like dogs over a chew toy." It occurred to me then that I could eavesdrop on his thoughts. "Give me a moment."

I focused on Thomas, opening up to receive whatever he was thinking.

Where's that damn file? Laurel must have taken it. Why not leave a copy on Jayden's hard drive? Has Laurel officially been assigned to take it over before I've even had a chance to make my case?

He rose and started clearing up his dishes, worrying over the file as he did.

She stole it. Laurel's so sure she's got the project, she swiped it. She was in Bernie's office for hours yesterday. He's given her the project.

"Have you been listening?" I asked Daniel.

"Yeah. Who's Bernie?"

"My boss. Why would he give Laurel the project? None of this makes sense. Thomas worked on it with me when an extra hand was required. He's familiar with it."

"You worked with him on it?"

"Not by choice. He was the one available."

"Is it a lucrative project?"

"Sure—for the company in revenues, and for the developer in bonuses and recognition."

"Must have been difficult to gather requirements."

"They sent a guy to liaise with me. He explained it, but he didn't tell me where he worked or what he did there."

"What was the project?"

"Data collection on whatever computer it was installed on. The data would then get sent to a server for processing. So, spyware. Also linked to wireless video and audio communication devices."

"Who were they spying on?"

"They didn't say. It's not my job to ask."

"Didn't you care?"

"All I was told was it was security software. If they lied to me, I didn't want to think about it." I gave a frustrated snort. "I minded my own business. You get used to keeping your mouth shut when you work with confidential, proprietary systems."

Daniel remained silent for a moment, watching Thomas dry his dishes and put them away. "Maybe Thomas pried into something dangerous."

"What do you mean?" However, I had a sick feeling and thought I knew. Had Thomas poked into this project, or another one as sensitive, and put himself at risk? "That's insane. Who'd murder a software developer?"

"Is that a rhetorical question?"

"That's not funny. He could be in danger." What had that idiot done? Had he no common sense? "We're assuming too much. He was only interested in taking over the project." But I couldn't stop thinking about all the times in the last few weeks that he'd peered over my shoulder, offered to help with testing, or in other ways insinuated himself into the project. He'd gone out of his way to be assigned to it as often as possible.

"He just wanted to work on it," I said, not certain if I was trying to convince Daniel or myself.

Dishes done, Thomas left the kitchen. I gave him a head start, tracing his path through the house. When he entered a bedroom on the second floor, I joined him, Daniel appearing beside me the moment I arrived.

The bedroom wasn't Thomas's. An elderly woman slept in the queen, four-poster bed. Red drapes, carpet, and velvet paper announced who'd done the decorating in this house.

"At least you know now that Thomas wasn't the one with the hideous taste," Daniel said.

"Don't count him out. We haven't seen his bedroom yet."

A woman in a nurse's uniform sat in a plush, black recliner, sipping a cup of tea. Knitting needles, a ball of yarn, and the beginnings of a scarf rested in her lap. She smiled a greeting at Thomas, and he nodded in acknowledgement.

"How was she today?" he asked, his voice a whisper.

"Fine. She sat up and read for a while."

Relief flooded his face. "That's great."

The nurse shook her head. "Her energy comes and goes. She's been asleep ever since she set down her book. I came in to sit with her until she woke up for her meds."

"Thank you. I've told you before it's not necessary to sit here when she sleeps."

"Aggie likes to see a friendly face when she wakes up, and it's my job to keep her happy."

"It's your job to take care of her, not to be her slave. You let her bully you." He spoke with affection, and he smiled indulgently, first at the nurse, and then at the woman in the bed who was obviously his mother.

In that moment, shame overwhelmed me. I'd worked with this man for four years. Never once had I asked him about his family. I hadn't cared what went on in his life or what burdens he had to bear. If I'd known he had a sickly mother to care for, I'd have been nicer to him.

"You think so?"

"I know so," I snapped at Daniel. "Obviously he has a heart. He never let me see it."

"Or you never let him show it to you."

"Are you saying it's my fault we didn't get along?"

"Are you denying it's your fault you didn't get along?"

I popped over to the bed and studied the old woman lying there. Her long, silver hair spread out on the pillow in waves. Tubes snaked from under the covers and into an IV stand. The blanket covered her up to her chin, hiding her body. The gaunt face and the slightness of the mound formed by her body told me she was not just thin but emaciated.

Cancer. It had to be.

"Her aura isn't black." I threw a puzzled gaze at Daniel.

"She's not going to die soon."

I looked over to where Thomas sat in an armchair next to the nurse. His aura surrounded him, black as ever.

"But Tom's is still black." I choked on the words. "We have to do something. His mother can't outlive him. We can't allow it."

"It's not up to us." Daniel's voice held compassion, his eyes, sorrow. "I'm sorry. In one, maybe two weeks, Thomas will be dead."

CHAPTER 14

Thomas's gentle laughter tugged me from the shock Daniel's words had induced. When I looked over, Thomas was patting the nurse's hand and assuring her she didn't have to remain in the room.

"Let her use the buzzer, Nora. You've done enough for one night."

"I'll give her another half hour. If she doesn't wake by then, I'll nudge her. She'll need her eight o'clock pills."

"All right." He rose and stretched, pressing his palms to his lower back. "I've got some work to do before I can relax. I'll be in my office."

Considering he shouldn't have work files here at home, I was interested to see what he planned to work on. While he kissed his mother's cheek, I got a bead on the location of his home office from his mind and popped on over. Daniel was only seconds behind me.

"What are you up to, Thomas?" I muttered, hovering over his desk. His computer monitor sat dark, the power bar underneath the desk switched off.

The office itself had a pleasant ambience. The walls were painted a neutral cream. A fireplace and recliner with floor lamp made a cozy reading nook in one corner, and a wet bar consumed half the east wall. An ergonomic leather chair faced a light oak desk clear of clutter.

"All the comforts of home," I said, envy tainting my voice.

My desk was always over-run with papers, stacks of books,

doodads and folderol, pens—half of them dry of ink—candles, and anything else I'd accumulated over the years that I'd needed or wanted close to me while playing around on my computer.

Most of my personal time on it was spent playing games, surfing the Net, writing, or studying. Tech skills had to be upgraded regularly or you risked falling behind. Thomas's desk showed no evidence he even used it. Impressive.

Bookcases lined the south wall. An examination revealed the books were mostly non-fiction.

"He has an interest in the paranormal." My voice betrayed shock.

"Why is that so strange?" Daniel asked.

"He's an engineer."

Daniel laughed. "So they can't believe in the paranormal?"

"He has a book on communicating with spirits. It's not very scientific."

"And yet, here we are."

To that, I had no response.

Thomas entered the room and went directly to the wet bar. He filled a kettle and plugged it in before striding to his desk and powering up the computer. When he opened the files he wanted to work on, I moved behind him and peered over his shoulder. For once, I would do the snooping.

He opened a journal.

"A diary," I said, answering the question Daniel had asked in his thoughts. "Maybe this'll tell me what's going on, otherwise, we may have to pay Laurel a visit."

He didn't reply, and his silence told me he wasn't thrilled with my plans.

"I have to know."

"I didn't say anything, Jayden."

"You didn't have to."

Another cigarette appeared in his hand, and he puffed on it. "I didn't even think anything."

"No. But whether you approve or not, we have to figure out what's going to kill Thomas. If it's preventable, I'll stop it."

When Daniel still refused to comment, I returned to scanning Thomas's file. Thankfully, the kettle shrieked then and he went to fix his tea. I wanted to read what was displayed before he scrolled away from it to begin today's entry.

September 30, 2016

Jayden wasn't in the office when I arrived this morning, which was highly unusual. She's always there before me. I wasn't concerned, assuming she had an appointment, but then Bernie called us all into the boardroom to tell us she'd had a heart attack and died.

I don't know how to handle this. She was a lovely woman—and I don't just mean her physical beauty, which she certainly had. When she was around, I wanted to be near her. I know I annoyed the hell out of her—she made that abundantly clear. But there was something about her that was gentle underneath and that I wanted to be around.

If only I hadn't spent so much time pestering her. But I knew she didn't like me, and it hurt, so I defaulted to arrogance. I loved telling her about the women I dated and treating her like one of the guys. Or hitting on her in ways that riled her.

I'll miss her and what might have been had we been different people.

The worst part is, she'll never know how much I tried to help her. That damn project. Good girl that she was, she towed the company line and didn't dig.

At that moment, Thomas returned and scrolled away from the entry. He entered the current date and wrote that he'd had no luck locating the project file and was relieved I hadn't taken it home.

Why?

I turned to Daniel. "Time to visit Laurel."

***

Laurel lived in Aurora in one of the new apartment complexes off Bayview Avenue. When Daniel and I appeared in her living room, she was in the midst of having after-dinner coffee and dessert with Bernie Dawson.

"Interesting. I didn't know she and Bernie were this cozy."

Laurel had always told me she didn't trust Bernie—that he held us back because we were women.

I'd never believed her. My dealings with him had been positive, and he'd never struck me as sexist or misogynistic. He wanted the right person for the job—not because he believed in fair play so much as he believed in making money. Get the best person who could do exceptional work fast and maximize profit.

"Maybe they're still working through their grief over your loss."

I started to laugh but cut myself off when I realized Daniel was serious.

"No, that's not it. Look how close they're sitting. It's so intimate."

He contemplated for a moment, and his expression told me he was picking up their thoughts.

"He has a wife."

The incredulity in his voice drove the chuckle from me. "When did that ever stop a guy?"

"My dear, were you always this cynical?"

I frowned at him, and he said, "I'm sorry. Did Rory cheat on you? I thought he met Clara after you'd divorced."

"After we separated. My cynicism isn't Rory's fault. It's life's fault, I guess. Too much misery and hurt everywhere." I scowled. "I never expected Laurel to be the other woman, though."

"How much will the new project net the company, Bern?" Laurel scooted closer to Bernie on the brown leather sofa and put a hand on his arm.

"At least a million."

"Same client?" Was that a hint of nervousness in her voice?

"Is that an issue for you?"

"After what happened to Jayden? Yes, it's an issue for me."

"What do you know about the client?" He squinted his eyes, studying her, suspicion lacing his voice.

"Nothing," she said, too quickly. When she continued, it was with a stammer. "I have no idea who the client is. Just the liaison. Jayden didn't know either."

"Jayden was snooping into things she shouldn't have been snooping into."

My stomach lurched. "Daniel, as God is my witness, I don't know what they're talking about."

"And Thomas?" said Laurel.

"Him too. I warned him—warned everyone who works at Dawson Data to stay out of the client's business. Jayden ignored that, and Thomas is ignoring that. Watch yourself, Laurel."

"What does that mean?" Daniel asked me. "What did you do?"

"What they told me to do. I communicated with one guy. All I knew about him was that his name was Gerry. I didn't even get a last name."

When he didn't reply, I said, "Was I murdered?" My voice shook. "How? The doctors said it was a heart attack. They said that!" I was getting hysterical, but I couldn't stop the babbling. "How could I have been murdered? You can't give someone a heart attack."

"It's okay." He put his arms around me. "We'll figure it out."

"Oh, God. What if whoever the client is thinks I have files at home? Thomas came looking. What if they hurt my kids? I have to get back to them. They have to be warned."

"Jayden—"

Whatever he said, I never heard. I was already back at my house.

***

The main floor of the house was dark and quiet. I followed Marc's thoughts to his room where he sat at his desk, working on his computer. When I peeked over his shoulder, I saw a lot of math and physics. A programming book lay open on his desk, and one on calculus rested open in his lap. Envy flared through me. I'd always enjoyed studying calculus. It would be nice to lose myself in it again.

Since Marc was all right, I turned my attention to Silver. She also was in her room, but she wasn't alone. Harrison was with her, which reassured me. They didn't seem agitated, so their talk with his parents must have gone well.

"They'll be fine." Daniel had joined me and stood behind me.

"I hope so. If anyone tries to hurt them, I'll—"

"—haunt them. Yes, I know."

"It's the truth. No one hurts my kids. No one." I hurled the words out in a torrent.

"Easy, girl. You have no reason to think anyone wants to." He put his arm around me again, and this time, I let it soothe me.

"What can we do?" I couldn't think. Yesterday, my worst problem had been that my teenage daughter was pregnant. Today, I was certain I'd been murdered. "I have to prove they killed me."

"If they've found a way to give someone a heart attack remotely, they're damn good," Daniel said.

"I was at home. Poison in my lunch? Would have been difficult. I make my lunch and keep it in a cooler bag by my desk. I mean, used to." It's difficult to think of yourself as dead when you still exist.

"What did you do that day? Where did you go?"

At that moment, Marc went rigid, and he rose from his chair. Shivering, he grabbed a sweater from his dresser. With a puzzled expression, he scanned the room.

"Mom? Are you here?"

"He feels me." I was unable to hide the excitement in my voice. "Marc!"

"Shouting doesn't help. They either hear you or they don't."

"Help me. Make him hear me." I turned a pleading gaze on him.

"What do you expect me to do?" he asked.

"I don't know!" I tried to stomp across the room and only managed to jump from one spot to the other. Chains appeared in my hands, and I rattled them, shaking the holy hell out of them.

"A bit cliché, don't you think?" The grin on Daniel's face made me bust out a laugh.

"I have to do something. They're cliché for a reason."

Marc returned to his desk and picked up his textbook again, but he didn't even glance at it. "I miss you, Mom—if you're here, I want you to know how much I love you. You always said it to me, but I didn't tell you enough. I regret that."

"Oh, baby, it's okay. I know you love me." The chains vanished—stupid idea, anyway—and I threw my arms around my boy. "Oh, God, it hurts you can't see me."

He shivered again, despite the sweater.

"Mom? I know you're here." He paused, and his frustration leaked out of him and into me. "You were at the visitation and the funeral, too. I sensed you. I could smell you."

I threw Daniel a horrified look. "I smell?"

"Everybody has a scent. You don't wear perfume, but your shampoo has a flowery scent. Lilacs?"

"Lavender—and it's the conditioner. The smell of my conditioner survived my death?" I shook my head. "It doesn't matter. What's important is Marc knows I'm here."

"When your vibration lowers, you are more physical, and those in the physical plane will more easily sense you."

"Then Silver will recognize my presence?" Hope surged into my heart. My girl would know me. I popped over to her room.

Daniel followed instantly. "Cut that out."

"What?" I gazed down at Silver and Harrison lying in her bed.

Both slept, Harrison's light snoring the only sound.

"Disappearing without informing me. I hate that."

"Sorry. I can't get used to how quickly things happen when all I do is think of them." I faced him. "I know where we need to go next."

CHAPTER 15

When I explained to Daniel who I wanted to see next, he argued. "If you follow the trail to the client now, you'll risk your family."

"I'm *dead*." That, ladies and gentlemen, explained everything. I'm dead. End of story. He wanted to tell me I should do this, or I couldn't do that? Wrong. I'm dead. Get it? When you're dead, you are master of your own domain. Queen of your castle. Go to the other side? Nope. Don't' want to. Don't have to. I'm dead. You want to tell me I can't track someone down? Sorry, I can do what I want. I'm dead.

"Jayden." His tone oozed patience, but his eyes flashed with irritation. "I understand you're angry."

"Angry," I said through clenched teeth, "doesn't begin to cover it."

He stroked a hand down my arm, clasping me by the wrist when he reached it. "Honey, the things you're thinking, the impulses compelling you to act, they're understandable."

I waited, the big, fat "but" hanging in the air as if he'd already said it.

"But it's rash. We can't interfere."

"We're here. No one can stop us."

"Do you think there'll be no consequences to our actions because we're not fully on the earth plane?"

That gave me pause. "You've been doing what you want for decades. Spirits can do whatever they want."

"So it would seem." He took my hand. "Come with me."

I gave him a reluctant nod, and we vanished from Silver's bedroom.

***

We appeared on the moon. The freakin' moon! Imagine it. Sure, I'd been reading minds and popping over to Hawaii, but I had no idea how broad my horizons really were. Dazed, I attempted to walk across the dusty terrain, but only popped from where I was to where I wanted to be.

"I want to walk!" It came out a wail of frustration. "Why can't I walk?"

Daniel strode to my side.

"Show-off."

"Give it time. You can go to the moon."

"Or anywhere in the universe?"

"Yes." He sounded so blasé.

"Why didn't you show me this before?"

He smiled. "I showed you Hawaii."

We'd stood on clouds. That should have tipped me off to our capabilities. "The sky's not the limit. Hey," I said, as something occurred to me. "I'm the first woman on the moon."

Daniel gave me a cheeky grin. "No, you're not."

"You brought other women here."

His smile broadened. "Best way I know to impress the ladies."

"You're hitting on women who've died?" My opinion of him lowered a little.

"It's not as bad as it sounds. You had a nice time when we went to Hawaii, didn't you?"

"Yes."

"You're my niece. I wanted to help you cope with what happened. It worked, didn't it?"

"Yes, I had an amazing time."

"I've helped others deal with the transition, and not all of them were my relatives. So I want to impress the ladies. Why is that so bad?"

"You're taking advantage of them."

He raised his hands towards the heavens where stars and uninterrupted blackness shimmered. "Look at it. It takes your breath away."

I scanned the darkness for the Earth and spotted it, a pale blue dot. "So beautiful."

"As you're so fond of saying, we're dead. When I bring a woman here, I simply want to share a special place and time with her. There's nothing sexual about it. It helps them gain perspective. Do you understand?"

The Earth floated, far away, a ball with swirling clouds, blue oceans, and brown lands.

"It's so beautiful," I repeated—and it was. The sight filled my heart with joy. I imagined new spirits coming here with Daniel, a strange new friend. A kind new friend. A friend to guide them through a disorienting new existence.

"I think I do," I replied. "What's down there," I said, pointing at the Earth, "all that activity, all the worry, means nothing out here."

We fell silent for a moment, and in the silence, he took my hand. His palm warmed mine, and its solidity released tension from my whole being.

"On the other side, these problems must seem even more vague and meaningless," I said.

"I don't think so," he replied. "I think they mean even more on many levels."

"Don't be so cryptic, Uncle." I smiled at him with affection. "Are you telling me there's a reason for what's happened? For what's happening?"

"And for what will happen," he concluded.

"You can't ask me to forget about everything they've done to me and my family."

"Would you agree there's a reason for everything?"

I considered it. When I was alive, I'd believed everything was random, coincidental, or pointless. The only one who controlled my fate was me. But someone else had decided I had to die, and I had been powerless in my ignorance to prevent it. My children—and my grandchildren—would suffer the consequences of what some faceless sociopath had orchestrated.

"Cause and effect," I finally said.

When I didn't say anything more, Daniel prompted me to continue. "Yes?"

"They messed with the wrong woman," I snarled. "What they did, they had no right to do. They've stepped on a landmine, and

I'm going to explode. They caused it. I'm the effect. If there's a reason for everything, then there's a reason they picked me and a reason I'm going after them. I want to know who did this. I have a right to know."

A noise behind me had me spinning around in time to see the portal that had followed me around for two days vanish from my sight.

"Well, what do you know?" I said, easing from tirade to smugness. "I'm trapped here. Eternity is mine, and I'm going to take advantage of it."

***

Gerry, the client's liaison for the project of death, was my logical go-to person now. I tapped into his thoughts by visualizing him and focusing. I shuddered when I picked up his thoughts, grim, black, and preoccupied with killing.

"This guy had me killed." Wonder, more than anything else, filled my voice. "How can someone kill in cold blood?"

"Sadly, too many people are capable of that," Daniel replied. "They justify it, though not all of them manage to sleep in peace after, no matter what they tell themselves."

"What happens to them when they die?" I returned my gaze to the Earth and grimaced at it as if I could see evil wafting from it like smog.

"Same thing that happened to us: they cross to the other side, are allowed to return for their final goodbyes, and then they leave through the portal."

"Aren't they punished?" If they weren't, then getting retribution on my killers was even more critical.

"I don't know what you expect to happen. You mean, are they sent to Hell? If you're looking for Divine retribution, you won't find it. What does happen, I've been told, is that everyone goes to the level of their vibration. This means those who aren't as spiritually evolved have a longer journey through the various levels, and it'll take more lifetimes to accomplish it. There's also a life review, and the worse your behaviour in life, the more unpleasant the review experience is. But you're the only one who judges your life."

"Great. So the monsters who slaughter innocents get to judge their own actions."

Would I be able to appear to Gerry as an avenging angel and terrify him? The moment the thought passed through my mind, I morphed. I must have appeared sufficiently terrifying because Daniel cried out in alarm.

When he caught his breath, he said, "Knock it off, Jayden. Obviously, you can appear any way you want. You're assuming, though. When you undergo a life review, you live it from the perspective of the other people involved, and you experience your actions firsthand from their point of view."

I returned to my own form.

"So Hitler experienced what his victims endured?" That was more like it.

"Yes. Kind of gives new meaning to 'do unto others,' doesn't it?"

Something niggled the back of my brain.

"Is that why you won't leave? You're afraid to relive what you did from your friend's and your girlfriend's perspective?"

When he averted his gaze and remained silent, I had my answer.

"Uncle, I'm sorry."

He must have suffered immensely when his loved ones had died, leaving him between this world and the next.

"Don't you think you've punished yourself long enough?"

"I can't leave," he whispered.

"Can't? Or won't?"

He again refused to respond, so I dropped it.

"We're paying Gerry a visit. If it means we can prevent him from harming anyone else, we have to. Maybe that's the reason for everything that's happened and for us meeting."

Daniel's eyes narrowed as he thought about it.

"Okay."

Arms linked, we left the moon and reappeared by Gerry's side.

He wasn't alone, and it was evident we'd stumbled onto something more terrifying than I'd imagined.

CHAPTER 16

We found Gerry in his office. At first glance, it appeared to be a typical office. The furniture was more expensive than what we had at Dawson's, but it was all your standard pieces for an executive office: desk with an ergonomic chair behind it and two chrome and leather chairs in front; a sideboard with coffee machine and tea service; and a round table with four chairs.

Then I spotted the terrifying features.

My picture, one of many, was thumbtacked to a board. A red 'X' marred it, as well as some of the others, but most were unmarked. Next to mine, hung Thomas's picture. It was unspoiled. The flagged ones were probably people already dead and the unmarked ones still living. Anyone seeing this would draw the same conclusion.

The man himself sat on the couch, ankle propped on knee, a mug of coffee in his fist.

Gerry, whose last name I still didn't know, wasn't an attractive man. He'd always had an icy stare, despite the fact that his eyes were brown—an eye colour I'd always associated with warmth. A bald spot crowned his noggin, and he kept the rest of his hair, which was salt and pepper, army trim.

Even when he wore a suit—and he always did whenever I saw him, including now—he carried himself as if he were wearing fatigues. When we'd worked together, I'd kept expecting him to tell me to drop and give him twenty. His mouth curved down even when he was relaxed, making his expression the male version of the resting bitch face.

On the couch next to him sat another man. The sight of him froze my blood.

This man was younger than Gerry and sexy in a rock star kind of way. He had full lips any woman would fantasize about kissing. His eyes, brown as acorns, held the warmth that was missing from Gerry's.

Black bangs that he'd brushed to the side drooped onto his forehead, giving him the air of a rebel. Even though he was sitting, I could tell he was tall. Despite the suit, I could see he was fit and muscular.

Death swirled around him. This man had killed, and he'd killed recently.

Pointing to the younger man, I said, "He's the man who murdered me."

Here sat my murderer, having coffee with the man who'd likely told him to do it.

"Why are you so sure?" Daniel asked.

"I just know. Gerry relayed the orders. This other man pulled the trigger."

"Pulled the trigger how? You had a heart attack."

"That's what we're here to find out."

The younger man rose and walked to the wall of targets. From his thoughts, I picked up the name "Michael Valiant."

Michael removed the thumbtack from Thomas's picture and studied the image.

"Did you send me the file?" he asked, his voice deep and soothing.

"Right before you got here. Check your email."

He nodded. "How?"

I shivered, nauseated. He wasn't asking how to check email.

"The ray." In his mind, an image of what looked like a laser pointer appeared.

"Two heart attacks in two weeks in people too young and healthy to have heart problems?" He tacked the photo back onto the board and perched on the edge of the desk.

Gerry shrugged. "No one will put it together. The average person won't have the smarts or the leverage to act on any suspicions. They'd probably suspect something in the office environment or work-related stress."

"Are there issues with the environment?"

"No, the building's too new."

"Then why—"

"It was a for instance, Mick. Relax. You're always over-thinking things." Gerry grinned, and, chillingly, the grin was affectionate.

Would he still qualify as a sociopath if he could feel affection for another person?

"Maybe he's not a sociopath," Daniel said.

"Then even more reason to be terrified. He believes in his mission then. He's a crusader."

"They're discussing the Tesla Ray."

"What's that? How do you know?"

"Picked it up from their minds. It's a death ray. Ever hear of physicist Nikola Tesla?"

"Of course," I replied.

"Some think he created a death ray machine that used a microwave beam to penetrate walls and cause damage."

"How do you know this?"

"Tesla's work fascinated me. Society gave him a raw deal. Rumour had it, the FBI stole his personal documents, and the plans to the death ray were in there."

I gasped. "How is it possible? The government created a death ray? That's crazy."

Daniel shook his head. "Tesla wanted his research used for society's benefit—to do good. The government wanted a deadlier weapon. I thought it was just another conspiracy theory. Guess I was wrong."

Michael returned to sit across from Gerry and checked his cell phone.

"When?"

I held my breath.

"We're waiting on some final surveillance reports to come in. If he's still snooping, you'll get the green light day after tomorrow," Gerry replied.

"I'll be ready." Michael rose and stretched, arching his back. "I'm going home. Jess has been complaining I don't spend enough time with her. If I leave now, I'll arrive in time to go to bed with her."

"You're whipped. You've always been whipped."

"She's not being unreasonable, and I want to spend more time with her. She's my wife, Torque."

Gerry, who apparently went by the nickname Torque—where do guys come up with these silly names?—seemed displeased at the reminder that Michael cared about his wife, but it made me strangely relieved.

If he could love another person, maybe there was hope for him.

***

Early the next day, Daniel and I followed Thomas to his cubicle at the office.

If we could force Thomas to stop his snooping, or, barring that, convince Gerry's spies that Thomas had backed off, we could save his life. I had to believe that.

Daniel disagreed. He was convinced this was a done deal, fated, which infuriated me. I refused to believe the future was set. If that's the case, then we should all give up striving for anything.

I also had a nagging feeling I'd missed something critical.

Gerry had said he was waiting on surveillance reports. If they didn't assassinate people willy-nilly, then something or someone had driven them to conclude they needed to eliminate me. But I hadn't done anything wrong.

When I tried to recall anything suspicious about my behaviour around Gerry at work, I drew a blank. I'd treated him the way I treated all clients: with respect and no interest taken in his personal life. I only asked questions about the job and nothing about his business.

So where had it all gone so fatally wrong?

Thomas booted up his computer and dove right into digging through the network files for information on my project. He'd accepted that Laurel now controlled it, but he persisted in his quest to track the files.

"Damn you." My irritation spiked when I tried again to pace and only succeeded in popping to one end of the room and back again. I hadn't realized how often I'd used pacing to work through my frustrations until I physically couldn't do it.

Desperate to stop Thomas, I appeared behind him and rammed my hand through his monitor. His computer was an all-in-one, which meant everything including the hard drive and processor were inside the monitor. It made a satisfying sizzle when my fist thrust through the screen and out the other side.

The odor of burning plastic wafted through the air, and the screen flickered and went dark. Thomas cursed. Even though he knew better, he pressed the power button in a useless attempt at turning it back on.

"No good, Tommy boy," I said.

His head jerked up as if he'd heard me, but if he suspected I was there, he didn't show it. He grabbed his phone and called for tech support.

My little stunt didn't slow him down for long. Within an hour, he had a replacement computer and was back on the network.

We never saved files to internal hard drives. Everything was saved to an external drive, which was backed up to the network and locked up at day's end. He hadn't lost anything but hardware.

Satisfying as it had been to affect something on the physical plane, repeatedly frying his electronics would be a useless exercise. However, it made me realize I was becoming physical enough to force him to recognize my presence.

I scanned the cubicle and spotted his coffee mug on the corner of his desk. The question was, could I affect solid objects as well as electronics?

"Daniel," I called out. "Help me fling this coffee mug across the room."

If we could get it soaring, Thomas couldn't explain it away. He'd have to consider paranormal involvement. Since I was his only recently dead acquaintance, he'd have to recognize I was behind it.

"You can do it." Daniel crossed his arms over his chest and prepared to observe the fun.

"Do I punch it?" I licked my lips and rubbed my hands together. *It's just a cup. How hard can it be?*

Impossible, I realized, if I didn't have a low enough vibration. I inhaled and braced for impact.

"Use your mind. Visualize the cup hitting the back wall over there." He pointed in the appropriate direction.

"Okay. Watch this."

I roared as I struck, imagining the mug splatting against the wall, coffee spraying everywhere.

It didn't even make it off the desk. The mug shifted an inch closer to the desk's edge and remained vertical, taunting me.

"Again!" Daniel shouted into my ear, and without thinking, I slammed it again.

This time, it hurled off the desk and into the wall, shattering, spraying glorious coffee everywhere.

A sudden craving had me manifesting a cup of dark Arabian brew in my hand, hot enough to raise steam. I inhaled its aroma and took an appreciative sip.

Thomas, meanwhile, lurched to his feet. He raced to where the remnants of his mug had fallen, scattered below the milky residue trickling down the wall.

"Tom?" Laurel peered over her side of the cubicle wall. "You okay?"

"I dropped my coffee." He continued to stare at it. *How the fuck did that happen?*

I winced at the use of the "f" word, but what could I do? He was a curser from way back. No matter how often I'd asked him to clean it up when in my presence, he'd never learned to control it. To be honest, I was seriously tempted to take up cursing myself after what I'd learned over the last two days.

"You dropped it against the wall?" Laurel raised her brows.

"Yes. I tripped. It flew. That's the result." Thomas waved his hand in the direction of the mess. Outwardly, his confidence hadn't wavered, though when I tapped into his thoughts, they were sprinkled with curses and laced with unease.

He can't deny something weird just happened. I skipped in place.

"Are you all right?" Laurel asked him.

"Fine." Thomas paused. "How's the project going? The one you inherited from Jayden?"

Laurel huffed out a breath. "It's difficult. Every time I work on it, I think about poor Jay. I'll never get over losing her."

Her eyes misted, but her thoughts betrayed her: *Jesus, Bernie's right. Tom's snooping. Idiot. Drop it.*

"Daniel, follow her for the day. Find out what she knows. See if you can pick up an explanation for why they killed me."

He nodded, understanding in his eyes. He disappeared, his destination Laurel's cubicle.

CHAPTER 17

Laurel chatted with Thomas as he cleaned up the mess with a whiskbroom, dustpan, and paper towels he'd had stashed in his desk drawer. Who kept cleaning supplies in their cubicle? This place had a nightly cleaning service. *I had no idea he was such a neat freak.*

"Tom." The seriousness and the hesitation in Laurel's voice made him look up and hold her gaze.

"What is it?"

The coffee-soaked paper towel sprinkled drops onto his shoe when he shifted his weight. He swore and tossed it into the garbage can by his desk.

"The project's close to completion. She did excellent work. You know how she was: thorough, perfectionistic. She put in a ton of hours."

"Yeah." He snatched another piece of paper towel from the roll and wiped his shoe. As he tossed the wadded paper into the trash, he said, "So?"

"The client was happy with the work. But with Jayden gone, they've decided to deal only with Bernie going forward."

"Why?" He soaked another wad of paper with bottled water, and proceeded to wipe down the remaining traces of coffee on the wall.

"Probably to maintain anonymity. Their work is highly sensitive. How much did Jayden explain to you?"

He shrugged. "Just that. I never met the client she liaised with."

"Good." She nodded. "She was always careful to maintain confidentiality."

Thomas chucked the last paper ball into the trash and fisted his hands on his hips. "What's this all about, Laurel?"

"I'm not shutting you out. Bernie thinks I should work alone on this. He'll communicate with the client and give me direction, but he wants me to work on it solo."

"That'll extend the deadline. Did you tell him that?"

"He knows. The client's aware. They said they can live with that. What's important is having as few eyes on it as possible. Okay?"

"Sure." He shrugged. "Less work for me. Good luck with it." He rested his hand on the top of the divider. "I'd better get back to work. Thanks for the update."

"Okay." She placed a hand on his arm. "It's for the best, Tom. You'll still get credit for work done. I can handle what's left."

She turned away, and he returned to his desk.

Determined to force him to sense me, I appeared behind him, leaned over, and hugged him. I nuzzled my face against his neck—hell, I would have licked it if it would get his attention.

Nothing.

He continued perusing the files on the network.

"They'll track you, you idiot! Stop it!"

I swatted his mouse. It flew across the desk and dropped to the floor.

Thomas leapt to his feet. He scanned the office, but no one had reacted.

I gripped him around the waist and squeezed without penetrating his body. That isn't as gross as it sounds—neither of us felt anything. People walked through me all the time, a side effect of being invisible and without substance.

This time, he shivered. He snatched his jacket off the back of his chair and slipped it on as he sat down again.

"It's Jayden!" My voice sounded mechanical and irritating, but desperation kept me screaming. "I'm here." I kept up a steady barrage of shrieks.

Thomas had gone pale, so maybe it was working. He recoiled in his chair. When he reached out to retrieve his mouse from the floor, his hand shook.

Jayden, are you around me? Do you see us?

At last, his thoughts travelled in the right direction. I searched the desk and almost went for the candy dish—a bowl full of chocolate kisses would be fun for him to pick off the floor—when I chose the light bulb in the desk lamp instead.

If the bulb had been an energy-efficient fluorescent one, I wouldn't have tried this. They contain mercury, and I was trying to save this weasel's life, not end it. Luckily, it was one of the old-style lightbulbs. Breaking it would only scare him, not make him sick or kill him.

I gripped the bulb and squeezed. For a moment, nothing happened. I screamed in rage. The glass shattered and the light went out, not only in Thomas's cubicle, but in the entire IT department. To finish the deal, I shoved my hand into the outlet where his power bar was plugged in. All the units in the department went down.

"To answer your question, Tom, yes, I'm here and I see you." I sat on top of his desk, legs crossed, and waited.

"Oh, my God," he whispered. *Jayden, if that was you ...*

Around us, pandemonium ensued, but Thomas remained in his seat, silently staring at his dark computer screen.

After a moment, he opened his desk drawer and removed a pad of paper and a pen. He set them on the desk.

Can you write?

Good question. Excellent idea if it worked.

My fingers struggled to grip the pen, but they kept slipping through it. Huffing with frustration, I swatted it, and it flew off the desk and crashed against the partition.

Okay, Thomas thought.

He picked up the pen and set the tip against the paper as if he wanted to jot down a note. Inhaling deeply, he closed his eyes.

Can you channel a message through me?

From where had this idea come? I was intrigued but didn't know what to do. How did mediums channel? Did a spirit take over their bodies? For lack of a better idea, I sat in his lap and let my body sink into his.

Instantly, I felt the pen gripped in his fist, and that was great. But I also felt his body encasing mine, and the shock propelled me to my feet.

It must have affected Thomas, too, because he tilted off his chair and collapsed on the floor in a dead faint.

CHAPTER 18

They sent him home.

After Thomas regained consciousness, he checked in at the nurse's station. The nurse told him he'd probably caught a stomach bug and needed to go home to recuperate. As he retrieved his bagged lunch and whatever else he'd stored in his cubicle for the day, Bernie stuck his head in to have a word. He kept his distance and didn't touch anything.

"Feeling okay to drive?" *God help me if he passes out at the wheel and kills someone. The last thing I need is a lawsuit from some family whose kid he killed.*

Nice, Bernie, I thought. *Very compassionate.*

"Yeah, I'm fine. Just need some rest."

In reality, Thomas had not only recovered, he was trying to hide his excitement. His thoughts rushed at me a mile-a-minute, and it was all I could do not to take over his body again to knock him out and shut him up.

I've got to get home. Jayden, stay with me. We have to communicate. It'll work out better next time. When I'm home, we'll be undisturbed.

And on and on and on it went. I had to hand it to him—most people would be losing their mind if a ghost took possession of their body. Thomas was revved up about it, but not in a bad way. He was excited and anxious for more.

Satisfied that he'd at least make it home okay without me riding along, I popped over to see how Daniel was doing with Laurel.

He lounged in a chair next to her desk, his long legs stretched

625

out, his feet propped up on the arm of her chair.

Laurel was nowhere in sight. She'd joined the others in the department for coffee in the kitchen while the electrician worked on the power outage. Most of the PCs in here would probably have to be replaced. That gave me some satisfaction.

"You look comfortable," I said.

Daniel dropped his feet to the floor and sat up straight. "She's not digging into anything she shouldn't now, but she was. According to her thoughts, she's the one who was snooping through your stuff and into the client files."

His eyes flared with anger, and he scowled. "She hacked into your computer from her desk and snooped from there."

"Oh, my God." I put a hand over my stomach. "She set me up?"

"Not deliberately. She covered her ass by exposing yours. You thought she was your friend, but she put you at risk to protect herself."

"Why was she digging?"

"She knew you had a lucrative contract and wanted to find out how much of a goldmine it really was. Once informed, she planned to confront Bernie and get a piece of the pie."

I perched on her desk. "She knows who the client is?"

Daniel shook his head. "She didn't get that far. Turns out, she didn't need to. All she had to do was seduce Bernie Dawson and the project was hers. Of course, you helpfully died first, and she convinced Dawson to pull the project from Thomas, who was at that point the most logical person to take over."

"I don't blame Thomas for trying to get the project back, but he can't continue to access the files. He's oblivious to how dangerous what he's doing is." I leaned forward, anxious. "We have to get to Tom's. I've managed to convince him I'm still around. We can save his life."

For the first time since I'd seen the black in Thomas's aura, I felt certain we could change the future.

***

Daniel and I arrived on Thomas's front porch as he pulled into the driveway. We went into the house while he parked the car in the garage and met him in the kitchen.

He scanned the room as if searching for me, so I moved next to him and hugged him. He shivered. Perhaps frequent exposure to me made him more sensitive to my energy.

"Jayden?" Thomas staggered and braced himself with a hand on the counter. He took a deep breath and exhaled. "I'm dizzy. I don't know if it's you or not, but my head is spinning."

I searched the room for a way to make my presence known. This time, I didn't want to cause a huge mess—I only wanted to let him know it was me.

"Knock on the wall," Daniel suggested.

"I can do that?"

"Well, sure. You hear about ghosts rapping on doors or tables all the time."

The kitchen table was solid oak.

"That'll do," I said and went to it.

First, I tried banging my fist on it. Both Daniel and I heard it loud and clear, but Thomas continued to stare into space with a hopeful expression.

"Harder."

"Okay, Coach." I grinned.

Daniel is the nicest dead uncle a girl could have. "I love you, Uncle. Thanks for helping me."

His face flushed pink, and he averted his eyes. "Thanks, Jayden. I love you, too."

"I had to say that. You never know when things will change."

He nodded. "No one ever learns that when they're alive."

I wasn't sure that was always true, but it was in my case. If I'd known my time was up, I'd have told a lot of people, especially my kids, how much I loved them. Maybe I'd even have gone out with Thomas, just once, and given him a chance. He wasn't so bad when you got to know him.

Throwing emotion into it, I pounded on the table. All the other times I'd managed to affect the environment, I'd been upset, angry, or in some way surging with emotion.

Thomas leapt to the table and gripped it with both hands, hard enough to turn the knuckles white.

"Is someone here? Do that again. One knock if it's Jayden, two if you're someone else."

This was good. We could at least do a question and answer session using yes and no. I gave another solid tap.

"Jayden, Oh, my God." He released the table and paced. "I wish I could see you. Okay, I have to test this. If this is Jayden, knock once for yes if your daughter's name is Patricia and twice for no."

I was impatient to get to the project-related stuff, but didn't blame him for wanting to verify. I banged twice.

"All right. Good." He paced some more. "Were you at your funeral?"

Bang.

"Were you watching us at the cemetery?"

Bang.

"The service was lovely. I'm happy you were there."

Impatient, I considered throwing something across the room so he'd get to the good stuff, when he changed his line of questioning.

"Do you know Laurel has control of your project?"

Bang.

"They've booted me off."

Don't tell me stuff I already know. How could I tell him not to keep digging? How could I explain anything? Why couldn't he hear my voice?

I did the only thing I could do: *Bang. Bang.*

"No?" He studied the table as if it held all the answers. "You want me to try to get back onto the project?"

A scream of frustration burst from me. "Damn it, no!"

Bang. Bang.

"Okay." He fell silent, deep in thought. To cut to the chase, I eavesdropped, so when he spoke again, I already knew what his idea was. It was a good one.

He explained he'd like to execute it at 3:00 o'clock in the morning. He thought he had to wait until the witching hour. *Cute.* I rapped once in agreement.

If we had the rest of the day to ourselves, I knew exactly who I wanted to visit next. I waved a hand to Daniel and saw approval in his eyes.

Together, we disappeared from Thomas's kitchen and went to find the enemy.

CHAPTER 19

We found Gerry in his boss's office, an elegantly furnished tribute to a long and lucrative career. Degrees, awards, and photographs of past triumphs and celebrity encounters adorned the wall. In the corner, a gas woodstove with a gold cooktop emitted a warm light and probably a comforting heat. It reminded me that fall was underway and, though Daniel and I didn't feel it, a chill was in the outside air.

Jim Cornell looked close in age to Gerry—maybe early fifties—and resembled a cartoon character. Cornell's cheeks were chubby, his head almost bald. He had a monk's fringe and sorrowful eyes that, combined with his horn-rimmed glasses, added a comical touch.

Gerry slouched on one of the armchairs in front of Cornell's desk. He looked more miserable than usual.

"I don't know what happened. Dawson says a power surge knocked everything out. They didn't lose any work."

"What about that new girl? Laurel Kincaid?"

"Dawson's got her on a short leash. He assures me there'll be no problems. She'll get the project completed."

"Does he still believe we're with the DND?" Cornell asked, referring to the Canadian Department of National Defence.

"Yeah. He doesn't pry, so other than at our first meeting, it's never come up again. All he cares about is the money we're paying. As long as we're giving him more than the work is worth, he'll remain uninterested."

Cornell leaned back in his chair, looking satisfied. "How's Mick?"

Gerry snatched his mug of coffee from the coaster on the desk and sipped before replying. His thoughts told me he was stalling for time. Interesting.

"Fine," Gerry said with a firm voice.

"No issues?"

"None that I can see." His tone dripped innocence, but he couldn't hide his internal unease from me.

I'd have to spend some time with this Michael person. Perhaps I could rock his solid little world enough to at least get him fired.

Daniel interrupted my plans. "That'd be playing a dangerous game."

"What? Getting a killer fired? Yeah, I'd be real sorry," I snapped in response.

Cornell spoke then, dragging us back to the main conversation.

"Bringing him into the office is a risk, Torque. I hope you're watching him."

I popped over to sit on Cornell's desk and faced Gerry. Here was the type of man who could sic a killer on someone without regret. His thoughts never turned to me, never considered how my family might be suffering while he enjoyed mid-morning coffee with his co-conspirator.

"Don't worry, Jim. Mick's demonstrated over the last five years that he's stable enough to join us here at headquarters."

A fabulous side benefit to tuning into people's private thoughts was that I could fill in the blanks as they retrieved information from memory. Sometimes, this remembering flashes by in images as it did now.

An image of a blonde by the name of Althaea flickered through Gerry's mind. Michael and this woman had worked together intimately, Gerry doing his best to push them together.

The plan had failed when Michael rejected Althaea, remaining loyal to his wife, and their partnership ended badly. Gerry worried that the incident had damaged Michael's dedication to their agency and had worked miracles to keep the extent of the debacle from Cornell.

"That old adage is wrong—there's no honour among thieves," I said.

"They're not thieves," Daniel replied.

"They stole my life." I popped over to join him behind Cornell's desk.

Our combined presence must have affected the air around Cornell, because he shivered and used the remote to turn up the thermostat on the fireplace.

"Gerry manipulates his partner, and he lies to his boss. What a hive of depravity we've got here." I vanished and reappeared to stand beside the thermostat. It currently read twenty-three degrees Celsius and was set to twenty-two degrees. Smiling to myself, I covered it with my hand and watched the indicator plummet.

"What are you doing?" Daniel asked.

"Just playing." I snickered. "Call me immature if you like, but they deserve at least some discomfort for what they've done."

The two men continued to talk and sip their coffee. I kept my hand on the thermostat, forcing the gauge to read far less than the actual temperature in the room.

After a while, both men removed their jackets, and Cornell again adjusted the thermostat to try and shut off the heat. Of course, the fire continued to burn brightly.

Finally, Gerry rose and strode over to the thermostat.

"Jesus, Jim, no wonder it's not shutting off. The gauge reads fifteen degrees."

Cornell stalked over to join him. "I'll have it checked. It's obviously broken."

He shut it off, but shivered when his hand slid through mine.

"There must be a cold spot here."

Fun as this had been, it was time to leave. I signalled to Daniel, and we left them tinkering with the thermostat.

***

Michael Valiant lived in an executive home in Aurora, Ontario. Since his job permitted him the flexibility to work from home, we found him there. He spent a good portion of his day locked in his office even when his wife was around.

The outside of the house was trim and professionally landscaped. They had money—murder for hire obviously pays better than software development. Of course, he had a spouse helping pay the bills, but I suspected he earned a great deal more than she did.

His wife, Jessica, wasn't home when Daniel and I arrived, but her energy was ubiquitous. She'd made the house a home with a few simple touches. Framed family photos lined the mantle of the fireplace, rose up the wall along the staircase, and stood propped on an occasional table.

A romance novel casually rested on the sofa in the family room, waiting for her to pick it up again. A trace of a floral scent hovered in their bedroom, remnants of the perfume she used. A patchwork quilt draped across the back of a recliner in the living room.

A note she'd left on the kitchen counter read "Don't forget to check on the roast in the slow cooker. I'll be home around 7:00. Love you."

The normality of this cold-blooded killer's family life shook me more than the sight of the gun strapped to his hip had. In their bedroom, I traced my finger down a photo of the two of them. Their arms were wrapped around each other, her lips pressed to his cheek and a radiant smile on his face. They both wore bathing suits, and behind them, ocean waves and white, sun-kissed sand formed a glorious vacation backdrop.

"He loves her," I said to Daniel. "How can he love someone but kill another human being?"

Daniel shrugged. "Don't bother to try and understand such a mind."

"I have to," I replied. If I understood why he'd killed me, perhaps I could find a way to forgive him.

"Why is that important?" Genuine puzzlement filled his voice.

"For me. For my kids. I hate him, Uncle, and I don't want to."

"I hate him, too, honey." His tone was gentle. "I can live with that."

His choice of words made me smile. "But he shouldn't kill."

"A lot of people do things they shouldn't."

I shook my head. "No, you misunderstand. Look around. Everything about their lives shows he makes room for love. How can such a person murder without remorse?" The question was rhetorical, so I answered it. "He shouldn't be able to. He ought to be wracked with guilt. Don't you feel the energy around him?"

"I don't get it."

"Come." I took him to the office where Michael sat hunched over a laptop. The screen displayed Thomas's picture.

I gasped at the sight, but forced myself to swallow my fear. If I

632

could prove my point to Daniel, perhaps I could find Michael's humanity and put a stop to his evil quest.

Michael's aura glowed with a golden light. The energy around him soothed rather than frightened. He used his right hand to click with the mouse and propped his chin on his left fist. As he stared at Thomas's picture and the stats that accompanied it, the air around him gradually transmuted. His posture grew rigid, his expression hard and cold. Even his aura darkened and muddied.

"Oh, my God," I said. It was as if he were turning into someone else. "What's happening?"

"He's thinking about his next assignment," Daniel replied.

"About killing." I switched positions and observed him from the front. No trace of warmth or kindness was left in his eyes. His lips curled into a sneer. He picked up his cell phone and made notes.

On an impulse, I smacked the phone from his hand, sending it sailing across the room. As it dropped to the floor, Michael sprang from his chair.

Before he could retrieve it, I squeezed it in my fist. Something inside it zapped, and a whiff of smoke curled up from it. A scent of ozone wafted through the air.

"Fucking great," Michael said. He kicked the phone against the wall, but then bent down and picked it up. In his head he rationalized what had just happened, telling himself he'd flung the phone by accident.

"Yeah, you tell yourself that, killer." I slammed into his empty chair and sent it spinning across the hardwood floor.

Michael staggered backwards until he crashed into the wall. His eyes showed surprise and annoyance rather than fear. His thoughts raced as he tried to reframe the incident, but the only option that fit was spirit activity.

He stared at his computer for a moment and contemplated getting back to work. Instead, he said, "I'm shutting it down. Okay? If you're listening, I won't work on anything. I'll power down."

"Clever," I said to Daniel. "He figures I won't zap his laptop if he's not on it."

"Will you?"

I shrugged and pointed to the laptop screen. "See that?"

Daniel leaned in. "What am I looking at?"

"He's working remotely. Everything he's accessed is stored on a server at his office building. It's probably backed up every night to an offsite server."

"Okay." Daniel wasn't going to argue. He had no personal experience with computers. By the time Bill Gates's dream of a computer on every desktop had become a reality, Daniel was long dead.

"I've seen enough," I said. "Let's go home."

CHAPTER 20

Promptly at 3:00 AM, Daniel and I appeared in Thomas's home office. Thomas sat at a round table, an Ouija board before him and a pad and paper beside his arm. The middle and index fingers of each hand rested lightly on the planchette. Two candles on a sideboard next to the table provided the only illumination.

His thoughts raced, and he inhaled a few deep, calming breaths. At first, I thought he was afraid of dabbling with a spirit board, but then I realized he was more excited than anything else.

"His arrogance serves him well tonight," I commented.

"Always a judgement with you," Daniel replied.

"I'm not judging." I migrated to the top of the table, sitting with legs crossed.

Daniel's hearty laugh made me glare in his direction.

"I was making an observation, not judging."

"All you've done since we met is criticize and condemn him for who he is." He joined me at the table, parking himself on one of the chairs.

It was a strange sight. The chair was pushed into the table, and Daniel's body was cut in two at the waist. His head, shoulders, chest, and abdomen seemed to grow out of the wooden tabletop.

Had I? I tried to recall all the times that I'd derided Thomas. Perhaps it had been frequent, but I'd been venting.

"He frustrated me when we worked together. Plus, I thought he disliked me." I gave Daniel a pleading look. What if he thought I was a horrible person? What if he left me?

"I wouldn't abandon you, sweetie. You're my flesh and blood."

We both smiled at the expression, technically incorrect on more than one level. However, it was the sentiment that mattered.

"Thank you," I said. His affection flowed into me like a warm breeze. "I had a lot of anger and resentment towards Tom when I died. He always knew how to annoy me."

"And he did it deliberately, right?"

I nodded.

"What does that tell you about him?"

I considered. "He wanted me to pay attention to him. It's a juvenile strategy."

"Agreed. But was your reaction any more mature?"

I had no reply. Daniel was correct, but I wasn't in the mood to admit it.

"Jayden? Are you here?" Thomas's question interrupted the discussion. "If you're here, move the planchette to yes."

"Me?" I glanced at Daniel, who nodded his encouragement.

"He doesn't know I'm here. Answer him."

After taking a deep breath, I placed my hands over Thomas's. He shivered.

I gathered an emotional charge and shoved the planchette towards "yes."

It nudged halfway to the goal. Before attempting another push, I focused on the yes, inhaled again, more deeply, and gathered more rage into me. Vaguely, I wondered if only negative emotions allowed me to interact with the physical plane.

The triangle-shaped disk slid smoothly onto the word yes.

"Awesome. Thank you." *Maybe that was me pushing it. God, I hope she's really here.*

I moaned in frustration. "He's going to wonder this for every answer I give."

Here I was, struggling to communicate with him, digging deep for emotion, dragging energy from him just to move the triangle three inches, and he doubted my presence.

"Okay, Jayden," Thomas said, sliding the planchette back to the centre. "Are you following me for a reason?"

I shoved it back to yes.

"Because you have a crush on me?"

"Oh, the arrogance," I said through gritted teeth.

No. If there were a way to add an exclamation to that, I

would've done it.

"Oh." He sounded disappointed. "You want to tell me something?"

Yes.

"Use the letters to spell it out."

Painstakingly, I moved the plastic triangle around until he had a word scribbled on his notepad: D-A-N-G-E-R.

Thomas stared at the word and frowned. "At home?"

I groaned, frustrated. It would be helpful if he were more intuitive. *No.*

"At work?"

Yes.

His eyes widened, and his lips pursed. "The project."

A statement, not a question. Good. *Yes.*

"Who is the client?"

"He's getting at the crux of it now," I remarked. "Maybe this won't take all night after all."

D-O-N-T-K-N-O-W.

I paused a moment, then continued.

K-I-L-L-E-R-S.

Thomas paled. "They killed you?" he whispered. "Oh, Jayden."

Grief flowed from him in waves, overwhelming me. Tears sprang to his eyes. "Why? You didn't do anything."

Suddenly, a look of horror crossed his face. "Oh, my God. It's my fault."

I swept the planchette to "no," quickly putting a halt to that line of thinking. By this point, his fingers weren't even touching it. Each letter displayed under the small window in the triangle for a moment, and, as soon as he wrote it down, I sailed to the next one.

In this way, I explained to him that he had to stay away from the project. When he spoke about calling the police, I told him to back off. Without explicitly saying so, I let him know that would endanger him even more.

As I finished, Thomas shivered, making the planchette tremble under his fingers. He scanned the room and reached for the sweater he'd slung on the back of the chair.

"Why'd he get cold? I haven't touched him?"

An aura of darkness seeped through the room.

"Jayden, honey," Daniel said. "We've got a problem."

CHAPTER 21

The temperature in the room dropped enough that Thomas's breath puffed out in soft, white clouds. He leapt from his chair, knocking it backwards onto the floor.

"Who's there? What's happening?"

In a panic, I rose and scanned the room, searching for whatever had interrupted our session. A hideous thought had my stomach sinking and my heart thudding.

"He opened himself up to everything in the spirit world, not just us, didn't he?"

Perhaps the superstitions about spirit boards were right.

"Yes." Daniel moved behind Thomas, prepared to defend.

In the centre of the room, a cloud of oily darkness coalesced into a human shape. Thomas didn't see it—his gaze bounced around the room, passing over the dark spot without lingering.

"There!" I pointed at the male figure. "What do we do?"

An anguished cry tore from the man's throat, and his gaze moved from me to Daniel to Thomas. The moment he realized Thomas was the one in the physical plane, he vanished and reappeared on the table in front of the board.

His eyes glowed red with hatred, and his lips curled into a sneer. He wore soiled jeans and no shirt. Lashes of congealed blood scored his back, chest, and arms. Easing into a crouch, he raised his fists and prepared to pounce.

Without thinking, I hurled myself onto his back. As he twisted and tried to shake me off, Daniel smashed the Ouija board off the table.

"Get Thomas out of here," I hollered at Daniel.

The moment the Ouija board soared across the room, Thomas backed against the wall. He blinked a few times, squinted in the gloom, and then struggled to make his way back to the table.

Was he crazy?

Daniel added his energy to mine, and we wrestled the dark man to the table.

"Damn it, Uncle, I appreciate your help, but I've got this. Get Thomas out of here."

Daniel replied through gasps as he struggled to help me hold Dark Man. "You don't have this. We don't have this." He jammed a knee into Dark Man's back, eliciting a howl.

The table shook and bounced from its place on the carpeted floor. The whole thing might have appeared comical to Thomas had he been able to see it. Or maybe not, I thought, catching a glimpse of the sores on Dark Man's back.

"Who are you?" I screamed at him.

He only grunted in response and vanished.

The moment he disappeared, Daniel and I dropped through the table onto the floor below and then, unnervingly, through it. My vision blurred, I screamed, and launched myself back up, Daniel duplicating the manoeuver right down to the girly yelp.

We huddled on the floor and he put an arm around me.

"Thomas never put up protection before using the spirit board. Damn it. He's opened a portal to some dark place, and we can't close it for him."

Fear balled in the pit of my stomach. "What does that mean? Why can't we?"

"Because he opened it on the physical plane. It'll stay open, and more of these spirits with toxic energy will find their way through."

I groaned. "Oh, God, that's all we need. How will we explain that to him?"

But we had to.

I popped over to the board and flipped it right-side up. "Bring the planchette here, please."

Daniel did as I asked, swatting it across the room. Thomas followed behind it, wide-eyed but swallowing his fear.

Newfound admiration for him made me want to redouble my efforts to save his sorry hide.

With effort that had me drained of energy by the time we finished, I explained to Thomas about the open portal and his need to close it. I also suggested he research the safe way to use the Ouija board.

I mentally kicked myself for not thinking of this and letting him mess unprotected with the spirit world.

"Don't blame yourself. We all should've considered it. If anyone's to blame, it would be me," Daniel said.

Our gazes met over the board. "Have you seen that spirit before?"

"No. But I've attended séances and the medium has always put up energetic protections. I should've remembered that step."

"Can we put up the protection ourselves?"

He shook his head. "Someone from the physical plane must do it."

"This is so frustrating. Talking to them is difficult." I'd never felt this exhausted on the spirit plane.

He moved to my side and put an arm around me. "Not much makes us tired here, but some things do drain our energy. Minor dabbling doesn't harm us, but when you spend time communicating and then battle a low-vibrating energy, you feel it."

"Dark Man was a low-vibrating energy?"

Daniel nodded. "Toxic energies vibrate at a lower frequency than energies from the light."

"Okay, I'll buy that." There was no time to contemplate the implications, so I let it go. I checked on Thomas.

He sat on the floor beside us, rereading the information we'd given him.

"Okay, I'll find a psychic who can help me," he said.

In the dim light from the candles, his aura remained blackened.

***

We spent another hour at Thomas's, and then Daniel and I went home to my kids. Both slept, Silver wrapped around Harrison as if he were a giant teddy bear. They'd be rousing soon, starting their day.

Daniel and I sat on the couch in the living room, biding our time. The sun hadn't brightened the sky yet, but it was on its way. Marc would return to university today, and Harrison had promised to move in here and stay with Silver.

His family hadn't protested, and I was relieved when I heard he'd be with her. While Silver's unplanned pregnancy would complicate their lives, they were at least taking the responsibility seriously. Money wouldn't be an issue for them—I'd left my kids plenty, and it would allow them to complete their education despite the delay for Silver while she went on maternity leave. She'd be fine.

Rory and Clara had told her to call them if she needed anything, and when I eavesdropped on their thoughts, I was reassured they meant it. They even showed excitement over the idea that they'd be grandparents. And Rory had put a ring on Clara's finger. She'd officially be Mrs. McQueen, grandma to Silver's baby.

"She'll never take your place, sweetie."

I could always count on Daniel to derail my self-pitying or negative thoughts.

"Maybe she won't mean to, but it's inevitable."

This time, I refused to give it up so easily. My grandchild would never know me. My heart split in two at the thought.

"This child will only know Clara." Tears slid down my face. A sob escaped as my shoulders shook.

"Oh, Jayden, no. It'll be okay. You'll see."

"How can it be okay?"

Upstairs, floorboards creaked as someone—I listened for thoughts and connected with Silver—walked to the bathroom.

"Your daughter will keep your memory alive."

"I know that."

He was right. Silver wouldn't forget me. She'd tell the baby stories about her grandma Jayden. Silver loved me. I should trust she'd ensure the baby knew me.

Silver appeared at the bottom of the stairs and made her way to the kitchen. I popped in to watch her make breakfast. She put coffee on for Harrison, but I was happy to see she put the kettle on for herself. She'd been a coffee fiend from the time she'd turned sixteen. At least she was making the sacrifice for her baby.

"You going to breathe down her neck over every little thing?"

"None of your business." My voice betrayed hurt. "She's my baby, and if I want to see how she does, I'm entitled. It's not like she'll know. She won't even know I care."

Daniel's face fell, and he rushed to me and hugged me.

"I'm sorry." He kissed the top of my head, and some of the tension eased from the pit of my stomach. "I didn't mean to hurt you."

Except for my sobs and the sound of Silver making toast and oatmeal, the kitchen was silent.

"I'm jealous." He said it gently, his voice barely cutting through my sobs.

I wiped the tears from my face and rubbed my eyes. "What?"

"You have a loving family—even your ex is stepping up. I never had that. I'm sorry. I don't mean to take my regrets out on you."

"Is that what compelled you to stay on this side?"

"Perhaps. She loved our baby so much. My family was fragmented. I never felt that kind of love from my parents. You have it for Silver and Marc. So does Rory."

"I'm sorry you missed out. I wish ..." But I couldn't complete that thought.

"What?" He stroked my hair, his arms holding me tight.

"I wish you hadn't died, and we'd have met earlier. I know I said it before, but I can't help it. Regrets are powerful, so I understand how you feel." I gazed up at him, giving him a rueful smile. "Silly, right? We can't change the past."

Harrison walked into the kitchen and interrupted our tender moment. He went over to Silver and put his arms around her from behind.

"What are you doing up so early?"

"I couldn't sleep, so I got up to make breakfast." She waved at the coffee maker. "Have a cup. It's fresh. Marc better get up soon or it'll scorch."

Harrison moved to the stove and lifted the lid on the pot that sat on the front burner. "Oatmeal."

"Just like Mom used to make." As soon as the words were out of her mouth, Silver's face contorted in grief. "Harry, oh, God."

She buried her head in her hands and sobbed.

Harrison dropped the cover back onto the pot and rushed to embrace her. "Oh, baby, it's okay."

She shook her head violently. "No, it isn't. It'll never be okay ever again." Convulsed with sobs, Silver crumpled into a chair at the kitchen table.

Harrison pulled up a seat next to her and drew her into his arms once more.

"Shh. Honey, I'm here." His eyes, too, brimmed with tears.

Silver raised her gaze to his, and when she saw the grief there, she cupped his face with her hands. "Thank you." Desire replaced anguish, and she kissed his lips.

"If they do it on the kitchen floor, I'm leaving."

"Daniel." I sounded exasperated, but I was amused, too, and above all, grateful to him for distracting me. Silver's grief had triggered mine, and Daniel's remark caught me a moment from a tear-filled meltdown.

"We should go anyway," I said. "Can't leave Thomas unsupervised for too long."

He chuckled in response, and we vanished from my home.

CHAPTER 22

Thomas spent the day working, and he didn't do anything at the office that he shouldn't be doing. Grateful for the probably temporary lull, Daniel and I took a mini-vacation to Greece. I'd always wanted to see the Mediterranean, and Daniel happily made my dream come true.

We toured Athens, Crete, and stood at the top of Mount Olympus. When I begged Daniel to cloud-walk with me again, he laughingly obliged. We played as we had on Mauna Kea, and then we settled for an afternoon of watching the ships in the harbour on one of the many islands.

Around the sea-view café we'd selected, whitewashed buildings clustered near sandy beaches. The water below us was dotted with sailboats, yachts, and cruise ships. Tourists strolled in and out of shops and restaurants.

We perched on the stucco wall overlooking a sea so blue and sparkling the beauty of it hurt my eyes and put an ache in my heart.

"I wish my kids could see this." Sighing with both contentment and wistfulness, I sipped on a café mocha I'd manifested. Between us sat a plate of Greek pastries, most of them made with phyllo dough and dripping with honey.

No matter how much I ate and drank, I discovered, I never felt overfull and never gained weight. With all the potential for pleasure on this in-between plane of existence, I was surprised the place wasn't packed with spirits who'd opted to stay.

Picking up on my thoughts, Daniel said, "Don't be so sure."

"How so?"

"Plenty of spirits remain earthbound. After a while, you get tired of it. Sooner or later, everyone finds their way home."

"You didn't."

"No." He selected a fat piece of baklava from the plate. Honey seeped from the sides, and it had a thick layer of nuts between wisps of phyllo. Daniel licked his lips and bit in, his eyes closing as he savoured the taste.

How would we manage to cross once we'd accomplished our mission?

I plucked another morsel for myself and we munched in companionable silence. The roar of the waves on the shore soothed me, and I could almost feel the breeze lapping at my skin. My eyes closed as I turned my face to the sun to drink in the moment. Even on this side of the veil, peace was fleeting.

Would I even want to leave this plane?

"We have to return to Thomas," I said. "I'm sorry, Uncle. Your world must have been lovely and peaceful before I burst in and disrupted it." I smiled, trying to mitigate the sadness bubbling up inside me.

He waved his hand and the plate of treats vanished along with the coffee and cigarette he'd held. "My dear, don't you know by now I wouldn't change it for the ability to step through the portal to return home right now?"

"But—"

"No buts," he replied, grinning. "I've had a lovely day. All my days since you've arrived have been lovely, if not busy." He took my free hand in his and pointed to the mug I held in the other hand. "Drink up, darling. You're right. We have to go."

***

We stood guard over Thomas the rest of the week, but everything remained quiet. If Gerry's spies were watching, Thomas didn't give them anything significant to report. He'd stayed away from the project files at work and spent his off-hours searching for a psychic to help him clear his home. Daniel and I hung out in Thomas's home office, stopping any low-vibrating-energy souls from crossing to our side.

By the weekend, visits from the darker side had become more

frequent, and I was drained more often than not. I craved an end to this, but at least by Saturday morning, Thomas announced he'd found his psychic.

While we hadn't had another Ouija session, Thomas talked to me whenever he was alone. When he finally announced he had an appointment, Daniel and I heaved sighs of relief.

He'd found the psychic at a store called The Green Witch, using an Internet search. The woman's name was Arla Hanson, and, according to the bio and testimonials on the site, she was knowledgeable, experienced, and accurate. She'd agreed to meet with Thomas at his home after she finished work.

As if preparing for a hot date, Thomas took pains with his appearance, changing his clothes three times before settling on black slacks and a burgundy dress shirt. He looked sexy, I begrudgingly admitted, annoyed that I felt a pang of jealousy as well.

"You do have a crush on him," Daniel teased.

I took it in the spirit in which he intended and laughed. "Maybe I prefer to hog all the attention."

"Did you notice he cleaned the whole house, including his bedroom?"

I had, and he'd prepared appetizers and uncorked a bottle of red wine from the cellar.

"That doesn't mean anything. I'd have cleaned my house, too. He has no idea if clearing the house means going into every room. Besides, he knows I'm watching. He's probably never going to have sex again."

"We could seriously damage his love life." Too much glee infused Daniel's eyes at the idea, and I laughed again.

"You were the practical joker in class, weren't you, Uncle?"

"Maybe."

The doorbell rang then, and we relocated to the door as Thomas set a platter of munchies on the coffee table in the living room.

A blonde goddess strode into the room. She flashed the bluest eyes I'd ever seen at Thomas and sashayed past him in a clatter of bracelets and bangles.

"She'll never sneak up on a ghost, that's for sure," I commented.

"Easy, girl, rein in the green-eyed dragon."

"I'm not jealous." I wasn't. "I'm stating a fact. She's a belled cat in that getup."

Arla twirled back around to face Thomas, her rainbow skirt swirling around her knees.

"Pleased to meet you. You must be Tom." She grinned, flashing perfect teeth. A hand, every finger sporting at least one ring, poked out from under the sparkly shawl around her shoulders.

Thomas clasped it in both of his and actually bowed.

"Oh, for the love of—" I cut myself off before I said something truly nasty.

"Welcome," Thomas said. "Let's go into the living room. You can put your bag down and tell me how you'd like to proceed."

She handed him her wrap, and he hung it on a hook behind the door. They walked together to the living room and settled side-by-side on the couch. Thomas poured tea while Arla explained the house-clearing process.

"Doesn't sound too scientific," Daniel said.

"Have you been through a house clearing before?" I asked. "Will she clear us out, too?"

"Yes and maybe." Before I could comment further, he said, "We'd be pushed out temporarily. For some reason, when someone on the earth plane burns sage, the air in that space becomes intolerable."

"Interesting."

How and why did that work?

I waited for Thomas to ask or for Arla to explain, but neither did.

"She takes it on faith, and he trusts her," Daniel said.

"Surely she knows how it works, though?"

As she talked, I started to warm up to her. Rather than flirty and outrageous, she came across as fun, friendly, and down-to-Earth— at least, as down-to-Earth as a psychic could get.

"You sounded a little panicked on the phone, Tom," Arla said. "Shall we get started? When I'm done, you can ask as many questions as you like."

I watched, unable to take my gaze off her as she unpacked an abalone shell with stand, a pouch of sage, a wild turkey feather, and a box of matches from her tote bag. She crumbled sage into the abalone shell and struck the match.

No sooner did the sage flame, smoke curling from it, than I

recoiled.

When I'd been alive, I'd loved the smell of incense and herbs, sage included. Now? All I wanted was to escape the eye-watering stench of it. Daniel and I sputtered and coughed.

"Before I take this around the house, I'll call on Archangel Michael to fill all the rooms with light, removing any trapped spirits and taking them to the other side." Arla set the shell on the stand she'd placed on the table and held her arms away from her body, her palms turned upward.

She said, "Archangel Michael, I call upon you now. Please fill this home with light and help any spirits trapped here cross to the other side."

"Oh, no," Daniel shouted. He grabbed my arm, and before I could respond, yanked me from Thomas's house.

CHAPTER 23

We reappeared at my house.

As always, the first thing I did was search for my children. Marc's thoughts placed him back in his dorm at university. Silver prepared dinner in the kitchen. She was alone, contemplating converting her room into a nursery and taking over the master bedroom.

Her mood was sedate, but beneath the calm, I sensed grief brewing. My girl wanted to be practical—the house had only three bedrooms, and she couldn't take over Marc's room—but her heart hurt at the blatant acceptance of my death.

I set that aside for a moment to ask Daniel what the hell had just happened.

"Why'd we have to go in such a rush? The sage?"

He shook his head. "She called on Archangel Michael. He'd have taken us to the other side."

Daniel said this so matter-of-factly I could only stare at him, stunned.

Finally, I asked, "Just like that?"

He looked sheepish.

"I don't know for sure," he admitted, "but I didn't want to take the chance. You heard what she said. If there are angels—and I'm not saying there are or there aren't—he'd have been able to bring the portal back for us and drawn us through."

I considered this information carefully before replying. "Is that what you think?"

"It's what I suspect."

"Angels use force?"

Daniel's brow furrowed, and he squinted at me. "They might require cooperation from us, but I didn't want to take the chance." His eyes widened. "Unless you're ready to go?"

"No," I replied quickly. "We can't leave without helping Thomas."

His aura retained that unsettling blackness. I refused to desert him until it either disappeared or he joined us on this side.

"Death isn't the worst thing to happen, is it?" I asked.

Daniel raised his brows. "You think Thomas might be better off dead?"

"No, of course not." I reclined on the sofa. Unsure how long Archangel Michael might linger, I figured we had time to chat. "But if we can't prevent it, he's not going to suffer."

"You're assuming his experience will be the same as yours."

"Wouldn't it be?"

He started to reply, but, with a huff of exasperation, I cut him off. "You don't know."

"No, but I can say the spirit we fought at Tom's had an experience different from ours."

"He was alive once?"

Daniel parked himself cross-legged on the coffee table in front of me.

"What did you think? That he was always like that?"

"He was in agony." We'd added to his torment by sending him back, I was sure of it, but we couldn't have let him stay here. "Rage and destruction were consuming him."

"Perhaps he'd been that way in life and couldn't shake it after death."

"And he never went through the portal."

Elbow on one knee, Daniel propped his chin on his hand. "I've seen some lower-vibrating spirits who refused to cross. Some are mean as hell."

He fell silent, and the uttered "hell" hung in the air between us.

Maybe there was no Heaven or Hell—not the way the Catholics meant it, anyway. Perhaps we made our own versions of it.

"It's not punishment from without, but from within," I said.

Going rigid, Daniel ended the discussion with a finger to his lips.

Swallowing loudly, I whispered, "What is it?"

"Come on."

He clutched my arm and, with me ignorant to our destination, we vanished once more.

***

Compared to Gerry's or Cornell's office, Michael Valiant's was less opulent. It lacked the fireplace, expensive furnishings, space, and view. Of course, Michael didn't spend as much time in his office as his partner or boss did. Michael's main job was field work—such as murdering me.

What had gotten Daniel worked up enough to drag me here turned out to be Michael's next assignment: he was preparing to hunt down and kill Thomas.

"Why?" I screamed it out, my voice panicked. "Thomas hasn't done anything."

"Neither did you," Daniel replied. "He killed you anyway."

"When they thought I was prying into their business." Is that why they were after Thomas now? Had something happened to make them believe he'd been snooping again? "Could it be Laurel?"

Daniel shook his head. "We should have checked in with her and Dawson."

"Do it. I'll stay with Valiant."

"Jayden," he said.

I gave him a questioning look.

"Take care."

"You too."

As soon as Daniel disappeared, I focused my attention back on Michael Valiant.

He'd already changed into jeans and a T-shirt and was gathering the tools of his trade into a black duffel bag he'd snatched from the closet. He then strapped on a shoulder holster. The gun he slipped into the holster looked like it could easily blow someone's head off.

But he wasn't done yet. From his thoughts, I picked up that he had to requisition the weapon required for the job: the death ray he'd used on me.

I didn't wait for him to sign it out but met him at his car in the parking garage. He drove a mid-size vehicle. It was black and the seats looked like leather. Seat warmers are helpful in Canadian winters unless you're a spirit, and he had them. The dashboard looked like the control panel on an airplane—not that I've seen one, but I could imagine—and it had a manual transmission. Show off.

Michael stuck the duffel bag on the back seat and slid behind the wheel. I rode shotgun. If he planned to use the death ray on Thomas today, then I wanted to be close enough to interfere.

Instead of pulling out of the parking spot, though, he pulled out a paperback and read.

After ten minutes, a white van with a cable company logo on it pulled up, Gerry behind the wheel. Michael transferred his bag into the back of the van and jumped into the passenger side. I found a place to sit right behind them.

"Everything all right?" Michael asked.

"Had to wait for them to release the van."

"Is that why you wanted me to meet you at my car?" Michael's underlying motive for asking the question wasn't curiosity or idle chatter. I sensed suspicion.

How long had they been partners? Gerry had pushed Michael towards his previous partner, so probably once the woman was out of the picture, Gerry took her place. Had Gerry manipulated the two so their partnership would implode and allow him to move in as Michael's partner, or was it an attempt to break up Michael's marriage? Maybe both. No wonder Michael didn't trust Gerry.

Perhaps there was a way to work that into Thomas's favour. I had to do something—Thomas's life was whittling down to hours, maybe minutes.

CHAPTER 24

Gerry parked the van on the street outside Thomas's house, and then he and Michael climbed into the back and fired up some impressive equipment. They had monitors displaying various rooms in the house. When Thomas received a phone call from a telemarketer, they listened to the conversation. If Thomas would've logged onto his laptop, they'd have monitored the activity on it.

This, as it turns out, provided Thomas a stay of execution.

Michael picked up activity on Thomas's office PC cracking into the project's database. Yet here was Thomas, relaxing at home, enjoying a glass of wine with Arla the psychic.

"Problem, Torque." Michael slid a finger along the screen of his laptop. "This traces a route through his office PC. See? I got a pingback from the database as soon as it was accessed. The IP routes through his office PC. I'd assume he was using remote access, but he's not on his computer. His laptop's not even powered up."

"What are you saying?" Gerry leaned into the screen as if that would help him understand.

"I'm saying," Michael replied, "Thomas Devereaux isn't your guy."

Why couldn't they have verified my innocence this way?

At least Michael was putting a stop to this. I popped into the house and peeked at Thomas's aura. The dark tinge remained.

Arla sat next to Thomas on the couch. A few nibbles remained on the appetizer tray, and the bottle of red wine was half-empty.

The newly acquainted couple gazed into each other's eyes, and both wore goofy grins. I could all but see floating hearts and twittering birds around their heads.

"Tom." Arla yanked her gaze from Thomas and focused it on me. "Someone's here."

If I could have staggered backwards, I would have. As it was, my knees shook and I almost crumpled to the floor. Could she see me? Hear my thoughts?

"I thought you said you'd cleared the house?" Thomas scanned the room, but his gaze passed right by me.

"Yes." Arla faced Thomas. "I banished whatever was stuck here and sealed the portal you'd opened, but this spirit is connected to you."

She turned back to me. "It's all right. I sense your presence and can communicate with you. My name is Arla Hanson."

"Can you hear me?" My voice, when I chose to use it, sounded tinny to my ears, but I could distinguish the words. Based on my family's reactions to it, I suspected most people heard a low buzzing sound but nothing resembling speech.

"I hear you fine. What's your name?"

"Jayden McQueen. I worked with Thomas." I changed location to the armchair. Arla continued to gaze at the spot from where I'd originally spoken.

"It's—"

Before she could finish, I cut her off.

"Stop. Don't say anything. Just listen." The place was bugged. If Gerry and Michael realized Arla was communicating with me, it would endanger her life as well.

Arla nodded at the armchair.

"What's going on?" Thomas squinted in my direction.

"I'll tell you in a moment," she replied.

I stood. "That's your little red car outside? Nod or shake your head."

She stared at Thomas, confusion clouding her face, but nodded.

I glanced at the half-finished bottle of wine. They hadn't had much, considering they'd been sitting here for at least two hours.

"Can you drive?"

She nodded.

"Tell Tom you want to take him for a drive. We'll go to your house. Don't ask any questions. I'll explain when we leave. Do you understand?"

Again, she looked at Thomas and nodded.

"Okay, now tell Thomas you'd like him to go back to your place with you."

She did as I asked.

Thomas hesitated. I tapped into his thoughts. He wrestled with the strangeness of her request and his attraction to her. Finally, he said, "I'll have to tell my mother's care provider I'm stepping out. She's gone to her quarters for the night."

Arla explained to Thomas on the drive to her home that I'd been the impetus for the change of location. I didn't say anything more until we arrived and Arla had ushered Thomas into the living room.

Her home was cozy, cute. She had witchy knickknacks that gave the place a goddess energy I loved. The sensation was new for me. In life, I'd have thought it all ridiculous.

A witch's broom, made of ash and willow, stood propped in a corner next to the woodstove. Statues of a Norse god and goddess ruled over a cloth-covered alter, surrounded by a small, lidded cauldron made of cast iron, a slim vase of flowers, and a three-candle candelabra.

The furniture was assembly-required pine with navy accents. Heavy on the feminine touches, it verified that Arla was a single woman living alone. A row of bookcases lined one wall, romance novels predominating.

"Jayden?"

I turned towards her.

Thomas and Arla huddled together on the couch, hands clasped. I had to admit, they made a cute couple. There was no way to predict if they'd end up together, but they deserved the chance to try. I relocated to the coffee table in front of them—an over-sized square that complemented the sectional where they sat.

"I'm here, Arla. Tell Tom."

She did, and he shifted his gaze to the coffee table. "Jayden, I'm so sorry for what happened to you. I can't believe you're dead."

"Tell him I'm not dead," I replied.

Instead of turning to Thomas, Arla continued to face me, worry etched on her face.

"Jayden ..."

"No, I understand I've passed. But I'm not dead. I'm here. To me, dead means gone, and I'm not gone."

"I understand." She repeated to Thomas what I'd said.

He silently digested the information. His thoughts were a confused jumble, skipping from one idea to the next, until settling on what we were doing at Arla's.

"Why are we here?" Thomas asked. "Why couldn't you talk to us at my house?"

With Arla's help, I explained that Thomas's place was bugged. I left out the threat of death around him—they both looked stricken enough at the news that someone was listening to them.

"Who are these men?" Arla asked.

Thomas provided an abridged explanation of the project we'd worked on together.

"Someone else has control of it now, and I've got nothing more to do with it." He faced me again. "I'm out of it. Whatever they're after, they can have it. I won't risk my life or anyone else's."

The wall of targets in Gerry's office flashed into my head.

"But there are other people who will get hurt."

Arla repeated my message to Thomas.

"What can we do?" he asked.

She rose and paced the room, envy for the ability growing in me with every step she took.

"It's not your business," she said to Thomas. "Stay out of it."

"I'm not arguing with you," he replied.

Arla halted and confronted him, hands on hips. "They'll hurt you."

He paled. "Are you sensing that? Is that a premonition?"

She hesitated, and I picked up from her thoughts that she wanted to tell him it was but didn't want to lie. At last, she said "no" and hung her head. When she looked up again, she went to sit beside him once more.

Taking his hands in hers, she said, "My recommendation to you, my client, is that you stay out of this. These men are dangerous—that's my intuition talking. You'll be okay if you keep your head down and do your work. I also suggest you find another job."

Before my eyes, Arla's aura darkened.

CHAPTER 25

My stomach churning and hands shaking, I stifled the groan that threatened to escape. Panicking Thomas and Arla wouldn't help anyone, and I was stumped. Everything I'd seen indicated that Thomas should no longer be a target, never mind that Arla wasn't. How could this have happened?

"I have to leave for a while," I said.

"Why?" Arla hugged herself, and her expression showed worry.

"It'll be okay," I lied. If Hell existed, I'd be burning in it for misleading them, but telling them the truth would only freak them out. "Stay inside and tell Thomas to stay out of the office servers."

She relayed the message, and he agreed readily enough. His face was white, and I'd never seen him so accommodating. Sorry I'd caused him such anxiety, I swore to myself I'd make it up to him.

"Arla?"

"Yes?"

"Tell Thomas to stay off his phone, too."

Without waiting for a response, I left Arla's and returned to Gerry's van, which was now heading back to Toronto.

***

As we reached highway 401, Daniel appeared in the captain's chair beside me. Before I could speak, he said, "It's not Laurel."

"Then who?" I slumped in my seat, emotionally drained.

"Someone from outside the company."

"Who?"

He shook his head. "Impossible to tell."

"Stop parsing me the information and tell me what happened."

He scowled, and when he replied, his words were clipped with frustration. "Someone was using Tom's PC. Remotely. No one was in the office. Okay?" His fingers tapped on the arm of the seat. "I found Laurel, but she wasn't on a computer. Neither was Dawson. They were together, by the way."

"Were they ...?" I didn't want to finish that thought in case I got a visual.

"Yeah. I didn't stick around to watch."

I'd never met Bernie's wife, but I felt sorry for her. No one deserved this kind of betrayal.

"He's using Laurel. He doesn't love her and won't leave his wife for her."

I frowned. "That makes it better?"

"No. I'm telling you what I picked up when I was with them. He's a slime. On that, we agree. But so is Laurel. They deserve each other."

"Never mind." The important thing was to find out who was messing around in Tom's computer. "We have a serious problem."

I told him what had happened with Thomas and Arla.

"Her aura darkened." My voice was close to hysterical by the time I finished. What if my interference had put her at risk? Guilt by association. If I'd stayed away from Thomas, he'd never have used the Ouija board, and he'd never have had a reason to contact Arla.

"They're going to kill her, too, and it's all my fault." I gripped the armrests of my seat.

Daniel covered my hand with his. "You don't know that. Maybe you were meant to get involved."

"Stop it. You know that's false. I'm to blame for this, so I have to fix it."

He stopped arguing, and as we fell silent, we realized Gerry and Michael were doing some disagreeing of their own.

"... killed an innocent man," Michael said.

"But you didn't," Gerry replied. His gaze was focused on the road ahead, so he didn't see the fury twisting Michael's face. And, of course, he wasn't privy to Michael's thoughts, which were ripe with rage.

"What's their definition of innocent?" I whispered.

"No idea. What did they think you were?" Daniel leaned forward so he could examine their faces. "Michael has doubts. If either one of them is likely to back out of killing Tom, he is."

"Have you listened to his thoughts? He's not thinking about killing either one of them." I frowned, puzzled. "He's not thinking about killing at all. Right now, all he cares about is that he might have killed without cause. He believes Tom is innocent."

"That's good, right?"

"Yes." I grabbed Daniel's arm. "But if he doesn't want to kill either of them, then why are their auras dark?"

"I don't know."

When we arrived at the office building, I searched for a sign or logo and didn't find one. The building looked like any one of a hundred other buildings that housed offices, but this one didn't announce proudly who owned it, while most of the others did.

"Downtown Toronto, so they can remain anonymous and lost in the crowd. No one's going to come in here without purpose. Check out the security." I waved my arm at the security desk in the lobby.

Banks of monitors displayed various locations in the building. Michael and Gerry buzzed themselves in and showed badges to the guard. Each pressed a thumb onto a scanner. After their identities were verified, they removed their weapons and stepped through a metal detector.

"Kind of ironic that they're checking killers for hidden weapons, don't you think?" I asked.

Daniel shrugged. "Routine. But I see your point."

"Watch this." I stood in the middle of the metal detector.

Within seconds, it zapped and sparked around me. When it went dark, the lights and monitors also went out.

"Cool." Daniel gave me a thumbs up and grinned. He wiped an imaginary tear from his eye. "I'm so proud of you."

The security guard was already using his cell phone to call for help. Michael and Gerry eyed the elevators and headed for the stairs. We stuck with Michael when the two reached the top and went to their respective offices.

I poked Daniel in the ribs and laughed. "Did you see how I made them take the stairs?"

He rubbed the top of my head with his hand and returned the

chuckle. "Too bad they didn't use the elevator. We could've had fun with that."

"If they don't back off, I'm going to have more than a little fun with them."

In Michael's office, we waited for him to power up his PC and open his files. He pulled up a report with Thomas's name on it and started typing. I leaned in behind him and observed.

"He's closing the case," I said, "and recommending they remove the surveillance equipment from Tom's home to focus on the office."

As Michael worked, I tapped into his thoughts. "He's determined to find out who's invading the system." I paused, listening to Michael's meanderings. "Terrorists. He hunts down terrorists."

The implications of that had me trembling with both fear and fury. He'd thought I was a terrorist. Who were these people who had the authority to mete out death without a fair trial?

Daniel leaned in closer to the screen, but a crackling sound made him pull back.

"Oops." He gave a wan smile. "Don't want to fry the CPU."

I put a hand on Daniel's arm, and when he raised his eyes and met my gaze, I said, "We have to find out who's hacking into Dawson's project and stop them."

CHAPTER 26

Anytime I wanted to locate a person, all I had to do was focus on the person's thoughts and draw my energy to that location. It was a matter of tapping into the person's aura and leveraging the personal connection. Since the moment of my death, I'd done this so many times it had become as automatic as breathing used to be.

However, tracking people I didn't know by name and had no connection to made locating them seemingly impossible. I refused to believe it couldn't be done.

Daniel suggested we begin from Thomas's office, which I agreed might be helpful. After ensuring neither Michael nor Gerry was likely to hunt down anyone that night, we headed to Dawson's.

At night, Dawson's offices are eerie and silent. During the day, there's always background noise, even if you tune it out. The IT department tends to be library quiet except for the whir of technology: printers, phones, fax machines, and such that testify to our productivity.

Now, all was quiet but for the almost imperceptible grind of Thomas's CPU as it executed whatever instructions our mystery person provided it.

"Thomas would be able to track the hacker, but I don't want him involved." I perched on top of the desk, glaring daggers at the blinking lights on the side of the monitor. "He's in there right now, and we can't get to him."

"Him?" Ensconced in Thomas's chair, Daniel stretched his legs out and rested his feet on the desktop.

"The generic 'him.' The hacker could be a woman, and it would be wise to remember it."

"Gerry's people are watching him. They'll find him for us."

I shook my head. "We have to find him first. If they locate him, he's dead."

Daniel nodded. "Likely. But maybe he deserves it."

"You mean if he's a terrorist?"

"Why else would he be doing this?"

"Gerry and Cornell jumped to that conclusion about me," I replied. "Obviously, they were wrong. They were wrong about Tom, too. At least they discovered that in time." Yet they weren't losing any sleep over my death, and, so far, no one had questioned whether they'd killed an innocent woman.

"Yeah," Daniel said. "You'd think someone would have been fired for it."

"Somehow, I think their definition of employee termination is different from ours." I hung my head. These men contained such potential for cruelty—too much to bear.

Daniel leaned forward and raised my chin with his finger. "Don't let what they are beat you down. If you do, they win."

"Thank you," I whispered, and, embarrassed that he'd seen weakness in me, turned my gaze to the monitor. The lights continued to blink and the CPU ground on.

To change the subject, I said, "What do we do now?"

He frowned at the blank monitor. "Find a way to connect to the person at the other end."

"He masked the IP address. If Gerry's team can't trace the route on the Internet, neither can we."

Daniel leaned his elbow on the desk and propped his chin on his hand.

"I'm not suggesting that. I don't understand the technology. But if we can sense his energy, we might be able to pick up thoughts. If we can do that, we can locate the hacker."

I must have looked puzzled because he gave me an affectionate smile. "Have you heard of remote viewing?"

"I've heard the term," I replied. "Seemed like hooey to me."

Daniel chuckled. "The US government studied it."

"How do you know?"

"Being dead gives me the highest security clearance."

I couldn't resist laughing out loud. "You spied on the US

government?"

"Not spied. I was trying to understand the limits of my abilities. I heard about their experiments and popped in to observe."

That would have been interesting. "Did they know you were there?"

He grinned. "No. All those psychics and not one of them sensed my presence."

Perhaps that meant they weren't psychic.

Daniel shrugged in response, though I hadn't vocalized it. "They weren't looking for spirits."

Much as I'd have enjoyed debating that, there wasn't time, so I let it slide. "Who ran the experiments? The CIA?"

"No, the US Army. The Stargate Project. That's not important. We can use remote viewing to find the hacker."

"All right. What's involved?"

Daniel pointed to the carpet. "Lie down. I'll talk you through it."

Uncertain, I moved to the floor and lay down on my back. Far above me, the black-dotted white ceiling attracted my gaze. "Should I close my eyes?"

"If you want."

I did.

"Think about the project. The hacker." Daniel's voice came from the floor next to me.

I peeked through half-closed lids.

He sat cross-legged by my shoulder, his gaze focused on the monitor.

"What do you see?" He spoke gently, his voice soothing. "Who's making the CPU work? Who's coming in over the network?"

I forced my mind to clear, pushing away thoughts of my kids, Thomas, Arla, my murderers, death, and everything else distracting my monkey mind. Someone had hacked into Dawson's network. Whoever it was had accessed protected files and was rooting around in them.

The vision of a slim hand popped into my head.

"A woman," I blurted out. "I see her hands."

The fingers were long and slender, the nails unpolished but filed neatly. She wore a wedding band and an engagement ring with a decent size diamond.

"She's married." Wonder filled my voice.

"You think married women can't be terrorists?"

"No. It's a shock, though."

Daniel put a hand on my shoulder. "Find her."

I focused on the hands, and the vision expanded to include the computer monitor. The project file was open in the window, and she was running the application.

"She's downloaded and installed the app," I said.

"What does that mean?" Daniel said.

"She's running the application. That means she snagged a copy of the source code or the compiled executable and installed it."

"So then—"

"She understands software development, or someone with her does."

"Locate her, Jayden."

I slipped back into meditation mode. Gradually, as though a curtain opened, I picked up thoughts. "She's frustrated. All she's viewed so far is test data. She can't trust any of what she's seen."

"Why?"

"I've located her. Come with me and I'll explain." I took his hand and we left Thomas's cubicle.

CHAPTER 27

Her name was Patty Richards, and she wasn't alone. She sat at a small desk in the basement of a closed bookstore, a blond-haired man perched on a stool beside her. The two hunched over the monitor and watched the data scroll past. A fan provided white noise and a breeze that would have made me shiver. As it was, Patty wore a cardigan over a turtleneck sweater, evidence that the fan wasn't there for comfort but concealment.

When Daniel and I arrived, the two were in the midst of a whispered conversation, as if terrified of being overheard even though the entire building was deserted.

"They're afraid the place is bugged."

I nodded my agreement. "It's her fault I'm dead."

"Jumping the gun a bit, aren't you?" Daniel stroked a hand down the back of my head, a reassuring gesture.

"What else can I conclude? If she wasn't the one who hacked her way into the system through my PC, then Gerry and friends have a serious security issue. How many people do you think are doing this? How many would have the skills?"

"What about Laurel?"

"Anything she's done was harmless by comparison. No wonder the activity on my computer raised flags."

"Maybe they really are terrorists."

I studied the couple. With her long, brown hair tied back in a ponytail and flawless skin, Patty looked youthful, but her hands betrayed her age. She was likely past forty-five.

The man appeared to be around the same age as Patty. A touch of grey showed in his hair, which was long enough to brush his collar. He wasn't fit, but he wasn't fat—he had that slightly doughy look men who don't exercise get as they age.

"His name's Ralph." Daniel moved to stand behind their stools. "He's a UFO nut. I assume she is, too. I haven't tapped into her yet."

"UFO nut?" I had a difficult time wrapping my head around that. "Not a terrorist?"

"Too soon to tell. I think we've uncovered something strange, though."

"Why would UFO nuts be after Dawson's project?"

"What's the data you're storing?"

"Nothing interesting. User info. Names, addresses, data from their PCs …" I trailed off, trying to understand what that meant. "Could be for anything. It seems innocuous enough, which is why they likely thought it was okay to farm it out. It's classified as spyware. It's monitoring software, like employers sometimes use."

"Seems like an awfully simple program to farm out."

"Bernie convinced them to turn it over to Dawson's. He's connected to Gerry. Friends, maybe. Gerry threw him the business, and I bet he got a kickback from Bernie for doing it."

"Don't you have to know what an application will be used for before you can design it?"

"Not in this case. They provided us with the requirements. All I had to do was create what they'd already spec'd out."

"That must have given you an excellent head start."

"I still had to develop the system. They had done the planning and analysis. But yeah, it gave me a head start." I considered the interface. "On one end, it's a simple data entry screen. Users can create reports from the data collected from the monitored device based on entered parameters."

The beauty of the application was the object-oriented code. Usage determined functionality in the classes.

"English, please. I can't understand anything you're saying. And thinking."

"Then quit eavesdropping." I smiled so he'd know I was kidding. "The system's design is generic. How a class is used determines how it behaves. It reduces code duplication and also allows it to be reused. The inputs are typical of most data entry applications."

"Then why didn't they buy something off the shelf? Why have it custom made and risk exposing themselves?" A cigarette appeared in Daniel's hand, and he puffed on it.

"They wanted something proprietary, and they bought the source code. That means they can take what we create and modify it to suit their needs. Doing it this way saves them having to do the bulk of the work but keeps the really sensitive stuff under their control."

A cell phone sounded, making Patty and Ralph jump.

Ralph gripped Patty's arm, calming her.

"It's okay. It's my disposable." He unclipped it from his belt and answered it. "Drummond ... Yes ... I'm sorry to hear that ... We didn't have a choice. It was easier to hack into Dawson's than the Agency ... No, stay where you are. Patty's with me ... Arnie's not here ... Yeah, bye."

"Your contact?" Patty asked when Ralph had put away the phone.

"Yeah. Log out and shut down."

Patty's eyes lit with fear, and her brows furrowed. Her mouth opened as if she wanted to question him, but then she hurriedly closed the application and powered down. When the screen was dark, she faced Ralph again.

"What happened?"

"The woman whose PC you used to access the app is dead."

Patty gasped and put her fist to her mouth. "Oh, God. When? How?"

"Last week. Heart attack." Ralph rose and paced the room. He didn't have much space—the room wasn't much larger than a broom closet, but he worked with what he had.

Once again, I envied the ability. Popping around a room wasn't as satisfying as walking it.

"A coincidence." She said it without conviction and hugged herself.

They fell silent, and the only sound in the room was the whoosh of the fan. I caught another whiff of Daniel's cigarette as he exhaled a long drag.

"It wasn't a coincidence." Ralph planted himself in front of her, hands fisted on hips. "They must know their files have been compromised."

"And we haven't learned a damn thing." Her eyes flashed with anger and frustration. "All that data we found? It's garbage. Dummy data."

"Did you expect them to provide real data?"

Patty sprang to her feet. "Then why'd we break into their servers?"

"To grab the app. Only the app. Data would've been a bonus, but I wasn't expecting to get it." Ralph dropped his arms to his sides but his hands remained fisted. "Hacking into the Dawson server was less risky—less chance of getting caught."

"Obviously, you were wrong about that."

"We weren't caught."

"That's not what it sounds like from the conversation you just had."

"Look, we're both stressed. Take a deep breath and calm down. We've got the app, now we can use it to interpret the data once they implement it on the Agency's server. Plus, we'll be able to set up alerts for it on our own systems. Now we know they're suspicious, we'll back off for a while."

"If they find out it's not a Dawson employee rooting around in there, they'll come after us." Patty sank back into her chair.

"Arnie knew what he was doing."

His aggrieved tone made her wince.

"Okay." It was said without conviction. She shook her head. "Arnie's good, Ralph, but they might be better. They have resources we don't. I told you that before we attempted this. You refused to listen."

"I listened. I refused to let it stop me. We can't live in fear of them or they win."

Beside me, Daniel swapped out the cigarette for a chocolate bar. How he could eat at a time like this baffled me.

"I always eat when nervous," he said.

"Oh, Uncle, these little things you do make me love you." I put an arm around him. "You're so you."

"What does that mean?"

"Nothing. Don't change."

He draped his arm around my shoulders. "Do they sound like terrorists to you?"

"Seems like they have a mission," I replied. Whatever it was, they'd gambled away my life for it, risked Thomas's and probably

Arla's, and were capping it off with their own.

I leaned against Daniel.

"We'll follow them. You stick to Ralph. I'll go with Patty. Maybe then we can figure out whose side we're on."

Daniel slanted me a puzzled look.

"If they're terrorists, Cornell and gang might be the good guys after all."

"They murdered you."

"By mistake."

"You're defending them?"

"No. I want to learn the truth."

When he agreed, a knot released in my gut. We were one step closer to dissecting this carcass and determining what was happening.

CHAPTER 28

An hour later, I found myself in a sprawling, brick bungalow in a comfortably middle-class neighbourhood in Aurora, Ontario. In one bedroom, Patty's teenage daughter, Michelle, and Michelle's boyfriend, Ian, studied for a math test. Fraser, Patty's husband, sprawled on the family room couch in front of the television. He'd just arrived home from a long day at the office where he held the position of CFO.

When Patty walked in the door, she called out to her family that she was home and headed to the kitchen. She leaned against the counter as she waited for water to boil for tea, tapping her finger nervously against her thigh. Based on her scattered thoughts, her husband had no idea she was involved with espionage of any kind. Her constant worry was that he'd become collateral damage if her covert activities were exposed.

I still couldn't figure out if that meant she was a terrorist. Everything about her home and her family spoke against that, but her actions and her behaviour belied it. She was involved in something lethal, but was she friend or foe? Was she fighting in the name of justice or revenge?

As the kettle whistled, her husband walked into the room.

"Hi, honey." He strode to her and hugged her in a way that told me this was the routine but she'd skipped it. "How come you didn't come say 'hi' when you got home?"

Her arms went around him but then dropped to her sides just as quickly. "I wanted to put the kettle on. Thought you might like some tea."

That was a lie. She hadn't given her husband a second thought when she'd walked in the door. Her entire focus had been on the app her group had stolen and on me. Even putting the kettle on had been done on autopilot. At least someone culpable was thinking about me with a measure of guilt.

The big question was why? Why feel guilty if she believed there was a greater good? Clearly, she believed that, or she wouldn't have been risking her own life and her family's future to do what she'd done. I sensed that what she'd done was even more serious than I knew. Whatever Patty and Ralph were up to, they'd been involved in it for a while.

"Thank you, I'd love a cup of tea," Fraser said. "Want some help? We can have it in the family room. I'm watching a show, but I can go back to it later."

She dropped a teabag into a teapot and poured the boiled water into it.

"No, you go ahead. I've got some work I want to do at my desk before I settle down for the night."

"You're spending a lot of time on UFO group stuff. Something up?"

"Oh, you know. The usual. I've got some recordings from the last sky watch Ralph's group did. He wants me to go through them. If I do that tonight, I'll get it out of my hair."

"Patty, you spent all evening with them."

"I'm sorry, Fraser. He needs me to review the video. It won't take long." Patty poured the tea into two mugs and handed him one. "I'll be less than an hour, I promise." She kissed him on the lips and left the room.

I met her in her office. She breezed in, shut the door, and locked it. After waiting by the door for a moment, listening for Fraser's footsteps, Patty strode to her desk. She set her tea by the monitor, but instead of powering on the computer, she pulled out her cell phone.

"Arnie? Patty." She dropped into her chair and yanked the elastic out of her hair. "Have you heard from Ralph?" Her gaze darted around the room. She picked up the lamp from the desk and examined it.

Amazed, I realized she was searching for anything out of place or for bugs.

"I'm fine. Anything unusual at your end?" She opened desk drawers and searched them. "I want you to meet me tomorrow, before the talk ... Yeah, at the coffee shop near the convention centre ... Eleven o'clock."

She powered up the computer as soon as she disconnected her call. When she was logged in, she opened her browser and went to the search box.

Once again, she'd lied to her husband about what she was up to. She wasn't reviewing any video recordings—she was searching for information about me.

A quick search on my name pulled up my obituary. Since it said only "passed away" without giving out the cause, she didn't have much to go on. Patty trolled through the photos that had been posted and studied my face, my kids, Rory.

Oh, God, we killed her. We killed that woman and now her kids have to live without their mother.

At least she felt bad, though she was taking on way too much guilt about it. She and Ralph hadn't killed me—Michael Valiant had. He'd pulled the trigger on the death ray that had stopped my heart.

I still didn't know why she'd risked my life, but it was some consolation that it disturbed her. Perhaps that meant she wasn't a terrorist.

As a software and web developer, I understood the value of occasionally doing an Internet search on myself to see what prospective employers or dates might find. I hadn't done that in a while, so when the results returned numbered in the hundreds of thousands, I would've staggered backwards had that option been available to me.

Of course, I'm not the only Jayden McQueen in the world, but, still, no one famous has that name. I leaned in close to examine the top links. My obituary was at the top, which made sense since Patty had recently visited that page.

After that, my social media profile links displayed, and then a bunch of images of me and other Jayden McQueens from around the web.

The effect was creepy.

I was dead, but I still lived on the Web. My family hadn't found all my social media links, and, while my Facebook page had a notice from Silver that I'd died, the profile was still active.

The Facebook page provided Patty with the most information on my death, including that I'd died of a heart attack. As soon as she spotted that tidbit, she whipped out her phone again.

"I verified McQueen died of a heart attack, Ralph," she said as soon as he picked up. "That rules out murder, right? She had a heart problem."

As my spirit heart sank in discouragement at the thought no one would know I'd been deliberately killed, she said, "A death ray? Are you crazy?"

Her thoughts turned to accusations of paranoia against Ralph and a willful blindness to what he was telling her. Nausea and fear fought with indignation and disbelief. Part of her believed whole-heartedly that a death ray could exist, but her rational mind refused to accept it.

"How is that possible? What do you think they are? Who comes up with this shit?" With every fibre of her being, Patty wanted to believe this was another crazy conspiracy theory.

"Yes, I'm on the disposable," she whispered. "Where are you?"

On his response, she said, "Did you check for bugs?"

Satisfied with his reply, she suggested he join her and Arnie, obviously a co-conspirator of theirs, at the coffee shop the next day.

"We have to figure out a way to get that data, otherwise, Jayden McQueen died for no reason."

How reassuring.

Patty said her goodbyes and disconnected her call. As she powered down her machine, the doorknob to her office rattled.

"Patty? You locked the door?" The voice was Fraser's.

Well, duh, dude, I thought.

Knots of anger and frustration roiled inside me, and it was all I could do not to zap the electricity in the house. Frying her computer would have been satisfying.

Patty scurried to the door and opened it, letting Fraser into the room. He looked annoyed, but when he noticed the worry on his wife's face, he softened.

"What's wrong, baby?" He brushed a lock of hair from her face and kissed the cheek against which it had lain.

"Nothing. A disagreement with Ralph."

Fraser flexed his biceps and wiggled his eyebrows. "Want me to have a talk with him?"

That got a laugh out of her, and her tension eased.

"No, you goof." She slipped her arm through his. "Come on. We'll watch some TV. I've done all I'm going to do tonight."

They left the room, and I zeroed in on Daniel. He was at Ralph's home, and after I locked onto the location, I followed him there.

CHAPTER 29

Ralph Drummond lived in a two-story brick home in an older section of the town of Aurora with his wife, Beth, and their two boys. Like Patty, he'd locked himself in his home office as soon as he'd arrived home. Like Fraser, Beth reacted with annoyance and frustration.

When I got there, Daniel was watching the couple argue about how much time Ralph devoted to his UFO group. Once again, Daniel puffed on a cigarette.

"Those things'll kill you, you know." I couldn't help myself. It popped out automatically. All my life I'd been programmed to say that.

He tossed an amused glance my way.

"Right. But maybe you should consider your next life. What if you reincarnate and the addiction carries into that life because you continued puffing away while you were dead?"

"You're reaching. I can't reincarnate—if there is such a thing—while I'm earthbound." He studied me, leaning his face into mine and squinting his eyes at me. "You okay? What happened at Patty's that got you so worked up?"

I sighed. "We're no further ahead now than we were before at figuring out what they're doing and who they are."

"They're UFO nuts."

"Yeah, I got that. But what's their mission? Why are they messing with Gerry and friends, and what the hell is the Agency?"

"We won't figure that out until Patty and Ralph learn what data

Gerry plans to store using that app."

A martini materialized in my hand. *May as well join him.* It wouldn't make me drunk, but at least I'd experience a placebo-effect destressing.

"That'll take time," I said. "First, the app has to finish the testing phase. Yeah, we completed programming, but it probably has bugs. Laurel will test it and fix bugs, and then Gerry will user-test it. If it passes, he'll take delivery, but if it doesn't, there'll be a round of bug fixes and testing."

"So? We've got time."

I stared at him, amazed that he'd so quickly forgotten lives were at stake.

"I haven't forgotten. Until implementation, Patty and Ralph won't push things. They've got a copy of the application."

"She doesn't know that much about software development if she doesn't realize they have a buggy version."

"I think all they care about is having any version."

"Makes me wonder, though. I think they not only stole the app but the source, too." Then they could do their own bug fixes, especially if they'd swiped copies of the documentation. If they had, they were damn good at hacking.

Beth and Ralph had kissed and made up by this time, though Beth continued to seethe inside. Ralph had promised to shut down his computer as soon as he'd posted a blog entry. She'd agreed to give him the space to do so, but she resented the concession. All of her thoughts revolved around feelings of neglect and loneliness. According to Beth, anytime Ralph wasn't at work, he was either with his UFO friends or locked in his home office working on UFO group business.

After Beth stormed from the room, Ralph turned his attention to his PC, which had gone into sleep mode. He activated it, and a window displaying a blank blog post appeared. While he pecked away at the keyboard using two fingers, Daniel and I read over his shoulder.

Ralph reported on a government conspiracy to cover up the existence of UFOs who come to Earth to experiment on people they abduct. I got the impression he wrote on this subject regularly and continued a previous thread.

From his thoughts, I picked up frustration at the lack of evidence of government collusion with extraterrestrials he'd been searching for with Dawson's app.

"Are you serious?" I hissed in a low voice. "They're cracking into government facilities or businesses who work with them to uncover UFO conspiracies?"

Daniel nodded. "Makes sense."

My head snapped around. "Makes sense? How?" What was wrong with these people? Why would they risk their lives, their families' lives, and my damn life to chase something that was about as real as a chimera?

"Calm down. I'm not saying they're right. What they're doing makes sense to them." Daniel put an arm around me and kissed my cheek. "What's a chimera?"

"A mythical creature. Part lion, part goat, part serpent."

"Sounds cool."

I laughed, which, as Daniel intended, released my tension.

"Let's get out of here," I suggested. "We're not going to learn anything more from him today, and I want to visit my friends and family. I need a break from all this."

Daniel readily indulged me, and we vanished, heading to my home where my daughter and Harrison would distract me for a while.

Funny how a single decision can change the course of your life—or in my case, death.

***

We took the rest of the month away from the UFO crazies. October remained mild and gorgeous, the leaves on the trees turning orange, red, and yellow, and then falling as softly as poppy petals.

Silver and Harrison often took walks through the local cemetery or along the trails that wind through Newmarket and Aurora. Sometimes, I'd follow them, reveling in my girl's pregnant glow. She suffered the occasional bout of morning sickness, but, for the most part, her pregnancy seemed to be going more smoothly than either of mine had.

This time of stillness, while nature wound down towards the darkness of winter, forced me to reflect on my life and what I'd done with it. To say I had a few regrets would be an understatement. That old chestnut about living every day as if it were your last haunted me as surely as I haunted my loved ones.

What did I regret? Touch. I should have savoured every touch, every hug, and every kiss that I'd ever shared with anyone, especially my children.

When they were babies, I'd tried to emblazon into my memory the soft feel of their skin, their baby-chick-down hair, their toothless smiles, how it felt to cuddle their warm bodies into the crook of my arm and feel the gentle tug at my nipple as they latched on. But as they grew, the newness wore off, and somehow, I forgot they were miraculous.

Oh, not always—there were times throughout their lives when I'd pause and impress a poignant moment onto my brain—but not often enough. As I watched Silver wander through her days, going to school, sharing her life with Harrison, I wished that I'd been more aware when I'd been on the physical plane.

Perhaps that's why I stole October for myself. We couldn't touch, but I could see and smell and hear, and that gave me as much of a second chance at appreciating those close to me as I could hope to get. It was a consolation and a comfort, though only Marc ever knew I was nearby, which made it bittersweet.

I even managed to slip away and visit my mother and sisters to fulfill my promise to provide proof of the afterlife. Daniel had suggested I visit during the night, while they slept. It's possible then to communicate with the living, though they often believe it's a dream.

My sister, Sarah, the skeptic, refused to believe it was anything more than a dream. Mom and Lois interpreted it as my spirit's farewell, which is likely true. Mustering energy for dream communication drained me, and I didn't want to try it again anytime soon.

A huge positive of my month off was the disappearance of the darkness in Thomas's and Arla's auras. Both cleared up, and that gave me the assurance I needed to let my guard down. However, as October eased into November, I discovered that while Daniel and I had been enjoying ourselves, Gerry and Michael had been busy.

We hadn't ignored those two—we just hadn't stalked them. Did I stop caring about what they were doing? No. But some things never change, even with the best of intentions, and I was never what you'd call an activist.

Was it possible this group that called themselves The Agency had some kind of agreement with extraterrestrials? Possibly, but I didn't really believe it. In all my life, I'd never believed in little grey men. I'd never bought that the crash in 1947 in Roswell, New Mexico was anything other than a weather balloon, just as the US military maintained.

Same with the sightings at Rendlesham Forest in the UK. The moving light reported could very well have been a nearby lighthouse.

What makes more sense? That extraterrestrials visit our planet, teasing us with light shows, exsanguinating cattle, and creating artistic designs in cornfields while the government covers for them? Or that attention-seekers get their fifteen minutes of fame by sharing their stories about sightings and abductions?

Some people make an excellent living from these stories. I refused to buy into them. Not this gal. You can't sell me swampland in Florida. I want solid proof. Heck, when I was a kid in Catholic school, and I heard the story of Doubting Thomas, I identified with Thomas. Show me the proof. There's nothing wrong with wanting to see the evidence.

What finally pulled my head out of the homey quilt I'd burrowed it into was a chance encounter with Patty Richards.

CHAPTER 30

I followed Silver to the mall after she finished school one Tuesday afternoon. She continued to work at her part-time job as a sales associate at Dressing Up, a clothing store selling the latest fashions for young adult women. In a few months, when she would begin to show, she planned to quit. At least the money she'd inherited from my estate would keep her afloat for a while.

Alone in the store, Silver worked on pricing items and stocking shelves. She admired the new fashions with more than a little regret that she'd be unable to wear them. Feminine laughter interrupted her work, and she greeted her new customers.

"Hi, may I help you?"

The mother and daughter could have passed for sisters, but I knew they weren't. Patty and her daughter, Michelle, returned my girl's smile.

"Daniel!" I couldn't hide the panic in my voice.

"It's all right. They're shopping." He placed a reassuring hand on my shoulder.

"Are they? She searched about me on the Internet."

He levelled his gaze at me. "Listen to her thoughts."

I exhaled the breath I'd been holding. "Of course."

Patty's thoughts focused on finding the ideal dress for her daughter. Michelle had plans to attend a musical in Toronto on the weekend with her boyfriend and wanted something new to wear.

A twinge of pain squeezed my heart. I'd never go shopping with Silver for the maternity clothes she'd need. I tilted my face to stare at the floor so Daniel wouldn't notice my grief.

"Honey, you can't hide it from me," he said. "I can sense what you're feeling even if I'm not eavesdropping on your thoughts."

Damn it.

He stroked my arm. "That's a good thing."

"Since when is lack of privacy a bonus?"

"Instead of viewing it that way, consider that I love you and am here for you. You want to cry?" He tapped his shoulder. "Right here."

Helpless to stop the grin, I beamed at him. "I can never be sad around you."

What would I have done without him?

"Well," he said, catching the sentiment, "you might have crossed over. You could be having tea with David Bowie right now."

Puzzled, I said, "Why Bowie?"

He shrugged. "Why not?"

By this time, Silver had pulled three dresses and a top and skirt combo from racks lining the store. Michelle, her face flushed with excitement, followed Silver to the dressing room, Patty taking up the rear.

Not wanting to peep on Michelle changing, I considered leaving but was reluctant to while Patty remained in the store. She hadn't come here to spy on Silver or put her at risk, but that didn't mean the risk wasn't there.

No sooner did that thought cross my mind than I noticed a woman in jeans and a T-shirt sitting on a bench outside the store. She appeared to be waiting for someone, but something about her made me tap into her thoughts.

"She's following Patty." I gripped Daniel's arm. "Oh, God, she's Agency."

I listened further, hoping to determine if Silver's identity registered on the woman's radar. Behind me, the women oohed and aahed over the dress Michelle modelled.

"You look beautiful in this one, honey," said Patty, her voice filled with pride and affection.

Immediately, Silver jumped in with a comment. "I agree. The colour is lovely on you."

"I don't know." But Michelle didn't sound dubious. "Yeah, I think so too."

Heart thudding in my chest, I popped from the store to stand beside Agency Lady. She looked like any other shopper hanging around waiting for a friend or spouse to finish up in another store.

Her face had minimal makeup, and with nothing to accentuate her features, she wouldn't stand out in a crowd. Even her bag was plain and cheap looking. She leaned forward, sliding her running-shoe-clad feet slightly under the bench.

After following Patty all day, she was bored but alert. The shopping trip had been a slight change in routine, but Agency Lady would have preferred finding evidence of terrorist activity. She hoped this assignment would lead to a promotion. She was all but packing her bags to go for training.

"There's a camp for assassins. They train them." I turned a horrified gaze on Daniel.

"I guess they'd have to." He shook his head. "If they're fighting terrorists, what else can they do?"

"Okay," I said grudgingly. "But does Patty look like a terrorist to you?"

"It's not like we know her well."

The excited voices inside the store drew nearer to the exit. Patty and Michelle were leaving, and Silver was encouraging Michelle to post photos of her in the dress on the company's social media pages.

That's my girl. What a fantastic sales person.

"Jayden."

Daniel nodded at the woman on the bench. "She's not the only one watching them." He waved at a coffee stand in the centre of the aisle.

A man leaned against a post, sipping a coffee.

Shocked, I recognized him as the man who'd been in the waiting room with my family when they'd received the news of my death. He'd been there to make sure I didn't survive. I wondered if Michael Valiant had been reprimanded for not killing me instantly. Or maybe they had to do this each time? Perhaps the ray hadn't been perfected enough to kill instantly.

When Patty and Michelle veered left as they exited the store, Agency Goon casually strode after them, giving Agency Lady a slight nod as he passed. She rose and strolled away.

"Shift change?" My words dripped disdain. Not expecting a reply from Daniel, I continued. "At least this probably means they're not interested in Silver."

"Agreed."

"What's the point of stalking Patty on a shopping spree?"

"Only one way to find out." He disappeared.

I waited, tracking Patty via her thoughts. The women were returning to the car, the shopping expedition completed. Patty's plans were to drop Michelle at her girlfriend's house so she could show off her new dress. Patty would continue on to meet Ralph.

And the Agency was hot on her heels.

I had to stop her.

From the backseat of Patty's car, I tried to figure out what to do. Daniel sat beside me, smoking a cigarette.

"You stressed, Uncle?"

"No, why?" He took a deep drag and exhaled the pungent smoke. "Does my smoking bother you?"

"No, but if you're stressed, there are better ways to relax." I gave him a rueful grin. "And I forgot again it won't harm you. Never mind."

He patted my hand, which gripped the back of Patty's seat. "You look like you could use a relaxant yourself. Are you afraid the Agency will harm Silver? They haven't been near your home or office for a month now."

"I know, but now I'm worried about Patty and Ralph—even Arnie."

We'd met Arnie a time or two over the last month when we'd checked in on Patty and Ralph. Not once had they exhibited terrorist activity. While I didn't agree with what they were doing, I didn't want them to pay for it with their lives.

Patty pulled up to a house in her neighbourhood and let Michelle out.

After giving her mother a quick hug and thanking her for the dress, Michelle raced from the car towards the house. Patty watched her daughter until she was safe inside and then turned the car around and drove to a nearby coffee shop.

When she pulled into the parking lot, Ralph and Arnie were visible through the window where they sat at a table.

"We're going in," I said.

CHAPTER 31

Patty bought herself a cup of coffee and joined her two friends. The trio huddled together, whispering about UFOs and government conspiracies. A few patrons, mostly teens, sat at various tables. Patty and friends camped at a table far enough away from others that they wouldn't be overheard by anyone still among the living.

Daniel and I stationed ourselves at a table beside them and conjured coffee and pastries for ourselves. While alive, I'd avoided junk food, being health conscious—for all the good it had done me. At least I'd been healthy and fit when I'd been murdered.

"Do you regret caring for your health?" Daniel asked.

"Not exactly." I bit into an éclair. "But I do regret ruining my enjoyment when I did have treats. Every time I indulged, I felt guilty about it. I should have savoured it."

He nodded knowingly.

"I was the opposite, indulging in everything. So hedonistic." His eyes filled with sorrow. "I should have gotten help for my alcohol problem."

"Too late to dwell on it now."

He raised his brows and cocked his head at me.

"Yes, that goes for me, too," I said. "At least we both know better now."

I studied the three people sitting next to us.

Arnie, in particular, attracted my gaze. He was yummier than even your typical hot hunk despite being a nerd by trade—a fellow software developer. I wasn't the only female in the room checking him out.

His eyes, blue and intense, drew me in first. I couldn't stop gazing into them. Taller than all the other men in the place, he carried his height with confidence. No slouching. His honey-coloured hair grazed the collar of his dress shirt, which was unbuttoned at the top. The sleeves were rolled up, exposing solid and sexy forearms. A light fuzz on his chin and cheeks that matched his hair in colour gave him a bad-boy allure. The unfortunate thing about this God's gift to women was his awareness and exploitation of it.

From his thoughts, I'd learned he was having an affair with a woman in his UFO group and had even slept with Patty once. When I'd first picked up on that, my disappointment in Patty bordered on rage. How could she? But every time I was around Arnie, I could understand, a little, how attention from him would be difficult to ignore.

And Patty didn't have the advantage of reading his mind. The guy was a hound inside, but outwardly? Irresistible charm.

My gaze still focused on Arnie, I spoke to Daniel. "Maybe we can help them realize their priorities are skewed before it's too late."

"That's not our job."

I frowned and shifted my gaze to meet Daniel's. "Why not?"

He opened his mouth to reply, but when nothing came out, I said, "We're here. We're aware. We've got the resources. If we aren't supposed to intervene, then why are we here?"

"Do you suddenly believe in fate?"

"No. I believe in taking charge." I waved my hand at the trio beside us. "They're playing a deadly game, and their families will pay the price for their stupidity. We can help them get past that."

Daniel squirmed, and a pained expression crossed his face.

"What?" Did he think what they were doing was okay?

"We don't know what'll happen. What if it's all true?"

"Aliens? Seriously?" I shook my head. "You don't believe that, do you?"

Or had he stumbled across evidence on this side of the spiritual divide?

"Have you seen ETs?" I pictured the little alien from Spielberg's movie and almost laughed out loud.

"I haven't seen evidence of extraterrestrials, but that doesn't mean they don't exist." He selected a double chocolate doughnut from the plate in front of us and bit into it. After he swallowed, he continued. "I've never concerned myself with UFOs or aliens. My concerns were more terrestrial. I watched over Grace and my daughter, their families. Sometimes I amused myself by appearing at a séance and startling the medium."

"You've never visited other planets?" I recalled our jaunt to the moon.

"No." He selected another pastry and chomped on it.

"Why?" Imagine seeing Saturn's rings up close, or checking out Venus or Jupiter—heck, any of the planets in and out of our solar system.

Daniel swallowed what was in his mouth and licked his lips. "Man, I haven't indulged like that since ..." He trailed off, and I picked up from his mind a vision of him sitting, invisible, next to Suzanne at a family gathering.

The little girl sat on the floor in front of the coffee table, legs crossed, holding a paper plate with a thick and gooey slab of vanilla-iced cake. She scooped delicate bites with a plastic fork, and licked her lips after chewing each morsel.

Across from her, Grace sat on the couch, her own piece of cake resting on a china plate.

Suzanne must have been about eight then, only two years away from death.

Daniel had duplicated a plate of delicacies for himself so he could eat with them. My heart ached, as his did, at the memory.

"I'm sorry, Uncle," I whispered.

"You tell yourself it's enough to be around them," he said, "but the torture of being unable to touch them or talk to them never goes away."

He wiped ghostly tears from his eyes with the heel of his hands. "Well, enough of that. Sorry to sidetrack you. Have you had enough?" He indicated the pastries.

When I nodded, they vanished.

"To answer your question," he said, "I've been afraid to venture out into space. It's not somewhere I want to see, especially not alone."

"We could go together. Find out if what they're trying to uncover is real or a hoax." Why hadn't the truth already come out?

Had no one in the spirit world cared enough to solve the mystery that had dogged us since at least Roswell?

"We wouldn't even have to leave the planet. All we'd have to do is explore Area 51. The evidence, if there is any, would be there. At the very least, there'd be clues to where we could look." A sense of excitement and adventure surged through me.

Daniel contemplated for a moment, staring at nothing, his head tilted down. "Maybe we don't even have to go that far. If the Agency is colluding with extraterrestrials, there'd be evidence on their premises. We could find it."

"And give it to Patty and Ralph," I concluded.

He snapped his head up. "Not unless there's a valid reason."

"Why would we keep it from them? They want answers."

Daniel pointed at Arnie. "This guy. Haven't you noticed? He's a loose cannon. If anyone betrayed them to the Agency, it was probably this guy."

"How so?" Maybe I'd let his appearance distract me, or maybe Daniel had spent more time following Arnie, but I hadn't noticed anything suspicious about his behaviour. As far as I saw, he was no more reckless than the other two.

"For one, he flirts with any woman within his line of sight. He's not fussy. That makes him the group's weak link. Listen to his thoughts. He's randier than a one-eyed raccoon."

I couldn't hold in the laughter, and coffee sprayed from my mouth.

Daniel dabbed at his face with a napkin but continued talking, unperturbed. "For another, he's mouthy on his blog. He's daring the government to notice him. That, more than anything, would have put them on the Agency's radar. You taunt the people in charge of the conspiracy the way he does, and you're asking to be taken down. He's arrogant, and it'll hurt them all."

"Okay," I admitted. "You have a valid point."

I refilled my now empty cup with more coffee. Perk number eighty-eight for being dead: bottomless cups of coffee for eternity.

"Arnie, I want you to take a copy of the app." Patty's words caught my attention, and I tuned in to their conversation.

"You have it with you?"

She nodded and dug in her purse. When she pulled her hand out, she held a compact. Opening it, she gave her face a quick once over, snapped the compact closed, and dropped it back in her bag.

Her fingers remained curled around something tucked in her palm.

They continued to chat until Patty stretched and then rose from her seat. "I need to run. Fraser's out, but he'll be home soon. I want to beat him there."

The guys rose to hug her. When she leaned in to peck Arnie's cheek, she slipped a memory stick into his jacket pocket.

"Whom should we follow?" I asked Daniel.

"You stick to Patty. I'll stay with the guys. If they separate, I'll go with Arnie and see what he does with that app."

"All right." I waved goodbye to Daniel and jumped to the passenger seat of Patty's car. As she pulled onto the street, I peeked into the rear-view mirror.

Behind us, the Agency vehicle followed.

CHAPTER 32

Even though Daniel and I followed Patty, Ralph, and Arnie around for a week, we couldn't find any evidence that they were terrorists. They never showed any desire to blow anything up or harm anyone. Their single-minded mission appeared to be finding evidence of the existence of extraterrestrials and suppressed collusion between aliens and the government—all governments.

The three believed governments from around the world were working with the extraterrestrials to exchange humans for experimentation for alien technology. To me, it sounded insane; to Daniel, it sounded plausible.

In the end, we decided the best strategy was to follow Gerry and Cornell around. If anyone was likely to lead us to evidence of alien conspiracies, it was these two. Again, we split up, Daniel following Gerry and me following Cornell.

Like Michael, Cornell was married, but unlike Michael, who had no children, Cornell had two boys.

On this particular day, Cornell arrived home late. This start-early-and-finish-late schedule seemed to be popular with Agency people. I couldn't figure out if it was because they loved their work so much (a terrifying thought), or if it was because they hated their family life so much.

Cornell's wife, Virginia, AKA Ginny, sat perusing a fashion magazine on the family room couch. The live-in housekeeper, Marnie, had already cleared away the dinner dishes and retired to her room. The boys, George and Wade, were up in their respective bedrooms doing homework or playing. Wade, eleven, was absorbed in a math assignment. George, only five, had no homework, so he sat on the carpet in his room, playing with his toy trucks.

I got the sense that these kids were typically out-of-sight-out-of-mind as far as their parents were concerned. If the boys needed anything, they'd bug the housekeeper before they'd dream of going to their parents. Their loneliness was a palpable ache.

After Cornell hung his coat in the closet and set his boots on the tray by the door, he headed for the wet bar in the living room. On his way past the family room, he stuck his head in to greet Virginia.

"How was your day?" she asked, though her voice was distracted. I could tell she wasn't interested. The conversation was a ritual and went the same way every day.

"Fine. Yours?"

"Good." She glanced up long enough to pantomime pouring a drink.

Receiving the message, he nodded.

He strode into the living room and fixed himself a scotch and soda and his wife a vodka martini. I decided to join them, and a cosmopolitan appeared in my hand. Amazing how it was tart, delicious, and perfectly mixed. If only I could study the mechanics of manifesting.

The new-agers in my life had crowed long and loud about how anyone could manifest their dreams. I'd always written it off as wishful thinking. Of course, things didn't work this well on the physical plane, but perhaps the love and light crowd had the right idea after all.

Cornell handed Virginia her drink. After giving him a cursory nod, she sipped and told him the martini was good. That's as far as their interaction went. He told her he'd be in his office and left the room.

I met him there and watched while he booted up his computer and settled in. As the others I'd spied on had done, he locked his door so no one could walk in unannounced. The first thing he pulled up on the computer screen was a file with reports from Michael and Gerry. The subject matter chilled me.

The reports described assassinations and kidnappings, some dating back ten years. Cornell was digging for something. He read, sorted, and filed. I stopped reading over his shoulder and lay down on the couch opposite the desk to track his progress via his thoughts. After a while, I realized he was reviewing everything Michael Valiant had worked on.

After an hour of this, I was ready to call it a night when Cornell's thought patterns changed. Up to this point, he'd been in work mode, routine. Now, he shifted to relaxation mode, as if he were getting into something that excited and interested him.

I moved to stand behind him, but when I peered over his shoulder, I must have leaned in too close, because he shivered. He went to the thermostat that controlled the gas fireplace and turned it up. In the meantime, I scanned the document he'd pulled up.

It looked like a medical file. The name at the top read "Carolyn Fairchild."

She was a healthy woman, late thirties. A photo embedded in the document showed a pretty blonde with electric-blue eyes. She wore a half-smile that hinted at self-deprecation or wry humour. Warmth and kindness radiated from her. Was it the photographer's skill that revealed such character, or was I sensing it psychically?

As Cornell slid back into his chair, pleasantness vanished, replaced by dark foreboding. He traced a finger over the woman's cheekbones, and lust emanated from him. His mind filled with a vision of her strapped naked to a table.

With rising nausea, I struggled to determine if this was something he'd dredged up from memory or from fantasy. Neither option was reassuring. I should find Daniel and report this new development. Cornell was some kind of pervert, and he used his power and authority to exploit at least one woman.

Tempting as it was to escape Cornell and his sordid thoughts, I forced myself to stay. To be any use to Carolyn Fairchild, I'd have to stay and learn what I could. How could I ignore what went on here? I'd be abandoning an innocent woman to victimization.

Teeth gritted, I resumed reading the document as he scrolled through it—and finally found evidence of extraterrestrial contact. The agent who'd provided the report described tests done on Carolyn by extraterrestrials and then by Agency scientists.

My stomach lurched at the description of invasive tests on her reproductive organs, including harvesting of her eggs. I shivered and my hand trembled when I raised it to swipe at a lock of hair that had fallen in my face.

This one report proved that contact with alien beings had been established. It also verified that the aliens were experimenting on humans with the help and permission of this secret organization. I still had to determine who ran the Agency, but I suspected government involvement.

Eyes closed, I attempted to connect to Daniel. I picked up his thoughts and located him with Gerry.

Come here, Uncle, please. I infused the plea with as much urgency and need as I could manage.

Barely had I finished the thought when Daniel appeared, his face anxious.

"Jayden?" His expression turned to relief when he spotted me. "What's going on?"

"I've found what we've been searching for." I waved a hand at the computer screen.

He leaned in close, and, once again, Cornell shivered. He glanced at the fireplace, which was lit, the blower on and circulating the warm air. With thoughts of a sweater and hot coffee in his head, Cornell left the room, shutting and locking the door behind him.

Daniel took Cornell's place in the chair and studied the file.

When you're a spirit, manipulating anything in the physical plane is difficult. It takes focus and energy, and, if it involves electronics, you have to take care not to zap them. The longer you're on the earth plane, the easier it gets, but it never matches what it was like when you were alive. Therefore, when Daniel tried to scroll up to view the top of the document, he failed on the first try.

He drew in a patient breath and concentrated, dragging his index finger along the mouse's scroll wheel. This time it worked, and the document shifted up. Carolyn's picture appeared in the window.

"She's attractive." Daniel dropped his elbow to the desk and propped his chin on the heel of his hand. "Can't believe they can do this."

"I can't believe they're able to erase it from her memory." According to the document, they wiped her memory at the end of every session.

"She's a psychic," he observed. "We could communicate with her."

"I don't know." The thought of going to her and telling her what they were doing made me nervous. How would I have reacted if some ghost had appeared to inform me aliens and government agents were experimenting on me and then erasing my memory?

"We can't. It'd destroy her. We have to figure out a better way."

Daniel attempted another scroll with the mouse and nailed it on the first try. The document swept two pages down.

A gasp behind us made me whirl around.

Cornell stood inside the doorway, his gaze taking in the scrolling window and the moving mouse.

CHAPTER 33

Daniel snatched his hand away from the mouse and leapt to his feet. As soon as our gazes met, we both laughed.

"Relax," I said. "He has no idea what's going on."

Cornell dropped to his knees in front of his desk and searched beneath it as if looking for hidden wires or magnets. The coffee cup he'd dropped on the floor had been full. The milky liquid was soaking into the carpet, unnoticed by the man who'd spilled it.

When he realized there was no trick, no smoke and mirrors, Cornell hauled himself into the chair. Working quickly, he backed out of the file and powered down the computer. He pushed away from the desk, skimming the chair across the coffee puddle and landing his stocking feet smack into it.

He spewed out a curse, and using an intercom, called the housekeeper to come clean it up.

"I've seen enough here." I wasn't going to stick around and watch him make someone else clean up his mess. "We can discuss things at my house."

Daniel took my hand, and we vanished.

***

At home, I discovered I could walk.

We were in the living room, Daniel on the couch with a coffee and cigarette, me standing at the large bay window. It was dark outside, but I stuck my face through the curtains and gazed out into the night.

Streetlights illuminated the front yard. Our neighbour, Mrs. Frankenhouser, stood on her front porch and whistled at her border collie, Percival, who'd escaped captivity and raced up and down the sidewalk. Occasionally, he veered onto the road. She was lucky the street was deader than I was.

Percival's antics made me smile but in a wistful way. We'd had a golden retriever when the kids were little, and I missed him. He'd passed away shortly after Rory and I had separated, leaving me emotionally drained. The kids had recovered enough after a month to ask for another dog, but I hadn't had the heart.

"I should've bought them a dog." Without thinking, I took a step in Daniel's direction. My face must have registered my shock because he chuckled.

"It's not a miracle, sweetie—just another step in your earthbound evolution." He moved to stand before me and clasped my hands in his. "Now, we can dance."

We spun around the room in a silent waltz, my heart soaring. There's freedom in movement that eclipses even playing in the clouds or standing on the moon.

Sometimes, it's the little things.

Daniel slowed our pace, released me, and bowed low. In return, I curtsied but wasn't ready to stop moving yet. I paced, and it was as satisfying as I remembered.

"You enjoy the strangest things, darling." Daniel parked himself on the couch again.

"It makes me feel almost alive."

Daniel produced another cigarette and dragged deeply on it. He puffed out a smoke ring. I followed its progress up to the ceiling.

Time to get back to business.

"We have to stop Cornell. He's evil."

"Surely you're not suggesting we kill him."

Horrified, I said, "Of course not. How could you think that?"

"I didn't seriously think so, but I can't see us doing anything else that ends with him giving up his career."

In a burst of inspiration, I said, "We could haunt him."

Daniel grinned. "You've been wanting to haunt someone ever since you got here. What makes you think that would halt his activities?"

"We'll interfere with everything he does."

"That can't go on indefinitely."

I halted, hands on hips, and grinned at him. "We've got nothing but time, so yes, it can."

He dragged on his cigarette and puffed out another smoke ring while he considered my suggestion. "I agree he should stop ..."

"But?"

He shook his head. "We can't interfere with what's meant to be."

"Meant to be? If you believed that, you'd be over on the other side. Did you or did you not choose to stay behind?"

"Yes, but—"

"No buts." I sat on the coffee table and met his gaze. "Aren't I here because I decided to stay here?"

"Yes, but—"

I cut him off again. "If we have no control over what happens, we might as well lie down and do nothing. I refuse."

"What do you intend to do? Stand next to him to keep him shivering and turning up the thermostat? Zap his electronics?"

I shrugged. "Maybe."

Daniel leaned back on the couch, and the cigarette in his hand disappeared. "Count me out."

"What?" Perhaps I hadn't heard him correctly.

"You're on your own on this. I'm bowing out. It's not our concern."

"How can you say that? You've seen what they're doing—what they've done. I'm a casualty of it. Doesn't that bother you?"

"Of course it does." He clasped my hands. "But if death is the worst thing that can happen to someone, is it so bad?"

"Some things are worse than death—having your eggs harvested without your consent, for one. Can you really sit there and tell me you won't do anything to help that poor woman?"

I yanked my hands from his and stood up to pace again. "Can you really sit idle and let them murder innocent people? Experiment on innocent people?"

"There's nothing we can do about it." He stood now, too, and went to the window. Thrusting the curtains to the side, he pressed his face to the glass. "Don't you think I tried? For years, I tried to make an impact."

I rushed to his side and put my arms around him. "You can affect the physical plane to a greater degree than I can. Together, we can stop Cornell."

He returned my hug, but then eased away from my embrace. His eyes were sad. "I can't help you."

"You mean you won't." I snapped the words out. "For once in your life, step up instead of avoid."

His expression became wounded as well as sad, and I regretted my harshness.

"I'm sorry, Uncle," I said, "but I can't ignore what's happening."

"What can we do? We'd fail and get others killed by interfering. Have you considered that?"

"No one else will be involved in this. Just Cornell, and if he's killed, it's because he deserves it."

Shock registered on his face. "Now you sound like them."

The words cut me deep inside. "How dare you? I'm standing up for what's right. For the innocent."

He shook his head. "You're after revenge."

"You're making assumptions about my motives? Did you pick that up from my thoughts?" I glared at him, daring him to say yes.

"You've expressed anger at your murder. Not only in your thoughts but out loud."

I forced myself to pause and count to ten. It was a trick I'd used when the kids were little and pushed the limits of my patience. If I didn't calm down, I'd say something else I'd regret.

"I hate that they murdered me, that they thought they had the right to decide when and how I should die. They stole me from my children. Stopping Cornell might get me some satisfaction for what they did to me and my family, but it wouldn't be as satisfying as preventing him from doing it to someone else."

"Who made you judge and jury on this? The living can look after themselves, and so they should." He stroked my cheek with his finger. "I'm out of this. If you feel you must intervene, then you'll do it without my help."

Before I could reply, he vanished, ending the conversation.

CHAPTER 34

Before I returned to Cornell's house, I took some time to visit with both my children.

Silver and Harrison spent their days at school. The pregnancy was still a secret kept to their immediate families, Silver's best friend, Marlene, the only exception.

I'd known Marlene since the two girls had met in junior kindergarten. They'd done everything together since then and were as close as sisters. Marlene would never betray my daughter.

Harrison kept his personal business personal and hadn't said anything to any of his guy friends. He was getting close to confiding in Alan, his best friend. Quite frankly, I hoped he would. I didn't believe in bottling things up. He needed input from a close male friend, so when he brought up the subject to Silver, I hoped she'd go along with it.

They were sitting at the table having dinner two nights after Daniel had abandoned me. Silver had made a simple meal of pasta with meat sauce and salad, and Harrison had added a garlic bread from the local pizza place.

He'd been edgy ever since they'd arrived home from school, and the air was fraught with tension. As they ate their meal in silence, he broached the subject.

"Al's dropping by after dinner."

Silver finished chewing a piece of garlic toast and nodded her head. "Okay. Any particular reason?"

"I invited him. We haven't been hanging out much lately."

"Sure." She kept her gaze on him but didn't push him for explanations.

"I'd like to tell him about the baby." He stuck his palm out as if to stop her from speaking, though she only sat, watching him. "We could tell him together. Marlene knows already, and Al's my best friend."

"All right." She spoke quietly, resigned that the news would slowly spread. While she didn't assume Alan would be the one to broadcast it, she expected that, one person at a time, it would get out.

For my part, I ached for what they'd go through, but compared to the Agency horrors I'd witnessed, these were minor, temporary problems. When Silver agreed to share her secret with Alan, something released in Harrison. His face brightened and his shoulders, which had been hunched up, relaxed.

He beamed a smile at Silver, and she returned it.

"Were you worried I wouldn't let you tell your best friend?"

"Sorry, I should have known better."

"Harry, I'm not looking forward to the news getting out, but I trust Alan. You have good taste in friends." She smiled. "And in girlfriends."

"That I do," he replied.

A sense of finality hovered over the evening, and I felt as though I were saying goodbye. Maybe I was—if not forever, then for a long time. Disgusted by these maudlin thoughts, I forced myself to shake them off and enjoy the time I spent with my daughter and her boyfriend.

Silver looked happy and healthy, and so did Harrison. They had family, friends, and solid finances. At least something good had come out of my death. Of course, if I hadn't died, she'd have had my direct help and my financial support. No matter how hard I tried to look on the bright side of what had happened, to find that silver lining, I couldn't do it.

While revenge wasn't my prime motivation for going after Cornell, I had to admit revenge featured prominently.

I remained with Silver and Harrison until Alan arrived, and then I carried on to Marc's dorm room at university.

He was studying, as always. The kid was a studying machine. It thrilled me to see him so passionate about school, and I knew he'd be successful in his field. I was proud of him, but sometimes, I wished he'd find himself a girlfriend, go out, and party.

As he had other times, he sensed my presence.

I sat on his bed, and he talked to me, telling me about his schoolwork and his job helping his profs with some research. It excited him. I wished with all my heart I could speak to him, but he couldn't hear me. I'd have to be content with the knowledge that he sensed me.

All too soon, I felt the tug to confront Cornell and had to leave. The longer I stayed with the kids, the greater became the urgency to get on with what must be done. Finally, the guilt became unbearable.

I didn't sleep, but neither did the Agency, and Cornell had to be stopped. I went to Marc and kissed his cheek. Tears falling, I vanished from his side.

***

Two days later, my torment of Cornell was in full swing at his office. He was on the phone, trying to talk to someone about property the Agency held in Peterborough. From the sound of it, they had property all over North America, much of it in rural pockets where they could work undisturbed. All they'd have to do is put up fences and "keep out" and "research facility" signs, and the average person would ignore them.

Except when it came to some UFO conspiracy nuts like Ralph, Arnie, and Patty.

After all the time I'd spent eavesdropping on them, I'd been able to pick up what had motivated each activist.

Ralph did it for his family's sake. He considered himself and his children abductees, and his memories held vague and confusing images of deer and raccoons. He considered these images to be screen memories, put there by aliens to disguise their identities. It sounded insane, except that I'd seen the evidence. In all probability, Ralph was correct.

Patty didn't consider herself an abductee but was militant about exposing the Agency and its secrets. She had a blog and spoke at conventions about government conspiracies and the UFO cover-up. Her reason for digging was to prove or disprove and then expose the findings.

At first, I thought Arnie was in it for the kicks or the chicks. On the surface, he came across as a committed horn dog and spotlight seeker, bleating loudly on issues for the attention it brought him, especially from women. But as I listened to his thoughts and picked up on his emotions, I realized that he was the most militant of them all. He was doing this both because he was an abductee and because he'd built up a rage and hatred for the governments he believed responsible for his suffering.

The more I learned about them, the more I wanted to help. Since I couldn't help them expose the conspiracy, I made a nuisance of myself to Cornell.

Every time he powered up his PC, I messed with the electricity. Lights flickered; the phone hissed when he picked it up and then went dead; I froze him until his lips turned blue. No matter how much he cranked the thermostat, he shivered, his extremities turning icy and numb.

When Gerry and Michael entered the room, I eased back on the chill and they roasted. The fireplace and blower were always working overtime.

At the moment, the phone crackled and hissed in Cornell's ear, and I could tell by the tone of his voice he was furious. He finally gave up the battle and disconnected the call. The intercom refused to respond when he pressed the button, and that made him snap.

Red-faced, sweating despite the chill, he leapt to his feet, his chair almost upending from the force he'd exerted. He stomped to the door and flung it wide. It crashed into the wall, and he grabbed it on the rebound.

"Helen, contact Zacharia White Wolf. Tell him I'm on my way to see him."

One glance at Cornell's face had Helen, Cornell's mousey assistant, hurrying to obey. She was already speaking to White Wolf before Cornell left the reception area.

***

Contrary to what Zacharia White Wolf's name might lead one to assume, he wasn't First Nation. Originally from England, he moved to Toronto to attend the University of Toronto as a young man and stayed after graduation. That must have been years ago because White Wolf now had a white mane, crow's feet around his eyes, jowls, and the sallow skin and red nose that suggested a long-time smoker and drinker.

He'd changed his last name from Patterson to White Wolf when he'd studied Shamanism in Peru. I couldn't pick up much more of his history than that, but I caught the name-change stuff from peeking at his documents and eavesdropping on his thoughts.

His training might have been legitimate, but his misleading name had me instantly suspicious of him—he was no Arla Hanson, that's for sure. The colours in his aura leaned towards the muddy— he truly was a shady character. That Cornell trusted him and turned to him for help added to my distrust. If White Wolf worked for the Agency, I'd have to be extra careful.

Cornell relayed to White Wolf what had been happening to him. He mentioned that he'd been feeling cold spots and sensing a presence before this, but it had really stepped up lately.

I mentally patted myself on the back for doing such an excellent job. He'd barely gotten any work done, and it interfered with getting through their hit list. As I'd discovered, not everyone on that list was slated to die. Some of them would be abducted—by the Agency, not the extraterrestrials.

Something was brewing, and it centred on the work Patty, Arnie, and Ralph were doing. Those three had kicked from slumber a vicious dog, and it was preparing to attack.

Cornell and White Wolf sat in White Wolf's home office. A part of his home had been designated for clients. Set up to resemble a spa, two rooms had massage tables, large crystals, a diffuser for aromatherapy, and candles. Aboriginal paintings hung on the walls, and Native carvings adorned tables and shelves—all to enhance the illusion, no doubt.

Another room had a sofa, armchairs, a round pedestal table where he could lay out cards for readings, and a desk with his computer and other equipment. This room also had diffusers, crystals, and candles, but most of his therapy work was done in the treatment rooms. The two men settled here, and I perched between them on the table.

Who the hell would trust this man to treat them? Obviously, quite a few people did, because his home was in an expensive part of Toronto. He lived in the Lawrence Avenue and Yonge Street area, in a sprawling ranch-style house on a large lot. The place must have been worth at least five million.

When Cornell arrived, the receptionist asked him to wait while

White Wolf finished with a client. Cornell ordered her to clear the schedule for an hour after the current appointment ended, and she did it without question.

That must have cost Cornell quite a chunk of change, especially when he paid her to go get lunch out.

As I listened to the two men talk, I observed White Wolf closely. He hadn't given any indication that he sensed me in the room until Cornell said he'd rushed over here when he couldn't take it anymore. Then White Wolf did two things: he blocked his mind so I couldn't read his thoughts, and he closed his eyes.

"She's here." White Wolf's voice was low and steady.

"A woman?" Cornell looked stumped. "Who is she?"

Now I'd see how good this guy really was. If I refused to speak to him, he wouldn't get far even if he had a gift for mediumship.

My name is Zacharia Patterson. Who are you, young lady?

I was surprised he'd provided his real name. Maybe it was a trick. I remained silent. Cornell shifted in his seat and leaned forward. White Wolf sat quietly, waiting. He didn't send me another thought, and he blocked from me any other access to his mind.

You have to identify yourself if you want me to help you. Tell me your name.

Almost blurting it out, I clamped my lips together. I swore to myself I wouldn't tell him anything, much less that I was a victim of the Agency.

A smile played on White Wolf's lips. "She's someone the Agency terminated."

He'd read my mind. I hadn't said anything—I'd only thought it—so he'd have had to have read my mind. I went through the process of blocking my thoughts from him. Why hadn't I done that first? Mentally, I kicked myself. Well, that's all he'd get from me.

Cornell's back had stiffened at the news that I was one of their targets.

"Recent?" he mused and then answered his own question. "It would have to be."

"She's closing herself off to me. She doesn't want to communicate."

"What can we do about it?" Cornell scanned the room as if he could find me. "Where is she?"

"Sitting on the table between us."

I scrambled up and bolted to the door—a silly response, considering I didn't need to use a door to exit.

"Don't go, dear." This time, White Wolf didn't think it at me. "I can't help you if you leave."

What should I do? If I told them who I was, it could have repercussions for my family, my friends, and, most likely, my coworkers.

I reached out to Daniel, and when he felt me in his thoughts, he bristled.

Please, Uncle, I begged. *I don't know what to do.*

Come here, Jayden. Right now.

He was right. I could return to harassing Cornell when he was alone. I followed Daniel's thoughts to his location.

CHAPTER 35

I found Daniel at the Toronto Zoo. He sat, smoking a cigarette, inside the cougar's habitat, a part of the Canadian animals exhibit. One big cat lay nearby in the snow. When I appeared, its ears twitched, but it didn't move.

Daniel waved a greeting to me. "Say 'hi' to Felix."

"Felix the cat? Really?" I studied the large cat's powerful body, the sleek, buff-coloured fur tinged with grey on the underside. He yawned at me, and I caught an impression of Daniel in the cage playing on the grass with him in the summertime.

"You play with the zoo animals?" What an intriguing thought. "We can communicate with them!"

"Sort of. Through images."

"He can see us," I said, wonder filling my voice. "Why doesn't it freak him out?"

"Animals here are used to people. They like it better when those of us who can understand them visit. Plus, it's a riot when people see a wild animal act like he sees something they don't. I can get Felix here to stare at me and growl. It's a hoot."

"You have a strange sense of humour." I took a seat in the snow beside Daniel. At least I didn't feel the effects of the cold.

"What happened?" He put an arm around me, and, relieved he wasn't angry with me, I snuggled into him.

"Cornell consulted a psychic. It frightened me."

Daniel kissed my cheek. "It's okay. You got away. Don't go back, and you'll be fine."

My heart sank. "I have to."

"Not this again." He snapped it out and his arm pulled away. "What did he say that scared you so much, and why would you go back for more?"

I shivered, chilled for the first time since I'd died. My shoulders missed his protective arm, and spirit tears slipped from my eyes.

Tired of arguing with him, I said, "Can you hold me again?"

"All right. Shh." He spoke gently and hugged me close. "If Cornell's called in a psychic, sweetie, then he knows a spirit is messing with him. You're putting yourself at risk for strangers. It might even put your friends and family at risk."

"I've thought about that." Tension eased from me. It felt so good to have Daniel's arm around me. I'd forgotten what it was like to have someone take care of me. Everyone needs it sometimes.

Sure, I could have turned to my parents anytime, but I never had after I'd moved away from home. Friends were a good backup, and so was Rory while we were married. Even after the marriage had ended, I could've turned to him in a time of need, but I hadn't. And here? After death? I had only Daniel, and I needed him now. It made me feel weak.

"You're not weak." He stroked my hair. "It's difficult here sometimes. You want to return to your family, to the way it used to be, but you can't. You go to them, but they can't see you. The longing, the ache to touch them and to have them touch you, can plunge you into a depression."

I raised my gaze to meet his. "Spirits can get depressed?"

"Oh, yes. Those of us who stay here experience all kinds of emotional upheaval. Why do you think we're supposed to cross? Honey, we're not meant to be here."

"If that were true, the option to leave would remain open."

He pressed his cheek against the top of my head.

"We chose to become earthbound. Our deliberate actions lowered our vibration and caused us to lose the option to depart. Until we find our way across, we'll remain here. But we're not supposed to stay. Regardless of how long it takes us to get to the other side, it'll remain our destination."

"In the meantime, I refuse to sit here and watch those psychopaths destroy lives. I can't play while they kill people. No one else should experience the kind of pain and devastation they forced on my family. Why won't you help me?" In despair, I pressed my palms to my face, squeezing my eyes shut.

What the hell was wrong with him? Why wouldn't he get involved?

"I can't. It's nothing personal. There's nothing I can do, and if we interfere, it'll cause problems for the very people we're trying to help."

Lifting my head, I glared at him. "Are you afraid?"

"Of course I'm afraid." Daniel met my gaze without flinching. "Cornell has called in a psychic. He'll hurt you." He put a hand on my shoulder. "Stay away from him. Okay?"

"No."

"Then at least spy on Cornell without letting him know you're there."

I shook my head. "If he doesn't know I'm there, what good does it do anyone? He needs to understand he hasn't gotten away with killing me and he won't get away with hurting others."

At that moment, Felix stepped through us and curled up at our knees. I tried to touch his sleek pelt, but my hand went through his body. Damn, I hated that. Just once, I'd like to touch something in the physical world and have good, solid contact with it.

"He's beautiful. Why'd you come here, Uncle Daniel?"

Daniel rested a hand on Felix's head. "I like him. He's the animal I relate to most. Felix never acts like I'm a spirit. Some of the others go wild, screech, or growl. Felix enjoys my company, and I enjoy his."

The simple explanation warmed my heart.

"I like him, too," I whispered.

This time when I touched the cat, I was careful to keep my hand controlled and steady. I couldn't feel his body under my palm, but I stroked him anyway. The motion soothed me.

"We're no longer part of this world. I told you it'd be difficult to stay and watch. You can't alter anyone's future. All you can do is observe what happens," Daniel said.

"You don't know that for sure."

"I do. I've tried to intervene. Do you think I wanted to watch Suzanne die?"

"She'd be with you then, away from all earthly problems."

"Did your worries disappear when you died?"

"No, but maybe if I were on the other side …"

He smiled. "People say 'rest in peace' when someone dies, but what's peace?" He continued in a rush. "Do you think peace is sleep? Nothingness? Oblivion? Because if so, then there is no resting in peace."

I had an urge to bury my face in Felix's side and sob until I felt better. Instead, I stood and paced. Felix bounced up and trotted to my side. When our gazes met, I caught an image of a large ball. Puzzled, I glanced at Daniel.

"He wants you to play ball with him."

"I don't have a ball."

Daniel laughed. "Get one."

"But I can't."

A cup of coffee appeared in Daniel's hand. "Yes, you can."

"But he won't be able to touch it." How could he? Nothing I manifested could be real on the earth plane. Could it?

"He can see us, he can feel us. It's the same with whatever you manifest."

"How?"

"Animals seem to have an ability to interact with the spirit world. Children, too, and some psychics."

I pondered that. "Arla couldn't see me, but White Wolf did." I whipped up a toy ball and kicked it to Felix, who swatted it with a paw. It bounced back to me, and I booted it at Felix again.

"That makes White Wolf even more dangerous. Stay away."

"I will." I had no reason to cross paths with White Wolf again. The promise was an easy one to make. "Thanks for helping me, Uncle."

His expression turned to panic. "Stay with me. There's so much we can do together. We can spend time with your kids."

I tapped into Cornell. He was at home. Night fell, and he hadn't bothered to return to the office after he'd left White Wolf's.

"Leave Cornell alone. Please. What's the point of getting him agitated? You'll slow him down, but you won't stop him. You'll enrage him and give him incentive to hurt you or your family."

"I'll stop him. Whatever his plans, I'll ruin them." I crossed my arms. "Look, I'll be more subtle. He won't know what's happening or who's doing it. But I won't quit."

When Daniel remained silent, I left.

CHAPTER 36

By the time I arrived at Cornell's home office, he'd already fixed himself and Virginia their evening cocktails. He sat at his desk sipping on a scotch and soda, the office door locked, the house silent. I couldn't even hear the drone of the television Virginia was watching or any sound from his kids.

The undercurrent in the silence was a walking-on-thin-ice fear. None of them wanted to anger him. While I sensed that he didn't hit them, there are other ways to instill fear, and Cornell obviously used them. Hate is a harsh word to describe feelings for another person, but I hated him.

I stood behind him, far enough away that he wouldn't sense my presence and get a chill, but close enough that I could view his monitor screen. As usual, he'd been reading a report. This one was on Patty Richards.

Agents continued their surveillance. Patty hadn't done anything damaging. Nor had the agents been able to locate proof that she had a copy of the app.

What a relief. She was either keeping a low profile or she was so good at hacking they couldn't catch her. I suspected if there was any superior hacking going on in that group, it wasn't Patty doing it. They probably weren't catching her in any suspicious computer activity because Arnie was the one behind it.

So, while I could feel some relief about what Patty had been up to, I couldn't trust that the group as a whole was behaving. My main problem now, though, was how to stop Cornell from pursuing them. If they didn't stop what they were doing, he'd eventually give the order to kill them.

I couldn't simply convince Patty and her friends to cease and desist. Stopping this group wouldn't save other Agency targets. Did the Agency stop any real terrorists? If so, I wouldn't want to decommission the entire organization, just the sociopath who included housewives and UFO buffs in his hit list.

Cornell closed his reports and opened another file. This one had information on psychic abilities and communicating with spirits. I probed Cornell's thoughts and hit a blank wall. I tried again with more force.

Nothing.

It was as if he'd set up protection.

White Wolf. He'd taught Cornell how to block his thoughts.

Then Cornell spoke aloud. "Are you here, watching me?"

I remained still and silent—not that I thought he'd be able to sense me. Cornell didn't have a psychic bone in his body.

He picked up a rectangular contraption small enough to hold in his hand. An LCD window showed 00.1 when he flipped it on. He waved it around, and the numbers went crazy when he passed it through my body.

I recoiled from it. An EMF Gauss meter—a gadget used to detect electromagnetic fields.

So, he wanted to play, did he? I stepped to the meter, and, before it could register my presence, I focused on setting the number displayed to zero. When that worked, I reset it to 00.1.

Whenever he waved it past me, I forced the numbers to remain at 00.1.

Ass. If a spirit could fry electronics, did he really think it couldn't influence the setting on an EMF meter?

To annoy him, I moved towards him until he shivered from the chill. I couldn't help laughing when his lips tinged blue and he raced to the thermostat to crank it up. The fireplace poofed on, cheering up the room with its orange glow.

"I know you're here. Tell me who you are. Let me see you."

As if.

He thumped the Gauss meter with his fist and glared at it when the numbers refused to budge. Still, he continued to wave it around. Every thirty seconds, I gave the numbers a nudge, but then as soon as he tried to read them, I reset them to 00.1.

I can do this all night, jackass.

His face reddening, Cornell stomped over to his desk and snatched up his cell phone. A moment later, he had his caller on the line.

"Zach? Jim. She's here."

I tried to tap into White Wolf's thoughts, but he was protecting them. Quickly, I blocked my own as well.

"The EMF meter I bought isn't working. It reads 00.1. I can't figure out where she is … Okay, but how do I make it show me her location?" He sank into the chair at his desk and leaned back in it. "So it's useless?"

Picking up his drink, he sipped and listened. Being unable to hear the other end of the conversation made me nervous. I could, of course, pop over to White Wolf's and listen from there, but I'd promised Daniel I'd stay away from the psychic.

Nevertheless, what he was telling Cornell might be important. I had to know. Before I could change my mind, I popped over to White Wolf's.

***

He sensed me as soon as I arrived, but I'd expected that.

"She's here with me, now," he said into the phone. His gaze hit me full on, and I realized I'd made a serious mistake. Panicked, I dropped out of sight behind the couch. Stupid, I know, but I couldn't think straight.

"Don't hide, girl. Come out. I won't hurt you."

Of course not. You can't. But I kept that to myself, my thoughts shielded.

"She's not speaking to me, Jim, so I'll take our conversation into my private room. It's shielded. If she doesn't want to talk to me, she has no right listening to our conversation."

He left the room, his footsteps telling me he headed right when he entered the hallway.

I followed, unable to help myself. How else would I know what he said to Cornell? He couldn't stop me from following him.

The door to his so-called private room was open—so much for privacy.

I stepped inside.

CHAPTER 37

The room was dimly lit with candles in hurricane lamps on otherwise bare walls. The walls themselves were black, which enhanced the creepiness factor. A round table dominated the centre of the room, a navy, star-spangled cloth draped over it. In the middle of this altar sat a crystal skull the size of a human head. A pearl-handle knife rested in front of the skull. Partially melted black candles in a three-candle holder stood behind the skull.

The only other furniture in the room was an enormous, dark oak armoire against the far wall with a three-seater burgundy couch next to it. I caught the hint of some kind of incense in the air—perhaps he'd burned sage because it irritated my nose and throat. Nausea niggled my gut, and the air pressed heavily on me. The room had no windows.

"Welcome." White Wolf gave me a toothy grin. He stood to the left of the door as if he'd been expecting me.

Oddly tired, I dragged my way to the couch and dropped onto it. He could leave the room, but I'd follow. Where was his privacy now? I bit my lip to stop the laughter.

"She followed me into my private room." He stepped from the room and closed the door behind him. I heard a lock snick into place.

How incompetent a psychic was he? Did he seriously think he was locking me in?

I visualized myself in the hallway. Nothing happened. Annoyed but not worried, I strode to the door and walked into it.

Into it, but not through it. The impact staggered me backwards. Panic set in. My hands shook, and I groped my way back to the sofa. I bashed into the altar on my way, knocking the candles onto the floor and jiggling the skull.

How was that possible? What had happened to me? Had White Wolf done this?

My head felt like it was stuffed with tissues. I tried to clear it and calm myself by gulping in deep breaths of air, but the lingering sage in the room made me gag.

Daniel, can you hear me? I tried to tap into his thoughts but got only silence. *No, this can't be happening. Daniel, please.*

I pulled my feet up onto the couch, hugged my shins, and rested my chin on my knees. Maybe if I focused on sending to Daniel he'd hear me and come help me. I closed my eyes and prepared to connect when a horrifying thought stopped me.

What if Daniel appeared here only to be trapped himself? It would be my fault, and he'd warned me to stay away from White Wolf. Why hadn't I listened? But how could I have known he'd be able to do this?

That was the problem—I hadn't known, and I'd let my guard down. Now I was trapped. What would he do to me? What could he do to me?

The door opened, and White Wolf stepped inside. He slammed shut the door behind him and used a key to lock it.

"Ready to talk, my dear?" he asked.

I dropped my feet to the floor and sat up straight to face him head on. "What have you done to me?"

"Excellent." He fluttered his fingers. Spotting the candles and holder on the ground, he emitted a hiss of frustration and crouched down to pick them up.

As he returned them to the table, he said, "I'm sure that was an accident, but you might be tempted to mess with my sacred tools when I'm not here." His gaze met mine. "I'll tell you once and expect you to remember: don't touch anything. I can torture you if I want. I'd rather not, but I do have the option."

"Torture?" I whispered it. He'd torture me? The whole situation was surreal.

Satisfied that everything on his altar was in its place, he walked over to the sofa and sat.

Terrified he'd touch me and I'd feel it, I jolted to my feet and

713

backed against the wall between the couch and the armoire.

"If torture's the only way to get what I want from you, I'll do it." He said this with an inflection of exasperation as if he were explaining the obvious to a moron.

"I'm dead." That meant he couldn't do anything more to me, didn't it? Isn't that why it had a reputation for being a sweet release?

"But not gone, and you've been earthbound for a while now. You were half in this world already, and I've ensured you're more fully in it now." He hadn't moved. His expression was bland, neutral, but underneath, a current of excitement charged him up. He enjoyed my discomfort, my fear.

That knowledge pushed my fear aside and replaced it with fury. I sauntered to the altar and stared pointedly at the skull. "So, you wouldn't want me to smash this against the wall, for example?"

His eyes narrowed. With obvious effort, he kept his seat. "Don't test me. You think you can't feel pain, but trust me, you can."

"Trust you?" I raised my brows in mock amusement. "That's cute. You work for a psychopath—you're probably one yourself—and you threatened me with torture. Why would I trust anything you say?"

"Sweetie, the confident act won't last long once I get started, so drop it."

He rose and approached me, his gaze fixed on mine.

"What do you want?" I asked.

"That's better." He took me by the arm, the jolt from his touch making me dizzy. "Sit. We have business to discuss. You might as well make it easy on yourself."

Before he could lead me away from the altar, I grabbed the knife off the table and swung at him.

He caught my wrist in a tight grip and pried the knife from my fingers. Before I could react, he'd twisted my arm behind my back and shoved upward. His other arm held me like a vise against his body. It didn't hurt, but I couldn't move.

"Why can you touch me? How is this possible?" I was talking more to myself than to him—it was difficult to get out of the habit of assuming the living couldn't hear me.

His laugh was a throaty rumble in my ear. "Iron, my pet."

I swallowed around the lump in my throat. "Iron?"

"I've lined the room with iron—all of it. You can't leave through floor, ceiling, door, or walls. Iron has been used for centuries to contain or repel spirits. When I had the room built, I had iron embedded in the material. My own little spirit dungeon."

He dragged me to the sofa, and, as one, we sat. Even when we were seated, he kept me pinned to him. He stroked a hand through my hair.

"Such a lovely girl. You died fairly young, am I right?"

I remained silent. No way would I make it easy for him to learn my identity.

"Come on, now. You might as well work with me. I can be kind as well as cruel."

"Fuck you." I struggled against him and tried to force his arm off me.

"I admire your spirit—if you'll pardon the pun." He guffawed, his breath blowing in my ear.

I twisted my head from side-to-side to escape it.

"You're so brave, trying to prevent me from learning who you are. But, sweetie, you don't have to tell me. I'll know soon enough."

No sooner had he said that than a knock sounded on the door.

"Ah," he said. "So it begins."

CHAPTER 38

White Wolf hollered "One moment" at the door and then hauled me to my feet. He dragged me to the armoire and wrestled it open while keeping me restrained with one arm.

I tried my best to make it difficult and frustrating for him, but, in the end, he achieved his goal. He grabbed a pair of iron restraints from one of the drawers and slapped the cuffs on my wrists. After dragging me to the wall, he attached the cuffs to a hook in the ceiling, stretching my arms above my head.

When he stepped away, I tried to roundhouse kick him—at least, what I imagined a roundhouse kick to be based on the name. I have no martial arts training.

Sadly, I missed. He saw it coming and shifted out of the way, laughing off my pathetic attempt at self-defence.

He strode to the door, shouting, "Coming. One moment."

Because I was restrained, he didn't have to hurry the newcomer into the room. White Wolf unlocked the door and swung it wide.

Cornell entered and immediately rushed to stand before me and study me. In the meantime, White Wolf once more secured the door.

"She's a ghost?" Cornell's voice held awe. With one hand, he stroked my body, testing its solidity. "Fascinating, Zach. I'm sorry I doubted you."

I shuddered at the invasion and lashed out with another kick. He jumped back at the last moment, and I almost kneecapped him.

He slapped me across the face, snapping my head back. This

time, I felt it, though only lightly. It seemed the longer I stayed in this room, the more solid I became. I responded by spitting at him, which failed miserably. Apparently, I wasn't corporeal enough to hock a loogie.

Give it time.

Cornell only smiled.

"Spirit, Jim." White Wolf appeared at Cornell's side.

"What?"

"You called her a ghost. The correct term is 'spirit.'"

Cornell slanted White Wolf a look. "What's the difference?"

"A spirit still has a soul; a ghost is a soulless entity—more energy than anything else. That's where hauntings come from."

"All right." Cornell drew nearer, but this time, he approached more cautiously. "I recognize her."

"Stop talking about me as if I'm not here." My tone betrayed rage. I'd fight them, resist them, however I could. If nothing else, they'd get a lesson in etiquette and learn I refused to be treated like an object.

Cornell met my gaze. "Jayden McQueen."

"James Cornell." I added a sneer for effect.

All that did was broaden his grin. "I had no idea you were such a hell cat. We appreciate your type at the Agency. Shame you had to be terminated." He waved a hand around the room. "I assume you figured out the real cause of your death and that's what this is about?"

"You almost got away with it," I replied. "You would have if you'd left well enough alone."

He raised his brows. "Explain."

Might as well answer and hopefully take any remaining focus away from Thomas.

"I was innocent, but you treated me as if I were guilty. You didn't bother to verify who was using my computer to hack into your system. That was shoddy, and when it continued, you went after another innocent person. I couldn't let you continue your rampage of death."

"We don't kill for no reason."

"You did this time."

"The evidence indicated you were part of it."

Horrified, I shouted at him. "What evidence? I didn't do anything!"

"The activity on your computer. You were recorded working on your computer while the server on our network was being hacked from your IP."

"Have you never heard of 'masking'? Your IT guys should be fired for not figuring out they hadn't traced it correctly."

Cornell twisted his lips into a frown. "They proved it. Discussion over."

"You made a mistake—you just refuse to admit it, because then you'd have to face the fact you murdered an innocent person."

"You're not innocent. You're nowhere near innocent."

"Fuck you. I've got nothing more to lose. If I'd hacked into your system, I'd be gloating about it—except there'd be no opportunity, because I'd still be alive. If I'd been the one to hack your server, you'd never have caught me."

"Interesting." He paused to contemplate.

I attempted to read his thoughts but was blocked. It didn't even feel like he was shielding. Instead, it felt as though I'd lost the ability. The implications terrified me. Even if I wanted to call Daniel, I couldn't.

Cornell glanced at White Wolf. "Can we use her?"

The moment his gaze was off me, I kicked out, squaring him in the nuts. My mamma had always taught me to use necessary force to defend myself, and victim wasn't part of my vocabulary. He'd retaliate, but I'd go down fighting.

"I'm right here. I warned you about talking over me."

Cornell crumpled to the floor clutching his crotch. White Wolf waded in and grabbed the foot I swung in his direction as he neared striking distance.

"You'll pay for that." His voice was low, menacing.

He punched me in the stomach. Even though it forced a gasp out of me and would've doubled me over if the chains hadn't held me up, it didn't hurt.

"Get it through your thick skull: eventually, the pain will come. In the meantime, I have other ways of making you suffer." He glanced at Cornell, who continued to clutch his jewels in the foetal position.

"Obviously, it's time for a demonstration."

***

I'd lived an ordinary life with a decent childhood—not great, but not terrible. So normal that nothing prepared me for hanging from a hook in a psychic's dungeon watching him and his sociopathic friend prepare to torture me.

White Wolf set up in silence, his motions choreographed, reverent. Cornell observed from a position on the couch. White Wolf would perform a ritual first, and he'd told Cornell to stay out of the way.

The three candles on the altar burned, their flames flickering unsteadily, at times flaring and sizzling. A small caldron filled with sand and a piece of charcoal White Wolf had retrieved from the armoire smoldered with pungent incense he'd scooped from a matchbox-sized container. Next to the skull, he'd crushed pieces of sage into an abalone shell resting on a three-legged holder.

The bastard planned to light the sage and torment me with it.

He kept his gaze focused on his altar, chanting under his breath as he moved around it. Into a silver goblet he poured the contents of a bottle of ale, then picked up a drum and wooden stick he'd set under the altar. His chanting grew louder, and he beat the drum.

Deciding I didn't have to be polite, I shouted, "Hey, numb-nuts. You're not even Indigenous. Consider yourself a shaman, do ya? More like charlatan!"

He ignored me, continuing to chant and dance. His steps mimicked the tiny hop-skip I'd seen Native dancers perform at a powwow I'd attended once in town. It angered me that he passed himself off as a medicine man.

I rounded on Cornell. "He's faking. It's a scam. He's a liar and playing you for a fool."

Cornell glanced at me, but then turned away to continue watching White Wolf's show.

Inspiration struck me, and I added my voice to the din by bursting into song—the song they'd played at my funeral—the one my sister Lois had told me channeled Archangel Michael.

"Listen to your heart; let the sunlight touch your soul ..."

White Wolf froze, his chanting cut off. His struggle to maintain focus was obvious. He glared in my direction, and I raised my voice.

"Let's find that place again ..."

"Shut her up," He barked at Cornell, who leapt to his feet and flung himself at me.

Avoiding my kicking feet, he managed to get behind me and press his hand to my mouth. I bit him. He grunted but kept his hand pressed against my lips.

"Stop it, you bitch," Cornell screamed in my ear.

White Wolf approached, smoke pouring from the shell he carried.

"This'll distract her."

Even before he reached me, my eyes stung and watered. Tendrils of smoke penetrated my nostrils, filled my head. All I wanted was to fly away from it, but the chains and Cornell and my physicality held me fast.

The smoke reached deep into my lungs, into my body. It spread through me, burning me from the inside out. My world was pain without hope of release. I opened my mouth and screamed, a long wail of agony and despair.

In a desperate attempt to escape the pain, I focused on the Archangel Michael song, drawing the words from deep in my soul. "Within this sacred space, it's time to find that place again."

Then Daniel's words from the day we'd run from Arla's cleansing of Thomas's home popped into my head: *She called on Archangel Michael. He'd have taken us to the other side.*

Spirits might be repelled by iron, but an Archangel should have the power to get through. If he existed.

Archangel Michael, I call you now.

Tears streamed from my eyes.

Take me home, please, take me home. I'm trapped. "Bring the light!"

Barely aware that I'd screamed that last part into Cornell's hand in a fit of delirium, I continued to writhe, tormented.

I don't know when everything changed, or how. Perhaps the light in the room grew brighter. Perhaps the pain diminished enough to allow me to return to awareness. Suddenly the room grew lovely and warm and filled with yellow light. Cornell and White Wolf were hollering, but I couldn't make out their words, only the rage behind them.

As the pain died away, love and peace filled me. I no longer heard the men's voices. Instead, a soft music filled the air. My lungs, nose, and eyes cleared, and I dragged in a healthy breath. Fatigue washed over me, and as I drifted off to sleep, I wondered at the miracle that brought me such peace.

CHAPTER 39

I awoke cradled in a puffy comforter and soft pillow on a bed in a familiar room. When I scanned my surroundings, I recognized the place as the house Suzanne had taken me to when I'd first died. She now sat on a chair next to my bed.

"I'm so happy you returned." Suzanne smiled and gently patted my hand. "Welcome back. I was afraid you'd remain there for years, like Daniel."

At the mention of Daniel's name, I rocketed into a sitting position.

"Daniel. Oh, no." He wouldn't know what had happened to me.

"You can visit him, but he knows you're here."

"I can go to him?" Anxious to see him, I started to rise, but Suzanne pressed her hand against my shoulder and stopped me.

"Not so fast." Her expression was kind, but her tone was firm. "You have to heal. You spent so much time on the other side you couldn't return without help from an archangel."

"Archangel Michael?" He was real?

"Yes, honey."

What should I ask first? Too many questions rattled around in my mind. I decided to start with Daniel.

"Uncle Daniel has been trapped on the earth plane for decades. Why hasn't Archangel Michael helped him to cross?"

"He's never been asked. The angels can't help us without our permission. We have free will for a reason. It's a sacred trust. Our decisions are our own. The consequences of those decisions are our own."

"In all this time, Daniel hasn't asked for help?"

"He's afraid."

"Of what?"

"He made decisions in the past that had horrible consequences. Daniel's been afraid to face judgement."

"You mean we're judged on this side?" Divine retribution exists?

Suzanne nodded. "Yes, but not the way you think—not by whom you think."

"Then by whom?"

"We judge ourselves. You'll see when you have your life review."

The life review was a real thing. I shifted, suddenly uncomfortable. I'd probably forgotten most shameful things I'd done, but I could recall some doozies.

"What happened to forgiving and forgetting?"

"You can't forgive yourself without recognizing what you've done. Not everything you've done was processed consciously." She winked at me. "And not everything you've done that you'll review will cause you to feel shame. This isn't an exercise in humiliation. It's a demonstration of compassion. But you'll see."

"Then Daniel's afraid for no reason?"

"He has his reasons. It's not for us to judge them or decide for him what he should do."

"Have you visited him?"

"Yes."

"Have you told him he can call for help?"

"He knows."

I thought about how quickly Daniel had dragged me away from Thomas's house when Arla called on Archangel Michael.

"I must return."

"Not yet. When you first passed away, you were still tied to the physical plane and could return to say farewell to your loved ones. Now you must remain here for a while. After you've healed, you may visit, but your vibration will never lower enough again to stay there or have any influence on anything there."

"But what about Patty? Ralph? Arnie? They're in trouble. I want to help them."

Suzanne shook her head. "I'm sorry."

"They'll suffer. Their families will suffer. How can we allow that? There was another woman—Carolyn Fairchild. Cornell will harm her. I want to stop him."

"You're so compassionate. I love that about you. But you can't interfere with their journey. It's out of your hands now."

"If I'd known that, I never would've called Archangel Michael. I'd have endured the torture."

"But that's not what happened, and now you're here. You've passed from the world. It'll go on without you."

"No. I shouldn't be here. I should've stayed." Tears streamed down my face. All those people. Oh, God, what would happen to them? The Agency had a whole list of victims. Weary, I met her gaze. "Why won't God stop these evil people?"

She didn't reply, so I said, "He doesn't exist?"

Still no reply.

"Free will? He'd rather sit back and watch torture, pain, and brutality to allow for free will?"

"Would you prefer to lose your freedom?"

"I'd prefer he didn't make assholes."

Suzanne said, her voice patient, "We—humans—make the assholes. We create our own monsters."

"But I have to try."

She smoothed a lock of hair from my face and tucked it behind my ear. "You were always so stubborn. In time, you'll realize that you've already helped."

She rose and offered her hand. I took it, and she helped me to my feet. Together, we walked outside into the yard with the blooming flowers and the buzzing bees. A glorious light shone in the distance, illuminating my grandparents, who waved joyfully when they spotted me.

Both looked young, maybe late twenties, but I recognized them from pictures I'd seen. My grandmother had shiny, black hair that curled around her face like you see in photos from the 1940s.

"Go ahead," Suzanne whispered. "They're waiting for you."

Love and peace flowed from the light, drawing me in. I walked towards it, and then, impatient to reach it, I ran. Music and the sound of singing reached my ears, and joy burst through me.

"I'm home, Gramma," I shouted, and threw myself into her arms.

CHAPTER 40

My healing took months, but the spirit plane is timeless, so I never noticed. I didn't forget those still among the living, but I learned to trust that whatever journey they each were on was theirs alone to take. I had lost my opportunity to change the outcome when I saved myself, but any guilt I carried over that dissipated in the face of the love that surrounded me. Forgiveness, especially of the self, cleanses and heals.

I returned to the earth plane on a bright spring day. It was warmer than usual—one of those days that makes you feel grateful simply to exist.

Daniel was the first person I searched for, and I found him at a sidewalk café in Toronto. We sat together and people-watched, sipped espresso, and ate chocolate cake.

He'd missed me, he said, and didn't accuse me of abandoning him. He continued to resist crossing to the other side—insisted he was where he belonged. If any spirit needed therapy, this one did, but he refused to admit he had a problem.

"I've been watching them," he said.

"The UFO group?"

"Yeah. And Thomas."

This was news. I gave him a sidelong glance. "Why?"

He shrugged. "Curiosity. And for you. I knew you'd want to know what's happening."

"Thanks." I was afraid of what might have happened while I was away. "Everything okay?"

"Yeah, with Thomas. He's dating Arla. They make a cute couple."

I wasn't sure how to react to that. "I hope they'll be happy."

Daniel ignored the comment and frowned. "Something's brewing."

"How so?"

"Gerry and Michael have forced Ralph into a psychiatric hospital."

I gasped. "How? What about his wife and kids?"

"They threatened his family. If they'd wanted him dead, they'd have killed him, I assume. It's telling that they handled him this way."

"And Beth?"

Daniel's eyes grew sorrowful.

"She's struggling to cope. Goes to work, takes care of her family, but it's crushing her."

"Poor woman." I had no other words. Whatever storm brewed was rolling in quickly, and there was no knowing who it would sweep away. Ralph was just the first, and Beth was collateral damage.

"I heard what happened with you and that psychic. Bastard."

"You haven't gone near him, I hope."

He shook his head. "I don't want on his radar. He saw you. He'd see me."

Relieved, I said, "Okay. Good."

Daniel set down his fork and a lit cigarette appeared in one hand.

Smiling, I said, "I love you, Uncle."

"What?"

"It's the little things. You're a dear." I sighed, remembering what we'd been discussing. "They'll go after them, won't they?"

He nodded, understanding I meant the hitmen from the Agency would go after Patty and Arnie.

"I can't prevent that." I dropped my fork. Half my cake remained, but I waved it back into oblivion. Where did this stuff go when we made it disappear? Was it destroyed? Had it even existed?

"I know," he replied. He wouldn't intervene either. He'd made that clear before.

"You were right," I said. "Whatever happens, it's not on us to try to change it."

"They taught you this over there?" he asked.

"Sort of. I learned by healing myself."

"Is there anything we can do?"

"Yes." I looked him in the eyes. "We can pray for them."

"Pray? You believe in that?"

I nodded. "Not in the way you think. It's a way of sending light energy to them, and that opens them up to communicate with their angels and guides."

He frowned. "I've never met any angels and guides."

"No. You can if you want to. All you have to do is ask."

He averted his gaze and smoked in silence, staring into space. At last, he asked, "Have you seen Silver?"

So the subject was changed.

"I wanted to find you first and make sure you were okay."

"I'm always okay."

"Yes, you are."

I smiled, but inside I was sad. He hadn't changed, and there was nothing I could do about it.

***

Silver was in the third trimester of her pregnancy. She was in the garden, working at clearing away the winter debris when I arrived. Harrison hovered around her, helping, trying to take the more physical jobs off her hands. She protested, insisting she was up to it, which meant the occasional tug-of-war over a yard waste bag or garden implement. It was a Saturday, so no school.

Marc opened the sliding doors and called out, "I'm putting the kettle on. Who wants tea?" He'd been back from university for a week now, final exams over. He'd work in Newmarket for the summer and then return to school in the fall a new uncle.

"Peppermint for me," Silver called out.

"Sure," Harrison said. "Regular for me."

Marc paused a moment and scanned the yard. He squinted in my direction, as though he'd spotted something he couldn't quite make out.

I grinned. He could still sense me. My vibration wasn't so high he couldn't tell I was there. I clapped my hands and squealed a little.

"Marc?" Silver said. "Something wrong?"

"No. I just ..." He trailed off. "It's nothing."

He slid the door closed.

"Hi."

Expecting to see a friend of Silver's approaching, I turned to face the speaker. But the young woman who had called the greeting was talking to me.

"You can see me?"

She smiled. "Of course."

"Oh, you're a spirit too?" Why was another spirit here with my family? I didn't recognize her, but she seemed vaguely familiar.

Her hair was the same chestnut as Silver's, but her cheeks were round and her eyes the same almond shape as Harrison's. I gasped.

She laughed. "Hi, Grandma."

"But ..." How could it be?

The young woman giggled, putting one dainty hand in front of her mouth.

"I can visit now that my mom is near the end of her pregnancy."

"Out of body?"

"Yes. Whenever my body is sleeping deeply."

"But you're not a baby."

"Thank goodness spirits can shift ages, don't you think? I see you're my age in spirit."

My grandkid was going to be a smartass like her mother.

"I'm so happy I could meet you," I said.

"Me too. When I sensed you here, I had to see you. I'm sorry I won't grow up with you, but maybe you can visit me. I'll know you're here."

I shook my head, and tears sprang to my eyes. "You won't. No one can see me."

"Marc has natural psychic ability. I'll have even more. This isn't my first rodeo, Grandma."

"You'll work on it?"

"Yes, but it'll complicate my life. Dark times are ahead. They'll need me."

"Dark times?" A sliver of fear spiked through my gut. Was Cornell going to harm my family?

"More global than that. We're all in for a rough ride." She smiled. "But don't worry. I'm here for a reason."

Everything happens for a reason. Daniel had believed that.

"What's your name?"

"They'll name me Rylan. This time around."

Marc stepped from the house carrying a tray with tea and biscuits. He set it on the round patio table on the back deck. Silver and Harrison dropped their gardening tools and hurried to claim their mugs.

"I'll visit," I said. "I'm so thrilled we met. I love you."

She hugged me, and I kissed her cheek. She vanished, returning to her tiny body in Silver's womb.

Daniel appeared, sporting a broad grin. "So, you've met the new addition to the family, I see."

"You've met?"

"Of course. While you were away."

We fell silent then, each reflecting on where I'd been.

"I have to return now." Regardless how long I stayed on this side, the risk of becoming earthbound was gone. But I wanted to go home. Absence from the Light brought a yearning for it I could only ignore for so long.

"Okay. I'll see you again?"

"Of course."

We hugged, and I vanished.

I reappeared inside a van parked across from Patty Richards's house. Michael Valiant and Gerry Muniz sat inside, eyes on a monitor displaying the interior of Patty's house.

It's beginning. Right now.

What these two men did here would reverberate through time. I tapped into Michael's thoughts. Uncertainty and doubt rolled off him in waves. As I watched, his aura shifted. Where it had been muddy, it lightened, acquiring a yellow tinge. Other colours bubbled up to the surface.

It's him. He's the key. Gently, I touched my palm to his face.

"I'll pray for you, too," I said and returned home.

The End

ABOUT THE AUTHOR

Val Tobin lives in Newmarket, Ontario with her husband, Bob, and Scully, their cat. She spends her days writing, reading, and searching for the perfect butter tart.

Her educational background includes a diploma in Computer Information Systems from DeVry Toronto, a B.Sc. in Parapsychic Science from the American Institute of Holistic Theology, a M.Sc. in Parapsychology from AIHT, Reiki Master/Teacher certifications, and Angel Therapy Practitioner® certifications.

CONNECT WITH VAL TOBIN

Facebook: https://www.facebook.com/valtobinauthor
Twitter: https://twitter.com/valandbob
Blog: http://bobandval.wordpress.com/
LinkedIn: http://www.linkedin.com/in/valtobin
Web Site: http://www.valtobin.com/

WATCH FOR THIS 2018 RELEASE

Poison Pen
Three wannabe authors suffering from various mental disorders find love in unexpected places when they interfere in the investigation of a colleague's murder. Part of the *About Three Authors* series, which includes *Whoever Said Love Was Easy?* by Patti Roberts and *Stolen Hearts & Muddy Pawprints* by Georgina Ramsey.

OTHER BOOKS BY VAL TOBIN

Angel Words by Doreen Virtue and Grant Virtue
Val contributed a story to Doreen and Grant Virtue's *Angel Words:*
Visual Evidence of How Words Can Be Angels in Your Life

The Valiant Chronicles Series
Prequel: *Earthbound*
A spirit becomes earthbound after refusing to cross over in order
to solve her murder and prevent more deaths, some of which
might be predestined.

Book One: *The Experiencers*
A black-ops assassin atones for his brutal past by trying to help an
alien abductee escape her fate.

Book Two: *A Ring of Truth*
A rogue assassin returns from the dead to rescue alien abductees
and triggers Armageddon.

The Valiant Chronicles are also available as a box set.

Injury
A young actress at the height of her career has her personal life
turned upside down when a horrifying family secret makes front-
page news.

Gillian's Island
A socially anxious divorcée confronts her greatest fears when she's
forced to sell her island home and falls for the dashing new owner.

Walk-In
A young psychic woman fights an attraction to a handsome but
skeptical novelist while she battles a power-hungry sorcerer
determined to make her his next conquest.

Made in the USA
Columbia, SC
09 February 2018